I0592093

John Wesley Hales

Longer English Poems

John Wesley Hales

Longer English Poems

ISBN/EAN: 9783744714921

Printed in Europe, USA, Canada, Australia, Japan

Cover: Foto ©Andreas Hilbeck / pixelio.de

More available books at **www.hansebooks.com**

LONGER ENGLISH POEMS

WITH NOTES

PHILOLOGICAL AND EXPLANATORY

AND AN

INTRODUCTION ON THE TEACHING OF ENGLISH

EDITED BY

J. W. HALES, M.A.

Late Fellow and Assistant Tutor of Christ's College, Cambridge
Barrister-at-law of Lincoln's Inn
Lecturer in English Literature and Classical Composition at King's College School, London
Co-editor of Bishop Percy's MS. Folio, &c.

London

MACMILLAN AND CO., Limited

NEW YORK : THE MACMILLAN COMPANY

1899

The Right of Translation and Reproduction is Reserved

1, OPPIDANS ROAD, PRIMROSE HILL.

April 20th, 1872.

DEAR MR. MACLEAR,

IT was you who suggested this book; and with your name I wish, with your kind permission, to connect it.

Everybody whose good fortune it is to work with you cannot but admire the self-denying energy and unostentatious devotion with which you discharge the onerous duties devolving upon you as the Head Master of King's College School, and sincerely congratulate you on the signal success which has crowned, and bids fair still to crown, your efforts in that capacity.

Amongst those who thus admire and congratulate, pray believe that not the least hearty is.

Very truly yours,

J. W. HALES.

CONTENTS.

	PAGE
PREFACE	ix
SUGGESTIONS ON THE TEACHING OF ENGLISH	xi

SPENSER.

PROTHALAMION	1

MILTON.

HYMN ON THE NATIVITY	6
L'ALLEGRO	14
IL PENSEROSO	17
LYCIDAS	22

DRYDEN.

MAC FLECKNOE	27
A SONG FOR ST. CECILIA'S DAY	32
ALEXANDER'S FEAST; OR, THE POWER OF MUSIC	34

POPE.

RAPE OF THE LOCK	39

JOHNSON.

LONDON	59
THE VANITY OF HUMAN WISHES	65

COLLINS.

THE PASSIONS	75

GRAY.
PAGE

Elegy written in a Country Churchyard 79
The Progress of Poesy 82
The Bard 86

GOLDSMITH.

The Traveller ; or, A Prospect of Society 91
The Deserted Village 101

BURNS.

The Cotter's Saturday Night 112
The Twa Dogs 117

COWPER.

Heroism 124
On the Receipt of my Mother's Picture out of Norfolk . 126

COLERIDGE.

The Ancient Mariner 130

SCOTT.

Cadyow Castle 148

WORDSWORTH.

Ode : Intimations of Immortality from Recollections of
    Early Childhood 154
Laodamia 159

BYRON.

The Prisoner of Chillon 165

KEATS.

The Eve of St. Agnes 176

SHELLEY.

Adonais 187

NOTES 201

INDEX 423

PREFACE.

THIS book, for reasons which need not here be specified, has been completed very slowly. Half of it was printed and in private use some two years ago. I only mention this fact here for the sake of explaining any differences of treatment that may seem to separate the earlier from the later pages. Probably, if I were to re-write the Introduction now (it was written and printed in the Christmas of 1869), I should alter some. things in it. No teacher or student, with an interest in his work, but must be perpetually reconsidering and modifying his views. We are often informed that Rome was not built in a day; but neither was the humblest and pettiest village that is: and so the theories of the most inconsiderable scholar as well as of the worthiest master, if there is any thinking and attention at all, are perpetually growing,—not, it is to be hoped, wild, but mature, or at least maturer.

With regard to the texts in this volume, it has not been thought right to tamper with the *orthography* of their authors. Whatever may be thought of such liberties in works designed for that volatile being "the general reader," there is surely no justification for them in manuals prepared for the student of literature and language. In every case except one, the latest edition published during the author's life has been followed. That one is Milton, whose pieces have been taken from the edition of 1645, as superior to that of 1673. In all cases the latest *readings* have been given. In one or two poems—in "Mac Flecknoe," "The Rape of the Lock," "London," "The Twa Dogs,"—slight omissions have been necessary, and in the latter two poems slight changes have been made, that the "reverence due to boys," to adopt Juvenal's phrase, might be well observed. Some of the later texts were revised by my friend Mr. Twentyman, late Fellow of Christ's College, Cambridge, now Vice-Master of King's College School, in whom indeed I hoped to have had a genial coadjutor in all the work to be done, had his other duties given him leisure.

And now, little book, whose compilation has taken me more time than would be thought, I send you forth into the world. Would you were something better; but it is late wishing when the very minute for parting has come. You must make the best of yourself; you must not mind scorings and defacements; no doubt you have much to learn. And still less must you mind much fingering and laceration; it may be that your ears may be made those of a dog; perhaps you may be cried over and called evil names and held an abomination. By these things be not troubled, O booklet; for they would mean, in spite of appearances, that you were really worthy. So this is the fortune I wish you; and if it is vouchsafed, then it cannot but be that you will be smiled as well as wept over, spoken of with some affection, deemed a sort of blessing.

SUGGESTIONS

ON

THE TEACHING OF ENGLISH.

. . . Σμικρὰ μὲν τάδ' ἀλλ' ὅμως
ἄχω . . .

I.

IT is certain that a great revolution is now taking place in the educational world. A discontent which has been growing for several generations is now reaching its culmination. For a long time Englishmen have been dissatisfied with their schools and universities ; they have felt that those well-designed institutions failed to do their proper work ; they have been made painfully conscious that the foster-children of them were to a great degree ignorant of what they ought to know, and accomplished in what was comparatively worthless; and at this state of things they have not unnaturally murmured. Not unfrequently they have done something more than murmur. There have arisen thoughtful and wise observers who have loudly and clearly protested against the existing system ; but no immediate hearing has been vouchsafed to them. The old idols have stood firm on their pedestals ; and no new divinities have been honoured with places by their side. But at last there seems to be come a time when those protests are to be heard, when school-doors and college-gates are to be thrown open to subjects that have long clamoured in vain for admission. This wonderful unbarring the present age appears destined to witness. When this century closes, the ordinary education

of an Englishman will be a very different thing from what it was
when the century began. The school of our grandchildren will not
closely resemble that of our grandfathers. It will exhibit new methods ;
it will comprehend fresh subjects; it will exalt other interests. We of
to-day should feel strange and unacquainted, were we seated on those
benches of the future. There will be sounds we know not of, text-
books to us incomprehensible, arrangements that with their novelty
would puzzle and perplex. There will perhaps be missing in these
future class-rooms something that is to us dear, and justly dear ;
there will certainly be found in them much on whose value we can
have no opinion, inasmuch as we are scarcely qualified by knowledge
to form any. For good or for evil a great revolution is taking place.
It is hard to think that it is all for evil, although many dear traditions
are being swept away. Doubtless it is hard to throw the brand
Excalibur into the mere. One cannot but see how richly gemmed
and jewelled it is ; one cannot but remember what noble services it
has wrought in its day, what famous home-thrusts it has dealt, what
safety and confidence it has given, still less that in the beginning it
was bestowed by Heaven : but for all these facts and memories it
may be better that it should now be flung away—that we should
"strongly wheel and throw it." At all events it may be well to
recognize that there are other weapons with which good work may
be achieved in our assaults upon the strongholds of Ignorance and
Dulness. Let the good sword be supported by other arms.

With whatever feelings we may regard this educational change, it is
certainly coming to pass. This nineteenth century seems likely to be
as memorable, or perhaps more memorable, in the history of education, than are the sixteenth and seventeenth centuries. As in those days
Greek and "the New Philosophy" at last found a place in our schools
and universities, so now Modern Languages and Natural Science
appear to be establishing themselves. It would perhaps be not unin-
structive for us to note what bitter opposition those old innovations
encountered. The introduction of Greek, for instance, was effected
in the teeth of the most furious hostility. The struggles described by
Homer as raging beneath Troy walls were neither so fierce nor so long
lasting as those which raged between the modern Greeks and Trojans,
as the combatants in the educational battle of the sixteenth century
called themselves. There were many then who from various points

of view echoed the sentiment expressed by the Duke of Norfolk in
1540. " *I never read the Scripture*," said that adherent of the departing age, " *nor never will read it. It was merry in England before
the new learning came up; yea, I would all things were as hath
been in times past.*" Who could laugh at these words of a strangely
troubled spirit ? Rather one might weep over them ; there is a certain
pathos in the helpless embarrassment and despair they reflect : but
one can see they were not wise, provident words ; one cannot regret
that the " new learning came up." But not altogether unlike is the
sentiment that may sometimes be heard in these days of like unsettle-
ment and transition.

'Ημεῖς τοι πατέρων μέγ' ἀμείμονες εὐχόμεθ' εἶναι.

But is this boast so well founded? Do we derive all the benefit that
is possible from their experience? Are we so much more catholic-
minded ?

Surely the wise course now is not to set our faces against the in-
coming studies, but to do our best to regulate and order their admission. Let us give these strangers a judicious welcome. Let us frankly
and generously examine what recommendations they have to advance
for themselves. Let us banish utterly and for ever from our minds
the notion of finality in education. Let us recognize that all our efforts
are but tentative, and that we are yet an immeasurable distance, not
only from absolute perfection, but from that degree of perfection which
is attainable. May it not be indeed that we are at present in an
extremely rudimentary stage of advancement in this momentous respect ?—that the question of education is yet in its veriest infancy?
Perhaps we are yet at the very foot of the mountain, and have not
really commenced the ascent. Not odder, it may be, in our eyes is
the educational system of the Middle Ages than our present system
will be according to the decisions of posterity. These possibilities
should surely make us, not reckless revolutionists, but thoughtful,
considerate reformers. The changes that are now making will in their
turn perhaps be modified or superseded. There is no such thing as
an educational canon which closes and is complete.

The subjects which especially concern us in this paper are English
Language and Literature. These subjects may be said to be now
finding places in our school *curricula*. That they will eventually be

admitted everywhere, there seems no reason to doubt. During the last ten years this important movement has advanced with hastening steps. The reign of Victoria will be as conspicuous in the history of our language in its connection with Education as is now the reign of Richard the Second. Between these two epochs—more than five hundred years apart—there is perhaps no other one of any ·comparable moment. In Richard the Second's time English was admitted into schools as the teaching medium ; it is now being admitted as a teaching subject. " John Cornwall," says an old chronicler in a well-known passage, " a master of grammar, changed the lore in grammar school and construction of French into English, and Richard Pencrich learned that manner teaching of him, and other men of Pencrich. So that the year of our Lord a thousand three hundred fourscore and five, of the Second King Richard, after the Conquest nine, in all the grammar schools of England children leave French and construe and learn in English."* To that innovation no doubt resistance was offered ; that same chronicler goes on to balance the advantage and the disadvantage : but it was effected. Some future historian will record of this present age that it witnessed the introduction into our schools—at least into some of them—of a careful study of our native tongue and the great works written in it. He will record that English boys and girls were for the first time instructed in the great classics of their country, that Shakspere and Milton and Scott were read and re-read along with Homer and Sophocles and Virgil, that a pernicious monopoly was for ever abolished. Why should we not know our Shakspere as the Greeks knew their Homer ? In Xenophon's *Symposium* one of the guests says of himself : ὁ πατὴρ ἐπιμελούμενος ὅπως ἀνὴρ ἀγαθος γενοίμην, ἠνάγκασέ με πάντα τὰ Ὁμήρου ἔπη μαθεῖν· καὶ νῦν δυναίμην αν Ἰλιάδα ὅλην καὶ Ὀδύσσειαν ἀπὸ στόματος εἰπεῖν. " My father, earnestly wishing that I should become a good man, made me learn all Homer's poetry ; and at this day I could say off by heart the whole Iliad and Odyssey." Not that we should servilely follow that method, and commit all Shakspere's poems and plays to memory; but why should our poet not have his proper place in our schools? There is room for him and for Homer too. There is no fatal incompatibility between these two supreme spirits. We do not love Homer less, but Shakspere more. It is a great loss to our national life that we do not more

* See Morris' *Specimens of Early English* (Clarendon Press Series), p. 339.

thoroughly study our great national poet. Do not let us flatter ourselves that at one time or another in our lives we do, as a nation,
study him. There is much talk of Shakspere; is there much real
knowledge? There is much pride in him; is it intelligent pride? To
the great majority of persons are his plays much more than names,
or at best but fine stories? It is no slight cause for rejoicing that the
time of this ignorance is no longer to be winked at; that our Shakspere is, to some extent at least, to be known, and receive a better
informed, a more discriminate, a more practical admiration.

11.

But it is not proposed here to enter into any general advocacy of
the teaching of English. This subject is rapidly becoming independent of any such support; its admission into schools is, as has
been already said, almost secured. What I propose in some sort to
deal with is rather the details of English teaching, not in the hope of
suggesting anything new or fresh to the many able teachers who have
of late turned their attention to this matter, but rather of showing
those who may still regard English as a subject somewhat barren of
such material as the teacher requires, how abundant and rich it is in
fact. Something of what follows has already been said in a paper
which appeared in the *London Student* magazine in July 1868, where
an attempt was made to treat one of Milton's sonnets mainly after the
same manner in which Scott's *Rosabelle* is to be treated here.

Before we proceed to our special work, let me make two general
observations :

(i.) *Nothing should be told a pupil which he can think out or find
out for himself.* The great function of education is not so much to
give information as to put the pupil in the way of getting it and recog-
nizing and using it justly when he has it. A man's knowledge is not
to be estimated by the number of facts which he has appropriated,
by the amount of books he has devoured, nor yet by the number of
principles which have been impressed upon his memory. A principle
mastered in such a way is, in an educational, a thought-developing
point of view, of no more worth than a fact. But knowledge is to be
gauged by the manner in which facts are arranged and combined, in
which principles have been arrived at. To teach how to arrange facts,

and to combine and to interpret—to impart real knowledge—is the schoolmaster's highest work. Of course the facts must be collected ; but this the memory, properly directed, easily accomplishes. Now with respect to English teaching, every pupil, however young, has already amassed a considerable store of facts : for instance, he can talk the language easily, he has a certain standard by which he talks it ; he has a vocabulary of no mean extent. The teacher should avail himself of this store ; he should aim at making the pupil the conscious master of it ; he should assist him to order and methodize it. It is not so much necessary at first to add to it. To create Kosmos out of Chaos no fresh material is wanted. Therefore let the pupil be led to observe and to order the stock of information he already possesses ; let him be made to turn that to good account ; let him be told nothing that he in fact knows though he is not sensible that he knows it. It may be questioned whether we always avoid the frightful example of the great Dunce Schoolmaster :

> " To ask, to guess, to know as they commence,
> As Fancy opens the quick springs of Sense,
> We ply the memory, we load the brain,
> Bind rebel Wit, and double chain on chain ;
> Confine the thought to exercise the breath,
> And keep them in the pale of words till death."

By all means let the pupil " ask ;" but let him first ask himself.

As for matters which he certainly does not know, or on which mere observation and reflection will not inform him, it is often good not directly to inform him, but to put him in the way of informing himself. Some personal exertion will endear to him the knowledge he acquires, and will impress it more deeply on his mind. The habit of independent search, conducted in however humble a way, is highly valuable.

(ii.) *With regard to the following paragraphs, it would not be advisable to give in every case equal importance to the various methods of study they indicate.* With a less advanced " form," certain of these methods might be omitted altogether ; with a more advanced one, certain others might be omitted. How many of them are made use of, and to what degree any one that is made use of should be carried, must depend upon circumstances : for instance, with a very low form it might be well to dwell simply on the story of what is read, to see that that is thoroughly understood and realized.

III.

To avoid vagueness, it may be well to take a particular piece of English writing, and apply what has to be said to it.   Let us take a piece of English poetry, of no extraordinary difficulty, on which to make our experiment.

ROSABELLE.

O listen, listen, ladies gay !
  No haughty feat of arms I tell ;
Soft is the note, and sad the lay
  That mourns the lovely Rosabelle.

" Moor, moor the barge, ye gallant crew !
  And, gentle lady, deign to stay !
Rest thee in Castle Ravensheuch,
  Nor tempt the stormy frith to-day.

" The blackening wave is edged with white :
  To inch and rock the sea-mews fly ;
The fishers have heard the Water-sprite,
  Whose screams forebode that wreck is nigh.

" Last night the gifted Seer did view
  A wet shroud swathed round lady gay ;
Then stay thee, Fair, in Ravensheuch ;
  Why cross the gloomy firth to-day ? "

" 'Tis not because Lord Lindesay's heir
  To-night at Roslin leads the ball,
But that my lady mother there
  . Sits lonely in her castle hall.

" 'Tis not because the ring they ride,
  And Lindesay at the ring rides well,
But that my sire the wine will chide
  If 'tis not fill'd by Rosabelle."

O'er Roslin on that dreary night
  A wondrous blaze was seen to gleam ;
'Twas broader than the watchfire's light,
  And redder than the bright moonbeam.

It glared on Roslin's castled rock,
  It ruddied all the copse-wood glen :
'Twas seen from Dryden's groves of oak,
  And seen from cavern'd Hawthornden.

Seem'd all on fire that chapel proud
  Where Roslin's chiefs uncoffin'd lie,
Each Baron, for a sable shroud,
  Sheath'd in his iron panoply.

b

Seem'd all on fire within, around,
 Deep sacristy and altar's pale ;
Shone every pillar foliage-bound,
 And glimmer'd all the dead men's mail.

Blazed battlement and pinnet high,
 Blazed every rose-carved buttress fair :
So still they blaze, when fate is nigh
 The lordly line of high Saint Clair.

There are twenty of Roslin's barons bold
 Lie buried within that proud chapelle :
Each one the holy vault doth hold,
 But the sea holds lovely Rosabelle.

And each Saint Clair was buried there,
 With candle, with book, and with knell ;
But the sea-caves rung, and the wild waves sung
 The dirge of lovely Rosabelle.

(i.) Let the piece be learned well by heart. This should be made a necessary part of the out-school work—of " preparation." While, as has been said above, something more than the memory is to be thought of, and a mere loading of that faculty is before all things to be depre- cated, the memory is not to be neglected. The memory is to be the servant of the mind ; it is to fetch and carry for it ; and it must be kept busy. One might say it should serve as a sort of library, which it were well to stock judiciously, with volumes well read and to be read again and again, not with shelves of works unintelligible to us. The learning a piece of good writing is placing a volume in that library. It is not enough to learn it, but it is a good beginning. Certainly, as has often been said, it is no trivial blessing to have the memory furnished in one's youth with what is worth remembering to the end of one's life, and grows more and more precious as we grow older and discern better its virtues.

Some attention should be paid to elocution. The piece learnt must be recited carefully and thoughtfully. When the pupil understands it better, as it is to be hoped he will do at the close of his " lesson," he will probably repeat it more intelligently ; but to repeat it with some intelligence, some proper feeling and emphasis, this must be one of the duties of his preparation for his work. How rare is good reading, at least among English men ! Ladies generally read better, because they have more practice in the art ; amongst men the art can scarcely be said to exist. Certainly much of the music of poetry and of rhythm is often lost or diminished, if the passage containing it is not read aloud. To be fully appreciated, it should be heard by the outer ear, and so by the inner. By younger persons, this music will probably be altogether unperceived and not understood, if they are not taught to feel and hear it. *Rosabelle* will be to them as a passage from one of Sir Richard Blackmore's Epics. They will miss its varying tones ; they will see the poet piping, so to say, but they will not hear the notes that flow from him ; he will pipe, but they will not dance ; he will mourn, but they will not lament. Let, then, their sense of the music of poetry be cultivated. Let them see that reading is in a manner interpretation.

(ii.) Now let the general meaning of the piece be considered. To turn to our instance, let the story of the poem be brought out. *Rosabelle*, it will be seen, divides into four parts : there is the introduction, the minstrel's proem ; then there is the group of figures on the frith shore, with the storm gathering over them ; then Roslin Chapel all ablaze ; then the two last stanzas connect, as it were, the two preceding scenes—connect the chief of those figures with that ominous blaze. To each of those two main scenes five stanzas are devoted ; so that in mere form they correspond together. These scenes. should be carefully realized ; the pupil should describe them in his own words. For younger pupils this realizing of the story might, as I have already said, be work enough. For them, old ballads and pieces like *Rosabelle*, or a chapter of one of the *Waverley Novels*, or a passage from Pope's *Iliad* would serve excellently ; or, which would require a little more power, they might read a play of Shakspere merely for the story. Of course with poems of a not merely narrative sort, greater difficulties would arise : take Wordsworth's lines on *The Daisy*, for instance, or Gray's *Ode on the Spring*. Perhaps few persons are fully conscious how very common most careless reading is, especially of poetry. Again and again the main point of a poem is missed : or, if the main point is caught, that is all. One may frequently meet devout admirers of Milton's *Lycidas* who understand scarcely a passage of that noble poem. They are lulled and pleased with *Lycidas* as one is with the sound of waves without knowing what they say. Gray's *Elegy* is, I suppose, a generally popular poem. How many of those who doat upon it follow the current of the thought, or at all comprehend certain parts ? Yet surely poetry read in this fashion is read most ineffectually. Poetry becomes a mere pleasant murmur. It is like hearing laughter without knowing the joke that moves it. Yorick, "a fellow of infinite jest," sets the table in a roar, and we roar with it ; but what was that "flash of merriment"? To these readers poetry is an inarticulate art, like music, but with inferior sensuous expression.

It is most important, therefore, that the general meaning of everything read should be asked after, even where it seems obvious. When this is well discovered, the meaning of the parts should be inquired into, and their relation to the main idea investigated ; that is, the *unity* of the piece should receive attention. It should be shown how in all artistic works of excellence one main idea rules and sways ; that there is one great centre towards which all the parts bend and converge ; that no part is really isolated and independent, however much it may seem so, but subserves that main idea. In what does the unity of *Rosabelle* consist? We have seen that this ballad presents us with two powerful pictures ; how are these pictures related ? Are they mere rivals jarring with each other ? Do they divide and distract the attention ? Or are they harmoniously subordinate to one idea, each serving to bring that idea into its full relief? Do their colours blend so as to leave one single impression? Questions of this sort may seem easy enough to the wise ; but they will certainly not be found so by the ordinary learner. To answer them will demand his best attention and thought. Again and again the teacher will discover that the part has been mistaken for the whole, that an aisle has been regarded as the cathedral.

It would frequently be advisable to direct one's pupils to make written abstracts of any piece of prose or poetry that is to be studied by them. These would serve as an evidence that the hours allotted to preparation had been rightfully employed ; secondly, they would thoroughly test the writer's comprehension of his work ; thirdly, they might be of use in teaching the scholar how to write his native tongue. With regard to the last suggested advantage, this mode of learning the art of composition is surely better, at least for younger persons, than that of what is called Essay writing. To exact "Essays" is perhaps to imitate that austere Egyptian master who insisted on bricks being produced though he declined to furnish straw. Even let it be supposed that a youth has knowledge enough to write an essay, yet the difficulty of transferring that knowledge to paper has to be overcome ;

and this is no slight difficulty. Many a fluent talker is a most tardy and labouring writer. All his powerful glibness goes at the sight of a pen.

> " Facunda parum decoro
> Inter verba cadit lingua silentio."

He cannot translate himself. He is like an undecipherable manuscript. Most persons, however ready scribes they may become eventually, have once experienced this helpless condition. Their minds have appeared to them *tabulæ rasæ* of as complete a kind as they were at the time of birth, according to Locke, or as the palpable unfilled sheet in front of them. They have no self-projecting power. They cannot cast any shadows. Abstract-making may teach how to express one's meaning without drawing too mercilessly on one's own resources. When the straw is provided, everybody may be expected to produce bricks of some sort. Much attention should be paid to the style, as well as to the matter, of these abstracts. They must be truthful ; they must be well turned.

The pupil should be encouraged to examine himself in his work. He should be taught to ask himself questions, and if he cannot answer any one of them he should be permitted to lay it before his teacher. Let him say to himself as he reads each passage : " Now do I understand that ? " Let him write down the difficulties he cannot overcome —in every case there should be some such—and bring them so written to his tutor. These questions would serve as another test of the pupil's having properly prepared his lesson. They could not fail to elicit his intelligence. They would place him in a position thoroughly to appreciate whatever instruction might be given him, and partly at least prevent that lavish throwing away of pearls of which many a class-room is the daily scene.

(iii.) Now let attention be given to minor, subsidiary matters—to allusions, to manners and customs, to historical and semi-historical details. The story having been well mastered, we must see how it is set forth and illustrated ; having observed the *form*, we must now regard the *colour*. What age does *Rosabelle* reflect? What habits, what superstitions, what rites, what creeds? Surveyed in this light, *Rosabelle* is full of interest. There is the old hall with its minstrel and its ladies gay ; then the water-sprite with its wreck-prophetic scream ; the Seer with his fearful vision ; the young lords bent on their knightly pastime; the dead barons lying in their quaint cerements; the funeral train with its torches, and, requiems, and tolling bells. All these are local and historical features that contrast with the permanent and abiding elements of the poem—with the deep human sympathy the sad tale stirs in us as in those "ladies gay" that heard it, or are fancied to hear it, long years ago ; with the filial affection which omens and storms cannot daunt from its pious purpose—a most fair sight, and one, thank Heaven, that has not passed away from the earth with the Middle Ages ; with the fond ever-cherished belief that the children of love and duty do not perish unnoticed by the higher powers, but that their

> " Death is mourned by sympathy divine."

Those temporary fashions contrast also with the unchanged and unchanging phenomena of nature. Nature might say with her bright daughter, the Brook :

> " Men may come, and men may go,
> But I go on for ever."

" The good knights are dust, And their swords are rust, And their souls are with the saints, we trust ;" the ladies gay have long since passed : the Seer has become a part of that world into which he was ever curiously gazing ; the torches of the priests burnt out ages ago ; but the sights and sounds of Nature are still fresh and vivid : waves still blacken foam-edged, winds still moan and wail.

The *water-sprite* is heard often in old poems, and the poems that imitate or refer to these. By Logan it is called the *water-wraith;* see his *Braes of Yarrow :*

> " Thrice did the *water-wraith* ascend,
> And gave a doleful groan thro' Yarrow."

And so Wordsworth in his *Yarrow Visited;* and so Campbell in his *Lord Ullin's Daughter* (a poem with a like catastrophe with *Rosabelle,* but of a different, less noble motive) :

> " By this the storm grew loud apace,
> The *water-wraith* was shrieking ;
> And in the scowl of heaven each face
> Grew dark as they were speaking."

But, according to Jamieson, this use of *wraith* is incorrect, *wraith* answering rather to the English *ghost.*

The *Seer* might be illustrated from many sources, as from Scott's *Legend of Montrose*, &c. A belief in *second sight* lingered late in Scotland, especially in the Highlands and the Isles—that is, amongst the Gaels. "Sawney," writes Addison, "was descended of an ancient family renowned for their skill in prognostics ; most of his ancestors were *second-sighted*, and his mother but narrowly escaped for a witch." This faculty was a power of discerning what was distant or future, just as it was or would be ; it could see through the curtains of space and time. See Dr. Johnson's account of it in his *Journey to the Hebrides*.

The ring they ride.—A ring was suspended, not tightly fastened, but so that it could easily be detached, from a horizontal beam resting on two upright posts. The players rode at full speed through the arch-way thus made, and as they went under, passed their lance-points, or aimed at passing them, through the ring, and so bore it off. (See Ellis's *Brand's Popular Antiquities*, just re-edited by Mr. Hazlitt.) Brand quotes from the *King of Denmark's Welcome*, 1606 : "On Monday, being the 4th day of August, it pleased our Kings Majestie himself in person, and the King's Majestie of Denmarke likewise in person, and divers others of his estate, to *runne at the ring* in the Tilt-yard at Greenwich, when the King of Denmarke approved to all judgements that majestie is never unaccompanied with vertue ; for there, in the presence of all his beholders, he tooke the ring fower severall times, and would I thinke have done the like four score times, had he runne so many courses."

St. 7. See Chambers's *Book of Days*—a most valuable repertory of antiquarian and other information—vol. i. 623-5 : "An old ' guide' at Roslin used to tell how when any evil or death was about to befall one of them [the Sinclairs] 'The chaipel aye appeared on fire the nicht afore.'" See also some account, with wood-cut sketches, of the "Apprentice's Pillar ; " compare st. 10.

With candle, with book, and with knell.—The priest in *Hamlet* (V. i. 257) speaks of the "bringing home of bell and burial," and below :

> "We should profane the service of the dead
> To sing a *requiem* and such rest to her
> As to peace-parted souls."

Romeo and Juliet :

> "All things that we ordained festival
> Turn from their office to black funeral ;

> Our instruments to melancholy bells ;
> Our wedding cheer to a sad burial feast ;
> Our solemn hymns to sullen dirges change," &c.

A Mayden's Song for her dead Lover (apud Brand) :

> " Come, you whose Loves are dead,
>   And whilst I sing,
>   Weepe, and wing
>   Every hand and every head ;
>   Bind with cypress and sad ewe
>   Ribbands black and *candles* blue ;
>   For him that was of men most true."

Dunbar's *Will of Maister Andro' Kennedy*—a reckless parody :

> " I will no priestis for to sing
>   Dies illæ,* dies iræ,
>   Nor yet no bellis for to ring,
>   Sicut solet semper fieri ;

> " But a bagpipe to play a spring,
>   Et unum alewisp ante me,
>   Instead of torches for to bring
>   Quatuor lagenas cervisiæ."

that is, " four flagons, or pots of beer."

With the last line but one compare in the *Tempest* :

> " Sea-nymphs lonely ring his knell—
>   Hark ! now I hear them,
>   Ding, dong, bell ! "

Where is Roslin ? Where Hawthornden ? Has the latter place any other poetical associations besides those which this ballad gives it ?

(iv.) In the next place the question of Prosody or of Rhythm might receive consideration. What is the metrical structure of *Rosabelle ?* How many accents are there in each line, and how do they fall, and is there any variety of fall ? Or, otherwise, how many syllables are there, and which are ordinarily accentuated, which extra-ordinarily ? How many rhyme-sounds are there in each stanza, and how often does each one occur, and in what order ? How does *Rosabelle* differ in this respect from the ordinary ballad-measure ? What is meant by *alliteration ?* Are there instances of it in *Rosabelle ?* All these and such questions may be answered by a little careful observation with but

---

* *Qu.* illa.

little assistance. And surely they are well worth studying and answering. Prosody is in poetry pretty much what Thorough-bass is in music. The real student will not be content to hear sweet sounds without inquiring somewhat as to how they are produced. The different measures in poetry are like the various musical instruments. Poetry, too, has its " trumpet's loud clangour," its flute for dying lovers, and " warbling lute " to whisper their dirge ; its " sharp violins," its organ-notes that " inspire holy love and wing their heavenly ways " up to the choirs of heaven.

Along, then, with those particular questions on the metre of *Rosabelle* might be combined some attention to the general subject of metre. In what are called classical schools, the ancient—the Latin and Greek —systems might be contrasted with the modern. What is the fundamental difference ? The youngest pair of eyes would easily notice some differences. Why is Rhyme agreeable to the ear ? It might be noticed how some nations have been satisfied with the recurrence of the same vowel sound, while others have desired a completer unison. What are the dangers of rhyme ? Milton's statement of them might be quoted, and illustrated from Spenser and other poets. What is the charm of Blank verse ? Might *Rosabelle* have been written in blank verse ? Could *Paradise Lost* have been effectively written in the metre of *Rosabelle ?* From such questions—and let reasons for the answers made them be given—it might be deduced that there is some profound connection between the form and the spirit of the poem— that the measure is not a mere accident, but the natural and proper vehicle of the thought.

> " So every spirit, as it is most pure
> And hath in it the more of heavenly light,
> So it the fairer bodie doth procure
> To habit in, and it more fairely dight
> With chearful grace and amiable sight ;
> For of the soule the bodie forme doth take ;
> For soul is forme, and doth the bodie make."

Most important in this high respect is the study of metrical form. Metres are the fit costumes of the various moods of the poetical spirit ; they are the figures which that mighty plastic force moulds, as it were, with its own hands.

IV.

(v.) And now something might be said about the author of our poem. Information given about an author before his works or some work of his is read, is not likely to be very interesting or useful. Handbooks of literature should not be read before something is known of the literature dealt with. What is the use of sign-posts, if one is not in, or is quite ignorant of, the country to whose roads they belong? But, having read *Rosabelle*, we may not unnaturally wish to know something of him who wrote it. Do we not always long to learn who the beauty is who charms us?—under what sweet influences she grew to her present sovereign loveliness?—what things and what persons have enjoyed the regard of her fair eyes? We cannot indeed interpret the secret of her fairness; but yet we would know what we may of its budding and its growth. Who, then, was the author of *Rosabelle*? What else did he write? When, and where did he live? What were the chief impulses of his times?

Is there anything in this little poem which connects it with its times?—or could it have been written at any time, and at any place? Suppose nothing was known of its origin, could anything be gathered from itself? Are there any features that might reveal the secret of its birth? Is there any tell-tale likeness? At first sight the poem may seem to carry us back into distant ages. The first stanza pictures us a minstrel in some old hall, singing and playing after the manner of his craft. "Feats of arms" were the great delight of men then; but now he sings not to men, but to "ladies gay," no martial trumpet-clanging triumphant story, but a soft-toned lay with a sad ending. Then there occur in the song, as we have seen, long extinct manners and customs and superstitions. Is, then, *Rosabelle* a voice from the old ages? Is it really an ancient ballad? A more careful study will show us signs of elaboration and refinement such as do not characterize genuine balladry. In the sense in which we speak of a "historical novel," it may be called a historical ballad. It is but an echo of these old days which it professes to portray. It is but a flash of "summer" lightning.

What age was it, then, that cared enough for those far-away times to try to reproduce them in literature?—that lent an ear to those voices that had seemed to die away in the distance and be forgotten? When did the old halls rise again from their ashes, and the minstrel once more strike his strings in them, and the "ladies gay" bow their fair heads and weep with eyes that had been lustreless for many a long day? When did old fancies and beliefs re-awaken, and bind men's minds with a fresh fascination?

From a study, then, of *Rosabelle* by itself, without any external help, much might be learnt of the circumstances of its appearing. We may learn the general character—or at least one highly significant characteristic—of the age when it appeared. To find the date of such an age as could have produced it we must turn to history. This necessity shows us how highly important it is to keep together, as far as possible, the studies of Literature and History. Do we really believe what is so perpetually repeated, that the literature of a nation reflects its life? Then why do we so obstinately put asunder the studies of History and Literature? Why do we not permit them to support and uphold each other? Even in schools, certainly with the higher pupils, this unhappy estrangement should as far as possible be ended by making the scholar in his History work study the same period to which his English Literature lessons belong. In this way a considerable economy of labour may be effected ; and certainly a much more thorough knowledge of what is studied—both of History and of Literature—may be gained.

V.

(vi.) And now it is time that we should turn to matters of Grammar. Grammar consists of two main parts—Accidence and Syntax. Let us accordingly observe first the inflections—the word-forms—that occur in our poem, and then the relation in which the words, both those that are inflected and those that are not, stand to each other—first each word, or each noteworthy word, by itself, and then in connection with its fellow words.

a. What "part of speech" is *that* in stanza 1, *still* in st. 11, *pale* in st. 10, &c. ? But first of all, this phrase "part of speech" should be clearly understood, and equivalents given for it. It is, in fact, a bit of old English which has lingered on in our language ; as if, though we have so completely changed our costume in other respects, we should still "slash" our sleeves, or deck our modern hats with a fine feather. We do not speak now of the "French *speech*" or "the study of *speech."* In what sense do we still retain the word? Then what is signified by "part"? Strictly, we ought to say, "To what part of speech does such a word belong?" Let, then, this phrase be made quite clear. Then how is the pupil to discover what "part of speech" any word is? Can he do so by looking at the word by itself? Are there cases where its form may guide him? Or may the grammatical definition of a word vary with its context? How many "parts of speech" may *still*, for instance, be? Let similar instances be quoted.

What part of the verb is *listen*, is *mourns*, is *cross* in st. 4, is *chide* in st. 6, *buried* in st. 12, &c.? These and such questions cannot be answered without an amount of care and attention which for a younger pupil would be considerable ; probably with regard to some of them he would need a helping hand. What case is *thee* in *rest thee*, and in *stay thee?* Compare such phrases as "he sat him down," "he lies him down," "he hies him home," "I followed me close" (Shaks. 1 *Henry IV.* II. iv. 240), &c. How are the pronouns in all these cases to be explained? Here, too, of course the student must be assisted ; but by all means let him feel, before he is so, what the difficulty is. What "case" is *Roslin's?* What does the apostrophe stand for? What wrong interpretation was once current, and is preserved in the *Book of Common Prayer?* Why was it wrong? What does the apostrophe stand for in *sheath'd?* Does it then always stand for *e?* Mention, with instances, other letters and letter-combinations which it occasion-ally represents. Then what is the effect of adding *ed* or *'d* to *sheath?* Or is there more than one effect that may be so produced ?—that is, is *sheathed* always a "preterite"? In what other way may a preterite be formed? Then the terms for the two methods of forming the preterite might be given, for they would now be felt to be useful. Do any verbs avail themselves of both methods? Let the pupil make as good a list as he can from his own observations. Are there any such verbs in *Rosa-belle?* Have any verbs two forms of the "strong" preterite? Is there difference in our present usage between *sang* and *sung*, *rang* and *rung* (see st. 13), &c.? In such a phrase as "he has seen," what is the tense? What part of the verb is *seen?* Is it correct to say "he has come"? What is the tense in "he did go"? What part of the verb is *go?* What part of the verb is *hold* in "doth hold" (st. 12)? What part is *doth?* What difference is there between *doth* and *does*, *hath* and *has*, &c.? In some such manner let the pupil be stimulated to observe and think for himself, and to arrange his thoughts and observations.   Many of these questions the pupil may be able to answer by the analogy of other languages—of German or French or Greek or Latin.

β. Now let the relations of the words to each other and in the sentence be considered.   What part of its sentence is *listen ?*   What part is *feats ?* &c.   If the terms *subject, predicate, object* are not thoroughly understood, let them be discussed.   The syllables *sub, ob, pre, ject* occur in a great many English words.   What is the force of each one ? Perhaps if the student made himself short lists of words in which they occur, he might, by comparing the words of each list together, gather that force ; and such an attempt at induction would be most valuable. *Dicate* might prove perplexing ; *indicate* might not lend help enough. So the pupil might turn to his dictionary ; or he might be told that *preach* is in fact but a corrupted form of *predicate*, and *preacher* of *predicator*, therefore *predicate* = preachment, or statement.   He must then learn how the use of the term is limited in grammar—how the " preachment " in grammatical usage is not the whole sermon, but only a certain essential part of it.   And so with regard to the terms *subject* and *object* as used in grammar, he must be instructed in their limitedness.   The subject is not the whole text, but only a certain part of it ; the object is, in fact, part of the preachment or predicate in the broadest sense of that term.   Now let the terms be applied to various sentences in *Rosabelle*.   How many sentences are there in stanza 3 ?   What are their various subjects?   What are the various predicates?   Which sentence contains an object ?   The general absence of inflections in English nouns, in the present state of our language, makes this sort of " parsing " something less of a mere mechanical process than it is apt to be where certain endings at once discover the " case."   Then what part of the third sentence is the last line ?   What part of the first is " with white " ?   What part of the second " to inch and rock " ?   In stanza 4 how many sentences are there ?   What relation do the words " last night " hold to the predicate?   In stanza 11 what part of its sentence is the clause—

" When fate is nigh
The lordly line of high Saint Clair ?"

&c. &c.   This analysis can be made as difficult or as easy as the teacher wishes.   Such questions as have just been suggested may admit of a ready solution ; but from time to time there will arise cases demanding the nicest delicacy, the most adroit management.

(vii.) It may often be well to submit the passage which is the lesson-subject to the formal processes of logic, which is the grammar of thought, as what is ordinarily called grammar is the grammar of words. The terms *subject* and *predicate* may be used in their logical sense ; the thought of the poem carefully examined ; the passage reduced to a series of propositions, and the proofs of these, where it is possible, thrown into a syllogistic form. Of course a purely narrative piece such as *Rosabelle*—a ballad—is not so well adapted for this treatment as one that is argumentative or quasi-argumentative, as, for instances, many passages of Wordsworth, of Shelley, of Pope, of Milton : yet even here there are parts where this method might be usefully followed. Why are "ladies gay" especially to listen to this lay ? What is the *major premiss* of the 1st stanza? What is that of the 4th stanza? What is the *conclusion* of the 5th and 6th stanzas ? This conclusion, it may be noticed, is, in accordance with the bold abrupt character of the poem, left to the imagination of the reader. It is, in fact, expressed by the impatient hurrying gesture which, so vivid is the picture, one sees Rosabelle making. If our thoughts are in danger of being obscure and confused until they are embodied in words—if our reason may grow morbid or deformed unless we give it plenty of air and exercise, then surely it is well to insist often on the transcription of those thoughts ; it is well to bring reason out into the light of the day, that any threatened malady or distortion may be averted. Surely it must be a good thing to make a student observe what his writer takes for granted and what use he makes of what he so takes, and so, by an obvious application, to bethink himself of what are the general propositions on which his own opinions and actions proceed.

Of course all terms new to the pupil must be closely investigated before he is allowed to employ them. Let him, as has been suggested above, be made sensible of this need before they are put into his mouth. Let him see that the word is created for the thing, not the thing for the word. This advice is not perhaps so superfluous as it might seem. Has no one, for instance, when the wonderful nomenclature in which the ancient scholiasts and grammarians delighted has been prematurely imposed on his memory, been left half in doubt whether the figure was made for the term, or the term for the figure ?—

whether Aposiopesis, Anacolouthon, Hyperbaton, Metonymy produced the poet, or the poet them? Has no one ever thought of these figures as at least influencing the writer, surrounding him with their various enticements, and winning a place in his heart? . Has one always regarded them as natural and spontaneous forms of speech that at a later period were to be classified and labelled by the Priscians and Quintilians? For the words *logic, syllogism, premiss*, &c. some such processes might be applied to them as has been suggested above for *subject* and *predicate*.

(viii.) The words of *Rosabelle* might now be considered with reference to their derivation and origin. With the assistance of a fair dictionary (*Chambers's Etymological English Dictionary* will serve well enough), the pupil might classify these words, or a certain portion of them, according to their etymology. He would soon find that our language consists of many various elements,—that in a most catholic spirit it has enriched its vocabulary from all accessible sources ; but he would also find that there is amongst these elements one that far surpasses all the others in its influence on our vocabulary—so far that it might well be inferred to be the basis of this composite language— to be, in fact, the original language itself. Its numerical superiority would suggest and illustrate this great fundamental fact ; other considerations, as the character, not only the number, of the words forming a great part of our language, and the study of English Grammar, would support and establish what that numerical superiority suggests. The pupil would see that, in whatever respects it may have changed, the language he reads and talks is really that which King Alfred read and talked, really that which some four centuries before Alfred's time was brought over from Northern Germany into this island, then called Britannia, to become its one permanent language, and from it to be spread to all the ends of the earth. This one great fact cannot be too much insisted upon, because it is so common to speak of English as a fusion of several languages. Nothing could be less true. A man does not cease to be master of his house because he entertains many guests. The Anglian invader did not drive the old Keltic tenant out of the house when he entered himself upon possession, but permitted him to live, in a lower capacity no doubt, where he had lived before; whether he would or not, he has received within his precincts many a stout foreigner who for a time perhaps had seemed to unseat and suppress him ; Danes and Norman-Frenchmen have rudely occupied the daïs of his hall, and he has been fain to eat at the lower table ; but yet the house has remained his through all these turbulent visitations : the tyranny has soon overpast, and the rightful master been seen sitting as of old at the head of his board. All this strange eventful history may be well illustrated from *Rosabelle*. It may be seen what English is, and to what influences it has with greater or less effect been exposed.

What other words have we in English cognate with *tell ?* What is the meaning of the termination of *lovely ?* Compare the German *lieblich*. In what relation does English stand to German ? What European language is yet nearer akin than German is ? What is the meaning of *to-day ?* Compare

> " Time to think on it then ; for thou'll be twenty *to weeäk*,"

in Tennyson's *Northern Farmer, New Style*. Compare also *to-morrow*. What is the meaning of *fore* in *forebode ?* Mention other words in which *fore* has the same meaning. Has it the same in *forego ?* in *therefore ?* in *before ?* What German prefix answers to it ? What is the derivation of *lonely ?* What of *moonbeam ?* Compare Lucretius' "tela diei," &c.

The Norman-French influence is, it may be noticed, strongly represented in this poem. The heroine's very name is Norman-French. "Haughty," " gay," "feat," " arms," " note," " deign," " sire," "chief," &c. are all highly significant Norman-French words. What is meant by *gentle lady ?* What is the etymon of *pinnet ?* of *battlement ?* What had battlements to do with churches ? What is the derivation of *chapelle ?* How is it that the *c* in *candle* is not softened in like manner ?

Ladies gay.—It is worth noticing that "ladies" is a native English word ; "dame," though it yet lives in the second " m " of "ma'am," did not finally supersede it. "Gay" was given us by the Norman-French. How much of deep interest do these two words suggest ! They might be treated in a history of the English language as a happily representative phrase.

Feat is etymologically the same word with *fact*. It might be useful to collect instances of similar pairs, as royal, regal, &c.—the one preserving almost intact the original Latin form, the other presenting that form all modified and corrupted.

Then there are ecclesiastical Latin words of interest : *dirge* (as we still speak of the *Te Deum*, the *Magnificat*, &c.) ; *sacristy* (observe the change in the first part, as it appears in *sexton*) ; *altar.*

Inch takes us back to the pre-English period. It is a Keltic word for island, or *iland*, as we ought to write (*isle* is quite a distinct word). The *Atlas* will show it attached to certain islands in the estuary of the Forth. Off the western coast of Ireland it appears in the dialectic form, *Inis.*

Firth, again, gives us a trace of the Northmen who broke in such fierce storms upon our sea-borders in the eighth, ninth, and tenth centuries. It is radically the same word as *ford* in Deptford and other names found on our coasts and up our rivers ; a different word from the *ford* in such inland names as Oxford, Bedford, &c. It is, in fact, *fiord*, perhaps a congener of the Latin *fretum*, &c.

And let us not forget that proper names, too, have, or have had, their meaning. To us they often seem mere symbols ; their voices are altogether meaningless ; but it was not always so. Every proper noun was once a common noun. Thus *Ravensheugh* denoted the raven's crag or steep. Compare *haughs* in Wordsworth's *Yarrow Unvisited :*

> "There's Galla Water, Leader *Haughs*,
> Both lying right before us ;"

and the old ballad *Willy drowned in Yarrow :*

> "O Leader *haughs* are wide and braid,
> And Yarrow *haughs* are bonny."

The composition of *Rosabelle* is obvious. *Roslin* is Keltic in both its parts : *Ros* is the Gaelic *ros*, a headland ; it occurs in the names *Ross* in Herefordshire, in Mont*rose*, *Ros*common, *Ross*neath, and in *Ross*-berg, Monte *Rosa*, *Rose*nlaui, in Switzerland. *Lin* is perhaps the Keltic *linn ;* compare King's *Lynn*, *Lin*coln, Dub*lin*, *Lin*lithgow. (See Taylor's *Words and Places.*) The *den* in Dry*den* and in Haw-thorn*den* is the same as that in Tenter*den*, and perhaps in Ar*den*nes and as the *dean* in Hazel*dean*. It is the oldest English (what is commonly called Anglo-Saxon) *dena* or *den*, a valley ;" we still use the word in a special sense—for a wild beast's lair. *Saint Clair* is the older form of the surname Sinclair ; so Saint Mawr of Seymour : compare the pronunciation of St. John. How could a family claim saintship for itself.

at least in its name ?   Perhaps in much the same way as in still older
ages men called themselves after Woden, and Thor, and other
primitive godheads.

The words must be looked at not only with reference to their origin,
but more particularly in respect of their meanings and of the meaning
each one bears in the passage immediately studied. Of course, in
deciding what the meaning is, the etymology will often be of para-
mount—it will generally be of some importance ; but a word sometimes wanders far away from the sense to which it was born, and
forms for itself quite new connections. The bare derivation of such
words as *villain, pagan, tawdry, assassin, bayonet,* &c. would not be
enough to explain the words to us. To connect a word's present sense
or senses with its origin will frequently require no little ingenuity ;
sometimes no little knowledge also.   There are, perhaps, no conspicuous specimens of this class of difficulties in *Rosabelle ;* but it
must not be forgotten. Certainly, whether it is advisable to search
after derivations or not, definitions must be perpetually asked for.
The furnishing them will often tax the pupil's powers of intelligent
expression to the utmost. There can be no better exercise for him
than to put into a lucid and complete shape the idea which is hovering
about his mind indistinct and formless. *Rosabelle* is easy in this
respect ; but let the pupil say—and let him express himself in full-
formed sentences, not by mere chips and fragments, by stammering
out some nounless verb or verbless noun—what is the exact force of
feat, of *panoply,* of *sable,* of *sable shroud* (a phrase borrowed from
Milton's *Lycidas,* l. 22), of *buttress,* of *pale,* of *gifted,* &c. A pupil's
knowledge is probably not of much value if he cannot reproduce it.
It may be truly said of him in one sense,

" Scire tuum nihil est nisi te scire hoc sciat alter."

What is meant by a *metaphor,* by a *simile,* by a *personification ?*
These are very important terms, because they represent ways of
speaking that are common in all languages, and not only common, but
universal. Nearly all words are, or were originally, metaphorical ;
though in a vast number the metaphorical colour has entirely faded
away. We talk poetry as unconsciously as Molière's immortal *parvenu*
talked prose. The word *metaphor,* which is Greek, corresponds as
nearly as possible to the Latin word *translation,* meta = trans,

phor = lation.* In what sense is a metaphor a translation? Now what metaphors occur in *Rosabelle ?* Mr. Abbott, in his *Shakespearian Grammar*, makes an excellent suggestion as to the treatment of metaphors, to this effect, that they should be "expanded." Thus such a phrase as "the ships plough the sea," in its expanded form becomes "As the plough turns up the land, so the ship acts on the sea." Then what is the difference between a *metaphor* and a *simile ?* Are there any *personifications* in *Rosabelle*, &c.?

VI.

(ix.) The subject-matter of the poem and the language of it having been carefully studied, some attempt at a criticism of it might be encouraged, at least with more advanced students. "They mistake the nature of criticism," says Dryden, in the Preface to his *State of Innocence*, "who think its business is to find fault." All the word means is a judgment—a verdict; judgments and verdicts are not always of condemnation. Now what are the merits of this imitation ballad? Perhaps its supreme virtue is the simple vigour with which its pictures are drawn. There is no personal intrusion; there are no vain cries and groans; there is no commenting and explaining. The pictures tell their own story, and tell it so vividly and thrillingly that nothing more is needed. The intensity of the piece would be destroyed by any words of commiseration. The deepest feelings are not the most garrulous. When the frightful news reached Macduff that his castle was surprised, his "wife and babes savagely slaughtered," he pulled his hat over his brows, and gave sorrow no words: a shallower grief would have "played the woman with its eyes and braggart with its tongue." This is the true secret of what power the old ballad poetry possesses. The writers conceive their situations so forcibly that they cannot indulge in any idle moanings; they cannot play with their agony; their sympathy is too profound for melodious sighs; their hands are so paralyzed with woe that they cannot tear their hair and beat their breasts. There is something awful in this plainness. You see the face of Necessity herself; you are spell-bound by her

---

* See Quintilian's *Inst. Orat.* VIII. vi. 4: "Incipiamus igitur ab eo [tropo], qui cum frequentissimus est tum longe pulcherrimus, *translatione* dico, quæ μεταφορά Græce vocatur." See also Cic. *de Orat.* iii. 38.

terrible eyes; you are raised beyond the vanity of tears in her tremendous presence. No, you cannot weep; " but yet the pity of it, Iago ! O Iago, the pity of it, Iago ! "

There is a certain statuesque force in these old scenes. Would any one put a scroll of written agony in Laocoön's mouth? Shall Niobe cry aloud," Me miseram ? " The figures are enough ; voices, sobs, shrieks are not wanted.

What can be more effective than that simple contrast which the last stanzas give between the two pictures already so vividly drawn ?— between the repose and the tossing, the stillness of the chapel and the wild sea-murmurs—the priestly services and the tumultuous ritual of Nature? With these lines the tenth canto of Tennyson's *In Memoriam* might be well compared or contrasted. Still more readily do they bring to one's mind the following exquisite lines, which harp on the same fancy, in a much different mood, and amidst different circumstances :—

> " The dismal yew and cypress tall
>   Weigh o'er the churchyard lone,
> Where rest our friends and fathers all
>   Beneath the funeral stone.
> In holy ground, our kindred sleep ;
>   O early lost, o'er thee
> No sorrowing friend shall ever weep,
> No stranger bend the knee.
>   Mocherna lorn am I !
> Hoarse dashing rolls the salt sea wave
> Over our perished darling's grave."

VII.

(x.) I have only further to suggest, that before passing on from one poem to another a rapid recapitulation of what has been said or done might be advisable. A careful paraphrase might now be asked for ; the pupil would find it good to note the difference between this his riper and better instructed work and his own unassisted effort : that is, the abstract which was recommended to be done by way of preparation. Once more the poem might be recited ; and, if elocution does indeed depend upon intelligence and comprehension, then in this matter too there ought to be seen a great improvement in the style in which the recital is executed.

Of course every piece studied cannot be explored in this minute manner ; but certainly occasional pieces might be so. As a rule, any one of the lines of study that have been suggested might be pursued singly, or at all events principally, and the others subordinated to it.

Of course much more may be added to what has been said. In the above essay many points of interest have been left untouched. The aim of these remarks has been to be suggestive, not exhaustive. But perhaps enough has been said to show to what educational account a not extraordinary piece of English writing may be turned. To the humble-minded and thoughtful teacher a common English song may prove as mind-stirring as " the meanest flower that blows " to the true poet ; and no teacher is likely to succeed in his great work, when his own mind is not stirred and excited by whatever is the subject of his instruction. After some such lesson as that just attempted, proper curtailments and expansions having been made, will not the intelligence of the pupil have been thoroughly exercised?—will not his previously acquired knowledge have been called into use and arranged better ?—will he not have added something to that better ordered store ?—will he not, while awaking to a pleasant consciousness of what the power of his mind is, and what apparent entanglements it can unravel if properly trained and directed, learn also how much there is that is beyond his reach, and how, of what lies within his reach, the better part may not be won " without dust and heat : "—learn the great lesson which concerns not only his schoolboy days, but all the days of his life, that there is nothing worthy to be achieved without sincere, undaunted, never-wearying industry ?

LONGER ENGLISH POEMS.

LONGER ENGLISH POEMS.

SPENSER.

PROTHALAMION.

CALME was the day, and through the trembling ayre
Sweete-breathing Zephyrus did softly play,
A gentle spirit, that lightly did delay
Hot Titans beames, which then did glyster fayre,
When I (whom sullein care,   5
Through discontent of my long fruitlesse stay
In Princes Court, and expectation vayne
Of idle hopes, which still doe fly away,
Like empty shaddowes, did afflict my brayne,)
Walkt forth to ease my payne   10
Along the shoare of silver streaming Themmes;
Whose rutty Bancke, the which his Riuer hemmes,
Was paynted all with variable flowers,
And all the meades adornd with daintie gemmes
Fit to decke maydens bowres   15
And crowne their Paramours
Against the Brydale day, which is not long.
   Sweete Themmes! runne softly, till I end my Song.

There, in a Meadow, by the Riuers side,
A Flocke of Nymphes I chaunced to espy,   20
All louely Daughters of the Flood thereby,
With goodly greenish locks, all loose vntyde,
As each had bene a Bryde;
And each one had a little wicker basket,
Made of fine twigs, entrayled curiously,   25
In which they gathered flowers to fill their flasket,

B

And with fine Fingers cropt full feateously
The tender stalkes on hye.
Of euery sort, which in that Meadow grew.
They gathered some, the Violet pallid blew,   30
The little Dazie, that at euening closes,
The virgin Lillie, and the Primrose trew,
With store of vermeil Roses,
To decke their Bridegromes posies
Against the Brydale day, which was not long.   35
  Sweete Themmes! runne softly, till I end my Song.

With that I saw two Swannes of goodly hewe
Come softly swimming downe along the Lee;
Two fairer Birds I yet did neuer see;
The snow, which doth the top of Pindus strew,   40
Did never whiter shew;
Nor Joue himselfe, when he a Swan would be,
For loue of Leda, whiter did appeare;
Yet Leda was (they say) as white as he,
Yet not so white as these, nor nothing neare; -   45
So purely white they were,
That euen the gentle streame, the which them bare,
Seem'd foule to them, and bad his billowes spare
To wet their silken feathers, least they might
Soyle their fayre plumes with water not so fayre,   50
And marre their beauties bright,
That shone as heavens light,
Against their Brydale day, which was not long.
  Sweet Themmes! runne softly, till I end my Song.

Eftsoones the Nymphes, which now had Flowers their fill,   55
Ran all in haste to see that siluer brood,
As they came floating on the Christal Flood;
Whom when they sawe, they stood amazed still
Their wondring eyes to fill;
Them seem'd they never saw a sight so fayre,   60
Of Fowles so louely, that they sure did deeme
Them heavenly borne, or to be that same payre
Which through the Skie draw Venus silver Teeme;
For sure they did not seeme
To be begot of any earthly Seede,   65
But rather Angels, or of Angels brecde;
Yet were they bred of Somers-heat, they say,

In sweetest Season, when each Flower and weede
The earth did fresh aray;
So fresh they seem'd as day,   70
Euen as their Brydale day, which was not long.
    Sweete Themmes! runne softly, till I end my Song.

Then forth they all out of their baskets drew
Great store of Flowers, the honour of the field,
That to the sense did fragrant odours yeild,   75
All which upon those goodly Birds they threw
And all the Waues did strew,
That like old Peneus Waters they did seeme,
When downe along by pleasant Tempes shore,
Scattred with Flowers, through Thessaly they streeme,   80
That they appeare, through Lillies plenteous store,
Like a Brydes Chamber flore.
Two of those Nymphes, meane while, two Garlands bound
·Of freshest Flowres which in that Mead they found,
The which presenting all in trim Array,   85
Their snowie Foreheads therewithall they crownd,
Whil'st one did sing this Lay,
Prepar'd against that Day,
Against their Brydale day, which was not long:
    (Sweete Themmes! runne softly, till I end my Song.)   90

" Ye gentle Birdes! the worlds faire ornament,
" And heauens glorie, whom this happie hower
" Doth leade unto your lovers blissfull bower,
" Joy may you haue, and gentle hearts content
" Of your loues couplement;   95
" And let faire Venus, that is Queene of loue,
" With her heart-quelling Sonne vpon you smile,
" Whose smile, they say, hath vertue to remoue
" All Loues dislike, and friendships faultie guile
" For euer to assoile.   100
" Let endlesse Peace your steadfast hearts accord,
" And blessed Plentie wait vpon your bord;
" And let your bed with pleasures chast abound,
" That fruitfull issue may to you afford,
" Which may your foes confound,   105
" And make your joyes redound
" Vpon your Brydale day, which is not long."
    Sweet Themmes! runne softlie, till I end my Song.

So ended she : and all the rest around
To her redoubled that her vndersong,   110
Which said their brydale daye should not be long :
And gentle Eccho from the neighbour ground
Their accents did resound.
So forth those joyous Birdes did passe along,
Adowne the Lee, that to them murmurde low,   115
As he would speake, but that he lackt a tong,
Yet did by signes his glad affection show,
Making his streame run slow.
And all the foule which in his flood did dwell
Gan flock about these twaine, that did excell   120
The rest, so far as Cynthia doth shend
The lesser starres. So they, enranged well,
Did on those two attend,
And their best seruice lend
Against their wedding day, which was not long.   125
   Sweete Themmes ! run softly, till I end my Song.

At length they all to mery London came,
To mery London, my most kyndly Nurse,
That to me gaue this Lifes first natiue sourse,
Though from another place I take my name,   130
An house of auncient fame.
There when they came, whereas those bricky towres
The which on Themmes brode aged backe doe ryde,
Where now the studious Lawyers haue their bowers,
There whylome wont the Templer Knights to byde,   135
Till they decayd through pride ;
Next whereunto there standes a stately place,
Where oft I gayned giftes and goodly grace
Of that great Lord, which therein wont to dwell,
Whose want too well now feeles my freendles case ;   140
But ah ! here fits not well
Olde woes, but joyes, to tell
Against the bridale daye, which is not long.
   Sweete Themmes ! runne softly, till I end my Song.

Yet therein now doth lodge a noble Peer,   145
Great Englands glory, and the Worlds wide wonder,
Whose dreadfull name late through all Spaine did thunder,
And Hercules two pillors standing neere
Did make to quake and feare.

Faire branch of Honor, flower of Chevalrie !   150
That fillest England with thy triumphes fame,
Joy haue thou of thy noble victorie,
And endlesse happinesse of thine owne name
That promiseth the same,
That through thy prowesse and victorious armes   155
Thy country may be freed from forraine harmes ;
And great Elisaes glorious name may ring
Through al the world, fil'd with thy wide Alarmes,
Which some braue muse may sing
To ages following   160
Vpon the Brydale day, which is not long.
   Sweete Themmes ! runne softly, till I end my Song.

From those high Towers this noble Lord issuing,
Like Radiant Hesper, when his golden hayre
In th' Ocean billowes he hath bathed fayre,   165
Descended to the Riuers open vewing,
With a great traine ensuing.
Aboue the rest were goodly to bee seene
Two gentle Knights of louely face and feature,
Beseeming well the bower of anie Queene,   170
With gifts of wit and ornaments of nature
Fit for so goodly stature,
That like the twins of Joue they seem'd in sight,
Which decke the Bauldricke of the Heauens bright.
They two, forth pacing to the Riuers side,   175
Receiued those two faire Brides, their Loues delight ;
Which, at th' appointed tyde,
Each one did make his Bryde
Against their Brydale day, which is not long.
   Sweete Themmes ! runne softly, till I end my Song.   180

MILTON.

HYMN ON THE NATIVITY.

I.

THIS is the month, and this the happy morn,
Wherein the Son of Heav'ns eternal King,
Of wedded Maid and Virgin mother born,
Our great redemption from above did bring;
For so the holy Sages once did sing :   5
   That he our deadly forfeit should release,
And with his Father work us a perpetual peace.

II.

That glorious form, that light unsufferable,
And that far-beaming blaze of majesty,
Wherwith he wont at Heav'ns high councel-table   10
To sit the midst of Trinal Unity,
He laid aside; and, here with us to be,
   Forsook the courts of everlasting day,
And chose with us a darksom house of mortal clay.

III.

Say, heav'nly Muse, shall not thy sacred vein   15
Afford a present to the Infant God?
Hast thou no vers, no hymn, or solemn strein,
To welcom him to this his new abode
Now while the Heav'n by the sun's team untrod
   Hath took no print of the approching light,   20
And all the spangled host keep watch in squadrons bright?

IV.

See how from far upon the eastern rode
The star-led Wisards haste with Odours sweet;
O run, prevent them with thy humble ode,
And lay it lowly at his blessed feet;   25
Have thou the honour first thy Lord to greet,
    And joyn thy voice unto the angel quire,
From out his secret altar toucht with hallow'd fire.

THE HYMN.

I.

It was the winter wilde,
While the Heav'n-born childe   30
    All meanly wrapt in the rude manger lies;
Nature in aw to him
Had doff't her gawdy trim,
    With her great Master so to sympathize;
It was no season then for her   35
To wanton with the sun her lusty paramour.

II.

Onely with speeches fair
She woo's the gentle Air
    To hide her guilty front with innocent snow,
And on her naked shame,   40
Pollute with sinfull blame,
    The saintly veil of maiden white to throw :
Confounded, that her Makers eyes
Should look so near upon her foul deformities.

III.

But he, her fears to cease,   45
Sent down the meek-eyed Peace;
    She, crown'd with olive green, came softly sliding
Down through the turning sphear,
His ready harbinger,
    With turtle wing the amorous clouds dividing,   50
And, waving wide her mirtle wand,
She strikes a universall peace through sea and land.

IV.

No war, or battails sound,
Was heard the world around;
  The idle spear and shield were high up hung;   55
The hooked chariot stood
Unstain'd with hostile blood;
  The trumpet spake not to the armed throng;
And kings sate still with awfull eye,
As if they surely knew their sovran Lord was by.   60

V.

But peacefull was the night
Wherin the Prince of Light
  His raign of peace upon the earth began;
The windes, with wonder whist,
Smoothly the waters kist,   65
  Whispering new joyes to the milde ocean,
Who now hath quite forgot to rave,
While birds of calm sit brooding on the charmed wave.

VI.

The stars, with deep amaze,
Stand fixt in stedfast gaze,   70
  Bending one way their pretious influence,
And will not take their flight
For all the morning light
  Or Lucifer that often warn'd them thence;
But in their glimmering orbs did glow,   75
Untill their Lord himself bespake, and bid them go.

VII.

And, though the shady Gloom
Had given day her room,
  The sun himself withheld his wonted speed,
And hid his head for shame,   80
As his inferiour flame
  The new-enlightn'd world no more should need;
He saw a greater sun appear
Then his bright throne or burning axle-tree could bear.

VIII.

The shepherds on the lawn   85
Or ere the point of dawn
  Sate simply chatting in a rustick row;
Full little thought they than
That the mighty Pan
  Was kindly com to live with them below;   90
Perhaps their loves, or else their sheep,
Was all that did their silly thoughts so busie keep,

IX.

When such musick sweet
Their hearts and ears did greet
  As never was by mortall finger strook,   95
Divinely warbled voice
Answering the stringed noise,
  As all their souls in blissfull rapture took;
The air, such pleasure loth to lose,
With thousand echo's still prolongs each heav'nly close.   100

X.

Nature, that heard such sound
Beneath the hollow round
  Of Cynthia's seat the airy region thrilling,
Now was almost won
To think her part was don,   105
  And that her raign had here its last fulfilling;
She knew such harmony alone
Could hold all Heav'n and Earth in happier union.

XI.

At last surrounds their sight
A globe of circular light,   110
  That with long beams the shame-fac't Night array'd;
The helmed Cherubim,
The sworded Seraphim
  Are seen in glittering ranks with wings displaied,
Harping in loud and solemn quire   115
With unexpressive notes to Heav'n's new-born Heir.

XII.

Such musick (as 'tis said)
Before was never made
   But when of old the sons of Morning sung,
While the Creator great   120
His constellations set,
   And the well-ballanc't world on hinges hung,
And cast the dark foundations deep,
And bid the weltring waves their oozy channel keep.

XIII.

Ring out, ye crystall sphears ;   125
Once bless our humane ears
   (If ye have power to touch our senses so),
And let your silver chime
Move in melodious time,
   And let the base of Heav'ns deep organ blow,   130
And with your ninefold harmony
Make up full consort to th' angelike symphony.

XIV.

For, if such holy song
Enwrap our fancy long,
   Time will run back, and fetch the age of Gold ;   135
And speckl'd Vanity
Will sicken soon and die,
   And leprous sin will melt from earthly mould ;
And Hell it self will pass away,
And leave her dolorous mansions to the peering day.   140

XV.

Yea, Truth and Justice then
Will down return to men,
   Orb'd in a rainbow; and, like glories wearing,
Mercy will set between,
Thron'd in celestiall sheen,   145
   With radiant feet the tissued clouds down stearing ;
And Heav'n, as at som festivall,
Will open wide the gates of her high palace hall.

XVI.

But wisest Fate sayes no ;
This must not yet be so ;   150
   The Babe lies yet in smiling infancy,
That on the bitter cross
Must redeem our loss,
   So both himself and us to glorifie ;
Yet first to those ychain'd in sleep   155
The wakefull trump of doom must thunder through the deep

XVII.

With such a horrid clang
As on Mount Sinai rang,
   While the red fire and smouldring clouds out brake ;
The aged Earth, agast,   160
With terrour of that blast,
   Shall from the surface to the center shake ;
When at the worlds last session
The dreadfull Judge in middle air shall spread his throne.

XVIII.

And then at last our bliss   165
Full and perfect is,
   But now begins ; for, from this happy day,
Th' old Dragon under ground,
In straiter limits bound,
   Not half so far casts his usurped sway ;   170
And, wroth to see his kingdom fail,
Swindges the scaly horrour of his foulded tail.

XIX.

The oracles are dumm ;
No voice or hideous humm
   Runs through the arched roof in words deceiving.   175
Apollo from his shrine
Can no more divine,
   With hollow shreik the steep of Delphos leaving.
No nightly trance, or breathed spell,
Inspires the pale-ey'd Priest from the prophetic cell.   180

XX.

The lonely mountains o're
And the resounding shore
   A voice of weeping heard and loud lament;
From haunted spring and dale
Edg'd with poplar pale   185
   The parting Genius is with sighing sent;
With flowre-inwov'n tresses torn
The nimphs in twilight shade of tangled thickets mourn.

XXI.

In consecrated earth,
And on the holy hearth   190
   The Lars and Lemures moan with midnight plaint;
In urns and altars round,
A drear and dying sound
   Affrights the Flamins at their service quaint;
And the chill marble seems to sweat,   195
While each peculiar power forgoes his wonted seat.

XXII.

Peor and Baälim
Forsake their temples dim,
   With that twise batter'd god of Palestine;
And mooned Ashtaroth,   200
Heav'ns queen and mother both,
   Now sits not girt with tapers holy shine;
The Lybic Hammon shrinks his horn;
In vain the Tyrian maids their wounded Thamuz mourn;

XXIII.

And sullen Moloch, fled,   205
Hath left in shadows dred
   His burning idol all of blackest hue;
In vain with cymbals ring
They call the grisly King
   In dismall dance about the furnace blue;   210
The brutish gods of Nile as fast,
Isis, and Orus, and the dog Anubis hast.

XXIV.

Nor is Osiris seen
In Memphian grove or green
   Trampling the unshowr'd grass with lowings loud,   215
Nor can he be at rest
Within his sacred chest ;
   Naught but profoundest hell can be his shroud;
In vain with timbrel'd anthems dark
The sable-stoled sorcerers bear his worshipt ark.   220

XXV.

He feels from Juda's land
The dredded Infant's hand ;
   The rayes of Bethlehem blind his dusky eyn;
Nor all the gods beside
Longer dare abide,   225
   Not Typhon huge ending in snaky twine:
Our Babe, to show his Godhead true,
Can in his swadling bands controul the damned crew.

XXVI.

So, when the Sun in bed
Curtain'd with cloudy red   230
   Pillows his chin upon an orient wave,
The flocking shadows pale
Troop to th' infernal jail ;
   Each fetter'd ghost slips to his severall grave;
And the yellow-skirted Fayes   235
Fly after the night-steeds, leaving their moon-lov'd maze.

XXVII.

But see the Virgin blest
Hath laid her Babe to rest ;
   Time is our tedious song should here have ending ;
Heav'ns youngest teemed star   240
Hath fixt her polished car,
   Her sleeping Lord with handmaid lamp attending ;
And all about the courtly stable
Bright-harnessed angels sit in order serviceable.

L'ALLEGRO.

HENCE, loathed Melancholy,
  Of Cerberus and blackest Midnight born
In Stygian cave forlorn
  'Mongst horrid shapes and shreiks and sights unholy ;
Find out som uncouth cell,   5
  Wher brooding Darknes spreads his jealous wings,
And the night-raven sings ;
  There, under ebon shades and low-brow'd rocks,
As ragged as thy locks,
  In dark Cimmerian desert ever dwell.   10
But com, thou Goddess fair and free,
In Heav'n ycleap'd Euphrosyne,
And by men heart-easing Mirth,
Whom lovely Venus at a birth
With two sisters Graces more   15
To ivy-crowned Bacchus bore ;
Or whether (as som sager sing)
The frolick wind that breathes the spring,
Zephir with Aurora playing
As he met her once a Maying,   20
There on beds of Violet blew
And fresh-blown roses washt in dew
Fill'd her with thee a daughter fair,
So bucksom, blith, and debonair.
  Haste thee, Nymph, and bring with thee   25
Jest and youthful Jollity,
Quips, and Cranks, and wanton Wiles,
Nods and Becks, and wreathed Smiles
Such as hang on Hebe's cheek,
And love to live in dimple sleek,   30
Sport that wrincled Care derides,
And Laughter holding both his sides.
Com, and trip it as ye go
On the light fantastick toe,
And in thy right hand lead with thee,   35
The mountain nymph, sweet Liberty ;

And, if I give thee honour due,
Mirth, admit me of thy crue
To live with her, and live with thee,
In unreproved pleasures free :   40
To hear the lark begin his flight,
And singing startle the dull Night
From his watch-towre in the skies,
Till the dappled Dawn doth rise,
Then to com in spight of sorrow,   45
And at my window bid good morrow
Through the sweetbriar, or the vine,
Or the twisted eglantine,
While the cock with lively din
Scatters the rear of Darknes thin,   50
And to the stack, or the barn dore,
Stoutly struts his dames before ;
Oft list'ning how the hounds and horn
Chearly rouse the slumbring Morn
From the side of som hoar hill,   55
Through the high wood echoing shrill ;
Som time walking not unseen
By hedge-row elms, on hillocks green,
Right against the eastern gate,
Wher the great Sun begins his state,   60
Rob'd in flames and amber light,
The clouds in thousand liveries dight,
While the plowman neer at hand
Whistles ore the furrow'd land,
And the milkmaid singeth blithe,   65
And the mower whets his sithe,
And every shepherd tells his tale
Under the hawthorn in the dale.
   Streit mine eye hath caught new pleasures,
Whilst the lantskip round it measures,   70
Russet lawns and fallows gray,
Where the nibling flocks do stray,
Mountains on whose barren brest
The labouring clowds do often rest,
Meadows trim and daisies pide,   75
Shallow brooks and rivers wide.
Towers and battlements it sees
Boosom'd high in tufted trees,
Wher perhaps som beauty lies,

The cynosure of neighbouring eyes.   80
Hard by, a cottage chimney smokes
From betwixt two aged okes,
Where Corydon and Thyrsis met
Are at their savory dinner set
Of hearbs and other country messes,   85
Which the neat-handed Phillis dresses;
And then in haste her bowre she leaves,
With Thestylis to bind the sheaves,
Or, if the earlier season lead,
To the tann'd haycock in the mead.   90
   Som times with secure delight
The upland hamlets will invite,
When the merry bells ring round,
And the jocond rebecks sound
To many a youth and many a maid   95
Dancing in the chequer'd shade !
And young and old com forth to play
On a sunshine holyday,
Till the livelong daylight fail;
Then to the spicy nut-brown ale,   100
With stories told of many a feat:
How fairy Mab the junkets eat:
She was pincht and pull'd, she sed;
And he, by friars lanthorn led,
Tells how the drudging goblin swet   105
To ern his cream-bowle duly set,
When in one night, ere glimps of morn,
His shadowy flale hath thresh'd the corn
That ten day-labourers could not end;
Then lies him down the lubbar fend,   110
And, stretch'd out all the chimney's length,
Basks at the fire his hairy strength,
And crop-full out of dores he flings,
Ere the first cock his mattin rings.
Thus don the tales to bed they creep,   115
By whispering windes soon lull'd asleep.
   Towred cities please us then,
And the busie humm of men,
Where throngs of knights and barons bold
In weeds of Peace high triumphs hold,   120
With store of ladies whose bright eies
Rain influence, and judge the prise

Of wit, or arms, while both contend
To win her grace whom all commend.
There let Hymen oft appear   125
In saffron robe, with taper clear,
And Pomp, and Feast, and Revelry,
With Mask and antique Pageantry,
Such sights as youthful poets dream
On summer eeves by haunted stream.   130
Then to the well-trod stage anon,
If Jonson's learned sock be on,
Or sweetest Shakespear, Fancies childe,
Warble his native wood-notes wilde.

  And ever against eating cares   135
Lap me in soft Lydian aires
Married to immortal Verse,
Such as the meeting soul may pierce
In notes with many a winding bout
Of lincked sweetnes long drawn out   140
With wanton heed and giddy cunning,
The melting voice thro' mazes running,
Untwisting all the chains that ty
The hidden soul of harmony ;
That Orpheus self may heave his head   145
From golden slumber on a bed
Of heapt Elysian flowres, and hear
Such streins as would have won the ear
Of Pluto to have quite set free
His half-regain'd Eurydice.   150
These delights if thou canst give,
Mirth, with thee I mean to live.

IL PENSEROSO.

HENCE, vain deluding Joyes,
  The brood of Folly without father bred!
How little you bested,
  Or fill the fixed mind with all your toyes!
Dwell in som idle brain,   5
  And fancies fond with gaudy shapes possess,

As thick and numberless
  As the gay motes that people the sun beams,
Or likest hovering dreams,
  The fickle pensioners of Morpheus train.   10
But hail ! thou Goddes sage and holy !
Hail ! divinest Melancholy !
Whose saintly visage is too bright
To hit-the sense of human sight,
And therefore to our weaker view   15
Ore laid with black, staid Wisdoms hue—
Black, but such as in esteem
Prince Memnons sister might beseem,
Or that starr'd Ethiope queen that strove
To set her beauties praise above   20
The sea nymphs, and their powers offended ;
Yet thou art higher far descended ;
Thee bright-haired Vesta long of yore
To solitary Saturn bore,
His daughter she (in Saturn's raign   25
Such mixture was not held a stain) ;
Oft in glimmering bowres and glades
He met her, and in secret shades
Of woody Ida's inmost grove,
While yet there was no fear of Jove.   30
  Com, pensive Nun, devout and pure,
Sober, stedfast, and demure,
All in a robe of darkest grain
Flowing with majestick train,
And sable stole of Cipres lawn   35
Over thy decent shoulders drawn !
Com, but keep thy wonted state,
With eev'n step and musing gate
And looks commercing with the skies,
Thy rapt soul sitting in thine eyes ;   40
There held in holy passion still,
Forget thy self to marble, till
With a sad leaden downward cast
Thou fix them on the earth as fast ;
And joyn with thee calm Peace and Quiet,   45
Spare Fast, that oft with gods doth diet,
And hears the Muses in a ring
Ay round about Joves altar sing ;
And adde to these retired Leasure,

That in trim gardens takes his pleasure;   50
But, first and chiefest, with thee bring
Him that yon soars on golden wing,
Guiding the fiery-wheeled throne,
The cherub Contemplation;
And the mute Silence hist along,   55
'Less Philomel will daign a song,
In her sweetest, saddest plight,
Smoothing the rugged brow of Night,
While Cynthia checks her dragon yoke
Gently o're th' accustom'd oke.   60
    Sweet bird, that shunn'st the noise of folly,
Most musicall, most melancholy!
Thee, chauntress, oft the woods among
I woo to hear thy eeven-song;
And missing thee, I walk unseen   65
On the dry, smooth-shaven green,
To behold the wandring moon
Riding neer her highest noon,
Like one that had bin led astray
Through the Heav'ns wide pathles way,   70
And oft, as if her head she bow'd,
Stooping through a fleecy cloud.
Oft on a plat of rising ground,
I hear the far off curfeu sound,
Over som wide-water'd shoar   75
Swinging slow with sullen roar;
Or, if the ayr will not permit,
Som still removed place will fit,
Where glowing embers through the room
Teach Light to counterfeit a gloom,   80
Far from all resort of mirth,
Save the cricket on the hearth,
Or the belman's drousie charm
To bless the dores from nightly harm;
Or let my lamp at midnight hour   85
Be seen in some high lonely towr,
Where I may oft out-watch the Bear
With thrice great Hermes, or unsphear
The spirit of Plato to unfold
What worlds or what vast regions hold   90
The immortal mind that hath forsook
Her mansion in this fleshly nook.

And of those dæmons that are found
In fire, air, flood, or under ground,
Whose power hath a true consent   95
With planet, or with element.
Som time let gorgeous Tragedy
In scepter'd pall com sweeping by,
Presenting Thebs or Pelops line
Or the tale of Troy divine,   100
Or what (though rare) of later age
Ennobled hath the buskind stage.
But, O sad Virgin, that thy power
Might raise Musæus from his bower,
Or bid the soul of Orpheus sing   105
Such notes as warbled to the string
Drew iron tears down Pluto's cheek,
And made Hell grant what Love did seek.
Or call up him that left half told
The story of Cambuscan bold,   110
Of Camball and of Algarsife,
'And who had Canace to wife,
That own'd the vertuous ring and glass,
And of the wondrous hors of brass
On which the Tartar king did ride;   115
And if ought els great bards beside
In sage and solemn tunes have sung,
Of turneys and of trophies hung,
Of forests and inchantments drear,
Where more is meant than meets the ear.   120
   Thus, Night, oft see me in thy pale career
Till civil-suited Morn appeer,
Not trickt and frounc't as she was wont
With the Attick boy to hunt,
But cherchef't in a comely cloud   125
While rocking winds are piping loud,
Or usher'd with a shower still
When the gust hath blown his fill,
Ending on the russling leaves
With minute drops from off the eaves.   130
And when the sun begins to fling
His flaring beams, me, Goddess, bring
To arched walks of twilight groves,
And shadows brown that Sylvan loves
Of pine and monumental oake,   135

Where the rude ax with heaved stroke
Was never heard the nymphs to daunt,
Or fright them from their hallow'd haunt;
There in close covert by som brook,
Where no profaner eye may look,   140
Hide me from Day's garish eie,
While the bee with honied thie,
That at her flowry work doth sing,
And the waters murmuring,
With such consort as they keep,   145
Entice the dewy-feather'd sleep;
And let som strange mysterious dream
Wave at his wings in airy stream
Of lively portrature display'd,
Softly on my eyelids laid;   150
And, as I wake, sweet musick breathe
Above, about, or underneath,
Sent by som spirit to mortals good,
Or th' unseen Genius of the wood.
But let my due feet never fail   155
To walk the studious cloysters pale,
And love the high embowed roof,
With antick pillars massy proof,
And storied windows richly dight
Casting a dimm religious light.   160
There let the pealing organ blow
To the full voic'd quire below
In service high and anthems cleer,
As may with sweetnes, through mine ear,
Dissolve me into extasies,   165
And bring all Heav'n before mine eyes.
     And may at last my weary age
Find out the peacefull hermitage,
The hairy gown and mossy cell,
Where I may sit and rightly spell   170
Of every star that Heav'n doth shew
And every herb that sips the dew;
Till old Experience do attain
To somthing like prophetic strain.
These pleasures, Melancholy, give,   175
And I with thee will choose to live.

LYCIDAS.

Yet once more, O ye Laurels, and once more,
Ye Myrtles brown, with Ivy never sear,
I com to pluck your berries harsh and crude,
And with forc'd fingers rude
Shatter your leaves before the mellowing year.   5
Bitter constraint, and sad occasion dear
Compels me to disturb your season due ;
For Lycidas is dead, dead ere his prime,
Young Lycidas, and hath not left his peer.
Who would not sing for Lycidas? he knew   10
Himself to sing, and build the lofty rhyme.
He must not flote upon his watry bear
Unwept, and welter to the parching wind
Without the meed of some melodious tear.
    Begin then, Sisters of the Sacred Well,   15
That from beneath the seat of Jove doth spring,
Begin, and somwhat loudly sweep the string.
Hence with denial vain and coy excuse ;
So may som gentle Muse
With lucky words favour my destin'd urn,   20
And, as he passes, turn
And bid fair peace be to my sable shrowd ;
For we were nurst upon the self-same hill,
Fed the same flock, by fountain, shade, and rill ;
Together both, ere the high lawns appear'd   25
Under the opening eyelids of the Morn,
We drove a field, and both together heard
What time the gray-fly winds her sultry horn,
Batt'ning our flocks with the fresh dews of night,
Oft till the star that rose at ev'ning bright   30
Towards Heav'ns descent had slop'd his westering wheel.
Mean while the rural ditties were not mute,
Temper'd to th' oaten flute,
Rough Satyrs danc'd, and Fauns with clov'n heel
From the glad sound would not be absent long,   35
And old Damætas lov'd to hear our song.

But O the heavy change, now thou art gon,
Now thou art gon, and never must return !
Thee, Shepherd, thee the woods, and desert caves
With wilde thyme and the gadding vine o'regrown   40
And all their echoes mourn.
The willows and the hazle copses green
Shall now no more be seen
Fanning their joyous leaves to thy soft layes.
As killing as the canker to the rose,   45
Or taint-worm to the weanling herds that graze,
Or frost to flowers, that their gay wardrop wear
When first the white thorn blows:
Such, Lycidas, thy loss to shepherds ear.
    Where were ye, Nymphs, when the remorseless deep   50
Clos'd o're the head of your lov'd Lycidas?
For neither were ye playing on the steep
Where your old bards, the famous Druids ly,
Nor on the shaggy top of Mona high,
Nor yet where Deva spreads her wisard stream.   55
Ay me ! I fondly dream !
Had ye bin there—for what could that have don?
What could the Muse her self that Orpheus bore,
The Muse her self, for her inchanting son,
Whom universal Nature did lament,   60
When by the rout that made the hideous roar
His goary visage down the stream was sent,
Down the swift Hebrus to the Lesbian shore?
    Alas ! what boots it with uncessant care
To tend the homely slighted shepherds trade,   65
And strictly meditate the thankless Muse?
Were it not better don, as others use,
To sport with Amaryllis in the shade,
Or with the tangles of Neæra's hair?
Fame is the spur that the clear spirit doth raise   70
(That last infirmity of noble mind)
To scorn delights, and live laborious dayes ;
But the fair guerdon when we hope to find,
And think to burst out into sudden blaze,
Comes the blind Fury with the abhorred shears,   75
And slits the thin-spun life. But not the praise,
Phœbus repli'd, and touch'd my trembling ears ;
Fame is no plant that grows on mortal soil,
Nor in the glistering foil

Set off to th' world, nor in broad Rumour lies, 80
But lives and spreds aloft by those pure eyes,
And perfet witnes of all-judging Jove ;
As he pronounces lastly on each deed,
Of so much fame in Heav'n expect thy meed.
  O fountain Arethuse, and thou honour'd flood, 85
Smooth-sliding Mincius, crown'd with vocall reeds,
That strain I heard was of a higher mood ;
But now my oat proceeds,
And listens to the herald of the sea
That came in Neptune's plea. 90
He ask'd the waves, and ask'd the fellon winds,
What hard mishap hath doom'd this gentle swain ?
And question'd every gust of rugged wings
That blows from off each beaked promontory ;
They knew not of his story, 95
And sage Hippotades their answer brings :
That not a blast was from his dungeon stray'd,
The air was calm, and on the level brine
Sleek Panope with all her sisters play'd.
It was that fatal and perfidious bark 100
Built in th' eclipse, and rigg'd with curses dark,
That sunk so low that sacred head of thine.
  Next Camus, reverend sire, went footing slow,
His mantle hairy and his bonnet sedge
Inwrought with figures dim, and on the edge 105
Like to that sanguine flower inscrib'd with woe.
Ah ! who hath reft (quoth he) my dearest pledge ?
Last came, and last did go,
The pilot of the Galilean lake ;
Two massy keyes he bore of metals twain 110
(The golden opes, the iron shuts amain) ;
He shook his miter'd locks, and stern bespake :
How well could I have spar'd for thee, young Swain,
Anow of such as for their bellies sake
Creep, and intrude, and climb into the fold ? 115
Of other care they little reck'ning make
Then how to scramble at the shearers feast,
And shove away the worthy bidden guest ;
Blind mouthes ! that scarce themselves know how to hold
A sheep-hook, or have learn'd ought els the least 120
That to the faithfull herdsmans art belongs !
What reeks it them ? What need they ? they are sped ;

And when they list their lean and flashy songs
Grate on their scrannel pipes of wretched straw;
The hungry sheep look up, and are not fed,   125
But swoln with wind, and the rank mist they draw,
Rot inwardly, and foul contagion spread;
Besides what the grim woolf with privy paw
Daily devours apace, and nothing sed;
But that two-handed engine at the door   130
Stands ready to smite once, and smite no more.
   Return, Alpheus, the dread voice is past
That shrunk thy streams; return, Sicilian Muse,
And call the vales, and bid them hither cast
Their bels, and flourets of a thousand hues.   135
Ye valleys low, where the milde whispers use
Of shades, and wanton winds, and gushing brooks,
On whose fresh lap the swart star sparely looks,
Throw hither all your quaint enameld eyes,
That on the green terf suck the honied showres,   140
And purple all the ground with vernal flowres.
Bring the rathe primrose that forsaken dies,
The tufted crow-toe, and pale gessamine,
The white pink, and the pansie freakt with jeat,
The glowing violet,   145
The musk-rose, and the well-attir'd woodbine,
With cowslips wan that hang the pensive hed,
And every flower that sad embroidery wears;
Bid Amaranthus all his beauty shed,
And daffadillies fill their cups with tears,   150
To strew the laureat herse where Lycid lies.
For, so to interpose a little ease,
Let our frail thoughts dally with false surmise,
Ay me! whilst thee the shores and sounding seas
Wash far away, where ere thy bones are hurl'd,   155
Whether beyond the stormy Hebrides,
Where thou perhaps, under the whelming tide,
Visit'st the bottom of the monstrous world,
Or whether thou to our moist vows deny'd
Sleep'st by the fable of Bellerus old,   160
Where the great vision of the guarded mount
Looks toward Namancos and Bayona's hold;
Look homeward, angel, now, and melt with ruth;
And, O ye Dolphins, waft the haples youth.
   Weep no more, woful shepherds, weep no more,   165

For Lycidas your sorrow is not dead,
Sunk though he be beneath the watry floar;
So sinks the day-star in the ocean bed,
And yet anon repairs his drooping head,
And tricks his beams, and with new-spangled ore   170
Flames in the forehead of the morning sky.
So Lycidas sunk low, but mounted high,
Through the dear might of Him that walk'd the waves,
Where other groves and other streams along,
With nectar pure his oozy lock's he laves,   175
And hears the unexpressive nuptiall song
In the blest kingdoms meek of Joy and Love.
There entertain him all the saints above
In solemn troops and sweet societies,
That sing, and singing in their glory move,   180
And wipe the tears for ever from his eyes.
Now, Lycidas, the shepherds weep no more;
Henceforth thou art the genius of the shore,
In thy large recompense, and shalt be good
To all that wander in that perilous flood.   185
    Thus sang the uncouth swain to th' okes and rills,
While the still Morn went out with sandals grey;
He touch'd the tender stops of various quills,
With eager thought warbling his Dorick lay;
And now the sun had stretch'd out all the hills,   190
And now was dropt into the western bay;
At last he rose, and twitch'd his mantle blew;
To-morrow to fresh woods and pastures new.

DRYDEN.

MAC FLECKNOE.

ALL humane things are subject to decay,
And, when Fate summons, monarchs must obey.
This Flecknoe found, who, like Augustus, young
Was call'd to empire and had govern'd long,
In prose and verse was owned without dispute   5
Through all the realms of Nonsense absolute.
This aged prince, now flourishing in peace
And blest with issue of a large increase,
Worn out with business, did at length debate
To settle the succession of the state ;   10
And pond'ring which of all his sons was fit
To reign and wage immortal war with wit,
Cry'd, " 'Tis resolved, for Nature pleads that he
" Should onely rule who most resembles me.
" Shadwell alone my perfect image bears,   15
" Mature in dulness from his tender years ;
" Shadwell alone of all my sons is he
" Who stands confirm'd in full stupidity.
" The rest to some faint meaning make pretence,
" But Shadwell never deviates into sense.   20
" Some beams of wit on other souls may fall,
" Strike through and make a lucid intervall ;
" But Shadwell's genuine night admits no ray,
" His rising fogs prevail upon the day.
" Besides, his goodly fabrick fills the eye   25
" And seems designed for thoughtless majesty,
" Thoughtless as monarch oakes that shade the plain
" And, spread in solemn state, supinely reign.

"Heywood and Shirley were but types of thee,
"Thou last great prophet of tautology.   30
"Even I, a dunce of more renown than they,
"Was sent before but to prepare thy way,
"And coursly clad in Norwich drugget came
"To teach the nations in thy greater name.
"My warbling lute, the lute I whilom strung   35
"When to King John of Portugal I sung,
"Was but the prelude to that glorious day,
"When thou on silver Thames did'st cut thy way,
"With well-tim'd oars before the royal barge,
"Swell'd with the pride of thy celestial charge,   40
"And, big with hymn, commander of an host;
"The like was ne'er in Epsom blankets tost.
"Methinks I see the new Arion sail,
"The lute still trembling underneath thy nail.
"At thy well-sharpned thumb from shore to shore   45
"The treble squeaks for fear, the basses roar;
"About thy boat the little fishes throng,
"As at the morning toast that floats along.
"Sometimes, as prince of thy harmonious band,
"Thou weildst thy papers in thy threshing hand.   50
"St. André's feet ne'er kept more equal time,
"Not ev'n the feet of thy own 'Psyche's' rhyme,
"Though they in number as in sense excell;
"So just, so like tautology, they fell
"That, pale with envy, Singleton forswore   55
"The lute and sword which he in triumph bore,
"And vowed he ne'er would act Villerius more."
Here stopped the good old syre and wept for joy,
In silent raptures of the hopefull boy.
All arguments, but most his plays, perswade   60
That for anointed dulness he was made.
    Close to the walls which fair Augusta bind,
(The fair Augusta much to fears inclin'd,)
An ancient fabrick rais'd to inform the sight
There stood of yore, and Barbican it hight;   65
A watch-tower once, but now, so fate ordains,
Of all the pile an empty name remains.
Near it a Nursery erects its head,
Where queens are formed and future hero's bred,
Where unfledged actors learn to laugh and cry,   70
And little Maximins the gods defy.

Great Fletcher never treads in buskins here,
Nor greater Jonson dares in socks appear ;
But gentle Simkin just reception finds
Amidst this monument of vanisht minds ;   75
Pure clinches the suburbian muse affords
And Panton waging harmless war with words.
Here Flecknoe, as a place to fame well known,
Ambitiously designed his Shadwell's throne.
For ancient Decker prophesi'd long since   80
That in this pile should reign a mighty prince,
Born for a scourge of wit and flayle of sense,
To whom true dulness should some "Psyches" owe,
But worlds of "Misers" from his pen should flow ;
"Humorists" and Hypocrites it should produce,   85
Whole Raymond families and tribes of Bruce.
    Now empress Fame had publisht the renown
Of Shadwell's coronation through the town.
Rows'd by report of fame, the nations meet
From near Bunhill and distant Watling-street.   90
No Persian carpets spread th' imperial way,
But scattered limbs of mangled poets lay ;
Much Heywood, Shirley, Ogleby there lay,
But loads of Shadwell almost choakt the way.
Bilkt stationers for yeomen stood prepar'd   95
And Herringman was captain of the guard.
The hoary prince in majesty appear'd,
High on a throne of his own labours rear'd.
At his right hand our young Ascanius sat,
Rome's other hope and pillar of the state.   100
His brows thick fogs instead of glories grace,
And lambent dulness plaied around his face.
As Hannibal did to the altars come,
Sworn by his syre a mortal foe to Rome :
So Shadwell swore, nor should his vow be vain,   105
That he till death true dulness would maintain,
And, in his father's right and realms defence,
Ne'er to have peace with wit nor truce with sense.
The king himself the sacred unction made,
As king by office and as priest by trade.   110
In his sinister hand, instead of ball,
He plac'd a mighty mug of potent ale ;
"Love's Kingdom" to his right he did convey,
At once his sceptre and his rule of sway ;

Whose righteous lore the prince had practis'd young   115
And from whose loyns recorded "Psyche" sprung.
His temples, last, with poppies were o'erspread,
That nodding seemed to consecrate his head.
Just at that point of time, if fame not lye,
On his left hand twelve reverend owls did fly.   120
So Romulus, 'tis sung, by Tyber's brook,
Presage of sway from twice six vultures took.
The admiring throng loud acclamations make,
And omens of his future empire take.
The syre then shook the honours of his head,   125
And from his brows damps of oblivion shed
Full on the filial dulness; long he stood,
Repelling from his breast the raging God;
At length burst out in this prophetick mood:
  "Heavens bless my son! from Ireland let him reign   130
"To far Barbadoes on the western main;
"Of his dominion may no end be known
"And greater than his father's be his throne;
"Beyond 'Love's Kingdom' let him stretch his pen!"
He paus'd, and all the people cry'd "Amen."   135
Then thus continu'd he: "My son, advance
"Still in new impudence, new ignorance.
"Success let others teach, learn thou from me
"Pangs without birth and fruitless industry.
"Let 'Virtuoso's' in five years be writ,   140
"Yet not one thought accuse thy toil of wit.
"Let gentle George in triumph tread the stage,
"Make Dorimant betray, and Loveit rage;
"Let Cully, Cockwood, Fopling, charm the pit,
"And in their folly show the writers wit.   145
"Yet still thy fools shall stand in thy defence
"And justify their author's want of sense.
"Let 'em be all by thy own model made
"Of dulness, and desire no foreign aid,
"That they to future ages may be known,   150
"Not copies drawn, but issue of thy own.
"Nay, let thy men of wit too be the same,
"All full of thee and differing but in name.
"But let no alien Sedley interpose
"To lard with wit thy hungry Epsom prose.   155
"And when false flowers of rhetoric thou would'st cull,
"Trust nature, do not labour to be dull;

" But write thy best and top ; and in each line
" Sir Formal's oratory will be thine.
" Sir Formal, though unsought, attends thy quill   160
" And does thy northern dedications fill.
" Nor let false friends seduce thy mind to fame
" By arrogating Jonson's hostile name ;
" Let father Flecknoe fire thy mind with praise
" And uncle Ogleby thy envy raise.   165
" Thou art my blood, where Jonson has no part ;
" What share have we in nature or in art ?
" Where did his wit on learning fix a brand
" And rail at arts he did not understand ?
" Where made he love in Prince Nicander's vein   170
" Or swept the dust in Psyche's humble strain ?
" When did his Muse from Fletcher scenes purloin,
" As thou whole Etheridge dost transfuse to thine ?
" But so transfused as oil on waters flow,
" His always floats above, thine sinks below.   175
" This is thy province, this thy wondrous way,
" New humours to invent for each new play :
" This is that boasted byas of thy mind,
" By which one way to dulness 'tis inclined,
" Which makes thy writings lean on one side still   180
" And, in all changes, that way bends thy will.
" Nor let thy mountain belly make pretence
" Of likeness ; thine's a tympany of sense.
" A tun of man in thy large bulk is writ,
" But sure thou'rt but a kilderkin of wit.   185
" Like mine, thy gentle numbers feebly creep ;
" Thy tragic Muse gives smiles, thy comic sleep.
" With whate'er gall thou sett'st thy self to write,
" Thy inoffensive satyrs never bite ;
" In thy fellonious heart though venom lies,   190
" It does but touch thy Irish pen, and dyes.
" Thy genius calls thee not to purchase fame
" In keen Iambicks, but mild Anagram.
" Leave writing plays, and choose for thy command
" Some peacefull province in Acrostick land.   195
" There thou may'st wings display and altars raise,
" And torture one poor word ten thousand ways ;
" Or, if thou would'st thy diff'rent talents suit,
" Set thy own songs, and sing them to thy lute."
He said, but his last words were scarcely heard,   .   200

For Bruce and Longville had a trap prepared,
And down they sent the yet declaiming bard.
Sinking he left his drugget robe behind,
Born upwards by a subterranean wind.
The mantle fell to the young prophet's part   205
With double portion of his father's art.

A SONG FOR ST. CECILIA'S DAY.

1.

FROM harmony, from heav'nly harmony
   This universal frame began.
   When Nature underneath a heap
    Of jarring atoms lay,
   And cou'd not heave her head,   · 5
The tuneful voice was heard from high :
   Arise, ye more than dead.
Then cold and hot and moist and dry
   In order to their stations leap,
   And Musick's pow'r obey.   10
From harmony, from heav'nly harmony
   This universal frame began ;
   From harmony to harmony
Through all the compass of the notes it ran,
The diapason closing full in Man.   15

2.

What passion cannot Musick raise and quell?
   When Jubal struck the corded shell,
   His list'ning brethren stood around,
    And, wond'ring, on their faces fell
   To worship that celestial sound;   20
Less than a god they thought there cou'd not dwell
   Within the hollow of that shell,
   That spoke so sweetly, and so well.
What passion cannot Music raise and quell?

3.

The trumpets loud clangor   25
    Excites us to arms
With shrill notes of anger
    And mortal alarms.
The double double double beat
    Of the thundering drum   30
    Cries, heark: the foes come!
Charge, charge, 'tis too late to retreat!

4.

The soft complaining flute
In dying notes discovers
The woes of hopeless lovers,   35
Whose dirge is whisper'd by the warbling lute.

5.

Sharp violins proclaim
Their jealous pangs and desperation,
Fury, frantick indignation,
Depth of pains and height of passion,   40
    For the fair, disdainful dame.

6.

But oh! what art can teach,
What human voice can reach
    The sacred organs praise?
    Notes inspiring holy love,   45
Notes that wing their heav'nly ways
    To mend the choires above.

7.

Orpheus cou'd lead the savage race,
And trees unrooted left their place,
    Sequacious of the lyre;   50
But bright Cecilia rais'd the wonder high'r:
When to her organ vocal breath was giv'n;
An angel heard, and straight appear'd,
    Mistaking earth for heav'n.

GRAND CHORUS.

As from the pow'r of sacred lays   55
  The spheres began to move,
And sung the great Creator's praise
  To all the bless'd above:
So, when the last and dreadful hour
This crumbling pageant shall devour,   60
The trumpet shall be heard on high,
The dead shall live, the living die,
And Musick shall untune the sky.

ALEXANDER'S FEAST;

OR, THE POWER OF MUSIC.

I.

'TWAS at the royal feast for Persia won
  By Philip's warlike son.
  Aloft in awful state
  The godlike hero sate
    On his imperial throne ;   5
His valiant peers were plac'd around,
Their brows with roses and with myrtles bound ;
  (So shou'd desert in arms be crown'd.)
The lovely Thais, by his side,
Sate like a blooming Eastern bride,   10
In flow'r of youth and beauty's pride.
  Happy, happy, happy pair !
    None but the brave,
    None but the brave,
  None but the brave deserves the fair.   15

2.

  Timotheus, plac'd on high
  Amid the tuneful quire,
With flying fingers touch'd the lyre ;
  The trembling notes ascend the sky,
  And heav'nly joys inspire.   20

The song began from Jove,
Who left his blissful seats above,
(Such is the pow'r of mighty love.)
A dragon's fiery form bely'd the god ;
Sublime on radiant spires he rode,   25
When he to fair Olympia press'd,
And while he sought her snowy breast ;
Then round her slender waste he curl'd,
And stamp'd an image of himself, a sov'raign of the world.
The list'ning crowd admire the lofty sound,   30
A present deity, they shout around ;
A present deity, the vaulted roofs rebound.
   With ravish'd ears
   The monarch hears,
   Assumes the god,   35
   Affects to nod,
  And seems to shake the spheres.

3.

The praise of Bacchus then the sweet musician sung,
Of Bacchus ever fair, and ever young.
  The jolly god in triumph comes ;   40
  Sound the trumpets, beat the drums ;
   Flush'd with a purple grace
   He shews his honest face ;
Now give the hautboys breath ; he comes, he comes.
  Bacchus, ever fair and young,   45
   Drinking joys did first ordain ;
  Bacchus blessings are a treasure,
  Drinking is the soldier's pleasure ;
   Rich the treasure,
   Sweet the pleasure,   50
  Sweet is pleasure after pain.

4.

 Sooth'd with the sound the king grew vain ;
  Fought all his battails o'er again ;
And thrice he routed all his foes, and thrice he slew the slain.
  The master saw the madness rise,   55
  His glowing cheeks, his ardent eyes ;
  And while he heaven and earth defy'd,
  Chang'd his hand, and check'd his pride.

He chose a mournful Muse,
   Soft pity to infuse ;   60
He sung Darius great and good,
   By too severe a fate
Fallen, fallen, fallen, fallen,
   Fallen from his high estate,
And weltring in his blood.   65
Deserted at his utmost need
By those his former bounty fed,
On the bare earth expos'd he lyes,
With not a friend to close his eyes.
With downcast looks the joyless victor sate,   70
   Revolveing in his alter'd soul
      The various turns of chance below:
   And, now and then, a sigh he stole,
   And tears began to flow.

5.

The mighty master smil'd to see   75
That love was in the next degree ;
'Twas but a kindred sound to move,
For pity melts the mind to love.
   Softly sweet, in Lydian measures,
   Soon he sooth'd his soul to pleasures.   80
War, he sung, is toil and trouble,
Honour but an empty bubble,
   Never ending, still beginning,
Fighting still, and still destroying ;
   If the world be worth thy winning,   85
Think, O think it worth enjoying ;
   Lovely Thais sits beside thee,
   Take the good the gods provide thee.
The many rend the skies with loud applause ;
So Love was crown'd, but Musique won the cause.   90
   The prince, unable to conceal his pain,
      Gaz'd on the fair
      Who caus'd his care,
   And sigh'd and look'd, sigh'd and look'd,
   Sighed and looked, and sighed again ;   95
At length, with love and wine at once oppress'd,
The vanquish'd victor sunk upon her breast.

6.

Now strike the golden lyre again ;
A lowder yet, and yet a lowder strain.
Break his bands of sleep asunder,   100
And rouze him, like a rattling peal of thunder.
    Hark, hark, the horrid sound
      Has rais'd up his head ;
      As awak'd from the dead,
    And amaz'd, he stares around.   105
    Revenge, revenge, Timotheus cries,
      See the Furies arise ;
      See the snakes that they rear,
      How they hiss in their hair,
    And the sparkles that flash from their eyes !   110
      Behold a ghastly band,
      Each a torch in his hand !
Those are Grecian ghosts, that in battail were slayn,
        And unbury'd remain
        Inglorious on the plain ;   115
        Give the vengeance due
        To the valiant crew.
Behold how they toss their torches on high,
    How they point to the Persian abodes,
And glitt'ring temples of their hostile gods.   120
The princes applaud with a furious joy ;
And the king seyz'd a flambeau with zeal to destroy ;
      Thais led the way,
      To light him to his prey,
And, like another Hellen, fir'd another Troy.   125

7.

      Thus long ago,
    'Ere heaving bellows learn'd to blow,
      While organs yet were mute,
      Timotheus, to his breathing flute
        And sounding lyre,   130
Cou'd swell the soul to rage, or kindle soft desire.
    At last divine Cecilia came,
    Inventress of the vocal frame ;
The sweet enthusiast, from her sacred store,
    Enlarg'd the former narrow bounds,   135

And added length to solemn sounds,
With Nature's mother-wit, and arts unknown before.
 Let old Timotheus yield the prize,
  Or both divide the crown:
 He rais'd a mortal to the skies: 140
  She drew an angel down.

POPE.

RAPE OF THE LOCK.

CANTO I.

WHAT dire offence from am'rous causes springs,
What mighty contests rise from trivial things,
I sing. This verse to CARYL, Muse! is due;
This, ev'n Belinda may vouchsafe to view;
Slight is the subject, but not so the praise, 5
If She inspire, and He approve my lays.
Say what strange motive, Goddess! could compel
A well-bred Lord t' assault a gentle Belle?
O say what stranger cause, yet unexplor'd,
Cou'd make a gentle Belle reject a Lord? 10
In tasks so bold, can little men engage?
And in soft bosoms dwells such mighty Rage?
Sol thro' white curtains shot a tim'rous ray,
And op'd those eyes that must eclipse the day;
Now lap-dogs give themselves the rousing shake, 15
And sleepless lovers, just at twelve, awake;
Thrice rung the bell, the slipper knock'd the ground,
And the press'd watch return'd a silver sound.
Belinda still her downy pillow prest,
Her guardian SYLPH prolong'd the balmy rest. 20
'Twas he had summon'd to her silent bed
The morning dream that hover'd o'er her head;
A Youth more glitt'ring than a Birth-night Beau,
(That ev'n in slumber caused her cheek to glow)
Seem'd to her ear his winning lips to lay, 25
And thus in whispers said, or seem'd to say:
" Fairest of mortals, thou distinguish'd care
Of thousand bright Inhabitants of Air!

If e'er one vision touch'd thy infant thought,
Of all the Nurse and all the Priest have taught—   30
Of airy Elves by moonlight shadows seen,
The silver token, and the circled green,
Or virgins visited by Angel pow'rs,
With golden crowns and wreaths of heav'nly flow'rs—
Hear and believe! thy own importance know,   35
Nor bound thy narrow views to things below.
Some secret truths, from learned pride conceal'd,
To Maids alone and Children are reveal'd.
What tho' no credit doubting Wits may give?
The Fair and Innocent shall still believe.   40
Know, then, unnumber'd Spirits round thee fly,
The light Militia of the lower sky;
These, tho' unseen, are ever on the wing,
Hang o'er the Box, and hover round the Ring.
Think what an equipage thou hast in Air,   45
And view with scorn two Pages and a Chair.
As now your own, our beings were of old,
And once inclos'd in Woman's beauteous mould;
Thence, by a soft transition, we repair
From earthly Vehicles to these of air.   50
Think not, when Woman's transient breath is fled,
That all her vanities at once are dead;
Succeeding vanities she still regards,
And tho' she plays no more, o'erlooks the cards.
Her joy in gilded Chariots, when alive,   55
And love of Ombre, after death survive.
For when the Fair in all their pride expire,
To their first Elements their Souls retire.
The Sprites of fiery Termagants in Flame
Mount up, and take a Salamander's name.   60
Soft yielding minds to Water glide away,
And sip, with Nymphs, their elemental Tea.
The graver Prude sinks downward to a Gnome,
In search of mischief still on Earth to roam.
The light Coquettes in Sylphs aloft repair,   65
And sport and flutter in the fields of Air.
Know farther yet: whoever fair and chaste
Rejects mankind, is by some Sylph embrac'd;
For Spirits, freed from mortal laws, with ease
Assume what sexes and what shapes they please.   70
What guards the purity of melting Maids,

In courtly balls and midnight masquerades,
Safe from the treach'rous friend, the daring spark,
The glance by day, the whisper in the dark,
When kind occasion prompts their warm desires, 75
When music softens, and when dancing fires?
'Tis but their Sylph, the wise Celestials know,
Tho' Honour is the word with Men below.
Some nymphs there are too conscious of their face,
For life predestin'd to the Gnomes embrace. 80
These swell their prospects and exalt their pride,
When offers are disdain'd, and love deny'd;
Then gay Ideas crowd the vacant brain,
While Peers, and Dukes, and all their sweeping train,
And Garters, Stars, and Coronets appear, 85
And in soft sounds, Your Grace salutes their ear.
'Tis these that early taint the female soul,
Instruct the eyes of young Coquettes to roll,
Teach Infant-cheeks a bidden blush to know,
And little hearts to flutter at a Beau. 90
Oft', when the world imagine women stray,
The Sylphs thro' mystic mazes guide their way;
Thro' all the giddy circle they pursue,
And old impertinence expel by new.
What tender maid but must a victim fall 95
To one man's treat, but for another's ball?
When Florio speaks what virgin could withstand,
If gentle Damon did not squeeze her hand?
With varying vanities, from ev'ry part,
They shift the moving Toyshop of their heart, 100
Where wigs with wigs, with sword-knots sword-knots strive,
Beaus banish beaus, and coaches coaches drive.
This erring mortals Levity may call;
Oh blind to truth! the Sylphs contrive it all.
Of these am I, who thy protection claim, 105
A watchful sprite, and Ariel is my name.
Late, as I rang'd the crystal wilds of air,
In the clear Mirror of thy ruling Star
I saw, alas! some dread event impend,
E're to the main this morning sun descend, 110
But heav'n reveals not what, or how, or where.
Warn'd by the Sylph, oh pious maid, beware!
This to disclose is all thy guardian can:
Beware of all, but most beware of Man!"

He said; when Shock, who thought she slept too long,   115
Leap'd up, and wak'd his mistress with his tongue.
'Twas then, Belinda! if report say true,
Thy eyes first open'd on a Billet-doux;
Wounds, Charms, and Ardors were no sooner read,
But all the Vision vanished from thy head.   120
  And now, unveil'd, the Toilet stands display'd,
Each silver Vase in mystic order laid.
First, rob'd in white, the Nymph intent adores,
With head uncover'd, the Cosmetic pow'rs.
A heav'nly image in the glass appears;   125
To that she bends, to that her eyes she rears.
Th' inferior Priestess, at her altar's side,
Trembling begins the sacred rites of Pride.
Unnumber'd treasures ope at once, and here
The various off'rings of the world appear;   130
From each she nicely culls with curious toil,
And decks the Goddess with the glitt'ring spoil.
This casket India's glowing gems unlocks,
And all Arabia breaths from yonder box;
The Tortoise here and Elephant unite,   135
Transform'd to combs, the speckled, and the white.
Here files of pins extend their shining rows,
Puffs, Powders, Patches, Bibles, Billet-doux.
Now awful Beauty puts on all its arms;
The fair each moment rises in her charms,   140
Repairs her smiles, awakens ev'ry grace,
And calls forth all the wonders of her face;
Sees by degrees a purer blush arise,
And keener lightnings quicken in her eyes.
The busy Sylphs surround their darling care,   145
These set the head, and those divide the hair,
Some fold the sleeve, whilst others plait the gown;
And Betty's prais'd for labours not her own.

CANTO II.

NOT with more glories, in th' etherial plain,
The Sun first rises o'er the purpled main,   150
Than, issuing forth, the rival of his beams
Lanch'd on the bosom of the silver Thames.
Fair Nymphs, and well-dresst Youths around her shone,

But ev'ry eye was fix'd on her alone.
On her white breast a sparkling Cross she wore,   155
Which Jews might kiss, and Infidels adore.
Her lively looks a sprightly mind disclose,
Quick as her eyes, and as unfix'd as those.
Favours to none, to all she smiles extends;
Oft' she rejects, but never once offends.   160
Bright as the sun, her eyes the gazers strike,
And, like the sun, they shine on all alike.
Yet graceful ease, and sweetness void of pride,
Might hide her faults, if Belles had faults to hide;
If to her share some female errors fall,   165
Look on her face, and you'll forget 'em all.
   This Nymph, to the destruction of mankind,
Nourish'd two Locks, which graceful hung behind
In equal curls, and well conspir'd to deck
With shining ringlets the smooth iv'ry neck.   170
Love in these labyrinths his slaves detains,
And mighty hearts are held in slender chains.
With hairy sprindges we the birds betray,
Slight lines of hair surprize the finny prey,
Fair tresses man's imperial race insnare,   175
And beauty draws us with a single hair.
   Th' advent'rous Baron the bright locks admir'd;
He saw, he wish'd, and to the prize aspir'd.
Resolv'd to win, he meditates the way,
By force to ravish, or by fraud betray;   180
For when success a Lover's toil attends,
Few ask, if fraud or force attain'd his ends.
   For this, e'er Phœbus rose, he had implor'd
Propitious heav'n, and ev'ry pow'r ador'd,
But chiefly Love—to Love an Altar built   185
Of twelve vast French Romances, neatly gilt.
There lay three garters, half a pair of gloves;
And all the trophies of his former loves;
With tender Billet-doux he lights the pyre,
And breathes three am'rous sighs to raise the fire.   190
Then prostrate falls, and begs with ardent eyes
Soon to obtain, and long possess the prize:
The pow'rs gave ear, and granted half his pray'r;
The rest the winds dispers'd in empty air.
   But now secure the painted vessel glides,   195
The sun-beams trembling on the floating tydes,

While melting music steals upon the sky,
And soften'd sounds along the waters die.
Smooth flow the waves, the Zephyrs gently play,
Belinda smil'd, and all the world was gay,   200
All but the Sylph ; with careful thoughts opprest,
Th' impending woe sat heavy on his breast.
He summons strait his Denizens of air;
The lucid squadrons round the sails repair :
Soft o'er the shrouds aërial whispers breath,   205
That seem'd but Zephyrs to the train beneath.
Some to the sun their insect-wings unfold,
Waft on the breeze, or sink in clouds of gold;
Transparent forms, too fine for mortal sight,
Their fluid bodies half dissolv'd in light,   210
Loose to the wind their airy garments flew,
Thin glitt'ring textures of the filmy dew,
Dipt in the richest tincture of the skies,
Where light disports in ever-mingling dyes,
While ev'ry beam new transient colours flings,   215
Colours that change whene'er they wave their wings.
Amid the circle, on the gilded mast,
Superior by the head, was Ariel plac'd;
His purple pinions opening to the sun,
He raised his azure wand, and thus begun :   220
    " Ye Sylphs and Sylphids, to your chief give ear !
Fays, Fairies, Genii, Elves, and Dæmons, hear !
Ye know the spheres and various tasks assigned
By laws eternal to th' aërial kind.
Some in the fields of purest Æther play,   225
And bask and whiten in the blaze of day.
Some guide the course of wandring orbs on high,
Or roll the planets thro' the boundless sky;
Some, less refin'd, beneath the moon's pale light
Pursue the stars that shoot athwart the night,   230
Or suck the mists in grosser air below,
Or dip their pinions in the painted bow,
Or brew fierce tempests on the wintry main,
Or o'er the glebe distill the kindly rain.
Others on earth o'er humane race preside,   235
Watch all their ways, and all their actions guide;
Of these the chief the care of Nations own,
And guard with Arms divine the British Throne.
Our humbler province is to tend the Fair,

Not a less pleasing, tho' less glorious care,   240
To save the powder from too rude a gale,
Nor let th' imprison'd essences exhale,
To draw fresh colours from the vernal flow'rs,
To steal from rainbows, e're they drop in show'rs
A brighter wash, to curl their waving hairs,   245
Assist their blushes, and inspire their airs,
Nay, oft', in dreams invention we bestow,
To change a Flounce, or add a Furbelo.
This day black Omens threat the brightest Fair
That e'er deserv'd a watchful spirit's care;   250
Some dire disaster, or by force, or slight;
But what, or where, the Fates have wrapt in night.
Whether the nymph shall break Diana's law,
Or some frail China jar receive a flaw,
Or stain her honour, or her new brocade,   255
Forget her pray'rs, or miss a masquerade,
Or lose her heart, or necklace, at a ball,
Or whether Heav'n has doom'd that Shock must fall.
Haste, then, ye spirits! to your charge repair:
The flutt'ring fan be Zephyretta's care;   260
The drops to thee, Brillante, we consign;
And, Momentilla, let the watch be thine;
Do thou, Crispissa, tend her fav'rite Lock;
Ariel himself shall be the guard of Shock.
To fifty chosen Sylphs, of special note,   265
We trust the important charge, the Petticoat:
Form a strong line about the silver bound,
And guard the wide circumference around.
Whatever spirit, careless of his charge,
His post neglects, or leaves the fair at large,   270
Shall feel sharp vengeance soon o'ertake his sins,—
Be stop'd in vials, or transfix't with pins,
Or plung'd in lakes of bitter washes lie,
Or wedg'd whole ages in a bodkin's eye;
Gums and Pomatums shall his flight restrain,   275
While clog'd he beats his silken wings in vain;
Or Alom stypticks with contracting pow'r
Shrink his thin essence like a rivell'd flower;
Or, as Ixion fix'd, the wretch shall feel
The giddy motion of the whirling Mill,   280
In fumes of burning Chocolate shall glow,
And tremble at the sea that froaths below!"

He spoke; the spirits from the sails descend.
Some, orb in orb, around the nymph extend;
Some thrid the mazy ringlets of her hair; 285
Some hang upon the pendants of her ear.
With beating hearts the dire event they wait,
Anxious, and trembling for the birth of Fate.

CANTO III.

CLOSE by those meads, for ever crown'd with flow'rs,
Where Thames with pride surveys his rising tow'rs, 290
There stands a structure of majestic frame,
Which from the neighb'ring Hampton takes its name.
Here Britain's statesmen oft' the fall foredoom
Of foreign Tyrants, and of Nymphs at home;
Here thou, great ANNA! whom three realms obey, 295
Dost sometimes counsel take—and sometimes Tea.
Hither the heroes and the nymphs resort,
To taste a while the pleasures of a Court.
In various talk th' instructive hours they past,
Who gave the ball, or paid the visit last. 300
One speaks the glory of the British Queen,
And one describes a charming Indian screen;
A third interprets motions, looks, and eyes;
At ev'ry word a reputation dies.
Snuff, or the fan, supply each pause of chat, 305
With singing, laughing, ogling, *and all that.*
Mean while, declining from the noon of day,
The sun obliquely shoots his burning ray;
The hungry Judges soon the sentence sign,
And wretches hang that jury-men may dine; 310
The merchant from the Exchange returns in peace,
And the long labours of the Toilet cease.
Belinda now, whom thirst of fame invites,
Burns to encounter two adventrous Knights,
At Ombre singly to decide their doom; 315
And swells her breast with conquests yet to come.
Strait the three bands prepare in arms to join,
Each band the number of the sacred nine.
Soon as she spreads her hand, the aërial guard

Descend, and sit on each important card: 320
First Ariel perch'd upon a Matadore,
Then each according to the rank they bore;
For Sylphs, yet mindful of their ancient race,
Are, as when women, wondrous fond of place.
　Behold four Kings in majesty rever'd, 325
With hoary whiskers and a forky beard,
And four fair Queens, whose hands sustain a flower,
Th' expressive emblem of their softer pow'r,
Four Knaves in garbs succinct, a trusty band,
Caps on their heads, and halberds in their hand, 330
And particolour'd troops, a shining train,
Drawn forth to combat on the velvet plain.
　The skilful Nymph reviews her force with care;
Let Spades be trumps! she said; and trumps they were.
　Now move to war her sable Matadores, 335
In show like leaders of the swarthy Moors.
Spadillio first, unconquerable lord!
Led off two captive trumps, and swept the board
As many more Manillio forced to yield,
And march'd a victor from the verdant field. 340
Him Basto followed, but his fate more hard
Gain'd but one trump and one Plebeian card.
With his broad sabre next, a chief in years,
The hoary Majesty of Spades appears,
Puts forth one manly leg, to sight reveal'd; 345
The rest his many-colour'd robe conceal'd.
The rebel Knave, who dares his prince engage,
Proves the just victim of his royal rage.
Ev'n mighty Pam, that Kings and Queens o'erthrew
And mow'd down armies in the fights of Lu, 350
Sad chance of war! now destitute of aid,
Falls undistinguish'd by the victor Spade!
　Thus far both armies to Belinda yield;
Now to the Baron fate inclines the field.
His warlike Amazon her host invades, 355
Th' imperial consort of the crown of Spades.
The Club's black Tyrant first her victim dy'd,
Spite of his haughty mien, and barb'rous pride.
What boots the regal circle on his head,
His giant limbs, in state unwieldy spread, 360
That long behind he trails his pompous robe,
And, of all monarchs, only grasps the globe?

The Baron now his Diamonds pours apace;
Th' embroider'd King who shows but half his face,
And his refulgent Queen, with pow'rs combin'd,   365
Of broken troops an easy conquest find.
Clubs, Diamonds, Hearts, in wild disorder seen,
With throngs promiscuous strow the level green.
Thus when dispers'd a routed army runs
Of Asia's troops, and Afric's sable sons,   370
With like confusion different nations fly,
Of various habit, and of various dye;
The pierc'd battalions dis-united fall,
In heaps on heaps; one fate o'erwhelms them all.
    The Knave of Diamonds tries his wily arts,   375
And wins (oh shameful chance!) the Queen of Hearts.
At this the blood the virgin's cheek forsook,
A livid paleness spreads o'er all her look;
She sees, and trembles at th' approaching ill,
Just in the jaws of ruin, and Codille.   380
And now (as oft in some distemper'd State)
On one nice Trick depends the gen'ral fate;
An Ace of Hearts steps forth; The King unseen
Lurked in her hand, and mourned his captive Queen:
He springs to Vengeance with an eager pace,   385
And falls like thunder on the prostrate Ace.
The nymph exulting fills with shouts the sky;
The walls, the woods, and long canals reply.
    Oh thoughtless mortals! ever blind to fate,
Too soon dejected, and too soon elate.   390
Sudden these honours shall be snatch'd away,
And curs'd for ever this victorious day.
    For lo! the board with cups and spoons is crown'd,
The berries crackle, and the mill turns round;
On shining Altars of Japan they raise   395
The silver lamp; the fiery spirits blaze;
From silver spouts the grateful liquors glide,
While China's earth receives the smoking tyde.
At once they gratify their scent and taste,
And frequent cups prolong the rich repaste.   400
Strait hover round the Fair her airy band;
Some, as she sipp'd, the fuming liquor fann'd,
Some o'er her lap their careful plumes display'd,
Trembling, and conscious of the rich brocade.
Coffee (which makes the politician wise,   405

And see thro' all things with his half-shut eyes)
Sent up in vapours to the Baron's brain
New Stratagems, the radiant Lock to gain.
Ah cease, rash youth! desist e'er 'tis too late,
Fear the just Gods, and think of Scylla's Fate!   410
Chang'd to a bird, and sent to flit in air,
She dearly pays for Nisus' injur'd hair!
   But when to mischief mortals bend their will,
How soon they find fit instruments of ill!
Just then Clarissa drew with tempting grace   415
A two-edg'd weapon from her shining case:
So Ladies in Romance assist their Knight,
Present the spear, and arm him for the fight.
He takes the gift with rev'rence, and extends
The little engine on his fingers' ends;   420
This just behind Belinda's neck he spread,
As o'er the fragrant steams she bends her head.
Swift to the Lock a thousand Sprites repair;
A thousand wings by turns blow back the hair;
And thrice they twitch'd the diamond in her ear;   425
Thrice she look'd back, and thrice the foe drew near.
Just in that instant, anxious Ariel sought
The close recesses of the Virgin's thought;
As on the nosegay in her breast reclin'd,
He watched th' Ideas rising in her mind,   430
Sudden he view'd, in spite of all her art,
An earthly Lover lurking at her heart.
Amaz'd, confus'd, he found his pow'r expir'd!
Resign'd to fate, and with a sigh retir'd.
The Peer now spreads the glitt'ring Forfex wide,   435
T' inclose the Lock; now joins it, to divide.
Ev'n then, before the fatal engine clos'd,
A wretched Sylph too fondly interposed;
Fate urg'd the shears, and cut the Sylph in twain
(But airy substance soon unites again).   440
The meeting points the sacred hair dissever
From the fair head, for ever, and for ever!
   Then flash'd the living lightning from her eyes,
And screams of horror rend the affrighted skies.
Not louder shrieks to pitying heav'n are cast,   445
When husbands, or when lapdogs breathe their last;
Or when rich China vessels fal'n from high,
In glittering dust and painted fragments lie.

Let wreaths of triumph now my temples twine,
The victor cry'd; the glorious Prize is mine!   450
While fish in streams, or birds delight in air,
Or in a coach and six the British Fair,
As long as Atalantis shall be read,
Or the small pillow grace a Lady's bed,
While visits shall be paid on solemn days,   455
When num'rous waxlights in bright order blaze,
While nymphs take treats, or assignations give,
So long my honour, name, and praise shall live!
What Time wou'd spare, from Steel receives its date,
And monuments, like men, submit to Fate!   460
Steel could the labour of the Gods destroy,
And strike to dust the imperial tow'rs of Troy;
Steel could the works of mortal pride confound,
And hew triumphal arches to the ground.
What wonder then, fair nymph! thy hair should feel   465
The conqu'ring force of unresisted steel?

CANTO IV.

BUT anxious cares the pensive nymph opprest,
And secret passions labour'd in her breast.
Not youthful kings in battel seiz'd alive,
Not scornful virgins who their charms survive,   470
Not ardent lovers robb'd of all their bliss,
Not ancient ladies when refus'd a kiss,
Not tyrants fierce that unrepenting die,
Not Cynthia when her manteau's pinn'd awry,
E'er felt such rage, resentment, and despair,   475
As thou, sad Virgin! for thy ravish'd Hair.
    For, that sad moment, when the Sylphs withdrew
And Ariel weeping from Belinda flew,
Umbriel, a dusky, melancholy sprite,
As ever sully'd the fair face of light,   480
Down to the central earth, his proper scene,
Repairs to search the gloomy Cave of Spleen.
    Swift on his sooty pinions flits the Gnome,
And in a vapour reach'd the dismal dome.
No chearful breeze this sullen region knows,   485
The dreaded East is all the wind that blows.

Here in a grotto, sheltred close from air,
And screen'd in shades from day's detested glare,
She sighs for ever on her pensive bed,
Pain at her side, and Megrim at her head.   490
Two handmaids wait the throne; alike in place,
But diff'ring far in figure and in face.
Here stood Ill-nature like an ancient maid,
Her wrinkled form in black and white array'd;
With store in pray'rs for mornings, nights, and noons,   495
Her hand is fill'd, her bosom with lampoons.
There Affectation, with a sickly mien,
Shows in her cheek the roses of eighteen,
Practis'd to lisp and hang the head aside,
Faints into airs, and languishes with pride,   500
On the rich quilt sinks with becoming woe,
Wrapt in a gown for sickness and for show.
The fair ones feel such maladies as these,
When each new night-dress gives a new disease.
A constant Vapour o'er the palace flies,   505
Strange phantoms rising as the mists arise,
Dreadful, as hermit's dreams in haunted shades,
Or bright, as visions of expiring maids:
Now glaring fiends, and snakes on rolling spires,
Pale spectres, gaping tombs, and purple fires;   510
Now lakes of liquid gold, Elysian scenes,
And crystal domes, and angels in machines.
Unnumber'd throngs on every side are seen,
Of bodies chang'd to various forms by Spleen.
Here living Tea-pots stand, one arm held out,   515
One bent; the handle this, and that the spout;
A Pipkin there, like Homer's Tripod, walks;
Here sighs a Jar, and there a Goose-pye talks;
Men prove with child, as pow'rful Fancy works,
And maids turn'd bottles call aloud for corks.   520
Safe past the Gnome thro' this fantastic band,
A branch of healing Spleenwort in his hand.
Then thus address'd the pow'r—"Hail, wayward Queen!
Who rule the sex to fifty from fifteen;
Parent of vapours, and of female wit,   525
Who give th' hysteric, or poetic fit;
On various tempers act by various ways,—
Make some take physic, others scribble plays;
Who cause the proud their visits to delay,

And send the godly in a pett to pray!   530
A nymph there is, that all thy pow'r disdains,
And thousands more in equal mirth maintains.
But, oh! if e'er thy Gnome could spoil a grace,
Or raise a pimple on a beauteous face,
Like Citron-waters matrons cheeks inflame,   535
Or change complexions at a losing game;
Or caus'd suspicion when no soul was rude,
Or discompos'd the head-dress of a prude,
Or e'er to costive lapdog gave disease,
Which not the tears of brightest eyes could ease,   540
Hear me, and touch Belinda with chagrin;
That single act gives half the world the spleen."
    The Goddess with a discontented air
Seems to reject him, tho' she grants his pray'r.
A wond'rous bag with both her hands she binds,   545
Like that where once Ulysses held the winds;
There she collects the force of female lungs,
Sighs, sobs, and passions, and the war of tongues.
A Vial next she fills with fainting fears,
Soft sorrows, melting griefs, and flowing tears.   550
The Gnome rejoicing bears her gift away,
Spreads his black wings, and slowly mounts to day.
    Sunk in Thalestris' arms the nymph he found,
Her eyes dejected, and her hair unbound.
Full o'er their heads the swelling bag he rent,   555
And all the Furies issued at the vent.
Belinda burns with more than mortal ire,
And fierce Thalestris fans the rising fire.
"O wretched maid!" she spread her hands, and cry'd,
(While Hampton's ecchoes "Wretched maid!" reply'd,)   560
"Was it for this you took such constant care
The bodkin, comb, and essence to prepare?
For this your locks in paper durance bound?
For this with tort'ring irons wreath'd around?
For this with fillets strain'd your tender head,   565
And bravely bore the double loads of lead?
Gods! shall the ravisher display your hair,
While the Fops envy, and the Ladies stare?
Honour forbid! at whose unrivall'd shrine
Ease, pleasure, virtue, all our sex resign.   570
Methinks already I your tears survey,
Already hear the horrid things they say,

Already see you a degraded toast,
And all your honour in a whisper lost !
How shall I then your helpless fame defend?   575
'Twill then be infamy to seem your friend!
And shall this prize, th' inestimable prize,
Expos'd through crystal to the gazing eyes,
And heighten'd by the diamond's circling rays,
On that rapacious hand for ever blaze?   580
Sooner shall grass in Hyde-park Circus grow,
And wits take lodgings in the sound of Bow ;
Sooner let earth, air, sea, to Chaos fall,
Men, monkeys, lapdogs, parrots, perish all."
    She said ; then raging to Sir Plume repairs,   585
And bids the Beau demand the precious hairs
(Sir Plume, of amber snuff-box justly vain,
And the nice conduct of a clouded cane.)
With earnest eyes, and round unthinking face,
He first the snuff-box open'd, then the case,   590
And thus broke out—"My Lord ! why, what the devil !
Zounds ! damn the lock ! 'fore Gad, you must be civil !
Plague on 't ! 'tis past a jest to plunder locks :
Give her the hair"—he spoke, and rapp'd his box.
    "It grieves me much," reply'd the Peer again,   595
" Who speaks so well should ever speak in vain ;
But by this lock, this sacred lock I swear,
(Which never more shall join its parted hair ;
Which never more its honours shall renew,
Clip'd from the lovely head where late it grew,)   600
That, while my nostrils draw the vital air,
This hand, which won it, shall for ever wear."
He spoke ; and speaking, in proud triumph spread
The long-contended honours of her head.
    But Umbriel, hateful Gnome ! forbears not so ;   605
He breaks the Vial whence the sorrows flow.
Then see ! the nymph in beauteous grief appears,
Her eyes half-languishing, half-drown'd in tears ;
On her heav'd bosom hung her drooping head,
Which, with a sigh, she rais'd ; and thus she said.   610
    " For ever curs'd be this detested day,
Which snatch'd my best, my fav'rite curl away!
Happy ! ah ten times happy had I been,
If Hampton-Court these eyes had never seen !
Yet am not I the first mistaken maid,   615

By love of Courts to num'rous ills betray'd.
Oh had I rather un-admir'd remain'd
In some lone isle, or distant Northern land,
Where the gilt Chariot never marks the way,
Where none learn Ombre, none e'er taste Bohea!   620
There kept my charms conceal'd from mortal eye,
Like roses, that in desarts bloom and die.
What mov'd my mind with youthful Lords to rome?
Oh had I stay'd, and said my pray'rs at home!
'Twas this, the morning omens seem'd to tell: 625
Thrice from my trembling hand the patch-box fell;
The tottering China shook without a wind;
Nay, Poll sat mute, and Shock was most unkind!
A Sylph too warn'd me of the threats of fate,
In mystic visions, now believ'd too late!   630
See the poor remnants of these slighted hairs!
My hands shall rend what ev'n thy rapine spares.
These, in two sable ringlets taught to break,
Once gave new beauties to the snowy neck;
The sister lock now sits uncouth, alone,   635
And in its fellow's fate foresees its own;
Uncurl'd it hangs, the fatal sheers demands,
And tempts once more thy sacrilegious hands.
Oh hadst thou, cruel! been content to seize
Hairs less in sight, or any hairs but these."   640

CANTO V.

SHE said; the pitying audience melt in tears;
But Fate and Jove had stopp'd the Baron's ears.
In vain Thalestris with reproach assails;
For who can move when fair Belinda fails?
Not half so fix'd the Trojan could remain,   645
While Anna begg'd and Dido rag'd in vain.
Then grave Clarissa graceful wav'd her fan;
Silence ensu'd, and thus the Nymph began:
    "Say, why are beauties prais'd and honour'd most,
The wise man's passion, and the vain man's toast?   650
Why deck'd with all that land and sea afford,
Why Angels call'd, and Angel-like ador'd?
Why round our coaches crowd the white-glov'd Beaus?

Why bows the side box from its inmost rows?
How vain are all these glories, all our pains,   655
Unless good sense preserve what beauty gains,
That men may say, when we the front box grace,
' Behold the first in virtue as in face !'
Oh! if to dance all night, and dress all day,
Charm'd the small-pox, or chas'd old age away;   660
Who would not scorn what huswife's cares produce,
Or who would learn one earthly thing of use?
To patch, nay ogle, might become a Saint;
Nor could it sure be such a sin to paint.
But since, alas! frail beauty must decay,   665
Curl'd or uncurl'd, since Locks will turn to grey;
Since painted, or not painted, all shall fade,
And she who scorns a man, must die a maid;
What then remains but well our pow'r to use,
And keep good-humour still whate'er we lose?   670
And trust me, dear! good-humour can prevail,
When airs, and flights, and screams, and scolding fail.
Beauties in vain their pretty eyes may roll;
Charms strike the sight, but merit wins the soul."
  So spoke the dame, but no applause ensu'd ;   675
Belinda frowned, Thalestris call'd her Prude.
"To arms, to arms!" the fierce Virago cries,
And swift as lightning to the combate flies.
All side in parties, and begin th' attack;
Fans clap, silks russle, and tough whalebones crack;   680
Heroes' and Heroins shouts confus'dly rise,
And base, and treble voices strike the skies.
No common weapons in their hands are found ;
Like Gods they fight, nor dread a mortal wound.
  So when bold Homer makes the Gods engage,   685
And heav'nly breasts with human passions rage;
'Gainst Pallas, Mars; Latona, Hermes arms;
And all Olympus rings with loud alarms;
Jove's thunder roars, heav'n trembles all around ;
Blue Neptune storms, the bellowing deeps resound;   690
Earth shakes her nodding tow'rs, the ground gives way,
And the pale ghosts start at the flash of day!
  Triumphant Umbriel, on a sconce's height,
Clap'd his glad wings, and sate to view the fight.
Prop'd on their bodkin spears, the Sprites survey   695
The growing combat, or assist the fray.

While thro' the press enrag'd Thalestris flies,
And scatters deaths around from both her eyes,
A Beau and Witling perish'd in the throng;
One dy'd in metaphor, and one in song.   700
"O cruel nymph! a living death I bear,"
Cry'd Dapperwit, and sunk beside his chair.
A mournful glance Sir Fopling upwards cast;
"Those eyes are made so killing"—was his last.
Thus on Mæander's flow'ry margin lies   705
Th' expiring Swan, and as he sings he dies.
　　When bold Sir Plume had drawn Clarissa down,
Chloe stepp'd in, and kill'd him with a frown;
She smil'd to see the doughty hero slain,
But at her smile the Beau reviv'd again.   710
　　Now Jove suspends his golden scales in air,
Weighs the Men's wits against the lady's Hair.
The doubtful beam long nods from side to side;
At length the wits mount up, the hairs subside.
　　See, fierce Belinda on the Baron flies,   715
With more than usual lightning in her eyes;
Nor fear'd the Chief th' unequal fight to try,
Who sought no more than on his foe to die.
But this bold Lord, with manly strength endu'd,
She with one finger and a thumb subdu'd.   720
Just where the breath of life his nostrils drew,
A charge of Snuff the wily Virgin threw;
The Gnomes direct, to ev'ry atome just,
The pungent grains of titillating dust.
Sudden with starting tears each eye o'erflows,   725
And the high dome re-echoes to his nose.
　　"Now meet thy fate," incens'd Belinda cry'd,
And drew a deadly bodkin from her side.
(The same, his ancient personage to deck,
Her great-great-grandsire wore about his neck,   730
In three seal-rings; which after, melted down,
Form'd a vast buckle for his widow's gown;
Her infant grandame's whistle next it grew,
The bells she gingled, and the whistle blew;
Then in a bodkin grac'd her mother's hairs,   735
Which long she wore, and now Belinda wears.)
　　"Boast not my fall," he cry'd, "insulting foe!
Thou by some other shalt be laid as low.
Nor think. to die dejects my lofty mind;

All that I dread is leaving you behind!   740
Rather than so, ah let me still survive,
And burn in Cupid's flames—but burn alive."
  "Restore the Lock!" she cries; and all around
"Restore the Lock!" the vaulted roofs rebound.
Not fierce Othello in so loud a strain   745
Roar'd for the handkerchief that caus'd his pain.
But see how oft' ambitious aims are cross'd,
And chiefs contend till all the prize is lost!
The Lock, obtain'd with guilt, and kept with pain,
In ev'ry place is sought, but sought in vain.   750
With such a prize no mortal must be blest,
So heav'n decrees! with heav'n who can contest?
  Some thought it mounted to the Lunar sphere,
Since all things lost on earth are treasur'd there.
There Hero's wits are kept in pondrous vases,   755
And Beau's in snuff-boxes and tweezer-cases.
There broken vows and death-bed alms are found,
And lovers' hearts with ends of riband bound,
The courtier's promises, and sick man's pray'rs,
The smiles of harlots, and the tears of heirs,   760
Cages for gnats, and chains to yoak a flea,
Dry'd butterflies, and tomes of casuistry.
  But trust the Muse—she saw it upward rise,
Tho' mark'd by none but quick poetic eyes;
(So Rome's great founder to the heav'ns withdrew,   765
To Proculus alone confess'd in view.)
A sudden Star, it shot thro' liquid air,
And drew behind a radiant trail of hair.
Not Berenice's Locks first rose so bright,
The heav'ns bespangling with dishevel'd light.   770
The Sylphs behold it kindling as it flies,
And pleas'd pursue its progress thro' the skies.
  This the Beau monde shall from the Mall survey,
And hail with music its propitious ray.
This the blest Lover shall for Venus take,   775
And send up vows from Rosamonda's lake;
This Partridge soon shall view in cloudless skies,
When next he looks thro' Galilæo's eyes;
And hence th' egregious wizard shall foredoom
The fate of Louis, and the fall of Rome.   780
  Then cease, bright Nymph! to mourn thy ravish'd hair,
Which adds new glory to the shining sphere!

Not all the tresses that fair head can boast,
Shall draw such envy as the Lock you lost :
For after all the murders of your eye,   785
When, after millions slain, your *self* shall die;
When those fair suns shall set, as set they must,
And all those tresses shall be laid in dust,
This Lock the Muse shall consecrate to fame,
And 'midst the stars inscribe Belinda's name.   790

JOHNSON.

LONDON.

THO' grief and fondness in my breast rebel,
When injur'd Thales bids the town farewel,
Yet still my calmer thoughts his choice commend,
(I praise the hermit, but regret the friend,)
Resolv'd at length, from vice and London far,   5
To breathe in distant fields a purer air,
And, fix'd on Cambria's solitary shore,
Give to St. David one true Briton more.
   For who woud leave, unbrib'd, Hibernia's land,
Or change the rocks of Scotland for the Strand?   10
There none are swept by sudden fate away,
But all whom hunger spares with age decay :
Here malice, rapine, accident, conspire,
And now a rabble rages, now a fire;
Their ambush here relentless ruffians lay,   15
And here the fell attorney prowls for prey ;
Here falling houses thunder on your head,
And here a female atheist talks you dead.
   While Thales waits the wherry that contains
Of dissipated wealth the small remains,   20
On Thames's banks in silent thought we stood,
Where Greenwich smiles upon the silver flood :
Struck with the seat that gave Eliza birth,
We kneel, and kiss the consecrated earth ;
In pleasing dreams the blissful age renew,   25
And call Britannia's glories back to view :

Behold her cross triumphant on the main,
The guard of commerce and the dread of Spain,
Ere masquerades debauch'd, excise oppress'd,
Or English honour grew a standing jest.   30
  A transient calm the happy scenes bestow,
And for a moment lull the sense of woe.
At length awaking, with contemptuous frown
Indignant Thales eyes the neighb'ring town.
  Since worth, he cries, in these degen'rate days   35
Wants ev'n the cheap reward of empty praise ;
In those curs'd walls, devote to vice and gain,
Since unrewarded science toils in vain ;
Since hope but sooths to double my distress,
And ev'ry moment leaves my little less ;   40
While yet my steady steps no staff sustains,
And life still vig'rous revels in my veins,
Grant me, kind heaven, to find some happier place,
Where honesty and sense are no disgrace ;
Some pleasing bank where verdant osiers play,   45
Some peaceful vale with nature's paintings gay,
Where once the harass'd Briton found repose,
And safe in poverty defy'd his foes ;
Some secret cell, ye pow'rs, indulgent give.
Let —— live here, for —— has learn'd to live.   50
Here let those reign, whom pensions can incite
To vote a patriot black, a courtier white ;
Explain their country's dear-bought rights away,
And plead for pirates in the face of day ;
With slavish tenets taint our poison'd youth,   55
And lend a lie the confidence of truth.
  Let such raise palaces, and manors buy,
Collect a tax, or farm a lottery ;
With warbling eunuchs fill our silenc'd stage,
And lull to servitude a thoughtless age.   60
  Heroes, proceed ! what bounds your pride shall hold ?
What check restrain your thirst of pow'r and gold ?
Behold rebellious virtue quite o'erthrown,
Behold our fame, our wealth, our lives your own.
To such the plunder of a land is giv'n,   65
When publick crimes inflame the wrath of heav'n :
But what, my friend, what hope remains for me,
Who start at theft, and blush at perjury ?
Who scarce forbear, tho' Britain's court he sing,

To pluck a titled poet's borrow'd wing;   70
A statesman's logic unconvinc'd can hear,
And dare to slumber o'er the Gazetteer;
Despise a fool in half his pension dress'd,
And strive in vain to laugh at Clodio's jest?
    Others, with softer smiles and subtler art,   75
Can sap the principles, or taint the heart;
With more address a lover's note convey,
Or bribe a virgin's innocence away.
Well may they rise, while I, whose rustick tongue
Ne'er knew to puzzle right, or varnish wrong,   80
Spurn'd as a beggar, dreaded as a spy,
Live unregarded, unlamented die.
    For what but social guilt the friend endears?
Who shares Orgilio's crimes, his fortune shares.
But thou, should tempting villany present   85
All Marlb'rough hoarded, or all Villiers spent,
Turn from the glitt'ring bribe thy scornful eye,
Nor sell for gold, what gold could never buy,
The peaceful slumber, self-approving day,
Unsullied fame, and conscience ever gay.   90
    The cheated nation's happy fav'rites see!
Mark whom the great caress, who frown on me!
London, the needy villain's gen'ral home,
The common sewer of Paris and of Rome,
With eager thirst, by folly or by fate,   95
Sucks in the dregs of each corrupted state.
Forgive my transports on a theme like this,
I cannot bear a French metropolis.
    Illustrious Edward! from the realms of day,
The land of heroes and of saints survey;   100
Nor hope the British lineaments to trace,
The rustick grandeur, or the surly grace,
But, lost in thoughtless ease and empty show,
Behold the warrior dwindled to a beau;
Sense, freedom, piety, refin'd away,   105
Of France the mimick, and of Spain the prey.
    All that at home no more can beg or steal,
Or like a gibbet better than a wheel,
Hiss'd from the stage, or hooted from the court,
Their air, their dress, their politicks import;   110
Obsequious, artful, voluble, and gay,
On Britain's fond credulity they prey.

All sciences a fasting Monsieur knows,
And bid him go to hell, to hell he goes.
   Ah! what avails it, that, from slav'ry far,   115
I drew the breath of life in English air;
Was early taught a Briton's right to prize,
And lisp the tale of Henry's victories;
If the gull'd conqueror receives the chain,
And flattery prevails when arms are vain?   120
   Studious to please and ready to submit,
The supple Gaul was born a parasite:
Still to his int'rest true, where'er he goes,
Wit, brav'ry, worth, his lavish tongue bestows;
In ev'ry face a thousand graces shine,   125
From ev'ry tongue flows harmony divine.
These arts in vain our rugged natives try,
Strain out with fault'ring diffidence a lie,   .
And get a kick for awkward flattery.
   Besides, with justice this discerning age   130
Admires their wond'rous talents for the stage:
Well may they venture on the mimick's art,
Who play from morn to night a borrow'd part;
Practis'd their master's notions to embrace,
Repeat his maxims, and reflect his face;   135
With ev'ry wild absurdity comply,
And view each object with another's eye;
To shake with laughter ere the jest they hear,
To pour at will the counterfeited tear,
And as their patron hints the cold or heat,   140
To shake in dog days, in December sweat.
How, when competitors like these contend,
Can surly virtue hope to fix a friend?
Slaves that with serious impudence beguile,
And lie without a blush, without a smile;   145
Can Balbo's eloquence applaud, and swear
He gropes his breeches with a monarch's air.
   For arts like these preferr'd, admir'd, caress'd,
They first invade your table, then your breast;
Explore your secrets with insidious art,   150
Watch the weak hour, and ransack all the heart;
Then soon your ill-plac'd confidence repay,
Commence your lords, and govern or betray.
   By numbers here from shame or censure free
All crimes are safe, but hated poverty.   155

This, only this, the rigid law pursues ;
This, only this, provokes the snarling muse.
The sober trader at a tatter'd cloak
Wakes from his dream, and labours for a joke;
With brisker air the silken courtiers gaze,   160
And turn the varied taunt a thousand ways.
Of all the griefs that harass the distress'd,
Sure the most bitter is a scornful jest;
Fate never wounds more deep the gen'rous heart,
Than when a blockhead's insult points the dart.   165
    Has heaven reserv'd, in pity to the poor,
No pathless waste, or undiscover'd shore?
No secret island in the boundless main?
No peaceful desert yet unclaim'd by Spain?
Quick let us rise, the happy seats explore,   170
And bear oppression's insolence no more.
This mournful truth is ev'ry where confess'd,
SLOW RISES WORTH, BY POVERTY DEPRESS'D:
But here more slow, where all are slaves to gold,
Where looks are merchandise, and smiles are sold ;   175
Where won by bribes, by flatteries implor'd,
The groom retails the favours of his lord.
    But hark ! th' affrighted crowd's tumultuous cries
Roll through the streets, and thunder to the skies:
Rais'd from some pleasing dream of wealth and pow'r,   180
Some pompous palace, or some blissful bow'r,
Aghast you start, and scarce with aching sight
Sustain the approaching fire's tremendous light;
Swift from pursuing horrors take your way,
And leave your little ALL to flames a prey ;   185
Then thro' the world a wretched vagrant roam,
For where can starving merit find a home?
In vain your mournful narrative disclose,
While all neglect, and most insult your woes.
    Should heaven's just bolts Orgilio's wealth confound,   190
And spread his flaming palace on the ground,
Swift o'er the land the dismal rumour flies,
And publick mournings pacify the skies ;
The laureat tribe in venal verse relate
How virtue wars with persecuting fate ;   195
With well-feign'd gratitude the pension'd band
Refund the plunder of the beggar'd land.
See ! while he builds, the gaudy vassals come,

And crowd with sudden wealth the rising dome;
The price of boroughs and of souls restore;   200
And raise his treasures higher than before:
Now bless'd with all the baubles of the great,
The polish'd marble, and the shining plate,
Orgilio sees the golden pile aspire,
And hopes from angry heav'n another fire.   205
    Could'st thou resign the park and play, content,
For the fair banks of Severn or of Trent;
There might'st thou find some elegant retreat,
Some hireling senator's deserted seat,
And stretch thy prospects o'er the smiling land, 210
For less than rent the dungeons of the Strand;
There prune thy walks, support thy drooping flow'rs,
Direct thy rivulets, and twine thy bow'rs,
And, while thy grounds a cheap repast afford,
Despise the dainties of a venal lord: 215
There ev'ry bush with nature's musick rings,
There ev'ry breeze bears health upon its wings;
On all thy hours security shall smile,
And bless thine evening walk and morning toil.
    Prepare for death, if here at night you roam,   220
And sign your will before you sup from home.
    Some fiery fop, with new commission vain,
Who sleeps on brambles till he kills his man,
Some frolick drunkard, reeling from a feast,
Provokes a broil, and stabs you for a jest.   225
    Yet ev'n these heroes, mischievously gay,
Lords of the street, and terrors of the way,
Flush'd as they are with folly, youth, and wine,
Their prudent insults to the poor confine;
Afar they mark the flambeau's bright approach,   230
And shun the shining train and golden coach.
    In vain, these dangers past, your doors you close,
And hope the balmy blessings of repose:
Cruel with guilt, and daring with despair,
The midnight murd'rer bursts the faithless bar;   235
Invades the sacred hour of silent rest,
And leaves, unseen, a dagger in your breast.
    Scarce can our fields, such crowds at Tyburn die,
With hemp the gallows and the fleet supply.
Propose your schemes, ye senatorian band,   240
Whose *ways* and *means* support the sinking land,

Lest ropes be wanting in the tempting Spring,
To rig another convoy for the king.
    A single gaol in Alfred's golden reign
Could half the nation's criminals contain ;   245
Fair Justice then, without constraint ador'd,
Held high the steady scale, but sheath'd the sword
No spies were paid, no special juries known :
Blest age ! but, ah ! how diff'rent from our own !
    Much could I add,—but see ! the boat at hand,   250
The tide retiring, calls me from the land :
Farewell !—When, youth and health and fortune spent,
Thou fly'st for refuge to the wilds of Kent,
And tir'd, like me, with follies and with crimes,
In angry numbers warn'st succeeding times ;   255
Then shall thy friend—nor thou refuse his aid—
Still foe to vice, forsake his Cambrian shade ;
In virtue's cause once more exert his rage,
Thy satire point, and animate thy page.

THE VANITY OF HUMAN WISHES.

LET observation, with extensive view,
Survey mankind, from China to Peru ;
Remark each anxious toil, each eager strife,
And watch the busy scenes of crowded life :
Then say how hope and fear, desire and hate,   5
O'erspread with snares the clouded maze of fate,
Where wav'ring man, betray'd by vent'rous pride
To tread the dreary paths without a guide,
As treach'rous phantoms in the mist delude,
Shuns fancied ills, or chases airy good ;   10
How rarely reason guides the stubborn choice,
Rules the bold hand, or prompts the suppliant voice ;
How nations sink, by darling schemes oppress'd,
When Vengeance listens to the fool's request.
Fate wings with ev'ry wish th' afflictive dart,   15
Each gift of nature and each grace of art ;
With fatal heat impetuous courage glows,
With fatal sweetness elocution flows,

F

Impeachment stops the speaker's pow'rful breath,
And restless fire precipitates on death. 20
 But, scarce observ'd, the knowing and the bold
Fall in the gen'ral massacre of gold ;
Wide-wasting pest ! that rages unconfin'd,
And crowds with crimes the records of mankind :
For gold his sword the hireling ruffian draws, 25
For gold the hireling judge distorts the laws :
Wealth heap'd on wealth nor truth nor safety buys ;
The dangers gather as the treasures rise.
 Let hist'ry tell, where rival kings command,
And dubious title shakes the madded land, 30
When statutes glean the refuse of the sword,
How much more safe the vassal than the lord ;
Low sculks the hind beneath the rage of pow'r,
And leaves the wealthy traitor in the Tow'r,
Untouch'd his cottage, and his slumbers sound, 35
Tho' confiscation's vultures hover round.
 The needy traveller, serene and gay,
Walks the wide heath, and sings his toil away.
Does envy seize thee ? Crush th' upbraiding joy,
Increase his riches, and his peace destroy : 40
New fears in dire vicissitude invade ;
The rustling brake alarms, and quiv'ring shade ;
Nor light nor darkness bring his pain relief, —
One shows the plunder, and one hides the thief.
 Yet still one gen'ral cry the skies assails, 45
And gain and grandeur load the tainted gales ;
Few know the toiling statesman's fear or care,
Th' insidious rival and the gaping heir.
 Once more, Democritus, arise on earth,
With cheerful wisdom and instructive mirth, 50
See motley life in modern trappings dress'd,
And feed with varied fools th' eternal jest.
Thou who couldst laugh where want enchain'd caprice,
Toil crush'd conceit, and man was of a piece ;
Where wealth unlov'd without a mourner dy'd ; 55
And scarce a sycophant was fed by pride ;
Where ne'er was known the form of mock debate,
Or seen a new-made mayor's unwieldy state ;
Where change of fav'rites made no change of laws,
And senates heard before they judg'd a cause ; 60
How wouldst thou shake at Britain's modish tribe,

Dart the quick taunt, and edge the piercing gibe!
Attentive truth and nature to descry,
And pierce each scene with philosophick eye.
To thee were solemn toys or empty show   65
The robes of pleasure and the veils of woe :
All aid the farce, and all thy mirth maintain,
Whose joys are causeless, or whose griefs are vain.
  Such was the scorn that fill'd the sage's mind,
Renew'd at ev'ry glance on human kind.   70
How just that scorn ere yet thy voice declare,
Search every state, and canvass ev'ry pray'r.
  Unnumber'd suppliants crowd Preferment's gate,
Athirst for wealth, and burning to be great ;
Delusive Fortune hears th' incessant call :   75
They mount, they shine, evaporate, and fall.
On ev'ry stage the foes of peace attend ;
Hate dogs their flight, and insult mocks their end ;
Love ends with hope ; the sinking statesman's door
Pours in the morning worshipper no more ;   80
For growing names the weekly scribbler lies,
To growing wealth the dedicator flies ;
From ev'ry room descends the painted face,
That hung the bright palladium of the place,
And smoak'd in kitchens, or in auction sold,   85
To better features yields the frame of gold ;
For now no more we trace in ev'ry line
Heroick worth, benevolence divine :
The form distorted justifies the fall,
And detestation rids th' indignant wall.   90
  But will not Britain hear the last appeal,
Sign her foes' doom, or guard her fav'rites' zeal?
Thro' Freedom's sons no more remonstrance rings,
Degrading nobles and controuling kings ;
Our supple tribes repress their patriot throats, 95
And ask no questions but the price of votes ;
With weekly libels and septennial ale,
Their wish is full to riot and to rail.
  In full-blown dignity see Wolsey stand,
Law in his voice, and fortune in his hand :   100
To him the church, the realm, their pow'rs consign,
Thro' him the rays of regal bounty shine,
Turn'd by his nod the stream of honour flows,
His smile alone security bestows :

Still to new heights his restless wishes tow'r,   105
Claim leads to claim, and pow'r advances pow'r;
Till conquest unresisted ceas'd to please,
And rights submitted left him none to seize.
At length his sov'reign frowns;—the train of state
Mark the keen glance, and watch the sign to hate.   110
Where-e'er he turns he meets a stranger's eye;
His suppliants scorn him, and his followers fly:
Now drops at once the pride of awful state,
The golden canopy, the glitt'ring plate,
The regal palace, the luxurious board,   115
The liv'ried army, and the menial lord.
With age, with cares, with maladies oppress'd,
He seeks the refuge of monastick rest.
Grief aids disease, remember'd folly stings,
And his last sighs reproach the faith of kings.   120
   Speak thou, whose thoughts at humble peace repine,—
Shall Wolsey's wealth, with Wolsey's end, be thine?
Or liv'st thou now, with safer pride content,
The wisest justice on the banks of Trent?
For why did Wolsey near the steeps of fate   125
On weak foundations raise th' enormous weight?
Why, but to sink beneath misfortune's blow,
With louder ruin, to the gulphs below?
   What gave great Villiers to th' assassin's knife,
And fix'd disease on Harley's closing life?   130
What murder'd Wentworth and what exil'd Hyde,
By kings protected, and to kings ally'd?
What but their wish indulg'd in courts to shine,
And pow'r too great to keep or to resign?
   When first the college rolls receive his name,   135
The young enthusiast quits his ease for fame;
Resistless burns the fever of renown,
Caught from the strong contagion of the gown:
O'er Bodley's dome his future labours spread,
And Bacon's mansion trembles o'er his head.   140
Are these thy views? Proceed, illustrious youth,
And Virtue guard thee to the throne of Truth!
Yet should thy soul indulge the gen'rous heat,
Till captive Science yields her last retreat;
Should Reason guide thee with her brightest ray,   145
And pour on misty Doubt resistless day;
Should no false kindness lure to loose delight,

Nor praise relax, nor difficulty fright;
Should tempting Novelty thy cell refrain,
And Sloth effuse her opiate fumes in vain;   150
Should Beauty blunt on fops her fatal dart,
Nor claim the triumph of a letter'd heart;
Should no Disease thy torpid veins invade,
Nor Melancholy's phantoms haunt thy shade;
Yet hope not life from grief or danger free,   155
Nor think the doom of man revers'd for thee:
Deign on the passing world to turn thine eyes,
And pause awhile from learning, to be wise;
There mark what ills the scholar's life assail—
Toil, envy, want, the patron, and the jail.   160
See nations slowly wise, and meanly just,
To buried merit raise the tardy bust.
If dreams yet flatter, once again attend,
Hear Lydiat's life and Galileo's end.
    Nor deem, when Learning her last prize bestows,   165
The glitt'ring eminence exempt from foes:
See, when the vulgar 'scape, despis'd or aw'd,
Rebellion's vengeful talons seize on Laud!
From meaner minds tho' smaller fines content,
The plunder'd palace or sequester'd rent,   170
Mark'd out by dang'rous parts he meets the shock,
And fatal Learning leads him to the block:
Around his tomb let Art and Genius weep,
But hear his death, ye blockheads, hear and sleep.
    The festal blazes, the triumphal show,   175
The ravish'd standard, and the captive foe,
The Senate's thanks, the gazette's pompous tale,
With force resistless o'er the brave prevail.
Such bribes the rapid Greek o'er Asia whirl'd;
For such the steady Romans shook the world;   180
For such in distant lands the Britons shine,
And stain with blood the Danube or the Rhine:
This pow'r has praise, that virtue scarce can warm,
Till fame supplies the universal charm.
Yet Reason frowns on War's unequal game,   185
Where wasted nations raise a single name,
And mortgag'd states their grandsires' wreaths regret,
From age to age in everlasting debt;
Wreaths which at last the dear-bought right convey
To rust on medals, or on stones decay.   190

On what foundation stands the warrior's pride,
How just his hopes, let Swedish Charles decide :
A frame of adamant, a soul of fire,
No dangers fright him, and no labours tire ;
O'er love, o'er fear, extends his wide domain,   195
Unconquer'd lord of pleasure and of pain ;
No joys to him pacifick scepters yield,—
War sounds the trump, he rushes to the field ;
Behold surrounding kings their pow'rs combine,
And one capitulate, and one resign :   200
Peace courts his hand, but spreads her charms in vain;
" Think nothing gain'd," he cries, " till naught remain,
" On Moscow's walls till Gothic standards fly,
" And all be mine beneath the polar sky."
The march begins in military state,   205
And nations on his eye suspended wait ;
Stern Famine guards the solitary coast,
And Winter barricades the realms of Frost :
He comes ; nor want nor cold his course delay ;—
Hide, blushing Glory, hide Pultowa's day :   210
The vanquish'd hero leaves his broken bands,
And shows his miseries in distant lands ;
Condemn'd a needy supplicant to wait,
While ladies interpose and slaves debate.
But did not Chance at length her error mend ?   215
Did no subverted empire mark his end ?
Did rival monarchs give the fatal wound ?
Or hostile millions press him to the ground ?
His fall was destin'd to a barren strand,
A petty fortress, and a dubious hand.   220
He left the name, at which the world grew pale,
To point a moral, or adorn a tale.
, All times their scenes of pompous woes afford,
From Persia's tyrant to Bavaria's lord.
In gay hostility and barb'rous pride,   225
With half mankind embattled at his side,
Great Xerxes comes to seize the certain prey,
And starves exhausted regions in his way.
Attendant Flatt'ry counts his myriads o'er,
Till counted myriads sooth his pride no more ;   230
Fresh praise is try'd till madness fires his mind,—
The waves he lashes, and enchains the wind ;
New pow'rs are claim'd, new pow'rs are still bestow'd,

Till rude resistance lops the spreading god.
The daring Greeks deride the martial·show,   235
And heap their vallies with the gaudy foe.
Th' insulted sea with humbler thoughts he gains ;
A single skiff to speed his flight remains ;
Th' encumber'd oar scarce leaves the dreaded coast
Through purple billows and a floating host.   240
   The bold Bavarian, in a luckless hour,
Tries the dread summits of Cæsarean pow'r,
With unexpected legions bursts away,
And sees defenceless realms receive his sway :
Short sway !—fair Austria spreads her mournful charms ;   245
The queen, the beauty, sets the world in arms ;
From hill to hill the beacon's rousing blaze
Spreads wide the hope of plunder and of praise ;
The fierce Croatian and the wild Hussar,
With all the sons of ravage, crowd the war.   250
The baffled prince in honour's flatt'ring bloom
Of hasty greatness finds the fatal doom,
His foes' derision and his subjects' blame,
And steals to death from anguish and from shame.
   Enlarge my life with multitude of days !   255
In health, in sickness, thus the suppliant prays ;
Hides from himself his state, and shuns to know,
That life protracted is protracted woe.
Time hovers o'er, impatient to destroy,
And shuts up all the passages of joy :   260
In vain their gifts the bounteous seasons pour,
The fruit autumnal and the vernal flow'r ;
With listless eyes the dotard views the store :
He views, and wonders that they please no more.
Now pall the tasteless meats and joyless wines,   265
And Luxury with sighs her slave resigns.
Approach, ye minstrels, try the soothing strain,
Diffuse the tuneful lenitives of pain :
No sounds, alas ! would touch th' impervious ear,
Though dancing mountains witness'd Orpheus near   270
Nor lute nor lyre his feeble pow'rs attend,
Nor sweeter musick of a virtuous friend ;
But everlasting dictates crowd his tongue,
Perversely grave or positively wrong.
The still returning tale and ling'ring jest   275
Perplex the fawning niece and pamper'd guest,

While growing hopes scarce awe the gath'ring sneer,
And scarce a legacy can bribe to hear;
The watchful guests still hint the last offence,
The daughter's petulance, the son's expence,   280
Improve his heady rage with treach'rous skill,
And mould his passions till they make his will.
    Unnumber'd maladies his joints invade,
Lay siege to life, and press the dire blockade;
But unextinguish'd Av'rice still remains,   285
And dreaded losses aggravate his pains:
He turns, with anxious heart and crippled hands,
His bonds of debt and mortgages of lands;
Or views his coffers with suspicious eyes,
Unlocks his gold, and counts it till he dies.   290
    But grant, the virtues of a temp'rate prime
Bless with an age exempt from scorn or crime;
An age that melts with unperceiv'd decay,
And glides in modest innocence away;
Whose peaceful day Benevolence endears,   295
Whose night congratulating Conscience cheers;
The gen'ral fav'rite as the gen'ral friend:
Such age there is, and who shall wish its end?
    Yet ev'n on this her load Misfortune flings,
To press the weary minutes' flagging wings;   300
New sorrow rises as the day returns,
A sister sickens, or a daughter mourns.
Now kindred Merit fills the sable bier,
Now lacerated Friendship claims a tear.
Year chases year, decay pursues decay,   305
Still drops some joy from with'ring life away;
New forms arise, and diff'rent views engage,
Superfluous lags the vet'ran on the stage,
Till pitying Nature signs the last release,
And bids afflicted worth retire to peace.   310
    But few there are whom hours like these await,
Who set unclouded in the gulphs of Fate.
From Lydia's monarch should the search descend,
By Solon caution'd to regard his end,
In life's last scene what prodigies surprise—   315
Fears of the brave, and follies of the wise!
From Marlb'rough's eyes the streams of dotage flow,
And Swift expires a driv'ler and a show.
    The teeming mother, anxious for her race,

Begs for each birth the fortune of a face :   320
Yet Vane could tell what ills from beauty spring ;
And Sedley curs'd the form that pleas'd a king.
Ye nymphs of rosy lips and radiant eyes,
Whom Pleasure keeps too busy to be wise;
Whom joys with soft varieties invite,—   325
By day the frolick, and the dance by night ;
Who frown with vanity, who smile with art,
And ask the latest fashion of the heart,
What care, what rules, your heedless charms shall save,
Each nymph your rival, and each youth your slave ?   330
Against your fame with fondness hate combines,
The rival batters, and the lover mines.
With distant voice neglected Virtue calls;
Less heard and less, the faint remonstrance falls :
Tir'd with contempt, she quits the slipp'ry reign,   335
And Pride and Prudence take her seat in vain.
In crowd at once, where none the pass defend,
The harmless freedom and the private friend.
The guardians yield, by force superior ply'd :
To Int'rest, Prudence ; and to Flatt'ry, Pride.   340
Here Beauty falls betray'd, despis'd, distress'd,
And hissing Infamy proclaims the rest.
    Where then shall Hope and Fear their objects find ?
Must dull Suspense corrupt the stagnant mind?
Must helpless man, in ignorance sedate,   345
Roll darkling down the torrent of his fate?
Must no dislike alarm, no wishes rise,
No cries invoke the mercies of the skies ?—
Enquirer, cease; petitions yet remain,
Which heav'n may hear; nor deem religion vain.   350
Still raise for good the supplicating voice,
But leave to heav'n the measure and the choice ;
Safe in his pow'r, whose eyes discern afar
The secret ambush of a specious pray'r.
Implore his aid, in his decisions rest,   355
Secure, whate'er he gives, he gives the best.
Yet when the sense of sacred presence fires,
And strong devotion to the skies aspires,
Pour forth thy fervours for a healthful mind,
Obedient passions, and a will resign'd ;   360
For love, which scarce collective man can fill ;
For patience, sov'reign o'er transmuted ill ;

For faith, that, panting for a happier seat,
Counts death kind Nature's signal of retreat :
These goods for man the laws of heav'n ordain ;　　　365
These goods he grants, who grants the pow'r to gain ;
With these celestial Wisdom calms the mind,
And makes the happiness she does not find.

COLLINS.

THE PASSIONS.

WHEN Music, heav'nly maid, was young
While yet in early Greece she sung,
The Passions oft, to hear her shell,
Throng'd around her magic cell,
Exulting, trembling, raging, fainting,　　　　　5
Possest beyond the Muse's painting;
By turns they felt the glowing mind
Disturb'd, delighted, rais'd, refin'd;
Till once, 'tis said, when all were fir'd,
Fill'd with fury, rapt, inspir'd,　　　　　10
From the supporting myrtles round
They snatch'd her instruments of sound;
And, as they oft had heard apart
Sweet lessons of her forceful art,
Each, for madness rul'd the hour,　　　　　15
Would prove his own expressive power.

First Fear his hand, its skill to try,
　Amid the chords bewilder'd laid,
And back recoil'd, he knew not why,
　Ev'n at the sound himself had made.　　　　　20

Next Anger rush'd; his eyes on fire
　In lightnings own'd his secret stings;
In one rude clash he struck the lyre,
　And swept with hurried hand the strings.

With woful measures wan Despair,　　　　　25
　Low sullen sounds, his grief beguil'd,

A solemn, strange, and mingled air ;
   'Twas sad by fits, by starts 'twas wild.

But Thou, O Hope, with eyes so fair,
   What was thy delightful measure?   30
Still it whisper'd promis'd pleasure,
   And bade the lovely scenes at distance hail!
Still would her touch the strain prolong,
   And from the rocks, the woods, the vale,
She call'd on Echo still thro' all the song ;   35
   And, where her sweetest theme she chose,
   A soft responsive voice was heard at ev'ry close,
And Hope enchanted smil'd, and wav'd her golden hair.
And longer had she sung, but, with a frown,
      Revenge impatient rose :   .   40
He threw his blood-stain'd sword in thunder down,
    And with a with'ring look
   The war-denouncing trumpet took,
   And blew a blast so loud and dread,
Were ne'er prophetic sounds so full of woe.   45
  'And ever and anon he beat
   The doubling drum with furious heat;
And tho' sometimes, each dreary pause between,
   Dejected Pity at his side
   Her soul-subduing voice applied,   50
Yet still he kept his wild unalter'd mien,
While each strain'd ball of sight seem'd bursting from his head.
Thy numbers, Jealousy, to nought were fix'd,
   Sad proof of thy distressful state ;
Of diff'ring themes the veering song was mix'd ;   55
   And now it courted Love, now raving call'd on Hate.
With eyes up-rais'd, as one inspir'd,
Pale Melancholy sate retir'd,
And from her wild sequester'd seat,
In notes by distance made more sweet,   60
Pour'd thro' the mellow horn her pensive soul ;
   And, dashing soft from rocks around,
   Bubbling runnels join'd the sound ;
Thro' glades and glooms the mingled measure stole,
   Or o'er some haunted stream with fond delay,   65
    Round an holy calm diffusing,
   Love of peace and lonely musing,
  In hollow murmurs died away.

But, O, how alter'd was its sprightlier tone,
When Chearfulness, a nymph of healthiest hue,   70
  Her bow a-cross her shoulder flung,
  Her buskins gem'd with morning dew,
Blew an inspiring air, that dale and thicket rung,
  The hunter's call to Faun and Dryad known !
  The oak-crowned sisters and their chast-eyed queen,   75
  Satyrs and sylvan boys, were seen,
  Peeping from forth their alleys green ;
Brown Exercise rejoic'd to hear,
  And Sport leapt up and seiz'd his beechen spear.
Last came Joy's ecstatic trial :   80
He, with viny crown advancing,
  First to the lively pipe his hand addrest,
But soon he saw the brisk-awak'ning viol,
  Whose sweet entrancing voice he lov'd the best ;
    They would have thought, who heard the strain,   85
    They saw in Tempe's vale her native maids,
    Amidst the festal sounding shades,
To some unwearied minstrel dancing,
  While, as his flying fingers kiss'd the strings,
  Love fram'd with Mirth a gay fantastic round ;   90
  Loose were her tresses seen, her zone unbound ;
  And he, amidst his frolic play,
As if he would the charming air repay,
Shook thousand odours from his dewy wings.
O Music, sphere-descended maid,   95
Friend of Pleasure, Wisdom's aid,
Why, Goddess, why to us deny'd
Lay'st thou thy antient lyre aside ?
As in that lov'd Athenian bow'r,
You learn'd an all-commanding pow'r,   100
Thy mimic soul, O Nymph endear'd,
Can well recall what then it heard.
Where is thy native simple heart,
Devote to Virtue, Fancy, Art?
Arise, as in that elder time,   105
Warm, energic, chaste, sublime !
Thy wonders, in that godlike age,
Fill thy recording Sister's page :
'Tis said, and I believe the tale,
Thy humblest reed could more prevail,   110
Had more of strength, diviner rage,

Than all which charms this laggard age,
Ev'n all at once together found
Cecilia's mingled world of sound.
O bid our vain endeavors cease,   115
Revive the just designs of Greece!
Return in all thy simple state!
Confirm the tales her sons relate!

GRAY.

ELEGY

WRITTEN IN A COUNTRY CHURCHYARD.

THE curfew tolls the knell of parting day,
    The lowing herd winds slowly o'er the lea,
The plowman homeward plods his weary way,
    And leaves the world to darkness and to me.

Now fades the glimmering landscape on the sight,   5
    And all the air a solemn stillness holds,
Save where the beetle wheels his droning flight,
    And drowsy tinklings lull the distant folds ;

Save that, from yonder ivy-mantled tow'r,
    The moping owl does to the moon complain   10
Of such as, wand'ring near her secret bow'r,
    Molest her ancient solitary reign.

Beneath those rugged elms, that yew-tree's shade,
    Where heaves the turf in many a mould'ring heap,
Each in his narrow cell for ever laid,   15
    The rude forefathers of the hamlet sleep.

The breezy call of incense-breathing Morn,
    The swallow twitt'ring from the straw-built shed,
The cock's shrill clarion, or the echoing horn,
    No more shall rouse them from their lowly bed.   20

For them no more the blazing hearth shall burn,
    Or busy housewife ply her evening care ;
No children run to lisp their sire's return,
    Or climb his knees the envied kiss to share.

Oft did the harvest to their sickle yield,   25
    Their furrow oft the stubborn glebe has broke ;

How jocund did they drive their team afield!
How bow'd the woods beneath their sturdy stroke!

Let not Ambition mock their useful toil,
  Their homely joys, and destiny obscure;
Nor Grandeur hear with a disdainful smile
  The short and simple annals of the poor.

The boast of heraldry, the pomp of pow'r,
  And all that beauty, all that wealth e'er gave,
Await alike th' inevitable hour.   35
  The paths of glory lead but to the grave.

Nor you, ye Proud, impute to these the fault,
  If Mem'ry o'er their tomb no trophies raise,
Where thro' the long-drawn isle and fretted vault
  The pealing anthem swells the note of praise.   40

Can storied urn, or animated bust,
  Back to its mansion call the fleeting breath?
Can Honour's voice provoke the silent dust,
  Or Flatt'ry sooth the dull cold ear of Death?

Perhaps in this neglected spot is laid   45
  Some heart once pregnant with celestial fire;
Hands, that the rod of empire might have sway'd,
  Or wak'd to extasy the living lyre.

But Knowledge to their eyes her ample page
  Rich with the spoils of time did ne'er unroll;   50
Chill Penury repress'd their noble rage,
  And froze the genial current of the soul.

Full many a gem of purest ray serene
  The dark unfathom'd caves of ocean bear:
Full many a flower is born to blush unseen,   55
  And waste its sweetness on the desert air.

Some village-Hampden, that, with dauntless breast,
  The little Tyrant of his fields withstood,
Some mute inglorious Milton here may rest,
  Some Cromwell guiltless of his country's blood.   60

Th' applause of list'ning senates to command,
  The threats of pain and ruin to despise,
To scatter plenty o'er a smiling land,
  And read their hist'ry in a nation's eyes,

Their lot forbad : nor circumscrib'd alone 65
  Their growing virtues, but their crimes confin'd ;
Forbad to wade through slaughter to a throne,
  And shut the gates of mercy on mankind,

The struggling pangs of conscious truth to hide,
  To quench the blushes of ingenuous shame, 70
Or heap the shrine of Luxury and Pride
  With incense kindled at the Muse's flame.

Far from the madding crowd's ignoble strife,
  Their sober wishes never learn'd to stray ;
Along the cool sequester'd vale of life 75
  They kept the noiseless tenor of their way.

Yet ev'n these bones from insult to protect
  Some frail memorial still erected nigh,
With uncouth rhimes and shapeless sculpture deck'd,
  Implores the passing tribute of a sigh. 80

Their name, their years, spelt by th' unletter'd Muse,
  The place of fame and elegy supply :
And many a holy text around she strews,
  That teach the rustic moralist to die.

For who, to dumb Forgetfulness a prey, 85
  This pleasing anxious being e'er resign'd,
Left the warm precincts of the chearful day,
  Nor cast one longing ling'ring look behind?

On some fond breast the parting soul relies,
  Some pious drops the closing eye requires ; 90
Ev'n from the tomb the voice of Nature cries,
  Ev'n in our ashes live their wonted fires.

For thee, who mindful of th' unhonour'd Dead
  Dost in these lines their artless tales relate ;
If chance, by lonely Contemplation led, 95
  Some kindred spirit shall inquire thy fate,

Haply some hoary-headed swain may say,
  "Oft have we seen him at the peep of dawn
Brushing with hasty steps the dews away,
  To meet the sun upon the upland lawn. 100

"There at the foot of yonder nodding beech,
  That wreathes its old fantastic roots so high,
His listless length at noontide would he stretch,
  And pore upon the brook that babbles by.

G

" Hard by yon wood, now smiling as in scorn,   105
    Mutt'ring his wayward fancies he would rove;
  · Now drooping, woeful wan, like one forlorn,
    Or craz'd with care, or cross'd in hopeless love.

" One morn I miss'd him on the custom'd hill,
    Along the heath and near his fav'rite tree;   110
  Another came; nor yet beside the rill,
    Nor up the lawn, nor at the wood was he;

" The next, with dirges due in sad array
    Slow thro' the church-way path we saw him borne.
  Approach and read (for thou canst read) the lay   115
    Grav'd on the stone beneath yon aged thorn."

THE EPITAPH.

Here rests his head upon the lap of Earth,
    A youth to Fortune and to Fame unknown:
Fair Science frown'd not on his humble birth,
    And Melancholy mark'd him for her own.   120

Large was his bounty, and his soul sincere,
    Heav'n did a recompense as largely send:
He gave to Mis'ry all he had, a tear,
  . He gained from Heaven ('twas all he wish'd) a friend.

No farther seek his merits to disclose,   125
    Or draw his frailties from their dread abode,
(There they alike in trembling hope repose,)
  The bosom of his Father and his God.

THE PROGRESS OF POESY.

I. I.

Awake, Æolian lyre, awake,
And give to rapture all thy trembling strings.
  From Helicon's harmonious springs
A thousand rills their mazy progress take :
The laughing flowers, that round them blow,   5
Drink life and fragrance as they flow.
Now the rich stream of music winds along,
Deep, majestic, smooth, and strong,
Thro' verdant vales, and Ceres' golden reign :
Now rowling down the steep amain,   10

Headlong, impetuous, see it pour ;
The rocks and nodding groves rebellow to the roar.

I. 2.

Oh! Sovereign of the willing soul,
Parent of sweet and solemn-breathing airs,
Enchanting shell! the sullen Cares   15
   And frantic Passions hear thy soft controul.
On Thracia's hills the Lord of War
Has curb'd the fury of his car,
And drop'd his thirsty lance at thy command.
Perching on the scept'red hand   20
Of Jove, thy magic lulls the feather'd king
With ruffled plumes, and flagging wing :
Quench'd in dark clouds of slumber lie
The terror of his beak, and light'ning of his eye.

I. 3.

Thee the voice, the dance, obey,   25
Temper'd to thy warbled lay.
O'er Idalia's velvet-green
The rosy-crowned Loves are seen
On Cytherea's day
With antic Sport, and blue-eyed Pleasures,   30
Frisking light in frolic measures ;
Now pursuing, now retreating,
   Now in circling troops they meet :
To brisk notes in cadence beating,
   Glance their many-twinkling feet.   35
Slow melting strains their Queen's approach declare :
   Where'er she turns, the Graces homage pay :
With arms sublime, that float upon the air,
   In gliding state she wins her easy way :
O'er her warm cheek, and rising bosom, move   40
The bloom of young Desire, and purple light of Love.

II. I.

Man's feeble race what ills await !
Labour and Penury, the racks of Pain,
Disease, and Sorrow's weeping train,
   And Death, sad refuge from the storms of Fate !   45

The fond complaint, my song, disprove,
And justify the laws of Jove.
Say, has he giv'n in vain the heav'nly Muse?
Night and all her sickly dews,
Her spectres wan, and birds of boding cry,   50
He gives to range the dreary sky;
Till down the eastern cliffs afar
Hyperion's march they spy, and glitt'ring shafts of war.

II. 2.

In climes beyond the solar road,
Where shaggy forms o'er ice-built mountains roam,   55
The Muse has broke the twilight-gloom
    To chear the shiv'ring native's dull abode.
And oft, beneath the od'rous shade
Of Chili's boundless forests laid,
She deigns to hear the savage youth repeat,   60
In loose numbers wildly sweet,
Their feather-cinctur'd chiefs, and dusky loves.
Her track, where'er the Goddess roves,
Glory pursue, and generous Shame,
Th' unconquerable Mind, and Freedom's holy flame.   65

II. 3.

Woods, that wave o'er Delphi's steep,
Isles, that crown th' Ægean deep,
    Fields, that cool Ilissus laves,
    Or where Mæander's amber waves
In lingering lab'rinths creep,   70
    How do your tuneful echos languish,
    Mute, but to the voice of Anguish!
Where each old poetic mountain
    Inspiration breath'd around;
Ev'ry shade and hallow'd fountain   75
    Murmur'd deep a solemn sound:
Till the sad Nine, in Greece's evil hour,
    Left their Parnassus for the Latian plains.
Alike they scorn the pomp of tyrant-Power,
    And coward Vice, that revels in her chains.   80
When Latium had her lofty spirit lost,
They sought, oh Albion! next thy sea-encircled coast.

III. 1.

Far from the sun and summer-gale,
In thy green lap was Nature's Darling laid,
What time, where lucid Avon stray'd,   85
    To him the mighty Mother did unveil
Her aweful face : The dauntless Child
Stretch'd forth his little arms, and smil'd.
"This pencil take (she said), whose colours clear
Richly paint the vernal year :   90
Thine too these golden keys, immortal Boy !
This can unlock the gates of Joy ;
Of Horror that, and thrilling Fears,
Or ope the sacred source of sympathetic Tears."

III. 2.

Nor second He, that rode sublime   95
Upon the seraph-wings of Extasy,
The secrets of th' Abyss to spy.
    He pass'd the flaming bounds of Place and Time :
The living Throne, the sapphire blaze,
Where Angels tremble, while they gaze,   100
He saw ; but, blasted with excess of light,
Clos'd his eyes in endless night.
Behold, where Dryden's less presumptuous car
Wide o'er the fields of Glory bear
Two Coursers of ethereal race,   105
With necks in thunder cloath'd, and long-resounding pace.

III. 3.

Hark, his hands the lyre explore !
Bright-ey'd Fancy, hovering o'er,
Scatters from her pictur'd urn
Thoughts that breathe, and words that burn.   110
But ah ! 'tis heard no more—
    Oh ! Lyre divine, what daring Spirit
    Wakes thee now? Tho' he inherit
Nor the pride, nor ample pinion,
    That the Theban Eagle bear,   115
Sailing with supreme dominion
    Thro' the azure deep of air :
Yet oft before his infant eyes would run

Such forms as glitter in the Muse's ray,
With orient hues, unborrow'd of the sun :   120
 Yet shall he mount, and keep his distant way
Beyond the limits of a vulgar fate,
Beneath the Good how far !—but far above the Great.

THE BARD.

I. I.

" RUIN seize thee, ruthless King !
 Confusion on thy banners wait ;
Tho' fann'd by Conquest's crimson wing,
 They mock the air with idle state.
Helm, nor hauberk's twisted mail,   5
Nor e'en thy virtues, Tyrant, shall avail
  To save thy secret soul from nightly fears,
  From Cambria's curse, from Cambria's tears !"
Such were the sounds that o'er the crested pride
 Of the first Edward scatter'd wild dismay, 10
As down the steep of Snowdon's shaggy side
 He wound with toilsome march his long array.
Stout Glo'ster stood aghast in speechless trance :
"'To arms !" cried Mortimer, and couch'd his quiv'ring lance.

I. 2.

On a rock, whose haughty brow   15
Frowns o'er old Conway's foaming flood,
 Rob'd in the sable garb of woe,
With haggard eyes the Poet stood
(Loose his beard, and hoary hair
Stream'd, like a meteor, to the troubled air), 20
And with a Master's hand and Prophet's fire
Struck the deep sorrows of his lyre.
 " Hark, how each giant-oak, and desert cave,
Sighs to the torrent's aweful voice beneath !
O'er thee, oh King ! their hundred arms they wave, 25
 Revenge on thee in hoarser murmurs breathe ;
Vocal no more, since Cambria's fatal day,
To high-born Hoel's harp, or soft Llewellyn's lay.

I. 3.

"Cold is Cadwallo's tongue,
That hushed the stormy main :   30
Brave Urien sleeps upon his craggy bed :
  Mountains, ye mourn in vain
  Modred, whose magic song
Made huge Plinlimmon bow his cloud-top'd head.
  On dreary Arvon's shore they lie,   35
Smear'd with gore, and ghastly pale :
Far, far aloof th' affrighted ravens sail ;
  The famish'd eagle screams, and passes by.
Dear lost companions of my tuneful art,
  Dear, as the light that visits these sad eyes,   40
Dear, as the ruddy drops that warm my heart,
  Ye died amidst your dying country's cries—
No more I weep. They do not sleep.
  On yonder cliffs, a griesly band,
I see them sit ; they linger yet,   45
  Avengers of their native land :
With me in dreadful harmony they join,
And weave with bloody hands the tissue of thy line.

II. I.

"Weave the warp and weave the woof,
The winding-sheet of Edward's race :   50
  Give ample room, and verge enough
The characters of hell to trace.
Mark the year, and mark the night,
When Severn shall re-echo with affright
The shrieks of death thro' Berkley's roofs that ring, 55
Shrieks of an agonizing king !
  She-wolf of France, with unrelenting fangs
That tear'st the bowels of thy mangled mate,
  From thee be born, who o'er thy country hangs
The scourge of heaven. What terrors round him wait ! 60
Amazement in his van, with Flight combined,
And Sorrow's faded form, and Solitude behind.

II. 2.

" Mighty Victor, mighty Lord !
Low on his funeral couch he lies !
  No pitying heart, no eye, afford   65
A tear to grace his obsequies.
  Is the sable warriour fled ?
Thy son is gone. He rests among the dead.
The swarm that in thy noontide beam were born ?
Gone to salute the rising morn.   70
Fair laughs the Morn, and soft the Zephyr blows,
  While proudly riding o'er the azure realm
In gallant trim the gilded vessel goes ;
  Youth on the prow, and Pleasure at the helm ;
Regardless of the sweeping Whirlwind's sway,   75
That, hush'd in grim repose, expects his evening-prey.

II. 3.

" Fill high the sparkling bowl,
The rich repast prepare,
  Reft of a crown, he yet may share the feast :
Close by the regal chair   80
  Fell Thirst and Famine scowl
  A baleful smile upon their baffled guest.
Heard ye the din of battle bray,
  Lance to lance, and horse to horse?
  Long years of havock urge their destin'd course,   85
And thro' the kindred squadrons mow their way.
  Ye towers of Julius, London's lasting shame,
With many a foul and midnight murther fed,
  Revere his Consort's faith, his Father's fame,
And spare the meek Usurper's holy head !   90
Above, below, the rose of snow,
  Twin'd with her blushing foe, we spread :
The bristled Boar in infant-gore
  Wallows beneath the thorny shade.
Now, brothers, bending o'er th' accursed loom,   95
Stamp we our vengeance deep, and ratify his doom.

III. I.

" Edward, lo ! to sudden fate
(Weave we the woof.   The thread is spun.)
   Half of thy heart we consecrate.
(The web is wove.   The work is done.)   100
Stay, oh stay ! nor thus forlorn
Leave me unbless'd, unpitied, here to mourn :
In yon bright track, that fires the western skies,
They melt, they vanish from my eyes.
But oh ! what solemn scenes on Snowdon's height   105
   Descending slow their glitt'ring skirts unroll?
Visions of glory, spare my aching sight !
   Ye unborn ages, crowd not on my soul !
No more our long-lost Arthur we bewail.
All hail, ye genuine kings, Britannia's issue, hail !   110

III. 2.

" Girt with many a baron bold
Sublime their starry fronts they rear ;
   And gorgeous dames, and statesmen old
In bearded majesty, appear.
In the midst a form divine !   115
Her eye proclaims her of the Briton-line ;
Her lion-port, her awe-commanding face,
Attemper'd sweet to virgin-grace.
What strings symphonious tremble in the air,
   What strains of vocal transport round her play,   120
Hear from the grave, great Taliessin, hear ;
   They breathe a soul to animate thy clay.
Bright Rapture calls, and soaring, as she sings,
Waves in the eye of Heav'n her many-colour'd wings.

III. 3.

" The verse adorn again   125
   Fierce War and faithful Love
And Truth severe—by fairy Fiction drest.
   In buskin'd measures move
Pale Grief, and pleasing Pain
With Horror, tyrant of the throbbing breast.   130

A voice, as of the Cherub-Choir,
Gales from blooming Eden bear ;
And distant warblings lessen on my ear,
   That lost in long futurity expire.
Fond impious man, think'st thou yon sanguine cloud,   135
   Rais'd by thy breath, has quench'd the orb of day?
To-morrow he repairs the golden flood,
   And warms the nations with redoubled ray.
Enough for me : with joy I see
   The different doom our fates assign :   140
Be thine Despair, and scept'red Care ;
   To triumph and to die are mine."
He spoke, and headlong from the mountain's height
Deep in the roaring tide he plung'd to endless night.

GOLDSMITH.

THE TRAVELLER;

OR, A PROSPECT OF SOCIETY.

REMOTE, unfriended, melancholy, slow,
Or by the lazy Scheld or wandering Po;
Or onward, where the rude Carinthian boor
Against the houseless stranger shuts the door;
Or where Campania's plain forsaken lyes,   5
A weary waste expanding to the skies;
Where'er I roam, whatever realms to see,
My heart untravell'd fondly turns to thee;
Still to my brother turns, with ceaseless pain,
And drags at each remove a lengthening chain.   10
   Eternal blessings crown my earliest friend,
And round his dwelling guardian saints attend:
Blest be that spot where cheerful guests retire
To pause from toil, and trim their ev'ning fire:
Blest that abode where want and pain repair,   15
And every stranger finds a ready chair:
Blest be those feasts, with simple plenty crown'd,
Where all the ruddy family around
Laugh at the jests or pranks that never fail,
Or sigh with pity at some mournful tale;   20
Or press the bashful stranger to his food,
And learn the luxury of doing good.
   But me, not destin'd such delights to share,
My prime of life in wand'ring spent and care;
Impell'd, with steps unceasing, to pursue   25
Some fleeting good that mocks me with the view;

That, like the circle bounding earth and skies,
Allures from far, yet, as I follow, flies;
My fortune leads to traverse realms alone,
And find no spot of all the world my own. 30
 Even now, where Alpine solitudes ascend,
I sit me down a pensive hour to spend; .
And plac'd on high above the storm's career,
Look downward where an hundred realms appear;
Lakes, forests, cities, plains extending wide, 35
The pomp of kings, the shepherd's humbler pride.
 When thus Creation's charms around combine,
Amidst the store should thankless pride repine?
Say, should the philosophic mind disdain
That good which makes each humbler bosom vain? 40
Let school-taught pride dissemble all it can,
These little things are great to little man;
And wiser he, whose sympathetic mind
Exults in all the good of all mankind.
Ye glitt'ring towns, with wealth and splendour crown'd; 45
Ye fields, where summer spreads profusion round;
Ye lakes, whose vessels catch the busy gale;
Ye bending swains, that dress the flow'ry vale;
For me your tributary stores combine:
Creation's heir, the world, the world is mine. 50
 As some lone miser, visiting his store,
Bends at his treasure, counts, recounts it o'er;
Hoards after hoards his rising raptures fill,
Yet still he sighs, for hoards are wanting still:
Thus to my breast alternate passions rise, 55
Pleas'd with each good that Heaven to man supplies:
Yet oft a sigh prevails, and sorrows fall,
To see the hoard of human bliss so small;
And oft I wish amidst the scene to find
Some spot to real happiness consign'd, 60
Where my worn soul, each wand'ring hope at rest,
May gather bliss to see my fellows blest.
 But where to find that happiest spot below
Who can direct, when all pretend to know?
The shudd'ring tenant of the frigid zone 65
Boldly proclaims that happiest spot his own;
Extols the treasures of his stormy seas,
And his long nights of revelry and ease:
The naked negroe, panting at the line,

Boasts of his golden sands and palmy wine,   70
Basks in the glare, or stems the tepid wave,
And thanks his gods for all the good they gave.
Such is the patriot's boast where'er we roam ;
His first, best country ever is at home.
And yet, perhaps, if countries we compare,   75
And estimate the blessings which they share,
Tho' patriots flatter, still shall wisdom find
An equal portion dealt to all mankind ;
As different good, by Art or Nature given,
To different nations makes their blessings even.   80
   Nature, a mother kind alike to all,
Still grants her bliss at Labour's earnest call :
With food as well the peasant is supply'd
On Idra's cliffs as Arno's shelvy side ;
And though the rocky crested summits frown,   85
These rocks by custom turn to beds of down.
From Art more various are the blessings sent ;
Wealth, commerce, honour, liberty, content.
Yet these each other's power so strong contest,
That either seems destructive of the rest.   90
Where wealth and freedom reign, contentment fails
And honour sinks where commerce long prevails.
Hence every state, to one lov'd blessing prone,
Conforms and models life to that alone.
Each to the favourite happiness attends,   95
And spurns the plan that aims at other ends :
'Till carried to excess in each domain,
This fav'rite good begets peculiar pain.
   But let us try these truths with closer eyes,
And trace them through the prospect as it lies :   100
Here for a while my proper cares resign'd,
Here let me sit in sorrow for mankind ;
Like yon neglected shrub at random cast,
That shades the steep, and sighs at every blast.
   Far to the right, where Apennine ascends,   105
Bright as the summer, Italy extends :
Its uplands sloping deck the mountain's side,
Woods over woods in gay theatric pride ;
While oft some temple's mould'ring tops between
With venerable grandeur mark the scene.   110
   Could Nature's bounty satisfy the breast,
The sons of Italy were surely blest.

Whatever fruits in different climes were found,
That proudly rise, or humbly court the ground;
Whatever blooms in torrid tracts appear,   115
Whose bright succession decks the varied year;
Whatever sweets salute the northern sky
With vernal lives, that blossom but to die;
These, here disporting, own the kindred soil,
Nor ask luxuriance from the planter's toil;   120
While sea-born gales their gelid wings expand
To winnow fragrance round the smiling land.
  But small the bliss that sense alone bestows,
And sensual bliss is all the nation knows.
In florid beauty groves and fields appear;   125
Man seems the only growth that dwindles here.
Contrasted faults through all his manners reign:
Though poor, luxurious; though submissive, vain;
Though grave, yet trifling; zealous, yet untrue;
And ev'n in penance planning sins anew.   130
All evils here contaminate the mind
That opulence departed leaves behind;
For wealth was theirs, not far remov'd the date
When commerce proudly flourish'd through the state;
At her command the palace learnt to rise,   135
Again the long-fallen column sought the skies,
The canvas glow'd, beyond e'en nature warm,
The pregnant quarry teem'd with human form;
Till, more unsteady than the southern gale,
Commerce on other shores display'd her sail;   140
While nought remain'd of all that riches gave,
But towns unman'd, and lords without a slave:
And late the nation found with fruitless skill
Its former strength was but plethoric ill.
  Yet still the loss of wealth is here supplied   145
By arts, the splendid wrecks of former pride;
From these the feeble heart and long-fall'n mind
An easy compensation seem to find.
Here may be seen, in bloodless pomp array'd,
The paste-board triumph and the cavalcade,   150
Processions form'd for piety and love,
A mistress or a saint in every grove.
By sports like these are all their cares beguil'd;
The sports of children satisfy the child.
Each nobler aim, represt by long controul,   155

Now sinks at last, or feebly mans the soul ;
While low delights, succeeding fast behind,
In happier meanness occupy the mind :
As in those domes where Cæsars once bore sway,
Defac'd by time and tottering in decay,   160
There in the ruin, heedless of the dead,
The shelter-seeking peasant builds his shed ;
And, wond'ring man could want the larger pile,
Exults, and owns his cottage with a smile.
  My soul, turn from them, turn we to survey,   165
Where rougher climes a nobler race display ;
Where the bleak Swiss their stormy mansions tread,
And force a churlish soil for scanty bread.
No product here the barren hills afford,
But man and steel, the soldier and his sword :   170
No vernal blooms their torpid rocks array,
But winter ling'ring chills the lap of May :
No Zephyr fondly sues the mountain's breast,
But meteors glare, and stormy glooms invest.
  Yet, still, even here content can spread a charm,   175
Redress the clime, and all its rage disarm.
Though poor the peasant's hut, his feasts tho' small,
He sees his little lot the lot of all ;
Sees no contiguous palace rear its head
To shame the meanness of his humble shed ;   180
No costly lord the sumptuous banquet deal
To make him loath his vegetable meal ;
But calm, and bred in ignorance and toil,
Each wish contracting fits him to the soil.
Chearful at morn he wakes from short repose,   185
Breathes the keen air, and carrols as he goes ;
With patient angle trolls the finny deep ;
Or drives his venturous plow-share to the steep ;
Or seeks the den where snow-tracks mark the way,
And drags the struggling savage into day.   190
At night returning, every labour sped,
He sits him down the monarch of a shed ;
Smiles by his chearful fire, and round surveys
His children's looks, that brighten at the blaze ;
While his lov'd partner, boastful of her hoard,   195
Displays her cleanly platter on the board :
And haply too some pilgrim, thither led,
With many a tale repays the nightly bed.

Thus every good his native wilds impart
Imprints the patriot passion on his heart ;
And e'en those ills that round his mansion rise   200
Enhance the bliss his scanty fund supplies.
Dear is that shed to which his soul conforms,
And dear that hill which lifts him to the storms ;
And as a child, when scaring sounds molest,
Clings close and closer to the mother's breast,   205
So the loud torrent and the whirlwind's roar
But bind him to his native mountains more.
    Such are the charms to barren states assign'd ;
Their wants but few, their wishes all confin'd.   210
Yet let them only share the praises due:
If few their wants, their pleasures are but few ;
For every want that stimulates the breast
Becomes a source of pleasure when redrest ;
Whence from such lands each pleasing science flies   215
That first excites desire, and then supplies ;
Unknown to them, when sensual pleasures cloy,
To fill the languid pause with finer joy ;
Unknown those powers that raise the soul to flame,
Catch every nerve, and vibrate through the frame.   220
Their level life is but a smould'ring fire,
Unquench'd by want, unfann'd by strong desire ;
Unfit for raptures, or, if raptures cheer
On some high festival of once a year,
In wild excess the vulgar breast takes fire,   225
Till, buried in debauch, the bliss expire.
    But not their joys alone thus coarsely flow :
Their morals, like their pleasures, are but low ;
For, as refinement stops, from sire to son
Unalter'd, unimprov'd, the manners run,   230
And love's and friendship's finely-pointed dart
Fall blunted from each indurated heart.
Some sterner virtues o'er the mountain's breast
May sit, like falcons, cow'ring on the nest ;
But all the gentler morals, such as play   235
Thro' life's more culter'd walks, and charm the way,
These, far dispers'd, on timorous pinions fly,
To sport and flutter in a kinder sky.
    To kinder skies, where gentler manners reign,
I turn ; and France displays her bright domain.   240
Gay, sprightly land of mirth and social ease,

Pleas'd with thyself, whom all the world can please,
How often have I led thy sportive choir,
With tuneless pipe, beside the murmuring Loire?
Where shading elms along the margin grew, 245
And freshen'd from the wave the Zephyr flew ;
And haply, though my harsh touch, faltering still,
But mocked all tune, and marr'd the dancer's skill,
Yet would the village praise my wonderous power,
And dance, forgetful of the noon-tide hour. 250
Alike all ages. Dames of ancient days
Have led their children through the mirthful maze,
And the gay grandsire, skill'd in gestic lore,
Has frisk'd beneath the burthen of threescore.
  So blest a life these thoughtless realms display ; 255
Thus idly busy rolls their world away ;
Theirs are those arts that mind to mind endear,
For honour forms the social temper here.
Honour, that praise which real merit gains,
Or even imaginary worth obtains, 260
Here passes current : paid from hand to hand,
It shifts in splendid traffic round the land ;
From courts to camps, to cottages, it strays,
And all are taught an avarice of praise.
They please, are pleas'd ; they give to get esteem ; 265
Till, seeming blest, they grow to what they seem.
  But while this softer art their bliss supplies,
It gives their follies also room to rise ;
For praise too dearly lov'd, or warmly sought,
Enfeebles all internal strength of thought, 270
And the weak soul, within itself unblest,
Leans for all pleasure on another's breast.
Hence ostentation here, with tawdry art,
Pants for the vulgar praise which fools impart ;
Here vanity assumes her pert grimace, 275
And trims her robes of frize with copper lace ;
Here beggar pride defrauds her daily cheer,
To boast one splendid banquet once a year ;
The mind still turns where shifting fashion draws,
Nor weighs the solid worth of self-applause. 280
  To men of other minds my fancy flies,
Embosom'd in the deep where Holland lies.
Methinks her patient sons before me stand,
Where the broad ocean leans against the land,

And, sedulous to stop the coming tide,   285
Lift the tall rampire's artificial pride.
Onward methinks, and diligently slow,
The firm connected bulwark seems to grow ;
Spreads its long arms amidst the watry roar,
Scoops out an empire, and usurps the shore.   290
While the pent ocean, rising o'er the pile,
Sees an amphibious world beneath him smile :
The slow canal, the yellow blossom'd vale,
The willow tufted bank, the gliding sail,
The crowded mart, the cultivated plain,—   295
A new creation rescu'd from his reign.
    Thus while around the wave-subjected soil
Impels the native to repeated toil,
Industrious habits in each bosom reign,
And industry begets a love of gain.   300
Hence all the good from opulence that springs,
With all those ills superfluous treasure brings,
Are here display'd. Their much-lov'd wealth imparts
Convenience, plenty, elegance, and arts :
But view them closer, craft and fraud appear ;   305
E'en liberty itself is barter'd here.
At gold's superior charms all freedom flies ;
The needy sell it, and the rich man buys ;
A land of tyrants, and a den of slaves,
Here wretches seek dishonourable graves,   310
And calmly bent, to servitude conform,
Dull as their lakes that slumber in the storm.
    Heavens ! how unlike their Belgic sires of old
Rough, poor, content, ungovernably bold ;
War in each breast, and freedom on each brow :   315
How much unlike the sons of Britain now !
    Fir'd at the sound, my genius spreads her wing,
And flies where Britain courts the western spring ;
Where lawns extend that scorn Arcadian pride,
And brighter streams than fam'd Hydaspis glide.   320
There all around the gentlest breezes stray ;
There gentle music melts on every spray ;
Creation's mildest charms are there combin'd,
Extremes are only in the master's mind !
Stern o'er each bosom Reason holds her state,   325
With daring aims irregularly great ;
Pride in their port, defiance in their eye,

I see the lords of human kind pass by;
Intent on high designs, a thoughtful band,
By forms unfashion'd, fresh from Nature's hand,   330
Fierce in their native hardiness of soul,
True to imagin'd right, above controul,
While even the peasant boasts these rights to scan,
And learns to venerate himself as man.
　　Thine, Freedom, thine the blessings pictur'd here ;   335
Thine are those charms that dazzle and endear:
Too blest indeed, were such without alloy:
But foster'd even by Freedom ills annoy :
That independence Britons prize too high
Keeps man from man, and breaks the social tie ;   340
The self-dependent lordlings stand alone,
All claims that bind and sweeten life unknown.
Here, by the bonds of nature feebly held,
Minds combat minds, repelling and repell'd ;
Ferments arise, imprison'd factions roar,   345
Represt ambition struggles round her shore,
Till, over-wrought, the general system feels
Its motions stop, or phrenzy fire the wheels.
　　Nor this the worst.　As nature's ties decay,
As duty, love, and honour fail to sway,   350
Fictitious bonds, the bonds of wealth and law,
Still gather strength, and force unwilling awe.
Hence all obedience bows to these alone,
And talent sinks, and merit weeps unknown:
Till time may come, when, stript of all her charms,   355
The land of scholars and the nurse of arms,
Where noble stems transmit the patriot flame,
Where kings have toil'd and poets wrote for fame,
One sink of level avarice shall lie,
And scholars, soldiers, kings, unhonour'd die.   360
　　Yet think not, thus when Freedom's ills I state,
I mean to flatter kings, or court the great :
Ye powers of truth that bid my soul aspire,
Far from my bosom drive the low desire.
And thou, fair Freedom, taught alike to feel   365
The rabble's rage and tyrant's angry steel ;
Thou transitory flower, alike undone
By proud contempt or favour's fostering sun,
Still may thy blooms the changeful clime endure !
I only would repress them to secure :   370

For just experience tells, in every soil,
That those who think must govern those that toil ;
And all that Freedom's highest aims can reach
Is but to lay proportion'd loads on each.
Hence, should one order disproportioned grow,   375
Its double weight must ruin all below.
  O then how blind to all that truth requires,
Who think it freedom when a part aspires !
Calm is my soul, nor apt to rise in arms,
Except when fast approaching danger warms ;   380
But when contending chiefs blockade the throne,
Contracting regal power to stretch their own,
When I behold a factious band agree
To call it freedom when themselves are free,
Each wanton judge new penal statutes draw,   385
Laws grind the poor, and rich men rule the law,
The wealth of climes where savage nations roam
Pillag'd from slaves to purchase slaves at home,
Fear, pity, justice, indignation start,
Tear off reserve, and bare my swelling heart ;   390
'Till half a patriot, half a coward grown,
I fly from petty tyrants to the throne.
  Yes, brother, curse with me that baleful hour
When first ambition struck at regal power ;
And thus polluting honour in its source,   395
Gave wealth to sway the mind with double force.
Have we not seen, round Britain's peopled shore,
Her useful sons exchanged for useless ore,
Seen all her triumphs but destruction haste,
Like flaring tapers brightening as they waste?   400
Seen opulence, her grandeur to maintain,
Lead stern depopulation in her train,
And over fields where scattered hamlets rose
In barren solitary pomp repose?
Have we not seen at pleasure's lordly call   405
The smiling long-frequented village fall?
Beheld the duteous son, the sire decay'd,
The modest matron, and the blushing maid,
Forc'd from their homes, a melancholy train,
To traverse climes beyond the western main ;   410
Where wild Oswego spreads her swamps around,
And Niagara stuns with thund'ring sound?
  Even now, perhaps, as there some pilgrim strays

Through tangled forests and through dangerous ways,
Where beasts with man divided empire claim,   415
And the brown Indian marks with murderous aim ;
There, while above the giddy tempest flies,
And all around distressful yells arise,
The pensive exile, bending with his woe,
To stop too fearful, and too faint to go,   420
Casts a long look where England's glories shine,
And bids his bosom sympathize with mine.
　Vain, very vain, my weary search to find
That bliss which only centers in the mind :
Why have I stray'd from pleasure and repose,   425
To seek a good each government bestows ?
In every government, though terrors reign,
Though tyrant kings or tyrant laws restrain,
How small, of all that human hearts endure,
That part which laws or kings can cause or cure ;   430
Still to ourselves in every place consign'd,
Our own felicity we make or find :
With secret course, which no loud storms annoy,
Glides the smooth current of domestic joy.
The lifted ax, the agonizing wheel,   435
Luke's iron crown, and Damien's bed of steel,
To men remote from power but rarely known,
Leave reason, faith, and conscience all our own.

THE DESERTED VILLAGE.

SWEET AUBURN ! loveliest village of the plain ;
Where health and plenty cheared the labouring swain,
Where smiling spring its earliest visit paid,
And parting summer's lingering blooms delayed :
Dear lovely bowers of innocence and ease,   5
Seats of my youth, when every sport could please,
How often have I loitered o'er thy green,
Where humble happiness endeared each scene !
How often have I paused on every charm,
The sheltered cot, the cultivated farm,   10
The never-failing brook, the busy mill,

The decent church that topt the neighbouring hill,
The hawthorn bush, with seats beneath the shade,
For talking age and whispering lovers made!
How often have I blest the coming day,   15
When toil remitting lent its turn to play,
And all the village train, from labour free,
Led up their sports beneath the spreading tree,
While many a pastime circled in the shade,
The young contending as the old surveyed;   20
And many a gambol frolicked o'er the ground,
And sleights of art and feats of strength went round.
And still, as each repeated pleasure tired,
Succeeding sports the mirthful band inspired;
The dancing pair that simply sought renown   25
By holding out to tire each other down;
The swain mistrustless of his smutted face,
While secret laughter tittered round the place;
The bashful virgin's side-long looks of love,
The matron's glance that would those looks reprove.   30
These were thy charms, sweet village! sports like these,
With sweet succession, taught even toil to please:
These round thy bowers their chearful influence shed:
These were thy charms—but all these charms are fled.
   Sweet smiling village, loveliest of the lawn,   35
Thy sports are fled, and all thy charms withdrawn;
Amidst thy bowers the tyrant's hand is seen,
And desolation saddens all thy green:
One only master grasps the whole domain,
And half a tillage stints thy smiling plain.   40
No more thy glassy brook reflects the day,
But, choaked with sedges, works its weedy way;
Along thy glades, a solitary guest,
The hollow sounding bittern guards its nest;
Amidst thy desert walks the lapwing flies,   45
And tires their ecchoes with unvaried cries;
Sunk are thy bowers in shapeless ruin all,
And the long grass o'ertops the mouldering wall;
And trembling, shrinking from the spoiler's hand,
Far, far away thy children leave the land.   50
   Ill fares the land, to hastening ills a prey,
Where wealth accumulates, and men decay:
Princes and lords may flourish, or may fade;
A breath can make them, as a breath has made:

But a bold peasantry, their country's pride,   55
When once destroyed, can never be supplied.
    A time there was, ere England's griefs began,
When every rood of ground maintained its man;
For him light labour spread her wholesome store,
Just gave what life required, but gave no more: 60
His best companions, innocence and health;
And his best riches, ignorance of wealth.
    But times are altered; trade's unfeeling train
Usurp the land and dispossess the swain;
Along the lawn, where scattered hamlets rose,   65
Unwieldy wealth and cumbrous pomp repose,
And every want to opulence allied,
And every pang that folly pays to pride.
These gentle hours that plenty bade to bloom,
Those calm desires that asked but little room,   70
Those healthful sports that graced the peaceful scene,
Lived in each look, and brightened all the green;
These, far departing, seek a kinder shore,
And rural mirth and manners are no more.
    Sweet Auburn! parent of the blissful hour,   75
Thy glades forlorn confess the tyrant's power.
Here, as I take my solitary rounds
Amidst thy tangling walks and ruined grounds,
And, many a year elapsed, return to view
Where once the cottage stood, the hawthorn grew,   80
Remembrance wakes with all her busy train,
Swells at my breast, and turns the past to pain.
    In all my wanderings round this world of care,
In all my griefs—and GOD has given my share—
I still had hopes, my latest hours to crown,   85
Amidst these humble bowers to lay me down;
To husband out life's taper at the close,
And keep the flame from wasting by repose:
I still had hopes, for pride attends us still,
Amidst the swains to show my book-learned skill,   90
Around my fire an evening groupe to draw,
And tell of all I felt, and all I saw;
And, as an hare whom hounds and horns pursue
.Pants to the place from whence at first she flew,
I still had hopes, my long vexations past,   95
Here to return—and die at home at last.
    O blest retirement, friend to life's decline,

Retreats from care, that never must be mine,
How happy he who crowns in shades like these
A youth of labour with an age of ease ;   100
Who quits a world where strong temptations try,
And, since 'tis hard to combat, learns to fly !
For him no wretches, born to work and weep,
Explore the mine, or tempt the dangerous deep;
No surly porter stands in guilty state,   105
To spurn imploring famine from the gate ;
But on he moves to meet his latter end,
Angels around befriending Virtue's friend ;
Bends to the grave with unperceived decay,
While resignation gently slopes the way;   110
And, all his prospects brightening to the last,
IIis heaven commences ere the world be past !
    Sweet was the sound, when oft at evening's close
Up yonder hill the village murmur rose.
There, as I past with careless steps and slow,   115
The mingling notes came softened from below ;
The swain responsive as the milk-maid sung,
The sober herd that lowed to meet their young,
The noisy geese that gabbled o'er the pool,
The playful children just let loose from school,   120
The watch-dog's voice that bayed the whispering wind,
And the loud laugh that spoke the vacant mind ;—
These all in sweet confusion sought the shade,
And filled each pause the nightingale had made.
But now the sounds of population fail,   125
No chearful murmurs fluctuate in the gale,
No busy steps the grass-grown foot-way tread,
For all the bloomy flush of life is fled.
All but yon widowed, solitary thing,
That feebly bends beside the plashy spring :   130
She, wretched matron, forced in age, for bread,
To strip the brook with mantling cresses spread,
To pick her wintry faggot from the thorn,
To seek her nightly shed, and weep till morn ;
She only left of all the harmless train,   135
The sad historian of the pensive plain.
    Near yonder copse, where once the garden smiled,
And still where many a garden flower grows wild ;
There, where a few torn shrubs the place disclose,
The village preacher's modest mansion rose.   140

A man he was to all the country dear,
And passing rich with forty pounds a year;
Remote from towns he ran his godly race,
Nor e'er had changed, nor wished to change his place;
Unpractised he to fawn, or seek for power,   145
By doctrines fashioned to the varying hour;
Far other aims his heart had learned to prize,
More skilled to raise the wretched than to rise.
His house was known to all the vagrant train;
He chid their wanderings but relieved their pain: 150
The long remembered beggar was his guest,
Whose beard descending swept his aged breast;
The ruined spendthrift, now no longer proud,
Claimed kindred there, and had his claims allowed;
The broken soldier, kindly bade to stay,   155
Sat by his fire, and talked the night away,
Wept o'er his wounds or tales of sorrow done,
Shouldered his crutch and shewed how fields were won.
Pleased with his guests, the good man learned to glow,
And quite forgot their vices in their woe;   160
Careless their merits or their faults to scan,
His pity gave ere charity began.
    Thus to relieve the wretched was his pride,
And e'en his failings leaned to Virtue's side;
But in his duty prompt at every call,   165
He watched and wept, he prayed and felt for all;
And, as a bird each fond endearment tries
To tempt its new-fledged offspring to the skies,
He tried each art, reproved each dull delay,
Allured to brighter worlds, and led the way.   170
    Beside the bed where parting life was laid,
And sorrow, guilt, and pain by turns dismayed,
The reverend champion stood. At his control
Despair and anguish fled the struggling soul;
Comfort came down the trembling wretch to raise,   175
And his last faultering accents whispered praise.
    At church, with meek and unaffected grace,
His looks adorned the venerable place;
Truth from his lips prevailed with double sway,
And fools, who came to scoff, remained to pray.   180
The service past, around the pious man,
With steady zeal, each honest rustic ran;
Even children followed with endearing wile.

And plucked his gown to share the good man's smile.
His ready smile a parent's warmth exprest ;   185
Their welfare pleased him, and their cares distrest :
To them his heart, his love, his griefs were given,
But all his serious thoughts had rest in heaven.
As some tall cliff that lifts its awful form,
Swells from the vale, and midway leaves the storm,   190
Tho' round its breast the rolling clouds are spread,
Eternal sunshine settles on its head.
   Beside yon straggling fence that skirts the way,
With blossom'd furze unprofitably gay,
There, in his noisy mansion, skill'd to rule,   195
The village master taught his little school.
A man severe he was, and stern to view ;
I knew him well, and every truant knew :
Well had the boding tremblers learned to trace
The day's disasters in his morning face ;   200
Full well they laughed with counterfeited glee
At all his jokes, for many a joke had he;
Full well the busy whisper circling round
Conveyed the dismal tidings when he frowned.
Yet he was kind, or, if severe in aught,   205
The love he bore to learning was in fault ;
The village all declared how much he knew :
'Twas certain he could write, and cypher too;
Lands he could measure, terms and tides presage,
And even the story ran that he could gauge :   210
In arguing, too, the parson owned his skill,
For, even tho' vanquished, he could argue still ;
While words of learned length and thundering sound
Amazed the gazing rustics ranged around ;
And still they gazed, and still the wonder grew,   215
That one small head could carry all he knew.
   But past is all his fame.   The very spot
Where many a time he triumphed is forgot.
Near yonder thorn, that lifts its head on high,
Where once the sign-post caught the passing eye,   220
Low lies that house where nut-brown draughts inspired,
Where grey-beard mirth and smiling toil retired,
Where village statesmen talked with looks profound,
And news much older than their ale went round.
Imagination fondly stoops to trace   225
The parlour splendours of that festive place :

The white-washed wall, the nicely sanded floor,
The varnished clock that clicked behind the door ;
The chest contrived a double debt to pay,
A bed by night, a chest of drawers by day ;   230
The pictures placed for ornament and use,
The twelve good rules, the royal game of goose ;
The hearth, except when winter chill'd the day,
With aspen boughs and flowers and fennel gay ;
While broken tea-cups, wisely kept for shew,   235
Ranged o'er the chimney, glistened in a row.
　　Vain transitory splendours ! could not all
Reprieve the tottering mansion from its fall ?
Obscure it sinks, nor shall it more impart
An hour's importance to the poor man's heart.   240
Thither no more the peasant shall repair
To sweet oblivion of his daily care ;
No more the farmer's news, the barber's tale,
No more the wood-man's ballad shall prevail ;
No more the smith his dusky brow shall clear,   245
Relax his ponderous strength, and lean to hear ;
The host himself no longer shall be found
Careful to see the mantling bliss go round ;
Nor the coy maid, half willing to be prest,
Shall kiss the cup to pass it to the rest.   250
　　Yes ! let the rich deride, the proud disdain,
These simple blessings of the lowly train ;
To me more dear, congenial to my heart,
One native charm, than all the gloss of art ;
Spontaneous joys, where Nature has its play,   255
The soul adopts, and owns their first born sway,
Lightly they frolic o'er the vacant mind,
Unenvied, unmolested, unconfined.
But the long pomp, the midnight masquerade,
With all the freaks of wanton wealth arrayed—   260
In these, ere triflers half their wish obtain,
The toiling pleasure sickens into pain ;
And, e'en while fashion's brightest arts decoy,
The heart distrusting asks if this be joy.
　　Ye friends to truth, ye statesman who survey   265
The rich man's joys encrease, the poor's decay,
Tis yours to judge, how wide the limits stand
Between a splendid and an happy land.
Proud swells the tide with loads of freighted ore,

And shouting Folly hails them from her shore;   270
Hoards e'en beyond the miser's wish abound,
And rich men flock from all the world around.
Yet count our gains. This wealth is but a name
That leaves our useful products still the same.
Not so the loss. The man of wealth and pride   275
Takes up a space that many poor supplied;
Space for his lake, his park's extended bounds,
Space for his horses, equipage, and hounds:
The robe that wraps his limbs in silken sloth
Has robbed the neighbouring fields of half their growth;   280
His seat, where solitary sports are seen,
Indignant spurns the cottage from the green:
Around the world each needful product flies,
For all the luxuries the world supplies;
While thus the land adorned for pleasure all   285
In barren splendour feebly waits the fall.
   As some fair female unadorned and plain,
Secure to please while youth confirms her reign,
Slights every borrowed charm that dress supplies,
Nor shares with art the triumph of her eyes;   290
But when those charms are past, for charms are frail,
When time advances, and when lovers fail,
She then shines forth, sollicitous to bless,
In all the glaring impotence of dress.
Thus fares the land by luxury betrayed: 295
In nature's simplest charms at first arrayed,
But verging to decline, its splendours rise;
Its vistas strike, its palaces surprize:
While, scourged by famine from the smiling land,
The mournful peasant leads his humble band,   300
And while he sinks, without one arm to save,
The country blooms—a garden and a grave.
   Where then, ah! where, shall poverty reside,
To scape the pressure of contiguous pride?
If to some common's fenceless limits strayed   305
He drives his flock to pick the scanty blade,
Those fenceless fields the sons of wealth divide,
And even the bare-worn common is denied.
   If to the city sped—what waits him there?
To see profusion that he must not share;   310
To see ten thousand baneful arts combined
To pamper luxury, and thin mankind;

To see those joys the sons of pleasure know
Extorted from his fellow-creature's woe.
Here while the courtier glitters in brocade,   315
There the pale artist plies the sickly trade ;
Here while the proud their long-drawn pomps display,
There the black gibbet glooms beside the way.
The dome where pleasure holds her midnight reign
Here, richly deckt, admits the gorgeous train :   320
Tumultuous grandeur crowds the blazing square,
The rattling chariots clash, the torches glare.
Sure scenes like these no troubles e'er annoy !
Sure these denote one universal joy !
Are these thy serious thoughts?—Ah, turn thine eyes   325
Where the poor houseless shivering female lies.
She once, perhaps, in village plenty blest,
Has wept at tales of innocence distrest ;
Her modest looks the cottage might adorn,
Sweet as the primrose peeps beneath the thorn :   330
Now lost to all ; her friends, her virtue fled,
Near her betrayer's door she lays her head,
And, pinch'd with cold, and shrinking from the shower,
With heavy heart deplores that luckless hour,
When idly first, ambitious of the town,   335
She left her wheel and robes of country brown.
    Do thine, sweet Auburn,—thine, the loveliest train,—
Do thy fair tribes participate her pain ?
Even now, perhaps, by cold and hunger led,
At proud men's doors they ask a little bread !   340
    Ah, no ! To distant climes, a dreary scene,
Where half the convex world intrudes between,
Through torrid tracts with fainting steps they go,
Where wild Altama murmurs to their woe.
Far different there from all that charm'd before.   345
The various terrors of that horrid shore ;
Those blazing suns that dart a downward ray,
And fiercely shed intolerable day ;
Those matted woods, where birds forget to sing,
But silent bats in drowsy clusters cling ;   350
Those poisonous fields with rank luxuriance crowned,
Where the dark scorpion gathers death around ;
Where at each step the stranger fears to wake
The rattling terrors of the vengeful snake ;
Where crouching tigers wait their hapless prey,   355

And savage men more murderous still than they;
While oft in whirls the mad tornado flies,
Mingling the ravaged landschape with the skies.
Far different these from every former scene,
The cooling brook, the grassy vested green,   360
The breezy covert of the warbling grove,
That only sheltered thefts of harmless love.
    Good Heaven! what sorrows gloom'd that parting day,
That called them from their native walks away;
When the poor exiles, every pleasure past,   365
Hung round the bowers, and fondly looked their last,
And took a long farewel, and wished in vain
For seats like these beyond the western main,
And shuddering still to face the distant deep,
Returned and wept, and still returned to weep.   370
The good old sire the first prepared to go
To new found worlds, and wept for others' woe;
But for himself, in conscious virtue brave,
He only wished for worlds beyond the grave.
His lovely daughter, lovelier in her tears,   375
The fond companion of his helpless years,
Silent went next, neglectful of her charms,
And left a lover's for a father's arms.
With louder plaints the mother spoke her woes,
And blest the cot where every pleasure rose,   380
And kist her thoughtless babes with many a tear,
And claspt them close, in sorrow doubly dear,
Whilst her fond husband strove to lend relief
In all the silent manliness of grief.
    O luxury! thou curst by Heaven's decree,   385
How ill exchanged are things like these for thee!
How do thy potions, with insidious joy,
Diffuse their pleasure only to destroy!
Kingdoms by thee, to sickly greatness grown,
Boast of a florid vigour not their own.   390
At every draught more large and large they grow,
A bloated mass of rank unwieldy woe;
Till sapped their strength, and every part unsound,
Down, down they sink, and spread a ruin round.
    Even now the devastation is begun,   395
And half the business of destruction done;
Even now, methinks, as pondering here I stand,
I see the rural virtues leave the land.

Down where yon anchoring vessel spreads the sail,
That idly waiting flaps with every gale,   400
Downward they move, a melancholy band,
Pass from the shore, and darken all the strand.
Contented toil, and hospitable care,
And kind connubial tenderness, are there;
And piety with wishes placed above,   405
And steady loyalty, and faithful love.
And thou, sweet Poetry, thou loveliest maid,
Still first to fly where sensual joys invade;
Unfit in these degenerate times of shame
To catch the heart, or strike for honest fame;   410
Dear charming nymph, neglected and decried,
My shame in crowds, my solitary pride;
Thou source of all my bliss, and all my woe,
That found'st me poor at first, and keep'st me so;
Thou guide by which the nobler arts excel,   415
Thou nurse of every virtue, fare thee well!
Farewell, and O! where'er thy voice be tried,
On Torno's cliffs, or Pambamarca's side, ·
Whether where equinoctial fervours glow,
Or winter wraps the polar world in snow,   420
Still let thy voice, prevailing over time,
Redress the rigours of the inclement clime;
Aid slighted truth with thy persuasive strain;
Teach erring man to spurn the rage of gain;
Teach him, that states of native strength possest,   425
Tho' very poor, may still be very blest;
That trade's proud empire hastes to swift decay,
As ocean sweeps the laboured mole away;
While self-dependent power can time defy,
As rocks resist the billows and the sky.   430

BURNS.

THE COTTER'S SATURDAY NIGHT.

My lov'd, my honor'd, much respected friend !
  No mercenary bard his homage pays :
With honest pride I scorn each selfish end,
  My dearest meed, a friend's esteem and praise :
To you I sing in simple Scottish lays   5
  The lowly train in life's sequester'd scene ;
The native feelings strong, the guileless ways ;
  What Aiken in a cottage would have been ;
Ah ! tho' his worth unknown, far happier there, I ween.

November chill blaws loud wi' angry sugh ;   10
  The short'ning winter-day is near a close ;
The miry beasts retreating frae the pleugh ;
  The black'ning trains o' craws to their repose :
The toil-worn Cotter frae his labour goes,
  This night his weekly moil is at an end,   15
Collects his spades, his mattocks, and his hoes,
  Hoping the morn in ease and rest to spend,
And weary, o'er the moor, his course does hameward bend.

At length his lonely cot appears in view,
  Beneath the shelter of an aged tree ;   20
Th' expectant wee-things, toddlin, stacher through
  To meet their Dad, wi' flichterin noise an' glee.
His wee bit ingle, blinkin bonnie,
  His clean hearth-stane, his thriftie wifie's smile,
The lisping infant prattling on his knee,   25
  Does a' his weary carking cares beguile,
An' makes him quite forget his labor an' his toil.

Belyve the elder bairns come drapping in,
  At service out amang the farmers roun';
Some ca' the pleugh, some herd, some tentie rin   30
A cannie errand to a neebor town:
Their eldest hope, their Jenny, woman-grown,
  In youthfu' bloom, love sparkling in her e'e,
Comes hame, perhaps, to shew a braw new gown,
  Or deposite her sair-won penny-fee,   35
To help her parents dear, if they in hardship be.

Wi' joy unfeign'd brothers and sisters meet,
  An' each for other's weelfare kindly spears:
The social hours, swift-wing'd, unnotic'd fleet;
  Each tells the uncos that he sees or hears;   40
The parents, partial, eye their hopeful years;
  Anticipation forward points the view.
The mother wi' her needle an' her sheers
  Gars auld claes look amaist as weel's the new;
The father mixes a' wi' admonition due.   45

Their master's an' their mistress's command
  The younkers a' are warned to obey;
An' mind their labours wi' an eydent hand,
  An' ne'er, tho' out o' sight, to jauk or play:
An' Oh! be sure to fear the Lord alway,   50
  'An' mind your duty, duely, morn an' night!
Lest in temptation's path ye gang astray,
  Implore His counsel and assisting might:
They never sought in vain that sought the Lord aright!'

But hark! a rap comes gently to the door;   55
  Jenny, wha kens the meaning o' the same,
Tells how a neebor lad cam o'er the moor
  To do some errands, and convoy her hame.
The wily mother sees the conscious flame
  Sparkle in Jenny's e'e, and flush her cheek;   60
With heart-struck, anxious care, inquires his name,
  While Jenny hafflins is afraid to speak;
Weel pleas'd the mother hears, it's nae wild, worthless rake.

Wi' kindly welcome Jenny brings him ben;
  A strappan youth; he takes the mother's eye;   65
Blythe Jenny sees the visit's no ill ta'en;
  The father cracks of horses, pleughs, and kye.

I

The youngster's artless heart o'erflows wi' joy,
  But, blate and laithfu', scarce can weel behave;
The mother, wi' a woman's wiles, can spy
  What makes the youth sae bashfu' an' sae grave;
Weel-pleas'd to think her bairn's respected like the lave.   70

O happy love! where love like this is found!
  O heart-felt raptures! bliss beyond compare!
I've paced much this weary, mortal round,——
  And sage experience bids me this declare——   75
'If Heaven a draught of heav'nly pleasure spare,
  One cordial in this melancholy vale,
'Tis when a youthful, loving, modest pair
  In other's arms breathe out the tender tale   80
Beneath the milk-white thorn that scents the ev'ning gale.'

Is there, in human form, that bears a heart——
  A wretch! a villain! lost to love and truth!
That can with studied, sly, ensnaring art
  Betray sweet Jenny's unsuspecting youth?   85
Curse on his perjur'd arts! dissembling smooth!
  Are honour, virtue, conscience, all exil'd?
Is there no pity, no relenting ruth,
  Points to the parents fondling o'er their child?
Then paints the ruin'd maid, and their distraction wild!   90

But now the supper crowns their simple board,
  The healsome parritch, chief o' Scotia's food:
The soupe their only Hawkie does afford,
  That 'yont the hallen snugly chows her cood;
The dame brings forth in complimental mood,   95
  To grace the lad, her weel-hain'd kebbuck, fell,
An' aft he's prest, an' aft he ca's it guid;
  The frugal wifie, garrulous, will tell,
How 'twas a towmond auld, sin' lint was i' the bell.

The cheerfu' supper done, wi' serious face   100
  They round the ingle form a circle wide;
The sire turns o'er wi' patriarchal grace
  The big ha'-Bible, ance his father's pride:
His bonnet rev'rently is laid aside,
  His lyart haffets wearing thin an' bare;   105

Those strains that once did sweet in Zion glide,
  He wales a portion with judicious care;
And 'Let us worship God!' he says, with solemn air.
They chant their artless notes in simple guise;
  They tune their hearts, by far the noblest aim;   110
Perhaps Dundee's wild warbling measures rise,
  Or plaintive Martyrs, worthy of the name;
Or noble Elgin beets the heav'nward flame,
  The sweetest far of Scotia's holy lays:
Compar'd with these, Italian trills are tame;   115
  The tickl'd ears no heart-felt raptures raise;
Nae unison hae they with our Creator's praise.

The priest-like father reads the sacred page,
  How Abram was the friend of God on high;
Or, Moses bade eternal warfare wage   120
  With Amalek's ungracious progeny;
Or how the royal Bard did groaning lie
  Beneath the stroke of Heaven's avenging ire;
Or Job's pathetic plaint, and wailing cry;
  Or rapt Isaiah's wild, seraphic fire;   125
Or other holy Seers that tune the sacred lyre.

Perhaps the Christian volume is the theme;
  How guiltless blood for guilty man was shed;
How He, who bore in heaven the second name,
  Had not on earth whereon to lay his Head;   130
How His first followers and servants sped;
  The precepts sage they wrote to many a land;
How he, who lone in Patmos banished,
  Saw in the sun a mighty angel stand;
And heard great Bab'lon's doom pronounced by Heaven's command.

Then kneeling down, to Heaven's Eternal King
  The saint, the father, and the husband prays:
Hope 'springs exulting on triumphant wing,'
  That thus they all shall meet in future days:
There ever bask in uncreated rays,   140
  No more to sigh, or shed the bitter tear,
Together hymning their Creator's praise,
  In such society, yet still more dear;
While circling Time moves round in an eternal sphere.

Compar'd with this, how poor Religion's pride,　　145
　　In all the pomp of method, and of art,
When men display to congregations wide
　　Devotion's ev'ry grace, except the heart!
The Pow'r, incens'd, the pageant will desert,
　　The pompous strain, the sacerdotal stole;　150
But haply, in some cottage far apart,
　　May hear, well pleas'd, the language of the soul,
And in his Book of Life the inmates poor enroll.

Then homeward all take off their sev'ral way;
　　The youngling cottagers retire to rest;　155
The parent-pair their secret homage pay,
　　And proffer up to Heav'n the warm request,
That He, who stills the raven's clam'rous nest,
　　And decks the lily fair in flow'ry pride,
Would, in the way His wisdom sees the best,　160
　　For them and for their little ones provide;
But chiefly in their hearts with grace divine preside.

From scenes like these old Scotia's grandeur springs,
　　That makes her lov'd at home, rever'd abroad:
Princes and lords are but the breath of kings,　165
　　'An honest man's the noblest work of God:'
And certes, in fair virtue's heavenly road,
　　The cottage leaves the palace far behind;
What is a lordling's pomp? a cumbrous load,
　　Disguising oft the wretch of human kind,　170
Studied in arts of hell, in wickedness refin'd!

O Scotia! my dear, my native soil!
　　For whom my warmest wish to Heaven is sent!
Long may thy hardy sons of rustic toil
　　Be blest with health and peace and sweet content!　175
And, Oh, may Heaven their simple lives prevent
　　From luxury's contagion weak and vile;
Then, howe'er crowns and coronets be rent,
　　A virtuous populace may rise the while,
And stand a wall of fire around their much-lov'd Isle.　180

O Thou! who pour'd the patriotic tide
　　That stream'd thro' Wallace's undaunted heart;
Who dar'd to nobly stem tyrannic pride,
　　Or nobly die, the second glorious part,

(The patriot's God peculiarly thou art, 185
 His friend, inspirer, guardian, and reward!)
O never, never, Scotia's realm desert,
 But still the patriot and the patriot-bard
In bright succession raise, her ornament and guard!

THE TWA DOGS.

'TWAS in that place o' Scotland's isle,
That bears the name o' Auld King Coil,
Upon a bonie day in June,
When wearing thro' the afternoon,
Twa dogs, that were na thrang at hame,   5
Forgather'd ance upon a time.
  The first I'll name, they ca'd him Cæsar,
Was keepit for his Honour's pleasure:
His hair, his size, his mouth, his lugs,
Shew'd he was nane o' Scotland's dogs;   10
But whalpit some place far abroad,
Whare sailors gang to fish for Cod.
  His locked, letter'd, braw brass collar,
Shew'd him the gentleman and scholar;
But tho' he was o' high degree,   15
The fient a pride—na pride had he;
But wad hae spent an hour caressin
Ev'n wi' a tinkler-gypsey's messin.
At kirk or market, mill or smiddie,
Nae tawted tyke, tho' e'er sae duddie,   20
But he wad stan't, as glad to see him,
An' stroan't on stanes and hillocks wi' him.
  The tither was a ploughman's collie,
A rhyming, ranting, raving billie,
Wha for his friend an' comrade had him   25
And in his freaks had Luath ca'd him,
After some dog in Highland sang,
Was made lang syne,—Lord knows how lang,
  He was a gash an' faithfu' tyke,
As ever lap a sheugh or dyke.   30

His honest, sonsie, baws'nt face,
Ay gat him friends in ilka place;
His breast was white, his touzie back
Weel clad wi' coat o' glossy black;
His gawcie tail, wi' upward curl, 35
Hung o'er his hurdies wi' a swirl.

 Nae doubt but they were fain o' ither,
An' unco pack an' thick thegither;
Wi' social nose whyles snuff'd and snowkit:
Whyles mice and moudieworts they howkit.; 40
Whyles scour'd awa in lang excursion.
An' worry'd ither in diversion;
Until wi' daffin weary grown,
Upon a knowe they sat them down,
And there began a lang digression 45
About the lords o' the creation.

CÆSAR.

 I've aften wonder'd, honest Luath,
What sort o' life poor dogs like you have;
An' when the gentry's life I saw,
What way poor bodies liv'd ava. 50
 Our Laird gets in his racked rents,
His coals, his kain, an' a' his stents;
He rises when he likes himsel;
His flunkies answer at the bell;
He ca's his coach; he ca's his horse; 55
He draws a bonie, silken purse
As lang's my tail, whare thro' the steeks
The yellow letter'd Geordie keeks.
 Frae morn to e'en, its nought but toiling
At baking, roasting, frying, boiling; 60
An' tho' the gentry first are stechin,
Yet ev'n the ha' folk fill their pechan
Wi' sauce ragouts and siclike trashtrie,
That's little short o' downright wastrie.
Our Whipper-in, wee blastit wonner, 65
Poor worthless elf, it eats a dinner,
Better than ony tenant man
His honour has in a' the lan:
An' what poor cot-folk pit their painch in,
I own it's past my comprehension. 70

LUATH.

Trowth, Cæsar, whyles they're fash't eneugh :
A cotter howkin in a sheugh,
Wi' dirty stanes biggin a dyke,
Baring a quarry, and siclike,
Himsel, a wife, he thus sustains,   75
A smytrie o' wee duddie weans,
An' nought but his han' darg, to keep
Them right and tight in thack an' rape.
    An' when they meet wi' sair disasters,
Like loss o' health, or want o' masters,   80
Ye maist wad think, a wee touch langer,
An' they maun starve o' cauld and hunger ;
But, how it comes, I never kent yet,
They're maistly wonderfu' contented ;
An' buirdly chiels an' clever hizzies   85
Are bred in sic a way as this is.

CÆSAR.

But then to see how ye're negleckit,
How huff'd, an' cuff'd, an' disrespeckit !
Lord, man, our gentry care as little
For delvers, ditchers, an' sic cattle,   90
They gang as saucy by poor folk,
As I wad by a stinking brock.
    I've notic'd, on our Laird's court-day,
An' mony a time my heart's been wae,
Poor tenant bodies, scant o' cash,   95
How they maun thole a factor's snash :
He'll stamp an' threaten, curse an' swear,
He'll apprehend them, poind their gear ;
While they maun stan' wi' aspect humble,
An' hear it a', an' fear and tremble !   100
    I see how folk live that hae riches :
But surely poor folk maun be wretches.

LUATH.

They're nae sae wretched's ane wad think,
Tho' constantly on poortith's brink :

They're sae accustom'd wi' the sight,   105
The view o't gies them little fright.
   Then chance an' fortune are sae guided,
They're ay in less or mair provided;
An' tho' fatigu'd wi' close employment,
A blink o' rest's a sweet enjoyment.   110
   The dearest comfort o' their lives,
Their grushie weans an' faithfu' wives;
The prattling things are just their pride,
That sweetens a' their fire-side.
   An' whyles twalpennie worth o' nappy   115
Can mak the bodies unco happy;
They lay aside their private cares,
To mind the Kirk and State affairs;
They'll talk o' patronage an' priests
Wi' kindling fury in their breasts,   120
Or tell what new taxation's comin,
An' ferlie at the folk in Lon'on.
   As bleak-fac'd Hallowmass returns,
They get the jovial, ranting kirns,
When rural life, o' ev'ry station,   125
Unite in common recreation;
Love blinks, Wit slaps, an' social Mirth
Forgets there's Care upo' the earth.
   That merry day the year begins
They bar the door on frosty win's;   130
The nappy reeks wi' mantling ream,
An' sheds a heart-inspiring steam;
The luntin pipe an' sneeshin mill
Are handed round wi' right guid will;
The cantie auld folks crackin crouse,   135
The young anes rantin thro' the house,—
My heart has been sae fain to see them,
That I for joy hae barket wi' them.
   Still it's owre true that ye hae said,
Sic game is now owre aften play'd.   140
There's monie a creditable stock
O' decent, honest, fawsont folk
Are riven out baith root an' branch,
Some rascal's pridefu' greed to quench,
Wha thinks to knit himsel the faster   145
In favour wi' some gentle Master,

Wha, ablins, thrang a parliamentin,
For Britain's guid his saul indentin—

CÆSAR.

Haith, lad, ye little ken about it;
For Britain's guid! guid faith! I doubt it.   150
Say rather, gaun as Premiers lead him,
An' saying *aye* or *no*'s they bid him :
At operas an' plays parading,
Mortgaging, gambling, masquerading :
Or maybe, in a frolic daft,   155
To Hague or Calais taks a waft,
To make a tour an' tak a whirl,
To learn *bon ton* an' see the worl'.
    There, at Vienna or Versailles,
He rives his father's auld entails;   160
Or by Madrid he taks the rout,
To thrum guitars, an' fecht wi' nowt ;
Or down Italian vista startles,
Love-making among groves o' myrtles :
Then houses drumly German water,   165
To mak himsel look fair and fatter.
For Britain's guid! for her destruction !
Wi' dissipation, feud, an' faction !

LUATH.

Hech, man! dear sirs! is that the gate
They waste sae mony a braw estate !   170
Are we sae foughten an' harass'd
For gear to gang that gate at last?
    O would they stay aback frae courts,
An' please themsels wi' countra sports,
It wad for ev'ry ane be better,   175
The Laird, the Tenant, an' the Cotter !
For thae frank, rantin, ramblin billies,
Fient haet o' them's ill-hearted fellows :
Except for breaking o' their timmer,
Or speaking lightly o' their limmer,   180
Or shootin o' a hare or moor-cock,
The ne'er-a-bit they're ill to poor folk.
    But will ye tell me, Master Cæsar,
Sure great folk's life's a life o' pleasure?

Nae cauld nor hunger e'er can steer them,   185
The vera thought o't need na fear them.

CÆSAR.

Lord, man, were ye but whyles whare I am,
The gentles ye wad ne'er envy 'em.
   It's true, they need na starve or sweat,
Thro' winter's cauld, or simmer's heat ;   190
They've nae sair wark to craze their banes,
An' fill auld age wi' grips an' granes :
But human bodies are sic fools,
For a' their colleges and schools,
That when nae real ills perplex them,   195
They mak enow themsels to vex them ;
An' ay the less they hae to sturt them
In like proportion less will hurt them.

   A country fellow at the pleugh,
His acre's till'd, he's right eneugh ;   200
A country girl at her wheel,
Her dizzen's done, she's unco weel :
But Gentlemen, an' Ladies warst,
Wi' ev'ndown want o' wark are curst.
They loiter, lounging, lank, an' lazy ;   205
Tho' deil haet ails them, yet uneasy :
Their days insipid, dull, an' tasteless ;
Their nights unquiet, lang, an' restless ;
   An' even their sports, their balls an' races,
Their galloping thro' public places,   210
There's sic parade, sic pomp an' art,
The joy can scarcely reach the heart.
   The men cast out in party-matches,
Then sowther a' in deep debauches.
Ae night they're mad wi' drink an' roaring,   215
Niest day their life is past enduring.
   The Ladies arm-in-arm in clusters,
As great an' gracious a' as sisters ;
But hear their absent thoughts o' ither,
They're a' run deils an' jads thegither.   220
Whyles o'er the wee bit cup an' platie
They sip the scandal potion pretty ;

Or lee-lang nights wi' crabbit leuks
Pore owre the devil's pictur'd beuks;
Stake on ·a chance a farmer's stackyard, 225
An' cheat like ony unhang'd blackguard.
   There's some exception, man an' woman;
But this is Gentry's life in common.

   By this, the sun was out o' sight,
An' darker gloamin brought the night; 230
The bum-clock humm'd wi' lazy drone,
The kye stood rowtin i' the loan;
When up they gat, an' shook their lugs,
Rejoic'd they were na *men* but *dogs;*
An' each took aff his several way, 235
Resolv'd to meet some ither day.

COWPER.

HEROISM.

THERE was a time when Ætna's silent fire
Slept unperceiv'd, the mountain yet entire;
When, conscious of no danger from below,
She tow'r'd a cloud-capt pyramid of snow.
No thunders shook with deep intestine sound   5
The blooming groves, that girdled her around;
Her unctuous olives and her purple vines,
(Unfelt the fury of those bursting mines)
The peasant's hopes, and not in vain, assured,
In peace upon her sloping sides matured.   10
When on a day, like that of the last doom,
A conflagration lab'ring in her womb,
She teem'd and heav'd with an infernal birth,
That shook the circling seas and solid earth.
Dark and voluminous the vapours rise,   15
And hang their horrors in the neighb'ring skies,
While through the Stygian veil that blots the day
In dazzling streaks the vivid lightnings play.
But oh! what muse, and in what pow'rs of song,
Can trace the torrent as it burns along?   20
Havoc and devastation in the van,
It marches o'er the prostrate works of man,
Vines, olives, herbage, forests disappear,
And all the charms of a Sicilian year.

Revolving seasons, fruitless as they pass,   25
See it an uninform'd and idle mass,
Without a soil t' invite the tiller's care,
Or blade that might redeem it from despair.

Ye time at length (what will not time achieve ?)
Clothes it with earth, and bids the produce live.   30
Once more the spiry myrtle crowns the glade,
And ruminating flocks enjoy the shade.
O bliss precarious, and unsafe retreats !
O charming paradise of short-lived sweets !
The self-same gale that wafts the fragrance round   35
Brings to the distant ear a sullen sound :
Again the mountain feels th' imprison'd foe,
Again pours ruin on the vale below ;
Ten thousand swains the wasted scene deplore,
That only future ages can restore.   40

Ye monarchs, whom the lure of honour draws,
Who write in blood the merits of your cause,
Who strike the blow, then plead your own defence,
Glory your aim, but Justice your pretence,
Behold in Ætna's emblematic fires   45
The mischiefs your ambitious pride inspires !

Fast by the stream that bounds your just domain,
And tells you where ye have a right to reign,
A nation dwells, not envious of your throne,
Studious of peace, their neighbours' and their own.   50
Ill-fated race ! how deeply must they rue
Their only crime, vicinity to you !
The trumpet sounds, your legions swarm abroad,
Through the ripe harvest lies their destin'd road,
At ev'ry step beneath their feet .they tread   55
The life of multitudes, a nation's bread ;

Earth seems a garden in its loveliest dress
Before them, and behind a wilderness ;
Famine, and Pestilence, her first-born son,
Attend to finish what the sword begun ;   60
And echoing praises such as fiends might earn,
And folly pays, resound at your return.
A calm succeeds ;—but plenty, with her train
Of heartfelt joys, succeeds not soon again,
And years of pining indigence must show   65
What scourges are the gods that rule below.

Yet man, laborious man, by slow degrees,
(Such is his thirst of opulence and ease)

Plies all the sinews of industrious toil,
Gleans up the refuse of the gen'ral spoil,   70
Rebuilds the tow'rs that smok'd upon the plain,
And the sun gilds the shining spires again.
   Increasing commerce and reviving art
Renew the quarrel on the conq'rors' part ;
And the sad lesson must be learn'd once more,   75
That wealth within is ruin at the door.

   What are ye, monarchs, laurel'd heroes, say,
But Ætnas of the suff'ring world ye sway?
Sweet Nature, stripp'd of her embroider'd robe,
Deplores the wasted regions of her globe,   80
And stands a witness at Truth's awful bar,
To prove you, there, destroyers as ye are.
   Oh place me in some heaven-protected isle,
Where peace and equity and freedom smile,
Where no volcano pours his fiery flood,   85
No crested warrior dips his plume in blood,
Where power secures what industry has won,
Where to succeed is not to be undone,
A land that distant tyrants hate in vain,
In Britain's isle, beneath a George's reign.   90

ON THE RECEIPT OF MY MOTHER'S PICTURE
OUT OF NORFOLK.

O THAT those lips had language ! Life has pass'd
With me but roughly since I heard thee last.
Those lips are thine—thy own sweet smiles I see,
The same that oft in childhood solaced me ;
Voice only fails, else how distinct they say,   5
"Grieve not, my child, chase all thy fears away !"
The meek intelligence of those dear eyes
(Blest be the art that can immortalize,
The art that baffles Time's tyrannic claim
To quench it !) here shines on me still the same.   10
   Faithful remembrancer of one so dear,
O, welcome guest, though unexpected here !
Who bidd'st me honour with an artless song,
Affectionate, a mother lost so long,

I will obey, not willingly alone, 15
But gladly, as the precept were her own :
And, while that face renews my filial grief,
Fancy shall weave a charm for my relief,
Shall steep me in Elysian reverie,
A momentary dream that thou art she. 20
   My mother ! when I learnt that thou wast dead,
Say, wast thou conscious of the tears I shed ?
Hover'd thy spirit o'er thy sorrowing son,
Wretch even then, life's journey just begun ?
Perhaps thou gav'st me, though unfelt, a kiss : 25
Perhaps a tear, if souls can weep in bliss—
Ah, that maternal smile ! It answers—Yes.
I heard the bell toll'd on thy burial day,
I saw the hearse that bore thee slow away,
And, turning from my nurs'ry window, drew 30
A long, long sigh, and wept a last adieu !
But was it such ?—It was.—Where thou art gone
Adieus and farewells are a sound unknown.
May I but meet thee on that peaceful shore,
The parting sound shall pass my lips no more ! 35
Thy maidens, griev'd themselves at my concern,
Oft gave me promise of thy quick return.
What ardently I wish'd I long believ'd,
And, disappointed still, was still deceiv'd.
By expectation every day beguil'd, 40
Dupe of *to-morrow* even from a child.
Thus many a sad to-morrow came and went,
Till, all my stock of infant sorrow spent,
I learnt at last submission to my lot ;
But, though I less deplor'd thee, ne'er forgot. 45
   Where once we dwelt our name is heard no more,
Children not thine have trod my nursery floor ;
And where the gard'ner Robin, day by day,
Drew me to school along the public way,
Delighted with my bauble coach, and wrapt 50
In scarlet mantle warm, and velvet capt,
'Tis now become a history little known,
That once we call'd the pastoral house our own.
Short-liv'd possession ! but the record fair
That memory keeps of all thy kindness there 55
Still outlives many a storm that has effac'd
A thousand other themes less deeply- trac'd.

Thy nightly visits to my chamber made,
That thou mightst know me safe and warmly laid;
Thy morning bounties ere I left my home, 60
The biscuit, or confectionary plum;
The fragrant waters on my cheek bestow'd
By thy own hand, till fresh they shone and glow'd;
All this, and, more endearing still than all,
Thy constant flow of love, that knew no fall, 65
Ne'er roughen'd by those cataracts and breaks
That humour interpos'd too often makes;
All this still legible in mem'ry's page,
And still to be so to my latest age,
Adds joy to duty, makes me glad to pay 70
Such honours to thee as my numbers may;
Perhaps a frail memorial, but sincere,
Not scorn'd in heaven, though little notic'd here.

Could Time, his flight revers'd, restore the hours,
When, playing with thy vesture's tissued flow'rs, 75
The violet, the pink, and jessamine,
I prick'd them into paper with a pin
(And thou wast happier than myself the while,
Wouldst softly speak, and stroke my head and smile),
Could those few pleasant days again appear, 80
Might one wish bring them, would I wish them here?
I would not trust my heart—the dear delight
Seems so to be desired, perhaps I might.—
But no—what here we call our life is such
So little to be lov'd, and thou so much, 85
That I should ill requite thee to constrain
Thy unbound spirit into bonds again.

Thou, as a gallant bark from Albion's coast
(The storms all weather'd and the ocean cross'd)
Shoots into port at some well-haven'd isle, 90
Where spices breathe, and brighter seasons smile,
There sits quiescent on the floods that show
Her beauteous form reflected clear below,
While airs impregnated with incense play
Around her, fanning light her streamers gay; 95
So thou, with sails how swift! hast reach'd the shore,
"Where tempests never beat nor billows roar,"
And thy lov'd consort on the dang'rous tide
Of life long since has anchor'd by thy side.
But me, scarce hoping to attain that rest, 100

Always from port withheld, always distress'd—
Me howling winds drive devious, tempest toss'd,
Sails ript, seams op'ning wide, and compass lost,
And day by day some current's thwarting force
Sets me more distant from a prosp'rous course.   105
But, oh the thought that thou art safe, and he !
That thought is joy, arrive what may to me.
My boast is not that I deduce my birth
From loins enthron'd and rulers of the earth ;
But higher far my proud pretensions rise—   110
The son of parents pass'd into the skies !
And now, farewell—Time unrevok'd has run
His wonted course, yet what I wish'd is done.
By contemplation's help, not sought in vain,
I seem t' have lived my childhood o'er again ;   115
To have renew'd the joys that once were mine,
Without the sin of violating thine :
And, while the wings of Fancy still are free,
And I can view this mimic shew of thee,
Time has but half succeeded in his theft—   120
Thyself remov'd, thy power to soothe me left.

COLERIDGE.

THE ANCIENT MARINER.

PART I.

IT is an ancient Mariner,
And he stoppeth one of three.
" By thy long grey beard and glittering eye,
Now wherefore stopp'st thou me?

" The Bridegroom's doors are opened wide,   5
And I am next of kin;
The guests are met, the feast is set:
Mayst hear the merry din."

He holds him with his skinny hand
" There was a ship," quoth he.   10
" Hold off! unhand me, grey-beard loon!"
Eftsoons his hand dropt he.

He holds him with his glittering eye—
The Wedding-Guest stood still,
And listens like a three years' child: 15
The Mariner hath his will.

The Wedding-Guest sat on a stone:
He cannot chúse but hear;
And thus spake on that ancient man,
The bright-eyed Mariner.   20

" The ship was cheered, the harbour cleared,
Merrily did we drop
Below the kirk, below the hill,
Below the lighthouse top.

" The Sun came up upon the left,   25
Out of the sea came he !
And he shone bright, and on the right
Went down into the sea.

" Higher and higher every day,
Till over the mast at noon——"
The Wedding-Guest here beat his breast,   30
For he heard the loud bassoon.

The bride hath paced into the hall,
Red as a rose is she;
Nodding their heads before her goes   35
The merry minstrelsy.

The Wedding-Guest he beat his breast,
Yet he cannot chuse but hear ;
And thus spake on that ancient man,
The bright-eyed Mariner.   40

" And now the storm-blast came, and he
Was tyrannous and strong :
He struck with his o'ertaking wings,
And chased us south along.

" With sloping masts and dipping prow,   45
As who pursued with yell and blow
Still treads the shadow of his foe,
And forward bends his head,
The ship drove fast, loud roared the blast,
And southward aye we fled.   50

" And now there came both mist and snow,
And it grew wondrous cold :
And ice, mast-high, came floating by,
As green as emerald.

" And through the drifts the snowy clifts   55
Did send a dismal sheen :
Nor shapes of men nor beasts we ken—
The ice was all between.

" The ice was here, the ice was there,
The ice was all around :
It cracked and growled, and roared and howled,   60
Like noises in a swound !

" At length did cross an Albatross.
Thorough the fog it came ;
As if it had been a Christian soul,   65
We hail'd it in God's name.

" It ate the food it ne'er had eat,
And round and round it flew.
The ice did split with a thunder-fit
The helmsman steered us through.   70

" And a good south wind sprung up behind ;
The Albatross did follow,
And every day, for food or play,
Came to the mariners' hollo !

" In mist or cloud, on mast or shroud,   75
It perched for vespers nine ;
Whiles all the night, through fog-smoke white,
Glimmered the white moon-shine."

" God save thee, ancient Mariner !
From the fiends that plague thee thus !   80
Why look'st thou so?"—" With my cross-bow
I shot the Albatross."

PART II.

" THE Sun now rose upon the right :
Out of the sea came he,
Still hid in mist, and on the left   85
Went down into the sea.

" And the good south wind still blew behind,
But no sweet bird did follow,
Nor any day for food or play
Came to the mariners' hollo !   90

" And I had done a hellish thing,
And it would work 'em woe :
For all averred, I had killed the bird
That made the breeze to blow.
' Ah wretch !' said they, ' the bird to slay,   95
That made the breeze to blow ! '

" Nor dim nor red, like God's own head
The glorious Sun uprist:
Then all averred, I had killed the bird
That brought the fog and mist.   100
' 'Twas right,' said they, ' such birds to slay,
That bring the fog and mist.'

" The fair breeze blew, the white foam flew,
The furrow followed free ;
We were the first that ever burst   105
Into that silent sea.

" Down dropt the breeze, the sails dropt down,
'Twas sad as sad could be ;
And we did speak only to break
The silence of the sea !   110

" All in a hot and copper sky,
The bloody Sun, at noon,
Right up above the mast did-stand,
No bigger than the Moon.

" Day after day, day after day,   115
We stuck, nor breath nor motion ;
As idle as a painted ship
Upon a painted ocean.

" Water, water, everywhere,
And all the boards did shrink ;   120
Water, water, everywhere,
Nor any drop to drink.

" The very deep did rot : O Christ !
That ever this should be !
Yea, slimy things did crawl with legs   125
Upon the slimy sea.

" About, about, in reel and rout
The death-fires danced at night ;
The water, like a witch's oils,
Burnt green, and blue, and white.   130

" And some in dreams assured were
Of the spirit that plagued us so ;

Nine fathom deep he had followed us
From the land of mist and snow.

"And every tongue, through utter drought,   135
Was withered at the root;
We could not speak, no more than if
We had been choked with soot.

"Ah! well-a-day! what evil looks
Had I from old and young!   140
Instead of the cross, the Albatross
About my neck was hung."

PART III.

"THERE passed a weary time.   Each throat
Was parched, and glazed each eye.
A weary time! a weary time!   145
How glazed each weary eye,
When, looking westward, I beheld
A something in the sky.

"At first it seemed a little speck,
And then it seemed a mist;   150
It moved and moved, and took at last
A certain shape, I wist.

"A speck, a mist, a shape, I wist!
And still it neared and neared:
As if it dodged a water-sprite,   155
It plunged and tacked and veered.

"With throats unslacked, with black lips baked,
We could nor laugh nor wail;
Through utter drought all dumb we stood!
I bit my arm, I sucked the blood,   160
And cried, A sail! a sail!

"With throats unslacked, with black lips baked,
Agape they heard me call:
Gramercy! they for joy did grin,
And all at once their breath drew in,   165
As they were drinking all.

"See! see! (I cried) she tacks no more!
Hither to work us weal;
Without a breeze, without a tide,
She steadies with upright keel!   170

"The western wave was all a-flame,
The day was well-nigh done!
Almost upon the western wave
Rested the broad bright Sun;
When that strange shape drove suddenly   175
Betwixt us and the Sun.

"And straight the Sun was flecked with bars,
(Heaven's Mother send us grace!)
As if through a dungeon grate he peered
With broad and burning face.   180

"Alas! (thought I, and my heart beat loud)
How fast she nears and nears!
Are those her sails that glance in the Sun,
Like restless gossameres?

"Are those her ribs through which the Sun   185
Did peer, as through a grate?
And is that Woman all her crew?
Is that a Death? and are there two?
Is Death that woman's mate?

"Her lips were red, her looks were free,   190
Her locks were yellow as gold:
Her skin was as white as leprosy,
The Nightmare Life-in-Death was she
Who thicks man's blood with cold.

"The naked hulk alongside came,   195
And the twain were casting dice;
'The game is done! I've won, I've won!'
Quoth she, and whistles thrice.

"The Sun's rim dips; the stars rush out;
At one stride comes the dark;   200
With far-heard whisper o'er the sea
Off shot the spectre-bark.

"We listened and looked sideways up!
Fear at my heart, as at a cup,

My life-blood seemed to sip!   205
The stars were dim, and thick the night,
The steersman's face by his lamp gleamed white;
From the sails the dew did drip—
Till clomb above the eastern bar
The horned Moon, with one bright star   210
Within the nether tip.

"One after one, by the star-dogged Moon,
Too quick for groan or sigh,
Each turned his face with a ghastly pang,
And cursed me with his eye.   215

"Four times fifty living men,
(And I heard nor sigh nor groan,)
With heavy thump, a lifeless lump,
They dropped down one by one.

"The souls did from their bodies fly,—   220
They fled to bliss or woe!
And every soul, it passed me by,
Like the whizz of my cross-bow!"

PART IV.

"I FEAR thee, ancient Mariner!
I fear thy skinny hand!   225
And thou art long, and lank, and brown,
As is the ribbed sea-sand.

"I fear thee and thy glittering eye,
And thy skinny hand, so brown."—
"Fear not, fear not, thou Wedding-Guest!   230
This body dropt not down.

"Alone, alone, all, all alone,
Alone on a wide, wide sea!
And never a saint took pity on
My soul in agony.   235

"The many men, so beautiful!
And they all dead did lie:
And a thousand thousand slimy things
Lived on; and so did I.

"I looked upon the rotting sea,   240
And drew my eyes away;
I looked upon the rotting deck,
And there the dead men lay.

" I looked to heaven, and tried to pray;
But or ever a prayer had gusht,   245
A wicked whisper came, and made
My heart as dry as dust.

"I closed my lids, and kept them close,
And the balls like pulses beat;
For the sky and the sea, and the sea and the sky, 250
Lay like a load on my weary eye,
And the dead were at my feet.

" The cold sweat melted from their limbs,
Nor rot nor reek did they:
The look with which they looked on me   255
Had never passed away.

" An orphan's curse would drag to hell
A spirit from on high;
But oh! more horrible than that
Is the curse in a dead man's eye!   260
Seven days, seven nights, I saw that curse,
And yet I could not die.

" The moving Moon went up the sky,
And nowhere did abide:
Softly she was going up,   265
And a star or two beside—

" Her beams bemocked the sultry main,
Like April hoar-frost spread;
But where the ship's huge shadow lay,
The charmed water burnt alway   270
A still and awful red.

" Beyond the shadow of the ship,
I watched the water-snakes:
They moved in tracks of shining white,
And when they reared, the elfish light   275
Fell off in hoary flakes.

" Within the shadow of the ship
I watched their rich attire :
Blue, glossy green, and velvet black,
They coiled and swam ; and every track　　280
Was a flash of golden fire.

" O happy living things ! no tongue
Their beauty might declare :
A spring of love gushed from my heart,
And I blessed them unaware :　　285
Sure my kind saint took pity on me,
And I blessed them unaware.

" The selfsame moment I could pray ;
And from my neck so free
The Albatross fell off, and sank　　290
Like lead into the sea."

PART V.

" Oh Sleep ! it is a gentle thing,
Beloved from pole to pole !
To Mary Queen the praise be given !
She sent the gentle sleep from heaven,　　295
That slid into my soul.

" The silly buckets on the deck,
That had so long remained,
I dreamt that they were filled with dew ;
And when I awoke, it rained.　　300

" My lips were wet, my throat was cold,
My garments all were dank ;
Sure I had drunken in my dreams,
And still my body drank.

" I moved, and could not feel my limbs :　　305
I was so light—almost
I thought that I had died in sleep,
And was a blessed ghost.

" And soon I heard a roaring wind :
It did not come anear ;　　310

But with its sound it shook the sails,
That were so thin and sere.

" The upper air burst into life !
And a hundred fire-flags sheen,
To and fro they were hurried about !   315
And to and fro, and in and out,
The wan stars danced between.

" And the coming wind did roar more loud,
And the sails did sigh like sedge ;
And the rain poured down from one black cloud,   320
The Moon was at its edge.

" The thick black cloud was cleft, and still
The Moon was at its side :
Like waters shot from some high crag,
The lightning fell with never a jag,   325
A river steep and wide.

" The loud wind never reached the ship,
Yet now the ship moved on !
Beneath the lightning and the Moon
The dead men gave a groan.   330

" They groaned, they stirred, they all uprose,
Nor spake, nor moved their eyes ;
It had been strange, even in a dream,
To have seen those dead men rise.

" The helmsman steered, the ship moved on ;   335
Yet never a breeze up blew ;
The mariners all 'gan work the ropes,
Where they were wont to do ;
They raised their limbs like lifeless tools—
We were a ghastly crew.   340

" The body of my brother's son
Stood by me, knee to knee :
The body and I pulled at one rope,
But he said nought to me."

" I fear thee, ancient Mariner ! "   345
" Be calm, thou Wedding-Guest !

'Twas not those souls that fled in pain,
Which to their corses came again,
But a troop of spirits blest:

For when it dawned—they dropped their arms,   350
And clustered round the mast;
Sweet sounds rose slowly through their mouths,
And from their bodies passed.

" Around, around, flew each sweet sound,
Then darted to the Sun;   355
Slowly the sounds came back again,
Now mixed, now one by one.

" Sometimes a-dropping from the sky
I heard the sky-lark sing;
Sometimes all little birds that are,   360
How they seemed to fill the sea and air
With their sweet jargoning!

" And now 'twas like all instruments,
Now like a lonely flute;
And now it is an angel's song,   365
That makes the heavens be mute.

" It ceased; yet still the sails made on
A pleasant noise till noon,
A noise like of a hidden brook
In the leafy month of June,   370
That to the sleeping woods all night
Singeth a quiet tune.

" Till noon we quietly sailed on,
Yet never a breeze did breathe:
Slowly and smoothly went the ship,   375
Moved onward from beneath.

" Under the keel nine fathom deep,
From the land of mist and snow,
The spirit slid: and it was he
That made the ship to go.   380
The sails at noon left off their tune,
And the ship stood still also.

" The Sun, right up above the mast,
Had fixed her to the ocean:

But in a minute she 'gan stir,   385
With a short uneasy motion—
Backwards and forwards half her length,
With a short uneasy motion.

"Then, like a pawing horse let go,
She made a sudden bound :   390
It flung the blood into my head,
And I fell down in a swound.

"How long in that same fit I lay,
I have not to declare ;
But ere my living life returned,   395
I heard, and in my soul discerned
Two voices in the air.

"'Is it he?' quoth one, 'Is this the man?
By Him who died on cross,
With his cruel bow he laid full low   400
The harmless Albatross.

"'The spirit who bideth by himself
In the land of mist and snow,
He loved the bird that loved the man
Who shot him with his bow.' ·   405

"The other was a softer voice,
As soft as honey-dew ;
Quoth he, 'The man hath penance done,
And penance more will do.'"

PART VI.

FIRST VOICE.

"'But tell me, tell me ! speak again,   410
Thy soft response renewing—
What makes that ship drive on so fast?
What is the ocean doing?'

SECOND VOICE.

"'Still as a slave before his lord,
The ocean hath no blast ;   415

IIis great bright eye most silently
Up to the Moon is cast—

"'If he may know which way to go;
For she guides him smooth or grim.
See, brother, see! how graciously   420
She looketh down on him.'

FIRST VOICE.

"'But why drives on that ship so fast,
Without or wave or wind?'

SECOND VOICE.

'The air is cut away before,
And closes from behind.   425

"'Fly, brother, fly! more high, more high!
Or we shall be belated:
For slow and slow that ship will go,
When the Mariner's trance is abated.'

"I woke, and we were sailing on   430
As in a gentle weather:
'Twas night, calm night, the moon was high;
The dead men stood together.

"All stood together on the deck,
For a charnel-dungeon fitter: 435
All fixed on me their stony eyes,
That in the Moon did glitter.

"The pang, the curse, with which they died,
Had never passed away:
I could not draw my eyes from theirs,   440
Nor turn them up to pray.

"And now this spell was snapt: once more
I viewed the ocean green,
And looked far forth, yet little saw
Of what had else been seen—   445

"Like one that on a lonesome road
Doth walk in fear and dread,

And having once turned round walks on,
And turns no more his head;
.Because he knows, a frightful fiend   450
Doth close behind him tread.

" But soon there breathed a wind on me,
Nor sound nor motion made :
Its path was not upon the sea,   .
In ripple or in shade.   455

"It raised my hair, it fann'd my cheek,
Like a meadow-gale of spring—
It mingled strangely with my fears,
Yet it felt like a welcoming.

"Swiftly, swiftly flew the ship,   460
Yet she sailed softly too :
Sweetly, sweetly blew the breeze—
On me alone it blew.

"Oh ! dream of joy ! is this indeed
The light-house top I see?   .465
Is this the hill? is this the kirk ?
Is this mine own countree?

" We drifted o'er the harbour-bar,
And I with sobs did pray—
O let me be awake, my God !   470
Or let me sleep alway.

" The harbour-bay was clear as glass,
So smoothly it was strewn !
And on the bay the moonlight lay,
And the shadow of the Moon.   '   475

"The rock shone bright, the kirk no less,
That stands above the rock :
The moonlight steeped in silentness
The steady weathercock.

" And the bay was white with silent light,   480
Till, rising from the same,
Full many shapes, that shadows were,
In crimson colours came.

"A little distance from the prow
Those crimson shadows were: .   485
I turned my eyes upon the deck—
Oh, Christ! what saw I there!

"Each corse lay flat, lifeless and flat,
And by the holy rood !
A man all .light, a seraph-man,   490
On every corse there stood.

"This seraph-band, each waved his hand,
It was a heavenly sight !
They stood as signals to the land,
Each one a lovely light ;   495

"This seraph-band, each waved his hand,
No voice did they impart—
No voice; but oh ! the silence sank
Like music on my heart.

"But soon I heard the dash of oars,   500
I heard the Pilot's cheer ;
My head was turned perforce away,
And I saw a boat appear.

"The Pilot and the Pilot's boy,
I heard them coming fast :   505
Dear Lord in heaven ! it was a joy
The dead men could not blast.

"I saw a third—I heard his voice :
It is the Hermit good !
He singeth loud his godly hymns   510
That he makes in the wood.
He'll shrieve my soul, he'll wash away
The Albatross's blood."

PART VII.

"THIS Hermit good lives in that wood
Which slopes down to the sea.   515
How loudly his sweet voice he rears !
He loves to talk with marineres
That come from a far countree.

"He kneels at morn, and noon, and eve—
He hath a cushion plump :
It is the moss that wholly hides
The rotted old oak stump.   520

"The skiff-boat neared : I heard them talk,
'Why, this is strange, I trow !
Where are those lights so many and fair,   525
That signal made but now ?'

"'Strange, by my faith !' the Hermit said—
'And they answered not our cheer.
The planks looked warped ! and see those sails,
How thin they are and sere !   530
I never saw aught like to them,
Unless perchance it were

"'Brown skeletons of leaves that lag
My forest-brook along ;
When the ivy-tod is heavy with snow,   535
And the owlet whoops to the wolf below,
That eats the she-wolf's young.'

"'Dear Lord ! it hath a fiendish look—
(The Pilot made reply)
I am a-feared.'—'Push on, push on !'   540
Said the Hermit cheerily.

"The boat came closer to the ship,
But I nor spake nor stirred ;
The boat came close beneath the ship,
And straight a sound was heard.   545

"Under the water it rumbled on,
Still louder and more dread :
It reached the ship, it split the bay :
The ship went down like lead.

"Stunned by that loud and dreadful sound,   550
Which sky and ocean smote,
Like one that hath been seven days drowned
My body lay afloat ;
But, swift as dreams, myself I found
Within the Pilot's boat.   555

L

"Upon the whirl, where sank the ship,
The boat spun round and round;
And all was still, save that the hill
Was telling of the sound.

"I moved my lips—the Pilot shrieked   560
And fell down in a fit;
The holy Hermit raised his eyes,
And prayed where he did sit.

"I took the oars: the Pilot's boy,
Who now doth crazy go,   565
Laughed loud and long, and all the while
His eyes went to and fro.
'Ha! ha!' quoth he, 'full plain I see,
The Devil knows how to row.'

"And now, all in my own countree,   570
I stood on the firm land!
The Hermit stepped forth from the boat,
And scarcely he could stand.

"'O shrieve me, shrieve me, holy man!'
The Hermit crossed his brow.   575
'Say quick,' quoth he, 'I bid thee say—
What manner of man art thou?'

"Forthwith this frame of mine was wrenched
With a woeful agony,
Which forced me to begin my tale;   580
And then it left me free.

"Since then, at an uncertain hour,
That agony returns:
And till my ghastly tale is told,
This heart within me burns.   585

"I pass, like night, from land to land;
I have strange power of speech;
That moment that his face I see,
I know the man that must hear me:
To him my tale I teach.   590

"What loud uproar bursts from that door!
The wedding-guests are there:

But in the garden-bower the bride
And bride-maids singing are :
And hark the little vesper bell,   595
Which biddeth me to prayer.

" O Wedding-Guest ! this soul hath been
Alone on a wide, wide sea :
So lonely 'twas, that God himself
Scarce seemed there to be.   600

"O sweeter than the marriage feast,
'Tis sweeter far to me,
To walk together to the kirk
With a goodly company !—

"To walk together to the kirk,   605
And all together pray,
While each to his great Father bends,
Old men, and babes, and loving friends,
And youths and maidens gay !

"Farewell, farewell ! but this I tell   610
To thee, thou Wedding-Guest !—
He prayeth well, who loveth well
Both man and bird and beast.

"He prayeth best, who loveth best
All things both great and small ;   615
For the dear God who loveth us,
He made and loveth all."

The Mariner, whose eye is bright,
Whose beard with age is hoar,
Is gone : and now the Wedding-Guest   620
Turned from the Bridegroom's door.

He went like one that hath been stunned,
And is of sense forlorn :
A sadder and a wiser man
He rose the morrow morn.

SCOTT.

CADYOW CASTLE.

WHEN princely Hamilton's abode
  Ennobled Cadyow's Gothic towers,
The song went round, the goblet flow'd,
  And revel sped the laughing hours.

Then, thrilling to the harp's gay sound,   5
  So sweetly rung each vaulted wall,
And echoed light the dancer's bound,
  As mirth and music cheer'd the hall.

But Cadyow's towers, in ruins laid,
  And vaults, by ivy mantled o'er,   10
Thrill to the music of the shade,
  Or echo Evan's hoarser roar.

Yet still of Cadyow's faded fame
  You bid me tell a minstrel tale,
And tune my harp of Border frame   15
  On the wild banks of Evandale.

For thou from scenes of courtly pride,
  From pleasure's lighter scenes, canst turn,
To draw oblivion's pall aside,
  And mark the long-forgotten urn.   20

Then, noble maid! at thy command,
  Again the crumbled halls shall rise;
Lo! as on Evan's banks we stand,
  The past returns—the present flies.

Where with the rock's wood-cover'd side   25
  Were blended late the ruins green,

Rise turrets in fantastic pride,
  And feudal banners flaunt between :

Where the rude torrent's brawling course
  Was shagged with thorn and tangling sloe,   30
The ashler buttress braves its force,
  And ramparts frown in battled row.

'Tis night—the shade of keep and spire
  Obscurely dance on Evan's stream;
And on the wave the warder's fire   35
  Is chequering the moon-light beam.

Fades slow their light; the east is grey;
  The weary warder leaves his tower;
Steeds snort; uncoupled stag-hounds bay,
  And merry hunters quit the bower.   40

The drawbridge falls—they hurry out—
  Clatters each plank and swinging chain,
As, dashing o'er, the jovial route
  Urge the shy steed, and slack the rein.

First of his troop, the chief rode on ;   45
  His shouting merry-men throng behind ;
The steed of princely Hamilton
  Was fleeter than the mountain wind.

From the thick copse the roe-bucks bound,
  The startled red-deer scuds the plain,   50
For the hoarse bugle's warrior-sound
  Has rouzed their mountain haunts again.

Through the huge oaks of Evandale,
  Whose limbs a thousand years have worn,
What sullen roar comes down the gale,   55
  And drowns the hunter's pealing horn ?

Mightiest of all the beasts of chace,
  That roam in woody Caledon,
Crashing the forest in his race,
  The Mountain Bull comes thundering on.   60

Fierce on the hunters' quiver'd band
  He rolls his eyes of swarthy glow,

Spurns with black hoof and horn the sand,
  And tosses high his mane of snow.

Aim'd well, the Chieftain's lance has flown;   65
  Struggling in blood the savage lies;
His roar is sunk in hollow groan—
  Sound, merry huntsmen! sound the *pryse!*

Tis noon—against the knotted oak
  The hunters rest the idle spear;   70
Curls through the trees the slender smoke,
  Where yeomen dight the woodland cheer

Proudly the Chieftain mark'd his clan
  On greenwood lap all careless thrown,
Yet miss'd his eye the boldest man   75
  That bore the name of Hamilton.

"Why fills not Bothwellhaugh his place,
  Still wont our weal and woe to share?
Why comes he not our sport to grace?
  Why shares he not our hunter's fare?"—   80

Stern Claud replied with darkening face,
  (Grey Pasley's haughty lord was he,)
"At merry feast, or buxom chace,
  No more the warrior shalt thou see.

"Few suns have set since Woodhouselee   85
  Saw Bothwellhaugh's bright goblets foam,
When to his hearths, in social glee,
  The war-worn soldier turn'd him home.

"There, wan from her maternal throes,
  His Margaret, beautiful and mild,   90
Sate in her bower, a pallid rose,
  And peaceful nursed her new-born child.

"O change accurs'd! past are those days;
  False Murray's ruthless spoilers came,
And for the hearth's domestic blaze   95
  Ascends destruction's volumed flame.

"What sheeted phantom wanders wild,
  Where mountain Eske through woodland flows?

Her arms enfold a shadowy child—
   Oh! is it she, the pallid rose? 100

" The wildered travell'r sees her glide,
   And hears her feeble voice with awe—
' Revenge,' she cries, ' on Murray's pride !
   And woe for injured Bothwellhaugh ! ' "

He ceased—and cries of rage and grief 105
   Burst mingling from the kindred band,
And half arose the kindling Chief,
   And half unsheath'd his Arran brand.

But who o'er bush, o'er stream and rock,
   Rides headlong with resistless speed, 110
Whose bloody poniard's frantic stroke
   Drives to the leap his jaded steed ;

Whose cheek is pale, whose eyeballs glare,
   As one some vision'd sight that saw,
Whose hands are bloody, loose his hair ?— 115
   'Tis he ! 'tis he ! 'tis Bothwellhaugh.

,From gory selle and reeling steed
   Sprung the fierce horseman with a bound,
And, reeking from the recent deed,
   He dash'd his carbine on the ground. 120

Sternly he spoke :— " ' 'Tis sweet to hear
   In good greenwood the bugle blown,
But sweeter to Revenge's ear,
   To drink a tyrant's dying groan.

" Your slaughter'd quarry proudly trod 125
   At dawning morn o'er dale and down,
But prouder base-born Murray rode   .
   Through old Linlithgow's crowded town.

" From the wild Border's humbled side
   In haughty triumph marched he, 130
While Knox relax'd his bigot pride,
   And smiled, the traitorous pomp to see.

" But can stern Power with all his vaunt,
   Or Pomp with all her courtly glare,

The settled heart of Vengeance daunt,   135
    Or change the purpose of Despair?

"With hackbut bent, my secret stand,
    Dark as the purposed deed, I chose,
And mark'd, where, mingling in his band,
    Troop'd Scottish pikes and English bows.   140

"Dark Morton, girt with many a spear,
    Murder's foul minion, led the van;
And clash'd their broad-swords in the rear
    The wild Macfarlanes' plaided clan.

"Glencairn and stout Parkhead were nigh,   145
    Obsequious at their Regent's rein,
And haggard Lindesay's iron eye,
    That saw fair Mary weep in vain.

"Mid pennon'd spears, a steely grove,
    Proud Murray's plumage floated high;   150
Scarce could his trampling charger move,
    So close the minions crowded nigh.

"From the raised vizor's shade his eye,
    Dark rolling, glanced the ranks along,
And his steel truncheon, waved on high,   155
    Seem'd marshalling the iron throng.

"But yet his sadden'd brow confess'd
    A passing shade of doubt and awe;
Some fiend was whispering in his breast,
    'Beware of injured Bothwellhaugh!'   160

"The death-shot parts—the charger springs—
    Wild rises tumult's startling roar!
And Murray's plumy helmet rings—
    —Rings on the ground, to rise no more.

"What joy the raptured youth can feel,   165
    To hear her love the loved one tell—
Or he, who broaches on his steel
    The wolf by whom his infant fell!

"But dearer to my injured eye
    To see in dust proud Murray roll;   170

And mine was ten times trebled joy,
    To hear him groan his felon's soul.

"My Margaret's spectre glided near;
    With pride her bleeding victim saw;
And shriek'd in his death-deafen'd ear,   175
    'Remember injured Bothwellhaugh!

"Then speed thee, noble Chatlerault!
    Spread to the wind thy banner'd tree!
Each warrior bend his Clydesdale bow!—
    Murray is fall'n, and Scotland free!"   180

Vaults every warrior to his steed;
    Loud bugles join their wild acclaim—
"Murray is fall'n, and Scotland freed!
    Couch, Arran! couch thy spear of flame!"

But, see! the minstrel vision fails—   185
    The glimmering spears are seen no more;
The shouts of war die on the gales,
    Or sink in Evan's lonely roar.

For the loud bugle, pealing high,
    The blackbird whistles down the vale,   190
And sunk in ivied ruins lie
    The banner'd towers of Evandale.

For Chiefs intent on bloody deed,
    And Vengeance shouting o'er the slain,
Lo! high-born Beauty rules the steed,   195
    Or graceful guides the silken rein.

And long may Peace and Pleasure own
    The maids who list the minstrel's tale;
Nor e'er a ruder guest be known
    On the fair banks of Evandale!   200

WORDSWORTH.

ODE.

INTIMATIONS OF IMMORTALITY FROM RECOLLECTIONS OF EARLY CHILDHOOD.

I.

THERE was a time when meadow, grove, and stream,
The earth, and every common sight
   To me did seem
  Apparelled in celestial light,
The glory and the freshness of a dream.   5
It is not now as it has been of yore ;—
   Turn wheresoe'er I may,
    By night or day,
The things which I have seen I now can see no more !

II.

  The rainbow comes and goes,   10
  And lovely is the rose ;
  The moon doth with delight
Look round her when the heavens are bare ;
  Waters on a starry night
  Are beautiful and fair ;   15
  The sunshine is a glorious birth ;
  But yet I know, where'er I go,
That there hath past away a glory from the earth.

III.

Now, while the birds thus sing a joyous song,
  And while the young lambs bound   20
   As to the tabor's sound,
To me alone there came a thought of grief ;
A timely utterance gave that thought relief,
   And I again am strong.

The cataracts blow their trumpets from the steep;   25
No more shall grief of mine the season wrong.
I hear the echoes through the mountains throng,
The winds come to me from the fields of sleep,
    And all the earth is gay;
        Land and sea   30
    Give themselves up to jolity,
        And with the heart of May
    Doth every beast keep holiday!
        Thou child of joy,
Shout round me, let me hear thy shouts, thou happy shepherd boy!
                        35

IV.

Ye blessed creatures, I have heard the call
    Ye to each other make; I see
The heavens laugh with you in your jubilee;
    My heart is at your festival,
      My head hath its coronal;   40
The fulness of your bliss, I feel—I feel it all.
      Oh, evil day! if I were sullen
      While the earth herself is adorning
        This sweet May morning;
      And the children are pulling,   45
        On every side,
      In a thousand valleys far and wide,
      Fresh flowers; while the sun shines warm
And the babe leaps up on his mother's arm:—
      I hear, I hear, with joy I hear!   50
      But there's a tree, of many, one,
A single field which I have look'd upon,
Both of them speak of something that is gone;
        The pansy at my feet
        Doth the same tale repeat.   .   55
Whither is fled the visionary gleam?
Where is it now, the glory and the dream?

V.

Our birth is but a sleep and a forgetting:
The soul that rises with us, our life's star,
      Hath had elsewhere its setting,   60
        And cometh from afar;
      Not in entire forgetfulness,
      And not in utter nakedness,

But trailing clouds of glory do we come
   From God, who is our home.   65
Heaven lies about us in our infancy!
Shades of the prison-house begin to close
   Upon the growing boy,
But he beholds the light, and whence it flows, —
   He sees it in his joy;   70
The youth, who daily farther from the east
  Must travel, still is Nature's priest,
   And by the vision splendid
   Is on his way attended;
At length the man perceives it die away,   75
And fade into the light of common day.

VI.

Earth fills her lap with pleasures of her own;
Yearnings she hath in her own natural kind,
And, even with something of a mother's mind,
   And no unworthy aim,   80
  The homely nurse doth all she can
To make her foster-child, her inmate man,
   Forget the glories he hath known,
And that imperial palace whence he came.

VII.

Behold the child among his new-born blisses,   85
A six years' darling of a pigmy size!
See, where 'mid work of his own hand he lies,
Fretted by sallies of his mother's kisses,
With light upon him from his father's eyes!
See, at his feet, some little plan or chart,   90
Some fragment from his dream of human life,
Shaped by himself with newly-learned art—
   A wedding or a festival,
   A mourning or a funeral;
    And this hath now his heart,   95
   And unto this he frames his song:
    Then will he fit his tongue
To dialogues of business, love, or strife;
   But it will not be long
   Ere this be thrown aside,   100
   And with new joy and pride
The little actor cons another part,

Filling from time to time his "humorous stage"
With all the persons, down to palsied age,   `
That Life brings with her in her equipage ;   105
  As if his whole vocation
  Were endless imitation.

VIII.

Thou, whose exterior semblance doth belie
  Thy soul's immensity ;
Thou best philosopher, who yet dost keep   110
Thy heritage ; thou eye among the blind,
That, deaf and silent, read'st the eternal deep
Haunted for ever by the eternal mind,—
  Mighty Prophet ! Seer blest !
  On whom those truths do rest,   115
Which we are toiling all our lives to find ;
In darkness lost, the darkness of the grave ;
Thou, over whom thy immortality
Broods like the day, a master o'er a slave,
A presence which is not to be put by ;   120
—Thou little child, yet glorious in the might
Of heaven-born freedom, on thy being's height,
Why with such earnest pains dost thou provoke
The years to bring the inevitable yoke,
Thus blindly with thy blessedness at strife?   125
Full soon thy soul shall have her earthly freight.
And custom lie upon thee with a weight,
Heavy as frost, and deep almost as life !

IX.

  O joy, that in our embers
   Is something that doth live,   130
  That Nature yet remembers
   What was so fugitive !
The thought of our past years in me doth breed
Perpetual benedictions, not indeed
For that which is most worthy to be blest—   135
Delight and liberty, the simple creed
Of childhood, whether busy or at rest,
With new-fledged hope still fluttering in his breast ;
  Not for these I raise
   The song of thanks and praise ;   140
  But for those obstinate questionings

Of sense and outward things,
Fallings from us, vanishings ;
Blank misgivings of a creature
Moving about in worlds not realised,
High instincts, before which our mortal nature
Did tremble like a guilty thing surprised:
But for those first affections,
Those shadowy recollections,
Which, be they what they may,
Are yet the fountain light of all our day,
Are yet a master light of all our seeing,
Uphold us, cherish, and have power to make
Our noisy years seem moments in the being
Of the eternal silence ; truths that wake,
To perish never ;
Which neither listlessness, nor mad endeavour,
Nor man nor boy,
Nor all that is at enmity with joy,
Can utterly abolish or destroy !
Hence in a season of calm weather,
Though inland far we be,
Our souls have sight of that immortal sea
Which brought us hither ;
Can in a moment travel thither,
And see the children sport upon the shore,
And hear the mighty waters rolling evermore.

X.

Then sing, ye birds, sing, sing a joyous song !
And let the young lambs bound
As to the tabor's sound !
We in thought will join your throng,
Ye that pipe and ye that play,
Ye that through your hearts to-day
Feel the gladness of the May !
What though the radiance which was once so bright
Be now for ever taken from my sight,
Though nothing can bring back the hour
Of splendour in the grass, of glory in the flower ;
We will grieve not, rather find
Strength in what remains behind,
In the primal sympathy

Which having been, must ever be ;
In the soothing thoughts that spring
Out of human suffering ;
In the faith that looks through death, 185
In years that bring the philosophic mind.

XI.

And O ye fountains, meadows, hills, and groves,
Forebode not any severing of our loves !
Yet in my heart of hearts I feel your might ;
I only have relinquished one delight, 190
To live beneath your more habitual sway.
I love the brooks, which down their channels fret,
Even more than when I tripp'd lightly as they :
The innocent brightness of a new-born day
      Is lovely yet ; 195
The clouds that gather round the setting sun
Do take a sober colouring from an eye
That hath kept watch o'er man's mortality !
Another race hath been, and other palms are won.
Thanks to the human heart by which we live, 200
Thanks to its tenderness, its joys and fears,
To me the meanest flower that blows can give
Thoughts that do often lie too deep for tears.

LAODAMIA.

" WITH sacrifice, before the rising morn,
Vows have I made, by fruitless hope inspired ;
And from the infernal gods, 'mid shades forlorn
Of night, my slaughter'd lord have I required ;
Celestial pity I again implore ;— 5
Restore him to my sight—great Jove, restore ! "

So speaking, and by fervent love endowed
With faith, the suppliant heavenward lifts her hands ;
While, like the sun emerging from a cloud,
Her countenance brightens, and her eye expands, . 10
Her bosom heaves and spreads, her stature grows,
And she expects the issue in repose.

O terror ! what hath she perceived ?   O joy !
What doth she look on—whom doth she behold ?
Her hero slain upon the beach of Troy ?   15
His vital presence—his corporeal mould ?
It is—if sense deceive her not—'tis he !
And a god leads him, winged Mercury !

Mild Hermes spake—and touched her with his wand
That calms all fear: "Such grace hath crowned thy prayer,   20
Laodamia ! that at Jove's command
Thy husband walks the paths of upper air :
He comes to tarry with thee three hours' space ;
Accept the gift ; behold him face to face ! "

Forth sprang the impassion'd queen her lord to clasp ;   25
Again that consummation she essayed ;
But unsubstantial form eludes her grasp
As often as that eager grasp was made.
The phantom parts—but parts to reunite,
And reassume his place before her sight.   30

" Protesilaus, lo ! thy guide is gone !
Confirm, I pray, the vision with thy voice ;
This is our palace,—yonder is thy throne ;
Speak, and the floor thou tread'st on will rejoice.
Not to appal me have the gods bestow'd   35
This precious boon, and blest a sad abode."

" Great Jove, Laodamia, doth not leave
His gifts imperfect :—Spectre though I be,
I am not sent to scare thee or deceive,
But in reward of thy fidelity ;   40
And something also did my worth obtain,
For fearless virtue bringeth boundless gain.

" Thou knowest, the Delphic oracle foretold
That the first Greek that touched the Trojan strand
Should die ; but me the threat could not withhold :   45
A generous cause a victim did demand ;
And forth I leapt upon the sandy plain,
A self-devoted chief—by Hector slain."

" Supreme of heroes—bravest, noblest, best !
Thy matchless courage I bewail no more,   50
Which then, when tens of thousands were deprest

By doubt, propelled thee to the fatal shore;
Thou found'st—and I forgive thee—here thou art—
A nobler counsellor than my poor heart.

"But thou, though capable of sternest deed,   55
Wert kind as resolute, and good as brave;
And he, whose power restores thee, hath decreed
Thou should'st elude the malice of the grave:
Redundant are thy locks, thy lips as fair
As when their breath enriched Thessalian air.   60

"No spectre greets me,—no vain shadow this;
Come, blooming hero, place thee by my side!
Give, on this well-known couch, one nuptial kiss
To me, this day a second time thy bride!"
Jove frown'd in heaven; the conscious Parcœ threw   65
Upon those roseate lips a Stygian hue.

"This visage tells me that my doom is past;
Nor should the change be mourned, even if the joys
Of sense were able to return as fast
And surely as they vanish. Earth destroys   70
Those raptures duly—Erebus disdains:
Calm pleasures there abide—majestic pains.

"Be taught, O faithful consort, to control
Rebellious passion; for the gods approve
The depth, and not the tumult, of the soul,   75
A fervent, not ungovernable, love.
Thy transports moderate; and meekly mourn
When I depart, for brief is my sojourn."

"Ah, wherefore?—Did not Hercules by force
Wrest from the guardian monster of the tomb   80
Alcestis, a reanimated corse,
Given back to dwell on earth in vernal bloom?
Medea's spells dispersed the weight of years,
And Æson stood a youth 'mid youthful peers.

"The gods to us are merciful—and they   85
Yet further may relent; for mightier far
Than strength of nerve and sinew, or the sway
Of magic, potent over sun and star,
Is love—though oft to agony distrest,
And though his favourite seat be feeble woman's breast.   90

"But if thou goest, 1 follow——" "Peace," he said—
She looked upon him and was calmed and cheered ;
The ghastly colour from his lips had fled ;
In his deportment, shape, and mien, appear'd
Elysian beauty, melancholy grace,   95
Brought from a pensive though a happy place.

He spake of love, such love as spirits feel
In worlds whose course is equable and pure ;
No fears to beat away—no strife to heal—
The past unsighed for, and the future sure ;   100
Spake of heroic arts in graver mood
Revived, with finer harmony pursued,

Of all that is most beauteous—imaged there
In happier beauty, more pellucid streams,
An ampler ether, a diviner air,   105
And fields invested with purpureal gleams,
Climes which the sun, who sheds the brightest day
Earth knows, is all unworthy to survey.

Yet there the soul shall enter which hath earned
That privilege by virtue.—" Ill," said he,   110
"The end of man's existence I discerned,
Who from ignoble games and revelry
Could draw, when we had parted, vain delight,
While tears were thy best pastime, day and night,

"And while my youthful peers, before my eyes,   115
(Each hero following his peculiar bent)
Prepared themselves for glorious enterprise
By martial sports,—or, seated in the tent,
Chieftains and kings in council were detained,
What time the fleet at Aulis lay enchained.   120

"The wished-for wind was given :—I then revolved
The oracle upon the silent sea ;
And, if no worthier led the way, resolved
That, of a thousand vessels, mine should be
The foremost prow in pressing to the strand,—-   125
Mine the first blood that tinged the Trojan sand.

"Yet bitter, ofttimes bitter, was the pang
When of thy loss I thought, beloved wife ;
On thee too fondly did my memory hang.

And on the joys we shared in mortal life,— 130
The paths which we had trod—these fountains,—flowers;
My new-planned cities, and unfinished towers.

" But should suspense permit the foe to cry,
' Behold, they tremble !—haughty their array,
Yet of their number no one dares to die'.?— 135
In soul I swept the indignity away :
Old frailties then recurred :—but lofty thought,
In act embodied, my deliverance wrought.

" And thou, though strong in love, art all too weak
In reason, in self-government too slow ; 140
I counsel thee by fortitude to seek
Our blest reunion in the shades below.
The invisible world with thee hath sympathised ;
Be thy affections raised and solemnised.

" Learn by a mortal yearning to ascend 145
Seeking a higher object :—Love was given,
Encouraged, sanctioned, chiefly for that end ;
For this the passion to excess was driven—
That self might be annulled ; her bondage prove
The fetters of a dream, opposed to love." 150

Aloud she shrieked !—for Hermes reappears !
Round the dear shade she would have clung—'tis vain :
The hours are past,—too brief had they been years ;
And him no mortal effort can detain :
Swift, toward the realms that know not earthly day, 155
He through the portal takes his silent way,
And on the palace-floor a lifeless corse she lay.

Thus, all in vain exhorted and reproved,
She perished ; and, as for a wilful crime
By the just gods whom no weak pity moved, 160
Was doomed to wear out her appointed time,
Apart from happy ghosts, that gather flowers
Of blissful quiet 'mid unfading bowers.

Yet tears to human suffering are due ;
And mortal hopes defeated and o'erthrown 165
Are mourned by man, and not by man alone,

M 2

As fondly he believes.—Upon the side
Of Hellespont (such faith was entertained)
A knot of spiry trees for ages grew
From out the tomb of him for whom she died ;   170
And ever, when such stature they had gained
That Ilium's walls were subject to their view,
The trees' tall summits withered at the sight—
A constant interchange of growth and blight !

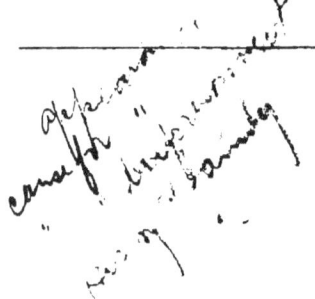

BYRON.

THE PRISONER OF CHILLON.

I.

My hair is grey, but not with years,
  Nor grew it white
  In a single night,
As men's have grown from sudden fears :
My limbs are bow'd, though not with toil,   5
  But rusted with a vile repose,
For they have been a dungeon's spoil,
  And mine has been the fate of those
To whom the goodly earth and air
Are bann'd, and barr'd—forbidden fare ;   10
But this was for my father's faith
I suffer'd chains and courted death ;
That father perish'd at the stake
For tenets he would not forsake ;
And for the same his lineal race   15
In darkness found a dwelling-place ;
We were seven—who now are one,
  Six in youth, and one in age,
Finish'd as they had begun,
  Proud of Persecution's rage ;   20
One in fire, and two in field,
Their belief with blood have seal'd,
Dying as their father died,
For the God their foes denied ;
Three were in a dungeon cast,   25
Of whom this wreck is left the last.

II.

There are seven pillars of Gothic mould
In Chillon's dungeons deep and old,

There are seven columns, massy and grey,
Dim with a dull imprison'd ray,   30
A sunbeam which hath lost its way,
And through the crevice and the cleft
Of the thick wall is fallen and left;
Creeping o'er the floor so damp,
Like a marsh's meteor lamp: 35
And in each pillar there is a ring,
  And in each ring there is a chain;
That iron is a cankering thing,
  For in these limbs its teeth remain,
With marks that will not wear away,   40
Till I have done with this new day,
Which now is painful to these eyes,
Which have not seen the sun so rise
For years—I cannot count them o'er,
I lost their long and heavy score   45
When my last brother droop'd and died,
And I lay living by his side.

III.

They chain'd us each to a column stone,
And we were three—yet, each alone;
We could not move a single pace,   50
We could not see each other's face,
But with that pale and livid light
That made us strangers in our sight:
And thus together—yet apart,
Fetter'd in hand, but join'd in heart,   55
'Twas still some solace, in the dearth
  Of the pure elements of earth,
To hearken to each other's speech,
And each turn comforter to each
With some new hope, or legend old,   60
Or song heroically bold;
But even these at length grew cold.
Our voices took a dreary tone,
An echo of the dungeon stone,
  A grating sound—not full and free,   65
  As they of yore were wont to be:
  It might be fancy—but to me
They never sounded like our own.

IV.

I was the eldest of the three,
  And to uphold and cheer the rest   70
  I ought to do—and did my best—
And each did well in his degree.
  The youngest, whom my father loved,
  Because our mother's brow was given
To him—with eyes as blue as heaven,   75
  For him my soul was sorely moved;
  And truly might it be distress'd
  To see such bird in such a nest;
For he was beautiful as day—
  (When day was beautiful to me   80
  As to young eagles, being free)—
  A polar day, which will not see
A sunset till its summer's gone,
  Its sleepless summer of long light,
The snow-clad offspring of the sun: 85
  And thus he was as pure and bright,
  And in his natural spirit gay,
  With tears for nought but others' ills,
  And then they flow'st like mountain rills,
  Unless he could assuage the woe   90
  Which he abhorr'd to view below.

V.

The other was as pure of mind,
But form'd to combat with his kind;
Strong in his frame, and of a mood
Which 'gainst the world in war had stood,   95
And perish'd in the foremost rank
  With joy:—but not in chains to pine:
His spirit wither'd with their clank,
  I saw it silently decline—
  And so perchance in sooth did mine: 100
But yet I forced it on to cheer
  Those relics of a home so dear.
He was a hunter of the hills,
  Had follow'd there the deer and wolf;
  To him his dungeon was a gulf,   105
And fetter'd feet the worst of ills.

VI.

Lake Leman lies by Chillon's walls :
A thousand feet in depth below
Its massy waters meet and flow ;
Thus much the fathom-line was sent   110
From Chillon's snow-white battlement,
    Which round about the wave enthralls,
A double dungeon wall and wave
Have made—and like a living grave
Below the surface of the lake   115
The dark vault lies wherein we lay,
We heard it ripple night and day ;
    Sounding o'er our heads it knock'd ;
And I have felt the winter's spray
Wash through the bars when winds were high   120
And wanton in the happy sky ;
    And then the very rock hath rock'd,
    And I have felt it shake, unshock'd,
Because I could have smiled to see
The death that would have set me free.   125

VII.

I said my nearer brother pined,
I said his mighty heart declined,
He loath'd and put away his food ;
It was not that 'twas coarse and rude,
For we were used to hunter's fare,   130
And for the like had little care :
The milk drawn from the mountain goat
Was changed for water from the moat,
Our bread was such as captive's tears
Have moisten'd many a thousand years,   135
Since man first pent his fellow men
Like brutes within an iron den ;
But what were these to us or him ?
These wasted not his heart or limb ;
My brother's soul was of that mould   140
Which in a palace had grown cold,
Had his free breathing been denied
The range of the steep mountain's side ;
But why delay the truth ?—he died.

I saw, and could not hold his head, 145
Nor reach his dying hand—nor dead,
Though hard I strove, but strove in vain,
To rend and gnash my bonds in twain.
He died—and they unlock'd his chain,
And scoop'd for him a shallow grave 150
Even from the cold earth of our cave.
I begg'd them, as a boon, to lay
His corse in dust whereon the day
Might shine—it was a foolish thought,
But then within my brain it wrought, 155
That even in death his freeborn breast
In such a dungeon could not rest.
I might have spared my idle prayer—
They coldly laugh'd—and laid him there:
The flat and turfless earth above 160
The being we so much did love;
His empty chain above it leant,
Such murder's fitting monument!

VIII.

But he, the favorite and the flower,
Most cherish'd since his natal hour, 165
His mother's image in fair face,
The infant love of all his race,
His martyr'd father's dearest thought,
My latest care, for whom I sought
To hoard my life, that his might be 170
Less wretched now, and one day free;
He, too, who yet had held untired
A spirit natural or inspired—
He, too, was struck, and day by day
Was wither'd on the stalk away. 175
Oh, God! it is a fearful thing
To see the human soul take wing
In any shape, in any mood :—
I've seen it rushing forth in blood,
I've seen it on the breaking ocean 180
Strive with a swoln convulsive motion,
I've seen the sick and ghastly bed
Of Sin delirious with its dread;
But these were horrors—this was woe
Unmix'd with such—but sure and slow; 185

He faded, and so calm and meek,
So softly worn, so sweetly weak,
So tearless, yet so tender—kind,
And grieved for those he left behind;
With all the while a cheek whose bloom   190
Was as a mockery of the tomb,
Whose tints as gently sunk away
As a departing rainbow's ray;
An eye of most transparent light,
That almost made the dungeon bright;   195
And not a word of murmur—not
A groan o'er his untimely lot,—
A little talk of better days,
A little hope my own to raise,
For I was sunk in silence—lost   200
In this last loss, of all the most;
And then the sighs he would suppress
Of fainting nature's feebleness,
More slowly drawn, grew less and less:
I listen'd, but I could not hear—   205
I call'd, for I was wild with fear;
I knew 'twas hopeless, but my dread
Would not be thus admonished;
I called, and thought I heard a sound—
I burst my chain with one strong bound,   210
And rush'd to him:—I found him not,
I only stirr'd in this black spot,
I only lived—*I* only drew
The accursed breath of dungeon-dew;
The last—the sole—the dearest link   215
Between me and the eternal brink,
Which bound me to my failing race,
Was broken in this fatal place.
One on the earth, and one beneath—
My brothers—both had ceased to breathe: 220
I took that hand which lay so still,
Alas! my own was full as chill;
I had not strength to stir, or strive,
But felt that I was still alive—
A frantic feeling when we know   225
That what we love shall ne'er be so.
          I know not why
          I could not die,

I had no earthly hope—but faith,
And that forbade a selfish death.   230

IX.

What next befell me then and there
I know not well—I never knew—
First came the loss of light, and air,
   And then of darkness too:
I had no thought, no feeling—none—   235
Among the stones I stood a stone,
And was, scarce conscious what I wist,
As shrubless crags within the mist;
For all was blank, and bleak, and grey;
It was not night—it was not day—   240
It was not even the dungeon-light,
So hateful to my heavy sight,
But vacancy absorbing space,
And fixedness—without a place;
There were no stars—no earth—no time—   245
No check—no change—no good—no crime—
But silence, and a stirless breath
Which neither was of life nor death;
A sea of stagnant idleness,
Blind, boundless, mute, and motionless!   250

X.

A light broke in upon my brain,—
   It was the carol of a bird;
It ceased, and then it came again,
   The sweetest song ear ever heard,
And mine was thankful till my eyes   255
Ran over with the glad surprise,
And they that moment could not see
I was the mate of misery;
But then by dull degrees came back
My senses to their wonted track;   260
I saw the dungeon walls and floor
Close slowly round me as before,
I saw the glimmer of the sun
Creeping as it before had done,
But through the crevice where it came   265
That bird was perch'd, as fond and tame,

And tamer than upon the tree;   *blue wings*
A lovely bird, with azure wings,
And song that said a thousand things,
   And seem'd to say them all for me!   270
I never saw its like before,
I ne'er shall see its likeness more:
It seem'd like me to want a mate,
But was not half so desolate,
And it was come to love me when   275
None lived to love me so again,
And, cheering from my dungeon's brink,
Had brought me back to feel and think.
I know not if it late were free,
   Or broke its cage to perch on mine,   280
But knowing well captivity,
   Sweet bird! I could not wish for thine!
Or if it were, in winged guise,
A visitant from Paradise;
For—Heaven forgive that thought! the while   285
Which made me both to weep and smile—
I sometimes deem'd that it might be
My brother's soul come down to me;
But then at last away it flew,
And then 'twas mortal—well I knew,   290
For he would never thus have flown,
And left me twice so doubly lone,—
Lone—as the corse within its shroud,
Lone—as a solitary cloud,
   A single cloud on a sunny day,   295
While all the rest of heaven is clear,
A frown upon the atmosphere,
That hath no business to appear
   When skies are blue, and earth is gay.

XI.

A kind of change came in my fate,   300
My keepers grew compassionate;
I know not what had made them so,
They were inured to sights of woe,
But so it was:—my broken chain
With links unfasten'd did remain,   305
And it was liberty to stride
Along my cell from side to side,

And up and down, and then athwart,
And tread it over every part;
And round the pillars one by one,   310
Returning where my walk begun,
Avoiding only, as I trod,
My brothers' graves without a sod;
For if I thought with heedless tread
My step profaned their lowly bed,   315
My breath came gaspingly and thick,
And my crush'd heart fell blind and sick.

XII.

I made a footing in the wall,
  It was not therefrom to escape,
For I had buried one and all   320
  Who loved me in a human shape;
And the whole earth would henceforth be
A wider prison unto me:
No child—no sire—no kin had I,
No partner in my misery;   325
I thought of this, and I was glad,
For thought of them had made me mad;
But I was curious to ascend
To my barr'd windows, and to bend
Once more upon the mountains high   330
The quiet of a loving eye.

XIII.

I saw them—and they were the same,
They were not changed like me in frame;
I saw their thousand years of snow
On high—their wide long lake below,   335
And the blue Rhone in fullest flow;
I heard the torrents leap and gush
O'er channell'd rock and broken bush;
I saw the white-wall'd distant town,
And whiter sails go skimming down;   340
And then there was a little isle,
Which in my very face did smile,
  The only one in view;
A small green isle, it seem'd no more,
Scarce broader than my dungeon floor,   345

But in it there were three tall trees,
And o'er it blew the mountain breeze,
And by it there were waters flowing,
And on it there were young flowers growing,
    Of gentle breath and hue. 350
The fish swam by the castle wall,
And they seem'd joyous each and all;
The eagle rode the rising blast,
Methought he never flew so fast
As then to me he seemed to fly; 355
And then new tears came in my eye,
And I felt troubled—and would fain
I had not left my recent chain;
And, when I did descend again,
The darkness of my dim abode 360
Fell on me as a heavy load;
It was as is a new-dug grave,
Closing o'er one we sought to save,—
And yet my glance, too much opprest,
Had almost need of such a rest. 365

XIV.

It might be months, or years, or days,
    I kept no count—I took no note,
I had no hope my eyes to raise
    And clear them of their dreary mote;
At last men came to set me free; 370
    I ask'd not why, and reck'd not where;
It was at length the same to me,
Fetter'd or fetterless to be,
    I learn'd to love despair.
And thus when they appear'd at last, 375
And all my bonds aside were cast,
These heavy walls to me had grown
A hermitage—and all my own!
And half I felt as they were come
To tear me from a second home: 380
With spiders I had friendship made,
And watch'd them in their sullen trade,
Had seen the mice by moonlight play,
And why should I feel less than they?
We were all inmates of one place, 385
And I, the monarch of each race,

Had power to kill—yet, strange to tell!
In quiet we had learn'd to dwell—
My very chains and I grew friends,
So much a long communion tends   390
To make us what we are :—even I
Regain'd my freedom with a sigh.

give facts of poem in order.
Stanzas 1, 2 3 4

outline 5 6 7 8 Island c

Look up "Gothic".
written lesson

Bring back these papers wit/
correct interpretations.

KEATS.

THE EVE OF ST. AGNES.

I.

St. Agnes' Eve—Ah, bitter chill it was!
The owl, for all his feathers, was a-cold ;
The hare limp'd trembling through the frozen grass,
And silent was the flock in woolly fold :
Numb were the Beadsman's fingers while he told   5
His rosary, and while his frosted breath,
Like pious incense from a censer old,
Seem'd taking flight for heaven without a death,
Past the sweet Virgin's picture, while his prayer he saith.

II.

His prayer he saith, this patient, holy man ;   10
Then takes his lamp, and riseth from his knees,
And back returneth, meagre, barefoot, wan,
Along the chapel aisle by slow degrees:
The sculptur'd dead on each side seem to freeze,
Emprison'd in black, purgatorial rails :   15
Knights, ladies, praying in dumb orat'ries,
He passeth by ; and his weak spirit fails
To think how they may ache in icy hoods and mails.

III.

Northward he turneth through a little door,
And scarce three steps, ere Music's golden tongue   20
Flatter'd to tears this aged man and poor ;
But no—already had his death-bell rung ;
The joys of all his life were said and sung :
His was harsh penance on St. Agnes' Eve :
Another way he went, and soon among   25
Rough ashes sat he for his soul's reprieve,
And all night kept awake, for sinner's sake to grieve.

IV.

That ancient Beadsman heard the prelude soft;
And so it chanc'd, for many a door was wide,
From hurry to and fro. Soon, up aloft,   30
The silver, snarling trumpets 'gan to chide:
The level chambers, ready with their pride,
Were glowing to receive a thousand guests :
The carved angels, ever eager-eyed,
Stared, where upon their head the cornice rests,   35
With hair blown back, and wings put cross-wise on their breasts.

V.

At length burst in the argent revelry,
With plume, tiara, and all rich array,
Numerous as shadows haunting fairily
The brain, new-stuff'd, in youth, with triumphs gay   40
Of old romance.   These let us wish away,
And turn, sole-thoughted, to one Lady there,
Whose heart had brooded, all that wintry day,
On love, and wing'd St. Agnes' saintly care,
As she had heard old dames full many times declare.   45

VI.

They told her how, upon St. Agnes' Eve,
Young virgins might have visions of delight,
And soft adorings from their loves receive
Upon the honey'd middle of the night,
If ceremonies due they did aright ;   50
As, supperless to bed they must retire,
And couch supine their beauties, lily white ;
Nor look behind, nor sideways, but require
Of Heaven with upward eyes for all that they desire.

VII.

Full of this whim was thoughtful Madeline :   55
The music, yearning like a God in pain,
She scarcely heard : her maiden eyes divine,
Fix'd on the floor, saw many a sweeping train
Pass by—she heeded not at all : in vain
Came many a tiptoe, amorous cavalier,   60
And back retir'd, not cool'd by high disdain,
But she saw not : her heart was otherwhere ;
She sigh'd for Agnes' dreams, the sweetest of the year.

VIII.

She danc'd along with vague, regardless eyes,
Anxious her lips, her breathing quick and short :   65
The hallow'd hour was near at hand : she sighs
Amid the timbrels, and the throng'd resort
Of whisperers in anger, or in sport,
'Mid looks of love, defiance, hate, and scorn,
Hoodwink'd with faery fancy, all amort,   70
Save to St. Agnes and her lambs unshorn,
And all the bliss to be before to-morrow morn.

IX.

So, purposing each moment to retire,
She linger'd still. Meantime, across the moors,
Had come young Porphyro, with heart on fire   75
For Madeline. Beside the portal doors,
Buttress'd from moonlight, stands he, and implores
All saints to give him sight of Madeline,
But for one moment in the tedious hours,
That he might gaze and worship all unseen,   80
Perchance speak, kneel, touch, kiss—in sooth such things have been.

X.

He ventures in : let no buzz'd whisper tell :
All eyes be muffled, or a hundred swords
Will storm his heart, Love's fev'rous citadel :
For him those chambers held barbarian hordes,   85
Hyena foemen, and hot-blooded lords,
Whose very dogs would execrations howl
'Against his lineage : not one breast affords
Him any mercy, in that mansion foul,
Save one old beldame, weak in body and in soul.   90

XI.

Ah, happy chance ! the aged creature came,
Shuffling along with ivory-headed wand,
To where he stood, hid from the torch's flame,
Behind a broad hall-pillar, far beyond
The sound of merriment and chorus bland :   95
He startled her ; but soon she knew his face,
And grasp'd his fingers in her palsied hand,
Saying, " Mercy, Porphyro ! hie thee from this place ;
They are all here to-night, the whole blood-thirsty race !

XII.

"Get hence ! get hence ! there's dwarfish Hildebrand ;　100
He had a fever late, and in the fit
He cursed thee and thine, both house and land :
Then there's that old Lord Maurice, not a whit
More tame for his grey hairs—Alas me ! flit !
Flit like a ghost away."—"Ah, Gossip dear,　　105
We're safe enough ; here in this arm-chair sit,
And tell me how "—"Good Saints ! not here, not here :
Follow me, child, or else these stones will be thy bier."

XIII.

He follow'd through a lowly arched way,
Brushing the cobwebs with his lofty plume ;　　110
And as she mutter'd "Well-a—well-a-day !"
He found him in a little moonlight room,
Pale, latticed, chill, and silent as a tomb.
"Now tell me where is Madeline," said he,
"O tell me, Angela, by the holy loom　　　115
Which none but secret sisterhood may see,
When they St. Agnes' wool are weaving piously."

XIV.

"St. Agnes ! Ah ! it is St. Agnes' Eve—
Yet men will murder upon holy days :
Thou must hold water in a witch's sieve,　　, 120
And be liege-lord of all the Elves and Fays,
To venture so : it fills me with amaze
To see thee, Porphyro !—St. Agnes' Eve !
God's help ! my lady fair the conjuror plays
This very night : good angels her deceive !　　125
But let me laugh awhile, I've mickle time to grieve."

XV.

Feebly she laugheth in the languid moon,
While Porphyro upon her face doth look,
Like puzzled urchin on an aged crone
Who keepeth closed a wond'rous riddle-book,　　130
As spectacled she sits in chimney nook.
But soon his eyes grew brilliant, when she told
His lady's purpose ; and he scarce could brook
Tears, at the thought of those enchantments cold,
And Madeline asleep in lap of legends old.　　135

XVI.

Sudden a thought came like a full-blown rose,
Flushing his brow, and in his pained heart
Made purple riot : then doth he propose
A stratagem, that makes the beldame start :
"A cruel man and impious thou art :   140
Sweet lady, let her pray, and sleep and dream
Alone with her good angels, far apart
From wicked men like thee. Go, Go! I deem
Thou canst not surely be the same that thou didst seem."

XVII.

"I will not harm her, by all saints I swear,"   · 145
Quoth Porphyro : "O may I ne'er find grace
When my weak voice shall whisper its last prayer,
If one of her soft ringlets I displace,
Or look with ruffian passion in her face :
Good Angela, believe me by these tears ;   150
Or I will, even in a moment's space,
Awake, with horrid shout, my foemen's ears,
And beard them, though they be more fang'd than wolves and bears."

XVIII.

"Ah ! why wilt thou affright a feeble soul?
A poor, weak, palsy-stricken, churchyard thing,   155
Whose passing-bell may ere the midnight toll ;
Whose prayers for thee, each morn and evening,
Were never miss'd." Thus plaining, doth she bring
A gentler speech from burning Porphyro,
So woeful, and of such deep sorrowing,   160
That Angela gives promise she will do
Whatever he shall wish, betide her weal or woe.

XIX.

Which was, to lead him, in close secrecy,
Even to Madeline's chamber, and there hide
Him in a closet, of such privacy   165
That he might see her beauty unespied,
And win perhaps that night a peerless bride,
While legion'd fairies paced the coverlet,
And pale enchantment held her sleepy-eyed.
Never on such a night have lovers met,   170
Since Merlin paid his Demon all the monstrous debt.

XX.

"It shall be as thou wishest," said the Dame :
"All cates and dainties shall be stored there
Quickly on this feast-night : by the tambour frame
Her own lute thou wilt see : no time to spare,   175
For I am slow and feeble, and scarce dare
On such a catering trust my dizzy head.
Wait here, my child, with patience kneel in prayer
The while : Ah ! thou must needs the lady wed,
Or may I never leave my grave among the dead."   180

XXI.

So saying she hobbled off with busy fear.
The lover's endless minutes slowly pass'd ;
The dame return'd, and whisper'd in his ear
To follow her, with aged eyes aghast
From fright of dim espial. Safe at last,   185
Through many a dusky gallery, they gain
The maiden's chamber, silken, hush'd and chaste ;
Where Porphyro took covert, pleas'd amain.
His poor guide hurried back with agues in her brain.

XXII.

Her falt'ring hand upon the balustrade,   190
Old Angela was feeling for the stair,
When Madeline, St. Agnes' charmed maid,
Rose, like a mission'd spirit, unaware :
With silver taper's light, and pious care,
She turn'd, and down the aged gossip led   195
To a safe level matting. Now prepare,
Young Porphyro, for gazing on that bed ;
She comes, she comes again, like ring-dove fray'd and fled.

XXIII.

Out went the taper as she hurried in ;
Its little smoke, in pallid moonshine, died :   200
She closed the door, she panted, all akin
To spirits of the air, and visions wide :
No utter'd syllable, or woe betide !
But to her heart her heart was voluble,
Paining with eloquence her balmy side ;   205
As though a tongueless nightingale should swell
Her throat in vain, and die, heart-stifled, in her dell.

XXIV.

A casement high and triple-arch'd there was,
All garlanded with carven imag'ries
Of fruits, and flowers, and bunches of knot-grass,   210
And diamonded with panes of quaint device,
Innumerable of stains and splendid dyes,
As are the tiger-moth's deep-damask'd wings;
And in the midst, 'mong thousand heraldries,
And twilight saints, and dim emblazonings,   215
A shielded scutcheon blush'd with blood of queens and kings.

XXV.

Full on this casement shone the wintry moon,
And threw warm gules on Madeline's fair breast,
As down she knelt for heaven's grace and boon;
Rose-bloom fell on her hands, together prest,   220
And on her silver cross soft amethyst,
And on her hair a glory, like a saint :
She seem'd a splendid angel, newly drest,
Save wings, for heaven :—Porphyro grew faint :
She knelt so pure a thing, so free from mortal taint.   225

XXVI.

Anon his heart revives: her vespers done,
Of all its wreathed pearls her hair she frees,
Unclasps her warmed jewels one by one,
Loosens her fragrant bodice ; by degrees
Her rich attire creeps rustling to her knees :   230
Half-hidden, like a mermaid in sea-weed,
Pensive awhile she dreams awake, and sees,
In fancy, fair St. Agnes in her bed,
But dares not look behind, or all the charm is fled.

XXVII.

Soon, trembling in her soft and chilly nest,   235
In sort of wakeful swoon, perplex'd she lay,
Until the poppied warmth of sleep oppress'd
Her soothed limbs, and soul fatigued away;
Flown, like a thought, until the morrow-day,
Blissfully haven'd both from joy and pain,   240
Clasp'd like a missal where swart Paynims pray,
Blinded alike from sunshine and from rain,
As though a rose should shut, and be a bud again.

XXVIII.

Stolen to this paradise, and so entranced,
Porphyro gazed upon her empty dress,   245
And listen'd to her breathing, if it chanced
To wake into a slumberous tenderness;
Which when he heard, that minute did he bless,
And breath'd himself : then from the closet crept,
Noiseless as fear in a wide wilderness   250
And over the hush'd carpet, silent, stept,
And 'tween the curtains peep'd, where, lo !--how fast she slept.

XXIX.

Then by the bed-side, where the faded moon
Made a dim, silver twilight, soft he set
A table, and, half anguish'd, threw thereon   255
A cloth of woven crimson, gold, and jet :—
O for some drowsy Morphean amulet !
The boisterous, midnight, festive clarion,
The kettle-drum, and far-heard clarionet,
Affray his ears, though but in dying tone :—   260
The hall-door shuts again, and all the noise is gone.

XXX.

And still she slept an azure-lidded sleep,
In blanched linen, smooth, and lavender'd,
While he from forth the closet brought a heap
Of candied apple, quince, and plum, and gourd,   265
With jellies soother than the creamy curd,
And lucent syrops, tinct with cinnamon,
Manna and dates, in argosy transferr'd
From Fez, and spiced dainties, every one,
From silken Samarcand to cedar'd Lebanon.   270

XXXI.

These delicates he heap'd with glowing hand
On golden dishes and in baskets bright
Of wreathed silver : sumptuous they stand
In the retired quiet of the night,
Filling the chilly room with perfume light.—   275
"And now, my love, my seraph fair, awake !
Thou art my heaven, and I thine eremite :
Open thine eyes, for meek St. Agnes' sake,
Or I shall drowse beside thee, so my soul doth ache."

XXXII

Thus whispering, his warm, unnerved arm   280
Sank in her pillow.   Shaded was her dream
By the dusk curtains :—'twas a midnight charm
Impossible to melt as iced stream :
The lustrous salvers in the moonlight gleam;
Broad golden fringe upon the carpet lies :   285
It seem'd he never, never could redeem
From such a steadfast spell his lady's eyes;
So mus'd awhile, entoil'd in woofed phantasies.

Awakening up, he took her hollow lute,—
Tumultuous,—and, in chords that tenderest be,   290
He play'd an ancient ditty, long since mute,
In Provence call'd "La belle dame sans mercy :"
Close to her ear touching the melody ;—
Wherewith disturb'd, she utter'd a soft moan :
He ceased—she panted quick—and suddenly   295
Her blue affrayed eyes wide open shone :
Upon his knees he sank, pale as smooth-sculptured stone.

XXXIV

Her eyes were open, but she still beheld,
Now wide awake, the vision of her sleep :
There was a painful change, that nigh expell'd   300
The blisses of her dream so pure and deep;
At which fair Madeline began to weep,
And moan forth witless words with many a sigh;
While still her gaze on Porphyro would keep;
Who knelt, with joined hands and piteous eye,   305
Fearing to move or speak, she look'd so dreamingly.

XXXV

"Ah, Porphyro!" she said, "but even now
Thy voice was at sweet tremble in mine ear,
Made tuneable with every sweetest vow ;
And those sad eyes were spiritual and clear :   310
How changed thou art ! how pallid, chill, and drear !
Give me that voice again, my Porphyro,
Those looks immortal, those complainings dear !
Oh leave me not in this eternal woe,
For if thou diest, my Love, I know not where to go."   315

XXXVI.

Beyond a mortal man impassion'd far
At these voluptuous accents, he arose,
Ethereal, flush'd, and like a throbbing star
Seen mid the sapphire heaven's deep repose;
Into her dream he melted, as the rose   320
Blendeth its odour with the violet,—
Solution sweet: meantime the frost-wind blows
Like Love's alarum pattering the sharp sleet
Against the window-panes; St. Agnes' moon hath set.

XXXVII.

'Tis dark: quick pattereth the flaw-blown sleet: 325
"This is no dream, my bride, my Madeline!"
'Tis dark: the iced gusts still rave and beat:
"No dream, alas! alas! and woe is mine!
Porphyro will leave me here to fade and pine.—
Cruel! what traitor could thee hither bring?   330
I curse not, for my heart is lost in thine,
Though thou forsakest a deceived thing—
A dove forlorn and lost with sick unpruned wing."

XXXVIII.

"My Madeline! sweet dreamer! lovely bride!
Say, may I be for aye thy vassal blest?   335
Thy beauty's shield, heart-shaped and vermeil dyed?
Ah, silver shrine, here will I take my rest
After so many hours of toil and quest,
A famish'd pilgrim,—saved by miracle.
Though I have found, I will not rob thy nest   340
Saving of thy sweet self; if thou think'st well
To trust, fair Madeline, to no rude infidel."

XXXIX.

"Hark! 'tis an elfin storm from faery land,
Of haggard seeming, but a boon indeed:
Arise—arise! the morning is at hand;—   345
The bloated wassailers will never heed:—
Let us away, my love, with happy speed;
There are no ears to hear, or eyes to see,—
Drown'd all in Rhenish and the sleepy mead:
Awake! arise! my love, and fearless be,   350
For o'er the southern moors I have a home for thee."

XL.

She hurried at his words, beset with fears,
For there were sleeping dragons all around,
At glaring watch, perhaps, with ready spears ;
Down the wide stairs a darkling way they found,   355
In all the house was heard no human sound.
A chain-droop'd lamp was flickering by each door ;
The arras, rich with horsemen, hawk, and hound,
Flutter'd in the besieging wind's uproar ;
And the long carpets rose along the gusty floor.   360

XLI.

They glide, like phantoms, into the wide hall !
Like phantoms to the iron porch they glide,
Where lay the Porter, in uneasy sprawl,
With a huge empty flagon by his side :
The wakeful bloodhound rose, and shook his hide,   365
But his sagacious eye an inmate owns :
By one, and one, the bolts full easy slide :—
The chains lie silent on the footworn stones ;
The key turns, and the door upon its hinges groans ;

XLII.

And they are gone : ay, ages long ago   370
These lovers fled away into the storm.
That night the Baron dreamt of many a woe,
And all his warrior-guests, with shade and form
Of witch, and demon, and large coffin-worm,
Were long be-nightmared. Angela the old   375
Died palsy-twitch'd, with meagre face deform :
The Beadsman, after thousand aves told,
For aye unsought-for slept among his ashes cold.

SHELLEY.

ADONAIS.

I.

I WEEP for ADONAIS—he is dead!
Oh, weep for Adonais! though our tears
Thaw not the frost which binds so dear a head!
And thou, sad Hour, selected from all years
To mourn our loss, rouse thy obscure compeers,　　　5
And teach them thine own sorrow; say: With me
Died Adonais; till the Future dares
Forget the Past, his fate and fame shall be
An echo and a light unto eternity!

II.

Where wert thou, mighty Mother, when he lay,　　　10
When thy son lay, pierced by the shaft which flies
In darkness? where was lorn Urania
When Adonais died? With veiled eyes,　　　.
'Mid listening Echoes, in her Paradise
She sate, while one, with soft enamoured breath,　　　15
Rekindled all the fading melodies,
With which, like flowers that mock the corse beneath,
He had adorned and hid the coming bulk of death.

III.

Oh, weep for Adonais—he is dead!
Wake, melancholy Mother, wake and weep!　　　20
Yet wherefore? Quench within their burning bed
Thy fiery tears, and let thy loud heart keep,
Like his, a mute and uncomplaining sleep;
For he is gone, where all things wise and fair
Descend:—oh, dream not that the amorous Deep　　　25
Will yet restore him to the vital air;
Death feeds on his mute voice, and laughs at our despair.

IV.

Most musical of mourners, weep again!
Lament anew, Urania!—He died,
Who was the Sire of an immortal strain,   30
Blind, old, and lonely, when his country's pride
The priest, the slave, and the liberticide
Trampled and mocked with many a loathed rite
Of lust and blood; he went, unterrified,
Into the gulf of death; but his clear Sprite   35
Yet reigns o'er earth, the third among the sons of light.

V.

Most musical of mourners, weep anew!
Not all to that bright station dared to climb:
And happier they their happiness who knew,
Whose tapers yet burn through that night of time   40
In which suns perished; others more sublime,
Struck by the envious wrath of man or God,
Have sunk, extinct in their refulgent prime;
And some yet live, treading the thorny road,
Which leads, through toil and hate, to Fame's serene abode. 45

VI.

But now, thy youngest, dearest one, has perished,
The nursling of thy widowhood, who grew
Like a pale flower by some sad maiden cherished,
And fed with true love tears instead of dew;
Most musical of mourners, weep anew!   50
Thy extreme hope, the loveliest and the last,
The bloom, whose petals nipt before they blew
Died on the promise of the fruit, is waste;
The broken lily lies—the storm is overpast.

VII.

To that high Capital, where kingly Death   55
Keeps his pale court in beauty and decay,
He came; and bought, with price of purest breath,
A grave among the eternal.—Come away!
Haste, while the vault of blue Italian day
Is yet his fitting charnel-roof! while still   60
He lies, as if in dewy sleep he lay;
Awake him not! surely he takes his fill
Of deep and liquid rest, forgetful of all ill.

VIII.

He will awake no more, oh, never more!
Within the twilight chamber spreads apace   65
The shadow of white Death, and at the door
Invisible Corruption waits to trace
His extreme way to her dim dwelling-place;
The eternal Hunger sits, but pity and awe
Soothe her pale rage, nor dares she to deface   70
So fair a prey, till darkness and the law
Of change shall o'er his sleep the mortal curtain draw.

IX.

Oh, weep for Adonais!—The quick Dreams,
The passion-winged Ministers of thought,
Who were his flocks, whom near the living streams   75
Of his young spirit he fed, and whom he taught
The love which was its music, wander not,—
Wander no more, from kindling brain to brain,
But droop there, whence they sprung; and mourn their lot
Round the cold heart, where, after their sweet pain,   80
They ne'er will gather strength, nor find a home again.

X.

And one with trembling hand clasps his cold head,
And fans him with her moonlight wings, and cries,
"Our love, our hope, our sorrow, is not dead;
See, on the silken fringe of his faint eyes,   85
Like dew upon a sleeping flower, there lies
A tear some Dream hath loosened from his brain."
Lost Angel of a ruined Paradise!
She knew not 'twas her own, as with no stain
She faded, like a cloud which had outwept its rain.   90

XI.

One from a lucid urn of starry dew
Washed his light limbs, as if embalming them;
Another clipt her profuse locks, and threw
The wreath upon him, like an anadem,
Which frozen tears instead of pearls begem;   95
Another in her wilful grief would break
Her bow and winged reeds, as if to stem
A greater loss with one which was more weak;
And dull the barbed fire against his frozen cheek.

Another Splendour on his mouth alit,   100
That mouth whence it was wont to draw the breath
Which gave it strength to pierce the guarded wit,
And pass into the panting heart beneath
With lightning and with music; the damp death
Quenched its caress upon its icy lips;   105
And, as a dying meteor stains a wreath
Of moonlight vapour, which the cold night clips,
It flushed through his pale limbs, and passed to its eclipse.

XIII

And others came,—Desires and Adorations,
Winged Persuasions, and veiled Destinies, 110
Splendours and Glooms and glimmering Incarnations
Of hopes and fears, and twilight Phantasies;
And Sorrow, with her family of Sighs,
And Pleasure, blind with tears, led by the gleam
Of her own dying smile instead of eyes,   115
Came in slow pomp;—the moving pomp might seem
Like pageantry of mist on an autumnal stream.

XIV

All he had loved, and moulded into thought
From shape, and hue, and odour, and sweet sound,
Lamented Adonais. Morning sought   120
Her eastern watch-tower, and her hair unbound,
Wet with the tears which should adorn the ground,
Dimmed the aerial eyes that kindle day;
Afar the melancholy thunder moaned,
Pale Ocean in unquiet slumber lay,   125
And the wild winds flew around, sobbing in their dismay.

XV

Lost Echo sits amid the voiceless mountains,
And feeds her grief with his remembered lay,
And will no more reply to winds or fountains,
Or amorous birds perched on the young green spray, 130
Or herdsman's horn, or bell at closing day;
Since she can mimic not his lips, more dear
Than those for whose disdain she pined away
Into a shadow of all sounds :—a drear
Murmur, between their songs, is all the woodmen hear. 135

XVI.

Grief made the young Spring wild, and she threw down
Her kindling buds, as if she Autumn were,
Or they dead leaves; since her delight is flown,
For whom should she have waked the sullen year?
To Phœbus was not Hyacinth so dear,   .   140
Nor to himself Narcissus, as to both
Thou, Adonais; wan they stand and sere
Amid the faint companions of their youth,
With dew all turned to tears, odour to sighing ruth

XVII.

Thy spirit's sister, the lorn nightingale,   145
Mourns not her mate with such melodious pain :
Not so the eagle, who like thee could scale
Heaven, and could nourish in the sun's domain
Her mighty youth with morning, doth complain,
Soaring and screaming round her empty nest,   150
As Albion wails for thee ; the curse of Cain
Light on his head who pierced thy innocent breast,
And scared the angel soul that was its earthly guest !

XVIII.

Ah, woe is me ! Winter is come and gone,
But grief returns with the revolving year;   155
The airs and streams renew their joyous tone ;
The ants, the bees, the swallows, re-appear;
Fresh leaves and flowers deck the dead Seasons' bier;
The amorous birds now pair in every brake,
And build their mossy homes in field and brere ;   160
And the green lizard, and the golden snake,
Like unimprisoned flames, out of their trance awake.

XIX.

Through wood and stream and field and hill and Ocean
A quickening life from the Earth's heart has burst,
As it has ever done, with change and motion, .   165
From the great morning of the world when first
God dawned on Chaos; in its stream immersed,
The lamps of Heaven flash with a softer light;
All baser things pant with life's sacred thirst,
Diffuse themselves, and spend in love's delight   170
The beauty and the joy of their renewed might.

XX.

The leprous corpse, touched by this spirit tender,
Exhales itself in flowers of gentle breath;
Like incarnations of the stars, when splendour
Is changed to fragrance, they illumine death,   175
And mock the merry worm that wakes beneath;
Nought we know dies. Shall that alone which knows
Be as a sword consumed before the sheath
By sightless lightning? th' intense atom glows
A moment, then is quenched in a most cold repose.   180

XXI.

Alas! that all we loved of him should be,
But for our grief, as if it had not been,
And grief itself be mortal! Woe is me!
Whence are we, and why are we? of what scene
The actors or spectators? Great and mean   185
Meet massed in death, who lends what life must borrow.
As long as skies are blue, and fields are green,
Evening must usher night, night urge the morrow,
Month follow month with woe, and year wake year to sorrow.

XXII.

He will awake no more, oh, never more!   190
"Wake thou," cried Misery, "childless Mother, rise
Out of thy sleep, and slake, in thy heart's core,
A wound more fierce than his with tears and sighs."
And all the Dreams that watched Urania's eyes,
And all the Echoes whom their sister's song   195
Had held in holy silence, cried: "Arise!"
Swift as a Thought by the snake Memory stung,
From her ambrosial rest the fading Splendour sprung.

XXIII.

She rose like an autumnal Night, that springs
Out of the East, and follows wild and drear   200
The golden Day, which, on eternal wings,
Even as a ghost abandoning a bier,
Has left the Earth a corpse. Sorrow and fear
So struck, so roused, so rapt Urania,
So saddened round her like an atmosphere   205
Of stormy mist, so swept her on her way,
Even to the mournful place where Adonais lay.

XXIV.

Out of her secret Paradise she sped,
Through camps and cities rough with stone, and steel,
And human hearts, which to her aery tread   210
Yielding not, wounded the invisible
Palms of her tender feet where'er they fell ;
And barbed tongues, and thoughts more sharp than they,
Rent the soft Form they never could repel,
Whose sacred blood, like the young tears of May,   215
Paved with eternal flowers that undeserving way.

XXV.

In the death-chamber for a moment Death,
Shamed by the presence of that living Might,
Blushed to annihilation, and the breath
Revisited those lips, and life's pale light   220
Flashed through those limbs, so late her dear delight.
"Leave me not wild and drear and comfortless,
As silent lightning leaves the starless night !
Leave me not !" cried Urania : her distress
Roused Death ; Death rose and smiled, and met her vain caress.
                                                      225

XXVI.

"Stay yet awhile! speak to me once again ;
Kiss me, so long but as a kiss may live ;
And in my heartless breast and burning brain
That word, that kiss shall all thoughts else survive,
With food of saddest memory kept alive,   230
Now thou art dead, as if it were a part
Of thee, my Adonais ! I would give
All that I am to be as thou now art !
But I am chained to Time, and cannot thence depart !

XXVII.

"O gentle child, beautiful as thou wert,   235
Why didst thou leave the trodden paths of men
Too soon, and with weak hands though mighty heart
Dare the unpastured dragon in his den ?
Defenceless as thou wert, oh ! where was then
Wisdom the mirror'd shield, or scorn the spear?   240
Or hadst thou waited the full cycle, when
Thy spirit should have filled its crescent sphere,
The monsters of life's waste had fled from thee like deer.

o

XXVIII

"The herded wolves, bold only to pursue,
The obscene ravens, clamorous o'er the dead,   245
The vultures, to the conqueror's banner true,
Who feed where Desolation first has fed,
And whose wings rain contagion,—how they fled,
When, like Apollo, from his golden bow,
The Pythian of the age one arrow sped   250
And smiled!—The spoilers tempt no second blow;
They fawn on the proud feet that spurn them lying low.

XXIX

"The sun comes forth, and many reptiles spawn;
He sets, and each ephemeral insect then
Is gathered into death without a dawn,   255
And the immortal stars awake again:
So it is in the world of living men;
A godlike mind soars forth, in its delight
Making earth bare and veiling Heaven, and when
It sinks, the swarms that dimmed or shared its light   260
Leave to its kindred lamps the spirit's awful night."

XXX

Thus ceased she; and the mountain shepherds came,
Their garlands sere, their magic mantles rent;
The Pilgrim of Eternity, whose fame
Over his living head like Heaven is bent,   265
An early but enduring monument,
Came, veiling all the lightnings of his song
In sorrow; from her wilds Ierne sent
The sweetest lyrist of her saddest wrong,
And love taught grief to fall like music from his tongue.   270

XXXI

'Midst others of less note, came one frail Form,
A phantom among men, companionless
As the last cloud of an expiring storm,
Whose thunder is its knell; he, as I guess,
Had gazed on Nature's naked loveliness,   275
Actæon-like, and now he fled astray
With feeble steps o'er the world's wilderness,
And his own thoughts, along that rugged way,
Pursued, like raging hounds, their father and their prey.

XXXII.

A pard-like Spirit beautiful and swift—   280
A love in desolation masked—a Power
Girt round with weakness—it can scarce uplift
The weight of the superincumbent hour ;
It is a dying lamp, a falling shower,
A breaking billow ;—even whilst we speak   285
Is it not broken ? On the withering flower
The killing sun smiles brightly ; on a cheek
The life can burn in blood, even while the heart may break

XXXIII.

His head was bound with pansies over-blown,
And faded violets, white, and pied, and blue ;   290
And a light spear topped with a cypress cone,
Round whose rude shaft dark ivy tresses grew
Yet dripping with the forest's noon-day dew,
Vibrated, as the ever-beating heart
Shook the weak hand that grasped it ; of that crew   295
He came the last, neglected and apart ;
A herd-abandoned deer, struck by the hunter's dart.

XXXIV.

All stood aloof, and at his partial moan
Smiled through their tears ; well knew that gentle band
Who in another's fate now wept his own ;   300
As in the accents of an unknown land
He sang new sorrow ; sad Urania scanned
The Stranger's mien, and murmured : "Who art thou ?"
He answered not, but with a sudden hand
Made bare his branded and ensanguined brow,   305
Which was like Cain's or Christ's. Oh! that it should be so !

XXXV.

What softer voice is hushed over the dead ?
Athwart what brow is that dark mantle thrown ?
What form leans sadly o'er the white death-bed,
In mockery of monumental stone,   310
The heavy heart heaving without a moan ?
If it be he, who, gentlest of the wise,
Taught, soothed, loved, honoured the departed one ;
Let me not vex, with inharmonious sighs,
The silence of that heart's accepted sacrifice.   315

XXXVI.

Our Adonais has drunk poison—oh!
What deaf and viperous murderer could crown
Life's early cup with such a draught of woe?
The nameless worm would now itself disown;
It felt, yet could escape the magic tone   320
Whose prelude held all envy, hate, and wrong,
But what was howling in one breast alone,
Silent with expectation of the song,
Whose master's hand is cold, whose silver lyre unstrung.

XXXVII.

Live thou, whose infamy is not thy fame!   325
Live! fear no heavier chastisement from me,
Thou noteless blot on a remembered name!
But be thyself, and know thyself to be!
And ever at thy season be thou free
To spill the venom when thy fangs o'erflow;   330
Remorse and Self-contempt shall cling to thee;
Hot Shame shall burn upon thy secret brow,
And like a beaten hound tremble thou shalt—as now.

XXXVIII.

Nor let us weep that our delight is fled
Far from these carrion-kites that scream below;   335
He wakes or sleeps with the enduring dead;
Thou canst not soar where he is sitting now.
Dust to the dust! but the pure spirit shall flow
Back to the burning fountain whence it came,
A portion of the Eternal, which must glow   340
Through time and change, unquenchably the same,
Whilst thy cold embers choke the sordid hearth of shame.

XXXIX.

Peace, peace! he is not dead, he doth not sleep—
He hath awakened from the dream of life —
'Tis we, who, lost in stormy visions, keep   345
With phantoms an unprofitable strife,
And in mad trance strike with our spirit's knife
Invulnerable nothings— *We* decay
Like corpses in a charnel; fear and grief
Convulse us and consume us day by day,   350
And cold hopes swarm like worms within our living clay.

XL.

He has outsoared the shadow of our night ;
Envy and calumny, and hate and pain,
And that unrest which men miscall delight,
Can touch him not, and torture not again ;   355
From the contagion of the world's slow stain
He is secure, and now can never mourn
A heart grown cold, a head grown grey in vain ;
Nor when the spirit's self has ceased to burn,
With sparkless ashes load an unlamented urn.   360

XLI.

He lives, he wakes—'tis Death is dead, not he ;
Mourn not for Adonais.—Thou young Dawn,
Turn all thy dew to splendour, for from thee
The spirit thou lamentest is not gone ;
Ye caverns and ye forests, cease to moan !   365
Cease ye faint flowers and fountains, and thou Air,
Which like a mourning veil thy scarf hadst thrown
O'er the abandoned Earth, now leave it bare
Even to the joyous stars which smile on its despair !

XLII.

He is made one with Nature : there is heard   370
His voice in all her music, from the moan
Of thunder to the song of night's sweet bird ;
He is a presence to be felt and known
In darkness and in light, from herb and stone,
Spreading itself where'er that Power may move   375
Which has withdrawn his being to its own ;
Which wields the world with never wearied love
Sustains it from beneath, and kindles it above.

XLIII.

He is a portion of the loveliness
Which once he made more lovely : he doth bear   380
His part, while the one Spirit's plastic stress
Sweeps through the dull dense world, compelling there
All new successions to the forms they wear,
Torturing th' unwilling dross that checks its flight
To its own likeness, as each mass may bear ;   385
And bursting in its beauty and its might
From trees and beasts and men into the Heaven's light.

XLIV

The splendours of the firmament of time
May be eclipsed, but are extinguished not;
Like stars to their appointed height they climb,   390
And death is a low mist which cannot blot
The brightness it may veil. When lofty thought
Lifts a young heart above its mortal lair,
And love and life contend in it, for what
Shall be its earthly doom, the dead live there,   395
And move like winds of light on dark and stormy air.

XLV

The inheritors of unfulfilled renown
Rose from their thrones, built beyond mortal thought,
Far in the Unapparent. Chatterton
Rose pale, his solemn agony had not   400
Yet faded from him; Sidney, as he fought
And as he fell and as he lived and loved,
Sublimely mild, a Spirit without spot,
Arose; and Lucan, by his death approved;
Oblivion as they rose shrank like a thing reproved.   405

And many more, whose names on Earth are dark,
But whose transmitted effluence cannot die
So long as fire outlives the parent spark,
Rose, robed in dazzling immortality.
"Thou art become as one of us," they cry;   410
"It was for thee yon kingless sphere has long
Swung blind in unascended majesty,
Silent alone amid a Heaven of song.
Assume thy winged throne, thou Vesper of our throng!"

XLVII

Who mourns for Adonais? oh come forth,   415
Fond wretch! and know thyself and him aright.
Clasp with thy panting soul the pendulous Earth;
As from a centre, dart thy spirit's light
Beyond all worlds, until its spacious might
Satiate the void circumference: then shrink   420
Even to a point within our day and night;
And keep thy heart light, lest it make thee sink
When hope has kindled hope, and lured thee to the brink.

XLVIII.

Or go to Rome, which is the sepulchre,
Oh, not of him, but of our joy : 'tis nought   425
That ages, empires, and religions, there
Lie buried in the ravage they have wrought ;
For such as he can lend,—they borrow not
Glory from those who made the world their prey ;
And he is gathered to the kings of thought   430
Who waged contention with their time's decay,
And of the past are all that cannot pass away.

XLIX.

Go thou to Rome,—at once the Paradise,
The grave, the city, and the wilderness ;
And where its wrecks like shattered mountains rise,   435
And flowering weeds and fragrant copses dress
The bones of Desolation's nakedness,
Pass, till the Spirit of the spot shall lead
Thy footsteps to a slope of green access,
Where, like an infant's smile, over the dead   440
A light of laughing flowers along the grass is spread.

L.

And grey walls moulder round, on which dull Time
Feeds, like slow fire upon a hoary brand ;
And one keen pyramid with wedge sublime,
Pavilioning the dust of him who planned   445
This refuge for his memory, doth stand
Like flame transformed to marble ; and beneath
A field is spread, on which a newer band
Have pitched in Heaven's smile their camp of death,
Welcoming him we lose with scarce extinguished breath.   450

LI.

Here pause : these graves are all too young as yet
To have outgrown the sorrow which consigned
Its charge to each ; and if the seal is set,
Here, on one fountain of a mourning mind,
Break it not thou ! too surely shalt thou find   455
Thine own well full, if thou returnest home,
Of tears and gall. From the world's bitter wind
Seek shelter in the shadow of the tomb.
What Adonais is, why fear we to become ?

LII

The One remains, the many change and pass;⠀⠀⠀⠀460
Heaven's light for ever shines, Earth's shadows fly;
Life, like a dome of many-coloured glass,
Stains the white radiance of Eternity,
Until Death tramples it to fragments.—Die,
If thou wouldst be with that which thou dost seek!⠀⠀465
Follow where all is fled!—Rome's azure sky,
⠀⠀Flowers, ruins, statues, music, words are weak
The glory they transfuse with fitting truth to speak.

LIII

Why linger, why turn back, why shrink, my Heart?
Thy hopes are gone before: from all things here⠀⠀470
They have departed; thou shouldst now depart!
A light is past from the revolving year,
And man, and woman; and what still is dear
Attracts to crush, repels to make thee wither.
The soft sky smiles,—the low wind whispers near:⠀⠀475
⠀⠀'Tis Adonais calls! oh, hasten thither,
No more let Life divide what Death can join together.

LIV

That light whose smile kindles the Universe,
That Beauty in which all things work and move,
That Benediction which the eclipsing Curse⠀⠀480
Of birth can quench not, that sustaining Love
Which, through the web of being blindly wove
By man and beast and earth and air and sea,
Burns bright or dim, as each are mirrors of
⠀⠀The fire for which all thirst, now beams on me,⠀⠀485
Consuming the last clouds of cold mortality.

LV

The breath whose might I have invoked in song
Descends on me; my spirit's bark is driven
Far from the shore, far from the trembling throng
Whose sails were never to the tempest given;⠀⠀490
The massy earth and sphered skies are riven!
I am borne darkly, fearfully afar;
Whilst, burning through the inmost veil of Heaven
⠀⠀The soul of Adonais, like a star,
Beacons from the abode where the Eternal are.⠀⠀495

NOTES

LONGER ENGLISH POEMS.

NOTES,

ETC.

EDMUND SPENSER.

Spenser was born in London (see lines 128–30 of the following poem) in the year 1552 ; but his family seems to have belonged to Lancashire. It was connected with the Spencers of Althorpe in Northamptonshire ; he dedicates various poems to his lady cousins of that house. Nothing is known of his earlier years. In 1569 he went up to Cambridge University, to Pembroke Hall (now College), as a sizar. In that same year were published, without his name, certain verses of his, translations from the Italian of Petrarch and the French of Du Bellay. At College he became acquainted with Gabriel Harvey and others who were subsequently of note. It is certain that he was a zealous student, and acquired a considerable knowledge of Latin and Greek literature, especially of Plato's writings ; but, perhaps fortunately for the world, he was not elected to a Fellowship, and so, on taking his M.A. degree, ceased to reside in Cambridge. For about a year he lived amongst his relations in Lancashire. During this period he fell deep in love with a lady whom in his poems he calls "Rosalind," but she preferred one "Menalcas" to him.

In 1578 he quitted the North for Penshurst, Sir Philip Sidney's residence, and for London, where Sidney introduced him to his uncle, the Earl of Leicester. In the following year he published his *Shepheards Calendar;* from that time he took his place among the chief poets of his day. In 1580 he was appointed Secretary to Arthur, Lord Grey of Wilton, the new Lord Lieutenant of Ireland. In Ireland he spent the rest of his life, two visits and a flight to England excepted. In 1581 he was appointed Clerk of Degrees and Recognizances in the Irish Court of Chancery, a post which he held seven years, when he was appointed Clerk to the Council of Munster. He probably lived at Dublin till he received the latter appointment, when, no doubt, he removed into Cork county, perhaps straight to the old castle so intimately associated with his name—to Kilcolman Castle. During all these years he was composing his great poem, the *Faerie Queene.* Sir Walter Raleigh, who visited him in 1589, persuaded him to accompany him to London, that he might publish the first three books. These books appeared in 1590, and won great applause. In 1591 he received a grant of land in the South of Ireland. This land was the estate on which he had, probably, been already residing. It was part of the forfeited Desmond estates. To it he returned, probably, towards the close of the year in which it became his own. He now proceeded with his great work. Probably about this time, being now a man of some substance, he resigned his Munster Council Clerkship. He seems to have been troubled by lawsuits urged by natives who denied and withstood his claims to certain properties. In the summer of 1594 he married one Elizabeth, probably the daughter of some neighbour settler, after a prolonged and almost desperate courtship. In 1596 he again visited England, and published the second three books of the *Faerie Queene.* In greater honour than ever, he returned to Ireland, purposing, no doubt, to resume and complete his yet but half-concluded labour. This purpose was fulfilled but to a very slight extent. In 1598 a furious insurrection, by no means the first or the last, was made by the

Irish. Spenser's castle was fired. It was all he could do to escape with his wife and children ; indeed, according to Ben Jonson, as reported by Drummond, one little child was left behind. In the beginning of the year 1599, in a state of great mental, if not other distress, he died in King Street, Westminster. He was buried in the neighbouring Abbey, not far from his great predecessor Chaucer.

Spenser was not only a great poet himself, but in a singular degree was the cause—that is, the immediate cause—of poetry in others. He did not, of course, make his readers poets, but in those of them who were so by nature he awakened a sense of their powers. In some such sense Milton, Thomson, Keats, and many others, called him father.

He was not a poet of the dramatic sort, as were Chaucer and Shakspere ; he had little or no sense of humour. He was a poet of conscious moral purposes ; also of abstract thoughts rather than of embodiments. His *persona* are rather virtues, ideas, essences, than living and breathing creatures of flesh and blood. As a poet, he lives and moves in a high, pure, spiritual world, wrapt in the contemplation of beauty and love, and other such fair existences.

The melody of his versification is especially remarkable. In a longer poem the incessant sweetness of his lines is apt to be somewhat cloying ; in a shorter one, especially when he writes in a bright happy mood, as in his *Epithalamium*, the effect is delightful.

Though he was but ten years senior to Shakspere, his language is *comparatively* obsolete. This is because in some respects he belonged to the age which was ending rather than to the great Elizabethan æra. The subject he chose for his great work drew him into the midst of the old times of chivalry, and the literature that belonged to them. With such a subject the older forms of the language seemed to consort better. To him too, perhaps, as to Virgil, the older words and word-forms seemed to give elevation and dignity. Moreover, an older dialect was probably to some extent his vernacular, as he had probably passed his youth in Lancashire. Lastly, the only great poet who had preceded him, his great model, the Tityrus of whom he "his songs did lere," was Chaucer. To him Chaucer's language may have seemed the one language of English poetry.

PROTHALAMION.

INTRODUCTION.

THIS is the last complete poem written by Spenser that is now extant. It was written and published towards the end of the year 1596, after the Earl of Essex's return from Spain. In that same year he published his *Hymns to Heavenlie Love and Heavenlie Beauty.*

There is no such word in Greek or Latin as "Prothalamium." The word for a marriage-song is Epithalamium—that which is sung at the bridal-chamber door. But this is no such song, but rather one in honour of a meeting of the happy pair—pairs in this case—before the bridal day has fully come. In Greece, and probably in Rome, a Hymenæan song was sung as the bridal procession moved along from the bride's house to that of the bridegroom (a custom as early as Homer's time ; see *Iliad*, xviii. 493): in Rome this song was called Talasius, or Talassio ; but this song does not answer to that, or one of those. Probably Spenser invented the word to express his purpose. The "Pro" may have a temporal force ; and the whole word mean " the song that preceded the nuptials." He himself calls it "a Spousall verse."

The happy pairs were "the two honourable and vertuous ladies the Lady Elizabeth and the Lady Catherine Somerset" (see l. 67) on the one hand, on the other " the two worthie gentlemen Mr. Henry Gilford and Mr. William Peter, Esquyers."

The text is here printed faithfully from the original edition, except that in l. 12 "the" is read for "he."

1. 3. *spirit.* Here, perhaps, in its radical sense. See on this word Max Müller's *Lect. on the Science of Language*, 2d Series, Lect. viii.

[What is meant by *lightly* here?]

delay = retard, impede ; and so, virtually, ward off.

1. 4. *Titans.* See *Class. Dict.*

fayre. In Anglo-Saxon, *adverbs* were sometimes but cases of nouns or adjectives specially used. All cases but the nominative were in fact so used ; but perhaps the case most commonly employed was the *dative.* The *e* at the end of *fayre* here is perhaps the *e* of the dative case used adverbially. This *e* had in Spenser's time lost both its sound and its meaning ; then, as now, *ly* was the usual adverbial sign ; so that what was really an adverb passed for an adjective adverbially used. For an instance of the old usage, see Chaucer, *Prol.* 94 :

> "Well cowde he sitte on hors and *faire* ryde."

glyster. Gray uses this form in his lines "On a favourite Cat drowned in a Tub of Gold Fishes : '

> " Know one false step is ne'er retrieved . . .
> Nor all that *glisters* gold."

5. It will be observed that the verb *afflict* in this sentence has two objects, viz. *whom* and *my brayne.* It has been proposed to read *whose* for *whom ;* but this is quite unnecessary. The latter object may be taken as in fact defining the former, and so standing in a sort of apposition to it. Or, the *whom* may be taken as used in a loose conjunctival way, as is not uncommon in Elizabethan English ; *e.g.* Shakspere's *Winter's Tale,* V. i. 136 ·

> " *Whom,*
> Though bearing misery, I desire my life
> Once more to look on *him.* '

Venus and Adonis, 935 :

> " *Who* when he lived, *his* breath and beauty set
> Gloss on the rose, smell on the violet."

See Abbott's *Shakespearian Grammar,* § 115.

6. See Spenser's *Life.* It is mentioned there that an estate was given him in Ireland ; but it was evidently surrounded with discomforts, and its position of course cut him off from the brilliant society and life of the time. No wonder he sought other preferment. Murmurs like that in this stanza are common in his poems. See below, l. 140, and *Mother Hubberd's Tale,* ll. 905–18.

8. [What is the force of *of* here ? Mention any other forces it may have.]

11. *Silver streaming Themmes.* See a fuller picture of the Thames in the *Faerie Queene,* B. IV. cant. xi., where his marriage with the Medway is described. Denham, too, mentions its extreme clearness, ironically it might seem to us ; see *Cooper's Hill :*

> "O could I flow like thee, and make thy stream
> My great example, as it is my theme !
> *Though deep yet clear,* though gentle yet not dull,
> Strong without rage, without o'erflowing full.

12. *rutty* = rooty, and so fruitful, flower-producing.

the which : so below, l. 47, &c. *Which* is partly adjectival in its nature. Etymologically it = who like. The very oldest form in which it is found—*i.e.* its Gothic form—is *hvêleiks.* Compare Anglo-Saxon *hwylc,* Old Frisian *hwelik,* the Scotch *quhilk.* Thus it answers to the Latin *qualis,* and the Greek πηλίκος, rather than to *qui* and ὅς. Therefore it can be used with the article, as other adjectives in English can be. We may say " the who-like [which] person," just as we say, " the like person," or, " the Cæsar-like person." This adjectival usage with " which " still prevailed when its etymology was quite forgotten, and the word had come to be used as if it was but a various form of ' who.' It has almost entirely died out now, *which* having come to be used as the neuter of *who.*

As *which* = who-like, so *such* = so-like: compare Gothic *svaleiks*, Scotch *swilk*. Hence in older English *which* was used correlatively to *such*, as in Chaucer's *Canterbury Tales*, 1:

> "Whan that Aprille . . . hath . . .
> . . . . bathud every veyne in *swich* licour
> Of *which* vertue engendred is the flour."

So in Shakspere, *passim*.

1. 13. [What is meant by *paynted* here?] Comp. Ovid, *Fast.* iv. 430 : "*Pictaque* dissimili flore nitebat humus."

variable. The termination *ble* has not in this word the force which it usually has in our modern usage. *Variable* generally = varying, changing, inconstant ; as in *Romeo and Juliet*, II. ii. 109:

> "O swear not by the moon, the inconstant moon,
> That monthly changes in her circled orb,
> Lest that thy love prove likewise *variable*."

So *merciable* in Chaucer's *Frankeleynes Tale* :

> "Lord Phebus, cast thy *merciable* eye
> On wrecche Aurilie, which that am forlorne."

"In Early English," says Marsh, "this termination [-*ble*] had by no means a uniformly passive force, and it formerly ended many words where we have now replaced it by -*al* and -*ful*." And he instances *medicinable* in the sense of medicinal, *vengeable* of vengeful, *powerable* of powerful. "Similar forms occur in Shakespeare." Comp. comfortable, changeable, impeccable, delectable, peaceable. In the text *variable* = our modern "various."

15. *maydens bowres.* See note, p. 66.

16. *paramours* = lovers, as elsewhere in Spenser, as *Shep. Cal.* xii. 139.

17. *against* = in opposition to, and hence so as to face, to meet, to provide for the bridal day. "To ride against the king or other noble person signified to ride to meet." (Halliwell's *Dict.*) See *Hamlet* :

> "Some say that ever, '*gainst* that season comes," &c.

So elsewhere in Spenser. So in Hooker, &c. Shakspere, *Midsummer Night's Dream*, III ii. 99:

> "I'll charm his eyes *against* she do appear."

So *Gen.* xliii. 25 ; *Exod.* vii. 15. Dryden uses the word in the same sense.

Brydale = bride's ale, *i.e.* feast. But this etymology had been long forgotten. Hence Spenser's "bridale feast," *Faerie Queene*, IV. xi. 9. Another meaning of *ale* is alehouse, as in *Piers the Ploughman*, Prol. 42, Ed. Skeat.

[What is the force of *long* here?]

20. *Flocke.* Properly of birds. See Marsh's *Eng Lang.* Ed. Smith.

21. [What does *thereby* mean here? What other meaning has it?]

22. *greenish locks.* Ovid speaks of the *carulei crines*, which may mean much the same, of the Sicilian nymph Cyane. (*Metam.* v. 432.)

Adjectives in *ish* were much more common in older English than they are now. Nowadays they belong nearly altogether to colloquial language.

See *Faerie Queene*, IV. xi. 11. Webster's *White Devil, or Vittoria Corombona*

> "Come, come, my lord, untie your folded thoughts,
> And let them dangle *loose as a bride's hair*."

On which Steevens notes: "Brides formerly walked to church with their hair hanging loose behind. Anne Bullen's was thus dishevelled when she went to the altar with King

Henry the Eighth." (But perhaps Steevens is confusing that unhappy Queen's marriage with her coronation. She rode through the streets to be crowned, "sitting in her hair.")

1. 25. *entrayled* (Old French) = intertwined. Spenser uses the word several times, as in *Faerie Queene*, II. iii. 27. In V. v. 2 he has "trayled."

26. *flasket*. A dim. from *flask*, from the same root as *flagon*. The word is still in use in Cornwall amongst the fishermen for the vessel with which the fish are transferred from the "seine" to the "tuck-net." See Murray's *Guide to Cornwall*.

Comp. the picture of Proserpine and her girl friends gathering flowers in the meadows of Enna, Ovid, *Fast.* iv. 429-42 ; and Europa with hers, Mosch. ii. 33 *et seq.*

2. 27. *feateously* = neatly, cleverly. From Old French *faictis* = Lat. *factitius*. See Chaucer, *Prol.* 157, Ed. Morris :

" Full *fetys* was hire cloke."

Comp. ' Foot it *featly*' (*Temp.* I. ii. 380).

28. *on hye* = in haste. So *hie thee* = haste thee

29. Comp. *Lycid.* 135 *et seq.*

33. *store*. Comp. *L'Alleg.* 121 : " *Store* of ladies."

34. *posy*. This word is very commonly used for a verse or motto inscribed on a ring : as in the *Merchant of Venice*, V. i. 147, where Gratiano speaks of

" A hoop of gold, a paltry ring
That she did give me, whose *posy* was
For all the world like cutler's poetry
Upon a knife, ' Love me and leave me not.' "

And generally for a legend, as in Webster's *Northward Ho*, III. ii. : " I'll have you make twelve *posies* for a dozen of cheese-trenches." (Cf. Massinger's *Old Law*, II. i.) As flowers had their language once in Western Europe (see *Hamlet*, IV. v. 175 ; Beaumont and Fletcher's *Philaster*, I. ii., &c.), as they have still in the East, it has been conjectured that the word *posy* was applied also to a nosegay as being significant and, so to speak, motto-containing. Others, regarding the nosegay in the same way, have derived its name from *pensée*, a thought. But neither of these derivations is quite satisfactory.

37. [What is meant by *With that* ?]

Swans were a very familiar sight on the Thames in Spenser's time, and before and after it. " Paulus Jovius, who died in 1552, describing the Thames, says : ' This river abounds in swans, swimming in flocks ; the sight of whom and their noise are vastly agreeable to the fleets that meet them in their course.'" (Knigh.'s *Cyclop. of London*.)

38. *Lee* = stream. This word, in various forms, occurs as a river-name in England (in Hertfordshire), in Ireland, in France, and other parts of Europe. Like nearly all European river-names, it is a Keltic word. We do not know of its occurring elsewhere than here as a common noun.

39. *yet*. See note on *Il Pens.* 30.

41. *shew* = appear. A very common sense in our older writers.

42. [What is the force of *would* here ?]

45. *nor nothing neare*. In Old English, one negative does not neutralize, but strengthens another in the same sentence. See *Piers Ploughman*, Prol. 30, Shakspere *passim*, &c. As late as Goldsmith we have instances of this double negative.

48. *to* = when brought near to, *i.e.* in comparison with. So Ben Jonson :

" All that they did was piety *to* this."

Hamlet, I. ii. 140 : " Hyperion *to* a satyr." Comp. Greek πρός.

49. *least . . plumes* = that they might soil their fair plumes in the least degree, *i.e.* that they might not soil them ; and so, for fear that they might soil them. So in Latin *ne* is

used without *ut*, in Greek μή without ἵνα. With the virtually negative force of *least* comp. that of Latin *minime*.

2. 55. *Eftsoones* = soon after, immediately. Eft = aft, a word still used in a special sense by sailors, properly = behind, and so following ; it is, in fact, the positive of *after.* The *s* in *eftsoons* was originally a genitive case-sign. So the *s* in else, unawares, needs. In the words *once, twice, thrice,* modern spelling has substituted *c :* in *Piers Ploughman* we have *onis, elles,* &c.

       their fill. Here an adverbial phrase of degree. So perhaps "a hundred fold" in Milton's Sonnet "Avenge, O Lord."

56. *all in haste* = altogether in haste, in great haste. Comp. *Il Pens.* 33 :

          "*All* in a robe of deepest grain," &c. &c.

The adverb *alle* occurs in Chaucer, &c.

58. *they stood amazed still.* Here the pred. is *they stood still ; amazed* serves for an adverb of manner. [In what other way might the sentence be analysed ?]

60. *them seem'd.* So *me thinks, him thought, him were lever* (Chaucer's *Frank. Tale*), &c. In all these, and such cases, the pronoun is the Old English dative, the verb is impersonal. So, too, is to be explained "if you please." At a later time these various verbs were used personally, and the nominative of the pronoun replaced the dative.

62. *heavenly borne* = heavenly by birth, and so in meaning = heaven-born. Analytically, *borne* is a quasi-adverb defining *heavenly,* which is part of the pred.

63. *Teeme.* See *Hymn on Nat.* 18 ; *Midsummer Night's Dream,* V. i. 391 ; *Romeo and Juliet,* I. iv. 57. It is cognate with the verb *teem.*

       Ovid (*Metam. x.* 708) describes Venus as "yoking her swans and so traversing the air."

65. Observe the word-play.

3 76. *goodly.* Observe what a favourite word this is with our older writers.

78. [What part of speech is *that* here ?]

79. Virgil (*Georg.* iv. 317) calls this vale "Peneus' Tempe."

       Tempes shore = the shore of, *i. e.* consisting of, Tempe. Tempe was the shore. Comp. Gray's *Long Story :*

          " In *Britain's isle*, no matter where,
             An ancient pile of building stands."

So "Siloa's brook," *Paradise Lost,* i. 11. *Shore* is often used of the banks of a river by our old writers. See *Il Pens.* 75 ; *Faerie Queene :*

          " Besides the fruitful *shore* of muddy Nile ;" &c.

80. Spenser seems here to invert the course of the Peneus. In fact, it rises in Thessaly. See *Atlas.*

83. *while* = time. It is still used for a space of time.

85. *trim. L'All.* 75.

92. See the personification in the beginning of *Adonais.*

93. *bower* = chamber ; radically, something built, *not* connected with *bough.* In Beowulf, and in the older romances, it is used especially of a lady's chamber or room, = *boudoir.* Tennyson uses it rightly in his *Godiva :*

          "Then fled she to her inmost *bower.*"

"Bower-maidens" in Scotch = ladies' maids.

95. *of* = out of, from. So *James* iv. 1. Bacon, *Ess.* 51 : "The even carriage between, two factions proceedeth not alwaies *of* moderation, but *of* a truenesse to a man's selfe, with end to make use of both." (Apud *Bible Word-Book.*) *Will. of Palerne* (E. E. Text S.), 1139 : " For she bade brought hem *of* bale bothe they seide," &c.

       your loves couplement = the union or marriage of your loves. *Couple* in the sense of to join in marriage occurs frequently in the Elizabethan and other writers; *e. g.* in *King John*, III. i. 228: "Married in league, *coupled*, and linked." As a substantive in *Paradise Lost*, iv. 339:

> "As beseems
> Fair *couple* link'd in happy nuptial league."

Armado, in *Love's Labour Lost* (V. ii. 537), addresses the King and Princess as "a most royal *couplement*." Some editions mistakenly read *complement* in this present passage.

3. 99. *All Loues dislike* = all dislike felt towards love. The so-called possessive case is here used objectively with regard to the substantive on which it depends. "The use of the possessive pronouns," says Marsh, "and of the inflected possessive case of nouns and pronouns was, until a comparatively recent period, very much more extensive than at present, and they were employed in many cases where the preposition with the objective now takes their place." Comp. *King's rebels, King's traitors* (Paston Letters), *Senecaes translation* (Lodge), *Sins poison, Graces antidote* (Fuller).

100. *assoile* = etymologically *absolve*.
[What is the meaning ?]

101. *accord.* Here used transitively. So in Sidney's *Arcadia:* "Her hands *accorded* the lute's music to the voice ; her panting heart danced to the music."

102. *wait vpon* = attend. Comp. *Psalm* cxxiii. 2: "So our eyes *wait vpon* the Lord our God." *Psalm* xxv. 3.
bord = table. See *As You Like It*, V. iv. 147:

> "Wedding is great Juno's crown—
> O blessed bond of *board* and bed."

Comedy of Errors, III. ii. 17, and V. i. 62, where Adriana says of "her poor distracted husband":

> "In bed he slept not for my urging it ;
> At *board* he fed not for my urging it."

105. Comp. *Psalm* cxxvii. 5.

4. 110. *to her* = according to, in accordance with her. So *Paradise Lost*, i. 550:

> "Anon they move
> In perfect phalanx *to* the Dorian mood
> Of flutes and soft recorders."

And *Ib.* 559–61:

> "Thus they,
> Breathing united force, with fixed thought,
> Moved on in silence *to* soft pipes."

vndersong = burden, refrain. So Browne, *Brit. Past.* ii. :

> "He thus began
> To praise his love, his hasty waves among,
> The frothy rocks bearing the *undersong*."

112. *neighbour* = neighbouring. So *Comus*, 484: "Some neighbour woodman." *Ib.* 576: "Some neighbour villager." *Love's Labour Lost*, V. ii. 94: "A neighbour thicket." *Hamlet*, III. iv. 212: "Neighbour room."

119. *in his flood.* We should rather say *on*. So in *Faerie Queene*: "*In* fresh summer's day," &c.

121. *shend*: Ang.-Sax. "*scendan*, to confound, shame, shend, reproach, revile, spurn" (Bosworth). Chaucer's *Man of Lawes Tale:*

> "But verrayly thou wolt his body *schende*."

Persoun's Tale: "He *schendeth* all that he doth." *Faerie Queene*, passim.

P

4. 122. *enranged.* Comp. arranged. See *Faerie Queene:*

> " As fair Diana, in fresh summer's day,
> Beholds her nymphs enranged in shady wood."

127. See Spenser's *Life.*

129. [What is meant by *sourse* here?]

132. When the order of the Knights Templar was suppressed in Edward the Second's reign, their London estate on the bank of the Thames was given over to the Knights of St. John; by these it was leased to the students of the Common Law, who not finding a home at Cambridge or Oxford were at that time in want of a habitation. At the Dissolution of the Religious Orders this arrangement was continued by the Crown, at least for some two-thirds of the estate; the third—what should have been the Outer Temple—was bestowed on a favourite. At a later time, in the reign of James I., the property was given to the lawyers.

135. *whilom,* an old dat.

byde = abide. Comp. bate, abate; maze, amaze; mend, amend; σκαίρω, ἀσκαίρω; ἀπαίρω, ἀσπαίρω; στάχυς, ἄσταχυς; στεροπή, ἀστεροπή; stella, ἀστήρ. Comp. also wake, awake; vouch, avouch; wait, await; *verus,* aver; down, adown; base, abase; but, abut; chief, achieve; Fr. *droit,* adroit. Comp. further, *sperare, espirer; spatium, espace; spiritus, esprit; species, espèce.*

137. The mansion here spoken of stood in the gardens of what should have been the Outer Temple. It covered the ground, where Essex Street now is. The two pillars which still stand at the bottom of Essex Street—those between which you pass in order to reach the river at the Temple Pier—belonged to some part or appurtenance of it. In this " stately place " the Earl of Leicester was living in 1580; one of Spenser's letters to his friend Harvey in that year is dated from it. Leicester is the " great Lord " mentioned in l. 140. He died in the autumn of 1588. After him the Earl of Essex occupied the house. It was from and in it that, in 1601, he attempted that rash insurrection against the Queen's advisers which involved him in ruin.

next whereunto. It was on the upper or western side of the Temple; not, as might seem from Spenser's description, on the lower.

139. *wont.* This word, as used here and often elsewhere in older English, is, in fact, the pret. of the old verb *won,* " Ang.-Sax. *wunian;* Dan. *wonen;* G. *wohnen,* to dwell, persist, continue " (Wedgewood). So in Waller's lines:

> " The eagle's fate and mine are one,
>   Which on the shaft that made him die
> Espy'd a feather of his own,
>   Wherewith he *wont* to soar so high."

And so in 1 *Henry VI.* I. ii. 14:

> " Talbot is taken, whom we *wont* to fear."

Comp. the disuse of *use* in the sense of " am accustomed," while *used* is common enough. This *pret.* came to be used itself as a quasi-*present;* so *ought—dare—durst—mind—wot— —ought—can—may—memini—*οἶδα. (See Latham.)

> " Through power of that, his cunning thieveries
>   He *wonts* to work that none the same espies."—*Faerie Queene.*

But much more commonly *wont* is a *part.,* with this peculiarity, that it is used only predicatively, never attributively. We say, " he was wont to be vigorous," but cannot speak of " his wont vigour." To pass on to a third sense, *wont* is sometimes a *subst.* The word *wonted,* which is used in the inverse way to *wont* the part.—*i.e.* is always an attributive, and not predicative—is perhaps an *adj.* derived from this *subst.* = customary; but it may be a *part.* formed from the secondary veib *wont.* Spenser has also an *adj. wontless* = unwonted, *Hymne in Honour of Beautie:*

> " What *wontlesse* fury dost thou now inspire
> Into my feeble breast when full of thee ?"

4. 140. "Of all English writers Spenser shows himself most independent of the laws of position." (Marsh.)

freendles. The privative termination *les* is more correctly spelt, as here, with only one *s.* It is quite distinct from the word *less.* It is a modernised form of Ang.-Sax. *-leas.* Thus friendless = Ang.-Sax. *freondleas.*

141. *fits.* So *Faerie Queene*, II. ii. 11 : " Here fits not tell." Comp. Sidney's *Arcad.*, where *it* is expressed :

> " How evil fits it me to have such a son."

In *methinks, them seemed,* &c. the *it* is omitted, as here.

146. Observe the alliteration.

147. See in Knight or Lingard an account of Essex's expedition against Spain in 1596. There are contemporary accounts by Camden, Stowe, Strype, Raleigh. It was a splendid feat of arms. Macaulay calls it, in his Essay on Bacon, " The most brilliant military exploit that was achieved on the Continent by English arms during the long interval which elapsed between the battle of Agincourt and that of Blenheim." There is a contemporary ballad on it given in Percy's *Reliques* from the Editor's " Folio MS." entitled " 'The Winning of Cales," *i.e.* of Cadiz.

148. *Hercules two pillors:* i.e. Calpe on the European, Abyla on the African coast, at the Fretum Gaditanum, our Straits of Gibraltar. This name for these facing projections is found first in Pindar (*Olymp.* 3, 77 ; *Nem.* 3, 35), who calls them variously the στηλαί and the κίονες of Hercules. They were said to have been erected by Hercules to mark the limit of his westward wanderings.

5. 154. Does he mean that *Devereux* " promises " he shall be *heureux?*

" Few noblemen of his age were more courted by poets [than was Robert, Earl of Essex]. From Spenser to the lowest rhymer he was the subject of numerous sonnets or popular ballads. I will not except Sidney. I could produce evidence to prove that he scarce ever went out of England, or even left London, on the most frivolous enterprise without a pastoral in his praise, or a panegyric in metre, which were sold or sung in the streets." (Warton.)

158. *Thy wide Alarmes* = the wide alarms excited by you. So the Wycliffite translation of *Gen.* ix. 2 : " And *youre* feer and *youre* trembling be upon all the beestis of the earth." Comp. the current version. See above on l. 99. So in Latin, as Ovid. *Her.* v. 149-50 :

> " Ipse repertor opis vaccas pavisse Pheræas
> Fertur, et a *nostro* saucius *igne* fuit."

So in Greek, as in Aristotle's Ode to Arete :

> σοῖς δὲ πόθοις 'Αχιλλεὺς Αἴας τ' 'Αίδαο δόμους ἦλθον.

Alarmes: orig. a French cry = "to arms." *Alarum* is the same word, the additional syllable in it having sprung perhaps from the full sound of the *r.* Comp. in *Havelok*, vv. 2408-9 (Ed. Skeat) :

> " And smot him thoru the rith *arum;*
> Therof was ful litel *harum.*"

159. *muse* = a poet ; as in *Faerie Queene*, IV. xi. 34 ; *Lycid.* 19. Shaksp. *Sonn.* 21 :

> " So is it not with me as with that *muse*,
> Stirred by a painted beauty to his verse."

Comp. Dryden's *Abs. and Ach.* Part I. :

> " Sharp-judging Adriel, the Muses' friend,
>   Himself a muse."

5. 173. [What is meant by *sight* here ?]

174. *bauldricke* = belt.   Lat. *balteus.*   O. Fr. *baudrê.*   O. H. G. *balderick.*   " A belt, girdle, or sash, of various kinds : sometimes a sword-belt." (Halliwell.)   It was sometimes merely a collar or strap passing round the neck ; but most commonly it passed over one shoulder and under the arm on the other side.   It was frequently used for a bugle-horn sash: as in Chaucer, *Prol.* 116, of the yeoman :

> " An horn he bar, the *bawdrik* was of grene."

Much Ado about Nothing, I. i. 242 : " But that I will have a recheat winded in my forehead, or hang my bugle in an invisible *baldrick*, the ladies shall pardon me." *The Bauldricke of the Heauens bright* = the Zodiac.

177. *which* is commonly used of persons in Older English, as in the *Lord's Prayer*, &c It is quite wrong to suppose it to be the neuter of *who*.   See above, l. 12.

JOHN MILTON.

Milton's life may be divided into three parts : (1) 1608–1639 ; (2) 1639–1660 ; (3) 1660–1672 (1) He was born in Bread Street, Cheapside, London, towards the close of the year 1608. Bread Street is close by Friday Street, in which was the Mermaid Tavern, where Shakspere and Jonson, and the other great wits of the day, used to meet together ; so that Milton may be said to have been born within sound of their famous merriments. His father seems to have been a man of a grave earnest nature, of high views on the subject of education and of the end of life, of strong religious convictions, himself well educated and accomplished, being a skilful and eager musician. Of his mother little is known. In very many respects he inherited his father's character.

He was very carefully educated at home under a private tutor, Thomas Young (his initials form part of *Smectymnuus*), at St. Paul's School, at Christ's College, Cambridge, at home again (Horton, Buckinghamshire), and lastly by a tour upon the Continent (in France, Italy, and Switzerland). Thus his formal education lasted down to his thirty-first year. The great number of the years thus occupied is to be accounted for by the fact that after he had once chosen his vocation of poetry, which he appears to have done at an early age, it seemed both to him and to his father above all things important that he should earnestly prepare himself for it. This first period of his life, then, may be called the period of preparation. During it he did not attempt any great work ; he only prepared himself to attempt one. At Christmas 1629 he wrote his *Hymn on the Morning of the Nativity*, his first considerable work ; seven years afterwards he wrote *Lycidas*, his last considerable minor work ; between these he wrote *L'Allegro* and *Il Penseroso* and *Comus*, besides some sonnets and other short pieces.

(2) It might seem that in 1639 Milton was at last ready to address himself to his great task : that "the mellowing year" (*Lycid.* 5) had come ; or to use another phrase (see Sonnet *On arriving to his Three-and-twentieth Year*), that he was sufficiently "endued" with that "inward ripeness" after which he had so sincerely and ardently aspired ; but he was now to be drawn away, perhaps for ever, from the object of his devotion. Poetry was to be abandoned for politics. Such was the condition of the times, that other services than those of a poet were required of him. He obeyed this call, and for more than twenty years he gave himself up to the urgent political and social questions of the day. He wrote on the Freedom of the Press, on Church Government, on Divorce, on Education, in defence of the English people when assailed by Saumase for the execution of their king. During all this period he wrote no poetry except a few sonnets. Of these sonnets several deal with the same matters which form the subjects of his prose works ; others give some insight into his social and personal life : the last one, written in 1658, reflects his profound grief for the loss of his second wife. By his first wife he had been made the father of three daughters. His incessant studiousness injured his sight, and at last produced blindness : the immediate cause of that affliction being his controversy with Saumase (see Sonnet to Cyriac Skinner on his Blindness).

(3) When the Republic fell and was superseded, Milton was no longer able to serve his country as a political writer. He could now once more, after an interval of some twenty-one

years, entertain and pursue the great idea of his life : he now set himself to compose his great epic poem. The subject which had once attracted him—King Arthur—now gave place to a strangely different one—the Fall of Man. That former subject was not consonant with Milton's nature, educed and developed as it had been during the Commonwealth days, nor with the circumstances amidst which he found himself and the spectacles he witnessed. It was not practical and real enough. In 1667 appeared *Paradise Lost*, in ten books. It was in that same year that Dryden brought out his *Annus Mirabilis*. Thus in that year the great poetic leader of the setting age and the leader of the rising age stood strikingly contrasted. Four years afterwards were published *Paradise Regained* and *Samson Agonistes*. In 1674 Milton passed away from the evil times and evil tongues upon which his life had fallen.

HYMN ON THE NATIVITY.

INTRODUCTION.

THIS hymn was written by Milton in the year 1629, when he was just twenty-one years of age. Hallam therefore is inaccurate in saying that we have nothing written by Milton earlier than his sonnet on "his being arrived to the age of twenty-three," which would be written in December 1631. The *Hymn* was written while he was yet an undergraduate. He gives some account of his writing it in one of his elegies—the sixth—which is a letter addressed to his friend Deodati—that same friend the news of whose death met him when he returned from his tour on the Continent, and whom he bewailed in his *Epitaphium Damonis* :

> " At tu siquid agam scitabere, si modo saltem
>   Esse putas tanti noscere siquid agam.
> Paciferum canimus cælesti semine regem,
>   Faustaque sacratis secula pacta libris ;
> Vagitumque Dei et stabulantem paupere tecto
>   Qui suprema suo cum patre regna colit ;
> Stelliparumque polum, modulantesque æthere turmas
>   Et subito elisos ad sua fana deos.
> Dona quidem dedimus Christi natalibus illa,
>   Illa sub auroram lux mihi prima tulit."

Which passage contains an excellent outline of the poem. Apparently he proposed to celebrate other great Christian events in a similar way. See the fragment on *The Passion*, and the ode on *The Circumcision*. With regard to the former he writes :—" This subject the author finding to be above the years he had when he wrote it, and nothing satisfied with what was begun, left it unfinished."

The metre of the introductory stanzas is that in which Spenser wrote his *Four Hymns*. It is a modification of the Italian eight-lined stanza, first made by Chaucer, who composed in it several of the Canterbury Tales. Chaucer modified the Italian stanza by the omission of a line ; Spenser in his *Faerie Queene* by the addition of one, that one of greater length than the others.

This hymn is the first considerable poem which Milton wrote.

   6. 2. *Wherein.* We should rather say *whereon.* See Spenser's *Prothal.* l. 119.

      4. *redemption* : here in sense, as etymologically, = ransom.

      6. *our deadly forfeit should release* = that he should remit, or rather cause to be emitted, the penalty of death to which we were liable.

6. 6. *deadly forfeit.* Comp. "penal forfeit," *Samson Agonistes,* 508, and *Paradise Lost,* xi. 195-8 :

> " or to warn
> Us, haply too secure of our discharge
> From penalty, because from death released
> Some days."

See *Measure for Measure,* V. i. 525 :

> " Thy slanders I forgive, and therewithal
> Remit thy other forfeits."

release is etymologically a modified form of *relax,* coming to us through the French ; = let go, quit, remit. See *Deut.* xv. 2 : "Every creditor that lendeth ought unto his neighbour shall *release* it." Comp. *Esther* ii. 18 : "He made a *release* to the provinces, and gave gifts, according to the state of the king."

7. *with.* Not the Lat. *cum,* but rather *apud,* or *inter.* Comp. Dryden :

> " Immortal powers the term of Conscience know,
> But Interest is her name *with* men below."

8. *unsufferable.* The old usage preferred the English prefix. So *un*possible (Ascham, &c.), *un*properlie (Ascham), *un*hospitable (Shakspere), *un*vulnerable (*ib.*), *un*cessant (Milton), &c. &c. In *Paradise Lost,* x. 256, occurs "unagreeable."

10. *wont.* See note on *Prothal.* l. 139.

11. *the midst* = rather "in the midst" than "the midmost one." [What part of speech is midst in *Paradise Lost,* v. 164-5 ?—

> " On earth join, all ye creatures, to extol
> Him first, him last, him *midst,* and without end."]

'The midst" is very common in older English as a substantive. On the "vulgarisms" *in our midst, in your midst,* see Marsh's *English Language,* Ed. Smith.

14. *darksom. Some* is a favourite adjectival termination in older English, = Early English *sum,* German *sam.* Thus, we find *laboursome, gaysome, ugsome, bigsome, longsome, toothsome,* &c. &c. See Trench's *English Past and Present.* In *Paradise Lost,* vii. 355, Milton uses *unlightsome.* This *some* is radically identical with the adjective *same.*

with us must not be taken in close connexion with the verb, but rather with the object. [What does *with* mean here ?]

15. *vein.* See *Paradise Lost,* vi. 628.

16. *afford. Afford* is commonly used in Elizab. English for to *give, present,* without any reference such as it now has to the means of the giver. *Paradise Lost,* iv. 46 :

> " What could be less than to *afford* him praise, &c. ? "

Ib. x. 271 ; · *Samson Agonistes,* 910 and 1,109 ; *Winter's Tale,* IV. iv. 16 ; *Henry VIII.* I. iv. 17. But it sometimes seems to have that reference, as in *Paradise Lost,* v. 316, &c. The stem is said to be the Latin *forum.*

19. *while* = during which time. *When* = at which time. In modern English we very commonly use *when* where *while* would be more exact, and where *while* would have been used by our forefathers : *e.g.* in l. 30.

20. *took.* So *Il Penseroso,* 91 : forsook, &c.

21. *spangled,* &c. is here an adjective, from the substantive *spangle,* rather than the participle of the verb *spangle.*

7. 23. See *Paradise Regained,* i. 249-54.

Wisards. -*Ard* had originally an intensive force, as in *sweethard* (corrupted into sweetheart), *drunkard, coward, braggart, laggard,* &c. It appears in some person-names, as *Leonard, Bernard, Everard.* It seems to have been very commonly appended to nouns of a contemptuous and depreciatory meaning. Most of the words ending in it that now survive are of this sort. Add to those already mentioned *bastard, sluggard, dotard;* Trench mentions others now obsolete (*English Past and Present*). In our text *wizards* perhaps means nothing more than the Wise Men, without anything of the later sense of magicians attached to it, although in the Middle Ages the three Eastern kings were undoubtedly regarded as "wizards" in the modern sense of the word, and that with all reverence. In *Comus,* 571, the modern sense appears, and so *ib.* 872. In *Lycid.* 55 the word is applied to the personified river Dee. Spenser calls the ancient philosophers "antique wizards" (*Faerie Queene,* IV. xii. 2).

7. 24. *prevent.* See *Psalms* cxix. cxlvii. &c. &c. See Trench's *Select Gloss.* Comp "prevenient," *Paradise Lost,* xi. 3; "prevention," *ib.* vi. 129.

27. *the angel quire.* See ll. 85-140; *Paradise Regained,* i. 242-5.

28. See *Isaiah* vi. 6, 7. He has the same allusion in his *Reason of Church Government.*

29. *born* is dissyllabic here.

31. *all.* See *Prothal.* l. 56.

32. *to him* is to be taken in connexion with *in awe,* rather than with *had dofft.*

41. *pollute* is the Latin participle pollutus, with its termination Anglicized.
blame. Comp. *Macbeth,* IV. iii. 122-5:

> "I
> Unspeak mine own detraction ; here abjure
> The taints and *blames* I laid upon myself
> For strangers to my nature."

42. *maiden white.* Comp. *maiden sword* (1 *Henry IV.* V. iv 134); *maiden walls* (*Henry V.* V. ii. 449); *maiden flowers* (*Henry VIII.* IV. ii. 169).

45. *cease.* Here causal. Comp. "shrink," *inf.* l. 203; *Lycid.* 133. So Bacon: "You may sooner by imagination quicken or slack a motion than raise or *cease* it." Comp. also Ascham's *Schoolmaster:*

> "Therefore, my heart, *cease* sighes and sobbes, *cease* sorowes seede to sow."

48. *The turning sphear.* Comp. *Paradise Lost,* iii. 416:

> "Thus they in heaven above *the starry sphere,*" &c.

In the Ptolemaic System the earth was the centre round which the heavens, with their stars, revolved. *Sphere* here means this great revolving framework.

On the words *orb, sphere, globe, ball,* see Smith's *Marsh's Lectures on the English Language.*

49. *harbinger.* Comp. German *herberger.* See *Paradise Regained,* i. 71:

> "Before him a great prophet to proclaim
> His coming is sent *harbinger,*" &c.

See also *Midsummer Night's Dream,* III. ii. 380; *Comedy of Errors,* III. ii. 12; *Macbeth,* I. iv. 46; and V. vi. 10; *Hamlet,* I. i. 122. Hawkins' *Life of Bishop Ken:* "On the remova. of the court to pass the summer at Winchester, Bishop Ken's house, which he held in the right of his prebend, was marked by the *harbinger* for the use of Mrs. Eleanor Gwyn," &c. (*Apud* Halliwell.)

For the form of the word, as *messenger* from message, *scavenger* from scavage, *porringer* from porridge, so *herbinger* from harb'rage ; see Wedgwood. In the *Ayenbite of Inwit* there is the form *herberyeres* for innkeepers, = harbourers. In Chaucer's *Man of Lawes Tale* herbergeour = harbinger:

> "The fame anon throughout the toun is born,
> How Alla King shal com on pilgrimage,
> By *herbergeours* that wenten him beforn," &c.

For *harbourage*, see *King John*, II. i. 234. In *Pericles*, I. iv. 100, "harbourage" is asked for "ourself, our ships." *Harbour* radically = a shelter for a host.

7. 50. See Collins' *Ode to Peace :*

> " O thou, who bad'st thy turtles bear
> Swift from his grasp thy golden hair,
>   And sought'st thy native skies ;
> When War, by vultures drawn from far,
> To Britain bent his iron car,
>   And bade his storms arise," &c.

52. *strikes* = produces with a stroke, *i.e.* instantaneously. So Dryden :

> " Take my Caduceus :
> With this th' infernal ghosts I can command,
> And *strike* a terror through the Stygian strand."

So *Richard III.* V. iii. ; 1 *Henry VI.* II. iii. Such, no doubt, is the force of the word here. Otherwise, one might comp. the Lat. *fœdus ferire*, &c.

About the time of the birth of Christ the Temple of Janus was shut ; *i.e.* there was peace in the Roman empire. See Merivale's *Romans under the Empire*, iii. 401, smaller Ed.

8. 56. *the hooked chariot* = *covinus*, variously described or referred to as *falcifer, falcatus, rostratus.* Comp. Spenser's *Faerie Queene*, V. viii. 28. It is said to have been a Keltic invention. The Romans adopted it, with certain natural changes, for their domestic use. Their *covinus* seems to have resembled our cabriolet. See Martial's enthusiastic apostrophe to it (xii. 24), &c. It is curious that so many Roman carriage-names are Keltic. *Essedum, petorritum, rheda*, are all so.

58. Comp. in Ovid's adjuration to Peace (*Fast.* i. 716) : "And let the wild trumpet sound no signal-blast save for the festal train."

59. *awfull*. So *Richard II.* III. iii. 76. It has its more usual sense in *Taming of the Shrew*, V. ii. 108 ; 2 *Henry VI.* V. i. 98, &c. *Awless*, in *King John* (I. i. 266), may have either an active or a passive meaning.

60. *sovran* Old French, *souverain.* Our erroneous modern spelling has probably arisen from the popular tendency to force strange word-forms into, or at least into some proximity to, familiar ones. Comp. beaf-eater, sparrow-grass, sweetheart, island, Charles' Wain, lanthorn, emerods, colleague, could, gooseberry, liquorice, frontispiece, shame-faced, Jerusalem artichoke, cray-fish, country-danse, Bag-o'-nails (as an inn name), Goat and Compasses (ditto), Bull and Mouth (ditto), loadstone, Billy Ruffian (as a ship's name), &c.

64. *whist* = hushed. So Spenser's *Faerie Queene*, VII. vii. 59. See *Tempest.* I. ii. 77-82 :

> " Come unto these yellow sands,
>   And then take hands ;
> Courtsied when you have and kissed,
>   The wild waves *whist*,
> Foot it featly here and there ;
> And, sweet sprites, the burthen bear."

where Johnson takes *whist* to be a verb = are silent ; but it is probably a participle, as in our text, the phrase *the wild waves whist* standing in an adverbial relation to the predicate, just as *thus done the tales* in *L'Allegro*, l. 115. No doubt the word is originally a sort of interjection commanding silence. Comp. the Latin *st*, Italian *zitto*, French *chut*. So our *hush, hist,* &c. Then *whist* is used as a verb = to say whist—*i.e.* to silence. It is also used = to be silent, as in Surrey's *Translation of Virgil:*

> " They *whisted* all, with fixed face intent."

Comp. *hush. Whisper* is from the same root. There is a provincial form *whister = whisper.* (Halliwell.) Then we have *whist* for the name of a game at cards, where the players are supposed to keep silence (it was frequently called *whisk*); *whist,* as an adjective, as in *Euphues and his England:* " So that now all her enimies are as *whist* as the bird attagen," &c. (H. & W.'s Nares.) The forms *whish* and *whisht* are also found.

8. 68. *birds of calm* = halcyons. See the story of Alcyone, told by Ovid, one of Milton's favourite authors, in *Metam.* xi. There was an ancient belief, that during the seven days preceding and the seven succeeding the shortest day of the year, at which time the alcyon was breeding, a great tranquillity prevailed at sea. When it "sat brooding," the "wave was charmed." Frequent allusions to this belief occur in the Classics, as in Aristophanes' *Birds* and his *Frogs,* in Theocritus, &c. &c. The Greeks spoke of "alcyon days" (ἀλκυονίδες ἡμέραι); the Latins, of *Alcedonia,* the halcyon time, *alcedo* being the old Latin name for the bird. Thus the Prologue-speaker of Plautus' play, the *Casina:* "There is a calm. All about the forum [= pretty much our "the City"] 'tis halcyon-tide;" *i.e.* there is no bustling and tumult. See "halcyon beaks" in *Lear,* II. ii. 84; "halcyon days," 1 *Hen. VI.* I. ii. 131.

70. *stedfast. Fast,* in the form *fæst,* is an Anglo-Saxon word, denoting firm. *Sooth-fast* = firm in truth, &c. In the modern editions of our Bible translation *shamefast* is corrupted into *shamefaced,* and *shamefastness* into *shamefacedness. Rootfast* has become obsolete.

71. *influence.* Here used in its original sense of the rays, or glances, or aspects, flowing from the stars to the earth. These aspects were believed to have a great mysterious power over the fortunes of men; and hence *influence* came to have its modern meaning. "The astrologers," says Bacon (*Essay* ix.), "call the evill *influences* of the starrs evil aspects." *Job* xxxviii. 31: "Canst thou bind the sweet *influences* of the Pleiades?" *Paradise Lost,* ii. 1034:

> " But now at last the sacred *influence*
> *Of light* appears."

Measure for Measure, III. i.: "the skiey *influences." King Lear,* I. ii. 135: "planetary *influence."* Comp. *L'Allegro,* l. 122.

Other astrological terms still surviving are "disastrous," "ill-starred," "ascendency," "lord of the ascendant," "jovial," "saturnine," "mercurial." (See Trench's *Study of Words.*) See what Gloucester and Edmund respectively say of the old faith, in *King Lear,* I. ii.; and this verse in Fletcher's lines *Upon an Honest Man's Fortune* (quoted in *Bible Word-Book*):

> " Man is his own star, and the soul that can
> Render an honest and a perfect man
> Commands all light, all *influence,* all fate;
> Nothing to him falls early, or too late."

So also *Paradise Lost,* x. 659. Fuller's *Scripture Observations,* xviii.

73. *for* = in spite of, notwithstanding. So frequently, as in Davies (*apud* Johnson):

> " But as Noah's pigeon, which return'd no more,
> Did show she footing found *for* all the flood," &c.

Probably the full phrase would be "for all the flood, or the morning light, or &c. &c *could do."* Certainly, the *all* does not qualify "the flood," or "the morning light," or &c.

74. *often.* As if Lucifer gave several separate admonitions, instead of, by his very appearance, one long one.

8. 75. Comp. *Midsummer Night's Dream,* III. ii. 61 :

> " Venus in her glimmering sphere."

76. *bespake* = spake.   So *Lycid.* 112 ; *Paradise Lost,* i. 43.   Sometimes the prefix *be* has its transitive-making force, as *e.g.* when Dryden writes :

> " Then staring on her with a ghastly look
> And hollow voice, he thus the queen *bespake.*"

Paradise Lost, ii. 849 :

> " No less rejoiced
> His mother bad, and thus *bespake* her sire."

Comp. bewail, bemoan, &c.

bid.   The weak preterite is here preferred to the strong form.   So *Paradise Lost,* ii. 514.   The form *bidde* occurs in *The Vision of Piers Ploughman.*   In the case of the preterite of *bite* the weak form has with us altogether superseded the strong form.   In *Piers Ploughman* we have *boot,* Ed. Wright, l. 2642 :

> " That he *boot* hise lippes. "

In that same poem both the forms *sitte* and *sat* are found.

77. Comp. Spenser's *Shep. Cal.* April.

78. *her* may refer either to shady gloom, *i.e.* night, or to day.

79. *withheld.*   Comp. *withdraw.*

81. *as.*   So commonly in modern English we should say *as if;* but in older English, when the force of the subjunctive was livelier, the *if* was not needed.

84. *axle-tree.*   Comp. *Comus,* 95-7.   *Tree* in Old English = wood, beam, &c.   So *dore-tree* = door-post, *Piers Ploughman,* roof-*tree,* &c.

9. 85. *lawn* = pasture ; commonly any open grassy space.   *Lawn* seems to denote radically a clear or cleared space, where the view is unobstructed.   So *launde* in *Piers Ploughman.*   Comp. *lane,* an opening, a passage between houses or fields (see Wedgewood).   Comp. *Paradise Lost,* iv. 252, where the groves of Eden are described :

> " Betwixt them *lawns* or level downs, and flocks
> Grazing the tender herb, were interposed," &c.

Pope :

> " Interspersed in *lawns* and opening glades,
> Thin trees arise that shun each other's shades."

With the sense here, comp. *L'Allegro,* l. 71.

86. *or ere* = before ever.   See *Daniel* vi. 24 ; *Hamlet,* I. ii. 147 ; *Psalm* xc. 2.   From the same root as *or* come our *ere, erst, early.*   *Or* is common enough in Old English, as in *Mirror for Magistrates :*

> " And, *or* I wist, when I was come to land."

This same form occurs in *Tempest,* I. ii. 11 ; *King John,* IV. iii. 20 (Ed. 1623), &c.   As for *ere,* in *or ere,* it probably stands for *ever :* it increases the force of the adverbial clause of time in which it appears ; thus in *King Lear,* II. iv. :

> " I have full cause of weeping ; but this heart
> Shall break into a hundred thousand flaws
> *Or ere* I'll weep : "

where the *ere* gives intensity. *Ere* in this and such cases has the same grammatical value as *twice*, in *Measure for Measure*, IV. iii. 92:

> " Ere *twice* the sun hath made his journal greeting
> To the under generation, you shall find
> Your safety manifested."

Or *yet* in *Paradise Lost*, x. 584:

> " Ere *yet* Dictæan Jove was born."

I.e. ever is an adverb of time. Hence the phrase *or ere*, = our mod. "ere ever," is nearly invariably used with a *clause*, and not as a preposition. We could say "ere long," "ere now," but not "ere ever long," "ere ever now." The phrase in our text is to be explained as parallel to "for all the morning light," "against their bridal day ;" where the full construction would demand a verb. (See notes, l. 73, and *Prothal.* l. 17.) It is, so far as we know, unique. Others interpret the *ere* in *or ere* as, in fact, a mere reiteration, the *ere* added as a sort of gloss, when the meaning of *or* had ceased to be generally known. In Greek, πρίν and πρότερον are found in the same sentence, πρότερον antecedent ; but this is obviously no parallel. Nor can the phrase "an if," which appeared for a time in our language, be said to justify the above explanation. Moreover, can we not say, "before ever," as "before ever he knew him, he acted nobly"? Does "ever" translate "before"?

9. 86. *point of dawn.* French, *point du jour.*

90. Warton quotes Spenser's *Shep. Cal.* May :

> " When *great Pan* account of shepheards shall ask."

92. *was.* The idea of the subject is singular, though the form is plural. So "the wages of sin *is* death," &c.

silly. A.-S. *sælig*, happy ; then simple, then foolish. Cf. German *selig.* The form *seely* is found in the *Faerie Queene*, &c. ; *sely* in Chaucer, *Leg. of Fair W.* :

> " O *sely* woman, full of innocence : "

and in *Piers Ploughman.* For the degradation of meaning, comp. *simple, innocent.* See Trench's *Study of Words*, and *Select Gloss.* Comp. εὐηθής.

95. *strook*, i.e. strook out. Of course, the word more properly applies to the notes of stringed instruments, as in Dryden's *Alexander's Feast*, 99:

> " Now *strike* the golden lyre again."

Other forms of the participle are stricken, strucken, struck. The form *strook* is found in *Piers Ploughman*, &c. Comp. the participial forms, took, forsook, &c.

as, though seemingly, is not really the relative, nor yet the subject, in this and such phrases. The relative is in fact omitted, as is not uncommon. The full phrase would be "as (music) *which* never was, &c."

96. *divinely warbled voice.* *Voice* = something uttered by the voice, as often Latin *vox.* Or perhaps, better, *warbled* = trilled, made to trill or quaver. Comp. *Arcad.* 87 :

> " Follow me, as I sing,
> And touch the *warbled* string."

In *Com.* 854 it means trilled forth, sung :

> " If she be right invoked in *warbled* song."

So, in the active form, in *Midsummer Night's Dream*, III. ii. 206 :

> " Both *warbling* of one song."

9. 96. Observe *s* sharp and *s* flat, according to our present pronunciation, rhyming together.

97. *noise.* Comp. *Faerie Queene,* I. xii. 39 :

> " During the which there was an heavenly *noise*
> Heard sownd through all the Pallace pleasantly."

Or perhaps here in its not uncommon Elizabethan sense of "a set or company of musicians." (Nares.) See "Sneak's *noise*," 2 *Henry IV.* II. iv. 12. Ben Jonson's *Masq. of Gyps.* : " The King has his *noise* of gypsies as well as of bear-wards and other minstrels," &c.

99. *loth* = in oldest English, hateful, our "loathed." Comp. *loathsome.* So *loathly*, Shakspere, &c.

100. *close.* So Dryden, *Fables :*

> " At every *close* she made, th' attending throng
> Replied, and bore the burden of the song."

Shakspere, *Richard II.* II. i. 12. So Herrick, *The Church:*

> " Sweet spring ! full of sweet days and roses,
>   A box where sweets compacted lie,
>   My music shows you have your *closes,*
>   And all must die."

102. As if the moon was but a bright spherical shell.

103. *Cynthia.* See *Proth., Il Pens.,* &c.

106. *here* = hereupon ; or = at this point of time, now. See Cowper's lines to Mary Unwin :

> " Thy needles, once a shining store,
>   For my sake restless *here*tofore," &c.

Comp. *there* in Shakspere, *Lover's Complaint :*

> " Even *there* resolved my reason into tears."

its. This passage, *Paradise Lost,* i. 254, and iv. 814, are said to be the only places where Milton uses this word. See note, l. 140.

107. [What are the two forces "alone" might have here ? and which has it ?]

108. [What is the force of the comparative here ?]

109. *their sight* = them as they look. Comp. " I pursue *thy lingering*" in *Paradise Lost,* ii. 702. So "thy wiseness," *Hamlet,* V. i. 286.

110. *globe* = a mass, a body ; or "circular" is tautological. Comp. *Hamlet's* "distracted *globe*" (I. v. 96).

111. *shame-fac't.* See note to *stedfast,* l. 70.

112. *Cherubim.* In his translation of *Psalm* lxxx. 5, Milton uses the English plural form. Shakspere generally uses *cherubim* for the singular (as in *Othello,* IV. ii. 63) ; but *cherub* occurs in *Hamlet,* IV. iii. 50. Knight reads *cherubims* in *Merchant of Venice,* V. i. 62. The Authorized Version of the Bible uses *cherubims. Cherubs* and *cherubims* now differ in meaning. Perhaps he does not mean to characterize, when he speaks of the *helms* of the cherubim and the *swords* of the seraphim. It was *cherubims* "with a flaming sword" that guarded the gates of Eden. Both orders are differently represented in the lines *At a Solemn Music.* Or he may mean that the *cherubim* were the more purely defensive spirits, the *seraphim* more active. Their "sword " may mean "the sword of the Spirit." (Comp. *Isaiah* vi. 6.)

113. *Seraphim.* "The great seraphic lords," *Paradise Lost,* i. 794.

9. 114. *with wings displaied.* See *Il Penseroso*, 149; *Faerie Queene*, I. xi. 20.
116. *unexpressive.* So in *Lyc.* 176. Shakspere, *As You Like It*, III. ii. 78.
10. 117. See *Paradise Lost*, vii. 565 *et seq.*
119. See *Job* xxxviii. 4–7.
122. *hinges* = support. See *Faerie Queene*, I. xi. 21 :

> " Then gin the blustring brethren boldly threat
> To move the world from off his steadfast *henge*."

Hinge is properly something to hang anything on, as a hook. Comp. Dutch *hengel*, a hook ;
German, *angel* The verb *to hang* has the form *hing* in the Scotch dialect.

The explanation of the two strong preterite forms which *hang* and many other
verbs have in modern English is that originally one was the *singular*, the other the *plural*
form. (See Latham.) This is exactly illustrated in this line from Chaucer's *Legende of Good
Women :*

> " And thus by reporte was hir name yshove
> That as they *woxe* in age, *wax* hir love."

123. Comp. the Lat. *jacere fundamenta.* Comp. *Faerie Queene :*

> " And shooting in the earth *casts* up a mount of clay."

2 Kings xix. 32 ; *Luke* xix. 43.
124. *weltring.* *Lyc.* 13 ; *Paradise Lost*, i. 78 ; Shelley's *In the Euganean hills.*
Ascham uses the forms *walter* and *waulter* in his *Scholemaster.* *Welter* is radically
connected with *wallow, waltz,* Latin *volvere*, &c. ; perhaps also with *walk*. (See
Wedgwood.)

oozy. *Lyc.* 175 ; Shelley's *Ode to the West Wind.* Comp. " *oozy* bed," *Tempest*,
V. i. 151 ; " *ooze* of the salt deep," *Ib.* I. ii. 252.
125. If the " music of the spheres " may ever be heard, the poet would it now should be.
On this music see *Arcad.* 62–7 ; *Paradise Lost*, v. 618 ; *Com.* 112–4, 241–3, 1,021. Comp.
At a Solemn Music, " *sphere-born* harmonious sisters, Voice and Verse." See also
Merchant of Venice, V. i. 61 :

> " There's not the smallest orb which thou behold'st
> But in his motion like an angel sings,
> Still quiring to the young-eyed cherubins," &c.

Twelfth Night, III. i. 120 ; *Antony and Cleopatra*, V. ii. 83 ; *Pericles*, V. i. 230. In *Hudibras*,
Part II. i. 617, the widow says a poet compares his mistress' voice to

> " *the music of the spheres*,
> So loud it deafens mortal ears,
> As wise philosophers have thought,
> And that's the cause we hear it not."

Dryden, in his *Ode to Mrs. Anne Killigrew*, declares that

> " Thy brother-angels at thy birth
>   Strung each his lyre and tuned it high,
>   That all the people of the sky
> Might know a poetess was born on earth ;
> And then, if ever, mortal ears
> Had heard the *music of the spheres*."

Shelley, in his lines *To a Lady with a Guitar:*

> " It had learnt all harmonies
> Of the plains and of the skies : .
> . . . .
> . . . . . . it knew   •
> That seldom-heard mysterious sound
> Which, driven on its diurnal round,
> As it floats through boundless day,
> Our world enkindles on its way."

This fancy is said to have originated with Pythagoras. For a minute account see the last book of Plato's *Republic*. The whorl of the distaff of necessity, as there described, consists of eight concentric whorls. These whorls represent respectively the sun and moon, the five planets known to the ancients, and the fixed stars. On each whorl sits a siren singing. Their eight *tones* make one exquisite "harmony." Milton here speaks of "your *nine*fold harmony ;" he adds a ninth sphere—the *primum mobile*—"that swift nocturnal and diurnal rhomb" (*Paradise Lost*, viii. 134). See also Plato, *Rep.* vii. 530. Cicero, in his *Nature of the Gods*, refers to the belief "ad harmoniam canere mundum," and again in his *Republic*, vi. 18

10. 127. Comp. *Merchant of Venice*, V. i. 76 :

> " Or any air of music touch their ears."

128. See *Paradise Lost*, xi. 559.

130. *organ.* See *Paradise Lost*, i. 708–9, xi. 560–3 ; *Song for St. Cecilia's Day.*
blow, in a quasi-passive sense. So Tennyson's *Princess:*

> " A moment while the trumpets *blow*
> He sees his brood about thy knee."

Comp. *beat* in that same song.

132. *Consort.* So *At a Solemn Music*, 27 ; *Il Penseroso*, 145 ; *Faerie Queene*, III. i. 40. (In *Solemn Music*, 6, "concent" occurs.) Elsewhere in Milton, as always in Shakspere, the word occurs in its ordinary sense.
to. See *Prothal.*

135. *fetch.* See Smith's *Marsh's Lectures on English Language.*
age of Gold. See Ovid's *Metam.* i. 89–112.

136. *speckl'd*, from speck. So handle, &c. &c. The *le* is also a diminutival termination. *Speckled* probably may mean here variegated, gaudy ; just as Spenser, Dryden, and Pope use it of a serpent and of snakes ; but it may mean "plague-spotted." Comp. Horace's "maculosum nefas" (*Od.* IV. iv. 23).

137. *sicken.* Nearly always *neuter* in Shakspere, as here. It is *transit.* in *Henry VIII.* I. i. 81.

138. *mould* is very commonly used by itself for the earth in the old romances, &c. See *Piers Ploughman*, 67, ed. Skeat : "The most mischiefe on *mold* is mountyng wel faste."

140. Obs. *her*self answering to "Hell *it*self." *Its* had not yet won a place in the written language. *His* originally served for both the masculine and neuter genders. When the old gender system decayed, and it became usual to decide on a word's gender by its *sense*, not by its form, or by some tradition of the language, then this *his* was felt to be inadequate. *It* was sometimes used in its place. But it was objectionable that the nominative and possessive should not differ in form. Hence arose the form *its*. This form was in Milton's time struggling for admission into the written language. He lived to see it established in it ; but in his earlier days that event seemed dubious. From this unsettled state of things arose confusions like the present. Men were not content with *his* as a neuter ; they did not yet

accept *its.*   Perhaps he uses *her* because amongst the Latins words for lands and countries were feminine.   *Hell* is, however, fem. in Anglo-Saxon.

10. 140. Comp. Homer's *Iliad,* v. 61; Virgil's *Æneid,* viii. 245;   Ovid's *Met.* ii. 560; Pope's *Rape of the Lock,* cant. v.

142. See the Story of Astræa.

143. *Orb'd in a rainbow,* i.e. of course semi-orbed.   See *Paradise Lost,* vii. 247 ; *Rev.* x. 1.

This is the reading of the 1673 edition.   That of 1645 reads :

" The enamelled arras of the rainbow wearing."

144. *set.*   So *Coriolanus,* I. ii. 27 :

" If they *set* down before us, for the remove
Bring up your army."

146. [What does *stearing* mean here ?]

147. *as* is radically but a contracted form of als = also = all so.

148. *her.*   The Anglo-Saxon *heofon* is feminine.

11. 152. *bitter cross.*   See Shakspere's 1 *Henry IV.* I. i. 27.

153. *redeem our loss* = recover what we have lost, as in *Ruth* iv. 6 ; or perhaps, less well, = ransom us lost ones.   Comp. "their sight" above.   *Redeem* has a personal object in *Paradise Lost,* iii. 281, &c. ; in iii. 214, it means " to pay the penalty of."

155. *ychain'd.*   So *yclept* in *L'Allegro.*   So in Chaucer—yblessed, ybete, yburied, ybrent, ycoupled, yfalle, yfonden, ygeten, yglewed, yhalved, yheered (= haired), yshove, ysette, &c. &c. ; in Spenser—yclad, yfraught, ybore, ymolt, &c.   This *y* is a corruption of the part. *ge,* which still survives in German.   Another form of this corruption is *i,* as in ifallen, ihorsed (*Roman of Partenay*), iarmed, ibene (= been), icorve (= carved), idight (= prepared), ifed, imaked (*William of Palerne,* ed. Skeat), &c. &c.   Another, according to some scholars, is *a,* as in *ago,* (Spenser has the forms ygo, ygoe) ; but the prefix in that word is perhaps a corruption of *of.*   In the very oldest stages of our language the prefix *ge* was not confined to the part.; *e.g.* in *William of Palerne* yknowe occurs as an inf.   " yshrilled " in Spenser's *Colin Clout's come Home again,* 62, is the pret.   But latterly it was so confined. Milton therefore shows an imperfect knowledge of the older language when he writes *y-pointing* in his *Epitaph on Shakspere.*

156. *wakefull.*   Here active.   See 1 *Thess.* iv. 16.

thunder.   See Max Müller's *Lectures on the Science of Language,* First Series. Allowing all that is said there, the root *t-n* may be itself onomatopœic.

158. See *Exod.* xix. *et seq.*

159. *brake.*   See note on *hung,* l. 122.

160. *The aged Earth.*   Comp. " the old beldam earth," 1 *Henry IV.* III. i. 32.

Agast.   So *Will. of Pal.* (re-ed. Skeat), 1777-8 :

" And he hem told tightly whiche tvo white beres
Hadde gon in the gardyn and him *agast* maked."

In the *Faerie Queene* the word occurs as a preterite :

" He met a dwarf that seemed terrifyde
With some late perill which he hardly past,
Or other accident which him *agast.*"

The participial form *agasted* is found.   The main part of the word is the Anglo-Saxon *gast ;* comp. German *Geist,* Old English *gost,* as in *Pierce the Ploughmans Crede,* 521, 529, 590 (ed.

Skeat). There occur the forms *agased* and *agazed*, evidently the results of a false derivation. (See Wedgwood.) See 1 *Henry VI.* I. i. 126, and *Chester Plays* (*apud* Halliwell):

> " The [= they] were so sore agased."

And Bishop Percy's *Folio MS.* iii. 154 (ed. Hales and Furnivall):

> " Whereatt this dreadfull conquerour
> Theratt was sore *agazed.*"

An adjective *gastful* occurs in the *Shep. Cal.*, and elsewhere.

11. 161.. *terrour.* This spelling is better than our modern way, as more significant of the channel through which the word came to us. So *honour* below.

162. *the center.* So *Com.* 382. *Hamlet,* II. ii. 159:

> " If circumstances lead me I will find
> Where truth is hid. though it were hid indeed
> Within *the centre.*"

So *Troilus and Cressida,* III. ii. 186.

In "the surface" and "the centre" the necessity of using either "his" or "its" is avoided. Comp. *Fardle of Facions,* 1555: "A certaine sede which groweth there of *the* owne accorde." (*Apud* Marsh.)

163. *session.* Though in appearance so different, "assize" and "session" are etymologically connected. Comp. royal, regal; French, *serment, sacrement; acheter, accepter; naif, native; chose, cause; etroit, strict,* &c. &c. We have also the word "sitting" in a cognate sense with session.

164. *spread his throne.* If we compare the Latin, *lectum sternere,* then the original notion would be the same as in our phrase "to *spread* a table;" that is, it would be to deck the throne with fit coverings: hence, to prepare, to set his throne. We may compare *Faerie Queene,* I. xii. 13:

> " And all the floore was underneath their feet
> Bespredd with costly scarlott of great name,
> On which they lowly sitt."

Comp. " his [Chaos'] dark pavilion *spread*" (*Paradise Lost,* ii. 960).

168. *Th' old Dragon.* See *Rev.* xii. 9.

170. *casts his usurped sway*—as if it were a net; as in 1 *Cor.* vii. 35, &c.

not half so far. A very common phrase in Shakspere. It has now become vulgar, so that a modern writer would hardly use it in a grave passage. Comp. "nor nothing near," in Spenser's *Prothal.*; "something like," *Il Penseroso,* 173.

171. *wroth.* Wrath in 1645 Ed. The form "wroth" is the substantive in Shakspere's *Merchant of Venice,* II. ix. 78:

> " I'l keep my oath
> Patiently to bear my *wroth.*"

172. *Swindges* = swings about, agitates violently. Comp. *Faerie Queene,* I. xi. 23:

> " His hideous tayle then hurled he about."

Comp. also *Ib.* 26:

> " The scorching flame sore *swinged* all his face."

Our verb *swing* is cognate with the German *schwingen,* &c. *Swinge* in the sense of to beat, to strike ("an act that is done with a swinging movement"—Wedgwood), occurs frequently in Old English (as in *Measure for Measure,* V. i. 130), and still survives in the North English dialects. It is associated by Cotgrave with "beat, lamme, bethwacke." See *Havelok* (re-ed. Skeat), and the *Mariage of Witt and Wisdome*, 1579 (*apud* Halliwell):

> "O the passion of God! so I shalbe *swinged;*
> So my boñes shalbe bang'd!
> The poredge pot is stolne ; what, Lob, I say,
> Come away and be hang'd."

For the word in our text comp. Waller's "Her tail's impetuous *swinge.*"

11. 172. *horrour.* So "sorrow" in *Lycid.* 166 ; and "vires" and "potentia," Virg. *Æn.* i. 664.

foulded = consisting of folds, spiral. So *mirrored* in *Adonais.*

173. Comp. *Paradise Regained*, i. 454-64. That the oracles ceased at and from the birth of Christ was a very general belief; but it was baseless. "Tacitus, Philostratus, Lucian, Strabo, Juvenal, Suetonius, Martial, Statius, Pliny the Younger, &c. &c., have incidentally mentioned oracular responses as existing in their own days." "Macrobius, in the reigns of Arcadius and Honorius, speaks of the '*Sortes Antianæ*' in words which distinctly prove that they were consulted as oracles in his time." (See *Occult Sciences*, a volume of the *Encycl. Metrop.*)

174. See the scene described in the beginning of the sixth book of the *Æneid.*

176. *from his shrine.* Comp. Æsch. *Choeph.* 497 (ed. Paley):

> φελλοὶ δ' ὡς ἄγουσι δίκτυον,
> τὸν ἐκ βυθοῦ κλωστῆρα σώζοντες λίνου.

Theoc. vi. 18: καὶ τὸν ἀπὸ γραμμᾶς κινεῖ λίθον. So, as Paley notes, the Greeks said, "The men out of the city fled," meaning, "The men who were in the city fled out of it." See Jelf's *Greek Gr.* § 647.

178. *hollow shreik*, i.e. unsubstantial, unreal, ghost-like, evanescent shriek ; the shriek of one who is so. Comp. "*hollow* fiend," *Twelfth Night*, III. iv. 101 ; "He will look as *hollow* as a ghost," *King John*, III. iv. 84 ; and the phrase "*hollow* laugh." Or the word may refer to "the dull sound of hollow things" (Wedgwood). Kilian, in his *Etymol. Teut. Ling.* glosses *holle stemme* as "vox fusca, non clara,"—a husky (as we should say), not clear voice. Comp. "his *hollow* whistling in the leaves" of "the southern wind," 1 *Henry IV.* V. i. 5. The former sense seems preferable.

Delphos. Milton prefers this form to the more usual *Delphi.* See *Paradise Regained*, i. 458. Shakspere, too, uses Delphos. (See *Winter's Tale.*) It was the mediæval form.

steep of Delphos. Comp. "Delphian cliff," *Paradise Lost*, i. 517. Gray has adopted this phrase, as so many others of Milton's. See his *Progress of Poesy*, l. 66. Delphi lay at the foot of the southern uplands of Parnassus, which end "in a precipitous cliff, 2,000 feet high, rising to a double peak, named the Phædriades, from their 'glittering' appearance as they faced the rays of the sun." (See Smith's *Ancient Geography.*)

"The oracle was consulted by Julian, but was finally suppressed by Theodosius." (Dr. Smith's *Dict. Geog.*)

179. *nightly* = nocturnal. Comp. *Il Penseroso*, 84 ; *Arcad.* 48, &c. So generally in Shakspere. In modern English the word generally means "night by night," as in Cowper's *Lines on the Receipt of my Mother's Picture*, &c.

180. *pale-ey'd.* Comp. *Romeo and Juliet*, III. v. 19, 20:

> "I'll say yon grey is not the morning's *eye*,
> 'Tis but the pale reflex of Cynthia's brow."

Shakspere uses "pale-faced," "pale-visaged." Or, better, *eye* may be used in its precise sense. Comp. *Henry V.* IV. ii. 47, where Grandpré, in his description of the English "jades," speaks of

> "The gum down-roping from their *pale-dead eyes.*"

11. 180. [How would you explain the *from ?*]

12. 181. [To what part of speech does *o're* here belong ?]

See Spenser's *Shep. Cal.* for May, note, where a quotation is made from Lavaterus' treatise, *de Lemuribus,* then newly translated into English (Warton). Lavaterus derived the story there quoted from him from Plutarch's " *booke of the ceasing of Oracles.*"

183. For the language comp. *Matt.* ii. 18.

185. *poplar pale.* Comp. Horace's " pinus ingens *albaque populus.*"

186. *parting.* Comp. "*part'ng* day " and "*parting* soul " in Gray's *Elegy.* In Old English, *part* occurs very commonly in the sense of our *depart.*

Genius. See *Il Penseroso,* 154.

sent = dismissed.

187. *flowre-inwov'n tresses torn.* This is a favourite arrangement of words with Milton. See "beckoning shadows dire," "every alley green," "thick and gloomy shadows damp," &c. &c.

188. *twilight.* Comp. "twilight groves" (*Il Penseroso,* 133).

the nimphs. See *Il Penseroso,* 137–8.

189. The words *in consecrated earth* refer to the *Lemures; on the holy hearth,* to the *Lars.*

consecrated = made " sacer." See Horace's *Sat.* I. viii. 13 ; Orelli quotes in his note the inscription " Dis Manibus locus consecratus," &c.

191. *Lemures* frequently denotes spectres, goblins ; but in Ovid—who, as has been already said, was a favourite writer with Milton—it is used convertibly with Manes. See *Class. Dict.*

192. [How would you parse *round* here ?]

194. *quaint* = nice, exact, &c. *Much Ado about Nothing,* III. iv. 22 : " But for a fine, *quaint,* graceful, and excellent fashion, yours is worth ten on't."

195. See Virg. *Georg.* i. 480.

196. *forgoes.* The "for" here = the "for" of *for*bear, *for*bid, *for*get, *for*give, *for*sake, *for*swear. Comp. German *ver.*

Comp. Virg. *Æneid,* ii. 351.

197. With the catalogue of deities which here follows comp. *Paradise Lost,* i. 376–521.

Peor. See *Numb.* xxv. 18, xxxi. 16 ; *Josh.* xxii. 17. It was one of the titles of Baal, "the supreme male divinity of the Phœnician and Canaanitish nations, as Ashtoreth was their supreme female divinity" (see Smith's *Smaller Bibl. Dict.*)—that is, it expressed one of the modifications of Baal's deity. Comp. *Baal-berith* (*Judges* viii. 33), *Baal-zebub* (2 *Kings* i. 2). But in *Paradise Lost,* i. 412, Peor is said to be the "other name" of Chemos.

Baälim. That is, Baal in all his various modifications: See preceding note. Comp. the various titles that were given to Jupiter by the Latins, to Zeus by the Greeks.

198. *temples dim.* He uses " dim " here in a less favourable sense than in *Il Penseroso,* 160. See *Paradise Lost,* i. 457–66, and *Samson Agonistes,* passim.

199. Dagon was the national god of the Philistines. See *Dictionary of the Bible ;* a'so 1 *Sam.* v.

200. *Mooned Ashtaroth.* See *Dictionary of the Bible.* It would seem more correct to identify this goddess with the planet Venus rather than the Moon. She was the Assyrian *Ishtar,* Greek and Roman *Astarte.* Certainly her worship was eventually identified with that of Venus.

201. *both.* Comp. the position of this word in *Twelfth Night,* V. i. 256 :

> " If nothing lets to make us happy *both,*
> But this my masculine-usurp'd attire," &c.

Selden says she was called "regina cœli," and " mater deum " (*De Diis Syriis*).

203. *Hammon.* See *Class. Dict.* s. v. *Ammon.* He was "originally an Æthiopian or

Lybian, afterwards an Egyptian, deity." His primitive function seems to have been to protect the flocks. He was variously represented as a ram, as a man with a ram's head, as a man with a ram's horns. The great seats of his worship were Meroë, Thebes, Ammonium.

12. 203. *shrinks.* See *Lycid.* 133.

204. *Thamuz* = Tammuz; properly "the Tammuz." See *Ezek.* viii. 14; *Paradise Lost*, i. 446-57. *Tammuz* has been identified with Adonis: "The worship of Adonis, which in later times was spread over nearly all the countries round the Mediterranean, was, as the story itself sufficiently indicates, of Asiatic or, more especially, of Phœnician origin. Thence it was transferred to Assyria, Egypt, Greece, and even to Italy, though of course with various modifications." See *Class. Dict.* The death of Adonis, and Aphrodite's grief over it, are frequently mentioned by the poets, both ancient and modern. Bion wrote a dirge on the subject. Ovid tells the story in the tenth book of his *Metam.* &c. &c. Shelley, weeping over the untimely fate of a young poet, killed, as he believed, by the stroke of a ruffian writer, thought of Adonis, and called his *in memoriam* poem *Adonais.* See Introd. to *Adonais.*

Tyrian maids. In *Paradise Lost*, l.c. "Syrian damsels."

205. *Moloch* = Molech. See *Bible Dict.* Moloch is represented as flying from his worshippers in the very midst of one of the services in his honour. "In Sandys' Travels, p. 186, ed. 1615, fol. a popular book in Milton's time, is a description of the sacrifices and image of Moloch, exactly corresponding with this passage and *Paradise Lost*, i. 392-6." (Warton.)

206. *In shadows dred.* Comp. *Paradise Lost*, i. 403-5:

> " And made his *grove*
> The pleasant valley of Hinnom, Tophet thence
> . And black Gehenna call'd, the type of hell."

207. "According to Jewish tradition, the image of Molech was of brass, hollow within, and was situated without Jerusalem."

burning is here what would be in Greek a present participle passive—so in such phrases as "the house is burning," "I saw it burning." Etymologically, the word is not a participle at all, though it looks like an imperfect participle. It is, in fact, an old verbal substantive, the preposition which once governed it having dropped out. In our older English writers, as still in the various dialects of the country, this preposition is frequently found. See 1 *Pet.* iii. 20, "while the ark was *a* preparing," &c. &c. This *a* is a corruption of *on*. See Chaucer:

> " *On* hontyng be they riden."

(Comp. *alive* = *on* live, &c.) For the -*ing*, a very common A. S. substantival termination was -ung or -*ing*, as *huntung, wonung, halgung, leorning, barning*, &c. &c. The -*ung* was subsequently corrupted into -*ing*. The -*ing* is often added to words that are themselves of Norman-French or Latin origin; *e.g.* preparing, &c. The identity of termination with that of our imperfect participle (itself a corruption from -*ande* or -*ende*), added to the loss of the preposition, and consequent danger of confusion, has led to the introduction of a cumbrous phrase, consisting of "being" followed by the perfect participle, as "the house was being built." But in many writers, and in many particular usages, the old form of expression still lingers.

all may be parsed as an adverb qualifying the adjectival phrase *of blackest hue.* See *Prothal.* 613.

208. Comp. *Paradise Lost*, i. 394.

209. *grisly* is cognate with the German *grässlich* = frightful. The word is used by Chaucer, often by Spenser, &c. See *Paradise Lost*, i. 670; ii. 704: "the grisly terrour," where either the original force of the word is unknown or forgotten, or the phrase is tautological. In iv. 821, occurs again "the grisly King."

211. *brutish* here of *form* and *shape* rather than, or as well as, of kind and nature.

12. 211. On the gods of Egypt, see Juvenal's fifteenth Satire, *beg.*, on which passage Mayor quotes Cic. *Tusc.* v. 78; Herod. ii. 69; Lucian *de Sacr.* 14. "The basis of the religion was Nigritian Fetishism, the lowest kind of nature worship." (*Dict. Bib.*) *as fast.* The correlative phrase is omitted, as in *Il Penseroso*, 44.

212. *Isis.* See *Class. Dict.* She was originally the Egyptian Earth goddess, the wife of Osiris, and mother of Horus ; subsequently she was worshipped as the goddess of the moon, and identified with Io (Juv. vi. 526); also, she was identified with Demeter, as Osiris with Dionysus. Those initiated in her mysteries wore in the public processions masks representing the heads of dogs.

Orus, or *Horus*, the Egyptian god of the sun.

the dog Anubis. Comp. Virg. *Æneid*, viii. 698 :

" Omnigenûmque deûm monstra, et latrator Anubis,
    Contra Neptunum et Venerem contraque Minervam
    Tela tenent."

Minucius Felix (21) calls him "Cynocephalus." Juv. xv. 8 : "Whole towns worship the dog." "Hence the oath of Socrates: μὰ τὸν κύνα τὸν Αἰγυπτίων θεόν, *Plat. Gorg.* p. 482, B." (Mayor.)

13. 213. Osiris here, as in Juv. viii. 29, stands for Apis, inasmuch as their godheads were in course of time identified. Apis was represented by a bull, which was kept with the utmost care at Memphis. When one bull died, or having been worshipped for a certain period was put to death, another was searched for which should fulfil the necessary conditions of colour and marks. When he was found, there was great joy. See Juv. l.c., and Mayor's quotations from Athenagoras and Minucius Felix. In iii. 27-29, Herodotus relates how Cambyses mocked and slew this deity, and in the following chapters what came of that ferocious act of impiety.

217. *his sacred chest = worship ark.* There is a sketch of an Egyptian ark in Wilkinson's *Ancient Egyptians.* Chaucer uses *chest* for coffin.

218. *shroud.* Etymologically = "what is cut up" (Bosworth), and so a garment. So generally a covering, and then a shelter, a hiding-place. See *Paradise Lost*, X. 1068 :

" The winds
Blow moist and keen . . . . .
. . . . . . which bids us seek
Some better *shroud*."

So *Tempest*, II. ii. 243 ; 3 *Henry VI.* III. i. 1 ; *Love's Labour Lost*, IV. iii. 479. "My sable shroud," in *Lyc.* 22 = my coffin.

220. *sable-stoled.* κυανόστολος. See note on *stole* in *Il Penseroso*, 35.

223. *eyn.* So Shakspere, *Antony and Cleopatra*, II. vii. 121 : " Plumpy Bacchus, with pink *eyne*." The *n* represents an old plural inflexion. In Chaucer we have *eyen* and *eyghen*; elsewhere *been, fon, shoon, lambren, sustren* (*Piers Ploughman*), &c. This inflexion still survives, or is traceable, in oxen, children, brethren, kine, swine ; also in welkin, chicken (see Trench's *English Past and Present*), which, though now used as singulars, are really plural.

224. *beside.* In modern English we prefer the form *besides.* So we say "sometimes" for "occasionally," in which sense "sometime" was once frequently used.

all the gods beside = all the other gods. *Beside* here holds an adjectival relation to *the gods.*

226. *Typhon.* See *Class. Dict.*

227. Comp. Hercules' feat while yet in his cradle, described by Theocritus in his *Herakliskus.*

231. Comp. *Midsummer Night's Dream*, III. ii. 379-87 ; *Paradise Regained*, iv. 426-38.

orient. Mr. Keightley refers to *Paradise Lost*, i. 546.

13. 234. *his severall grave.* So *Much Ado about Nothing*, V. iii. 29. *His several* = his particular, his own, his respective. In modern English *several* generally = various, divers, and hence is joined only with a plural noun. Etymologically *several* = *separate*.

    his = its. See above. l. 106.

    235. Comp. *Paradise Lost,* i. 781-8.

    Fayes = *Fées.* The Italian form *fate* points to a derivation from *fatum.* On the various meanings of the word *fairy* or *faery,* see Keightley's *Fairy Mythology.*

    236. *the night-steeds.* Statius speaks of "Night's horses" (*Theb.* ii. 60); Shakspere of "Night's swift dragons" (*Midsummer Night's Dream*, III. ii. 379). In *Il Penseroso*, Milton speaks of Cynthia's "dragon yoke."

    moon-lov'd. See *Paradise Lost,* i. 784.

    maze = intricate dance; elsewhere, of the tangles of a forest, as in *Paradise Regained,* ii. 246; *Com.* 181.

    240. See l. 19.

    youngest teemed = last born.

    241. That is, had taken up her station; no longer moves.

    242. Comp. *Matt.* xxv. ; *Sonnet to a Virtuous Yô ing Lady.*

    244. *bright-harnessed. Harness,* now used of the gear of horses, in older English signifies men's armour. See *Paradise Lost*, vii. 202; *Macbeth*, V. v. 52:

> "At least we'll die with *harness* on our back."

"*Harnessed* masque," *King John*, V. ii. 132. *Exod.* xiii. 18.

    244. Comp. *Sonnet on his Blindness:*

> "They also serve who only stand and wait."

L'ALLEGRO AND IL PENSEROSO.

INTRODUCTION.

L'ALLEGRO and IL PENSEROSO, to be properly understood, must be read together. The likings and tastes expressed are meant to be contrasted. The one poem is the counterpart of the other. The one celebrates the charms of "Mirth;" the other those of "Melancholy." The advocate of Mirth bids Melancholy begone to the realm of Darkness, bids "heart-easing Mirth" come to him with a retinue of kindred spirits; he would fain hear the lark singing and enjoy all other cheery sights and sounds of the bright morning-time; he would be present at the merrymakings of the village and listen to its marvellous tales; he rejoices in the life of the town—in all its gay gatherings; he goes to see great comedies acted; above all things he would be surrounded by the sweet singing of exquisite verses. On the other hand, the melancholic man will not allow "vain deluding joys" to be near him; he bids Melancholy hail, and she is to bring with her a fitting company; his pleasure is in the song of the nightingale, in walks beneath the moon, in the sounds and in the quiet proper to the night, in calm studies through its watches—readings of philosophy, of poetry, of high romances; the night is the season he loves; when it must end, let the daybreak be cloudy and rain-dripping; when the sun at last will shine out, let some undisturbed grove screen him from its blaze; there let him slumber, to wake with sweet music in his ears; let him ofttimes pace some old Gothic cathedral, and listen to rich anthems; at the end, let him pass away his years in some peaceful hermitage, still gathering wisdom.

This meagre outline of the two poems should be carefully filled in. Observe who are to be the companions of Mirth, who of Melancholy; what kind of music suits either speaker; in what different ways Orpheus is mentioned; how one man looks on to the end, the other's sight is shorter; what diverse daybreakings are preferred; what diverse kinds of literature, and how the one of these is to be communicated orally, the other through no living medium, but through books; how various are the tastes described with regard to natural scenery. To these many other observations might be added.

It is evident, if these two poems are carefully examined, that the respective characteristics of the speakers are by no means what we should call mirthful and melancholic. There is nothing mirthful in our sense of the word in a wide landscape; there is nothing melancholy in reading Chaucer. The two characters are, perhaps, most sharply distinguished in respect of sociality. The one is eminently social; he delights to associate with the "kindly race of men." The other likes better to be left with his own thoughts, with no human intrusion. The one is light-hearted; the other not of a sad but rather of a grave spirit. The eyes of the one look outward, and brighten at the sight of the fair images of nature; the eyes of the other rather look inward, at the fine forms which the mind can present. There are several points in common between Il Penseroso and Jacques in *As You Like It;* but Jacques' melancholy is dashed with a certain cynicism not to be found in the character sketched by Milton. Perhaps Milton felt that no two English words he could think of would serve him as titles, and therefore adopted the Italian words by which the poems are known. There can be little doubt as to which of the two characters he portrays was after his own heart. He portrays L'Allegro with much skill and excellence; but he cannot feign with him the sympathy he genuinely feels with the other; into his portrait of Il Penseroso he throws himself, so to speak, with all his soul. He is indeed not altogether at home in the poem describing the former: he distinguishes the sweet-briar from the eglantine, whereas they were one and the same; larks do not visit even poets' windows to say good-morrow, but rather "singing ever soar and soaring ever sing;" he had never seen, it is believed, barren-breasted mountains; and generally we think that the wings of his Mirth are somewhat constrained in their flight. But in the other poem his whole nature appears. The limits in point of length, previously sufficing, are now exceeded. He cannot content himself with so brief a description of his "Melancholy" as of "Mirth." He refers no less than thrice to music, his darling delight. He refers, at length, to the studies that were always for him of supreme interest—amongst them to the works of Spenser, whom, as he told Dryden, he regarded as his poetical father—thus illustrating well the line in one of his letters to Deodati,

> "Totum rapiunt libri me, mea vita, libri."

He is charmed by the nightingale, to which bird on another occasion he addressed a sonnet. He gives several hints which he afterwards expanded in his greater works. And he proposes as the close of Il Penseroso's life that which he ever aspired after as the glorious maturity of his own—that he should

> "Attain
> To something like prophetic strain;"

for it was a poet of the Hebrew sort—a *vates*—that Milton was ambitious to be.

It seems pretty certain that these two poems were written after Milton had left Cambridge, during his six years' residence at his father's house at Horton, in Buckinghamshire—that is, between 1632 and 1638. They were probably written in some earlier year of this period, for in *Lycidas,* which was composed in 1637, he speaks as one that only writes poetry under the compulsion of "bitter constraint and sad occasion dear." It appears likely they were written before *Comus,* which was acted at Ludlow Castle in 1634. So, to connect these pieces of national literature with our national history, they were in all probability written in the earlier part of the period when Charles I. attempted the fatal experiment of governing without a parliament.

There can be little doubt that Milton drew some suggestions for the leading idea of his two poems from Burton's *Anatomy of Melancholy*, and from a song in the play of *The Nice Valour*. In the "Author's Abstract of Melancholy," certain verses prefixed to Burton's work, *pros* and *cons* with regard to melancholy are alternately stated. The song in *The Nice Valour*, a play composed by Fletcher and some unknown person, is as follows :—

> "Hence, all you vain delights,
>   As short as are the nights,
>   Wherein you spend your folly !
> There's nought in this life sweet,
>   If man were wise to see't,
>   But only melancholy ;
>   Oh, sweetest melancholy !

> "Welcome, folded arms and fixed eyes,
>   A sigh that piercing mortifies,
>   A look that's fasten'd to the ground,
>   A tongue chain'd up, without a sound !

> "Fountain-heads, and pathless groves,
>   Places which pale passion loves !
>   Moonlight walks, when all the fowls
>   Are warmly housed, save bats and owls !
>   A midnight bell, a parting groan !
>   These are the sounds we feed upon ;
> Then stretch our bones in a still gloomy valley ;
> Nothing's so dainty sweet as lovely melancholy."

The Nice Valour was not printed till 1647, two years after *L'Allegro* and *Il Penseroso* were printed, many years after they had been written ; but this song had probably been composed and known very many years before the appearance of the play in which it was inserted. It is said to have been written by Beaumont, Fletcher's great co-worker, who died in the same year as Shakspere, 1616.

Perhaps *Il Penseroso* was written first. Fletcher's poem suggested it, and then the counterpart was written. "Not unseen," in *L'Allegro*, must have been written after the "unseen" of *Il Penseroso*.

L'ALLEGRO.

14. 1. *Hence.* In a similar verbal manner are used "away," "down," "out," "up," "forward," &c. The verb is in fact absorbed into the adverb.

2. This amour is Milton's own invention. In Grecian mythology, Erebus is the spouse of Night, and, by her, father of Æther and Hemera : the dog Cerberus has no offspring. Not that Milton makes a blunder. He is altering the old story consciously. Here, as elsewhere, he modifies the ancient mythology after his pleasure, with the same independence and right of variation as mark the treatment of it by the old Greek poets. He was one of those poets in spirit, and claimed for himself the same licence. He not only modifies the classical tales ; he sometimes mythologizes on his own account. Comp. below, ll. 18–24.

Cerberus. See *Class. Dict.*

3. In some such cave as Cerberus' own, which, according to Virgil, faced the landing place of spirits on the further bank of the Styx. When Æneas stepped ashore, the monster made the nether realms ring again with his "three-mouthed barking :"

> "Adverso recubans immanis in antro."—*Æn.* vi. 418.

14. 4. *shapes.* *Com.* 207. Comp. Virg. *Æn.* vi. 285.

5. *uncouth cell.* Elsewhere Milton speaks of "the uncouth swain" (*Lyc.* 185), "a voyage uncouth" (*Paradise Lost,* v. 98); "this uncouth dream." Radically, *uncouth* = unknown. Couth or couthe or cowthe occurs as a pres., as a pret., and as a part. As a pres. it has in *Piers Ploughman,* Ed. Skeat, v. 181, a causative force:

"I *couth* it in owre cloistre, that al owre couent wo:e it."

As a pret. we still retain it in our *could.* (Comp. *Lycidas:* "he *knew* himself to sing" = he could sing.) As a part. in *Sir Gawayne and the Green Knight,* Ed. Morris, 1490, &c. Strictly it is the pret. of Ang.-Sax. *cunnan;* see note on *wont, Prothal.* 139. *Uncouth* survives in Lowland Scotch as "unco'."

6. *brooding:* not literally so, as in *Paradise Lost,* i. 21, or it would be *her,* not his, jealous wings: but as it were in a brooding, *i.e* overcovering, attitude. So *incubo* in Latin, as *Æn.* i. 89: "Ponto nox *incubat* atra;" vi. 610: "Qui divitiis soli *incubuere* repertis." There is another secondary meaning the word sometimes has, viz. to meditate or ponder mischievously or sullenly. Except when used literally it has seldom or never a good sense.

his. See note on *Hymn Nat.* 106. Probably in using "his" with reference to Darkness he has in mind the classical Erebus.

7. See 2 *Henry VI.* III. ii. 40:

"Came he right now to sing a raven's note,
Whose dismal tune bereft my vital powers," &c.

Macb. I. v. 40; *Tit. Andr.* II. iii. 97; Spenser's *Shep. Cal.* June, l. 23:

"Here no *night-ravens* lodge, more black than pitche."

8. *ebon* = "black as ebony" (*Love's Labour Lost,* IV. iii. 247). So "amber hair," *Love's Labour Lost,* IV. iii. 86; "raven locks," "eagle eye," &c.

9. *low-brow'd locks* = beetle-browed, overhanging.

ragged. See *Isaiah* ii. 21.

10. *dark Cimmerian.* Milton's earlier style is occasionally not altogether free from tautology. See Ovid's *Met.* xi. 592: "Est prope Cimmerios longo spelunca secessu mons cavus." Warton quotes from one of Milton's *Prolusiones:* "Dignus qui Cimmeriis occlusus tenebris longam et perosam vitam transigat." See Hom. *Od.* xi. 14; *Tibull.* IV. i. 65.

12. *ycleap'd.* See note on ychain'd, *Hymn Nat.* 155. See *Love's Labour Lost,* I. i. 242: "It is *ycleped* thy park;" and V. ii. 602:

"Judas I am, *ycliped* Maccabæus."

where Dumain puns:

"Judas Maccabæus clipt is plain Judas."

Clepe occurs in various forms in Chaucer, and in Spenser. Palsgrave has, "I clepe, I call, *je huyscke;* this terme is farre Northerne." This verb is still used by boys at play in the Eastern counties, who "*clape* the sides at a game." (Halliwell.) The word survives also in the Scotch *clep,* and, as some think, in the English *clap*-trap.

14. *at a birth.* *A,* which is but a corruption of one, here has its full etymological force, as in many current phrases: "one at *a* time," "*a* shilling a [on] piece," &c.

The most common account makes the Graces daughters of Zeus, by whom is not agreed. Another derives them from Apollo, by either Ægle or Euanthe. Lastly, there is the account here adopted by Milton, which is said to be given only by Servius in a comment on *Æn.* i. 720.

17. *som sager,* so far as is known, = Milton's self. Some late editions read "sages," corruptly.

Comp. Soph. *Œd. Tyr.* 1098.

14. 18. *frolick.* Here an adjective, as in *Midsummer Night's Dream*, V. i. 394: "We fairies
. . . now are *frolick."* *Com.* 59: "Ripe and *frolick* of his full-grown age." So Tennyson's
Ulysses, "with a frolic welcome." At the close of the seventeenth century it was commonly
used, as it now is, as a substantive. A second adjective was presently formed from it—*frolic-
some.* (Comp. gamesome.) Shakspere, Spenser, and others use it also as a verb, as it is
still used. The word is of course radically the same with the German *fröhlich.* Indeed the fact
of its not occurring in Ang.-Sax. and its form suggest, that it is simply *fröhlich* imported into
English, the *c* representing the guttural. The term *lic* is not uncommon in Ang.-Sax., as
gastlic (comp. German *geistlich*), but in later English it is generally softened away into *ly:*
thus *gastlic* becomes ghastly, *nihtlic* nightly, &c.

20. *a Maying.* This *a* is a corruption of *on.* See note on *Hymn Nat.* l. 207. So in
"a dying," *Luke* viii. 42; Shakspere's *Richard II.* II. i. 90; "a fishing," *John* xxi. 3. In the
words *alive, aloft, apart, aslant, abroad, away, aground,* the prep. and its noun are fused
together, as also in the wholly or partly obsolete words *abed, afire, afoot, athirst, acold,
acool, aflame, agape.*

Maying. See Chaucer's *Knight's Tale;* Herrick's *Hesperides,* passim, &c. For
some account of the old May-day customs see Ellis's *Brand's Popular Ant.* Warton well
refers to Ben Jonson's *Masque* at Sir W. Cornwallis' house at Highgate, 1604.

[What is the force of *once* here? What other forces has it?]

21. [What is meant here by *there?*]

22. See *Taming of the Shrew,* II. i. 173:

> " I'll say she looks as clear
> As morning roses newly wash'd in dew."

24. [Explain the *so* here.]

bucksom. This word is here, as many a time since, used somewhat vaguely. It is
the Ang.-Sax. *bocsum,* and means radically *bow-some,* flexible, pliant; German, *beugsam,
diegsam.* Then it means yielding, and so obedient, in which senses it is frequently used by
Chaucer and our older writers. Thus, Spenser, *View of the State of Ireland:* "Thinking
thereby to make them the more tractable and *buxom* to his government." "In an old form of
marriage used before the Reformation the bride promised to be obedient and *buxom* in bed
and board." (Johnson.) See other instances in Trench's *Sel. Gloss.* See also *Will. Pal.* Ed.
Skeat, 2943:

> " The proddest of them alle
> Schul be *buxum* at your wille."

In the *Vision of Piers Ploughman* is found *unbuxome* for disobedient. See also *Faerie
Queene,* I. xi. 37:

> " Then gan he tosse aloft his stretched traine,
> And therewith scourge the *buxome* aire so sore,
> That to his force to yielden it was faine."

(Which phrase occurs also in *Paradise Lost,* ii. 842 and v. 270; comp. Horace's "sedentem
aëra," Sat. II. ii. 13.) *Faerie Queene,* III. ii. 23:

> " Imperious Love . . . . .
>   . . . tyrannizeth in the bitter smarts
> Of them that to him *buxome* are and prone."

Perhaps because obedience was in the old days considered the great charm of a woman (see
Taming of the Shrew), the word came to be used in a general complimentary sense. Gower,
in Shakspere's *Per.* I. i. 23, speaks of

> " A female heir
> So *buxom,* blithe, and full of face
> As heaven had lent her all his grace;"

from which passage probably Milton borrows here. Other old forms of the word are bugh-som, bousom. *Buxumness* is used for obedience in *Piers Ploughman*, and elsewhere.

14. 24. *debonair.* See *Faerie Queene*, I. ii. 23:

"Was never Prinçe so meeke and *debonaire*;"

and elsewhere. In the *Boke of Curtasye*, 191 (Ed. Furnivall), there is the form *boner*:

"Gyf hym *boner* wordys on fayre manere."

25. *Haste thee.* So "Hie thee," "lie thee down," "fare thee well," &c. In these and all such phrases the pronoun is the ethic dat., as in "he plucked *me* ope his doublet," &c. Compare "I followed me close," 1 *Henry IV.* II. iv. 240. "I have writ me here a letter," *Merry Wives of Windsor*, I. iii. 65, &c. See Fiedler and Sach's *Gramm. Eng.* ii. 265. So Chaucer's *Cant. T.* 14,078:

"These riottoures thre
Were set *hem* in a tavern for to drinke."

Piers Ploughman, Ed. Skeat, Prol. 7:

"I was wery forwardred, and went *me* to reste."

Bowle quotes from Buchanan:

"Vos adeste rursus
Risus, Blanditiæ, Procacitates,
Lusus, Nequitiæ, Facetiæque
Joci Deliciæque et Illecebræ."

Comp. Stat. *Sylv.* II. vii.

26. *Jollity.* See *Com.* 102-4.

27. *Quips.* See *Alex. and Camp.* apud Nares:

"Ps. Why what's a *quip?*
"MA. We great girders call it a short saying of a sharp wit, with a bitter sense in a sweet word."

Two Gentlemen of Verona, IV. ii. 12; *As You Like It*, V. iv. 79. Greene called a satirical tract he wrote on the affectations of the fine gentlemen of his time "A Quip for an Upstart Courtier." The word occurs also as a verb. See *Janua Linguarum*, Ed. 1667, § 916: "Be not a fleering jiber at other men: and if by way of discourse thou comest out with any pleasant matter, let them be witty jests (squibs), not scoffing taunts; glance at (allude) but do not gird," where the margin gives for "gird" "*quip*, twitch, carp." Spenser, *Faerie Queene*, VI. vii. 44, where Scorn,

"Having in his hand a whip,
Her therewith yirks, and still, when she complaines
The more he laughes, and does her closely *quip*
To see her sore lament and bite her tender lip."

It is perhaps etymologically but another form of *whip*. Comp. *quirk, twit.*

cranks. In Shakspere's *Coriolanus*, I. i. 141, this word is used for winding passages. In the *Faerie Queene*, VII. vii. 52, Mutability, speaking of certain planets, says:

"So many turning *cranks* these have, so many crookes."

Milton speaks of "the ways of the Lord" as "straight and faithful," "not full of cranks and contradictions." Here it seems to mean turnings, inversions, distortions of what is said: *e.g.* puns, designed misconstructions, deliberate crooked answers. Comp. the Clown's remark in *Twelfth Night*, III. i. 13: "A sentence is but a cheveril glove to a good wit; how quickly the wrong side may be turned outward."

14. 28. Warton quotes from Burton's *Anat. of Mel.*:

> " With becks and nods he first began
> To try the wench's mind ;
> With becks, and nods, and smiles again
> No answer did he find."

wreathèd smiles. The faces of the personified Smiles are all lined and puckered with laughing. Contrast *wrinkled care.* Both joy and grief furrow the face, but these furrows are spoken of in very different terms.

29. *Hebe.* See *Class. Dict.*

30 *love to live* = are wont to live. So *amo* in Latin, φιλέω in Greek.

32. Comp. Shakspere's *Cymbeline*, I. vi. 67 :

> " Whiles the jolly Briton—　　··
> Your lord, I mean—laughs from's free lungs, cries ' *O,*
> *Can my sides hold* to think,'" &c.

Midsummer Night's Dream, II. i. 55.

33. *trip it.* In *Cymbeline*, to map it, to prince it : and elsewhere, to go it, to drop it, dance it (" dance it trippingly," *Midsummer Night's Dream,* V. i. 403), lord it, saint it, sinner it, queen it, feast it, wive it, devil-porter it (*Macbeth,* II. iii. 19), battle it, career it, mouth it, virgin it, clown it, &c. &c. Perhaps the " it " in this usage stands in the place of a cognate accusative ; *e.g.* " trip it " = trip a tripping ; but this being a somewhat cumbrous phrase the substantive is displaced by the pronoun. In other words, the " it " represents a substantive implied in the governing verb (so, in Greek ἴσην γ' ἔτισεν, Soph. *Œd. Tyr.* 810, ἴσην agrees with τίμην contained in ἔτισεν, &c.).

34. Contrast " the even step and musing gate" in *Il Penseroso,* 38. Comp. *Com.* 144 :

> " Beat the ground
> In a light fantastic round ; "

and 962 :

> " Here be, without duck or nod,
> Other trippings to be trod
> Of lighter toes."

36. Is he thinking of Wales, Switzerland, Greece, and other mountainous countries, in which the heights have proved the great strongholds of freedom ? Or does he refer to the absence of conventional restraints and general sense of unconfinement that belong to mountains? Comp. Keble's *Christian Year:*

> " What liberty so glad and gay,
> As where the mountain boy,
> Reckless of regions far away,
> A prisoner lives in joy," &c.

No such nymph is found amongst the acknowledged Oreads and Orodemniads of the Greeks. Libertas had a temple built to her on the Aventine Hill at Rome. But the first interpretation suggested is probably the correct one. Comp. Byron's

> " The mountains look on Marathon,
> And Marathon looks on the sea,"

with Wordsworth's

> " Two Voices are there—one is of the sea,
> One of the mountains— each a mighty voice :
> In both from age to age thou didst rejoice,
> They were thy chosen music, Liberty," &c.

Add Tennyson's

> " Of old sat Freedom on the heights,
> The thunder breaking at her feet ;
> Above her shook the starry lights,
> She heard the torrents meet."

15. 38. *crue*. Crew signifies radically any gathering or assembly. It is probably connected with crowd. In modern English it has mostly a bad sense, when used generally.

40. *unreproved* = unreprovable. So in Spenser, "unreproved truth." Comp. the use of *invictus* in Latin.

unreproved pleasures free. On this favourite word-order of Milton see *Hymn Nat.* 187.

42. Comp. Shakspere's *Henry V.* IV. i. 11 :

> " Piercing the night's dull ear."

43. Comp. " From his high watch-tower in the heavens." (Milton's *Reformation touching Church Discipline in England.*)

44. Comp. Shakspere's *Much Ado About Nothing*, V. iii. 25 :

> " The gentle day,
> Before the wheels of Phœbus, round about
> *Dapples* the drowsy East with spots of grey."

45. The verb "to come" depends upon the verb "to hear" in l. 41. He wishes to hear the lark begin its flight, and then to hear it come to his window and give him " good morning." The "to" before "come" is made necessary by the distance between it and the governing verb ; otherwise, it would be omitted according to our usage after "*hear*", just as after *may, can, see,* &c. (We say "I made him come ;" but "I compelled him to come.") The lark, then, is to greet the poet. Comp. a sprightly song by T. Heywood, apud *The Golden Treasury* :

> " Pack, clouds, away, and welcome day,
> With night we banish sorrow ;
> Sweet air, blow soft, mount larks aloft
> To give my love good morrow."

In *Paradise Regained*, ii. 279–281, the lark is to salute the Morning's self :

> " And now the herald lark
> Left his ground-nest [comp. *Com.* 317], high towering to descry
> The Morn's approach, and greet her with his song."

Other interpretations of this passage have been suggested by those reluctant to allow the ignorance of a lark's habits—the untruthfulness to nature—shown by Milton, if the above construction be adopted. The "to come" has been made dependent upon "admit me," in l. 38, and it has been maintained that it is the poet who is to say "good morrow." The poet is supposed to be out of doors, and to visit his own window. But (1) "at my window" should rather be "at my own window ;" (2) to whom is he to bid good morrow? Another suggestion supposes him to be *in* doors, to go to his window, and bid good morrow to the world at large! No ; the poet evidently means that the lark is to descend and perch for a moment upon his window-sill.

Warton quotes from Sylvester's *Du Bartas* in the Cave of Sleep :

> " Cease, sweet chantecleere,
> To bid good morrow."

and

> " But cheerful birds chirping him sweet good morrows.

15. 45. *in spight of sorrow* = out of a spirit of spite towards sorrow, and so = to spite sorrow.

47. The eglantine and sweet-brier are said to be one and the same. See Warton's and Mr. Keightley's notes. Etymologically "eglantine," of the same root with French *aiguille*, denotes something prickly. Spenser, in *Faerie Queene*, II. v. 29, describes an "arber,"

> " Through which the fragrant eglantine did spred
> His prickling arms, entrayled with roses red,
> Which daintie odours round about them threw."

" Eglantine " is distinguished from "woodbine" or "honeysuckle" by Oberon in *Midsummer Night's Dream*, II. i. 251. Perhaps by the epithet *twisted* Milton means to express some special species of sweet-brier. Else, he is inaccurate here too. His master, Spenser, is frequently careless and inexact in the details of his descriptions of nature : incompatible trees and flowers appear together. See *Faerie Queene*, I. i. 9 ; *Prothalam.* 130.

49. Comp. the picture of Chaunticlere in Chaucer's *Nonne Prestes Tale*, 16335.

50. [From what is the metaphor here taken ?]

51. [How do you read this line ?]

54. Comp. Gray's *Elegy*, 17–20. The influence of Milton upon Gray's language is conspicuous in all that poet's writings.

55. *hoar* = rime-white.

56. [What is meant by *high wood* ?]

57. *not unseen.* Comp. *Il Penseroso*, 65.

59. Comp. *Samson Agonistes*, 547 :

> " Wherever fountain or fresh current flow'd
> Against the eastern ray," &c.

See *Midsummer Night's Dream*, III. ii. 391.

      the eastern gate. Comp. " Heaven's gate " in the song in Shakspere's *Cymbeline*, II. iii. 21. Gray borrows the phrase in his *Descent of Odin*.

62. *liveries* here has its modern sense. In older English it was not confined to clothes, but signified any dole or allowance made to dependents. Cotgrave defines *La Livrée des Chanoines* to be " their liverie or corrodie ; their stipend, exhibition, dailie allowance in victuals or money." The *Boke of Curtasye* speaks " of candel liueray " = a livery of candles. (Ed. Furnivall, v. 839.) In *Bishop Percy's MS. Folio* there occurs *livere* for wages, pay ; *liverye* for allowance of food ; as *Gay and Colebrande*, 534–6 :

> " And euery day when the noone bell rang
> The litle ladd to the towne must gang
> To ffeitch the ladyes *liuerye*."

See Trench's *Select Gloss.*

      dight. Il Pens. 159. It is derived from the A.-S. verb *dihtan*, to dispose, arrange. It is common enough in our older writers, in Chaucer, Spenser, &c. See *Faerie Queene*, I. iv. 6 :

> " Thence to the hall, which was on every side
> With rich array and costly arras *dight*."

In II. i. 18 a steed is spoken of,

> " Whose sides with dapled circles weren *dight*."

See Warton's quotations from one of Milton's *Prolusiones*, and from *Britannia's Pastorals*, IV. iv.

67. *tells his tale* = counts his flock. This is undoubtedly the meaning, although it may be, as Mr. Keightley says, that the phrase occurs nowhere else in older English in this sense. Milton is, perhaps, more than any other poet fresh and original in his phraseology. *Tell*

occurs frequently in the sense of "to count." This is one of the senses of the A.-S. *tellan*. Cotgrave in his *French Dict.* writes "*compter*, to count, account, reckon, *tell*, number." See *Gen.* xv. 5; *Ps.* xxii. 17, xlviii. 12. *Tale* occurs often in the sense of that which is told or counted, a number: A.-S. *tal*, Germ. *Zahl.* See *Exod.* v. 8 and 18; 1 *Sam.* xviii. 27; 1 *Chron.* ix. 28. The *Bible Word-Book* quotes from Udal's Erasmus, *Luke*, fol. 103, *b:* "He hath even the verai heares of your heades noumbred out by *tale*." Dryden writes :

> " Both number twice a day the milky dams,
> And once she takes the *tale* of all the lambs."

Robert of Gloucester speaks of "folc without *tale*." It has been suggested that *tells his tale* = tells the story of, avows his love. But (1) this would be a somewhat abrupt use of the word *tale*. (2) The *every* shows that some piece of business is meant. (3) The context too shows that. (4) The early dawn is scarcely the time for love-making. Some of these objections, but not all, are obviated by taking *tale* in a general sense. See Mr. Keightley's note, who refers to *Nat.* 85, Virg. *Ecl.* vii. 1. For the hawthorn, see 3 *Hen. VI.* II. v. 42 :—

> " Gives not the hawthorne bush a sweeter shade
> To shepherds looking on their silly sheep," &c.

Warton quotes appositely from W. Browne's *Shepheard's Pipe*, when the dawn is being described :—

> " When the shepheards from the fold
> All their bleating charges *told*,
> And, full careful, search'd if one
> Of all the flock was hurt or gone," &c.

15. 69. *Streit* = straightway, as in *Hamlet*, V. i. 2.

70. *lantskip.* This is nearer to the A.-S. form (*landscipe*) than our present orthography. The scipe or skipe is of the same root as the A.-S. *scapan*, our shape. A landscape is simply a *land-shape*, the *c* not having been softened away into *h*, as so frequently happens in our modern English forms as compared with the original ones. The A.-S. word for a poet is *scop* = a shaper.

71. It would seem that he here puts together two different autumnal appearances of the pasturages, the morning appearance (comp. *hoar hill*, in l. 55) and one belonging to a later time of the day, when the grey of the rime has vanished and the dun colour of the ground is visible ; or perhaps he may refer to different pasturages, one rime-covered, the other showing its natural brown, the difference in colour being due to their different positions, one exposed, the other sheltered. On *lawns*, see *Hymn Nat.* 85. *Fallow* is not used here in its radical sense. It denotes here, as elsewhere, land which has long lain unploughed and is grass-overgrown.

72. *stray*, as *errare*, in Virg. *Ecl.* i. 9.

75. *trim.* *Il Pens.* 50; *Hymn Nat.* 33; *Com.* 120. This word occurs commonly in Shakspere and elsewhere as a substantive, as an adjective, as a verb.

daisies pide. See Song in *Love's Labour Lost*, V. ii. 903. Shylock speaks of "all the eanlings which were streak'd and *pied*" (*Merchant of Venice*, I. iii. 82). Shelley's *Adonais*, stanza 33 :

> " Faded violets, white, and *pied*, and blue."

The root survives in "mag *pie*," "*pie*bald."

76. *Runlets* abound at and near Horton. For rivers, there are the Thames and the Coln, which about a mile from the village pours itself into the Thames.

77. Is he thinking of Harefield Place, the residence of the Dowager Countess of Derby (a cousin of Spenser the poet), in whose honour his *Arcades* were written ? or, rather, of what is the great commanding feature of the landscape around Horton—of Windsor Castle ?

15. 78. [What is the exact meaning of *boosom'd* here, and of *tufted?*]   See *Paradise Lost,*
v. 127, and *Com.* 225.

79. *lies* = dwells, as very commonly in Old English.   See 1 *Henry VI.* II. ii. 41 · *Othello,*
III. iv. 1, &c.

16. 80. *cynosure.*   See *Class. Dict.*   Ovid, *Fast.* iii. 107.   *Com.* 341 :

> " And thou shalt be our star of Arcady,
>   Or Tyrian *Cynosure.*"

Comp. "lode-star" in *Midsummer Night's Dream,* I. i. 183.

81. *hard by.*   ".The idea is from hard substances being usually compact, close in
texture." (*Bible Word-Book.*)   Compare *close by, fast by.*

85. *messes.*   See *Gen.* xliii. 34; 2 *Sam.* xi. 8.   Comp. Virg. *Ecl.* ii. 10.

86. *neat-handed.*   "He uses *neat-fingered* of a cook in *Animadversions.*"   (Mr.
Keightley.)

87. *bowre.*   See note, *Prothal.* 15.

90. This line may be connected immediately with *lead,* in which case must be understood "She goes there," or something of that sort; or, better, it may be loosely connected
with *her bowre she leaves,* which phrase conveys the notion of going : i.e. *her bowre she leaves*
is used zeugmatically.

91. [What are the derivation, the first meaning, the classical use, of *secure?*]

92. *upland hamlets,* opp. to *towred cities,* v. 117.   *Upland* = country as opp. to town.
Strictly it means "highland," Germ. *oberland,* and derives that other force from the fact that
large towns belong to the plains.   A third meaning naturally is rude, illiterate, unrefined,
savage.   See Trevisa's Higden's *Polych.* apud Mr. Morris's *Spec. Early Eng.:* "*Uplond-
ysche* men wol lykne hamsylf to gentile man," &c.   Gray in his *Elegy* seems to use the word
loosely for "on the higher ground."   Perhaps he took it from Milton without quite understanding in what sense Milton used it.   So Johnson says, that it means here "higher in
situation."   So Mr. Keightley, &c.

94. *rebecks.*   "Hugh Rebeck" is one of the musicians in *Romeo and Juliet,* IV. v. 135.
It was "an instrument of music having catgut strings, and played with a bow ; but originally
with only two strings, then with three, till it was exalted into the more perfect violin with four
strings." (*Nares.*)   See Chappell's *Popular Music of the Olden Time.*

96. Comp. *Titus Andronicus,* II. iii. 15.

97. [What part of the verb is *com* here?]

98. See *Com.* 959.

100. *the spicy nut-brown ale* = Shakspere's "gossips' bowl" (*Midsummer Night's Dream,*
II. i. 47), says Warton.   This beverage consisted of " ale, nutmeg, sugar, toast, and roasted crabs
or apples ; it was called Lamb's Wool.   In Fletcher's *Faithful Shepherdess* it is styled ' the
spiced wassail-bowl.' "

> *to the,* &c.   Comp. v. 90.

102. *fairy Mab.*   See Mercutio's description of her in *Romeo and Juliet,* I. iv. 54.
See also Keightley's *Fairy Mythology.*

> *junkets,* also written juncates, = sweetmeats, dainties.   Cotgrave, in his definition
of *dragée,* speaks of "*jonkets,* comfits, or sweetmeats, served in the last course for stomach
closers."   Then = any delicacy.   See *Taming of the Shrew,* III. ii. 250.   *Faerie Queene,*
V. iv. 49 :

> " And beare with you both wine and *juncates* fit,
>   And bid him eate."

Comp. Ital. *giuncata* = cream-cheese.   Then = a feast, a merrymaking.   So the verb.
"Job's children," says South, *apud* Johnson, "*junketed* and feasted together often," &c. :
and ."the Apostle would have no revelling or *junketing.*"   In Devonshire and Cornwall
junkets is still in use, for curds and clouted cream.

16. 103. See *Merry Wives of Windsor*, V. v. 95 :

" As you trip, still pinch him to your time."

According to the old ballad of *Robin Goodfellow*, servant-maids were only so pinched if they deserved it :

" When house or hearth doth sluttish lie,
I pinch the maids both black and blue,
And from the bed the bedcloths I
Pull off, and lay them nak'd to view."

See also Butler's *Hudibras*, III. i. 1413 ; and especially Ben Jonson's *Entertaynment* at *Althorpe* :

" When about the cream-bowles sweete," &c.

On the other hand, clean and tidy servants were rewarded. See Dryden's *Fables*, *The Wife of Bath, her tale* :

" The dairy maid expects no fairy guest
To skim the bowls, and after pay the feast ;
She sighs and shakes her empty shoes in vain,
No silver penny to reward her pain."

On which Bell quotes from Bishop Corbett's ballad, *The Faerye's Farewell* :

" And though they sweepe theyr hearths no less
Than mayds were wont to doe,
Yet who of late for cleanliness
Finds sixpence in her shoe?

Compare particularly in *Midsummer Night's Dream*, II. i., the conversation between Fairy and Puck.

104. Two stories seem here run into one *as regards the grammar*: (1) the story of how Will o' the Wisp misled the swain ; (2) the story of the servant spirit. Otherwise, if *led* is to be taken as a predicate, there is no subject to *tells*. But the confusion of the two stories is so awkward, that it is perhaps better to take *led* so. Milton might use " tells " for " he tells,"— that is, might regard the pronoun as superfluous, as indeed it etymologically is (for the final *s* is the sign of the third person in the present tense), and in Latin and Greek is practically. In *Par. Reg.* i. 85 he uses *am* for *I am*. So *dost* is used for *dost thou ;* so *hast, didst,* &c.

The 1645 Edition reads :

" And by the Friar's lantern led."

friars lanthorn. According to Mr. Keightley, Milton is guilty here of confounding two very different beings, viz. Friar Rush and Jack o' the Lanthorn. " It was probably the name Rush, which suggested rushlight, which caused Milton's error." Scott, in a note on *Marmion*, makes a like blunder : " Friar Rush, *alias* Will o' the Wisp." Friar Rush " haunted houses, not fields." " He is the Brüder Rausch of Germany, the Broder Ruus of Denmark." For *Jack o' the Lanthorn* (the Scotch Spunkie) see *Comus*, 432 ; *Paradise Lost*, ix. 634-42. This *ignis fatuus* was also called Meg with the Wad.

105. Comp. Butler's *Hudibras*, III. i. 1407 :

" Thou art some paltry blackguard spright
Condemn'd to drudgery in the night," &c.

Burton's *Anat. Mel.* I. ii. 1, subsect. 1: "A bigger kind there is of them ["terrestrial devils "], called with us *hobgoblins* and *Robin Goodfellows*, that would in those superstitious

R

times grind corn for a mess of milk, cut wood, or do any kind of drudgery work," &c. &c. Comp. Scotch "brownie." See Reginald Scott's *Discoverie of Witchcrafte,* IV. ch 10; Warner's *Albion's England,* ch. 91.

16. 105. [*Swet.* Explain this form of the pret.]

107. *ere.* See note, *Hymn Nat.* 86.

108. *hath.* The old Southern inflection survived in this word after it had for the most part disappeared from the written language. Milton does not use the form *has.*

In *Grim, the Collier of Croydon,* Robin Goodfellow " enters with a flail."

109. [What does *end* mean here ?]

110. *lies him down.* So "sits him down," &c. See above, line 25.

lubbar. See *Fairy Myth.* The fairy in *Midsummer Night's Dream* addresses Puck as " Thou *lob* of spirits," II. i. 16. In Fletcher's *Knight of the Burning Pestle,* III. i. : " There is a pretty tale of a witch that had a giant to be her son, that was called Lob Lie-by-the-fire." (Comp. "stretch'd out all the chimney's length.") Connect with it loby, looby, lubbard, lubberkin, lob-cock, lob-coat.

111. *chimney* = fire-place. Comp. chimney-piece. So Shakspere, *Cymbeline,* II. iv. 80: "The *chimney* is south the chamber." The word comes to us through the French, from the Latin *caminus.* In the *Turke and Gowin* (*Bishop Percy's MS. Fol.* i. 98) it is used for a *grate,* a sort of huge brazier:

> " Then there stood amongst them all
> A *chimney* in the kinges hall
> With barres mickle of pride ;
> Then was laid on in that stond
> Coals and wood that cost a pound,
> That upon it did abide."

113. *crop-full.* Specially, *crop* is the craw or first stomach of fowls.

114. See *Paradise Lost,* v. 7.

115. *Thus don the tales.* For grammatical construction compare Shakspere, *Tempest,* I. ii. 379.

116. [In what grammatical relation does this verse stand to *creep* ?]

117. Milton himself showed this variety of taste. His residence at the "upland hamlet" of Horton was diversified by visits to the " towered city" of London.

then (not when the tales are over and the tellers in bed, but) = at some other time. He is not describing one long day, but the pleasures which one day or another might entertain *L'Allegro.*

120. *weeds.* This word was not confined to a widow's dress in the seventeenth century. See Shakspere, *passim.* The phrase "weeds of peace" occurs in *Troilus and Cressida,* III. iii. 239.

triumphs = " public shows or exhibitions, such as masques, pageants, processions. Lord Bacon, describing the parts of a palace, says of the different sides : ' The one for feasts and *triumphs,* and the other for dwelling.' " (*Nares.*) See Bacon's *Essay on Masques and Triumphs. Sams. Agon.* 1312.

121. *store.* See *Prothal.* l. 33.

122. *influence.* See note, *Hymn Nat.* 71.

17. 123. Probably the poet is here drawing from what he had read rather than from anything he had seen or heard. What the Tournaments were for " arms " in the old Romance days, that were the Parliaments of Love for " wit."

125. As a specimen of the marriage galeries here referred to, see Ben Jonson's *Hymenæi, or the Solemnities of Masque and Barriers at a Marriage.* See also the last scene of *As You Like It.*

126. See Jonson's *Hymen. :* " Entered Hymen . . . in a saffron-coloured robe, his under

vestures white, his socks yellow, a yellow veil of silk on his left arm, his head crowned with roses and marjoram, in his right hand a torch of pine-tree."

17. 126. *taper.* See *Hymn Nat.* 202.

127. *Pomp,* &c. These were various forms of entertainment highly popular in the early part of the seventeenth century. They were all the rage at the court. Inigo Jones, Ben Jonson, and others, each in his way, assisted in the "getting-up" of them. The Queen of James I. delighted to take a part in them. See especially Jonson's *Entertainments.* See also Shakspere, *Tempest,* IV. i. ; *Henry VIII.* I. iv. ; *Romeo and Juliet,* I. iv. ; *Winter's Tale,* IV. iv. "The King," says Armado, in *Love's Labour Lost,* V. i. 117, "would have me present the princess, sweet chuck, with some delightful ostentation, or show, or pageant, or antique, or firework." See also Milton's own *Comus* and *Arcades.*

Revelry. Revels was both a special and a generic term. In the general sense, "a master of the revels was appointed at the court in 1546." Todd quotes Minshen's definition of revels : " sports of daouncing, masking, comedies, tragedies, and such like, used in the king's house, the houses of court or of other great personages."

128. See Warton's *Hist. Eng. Poet.* ii.

130. See *Hymn Nat.* 183.

132. Jonson, educated at Westminster School, and for a time at Cambridge, and much given to classical studies subsequently, was held in high esteem for his learning. He had attempted to introduce into the English drama the observance of the so-called unities, so great was his affection for the classical drama. His learning is not unfrequently so lavishly displayed as to render him liable to the charge of pedantry. At the time *L'Allegro* was written, he had outlived his popularity as a play-writer. His *New Inn,* brought out in 1630, was received with derision. But he was still the leading figure in the world of letters. He died in 1637.

sock. Lat. *soccus.* Contrast " buskin'd stage," *Il Pens.* 102. " Or when thy socks were on " occurs, as Warton notes, in Ben Jonson's recommendatory verses prefixed to the Shakspere Folio of 1623.

133. Gray writes in the same strain. See *Progress of Poesy,* l. 84. The one recognised form of learning in the seventeenth and eighteenth centuries was the classical. Shakspere, having comparatively little of that, was regarded as altogether unlearned. He was " Fancy's child." The romantic drama, of which he was the supreme master, differed much from that drama which the scholarship of Milton's day admired : it seemed lawless and rude. Hence "his native wood-notes *wilde*" are spoken of. At the same time, that Milton admired him profoundly appears from his *Epitaph on the admirable dramatic poet William Shakspeare.* See also what is said of Shakspere in the *Theatrum Poetarum,* by Milton's nephew, who was probably assisted by his uncle, 1675. See Pope's *Imitat. of Horace's Ep.* II. i. :

> " Not one but nods and talks of *Jonson's art,*
> Of *Shakespear's nature,* and of Cowley's wit."

134. *warble.* See *Hymn Nat.* 97.

135. *eating cares.* Horace's "mordaces sollicitudines."

136. *lap.* " Lapt in proof," *Macbeth,* I. ii. 54, &c. Spenser, too, uses the word.

Lydian aires. Of the three prevailing Greek " modes," or musical styles (the Lydian, the Phrygian, the Dorian), the Lydian was soft and voluptuous. See Dryden's *Alexander's Feast,* l. 79. Spenser's *Faerie Queene,* III. i. 40 :

> " And all the while sweet Musicke did divide
> Her looser notes with *Lydian harmony.*"

137. Comp. Horace's "Verba loquor socianda chordis " (Od. IV. ix. 4).

139. *bout* = bend, turn : here a musical passage.

140. [What part of the sentence is *long* ?]

141. [How would you explain the apparent contradiction between " wanton " and " heed," between " giddy " and " cunning ? "]

17. 143. In every soul—indeed in all creation—there is harmony, but for the most part it lies imprisoned and bound, so that it cannot be heard. The sweetness of the music described in the text is to be such that it shall set free this prisoner, and make its voice audible. See Hooker's *Eccles. Pol.* v. 38 : "Touching musical harmony, whether by instrument or voice, it being but of high and low in sounds a due proportionable disposition, such notwithstanding is the force thereof, and so pleasing effects it hath in that very part of man which is most divine, that some have been hereby induced to think that the soul itself by nature is, or hath in it, harmony." By "some" Hooker means Plato. See *Phæd.* cap. xxxviii. *Merchant of Venice*, V. i. 61 :

> " There's not the smallest orb which thou behold'st
> But in his motion like an angel sings,
> Still quiring to the young-eyed cherubins ;
> Such harmony [*i.e.* a like harmony] is in immortal souls,
> But whilst this muddy vesture of decay
> Doth grossly close it, we cannot hear it."

See also *Hymn Nat.* stanza 13.

145. *self* is here, as it seems to be primarily, a substantive.

heave his head. *Samson Agonistes*, 197 ; *Paradise Lost*, i. 211 ; *Comus*, 885.

149. In our older English writers, as in our modern colloquial language, the perfect infinitive is used to express a result or a purpose which has not been attained. See *Hamlet*, V. i. 268 :

> " I thought thy bride-bed *to have deck'd*, sweet maid."

Paradise Lost, i. 40:

> " He trusted *to have equall'd* the most High,
> If he opposed."

Ivanhoe : " It was his purpose to have rendered the experiment as complete as possible."

150. *Eurydice.* See *Il Pens.* The story is exquisitely told by Virgil in *Georg.* iv. It is prettily retold by some old late medieval poet in a strange romantic form.

151. Comp. close of Marlowe's *Passionate Shepherd to his Love*, in the *Golden Treasury.*

IL PENSEROSO.

1. BOWLE quotes from Sylvester, the translator of *Du Bartas*:

> " Hence, hence, false pleasures, momentary joyes,
> Mocke us no more with your illuding toyes."

2. That is, the offspring of unmixed folly. So in Hesiod's *Theogony* the brood born of Night have no father : " She bare loathed Fate and black Destiny, and Death ; and she bare Sleep, and ever and anon the tribe of Dreams."

> " οὔτινι κοιμηθεῖσα θεὰ τέκε Νὺξ ἐρεβεννή."

(*Theog.* 211–13.) She bare others also ; and so too, it would seem, one of her daughters, Eris, bare children, having neither husband nor paramour.

3. *bested.* This word is usually a participle, as in *Isaiah* viii. 21 : "They shall pass through it, hardly *bestead* and hungry." So in Chaucer, Gower, Spenser, Shakspere, &c. See *Bible Word-Book.* In the sense of it the simple verb also is commonly used, as in Shakspere, *Two Gentlemen of Verona*, II. i. 119 ; *Measure for Measure*, I. iv. 18, &c. ; or to stand instead, as in 1 *Henry VI.* IV. vi. 31 :

> " The help of one stands me in little *stead.*"

Except in certain phrases, *stead*, both as a substantive and a verb, has fallen out of use. It survives in compos. in *stead*fast, home*stead*, *steady*, in*stead*, Hamp*stead*, bed*stead*.

17. 4. *fixed.* See *Faerie Queene*, IV. vii. 16.

6. *fond* = foolish, as usually in Old English, and still in the North. "Thou *fond* mad woman." (*Richard II.* V. ii. 95.) So *Coriol.* IV. i. 26. "Fondling" is used both as a term of endearment, and for a fool. In Wickcliffe and in Chaucer occurs the form *fonned*, which is the participle of *fonnen*, to be foolish (found in Chaucer, the *Townley Mysteries*, &c. Scotch *fon*). Then *fond* = foolishly affectionate, "loving not wisely." In our present usage the word has acquired a better meaning, the idea of folly originally so predominant in it being diminished. The first meaning of *dote* is to be silly. "Most loving mere folly," sings Amiens, in *As You Like It*, II. vii. 181. As to the passive participle being used (*i.e. fonned*, not *fonnend*, or *fonning*), comp. "dot*ed* ignorance," in *Faerie Queene*, I. viii. 34. On the other hand, from "mad," = to be mad, we have "madding," as in *Paradise Lost*, vi. 210; Gray's *Elegy*, &c.

shapes. See *L'Allegro*, 4.

18. 7. Warton refers to Sylvester's Cave of Sleep in *Du Bartas*.

thick. Comp. Knolles *apud* Johnson : "They charged the defendants with their small shot and Turkey arrows as *thick* as hail." [What other meanings has *thick*?]

9. *likest. Like*, though a monosyllable, does not in our present English form its degrees of comparison by inflection.

10. *Morpheus.* See *Class. Dict.*

Morpheus train = what Ovid calls "populus natorum mille suorum" (*Metam.* xi. 634).

pensioners. See *Midsummer Night's Dream*, II. i. 10.

12. Bowle thought that Milton took the idea of his Melancholy from Albert Dürer's design of Melancholia.

15. Comp. *Exod.* xxxiv. 29–35.

18. *Prince Memnons sister:* i.e. some beautiful Ethiopian princess. Another son of Tithonus and Eos, viz. Emathion, is mentioned, but, it would seem, no daughter. Memnon was famous for his beauty.

19. = Cassiepea, Cassiopea, or Cassiope, as the name is variously written. The usual story is that it was her daughter Andromeda's beauty that she declared to surpass that of the Nereides, for which presumption her country was visited with a deluge and a sea monster, and these curses withdrawn only on the condition that Andromeda should be given up to the monster. See Ovid. *Met.* iv. 670: "The unpitying Ammon had bidden that innocent Andromeda should there pay the penalty for her mother's tongue." The story, as told by Milton, is given by Apollodorus. For so boasting of herself "she was represented, when placed among the stars, as turning backwards." Manilius, in his *Astronomics* (i. 352), speaks of her punishment, not of her crime :

"Cassiepia
In pœnas signata suas."

starr'd, not star-crowned, but made or transformed into stars. Aratus describes this constellation. See Cicero's translation, 187 *et seq.*

22. *higher far.* [What part of speech is *higher* here? Comp. "high-born."]

23 Milton here mythologizes for himself. See *L'Allegro*, l. 2.

of yore. Comp. "of late," "of old," &c.

25. *Solitary Saturn.* According to the old story he made himself so, as a father, by devouring his offspring.

Hesiod, in his *Theogony*, 454, mentions Histia as one of his children by Reia.

29. *Ida.* See *Class. Dict.* There were several mountains of this name. [Which one is meant here?]

30. *yet.* In our present English, when *yet*, in the sense it has here, [what is that? and

what other senses has *yet ?*] is placed before the verb of its sentence, we qualify it by prefixing *as*. We could say either "while there was not yet any fear of Jove," or "while as yet there was no fear of Jove." This *as* serves to distinguish the sense of *yet*. (In the other case the position of the word distinguishes its sense.) For the older English usage, comp. with this passage, *Taming of the Shrew*, Induct. i. 96: "For *yet* his honour never heard a play," &c. So A. Phillips to Charlotte Pulteney (apud *Golden Treas.*):

> " Simple maiden, void of art,
> Babbling out the very heart,
> *Yet* abandon'd to thy will,
> *Yet* imagining no ill,
> *Yet* too innocent to blush."

18. 30. *i.e.* during the Golden Age. Comp. *Paradise Lost*, x. 584. For a picture of Saturn after the fear of Jove had been realized, see Keats' *Hyperion*.

32. *stedfast*. See notes on *bested, Il Pens.* 3; *shamefac't, H. Nat.* III.

demure. Comp. Spenser's "With countenance *demure* and modest grace." In form and derivation, comp. *debonair*. See note, *L'All.* 24. The root of the latter part of the word appears in "moral," &c. It is quite distinct from that of "demur." See Trench's *Select Gloss*.

33. *all* may be an adjective here : comp. Horace's "*totus* in illis" (1 *Sat.* ix. 2): or it may be an adverb (see note, p. 66), qualifying the adjectival phrase *in a robe of*.

darkest grain = "not, as Webster supposes, a mourning black, or a dull neutral tint, but the violet shade of purple." See especially Marsh's *Lect. on the Eng. Lang.* 1st Ser. *Grain* originally = a seed, or kernel, then a small seed-like object, then any minute thing, then an insect of the genus *coccus*, "the dried body or rather ovarium of which furnishes a variety of red dyes," then one of the dyes so procured. Hence *grain* is used by Milton and other English poets for Tyrian purple. See *Paradise Lost*, xi. 240–4 :

> " Over his lucid arms
> A military vest of purple flow'd,
> Livelier than Melibœan, or the *grain*
> Of Sarra, worn by kings and heroes old
> In time of truce : Iris had dipt the woof."

Ib. v. 285, *Com.* 750 ; Chaucer's "scarlet *en grayn* ;" Shakspere's "purple *in grain*" (*Midsummer Night's Dream*, I. ii. 95). As "the colour obtained from kermes, or grain, was peculiarly durable, or, as it is technically called, a fast or fixed dye," *in grain* was used for deep-dyed, "fast," fixed.

35. *stole*. The *stola* was the characteristic robe of the Roman lady. Exactly, it was a "tunic," short-sleeved, flounced, made so long that it reached the ground, and also fell in a broad fold over the girdle. (Under it was worn the *tunica interior*, over it, out of doors, the *palla*.) But Spenser, as Mr. Keightley remarks, uses *stole* for hood or veil (see *Faerie Queene*, I. i. 4 ; *Colin Clout's come Home again*, 495 ; and in that sense, probably, Milton uses it here. He has already mentioned a robe "flowing with majestic train." The ecclesiastical stole was, and is, something very different—"a long narrow scarf, with fringed ends." (See *Morte D'Arthur*, Globe Edition, p. 373 : "And then the good man and Sir Launcelot went into the chapel, and the good man took a *stole* about his neck," &c.) The robe which the priests of Isis wore was the Roman *stola*. Comp. *Hymn Nat.* 220.

Cipres lawn = crape. Crape may not be derived from "Cipres" (= Cyprus), as some say (but rather from Fr. *crêpe*, Lat. *crispus*), but the two words seem to have denoted the same thing. See *Twelfth Night*, III. i. 132. "Both black and white were made, as at present, but the black was more common, and was used for mourning, as it is still" (*Nares*). See Jonson's *Every Man in his Humour*, I. iii. &c. See Webster's *Malcontent*, III. i. :

"Why, dost think I cannot mourn, unless I wear my hat in *cipres*, like an alderman's heir ?" Shirley's *Love Tricks :*

> "*Gong.* Goddess of Cyprus——
> *Bub.* Stay, I do not like that word Cyprus, for she'll think I mean to make hatbands of her."

Lawn is here used generally, not in its technical sense. It is often distinguished from *cyprus*, as in Autolycus' song, *Winter's Tale*, IV. iv. 220 :

> " *Lawn* as white as driven snow,
> *Cyprus* black as e'er was crow."

" Cobweb lawn, or the very finest lawn," says Nares, "is often mentioned with Cyprus, and, what is singular, Cotgrave has made *crespe* signify both." See Jonson's *Epig.* 73. Comp. at a later time Pope's *Mor. Ess.* i. 135-6 :

> " 'Tis from high life high characters are drawn,
> A saint in *crape* is twice a saint in *lawn;*"

lawn being used for bishops, *crape* for the other clergy.

18. 36. [What is meant by *decent ?*] Comp. Horace's "gratiæ *decentes*" (*Od.* I. iv. 6), "decentes malas " (*Od.* III. xxvii. 53),

39. Comp. Cicero's *Tusc. Disp.* V. xxiii. 65 : " Quis est omnium qui modo *cum Musis*, id est cum humanitate et cum doctrina, *habeat aliquod commercium*, qui se non hunc mathematicum [Archimedem] malit quam illum tyrannum [Dionysium]." Ovid's *Tristia*, V. x. 35 :

> " Exercent illi *sociæ commercia linguæ;*
> Per gestum res est significanda mihi."

Hamlet, III. i. 110 : " Could beauty, my lord, have better *commerce* than with honesty ?"

41. [What part of speech is *still* here ?]

42. See *Epitaph on William Shakspere.*

43. Comp. Gray's *Ode to Adversity :*

> " With leaden eye that loves the ground."

Spenser's *Epithal.* 234.

10. 50. See Bacon's *Essay on Gardens :* " God Almighty first planted a garden ; and indeed it is the purest of human pleasures ; it is the greatest refreshment to the spirits of man." In Marvell's *Thoughts in a Garden* (given in the *Golden Treasury*), one seems to see Retired Leisure recreating in its garden. Comp. *Com.* 375-80.

his. See note, *Hymn Nat.* 106.

52. *yon.* Here an adverb. The A.-S. form is *geond.* Shakspere uses the form *yond* in *Tempest*, I. ii. 409, Fol. 1623 :

> " And say what thou see'st *yond."*

The usual form, both adverb and adjective, is now "yonder." In Shakspere and Milton *yon* as an adjective is about as common as yonder. Spenser has "that yond *same*," in *Faerie Queene*, VI. xii. 18. For the dropping off of the *d*, comp. "fon," a form for "fond."

The vision is described at greater fulness in *Paradise Lost*, vi. 750-9. For the original, see *Ezek.* x.

54. Spenser's Contemplation is an old man. See *Faerie Queene*, I. x. 46.

55. *hist along* = bring silently along. See note on *Hymn Nat.* 64.

58. Comp. Horace's "Explicuit vino contractæ seria frontis " (*Sat.* II. ii. 125). *Com.* 251-2.

59. *Cynthia.* See *Class. Dict.* Spenser's *Faerie Queene*, VII. vii. 50.

19. 59. *dragon yoke.* Night's, not the Moon's, dragons are often spoken of, as in Shakspere, *Midsummer Night's Dream*, III. ii. 379: "Night's swift dragons." *Troilus and Cressida*, V. viii. 17: "The dragon wing of night." *Cymbeline*, II. ii. 48: "Yon dragons of the night." By the Latin poets Ceres is described as dragon-drawn: see Ovid, *Fast.* iv. 497: "frenatos curribus angues jungit;" and 561: "inque dracones transit." Not only here does Milton give the moon dragons; see in his *Silvarum Liber* the lines, *In obitum præsulis Eliensis*, l. 56:

> " Vidi triformem dum coercebat suos
> Frenis dracones aureis."

Ovid speaks of the moon's snow-white horses (*Fast.* i. 374).

60. *th' accustom'd oke.* The article seems to show that the poet has in his mind some particular landscape.

61. *noise.* See note, *Hymn Nat.* 97.

63. *chauntress.* Wotton calls birds "yon curious *chanters* of the wood." Comp. *Chant*icleer.

64. *eeven-song.* Comp. the cock's *matin*, *L'Allegro*, 114.

65. *unseen.* Contrast *L'Allegro*, 57.

66. *smooth-shaven green.* Comp. "short-grass'd green," Shakspere's *Tempest*, IV. i. 83. Shakspere uses both participial forms: *shaved* in 1 *Henry IV.* III. iii. 68; *shaven* in *Much Ado about Nothing*, III. iii. 145.

67. *the wandring moon.* Comp. Shelley's "Art thou pale for weariness," &c.

68. *neer her highest noon* = nearly full. Or perhaps rather in the middle of the night that is, of the moonlit hours of the night; near her highest point of ascension.

73. *plat* is a various form of plot. We still speak of a "grass plat." Comp. *flat*, *plat-form*, *plate.*

74. *curfeu* = strictly, fire-cover. See Bacon *apud* Johnson: "But now for pans, pots, *curfews*, counters, and the like, the beauty will not be so much respected so as the compound stuff is like to pass." It was commonly used for the fire-cover bell—*i.e.* the bell at whose ringing all household fires were to be put out for the night, as in *Tempest*, V. i. 40; *Lear*, III. iv. 120. In *Romeo and Juliet*, IV. iv. 4, *curfew bell* is used generally for a bell.

[What part of speech is *sound* here?]

75. = over some shore and the wide piece of water it edges.

wide-water'd. Our older writers often speak of "a water," meaning a lake or a river. See *Morte D'Arthur.* Tennyson has revived the phrase in his *Morte D'Arthur* :

> " On one side lay the ocean, and on one
> Lay a great *water*, and the moon was full."

Milton here may be thinking of the Thames.

80. Comp. *Paradise Lost*, i. 62-4.

83. *The belman* = the watchman of a later time, down to the establishment of the present police system. Herrick in one of his poems blesses his friends in the character of a bellman :

> " From noise of scare fires rest ye free,
> From murders benedicite ;
> From all mischances that may fright
> Your pleasing slumbers in the night ;
> Mercie secure ye all and keep
> The goblin from ye, while ye sleep.
> Past one o'clock, and almost two,
> My masters all, good-day to you."

For other "bellman's verses," see Chambers' *Book of Days*, i. 496.

*9. 83. *nightly* = during the night, not night by night See note on *Hymn Nat.* 179.

88. *thrice great Hermes* = Hermes Trismegistus = the Egyptian Thot or Theut, with whom the Greek Hermes was identified. This Egyptian Hermes was held in great reverence by the Neo-Platonists : he was the Word (ὁ λόγος) incarnate ; he was the source of Plato's knowledge, and of that of Pythagoras. Certain works ascribed to him (really written probably in the fourth century of our æra) were much pored over. The Hermetical Philosophy was so called after him. Probably Milton here is thinking of his *Pœmander,* a work discussing the creation of the world, the deity, the human soul, &c.

unsphear : so unthrone, *Paradise Lost,* ii. 231, &c.

90. See Plato's *Phæd. passim.*

91. *forsook.* See note, *Hymn Nat.* 98.

20. 93. = Salamanders, sylphs, nymphs, and gnomes. See *Rape of the Lock,* i. 60-4.

95. *consent.* Compare Shakspere, 1 *Henry VI.* I. i. 2-4 :

> " Ye comets,
> . . . . . scourge the bad revolting stars
> That have *consented* unto Henry's death."

Hor. *Od.* II. xvii. 22.

96. *with planet.* There was a very general belief in astrology throughout the seventeenth century. Then lived Dee, Forman, Napier, Lilly, and others of like pretensions. See Shakspere, *passim ;* Butler's *Hudibras,* &c. Dryden was a believer in the art. See Disraeli's *Curiosities of Literature.*

98. *scepter'd pall* = royal robe ; *scepter'd* may answer to Horace's " honesta " (*Ars Poet.* 278). Or perhaps the phrase = with sceptre and with pall—*i.e.* two things are expressed as one, just as often one thing is expressed as two, which latter figure is called Hendiadys. The former figure is δύο δι' ἑνός. Comp. above, l. 75.

pall is = the Latin *palla.* See Hor. *Ars Poet.* 8. The great tragedy robe was called ξυστίς.

99. Œdipus and Pelops and their respective houses, and the various heroes who fought before Troy, formed the three most popular subject-matters of Attic Tragedy.

100. [What is meant by the epithet of *divine* applied to Troy ?]

101. It may be supposed that Milton has in his mind's eye *Othello, King Lear, Hamlet.*

102. *buskind* = Latin *cothurnatus.* The Greek κόθορνος, Latin *cothurnus,* was a boot with high heels designed to add to the stature, and so to the dignity, of the Tragic Actor. The comic *soccus* was a sort of slipper. Horace uses these words to represent the dramas to which they respectively belonged ; as in *Ars Poetica,* 80 :

> " Hunc *socci* cepere pedem grandesque *cothurni.*"

i.e. both comedy and tragedy adopted the iamb. See *Ib.* 280, 1 *Sat.* I. v. 64. The *cothurnus* or buskin was also worn by hunters, and so by Diana and her nymphs. Hence "silver-buskin'd nymphs" in *Arcades,* 33.

104. *from his bower.* Comp. "the Muses' bower" in Sonnet III.

105. *Orpheus.* See *L'Allegro,* 145.

109. Chaucer's *Squire's Tale* breaks off in the middle. Spenser continues and finishes the story in his own style in *Faerie Queene,* IV. ii. and iii. It was also finished by one John Lane, a friend of Milton's father ; of which version there are MS. copies in the British and in the Ashmolean Museums. (See Masson's *Life of Milton,* p. 42.) This tale, then, must have been particularly well known to Milton. Amongst the *Canterbury Tales* it is conspicuous for a certain Oriental richness of invention and of ornament.

110. *Cambuscan.* The accentuation of this word here is strange. Of course the word = Cambus Khan. Chaucer, though he writes the two words as one, gives no accent to the middle syllable, *e.g. :*

> " This noble King was cleped Cambuscan."

20. 111. See Chaucer, 10,340:

> " This noble Kyng, this Tartre, this Cambynskan,
> Hadde tuo sones by Eltheta his wyf,
> Of which the eldest highte Algarsyf,
> That other was icleped Camballo ;
> A doughter had this worthi King also
> That yongest was, and highte Canace," &c.

112. *to wife.* Comp. *Hamlet,* I. ii. 14 ; *Exod.* ii. 1 ; Bunyan: " He hath a pretty young man *to his son ;" Faerie Queene,* I. i. 28 : "With God *to friend ;"* I. x. 66 :

> " Whereof Georgos he thee gave *to name,"* &c.

113. *vertuous.* See *Mark* v. 30, *Luke* vi. 19. *Com.* 165, "The virtue of this magic dust," &c. We still say " by virtue of" = by the power of.

By virtue of the *ring* the wearer could understand the language of birds and the medicinal power of all herbs. The *mirror* would reflect the falseness of subjects and of lovers. The *steed* could convey any one who knew how to manage it any distance in one day. Besides these wonders there was a sword which could cut through anything, and the wounds inflicted by which could be healed only by being stroked with the flat of it.

115. *did ride.* "The words *do* and *did*, which so much degrade in present estimation the line that admits them, were in the time of Cowley little censured or avoided." (Johnson.)

116. *great bards beside* = Boiardo, Ariosto, Tasso, Spenser, &c. Milton in his youth was deeply read in these poets of romance : he purposed to adopt a romantic subject for his own great poem ; see his Latin poem to Mansus in his *Sylvarum Liber.* His acquaintance with these writers appears often ; see *Paradise Lost,* i. 580–7, ix. 25–43.

120. See Spenser's Letter to Sir W. Raleigh, "expounding his whole intention" in the course of the *Faerie Queene.* Milton, in his *Areopagitica,* speaks of Spenser as " our sage and serious Spenser, whom I dare be thought to hold a better teacher than Scotus or Aquinas." The Italian romantic poets profess a high moral purpose. " Both Tasso and Ariosto pretend to an allegorical and mysterious meaning ; and Tasso's *Enchanted Forest,* the most conspicuous fiction of the kind, may have been here intended." (Warton.)

Bowle quotes from Seneca, *Epist.* 114 : " In quibus plus intelligendum est quam audiendum."

121. *pale career.* Comp. "pale rage," *Adonais,* 70, &c. Strictly speaking, these epithets are placed with the wrong substantives. Comp. Æschylus' *Agam.* 152 : "νεικέων τέκτονα σύμφυτον," &c.

122. Contrast *L'Allegro,* 61, 62. See *Romeo and Juliet,* III. ii. 10 ·

> " Come, *civil* night,
> Thou sober-*suited* matron all in black," &c.

123. *trickt.* See *Lyc.* 170. Sandys *apud* Johnson:

> " Their heads are *trickt* with tassels and with flowers."

Locke " People lavish it profusely in *tricking* up their children in fine cloathes, and yet starve their minds." " Trick't and blaz'd " is a heraldic phrase ; see Beaumont and Fletcher's *Night-Walker,* II. vii.

frounc't = frizzled and curled. See *Faerie Queene,* I. iv. 14:

> " Some *frounce* their curled heare in courtly guise ;
> Some pranke their ruffes ; and others trimly dight
> Their gay attyre."

French *froncer,* to wrinkle, plait ; originally perhaps to wrinkle the brow, from Latin *frons*

Flounce is but another form of *frounce*. In the *Romaunt of the Rose*, 860, we have "her forehead *frounceles.*"

20. 124. *Attick boy* = Cephalus. See Ovid's *Metam.* vii. 701-4.

125. *cherchef't* = kerchiefed. The *ker* = cur, in curfew. See *Merry Wives of Windsor*, III. iii. 62: "A plain *kerchief*, Sir John; my brows become nothing else."

127. *usher'd.* See *Paradise Lost*, iv. 355.

128. [What part of the sentence is *his fill?*]

132. *flaring* = strictly, fluttering. Comp. German *flackern*. Comp. flaunt.

133. *twilight groves.* See *Hymn Nat.* 188, "twilight ranks;" *Arcad.* 99.

134. *Sylvan.* See *Paradise Lost*, iv. 705:

> " In shadier bower,
> More sacred and sequester'd, though but feign'd,
> Pan or *Sylvanus* never slept; nor nymph
> Nor Faunus haunted."

Com. 268. Virg. *Georg.* ii. 493:

> " Fortunatus et ille, deos qui novit agrestes,
> Panaque Silvanumque senem Nymphasque sorores."

shadows brown. See Pope *apud* Johnson:

> " From whence high Ithaca o'erlooks the floods,
> Brown with o'erhanging shades and pendent woods."

135. *monumental oake.* Chaucer (*Assembly of Fowles*, 175), and Spenser after him (*Faerie Queene*, I. i. 8), calls it "the builder oak."

21. 136. *with heaved stroke.* See v. 121.

140. *profaner* = somewhat, or at all profane; = profan-*ish*, if there were such a word. Such is frequently the force in Latin also of what is called the comparative degree: thus *senior* = somewhat old, elderly, &c.

141. *gareish.* See *Romeo and Juliet*, III. ii. 25: "the garish sun." Lilly, Drayton, and others use the word in a good sense. (See *Halliwell.*) There is an old English verb *gare*, to stare. "It is a favourite word with Drayton." (Todd.)

142. See the description of the sleep-enticements in the palace of Morpheus, *Faerie Queene*, I. i. 41. Amongst these there is a

> " Murmuring winde, much like the sowne
> Of swarming bees."

See Virg. *Ecl.* i. 56. Comp. *Paradise Regained*, iv. 247.

144. *sing.* This verb has a very comprehensive force. Comp. Shaksp. *Rich. II.* II. i. 263:

> " We hear this fearful tempest *sing.*"

145. *consort.* See *Hymn Nat.* 132. [Who are *they?*]

146. Comp. Ovid, a favourite author with Milton, *Metam.* xi. 602-4:

> " Saxo tamen exit ab imo
> Rivus aquæ Lethes, per quem cum murmure labens
> Invitat somnos crepitantibus unda lapillis."

dewy-feather'd. For *dewy* comp. Shakspere's "golden dew of sleep" (*Richard III.* IV. i. 84), "the honey-heavy dew of slumber" (*Julius Cæsar*, II. i. 230), &c. Explain this metaphor. For *feathered*, comp. Virgil's "volucris somnus," *Æn.* ii. 794, vi. 702. Ovid (*Met.*

xi. 650) speaks of the noiseless wings of Morpheus, who in his account is one of the subalterns of Somnus :

> " Ille volat, nullos strepitus facientibus alis,
>   Per tenebras."

These wings are in ancient bas-reliefs sometimes those of a butterfly (some say, a bat), sometimes those of an eagle ; they are sometimes attached to Sleep's temples as well as his shoulders. See a paper by Bishop Thirlwall in *Philolog. Mus.* ii. 471, on the address to Sleep in the *Philoctetes* of Sophocles. Though the words *dewy* and *feathered* are printed as one, yet it is possible they may not make a compound idea. In other words, *dewy* is not an epithet of *feathers* contained in *feathered*, but rather a co-equal epithet of sleep. Comp. *Com.* 553, where *drowsy* does not qualify or modify *frighted*, but is, co-ordinately with *frighted*, an epithet of *steeds*. It is possible, however, that a compound idea may be meant ; i.e. *dewy-feather'd sleep* = sleep with dewy feathers, that is, with feathers that scatter or besprinkle with dew, like the sleep god's bough in *Æn.* v. 854 : " Lethæo rore madens vique soporatus Stygia." Comp. *Paradise Lost*, v. 285-7 :

> " Like Maia's son he stood
> And shook his plumes, that heavenly fragrance fill'd
> The circuit wide."

21. 147. Sleep is generally described by poets as sending forth Dreams as his ministers. See Ovid, *Met.* xi. *sub fin.* ; Spenser's *Faerie Queene*, I. i. 39-44. (In *Macbeth*, II. i. 50, Dreams and Sleep are in opposition.) Here he comes himself, attended by a Dream. This Dream he bears on his wings, just as the Sprite sent by Archimago bears the Dream with which Morpheus provides him (*F. Q.* I. i. 44) :

> " And on his litle wings the dreame he bore
>   In hast unto his Lord."

As he stands over the reposing poet, the Dream is to hover to and fro before him, and present various images to the eyes of the sleeper. Such seems to be the meaning of this extremely difficult passage ; but it does not satisfactorily explain *at his wings*. If only it were possible, it would be better to take the whole four lines as referring to the Dream only, *i.e.* to take *his wings* = the Dream's wings, and *displayed* as qualifying *wings* ; but *at* makes a seemingly insuperable impediment. *Wave at* could scarcely be used for " wave at me " = wave near. Warton proposes to strike out *at !* Budgell, who in *Spect.* No. 425 quotes admiringly this passage, writes " wave *with* his wings," without authority. See a valuable note by Mr. Payne in *Notes and Queries* for July 1868.

   151. [What part of the verb is *breathe* here ?]
   153. [What is the force of *good* here ? What substantive does it qualify ? See *Lycid.* 184.]
   154. See *Arcades*, where a " Genius of the Wood " describes his functions, and also " sweet music breathes " in two songs.
   155. [What is the force of *due* here ?]
   156. *the studious cloysters pale* = the precincts of some retirement which is devoted, or should be so, to study and learning, and also, as he goes on to describe, to religious services = a university, or a cathedral establishment. He is probably thinking of old 'St. Paul's. St. Paul's cloisters in the strict sense of the word (described by Stowe) were pulled down in 1549, by orders of the Duke of Somerset, who, it is said, wanted the stones from them for a palace in the Strand (the old Somerset House).

   pale = enclosure. We still speak of " the English *pale* " in Ireland, and of " the *pale* of the Church."
   157. [What is the grammatical subject of *love* ?]
   high embowed roof, &c. Is he thinking of old St. Paul's, or of Westminster Abbey ?

The details scarcely suit King's College Chapel. Milton was one of the latest true lovers of Gothic architecture when the taste for it was declining, as Gray was one of the earliest when the taste was reviving.

21. 157. Comp. a once widely popular passage of Congreve's *Mourning Bride*:

> " How reverend is the face of this tall Pile,
> Whose ancient Pillars rear their marble heads
> To bear aloft its arch'd and pond'rous roof,
> By its own weight made stedfast and immoveable,
> Looking tranquillity."

158. *massy.* Milton and Shakspere do not use the form *massive.*

proof, i.e. proof against (= able to bear) the enormous weight of the roof. Comp. *Coriolanus*, I. iv. 25, "with hearts more *proof* than shields." Sometimes with an adverb or adjective so used, as in *Samson Agonistes*, 134, of "a frock of mail," " adamantean proof:" with which compare *Paradise Regained*, iv. 533:

> " *Proof* against all temptation as a rock
> Of adamant."

Some editors read in the text *massy-proof.* More commonly, that against which what is spoken of is proof is mentioned, as " shame-proof," *Love's Labour Lost*, V. ii. 513 ; "star-proof," *Arcad.* 88: see also *Paradise Lost*, ix. 298 ; x. 882, &c.

159. *storied.* See *Com.* 516 ; Shakespere, *Cymb.* I. iv. 36.

dight. See *L'Allegro*, 62.

160. [What is meant by *religious* here ?] Collins borrows the word in his *Ode to Evening.* He speaks of evening's " *religious* gleams."

161. *the pealing organ.* See *Paradise Lost*, i. 708-9 ; xi. 560 ; *Hymn Nat.* 130.

blow. See *Hymn Nat.* 130.

163. *anthems.* This word radically is identical with antiphons = amœbean or alternate chanting.

164. *as* = such as, or in such a way as.

168. *the.* The article is here used generically, as in v. 156, as in our phrase "he went up to *the* university."

Hermits and hermitages are perpetually mentioned in the old romances. See *Morte D'Arthur* (Globe Ed.), p. 423, &c. ; *Faerie Queene*, &c.

172. See *Epitaph. Damon.* 150.

173. *do*, subjunctive. So above, ll. 44 and 122. In *L'Allegro*, 44, there is the indicative.

LYCIDAS.

INTRODUCTION.

Lycidas was written in the autumn of 1637, and published at Cambridge in the following year, along with other *In Memoriam* poems, some in Latin, some in Greek, some in English, by various members of the University. It would seem, from the opening lines, that Milton had previously formed a resolution to write no more poetry for the present—to write no more till he thought himself better fitted to do so ; but "bitter constraint and sad occasion dear" made him break that resolution. Probably, the last piece he had produced was *Comus*, which was "presented" at Ludlow Castle in 1634.

He whose untimely death he laments in *Lycidas* was one King, a fellow-collegian and an intimate friend. King, too, was something of a poet (only Latin pieces by him are extant).

See l. 10. He was a fellow and tutor of his college, and otherwise, it would seem, a notable member of his university ; hence Father Cam is one of his chief mourners. He was designed for holy orders, as Milton himself had been once ; hence St. Peter's grief for his loss. He was drowned crossing over to Ireland. The account given in the Cambridge *In Memoriam* volume is that "haud procul a littore Britannico, navi in scopulum allisa et rimis ex ictu fatiscente, dum alii vectores vitæ mortalis frustra satagerent, immortalem anhelans in genu provolutus oransque una cum navigio ab aquis absorptus, animam deo reddidit iiii. eid. Sextilis anno Salutis MDCXXXVII. Ætatis xxv." = "not far from the British shore, when the ship was dashed on to a rock, and through the blow leaked and gaped, while the other voyagers busied themselves in vain with mortal life, he, aspiring after the immortal, threw himself upon his knees, and as he so prayed was swallowed up by the waters along with the vessel, and gave his life to God, on the 10th of August, in the year of salvation 1637, of his life twenty-five." The account Milton appears to follow in his Elegy is, that the vessel was unseaworthy, and foundered in a tranquil ocean.

This poem is full of biographical and historical, besides its high poetic, interest. It reflects clearly the dark and threatening condition of things ecclesiastical ; it portrays the frivolous state of literature ; but most especially it brings before us the poet in the great transitional stage of his life. Milton's earlier style and his later are both visible in this poem ; the author of *Comus* is perceivable, but so also is the author of *Paradise Lost*; there may be heard the sweetness of his youthful, the grandeur of his maturer notes.

22. 1. MILTON'S conceptions of a poet's work, and of the preparation needed for it, were of the highest. He was ever striving after "inward ripeness" (see *Sonnet II.*), and conscious how far he was from attaining it. This sense of his unfittedness to perform as yet a poet's high duties had determined him to write no more till he was sensible of being maturer—till "the mellowing year" had dawned. But the death of his dear friend forced him to intermit this resolve. Therefore "yet once more" would he write ; he would yet again play the poet, though he knew well his proper hour had not yet come. This seems to be the true interpretation of these often misunderstood lines. As to that resolution to preserve a poetical silence for a time, see what he says even as late as 1641, in his *Reason of Church Government :*

" Neither doe I think it shame to covnant with any knowing reader, that for some few yeers yet I may go on trust with him toward the payment of what I am now indebted, as being a work not to be rays'd from the heat of youth, or the vapours of wine, like that which flows at wast from the pen of some vulgar amorist, or the trencher fury of a riming parasite ; nor to be obtain'd by the invocation of Dame Memory and her Siren daughters, but by devout prayer to that eternall Spirit who can enrich with all utterance and knowledge, and sends out His seraphim with the hallow'd fire of His altar, to touch and purify the lips of whom He pleases. To this must be added industrious and select reading, steddy observation, insight into all seemly and generous arts and affaires ; till which in some measure be compast, at mine own peril and cost, I refuse not to sustain this expectation from as many as are not loath to hazard so much credulity upon the best pledges that I can give them."

A little attention will show how these opening words cannot well be taken to mean, as by some readers and editors they are taken, "I am about to write another *In Memoriam* poem." It is true Milton had written a piece *On the Death of a fair Infant dying of a Cough,* and also *An Epitaph on the Marchioness of Winchester;* but there is no manner of allusion to either of those poems here : laurels, and myrtles, and ivy are not funereal emblems. He should say, "I come to pluck your leaves, cypresses," if he wished to mention some sad sepulchral property : or "I come to cull flowers ' that sad embroidery wear.'" What he does say must mean, "Once more I must wear the poet's garland." (Comp. *Reas. of Ch. Gov. :* "For although a poet, soaring in the high reason of his fancies, with his *garland* and singing robes about him," &c.)

yet once more. Comus was acted at Ludlow Castle in 1634; *Arcades* at Harefield Court, probably a little earlier.

22. 1. *Laurels.* Horace calls the bay "Apollinaris" (*Od.* IV. ii. 9). See *Faerie Queene,* I. i. 9.

2. *ye Myrtles brown.* At a Greek banquet a myrtle bough was held by each guest as in his turn he sung ; *e.g.* see Aristophanes' *Clouds,* 1364 :

> "ἔπειτα δ' ἐκέλευσ' αὐτὸν ἀλλὰ μυρρίνην λαβόντα
> τῶν Αἰσχύλου λέξαι τί μοι."

and the famous Scolium :

> "ἐν μύρτου κλαδὶ τὸ ξίφος φορήσω," κ.τ.λ.

For the *brown,* comp. Horace's "pulla myrtus" (*Od.* I. xxv. 18), *à propos* of which Orelli quotes Jacob's quotation from Goethe's *Italian Travels,* "niedrige graulichgrüne Myrten," and Ovid's "nigra myrtus" (*Art. Amat.* iii. 690).

ivy. "Doctarum hederæ præmia frontium" (Hor. *Od.* I. i. 29). See Virg. *Eclog.* vii. 27, and viii. 13 :

> "Hanc sine tempora circum
> Inter victrices hederam tibi serpere lauros."

It was sacred to Bacchus.

3. *crude.* Originally = bleeding, raw, and then in various derived senses, as uncooked, unripe, &c. *Cruel* is of the same root.

4. *forc'd.* See l. 6.

5. *shatter.* See *Paradise Lost,* x. 1065 :

> "While the winds
> Blow moist and keen, *shattering* the graceful locks
> Of these fair-spreading trees."

"Here," says Warton, "is an inaccuracy of the poet ; the 'mellowing' year could not affect the leaves of the laurel, the myrtle, and the ivy ; which last is characterised before us 'never sere.'" The fact is, Milton is thinking more of "the meaning" than "the name" (see *Paradise Lost,* vii. 5) ; he is thinking more of what these leaves and berries represent—that is, poetical fruit—than of the berries and leaves themselves.

6. *Sad occasion dear.* Comp. Spenser's *Faerie Queene,* I. i. 53 : "deare constraint." Shakspere, *Hamlet,* I. ii. 182 :

> "Would I had met my *dearest* foe in heaven,
> Ere I had seen that day."

As You Like It, I. iii. 34 :

> "My father
> Hated his father *dearly.*"

Julius Cæsar, III. i. 196 :

> "Shall it not grieve thee *dearer* than thy death?"

Where see Craik's note. Horne Tooke proposes to connect the word with Ang.-Sax. *derian,* to hurt, and to make its sense of "precious" a secondary one : but *dear* is without doubt the Anglo-Saxon *deore,* cognate with Old German *tiur,* Modern German *theuer.* Perhaps, as Craik suggests, it may be supposed "that the notion properly involved in it of love, having first become generalized into that of a strong affection of any kind, had thence passed on into that of such an emotion the very reverse of love."

7. [How is the verb here in the singular ?]

to disturb your season due : i.e. to anticipate your proper season.

10. Comp. Virg. *Eclog.* x. 3.

11. *to build the lofty rhyme.* Comp. Latin "condere carmen" (Hor. *Ep.* I. iii. 24); *Ars Poet.* 436 ; and Aristophanes' πυργώσας ῥήματα σεμνά (*Frogs,* 1004). So Eur. *Suppl.* 997.

22. 11. *rhyme.* The orthography of this word arises from a false notion of a connexion between the English *rime* and the Greek *rhythm.*

Only Latin verses of King's are extant. There is a copy of Latin iambics in the *Anthologies* on the King's recovery, *Cantab.* 1632. See Warton's note.

13. *welter.* See *Hymn Nat.* 124.

to. See *Hymn Nat.* 132. Comp. Greek ὑπό with genitive or dative, and the phrase "made *to* order." Of ships *before* is generally used, as in 3 *Henry VI.* I. iv. 4.

14. *melodious tear.* The epithet may be justified by noting that Spenser calls the songs in which the Muses lament the condition of his times "the *tears* of the Muses."

15. *the Sacred Well.* See *Paradise Lost,* iii. 28. In the mountain range of Helicon, in Western Bœotia, there were two fountains sacred to the Muses, Aganippe and Hippocrene. Aganippe was the more famous. Near it was the grove of the Muses. Virgil mentions " Aonie Aganippe " (Aonia was the name of that part of Bœotia where Helicon was) as one of the special haunts of the Muses. (*Eclog.* x. 12.) Propertius sings of his mistress, that she is

" Par Aganippeæ ludere docta lyræ."

"She has skill to play as sweetly as the lyre of Aganippe :" that is, as well as the Muses. In our Elizabethan writers Helicon is very often spoken of as it were the well : *e.g.* Browne, in his *Brit. Past.*, calls it "the sacred well " (I. v. *end*). Milton seems to speak of it correctly in his *Epitaph on the Marchioness of Winchester,* 55-6 :

" Here be tears of perfect moan
Wept for thee in Helicon."

Comp. the former burden of *Theocritus'* first Idyl :

" ἄρχετε βωκολικᾶς, Μῶσαι φίλαι, ἄρχετ' ἀοιδᾶς."

and the burden of the *Epitaph. Bionis,* ascribed to Moschus :

" ἄρχετε, Σικελικαί, τῶ πένθεος ἄρχετε, Μοῖσαι."

Milton probably has in his mind in this passage the opening lines of Hesiod's *Theogony*

" Μουσάων Ἑλικωνιάδων ἀρχώμεθ' ἀείδειν,
αἵθ' Ἑλικῶνος ἔχουσιν ὄρος, μέγα τε ζάθεόν τε,
καί τε περὶ κρήνην ἰοειδέα πόσσ' ἁπαλοῖσι
ὀρχεῦνται καὶ βωμὸν ἐρισθενέος Κρονίωνος," κ.τ.λ.

" With the Muses of Helicon let us begin to sing, with them who haunt the mountain, vast and divine, of Helicon, and with tender feet dance round the dark-coloured fountain [Aganippe] and *altar of the mighty Son of Kronos*," &c. The "seat of Jove" is this altar. Curiously enough, this altar does not seem to be mentioned elsewhere. See Göttling's note on Hes. l. c. Many of Milton's commentators, not having observed, or unaware of even, Hesiod's mention of it, have accused their author of blundering. In fact, the passage gives us a very remarkable instance of the carefulness of Milton's reading. No doubt, in availing himself of Hesiod's hint, the poet wished to closely connect the Muses and their well with their great father—to connect the ministers of inspiration with its supreme author. See the extract given above from his *Reason of Church Government.* In *Paradise Lost,* i. 10-12, and iii. 25-32, he institutes a sort of analogy between the Aonian Mount and its waters, on the one hand, and Zion and its waters on the other. As "Siloa's " brook "flows fast by the Oracle of God," so here he makes the Gentile stream spring from beneath the seat of Jove.

17. *sweep the string.* So Pope :

" Descend, ye nine,
. . . and sweep the sounding lyre," &c.

22. 18. *hence.* See note, *L'Allegro,* 1.

Warton quotes "a *coy* flirting style," from the *Apology for Smectymnius.*

19. Comp. Gray's *Elegy,* st. 24.

Muse = poet. Else it would not be *he* in l. 21. See note on *Proth.* 159.

20. *lucky words* = words that wish me good luck, wish it may be well with me. See l. 22. Comp. the old Roman wish : " Sit tibi terra levis."

urn. See Ovid's *Heroid.* xi. 124, &c.

21. *as he passes.* Comp. Gray's "*passing* tribute of a sigh" (*Elegy,* st. 20). Gray was a profoundly admiring student of Milton's works.

22. *my sable shrowd* = " my black coffin" in *Twelfth Night,* II. iv. 61 ; what he has just called metaphorically "his destin'd urn." Todd quotes from a funeral Elegy of Sylvester:

" From my sad cradle to my *sable chest,*
Poore pilgrim I did finde few months of rest."

In Chaucer *chest* = coffin. Sylvester's translation of *Du Bartas* has "sable tomb." Todd notes that Sylvester, in his *Bethulian's Rescue,* uses the very phrase *sable shrowd,* but in a different sense :

" Still therefore, cover'd with *a sable shrowd,*
Hath she kept home as to all sorrow vow'd."

On *shrowd,* see *Hymn Nat.* 218.

23. *I.e.* they had been members of the same college.

25. *the high lawns.* Comp. Gray's "upland lawn" (*Elegy,* st. 7).

26. Comp. "the grey-eyed morn," *Romeo and Juliet,* II. iii. 1. See *Job* iii. 9, *marg.*

27. *we drove a field.* Gray adopts this phrase : *Elegy,* st. 7.

a field. See note on "a Maying," *L'Allegro,* 20, and *Hymn Nat.* 207.

28. The object of the principal verb is here made the subject of the dependent one. See Gray's *Elegy,* and Collins' *Ode to Evening :*

" Now air is hush'd, save where the weak-eyed bat
With short shrill shriek flits by on leathern wing,
Or where the beetle winds
His small but sullen horn,
As oft he rises 'midst the twilight path,
Against the pilgrim borne in heedless hum."

Macbeth, III. ii. 40–4 :
" Ere the bat hath flown
His cloister'd flight, ere to black Hecate's summons
The shard-borne beetle, with his drowsy hums,
Hath rung night's yawning peal," &c.

The gray-fly, also called the trumpet-fly, hums sharply at noon, or the hottest part of the day. " But by some this [Milton's gray-fly] has been thought the chaffer, which begins its flight in the evening." (Warton.) Perhaps it is better to understand noon to be meant here, the "battening," &c., referring to the evening—to something subsequent to the hearing of the gray-fly. Comp. *L'Allegro :*

" Thus done the tales, to bed they creep,
By whispering winds soon lull'd asleep."

29. *batt'ning* is of the same root as " better." It is often intransitive, as in *Coriolanus,* IV. v. 35.

22. 30. Milton wrote originally (see the first edition of *Lycidas*):

> " Oft till the ev'n-starre bright
> Towards heaven's descent had slop'd his burnisht wheel."

31. *westering.* See Chaucer's *Troil. and Cress* ii. 905. Comp. *west* in *Faerie Queene*, v *Introd.* 8

32. *ditties.* See *Paradise Lost,* "am'rous ditties."

33. *temper'd* = modulated, "set." See *Paradise Lost*, vii. 598. Warton quotes from Phineas Fletcher's *Purple Island,* IX. iii. ;

> " Tempering their sweetest notes unto thy lay."

See Hor. *Od.* IV. iii. 16, 17.

to. See l. 13.

th' oaten flute = Latin *avena.* See Virgil, *Ecl.* i. 2 :

> "Sylvestrem tenui Musam meditaris avena,"

&c. Elsewhere "arundo" (*Ecl.* vi. 8), "calamus agrestis" (*Ecl.* i. 10), "stridens stipula," in a disparaging sense (*Ecl.* iii. 27). Comp. Collins' *Ode to Evening* :

> " If aught of *oaten stop* or pastoral song," &c.

Love's Labour Lost, V. ii 913 :

> "When shepherds pipe on *oaten straws*," &c.

Hall, in his first *Satire*, says he cannot

> " Under everie bank and everie tree
> Speake rimes unto mine *oaten minstrelsie.*"

In that same *Satire* he uses "reeds" to denote Pastoral poetry.

oaten. The adjectival termination *en*, denoting "made of," was more commonly used in older English than it is now, when we use the substantive itself in the sense of the adjective formed by that addition. Of those adjectives many are obsolete ; those that survive have changed their meaning : *e.g.* silvern, leathern, golden, earthen, ashen, silken, milken, stonen, thornen, leaken, elmen, glazen. See Fielder and Sachs (*Wissensch. Grammat. der Eng. Sprache*, i. 172).

34. The *Fauni* were rural Latin gods, corresponding in many respects to the Greek *Satyrs*, and in time regarded as identical with them. Faunus, the chief of them, was identified with Pan.

with clov'n heel Faunus was represented with horns (hence Ovid calls him *bicornis*), and goat's feet. Hence Ovid (*Fast.* v. 101):

> "*Semicaper*, coleris, cinctutis, Faune, Lupercis,
> Cum lustrant celebres vellera secta vias."

Satyrs and Fauns. Comp. Virg. *Ecl.* vi. 27. This is a pastoral way of describing the University men of his time.

36. *old Damœtas* = probably W. Chappell, the Tutor of Christ's College in Milton and King's time.

23. 38. *must.* Perhaps there is a certain fine courtesy in the use of this word here instead of "mayest." The poet, having to say that his friend will never return, says that, "he is not compelled to return," rather than "he is not permitted to return." Or perhaps must = art appointed or ordained. Comp. *Hymn Nat.* 151.

> "This *must* not yet be so ;"

and *ib.* 156:
> " The wakeful trump of doom *must* thunder through the deep."

23. 39. Comp. Ov. *Met.* xi. 43.

40. *gadding.* " Envy," says Bacon, " is a *gadding* passion, and walketh the streets, and doth not keep home."

41. *echoes.* See Song to Echo in *Comus. Epitaph. Bionis,* 30 :

> " ἀχὼ δ' ἐν πέτρῃσιν ὑδύρεται ὅττι σιωπῇ
> κοὐκέτι μιμεῖται τὰ σὰ χείλεα."

Shelley's *Adonais,* stanza 15 :

> " Lost Echo sits amid the voiceless mountains,
> And feeds her grief with his remembered lay," &c.

Comp. Milton's *Ode on the Passion,* stanza 8. In Wordsworth's *Ode on Intimations of Immortality,* &c. these echoes are not "imagines " of the poetic voice, but, it would seem, of the various voices of nature :

> " I hear *the echoes* through the mountain throng."

42. *hazle copses green.* On this arrangement of words, see note to *Hymn Nat.* 187.

44. *to.* See above, l. 33.

45. *canker.* Originally the same word with cancer. It is sometimes made more precise by the addition of "worm," as in *Joel* i. 4 ; just as *taint* in the following line.

46. *weanling* = yeanling, or eanling, as is variously read : *Merchant of Venice,* I. iii. 80 ; *Paradise Lost,* iii. 434. For the first letter, comp. the pronunciations of *once, who, whole, whoop,* with their spelling : *whole* and *hale, whirl* and *hurl, worm* and *Orme's* Head ; *old* = *wold,* in *King Lear,* III. iv. 125. Sir Hugh Evans calls *woman* " oman" (*Merry Wives of Windsor,* passim). For the *ling,* comp. first*ling,* year*ling,* kit*ling,* nest*ling,* nurse*ling,* found*ling.* [Add others to this list.]

47. *wardrop.* Chaucer uses the form "ward-rope." That form is still in use in Yorkshire. (See *Halliwell.*) The order of the ingredient words in this compound is noticeable. Comp. flour-bin, fire-guard, reading-desk, &c. &c. [What is the law observable in these and such words?] The varying from the usual order in *wardrobe* is accounted for by the fact that the word comes to us in an already compounded state from the French *garde robe* (the Low Latin *garda roba*).

49. *such* = so killing.

50. Comp. *Theocr.* i. 65–9 ; Virg. *Ecl.* x. 9–12.

52. *the steep* = probably Penmaenmawr. Gray's bard stood

> " On a rock, whose haughty brow
> Frowns o'er old Conway's foaming flood."

= this steep, probably ; but the topography of *The Bard* will not bear investigation " For the Druid sepulchres, at Kerig y Druidion, in the mountains of Denbighshire, he consulted Camden's *Britannia.*" (Warton.)

54. *Mona* = certainly Anglesey here, not the Isle of Man. "It was not unfrequently described as Môn mam-Gymru : *i.e.* Mona, the nursing mother of Wales, in allusion either to its former fertility, or to its being the residence of the Druids." (*Black's Guide to North Wales.*) See the picture Tacitus gives of the Druids there urging their countrymen to oppose the Romans : " Preces diras sublatis ad cælum manibus fundentes."(*Annal.* xiv. 30.) Cromlechs abound in the island. For *shaggy top,* "it was called by the bards 'the shady island,' because it formerly abounded with groves and trees : but there is now little wood, except along the bank of the Menai." Tacitus speaks of "luci sævis superstitionibus sacri " being cut down

for purposes of defence. For the *high*, Parys Mountain is the highest eminence of the island.
" In Drayton's *Polyolbion*, Mona is introduced reciting her own history, when she mentions
her thick and dark groves as the favourite residence of the Druids." Warton takes Mona to
be the Isle of Man.

23. 55. See *A Vacation Exercise*, 98: "ancient hallow'd Dee." Spenser's *Faerie Queene*,
IV. xi. 39:

> " Dee, which Britons long ygone
> Did call divine, that doth by Chester tend."

See also *Faerie Queene*, I. ix. 4. Drayton speaks of "Dee's holiness;" he calls it
"hallowed," "the ominous flood." Higden's *Polychronicon* mentions certain wizard-like
features in this river: "Under the cite of Chestre," says John de Trevisa's translation,
"corneth [runs] the river Dee, that now to-deleth [parts] Engelond and Wales; that ryver
everych monthe chaungeth his fordes, as men of the contray tel!eth, and leveth ofte the
chanel. Bote whether the water drawe more toward Engelond other toward Wales, to what
syde that hyt be that yer, men schal habbe the wors ende and be overset, and the men of the
other syde schal habbe the betre ende and be at here above. Whanne the water chaungeth
so hys cours, hyt bodeth such happes." (*Apud* Morris' *E. E. Specimens.*) The Tiber
was thought sacred by the Latins. (See *Æn.* viii. 72.) See Tenth Song of Drayton's
Polyolbion.

wisard. See note on *Hymn Nat.* 23. Drayton calls the Weever "the wizard
river."

56. *fondly.* See note, *Il Pens.* 6.

58. [Who was this Muse?] See *Paradise Lost*, vii. 34–8.

59. *inchanting son.* See the song, "Orpheus with his lute made trees," in Shakspere s
Henry VIII. III. i. 3. Hor. *Od.* I. xii. 7–12, &c. &c.

61. See Virg. *Georg.* iv. 517–27; Ovid, *Met.* xi. 1–89, esp. 50–5:

> " Caput, Hebre, lyramque.
> Excipis . . . . .
> Jamque mare invectæ flumen populare relinquunt,
> Et Methymnææ potiuntur littore Lesbi."

the hideous roar. "The" was more emphatic in older English than it is now.

63. *swift Hebrus.* See Virg. *Æn.* i. 321. Servius blames the epithet: "Nam
quietissimus est etiam cum per hyemem crescit."

64. Shakspere, Beaumont, Fletcher, Massinger, and other bright lights of the Elizabethan age, had for some years passed away. The last representative of that great race—Ben
Jonson—had just been gathered to his fellows. The race of poets which had succeeded were of
a different breed. The dramatic period was over. There arose a tribe of light lyric poets
—Herrick, Suckling, Donne, Lovelace, Wither. It is easy to understand how, to one of
Milton's high poetic theory and purpose, the popularity of these triflers must have suggested
despair for himself and for his time.

uncessant. See *Hymn Nat.* 8.

65. *shepherd.* The metaphor is used in a different sense below, ll. 113–31.

66. Part of this phrase is Virgil's. See *Ecl.* i. 2.

thankless. Comp. Virg. *Æn.* vii. 425.

Here Milton shows what his theory was of a poet's duty in the way of preparation
for his work. See note on the opening lines of this poem.

67. *use.* This present is now almost obsolete. The pret. survives. See note on *wont*
in *Prothal.* 135.

68. As Tityrus with her name, in Virgil's *Ecl.* i. 4:

> " Tu, Tityre, lentus in umbra
> Formosam resonare doces Amaryllida sylvam."

23. 69. Comp. Lovelace's

> " When I lie tangled in her hair,
> And fetter'd to her eye,
> The birds that wanton in the air
> Know no such liberty."

Warton thinks Milton refers to certain poems of Buchanan addressed to Amaryllis and Neæra, which were well known at this time.

70. " Reward is the spur of virtue in all good acts, all laudable attempts; and emulation, which is the other spur, will never be wanting when particular rewards are proposed." (Dryden.)

71. Comp. Tac. *Hist.* iv. 6 : " Erant quibus adpetentior famæ videretur quando etíam sapientibus cupido gloriæ novissima exuitur."

74. See the discussion on " glory" in *Paradise Regained*, iii. 21–150; esp. ll. 47–70.

blaze. " For what is glory but the *blaze* of fame?" (*Paradise Regained,* iii. 47.)

75. *Fury.* It was one of the Fates or Μοῖραι or Parcæ, viz. Atropos, not one of the Furies, who was fabled to cut one's thread of life. Shakspere speaks of "the shears of Destiny." (*King John*, IV. ii. 91.) Perhaps Milton uses the word Fury here not in its special, but a general sense.

76. *thin-spun life.* See Tibull. *Eleg.* I. vii. 1, 2 :

> " Parcæ fatalia nentes
> Stamina, non ulli dissoluenda deo."

life : i.e. thread of life.

77. See Virg. *Ecl.* vi. 3 :

> " Cynthius aurem
> Vellit, et admonuit," &c.

Georg. iv. 6, 7.

79. *foil.* French *feuille*, Latin *folium.* See Spenser's *Faerie Queene*, I. iv. 4 :

> " Whose [a stately palace's] wals were high, but nothing strong or thick,
> And golden *foile* all over them displaied.'

Warton quotes Shakspere, 1 *Henry IV.* I. ii. 239 ; but the sense there is different. Perhaps it is better to connect *in the glistering foil*, &c., with *lies.*

24. 81. [What is the force of *by* here?]

82. *perfet.* This is from the French form *parfait.* So *feat* and *fact.*

84. *meed.* See l. 14.

85. *Arethuse.* See *Class. Dict.* In *Arcades* he speaks of

> " Divine Alpheus, who by secret sluice
> Stole under seas to meet his *Arethuse*."

Shelley's " Arethuse arose," &c. Virg. *Ecl.* x. 1 :

> " Extremum hunc, Arethusa, mihi concede laborem."

Æn. iii. 694, &c. *Mosch. Fr.* v. 1–8, Ed. Ahrens.

[Why *honour'd?* See *Class. Dict.* See also Virg. *Georg.* iii. 13–15.]

86. *reeds.* See l. 33.

88. *My oat proceeds, And listens,* &c. There is a carelessness of style here. Comp. *L'Allegro*, 121–2 ; *Il Penseroso*, 155–7.

90. [What is meant by *in Neptune's plea?*]

24. 93. *Every—each.* Milton often uses both these words in the same sentence, merely, it would seem, for the sake of variety. *Com.* 19:

> " Of *every* salt flood and *each* ebbing stream."

Ib. 311 :

> " I know *each* lane and *every* alley green."

Etymologically, every = ever each. [What difference is there between the usages of *each* and *every* ?]

96. *Hippotades.* See Homer's *Odyss.* x. 2 ; Ov. *Met.* xiv. 86.

97. *his dungeon.* See Virg. *Æn.* i. 50–63.

was strayed. So "was dropt," l. 191 ; " is run," *Julius Cæsar,* V. iii. 25, &c. See Abbott's *Shakesp. Gr.* § 158. This older usage is more strictly correct than our present one, which admits the transitive auxiliary " have " with these participles of intransitive verbs. The French still say " Je suis arrivé." On German usage see Wittich's *G. Gr.* § 120.

99. *Panope.* Virgil calls her Panopea, *Æn.* v. 240. [Who were her sisters? See *Georg.* i. 437. Hesiod gives their names in his *Theogony,* 240 *et seq.* See also *Faerie Queene,* IV. xi. 49.]

101. *th' eclipse.* [What is the force of *the* here?]

with may = along with, in the midst of; or, better, by a bold poetical figure, it may be instrumental.

Eclipses were believed, both by the ancients and in later ages, to be times of evil omen, and to bring a curse upon everything done during them. Thus Gloucester, in *King Lear,* I. ii. 112 *et seq.* : " These late eclipses in the sun and moon portend no good to us," &c. As to the distress with which these " swoonings " of the greater lights were regarded, see Ellis's Brand's *Popular Antiquities.* Comp. *Paradise Lost,* i. 596–9, of the sun when

> " from behind the moon
> In dim eclipse disastrous twilight sheds
> On half the nations, and with fear of change
> Perplexes monarchs."

See *Macbeth,* IV. i. 28. They were supposed to be caused by the spiteful power of witches. See *Paradise Lost,* ii. 665.

Comp. Hor. *Od.* II. xiii. and *Epod.* x. 1.

103. *went.* In our present usage *go* is opposed to *come,* and *went* to *came;* but that opposition is not radical. The old verb *wend* is connected radically with *wind,* and means merely to wind or turn. The original sense, therefore, would be to move in a serpentine manner. Comp. the use of *wind,* as in *Paradise Lost,* iii. 563–4 :

> " and *winds* with ease
> Through the pure marble air *his oblique way*
> Amongst innumerable stars."

Here *went* = simply "passed along." *Wend* and *yode* having fallen out of use, *go* and *went* serve respectively as present and perfect to each other. Comp. *am* and *was,* Latin *fero* and *tuli, tollo* and *sustuli,* Greek φέρω, ἔνεγκα, ἐνήνοχα, &c.

footing. See *Pilgrim's Progress* : " I warrant you he footed it right merrily." To insert the " it " would not suit the gravity of the present passage. See note on " *trip it,*" *L'All.* 33.

104. See description of Thamis in *Faerie Queene,* IV. xi. 27, 28: he was

> " All decked in a robe of watchet [pale blue] hew,
> On which the waves, glittering like christall glas,

> So cunningly enwoven were, that few
> Could weenen whether they were false or trew ;
> And on his head like to a coronet
> He wore, that seemed strange to common view,
> In which were many towres and castels set,
> That it encompast round as with a golden fret."

24. 104. *bonnet*, in older English, as in Scotch still, denoted a man's head-covering. See *Richard II.* I. iv. 31; *Hamlet*, V. ii. 95; *Coriolanus*, III. ii. 74. Comp. French *bonnet-à-poil, bonnet-de-police*.

    sedge. See *Tempest*, IV. i. 130:

> " You nymphs, call'd Naiads, of the windring brooks,
> With your *sedged crowns* and ever-harmless looks, &c."

105. What *figures* are here meant, has not yet been satisfactorily explained. Warburton says allusion is made "to the fabulous traditions of the high antiquity of Cambridge ;" others think, to certain natural streaks on sedge-leaves or flags "when dried, or even beginning to wither."

    106. *that sanguine flower*, &c. = the hyacinth. See Ovid, *Met.* x. 215. Phœbus, mourning for Hyacinthus dead, is not content that he should be metamorphosed into a flower:

> " Ipse suos gemitus foliis inscribit, et ai ai
> Flos habet inscriptum, funestaque littera ducta est."

    [Does *like* apply to *bonnet* or *figures* ?]

107. *pledge* = child. So *pignus* in Latin. Comp. *Titus Andronicus*, III. i. 292.

    quoth he. So "says he," "said he." The position of the pronoun in these cases serves to illustrate the meaning discovered by philology of the various endings of verbs in the numbers of each tense. These endings are, in fact, but personal signs, which have become amalgamated with the verb. "Quoth he," and such phrases, show the tendency there is to place the pronoun *after* the verb.

    109. = St. Peter.

    Archbishop Laud was at this time at the height of his power. The 'policy of "thorough" was being vigorously pursued in the state ; a kindred policy was being carried out with no less vigour in the Church. A Ritualistic reform was in course of enforcement both in England and Scotland. Against this and against all Laud's proceedings the Puritanism of this country was vehemently opposed ; and this Puritanism was the great growing, nearly full-grown, power of the day. Milton here for the first time speaks out his sympathy with that party with which he was afterwards to be so conspicuously associated.

    110. *twain*. In the Elizabethan writers *twain* is used (1) predicatively ; (2) when the substantive is placed first ; (3) substantively.

    111. *amain*. See *Paradise Lost*, ii. 165, 1024, &c. Shakspere, *Tempest*, IV. i. 75, &c. Spenser has the form "mainly." [What is the force of the word ?]

    112. *bespake*. See *Hymn Nat.* l. 76.

    114. *anow* = enow. *Paradise Lost*, ii. 504: "hellish foes *enow*." This form is generally said to be the plural of *enough*. See quotations from Sidney, Hooker, and Dryden, Addison *apud* Johnson.

    115. Comp. *Paradise Lost*, iv. 192. *Sonnet to Cromwell*. *St. John* x. 12, 13. . One of Milton's pamphlets was entitled, *The Likeliest Means to remove Hirelings out of the Church.* See also his *Of Reformation.*

    116. *Of other care*. [What should we say in our present English ?]

    119. *Blind mouthes*, &c. Comp. l. 88. *Paradise Lost*, v. 711, 718. Milton is indifferent to the verbal incongruity ; there is none in sense. *Mouths* = gluttons. Comp. *gula* in Latin. See Hor *Sat.* II. ii. 40.

24. 119. *know how to hold.* In l. 10 we have " knew to sing."

120. *the least.* [In what two ways may this phrase be parsed? Which is the better?]

121. *faithfull.* In Elizabethan writers *full* in composition retains all its letters; its independent force was still fresh.

heardsman " has a general sense in our older writers, and often occurs in Sydney's *Arcadia,* a book well known to Milton. In our old Pastorals heard-groome sometimes occurs for shepherd." (Warton.)

122. *sped.* See *Merchant of Venice,* II. ix. 72 : " So be gone ; *you are* sped." *Romeo and Juliet,* III. i. 95. Knolles *apud* Johnson : " Barbarossa, *sped* of all he desired, staid not long at Constantinople." As a preterite the word occurs in Shakspere, *Merry Wives of Windsor,* III. v. 67, &c. In *Measure for Measure,* IV. v. 10, and *Paradise Regained,* iii. 267, there is the longer form of the participle, viz. *speeded.* So "lift" has two participial forms, lift and lifted. [Mention other verbs that have two.] *Speed* was used much more frequently and more variously in older English than it is now. Comp. "God *speed* the Parliament " in Shakspere, 1 *Henry VI.* III. ii. 60; "an honest tale *speeds* best," *Richard III.* IV. iv. 358, &c.

25. 123. *list* is akin to German and Old English *lust* = pleasure. It survives in *list*less, as *reck* in reckless. It was originally used impersonally : thus, " if the list," Chaucer, *Canterbury Tales,* 1185; "what them listeth," Hooker, &c. So *please, reck,* &c. were originally impersonal.

flashy. " Distilled books are like common distilled waters, *flashy* things." (Bacon's *Essays.*) [What does the word mean?]

124. *grate.* So *blow, Il Penseroso,* 161.

Comp. Virg. *Ecl.* iii. 26 :

> " Non tu in triviis, indocte, solebas,
> Stridenti miserum stipula disperdere carmen ?' "

scrannel is used in Lancashire for "a lean person" (Halliwell). "Scranny" is a common provincial word for "lean." The metaphor, therefore, is the same as in "*lean* and flashy songs." Comp. Cicero's "*tenuis* exsanguisque sermo" (*De Or.* I. xiii. 57).

125. See Spenser's *Eclogue* for May.

126. *draw.* So *Paradise Lost,* viii. 284: "From where I first *drew* air." We still speak of a "draught." Comp. Latin *haurio, haustus.*

128. There were many perversions to the Church of Rome about this time. See Masson's *Life of Milton,* i. 638.

129. *and nothing sed.* [How would you parse this phrase?]

130. Comp. *St. Matth.* iii. 10; *St. Luke* iii. 9. Raleigh *apud* Johnson : "The sword, the arrow, the gun, with many terrible *engines* of death, will be well employed." The word *engine* is radically connected with "ingenious," "ingenuity," and means simply something clever. For *two-handed* Shakspere has "a two-hand sword," 2 *Henry VI.* II. i. 49. (See a description of one in Scott's *Monastery.*) Comp. *Paradise Lost,* vi. 251.

He means to say, generally, that the time of retribution is at hand. Some commentators, unwisely in my opinion, take the words as a definite prophecy of Laud's execution (in 1645). Certainly they could never have been understood in that sense at the time of the poem's first publication, " under the sanction and from the press of one of our universities," and " when the proscriptions of the Star Chamber and the power of Laud were at their height." In his *Of Reformation in England* he speaks of "the axe of God's reformation hewing at the old and hollow trunk of papacy."

132. *Alpheus.* See *Class. Dict.*

133. *shrunk.* See *Hymn Nat.* 203. Comp. Rowe's *Jane Shore,* I. i. :

> " Our common foes
> The Queen's relations, our new-fangled gentry,
> Have *fall'n* their haughty crests."

25. 133. *Sicilian Muse.* See above, l. 85. Virg. *Ecl.* vi. 1; iv. 1. *Epitaph. Bion.* attributed to Moschus.

Comp. *Psalm* civ. 7.

"The dread voice," and another equally dreadful, afterwards "shrunk the streams" of poetry for Milton for nearly thirty years. After writing *Lycidas*, in 1637, Milton wrote scarcely any more poetry till after the Restoration. *Paradise Lost* was published in 1667. Between it and *Lycidas* he had produced in poetry only a few sonnets. During nearly all that interval he abandoned, at the call of duty, his proper vocation of poet, and gave all his energies to politics. See *Reason for Church Government against Prelaty.*

134. *hither cast* = come hither and cast. Comp. Soph. *Œd. Col.* 23:

> " ἔχεις διδάξαι δή μ' ὅποι καθέσταμεν;"

Ib. 1253: " πάρεστι δεῦρο Πολυνείκης ὅδε."

Ant. 42: " ποῖ γνώμης ποτ' εἶ;"

135. *bels.* See *Tempest*, V. i. 89:

> " In a cowslip's bell I lie."

Comp. *bel*-flower, blue-*bell*.

of a thousand hues. So in l. 93, "Of *rugged* wings."

[*flowrets.* Mention other substantives with this dimin. termination.]

136. *use.* See l. 67.

milde whispers. Comp. Theocritus' " ψιθύρισμα" (*Id.* i. 1).

138. *fresh lap.* See *Richard II.* V. ii. 47: "the green *lap* of the new-come spring." *Ib.* III. iii. 47:

> " The *fresh* green *lap* of fair King Richard's land."

the swart star: i.e. swart-making (tanning, brown-dyeing) star. So "*albus* Notus" in Hor. *Od.* I. vii. 15 = white- or clear-making (comp. *Od.* III. xxvii. 19). Homer's "ἀργεστής," *Il.* xi. 306; Virgil's "*clarus* Aquilo," *Georg.* i. 460. Comp. "dim" in *Paradise Lost*, iii. 26, &c. The star meant is, of course, Sirius or Canicula, a star just in the mouth of the constellation Canis (Orion's dog). It rose at Athens about the time of the greatest heat, and was therefore supposed to cause that heat. See Æschylus' *Agam.* 939-40 (Ed. Paley):

> " ῥίζης γὰρ οὔσης φυλλὰς ἵκετ' ἐς δόμους
> σκιὰν ὑπερτείνασα Σειρίου κυνός."

The Latins echo this theory. See Horace, *passim.* His "rubra Canicula," in *Sat.* II. v. 39, probably = *flagrans.*

Comp. Hor. *Od.* III. xiii. 9.

sparely. Comp. Horace's "parcius," *Od.* I. xxv. 1.

139. *quaint.* See *Hymn Nat.* 194.

enameld. "The materials of glass melted with calcined tin compose an undiaphanous body. This white *amel* is the basis of all those fine concretes that goldsmiths and artificers employ in the curious art of enamelling." (Boyle on Colours, *apud* Johnson.)

142–51. Comp. Shakspere, *Cymbeline*, IV. ii. 220-30. Comp. also Spenser's *Ecl.* April.

142. *rathe.* The root of this word yet appears in "rather" = earlier, sooner. (Holofernes uses "ratherest" in *Love's Labour'Lost*, IV. ii. 19.) Tennyson has revived the word itself. (*In Mem.* cix.)

Comp. Shakspere's "Primroses that die unmarried," &c. (*Winter's Tale*, IV. iv. 122.)

25. 143. *crow-toe*. Comp. the name "crow-foot" (the ranunculus).

144. *freakt*. Freckle is a dim. of *freak*, the substantive. Comp. "*freckled* cowslip," *Henry V*. V. ii. 49.

146. *well attir'd* = well covered with leaves; or, perhaps, = fair-flowered, well head-dressed, as it were. The head-dresses of Elizabethan ladies were called "attiers." It may be noticed that *attire* has been adopted by botanists as a technical term. See Johnson.

149. *his*. See note, *Hymn Nat.* 106.
[What part of the verb is *shed* here?]

150. *daffadillies*. Constable uses this form with an addition, viz. "daffadowndilly." See a song by him in the *Golden Treasury*, No. XV.

151. *laureat* may allude to Lycidas' being a poet, or rather to his being lamented by poets. Comp. *Epitaph on Marchioness of Winchester*, 55-9 :

> " Here be . . . .
> . . . some flowers, and some *bays*
> For thy herse, to strow the ways,
> Sent thee from the banks of Cam."

See l. 1.

herse = tomb. So in Ben Jonson's well-known Epitaph, "Underneath this marble *hearse*," &c. Comp. *Hamlet*, I. iv. 47 : "*hears'd* in death," &c. According to Wedgwood, it was originally "a triangular framework of iron used for holding a number of candles at funerals and Church ceremonies;" then a funeral monument—in particular, a temporary cenotaph.

152. [What does *so* mean here? How otherwise might this passage be punctuated? What would *so* mean then?]

154. [What is the predicate to *shores*?] Comp. Virg. *Æn*. vi. 362.

158. *monstrous* here to be taken literally (not as, for instance, in *Othello*, III. iii. 427). So *Paradise Lost*, ii. 624-5 :

> " Nature breeds,
> Perverse, all *monstrous*, all prodigious things," &c.

There is a powerful picture of this " monstrous world " in the old poem of *Beowulf*, where the hero invades Grendal's dam in her den at the sea-bottom. (See ll. 2820-3028, Ed. Thorpe.) For another, see Clarence's dream in *Richard III*. I. iv. 16-33. See Virg. *Æn*. vi. 729.

159. [*our moist vows*. What is the substantive qualified *in sense* by *moist*?]

160. [In what sense is *fable* used here?]

Bellerus = one of the old Cornish giants. "No such name occurs in the Catalogue of the Cornish giants, but the poet coined it from Bellerium. At first he had written Corineus." (Warton.) Corineus was a giant who came into Britain with Brute. See *Faerie Queene*, II. x. 10 and 12. Diodorus Siculus speaks of Belerium ; Ptolemy of Bolerium. On the old Giants see *Faerie Queene*, II. x. 7-12.

161. Camden tells us that Land's End is "the only part of our island that looks directly towards Spain." (Warton.) See Drayton's *Polyolb*. xxiii.

the great vision, &c. "A stone lantern in one of the angles of the church" built on St. Michael's Mount "is called St. Michael's Chair. There is still a tradition that a vision of St. Michael seated on this crag, or St. Michael's chair, appeared to some hermits." Warton also takes "guarded" to refer to "a strong fortress, regularly garrisoned," that was built on the Mount ; but it seems better to understand it of the watch kept by the angel. (Comp. Hamlet's "heavenly *guards*.")

162. *Namancos*. It used to be thought that the ancient Numantia was here meant ; but this was an error. Todd found, in Mercator's *Atlas*, ed. fol. Amst. 1623, and in the ed. of

1636, in the map of Galicia, near Cape Finisterre, "Namancos T." (*i.e.* Turris). "In this map the castle of Bayona makes a very conspicuous figure."

25. 163. *angel:* i.e. St. Michael.

[*ruth.* What derivative of this word is still in use ? What cognate verb ?]

164. *O ye Dolphins,* &c. As in the old days a dolphin had borne Arion safely through the seas to land. See Herod. I. i. 24 ; Ovid, *Fast.* ii. 83–118 ; Wordsworth's *Power of Sound,* ix.

waft, "to carry through the air *or the water.*" (Johnson.) See *King John,* II. i. 71–3 :

> "In brief, a braver choice of dauntless spirits
> Than now the English bottoms have *waft* o'er,
> Did never float upon the swelling tide," &c.

165. Warton compares Spenser's *Ecl. Nov.*; *Epith. Damonis,* 201–8 ; *Ode on the Death of a fair Infant,* stanza x.

26. 166. *your sorrow.* So love, care, joy, delight, pride, hope, are used in a concrete sense. So in Latin and Greek *amor, spes,* πόνος, ὠδίς, &c.

167. *watery floor.* Comp. Shakspere's "*floor* of heaven," *Merchant of Venice,* V. i. 58.

168. *the day-star* = the sun. So "diurnal star," *Paradise Lost,* x. 1069.

169. Comp. Gray's *Bard,* of the "orb of day" :

> "To-morrow he repairs the golden flood."

170. *tricks.* See *Il Pens.* 123.

spangled. See *Hymn Nat.* 21.

ore = metal. So *Paradise Lost,* i. 673.

173. See *St. Matthew* xiv. 22.

that walk'd the waves. So Spenser :

> "She wander'd many a wood."

Paradise Lost, i. 520 :

> "And o'er the Celtic roamed the utmost isles."

v. 272, "a phœnix gazed by all." So in Shakspere, "muse," "smile," &c. &c., govern accusatives. So "myself was then travelling that land," Tennyson's *Golden Supper.*

174. Comp. Virg. *Æn.* vi. 641 ; Wordsworth's *Laodamia.*

175. Comp. Hor. *Od.* III. iv. 61.

oozy. *Hymn Nat.* 124.

176. *unexpressive.* *Hymn Nat.* 116. So "inenarrabile carmen," in his poem *Ad Patrem.* Comp. "insuppressive," Shakspere, *Julius Cæsar,* II. i. 134.

nuptiall song. See the *Revelation* xxii. 17.

179. Comp. *Paradise Lost,* xi. 82.

"Milton's angelic system . . . is to be seen at large in Thomas Aquinas and Peter Lombard." (Warton.)

181. See *Isaiah* xxv. 8 ; *Rev.* vii. 17.

183. Comp. the story of Melicerta or Palæmon. Ov. *Met.* iv. 522 ; *Fast.* vi. 485 ; Virg. *Georg.* i. 436.

184. *In thy large recompense.* [What is the force of *thy* here ?] See Spenser's *Prothal* 158.

good. See *Il Pens.* 153 ; cf. Virg *Ecl.* v. 65.

185. *in.* We should say "on" or "o'er."

186. *uncouth.* See *L'Allegro,* l. 5.

187. *still.* This is a favourite word with Milton. See *Il Pens* 127.

Comp. the description of evening in *Comus,* 188–90.

26. 188. *stops* = "these ventages" in *Hamlet*, III. ii. 372.

quills. Comp. Dryden :

> " His flying fingers and harmonious *quill*
> Strike seven distinguish'd notes, and seven at once they fill."

189. *warbling.* Another of Milton's favourite words.

Dorick lay = poem in the pastoral style. Theocritus, Bion, Moschus, wrote in the Doric dialect.

190. *the hills*, that is, their shadows. Comp. Virg. *Ecl.* i. 83.

191. *was dropt.* See above, l. 97.

192. *twitch'd.* Comp. Juvenal's "Tyrias humero revocante lacernas " (*Sat.* i. 27).

mantle blew. Blue was the colour of a shepherd's dress, and the poet here personates a poetic shepherd. It was also a common colour for servant-men. Ben Jonson speaks of servants as "the blue order ;" also of "a blue waiter." In Beaumont and Fletcher a footman is called "a blue-bottle," a familiar phrase still.

193. Comp. Theocr. *Id.* i. 145 :

> "χαίρετ'· ἐγὼ δ' ὔμμιν καὶ ἐς ὕστερον ἅδιον ᾆσω."

DRYDEN.

1. JOHN DRYDEN was born on the 9th of August, 1631 (the year before Locke was born), probably in the house of his maternal grandfather, at Aldwincle All Saints, near Oundle, in Northamptonshire. His father, of a family belonging originally to Cumberland, was the proprietor of a small estate at Blakesley, a village near Aldwincle All Saints. In course of time he was sent to Westminster School, then under the superintendence of Dr. Busby, and subsequently to Trinity College, Cambridge. Leaving the University in 1657, without, it would seem, having specially distinguished himself there, he went up to London, and devoted himself to politics and to literature. Amongst his family connexions were certain important members of the Puritan party. The death of Cromwell soon provided him with a poetical subject. His writing an elegy on that occasion did not prevent him, any more than Waller, and other poets of the day, from welcoming back with a poem Charles the Second. With the Restoration a new field was thrown open to the wits of the time in the shape of the stage, which for some eighteen years had been altogether, or partially, shut up. Dryden turned play-writer. He wrote comedies, tragedies, tragi-comedies : the comedies, in prose ; the tragedies, the earliest in blank verse, then some in rhyme, on the model of the French tragic drama, the latest in blank verse. His subjects he drew mostly from the old romances, and from history. He reproduced three of Shakspere's plays, *Troilus and Cressida*, *Antony and Cleopatra* (which he called *All for Love*), and *The Tempest*. In 1671 his plays were heartily, and not undeservedly, ridiculed in the *Rehearsal*, written by the Duke of Buckingham, assisted, it is said, by " Hudibras " Butler, and others. All this time he was winning more lasting fame by the various critical essays with which his plays, when published, were frequently prefaced. In 1663 he married the Lady Elizabeth Howard, a daughter of the Earl of Berkshire, who by no means proved a congenial consort.

2. It was not till Dryden was some fifty years old that he fully discovered where his strength lay. Before 1681 he had written other poetical pieces, as his *Annus Mirabilis* (published in 1667, the same year with *Paradise Lost*), besides his plays, and everything he had written had been marked by a certain power and might ; but in that year his *Absalom and Achitophel* displayed his characteristic talents in their fullest and completest vigour. The nation was at that time in a state of profound excitement ; the struggle between Absolutism and Constitutionalism was rapidly nearing its final crisis ; the contest between the Court party and the Exclusionists, an important passage in that other all-comprehensive struggle, had just reached its utmost fury. Dryden stood forth as the champion of the Court party ; in his *Absalom and Achitophel* he dealt the Exclusionists the severest blows his genius could inflict, and they were terribly effective. That poem was speedily followed by another, *The Medal*, aimed at that same Achitophel ; and this by another, *Mac Flecknoe*, aimed at Shadwell, the chief poet of the Whig side. At this same memorable period of his life he wrote also *Religio Laici*, to vindicate Revelation against Atheism, and Protestantism against Tradition. How well the Stuarts rewarded his great services appears from the fact that it was only with much appealing and difficulty he could procure the payment of the salary due to him as Poet Laureate. Not

long after the succession of James II. he became a Roman Catholic ; with his usual fervour and brilliancy he in 1686 wrote his *Hind and Panther* (published the following year), in which he defended that tradition of which in the *Religio Laici* he had made so light. When the boy was born who was afterwards known as "the Pretender," Dryden celebrated the event in his *Britannia Rediviva ;* but that birth was in fact the signal for the combined action of a justly indignant nation, and the irreparable fall of the Stuart dynasty.

3. Dryden fell with his patrons. Whatever may be thought of the consistency of his previous life, he certainly refused overtures now made to him by the triumphant Protestant party. His political life ended ; his literary activity was as intense as ever. He now set himself to the translation of certain classical poets. His version of Persius and Juvenal was published in 1693 ; that of the *Æneid* in 1697, in which same year he wrote also his now best-known poem, his *Alexander's Feast.* His modernizations of Chaucer and other pieces—his *Fables* —appeared in 1700. Thus his vigour remained to the end, for in 1700 he died.

Of his twenty-eight plays scarcely any one is now at all known ; and perhaps not much more deserves to be known. The comedies abound in wit, those written in the heroic metre in fine versification ; but Dryden was wanting in dramatic power, he was wanting in humour, in tenderness, in delicacy. He could describe in a masterly manner, but this is not the dramatist's great function ; he had not the art of making his characters develop themselves —describe themselves by their actions, so to speak. He could lay bare all the motives that actuated them, but he could not show them in a state of action obedient to those motives : in short, his power was rather of the analytical kind.

His descriptive power was of the highest. Our literature has in it no more vigorous portrait-gallery than that he has bequeathed it. He succeeds better in his portraits of enemies than of friends ; perhaps because, as it happened, the Whig leaders excited in him more disgust than the Tories admiration. The general type of character which that age presented was in an eminent degree calculated not to stir enthusiasm. Dryden fell upon evil times. What he for the most part saw was flagrant corruption in Church and in State, and in society : he lived the best years of his life in the most infamous period of English history ; he was getting old when a better time began. The poet reflects his age : there was but little noble for Dryden to reflect. Naturally, he turned satirist.

His power of expression is beyond praise. There is always a singular *fitness* in his language : he uses always the right word.

He is one of our greatest masters of metre : metre was, in fact, no restraint to him, but rather it seems to have given him freedom. It has been observed that he argues better in verse than in prose : verse was the natural costume of his thoughts. As a prose-writer he is excellent ; but verse-writing was his proper province.

MAC FLECKNOE.

INTRODUCTION.

THIS piece was directed against Shadwell, the leading Whig poet of the day, as Dryden was the Tory. It was published in October 1682. Johnson therefore mistakes when he says that it was occasioned by Shadwell's being appointed to succeed Dryden as Poet Laureate (see his *Life of Dryden*) ; for that superseding did not take place till after the Revolution.

In spite of what is said in the following Satire, Shadwell was a comic poet of no mean power, and but for his lavish indecency would well deserve to be read. He was certainly a better play-writer than his satirist. Dryden and he had once been friends, and indeed fellow-workers, and in those days Dryden had not been blind to his merits. In the Epilogue to the *Volunteers*, one of Shadwell's plays, he speaks of him as

> " The great support of the comic stage,
> Born to expose the follies of the age,
> To whip prevailing vices, and unite
> Mirth with Instruction, Profit with Delight ;
> For large ideas and a flowing pen
> First of our times, and second but to Ben."

This praise must have been particularly welcome to Shadwell, not only as coming from whom it did come, but for its form ; for Shadwell modelled himself upon Ben Jonson. He, too, aimed at representing "humours." He is said to have resembled him somewhat in person. He found no difficulty in resembling him in his affection for the tavern. Had he lived some half-century sooner he would no doubt have gladly been enrolled in what Jonson himself called "the tribe of Ben." If Jonson wrote *Masques*, Shadwell wrote an opera, *Pysche*. In course of time Dryden and he became enemies. Dryden had spoken disparagingly of Ben Jonson (see his *Essay on Dramatic Poetry*) ; Shadwell sneered at *Aureng-zebe*. When the fearful factious excitements connected with the Exclusion Bill and the Popish Plot came to a head in 1678, and the two following years, Dryden and Shadwell were ranged on opposite sides. Shadwell answered the *Medal* with his *Medal of John Bayes;* he took part also in a lampoon called *The Tory Poets*, aimed at Dryden and Otway. In October 1682 appeared *Mac Flecknoe : A Satire on the True Blue Protestant Poet, T.S.;* and in the following month the Portrait of Shadwell under the name of Og in the Second Part of *Absalom and Achitophel*.

For the name, Shadwell would have been proud to be called the "Son of Ben ;" Dryden calls him the "Son of Flecknoe," the heir of one of the meanest versifiers of the century. Of this poor poetaster, Flecknoe, the very name would now barely be known but for the immortality Dryden thus gave him. Dryden plucked him from oblivion to become a proverb of badness. Thus Swift writes in his *On Poetry, a Rhapsody*, 1744 :

> " Remains a difficulty still
> To purchase fame by writing ill.
> From *Flecknoe* down to Howard's time,
> How few have reached the low sublime ! "

Besides its great intrinsic merit, *Mac Flecknoe* has the additional interest of having mainly suggested the form of Pope's *Dunciad*. "I doubt not," says Pope himself in a note to "Flecknoe's Irish Throne" (*Dunciad*, ii. 2), "our author took occasion to mention him in respect to the poem of Mr. Dryden, to which this bears some resemblance, though of a character more different from it than that of the *Æneid* from the *Iliad*, or the *Lutrin* of Boileau from the *Défait de Bouts Rimées* [sic] of Sarazin."

27. 3. *Flecknoe.* See *Introduction.*

Augustus was just thirty-three years of age when he overthrew his formidable rival Antony, and became the undisputed master of the Roman world. He held that mastership for forty-four years. See *Class. Dict.* or *Hist. Rom.* [In what year did he accept the *imperium proconsulare ?* In what year did he die ?]

8. [Explain the exact meaning of *a large increase.* In what relation do the words stand to *issue ?*]

increase is often used particularly for family or progeny. See 1 *Sam.* ii. 33. So Shakspere's *Coriolanus*, III. iii. 114 ; Pope's *Odyssey :*

> " Him young Thoosa bore, the bright *increase*
> Of Phorcys."

Comp. Latin *incrementum.* Often it is used generally for *produce.* See Shakspere's *Tempest,* IV. i. 110; 3 *Henry VI.* II. ii. 164, &c.

27. 10. *to settle* = the settling. So

> " For not to have been dipt in Lethe's lake
> Could save the son of Thetis from to-die."

(*Two Gentlemen of Verona,* III. i. 182.) " I leave *to be*," &c. Or *debate to settle* may = debate how to settle; comp. Milton's *Lyc.* 10. Comp. " to subdue any that in anywise denied to do it." (Bunyan's *Holy War.*)

    The settling of the succession of the political state was an only too familiar question at this time. It had troubled Cromwell; it was now pressing upon Charles the Second, if anything could press upon him; it was certainly vexing the whole nation. Thus Flecknoe's position was easy to realize.

    13. Observe the force of the metre here.

    'Tis resolved. Comp. beginning of *Alexander's Feast.*

    14. [What " part of speech " is *onely* here? What does it qualify? Where ought it, strictly, to be placed? Quote or find similar instances of careless arrangement.]

    22. " The long dissensions of the two houses, which although they had had *lucid intervals* and happy pauses, yet they did ever hang over the kingdom ready to break forth."; (Bacon.)

    intervall here, as etymologically, of space. Shakspere uses the Latin form in 2 *Henry IV.* V. i. 85, " a' shall laugh without *intervallums.*"

    23. [What is meant by *genuine night?*]

    24. In a moral sense we still say " prevail upon," = persuade; so " prevail with." In a material sense perhaps we should rather say " prevail over." See Shakspere's *Richard III.* III. iv. 64. Comp. " prevail against." Comp. also *Daniel* iii. 27: " These men *upon* whose bodies the fire had no power."

    [Has *rising* any *present* force here?]

    25. See *Introd.*

    fabrick. The comparison of a body to a building is common enough: see St. Paul's *Second Epistle to the Corinthians,* v. 1. It is the leading idea of Howe's *Living Temple.* (See 1 *Cor.* iii. 16, &c.)

    26. [Is *majesty* used here in an abstract or a concrete sense?]

    28. *supinely.* Keats used *supine* in its original sense in *Eve of St. Agnes.*

    28. 29. *Heywood* was one of the " Elizabethan " dramatists. Of the details of his life little is known. He died some time in the reign of Charles I. He would seem to have been a writer of wonderful fertility, for he boasts of having had " an entire hand, or at the least a main finger," in 220 plays. He was a writer of far greater merit than might be supposed from this mention of him by Dryden. See some extracts from his plays in Lamb's *Specimens of English Dramatic Poets.* Lamb, a most discerning critic, says of him that he is " a sort of *prose* Shakspeare. His scenes are to the full as natural and affecting. But we miss *the Poet,* that which in Shakspeare always appears out and above the surface of *the nature,*" &c.

    Shirley, born probably in 1594, died in 1666. Neither to him does Dryden here quite do justice; see specimens of his plays in the selection just mentioned. Lamb says of him, that he claims a place amongst the worthies of this period not so much for any transcendent genius in himself as that he was the last of a great race, all of whom spoke nearly the same language, and had a set of moral feelings and notions in common. A new language and quite a new turn of tragic and comic interest came in with the Restoration." Dryden, as the great superseder of this school of which Shirley was the last notable member, not unnaturally failed to appreciate what merits he had.

    31. *dunce.* Duns Scotus (he was born about the same time as Dante, died in 1308,) was a man of an acute intellect, and of great erudition; but, when that school of learning to which he belonged fell into contempt, his name became a by-word for ignorance: thus his very

eminence in his own age placed him in a low and contemptible position in another age. See Trench's *Study of Words.*

28. 33. *Norwich drugget.* He wrote first "rusty-drugget." (Todd.) Norwich was known for its woollen manufactures from the time of Henry I., when a colony of Flemings settled in the neighbourhood of Worstead. "Others, settlers from the same country, joined their brethren in the reign of Henry VI. and Elizabeth." (*Pop. Encycl.*) "Worsted," "Lindsey Wolsey," and "Kerseymere" are said to be so called from East Anglian villages noted for their woollen productions: see Taylor's *Words and Places.* For the term *drugget,* "it is said that drugget or droget was first made at Drogheda in Ireland."

35. *warbling.* See *Hymn Nat.* 96.

lute. See *Ode for St. Cecilia's Day,* 36.

whilom. Scotch "quhylum." This is an old dat. case ; so "seldom." With the help of a prep. was formed from the same stem the adverb "umwhile," Scotch "umquhile :" see *Piers Ploughman,* Ed. Skeat, v. 345.

36. See *Introd.*

38. *silver Thames.* See Spenser's *Prothal.* l. 11.

39. [What other meaning has *well-tim'd* ?]

barge = pleasure boat. In a "barge" Cleopatra sailed down the Cydnus ; see *Antony and Cleopatra,* II. ii. 196.

40. [What is the force of *of* here ?]

42. That is, "such a scene was never depicted even in one of your own nonsensical plays." Shadwell had written a play called *Epsom Wells.* The virtue of the springs at Epsom was discovered in 1618.

43. *Methinks.* See note, *Prothal.* 60.

45. *well-sharpned thumb.* As if his thumb was a sword inflicting cruel cuts on the trebles and the basses. Comp. Juvenal's "stricto pane" (*Sat.* v. 169). Shadwell is the *leader* of the band.

[Why do *nail* and *thumb* make the description ludicrous?]

49. As they might be supposed to have thronged around Arion ; but in fact fishes, except seals, are said to be insensible to the charms of music. Comp. with this passage an old ballad on the death and funeral of Queen Elizabeth (quoted here from memory) :

> " The Queen was brought by water to Whitehall,
> At every stroke the oars did tears let fall ;
> Some clung about the boat ; the fishes under water
> Wept out their eyes of pearl, and swam blind after."

No doubt one great amusement of leisurely voyagers up and down the Thames in the days of pleasure barges would be throwing over pieces of bread and toast and watching the eager contentious pursuit of the little fishes. Or, more probably, this passage refers to fragments of the *morning toast* which, thrown out for the benefit of the swans (a great number of these were kept on the river in the old days), became objects of desire and pursuit to the fishes.

50. *thy threshing hand,* i.e. the hand which you move as if you were threshing = with which you beat time. His roll of "papers" served him as a *bâton.*

51. *St. André* was a well-known French dancing-master of the day.

52. *Psyche.* See *Introd.*

54. [What is meant by *they* ? and what by saying *they fell like tautology* ?]

55. *Singleton* is said to have been the leader of the King's private band. Pepys mentions once, in 1660, the king "did put a great affront upon his music, bidding them stop and make the French music play." He was also an actor, as the present passage shows. *Villerius* is a *persona* in Sir W. D'Avenant's *Siege of Rhodes.* With regard to the *lute and sword,* see the Fifth Act of *The Rehearsal,* where that play is parodied. The stage direction runs : "Enter at several doors the General and Lieutenant-General arm'd Cap-a-pea, with

T

each of them a lute in his hand and his sword drawn, and hung with a scarlet ribbon at his wrist." Villerius' part required both military valour and musical skill; hence his double equipment.

28. 59. [What is the force of *of* here?]

62. *Augusta.* As it was the fashion to speak of Charles the Second as Cæsar (see Dryden's lines *To his Sacred Majesty*) and as Augustus (see *e.g.* his *Threnodia Augustalis*), the capital city of his kingdom came to be called by the affected name of Augusta. It was, in fact, an old name revived. Augusta was a common title in the Roman Empire for cities founded or specially patronized by the first of the Emperors; thus there were Augusta Rauracorum (the modern Aust), Augusta Trevirorum (now Trèves), Augusta Eminta (now Merida), Augusta Prætoria (Aosta), Augusta Taurinorum (Turin), &c. Ammianus Marcellinus informs us that London enjoyed this title. He speaks of "Lundinium, an old town to which posterity gave the title of Augusta." In the *Notitia Dignitatum* mention is made of a " Præpositus Thesaurorum *Augustensium* in Britanniis;" "in the Chorography of Ravenna the complete form Londinium Augusta is given." (Smith's *Dict. Greek and Rom. Geography*, s. v. "Londinium.") See Gay's *Trivia*, III.

> "Happy *Augusta!* law-defended town," &c.

Swift, *On Poetry, a Rhapsody:*—

> "For poets (you can never want them)
> Spread through *Augusta Trinobantum,*
> Computing by their pecks of coals,
> Amount to just nine thousand souls."

the walls which, &c. The old line of the walls may be traced by the gates, whose position is still recorded in certain street names, as Lud-*gate*, New-*gate*, Cripple-*gate*, &c. Just south of the church of St. Giles', Cripplegate, near the street called *London Wall*, a considerable piece of them yet stands.

63. The strange vicissitudes of the Civil War time, the Plague, the Fire, the suspected instability of the Government, had made London nervous—hysterical, so to speak. Hence its wild readiness to believe in Popish plots, &c. See history of Charles II.'s reign

65. *Barbican.* "Propugnaculum exterius quo oppidum aut castrum, præsertim vero eorum portæ aut muri muniuntur." (Du Cange.) "It was generally a small round tower for the station of an advanced guard placed just before the outward gate of the castle-yard or ballium." (Halliwell and Wright's Nares' *Gloss.*) It frequently stood on the other, *i.e.* the outer, side of the foss. (See *Ivanhoe.*) It served especially as a watch-tower. Comp. "raised to inform the sight," &c. in our text Spenser's *Faerie Queene*, II. ix. 25:

> "Within the *barbican* a porter sate
> Day and night duly keeping watch and ward."

Where see Mr. Kitchin's note. "Chaucer useth the word for a watch-tower, which in our Saxon tongue was called a *burgh-kenning.*" (Cotgrave.) For the derivation and first meaning of the word, see Wedgwood's *Dict. Eng. Etym.*, according to which barbican and balcony are both but various forms of a combination of two Persian words, meaning an upper chamber. The particular barbican here referred to was the advanced post of Cripplegate. (Ludgate too had its barbican.) Stowe says that from it "a man might behold and view the whole city towards the south, and also into Kent, Sussex, and Surrey, and likewise every other way east, north, or west." See Timbs' *Curiosities of London.* In the street still named after it Milton at one time lived.

hight = was called. Sometimes it has a present sense, sometimes it is a participle. Spenser uses it frequently in all these ways. See Halliwell and Wright's Nares' *Gloss.* It is a later form from the A.-S. *hatan* (pret. *hatte*), which has both an active and passive sense; so German *heissen*, which is of the same root: hence the double use of *hight* in later English both as a passive participle and as a verb of active form and passive meaning. With it in this latter usage comp. apparently Lat. *veneo, fio, cluo, vapulo;* A.-S. *weorthan,* to be made, &c. "Properly it was a passive form of the verb, as shown by Mœso-Goth. *haitith,* he calls ; *haitada,* he is called ; as in 'Thomas saei haitada Didimus,' Thomas who is called Didymus." (See Skeat's *Piers Ploughman,* Clar. Press Ed. *Gloss.*) See *Piers Ploughman, Canterbury Tales, Faerie Queene,* passim. See *Midsummer Night's Dream,* V. i. 140 ; *Love's Labour Lost,* I. i. 171 ; *Pericles,* IV. Gower, l. 17. Milton does not use it, at least in his poems. The form *highteth* occurs in an old play called *Ordinary*: "How *highteth* she, say you ?" There was another A.-S. verb *hatan,* to command ; the preterite of which (*het*) is often confounded with that of *hatan,* to call : see Morris' Chaucer's *Prologue,* Clar. Press Ed. Hence the various senses of *hight* as used by Spenser. See Halliwell and Wright's Nares' *Gloss.*

28. 68. *a Nursery:* a place where youthful would-be actors, and perhaps would-be playwrights, made their first attempts, and so the head-quarters of inferior theatrical art. See *The Rehearsal,* II. iii. : "Igad," says Mr. Bayes of his actors, "these fellows are able to spoil the best things in Christendom. I'll tell you, Mr. Johnson, I vow to gad I have been so highly disoblig'd by the peremptoriness of these fellows that I am resolv'd hereafter to bend all my thoughts for the service of the *Nursery,* and mump your proud players, Igad." It received letters patent from the King in 1662 ; its object was to train boys and girls in the art of acting.

71. *Maximins.* Maximin was the god-defiant hero of Dryden's *Tyrannic Love.*

29. 72. Fletcher seems to have been in Charles II.'s reign more popular than Shakspere. In his own day he was placed very near him. His name may be said to stand as for Beaumont and Fletcher. In the plays written during Beaumont's life it appears almost impossible to separate his work from that of his colleague, and in those which came out after Beaumont's death (Beaumont died in 1616, Fletcher in 1625) there are probably posthumous parts. Certainly the strength of these dramatists lay in comedy, in spite of Dryden's *buskins* in our text ; and their strength was great.

buskins. See *Il Penseroso,* l. 102.

73. See *L'Allegro,* l. 132.

74. *gentle Simkin* was a cobbler in an interlude of the day. Shoemaking was especially styled "the gentle craft." Compare this title of a book published in 1758: "The Delightful, Princely, and entertaining History of the Gentle Craft, very pleasant to read, shewing what famous men have been Shoemakers, shewing why it was called the Gentle Craft, and how a Shoemaker's Son is a prince born, with the Merry Pranks of the Green King, the Shoemaker's Glory," &c.

75. *vanished minds* = of intellects departed, of idiotcy. Comp. Tennyson's

> " O for the touch of a *vanish'd* hand ; "

and "a *vanished* life," in *In Mem.*

76. *clinches.* In Taylor's *Wit and Mirth* "clinch" is used for a clencher, "an unanswerable reply." (Halliwell and Wright's Nares' *Gloss.*) It was used also for a witty saying, a repartee. (Halliwell's *Dict.*) Johnson defines it "a word used in a double meaning, a pun, an ambiguity," &c., and quotes, besides *Mac Flecknoe,* Boyle : " Such as they are, I hope they will prove without a *clinch,* luciferous : searching after the nature of light." Dryden says of Shakspere : "He is many times flat and insipid ; his comic wit degenerating into *clenches,* his serious swelling into bombast." Comp. *Dunciad,* i. 63 :

> " Here one poor word an hundred *clenches* makes."

suburbian. So "robustious" in *Sams. Agon.* 569 ; "monstruous," *Faerie Queene,* II. xii. 85.

77. Panton is said to have been a noted punster of the day.

29. 80. *Decker.* Thomas Dekker was one of the great Elizabethan dramatists. Jonson is supposed to have satirised him in his *Poetaster*, a compliment which he returned in his *Satiromastix.* Dryden introduces him here because he was a " City poet." Dryden seems scarcely to have estimated him at his proper worth. There is a singularly musical and otherwise exquisite song by him,

> " Art thou poor, but hast thou golden slumbers,"

quoted in the *Golden Treasury.*

83. *Psyche—The Miser—The Humorists,* are plays by Shadwell.

86. *Raymond* is one of the characters in the *Humorists,* "a gentleman of wit and honour."

> *Bruce* is a character in *The Virtuoso,* "a gentleman of wit and sense."

90. *Bunhill—Watling-street.* See map of London.

91. Comp. Æsch. *Agam.* 881–2 (Ed. Paley).

92. Comp. Horace's " disjectaque membra poetæ."

93. *Ogleby,* at first a dancing-master, translated the *Iliad,* the *Odyssey,* and the *Æneid,* besides producing some original poetry and writing a *History of China.* See *Dunciad,* i. 141 and 328.

95. *Bilkt:* who had been defrauded of their due payments.

> *stationers* = booksellers. This was the original force of the word, and was still its force in Dryden's time. See Trench's *Sel. Gloss.; Dunciad,* ii. 30.

> *yeomen.* "He instituted for the security of his person a band of fifty archers under a captain to attend him, by the name of yeomen of his guard." (Bacon's *Henry VII.*) This word is variously connected with Fris. *gaeman,* a village ; A.-S. *gemæne,* common ; A.-S. *yeonge,* young ; A.-S. *geongra,* a vassal ; fancifully with *yew.*

96. *Herringman* was a well-known publisher of Charles II.'s reign. Dryden, in the earlier part of his career, had been connected with him. He was the " bookseller " meant by Shadwell in his *Medal of John Bayes :*

> " He turned a journeyman to a bookseller,
> Writ prefaces to books for meat and drink,
> And as he paid he would both write and think."

98. *throne:* " state " in the first edition. " The state was a raised platform, on which was placed a chair with a canopy over it." See Glossary to Cunningham's *Massinger.*

[What is meant by *of his own labours ?*]

99. *Ascanius.* See *Æneid,* passim. Dryden did not produce his translation of Virgil's great poem till some fifteen years after the coming out of *Mac Flecknoe,* but he was already thoroughly familiar with it, as indeed all his age was.

100. *Rome's other hope* = spes altera Romæ (*Æn.* xii. 168).

101. *glories.* See Keats' *Eve of St. Agnes.*

102. Comp. *Æn.* ii. 680, and old Romance of *Havelok.*

103. See *Class. Dict.* and *Hist. Rome;* Livy's *Hist.* xxi. 1.

104. [What does *sworn* mean here ?]

107. [What is meant by *his father's right ?*]

108. [What is the government of *to have,* &c. ?]

109. *made* = performed.

111. *ball.* " Hear the tragedy of a young man that by right ought to hold the *ball* of a kingdom ; but by fortune is made himself a ball, tossed from misery to misery, from place to place." (Bacon *apud* Johnson.)

113. *Love's Kingdom:* a play by Flecknoe. Derrick says he wrote four plays, but " could get only one of them acted, and that was damned."

> *convey* is used here in its technical sense. " The Earl of Desmond, before his

breaking forth into rebellion, *conveyed* secretly all his lands to feoffees in trust." (Spenser.) Comp. *The Medal*, of Shaftesbury's political doctrine :

> " He preaches to the crowd that power is lent,
> But not *conveyed*, to kingly government."

80. 116. *recorded* = above mentioned ; or rather = sung, for *Psyche* was an opera. Comp. Fairfax :

> " They long'd to see the day, to hear the lark
> *Record* her hymns and chaunt her carols blest."

"*Record*, to sing ; applied particularly to the singing of birds." (Darley's *Beaumont and Fletcher*, Gloss.) A recorder was a flageolet.

121. See Ovid's *Fast.* iv. 817.

125. *the honours of his head.* Comp. Valerius Flaccus' *Argonautics*, vi. 296 :

> " Populeus cui frontis *honor*, conspectaque glauco
> Tempora nectuntur ramo."

126. [What is meant by *damps of oblivion* ?]

127. [What is the force of *full* here ?]

128. *the filial dulness.* Comp. Horace's " mitis sapientia Læli," &c. Comp. *Æneid*, vi. 79.

134. [What are the ludicrous points of this line ?]

136. Comp. *Æn.* vi. 95.

138. *He* is parodying *Æn.* xii. 435.

140. " While Dryden accuses Shadwell of slowness in composition, Rochester attributes his faults to haste." See *Allusion to Tenth Satire of First Book of Horace.* (Note in the forthcoming Globe Edition of Dryden's works.)

142. *George* = Sir George Etheredge, a man of fashion, a diplomatist, a poet, a comedy writer. He died at Ratisbon, where he was Minister Resident, in 1694. See Dryden's *Poetical Epistle* addressed to him at Ratisbon, and also the *Epilogue* which Dryden wrote for his most popular play, *The Man of the Mode*, or *Sir Fopling Flutter.* See below, l. 144.

143. *Dorimant, Loveit*, &c., are characters in Etheridge's plays, *The Man of the Mode*, and *Love in a Tub.*

154. *Sedley.* Sir Charles Sedley was one of the wits and the poets and the dramatists that sparkled in the court of Charles II. See his songs, "Ah ! Chloris, could I now but sit," and " Not, Celia, that I juster am " (given in the *Golden Treasury*). He wrote the prologue for Shadwell's *Epsom Wells* (1672).

155. *hungry* = lean, " scrannel." See *Lycidas*, 125.

Epsom prose refers to Shadwell's *Epsom Wells.*

81. 158. *top.* Comp. *The Rehearsal*, III. i. : "he does not *top* his part," where the *Key* of 1704 notes that "it was a great word with Mr. Edward Howard."

159. Sir Formal Trifle is a verbose oratorical person in Shadwell's *Virtuoso.*

161. " By the *northern dedications* are meant Shadwell's frequent dedications to the Duke of Newcastle ; he dedicated also to the Duchess and to their son the Earl of Ogle." (Note in the Globe Edition of Dryden's *Works*.)

163. See *Introd.*

170. *Nicander* is a character in *Psyche.*

174. Observe the rhyme between *purloin* and *thine.* So *join* was sounded *jine*, &c. *Noise* rhymes with *cries* in *Dunciad*, ii. 221–2.

178. *byas.* See Shakspere, *Richard II.* III. iv. 5 ; *Hamlet*, II. i. 65. So *The Medal* :

> " To his first *bias* longingly he leans."

31. 183. *tympany:* i.e. no healthy normal growth, but a dropsical expansion. The meaning is exactly illustrated by what Macaulay says of Dryden's own plays in his Essay on Dryden: "The swelling diction of Æschylus and Isaiah resembles that of Almanzor and Maximin no more than the tumidity of a muscle resembles the tumidity of a boil. The former is symptomatic of health and strength, the latter of debility and disease."

184. Comp. Chaucer's "tonne-gret."

185. [How do you read this line ?]

[*kilderkin.* Quote other instances of this diminutival termination. What other dim. termns. are there in English ?]

191. [What does *dyes* mean here ?]

193. *keen Iambicks:* that is, satirical poetry such as Archilochus wrote, "proprio iambo." See Hor. *Ars Poet.* 79; Arist. *Poet.* iv. 9: "Hence also the Iambic verse is now so called, because in this metre they used to *Iambize* [i.e. satirize] each other."

mild Anagram. See *Spect.* Nos. 58 and 60, where these lines are quoted, and chronograms and "*bouts rimez*" also are discussed ; but anagrams and acrostics were much older than Addison supposed. See also Disraeli's *Curiosities of Literature,* on "Literary Follies :"—"I shall not dwell on the wits who composed verses in the forms of hearts, wings, altars, and true-love knots ; or, as Ben Jonson describes their grotesque shapes,

> ' A pair of scissors and a comb in verse.'

Tom Nash, who loved to push the ludicrous to its extreme, in his amusing invective against the classical Gabriel Harvey, tells us that ' he had writ verses in all kinds : in form of a pair of gloves, a pair of spectacles, and a pair of pot-hooks,' &c." See Puttenham's *Arte of English Poesie,* pp. 104–25 of the *English Reprints* Edition ; where the critic speaks of poems in the shape of "lozanges," "spindles," "spheres," "eggs," &c. &c.

32. 201. Bruce and Longville, in the *Virtuoso,* make Sir Formal Trifle disappear through a trap-door in the midst of his speechifying.

A SONG FOR ST. CECILIA'S DAY.

INTRODUCTION.

THIS song was written for the festival of St. Cecilia, 1687. The celebration of that festival by lovers of music was commenced (or revived, if, as is probable, it was kept in some sort before the Reformation) in 1683, in which year Purcell "set" the song that was written for the occasion. In 1684 Oldham wrote the anniversary song, in 1685 Nahum Tate ; in the following year the festival was not observed ; in 1687 Dryden wrote the song given in the text. He wrote another, his *Alexander's Feast,* ten years afterwards. Pope wrote in 1708.

It is not clear how St. Cecilia came to be regarded as the patron saint of music. In her legend, as told in the *Legenda Aurea* (written towards the close of the thirteenth century), almost literally translated by Chaucer in his *Secounde Nonnes Tale,* she is not so spoken of. All that is said there of music is that "Cantantibus organis illa in corde suo soli Domino cantabat," &c. ; or in Chaucer's words, 12,062–5, ed. Wright :

> "And whil the organs made melodie,
> To God alloon in herte thus sang sche :
> ' O Lord, my soul and eek my body gye
> Unwemmed, lest that I confounded be.' "

Of course, however, the Latin words might be translated, "while her organs were sounding ;" that is, "while she was playing." The legend goes on to say, that this "mayden bright Cecilie" was under the immediate and present protection of an angel. In this passage of her story may perhaps be seen the beginning of the tradition referred to in *Alexander's Feast*, and so exquisitely painted by Raphael and others, that "she drew an angel down ; " but in the old story not her sweet playing, but her spotless purity, brought the angel near her, not to listen, but to be a "heavenly guard." He is seen by her husband too, when he becomes a Christian :

> " Valirian goth home and fint Cecilie
> Withinne his chambre with an aungel stonde.
> This aungel had of roses and of lilie
> Corounes tuo, the which he bar in honde ;
> And first to Cecilie, as I understonde,
> He gaf that oon, and after can he take
> That other to Valirian hir make."

She and he are said to have suffered martyrdom in the year 220. All, then, that the legend certainly shows to the purpose is, that St. Cecilia was one over whom music had great influence —that it inspired in her high religious emotion. It may show further that she was herself a skilful musician. The fame of her deep passion for sacred music, and possibly of her skill in it, might well at a later time give countenance, if it did not give rise, to the tradition that she invented the grand instrument of Church music.

As for this said instrument, its early history is obscure. "Some derive its origin from the bagpipe ; others, with more probability, from an instrument of the Greeks, though a very imperfect one—the water-organ—as it is known that the first organs used in Italy came thither from the Greek empire. It is said that Pope Vitellianus (died 671) caused organs to be set up in some Roman churches in the seventh century. Organs were at first portable. The organs now in use are considered an invention of the Germans, but respecting the time of this invention opinions differ. . . . It is certain that the use of organs was not common before the fourteenth century." (*Pop. Cycl.*) That the name is Greek is a strong confirmation of its Greek origin. "The only incident of religious history," runs a paragraph in Chambers' *Book of Days* (i. 495), "connected with the 10th of April that is noticed in a French work resembling the present, is the introduction, by King Pepin of France, of an organ into the church of St. Corneille at Compiègne in the year 787."

32. 1. This was an opinion said to have been held by Pythagoras. "We find running through the entire Pythagorean system the idea that order or harmony of relation is the regulating principle of the whole universe." (Smith's larger *Biog. Myth. Dict.*) It was not only "the regulating," but in the first instance the creative principle ; it brought into union opposing elements, "jarring atoms." The music of the spheres was a Pythagorean notion. See Milton's *Hymn Nat.* 125.

[What does *heavenly* mean here ?]

2. *frame.* This was a favourite word with poets about the close of the seventeenth century. See "vocal *frame*," in *Alexander's Feast ;* "a shining *frame*" in Addison's

> " The spacious firmament on high," &c.

began from, &c. So *Alexander's Feast*, 25 :

> " The song began from Jove."

Comp. Virgil's "a Jove principium" (*Ecl.* iii. 60) ; Theocritus' ἐκ Διὸς ἀρχώμεσθα (*Id.* xvii. 1, ed. Paley).

4. Comp. Ovid's picture of Chaos :

> " Rudis indigestaque moles,
> Nec quidquam, nisi pondus iners, congestaque eodem
> Non bene junctarum discordia semina rerum."

See the whole passage in his *Metam.* i. 5-20. See also *Paradise Lost*, ii. 890-916.

32. 5. *heave her head.* See *L'Allegro*, 145. Miltonic words and phrases are very common in Dryden's writings. Pope, too, has this phrase, *Dunciad*, ii. 256:

> " Roused by the light, old Dulness *heav'd the head.*"

[In what sense do we use *heave* now ?]

6. [What is the force of *The* here ?]

voice = words uttered by the voice. So frequently *vox*, in Latin, as in Horace's "nescit *vox* missa reverti." (*Ars Poet.* 390.)

[Fully explain the construction of the phrase *ye more than dead.*]

8. See *Paradise Lost*, ii. 898.

14. *the notes :* i.e. of the first seven notes of the octave.

15. *the diapason.* "Diapason denotes a chord which includes all tones ; it is the same with what we call an eight or an octave ; because there are but seven tones or notes, and then the eight is the same again with the first." (*Har.* apud Johnson.) *Diapason* = (i,) διὰ πασῶν (χορδῶν συμφωνία). One of Aristotle's *Problemata* is : " διὰ τί ἡ διὰ πασῶν συμφωνία ᾄδεται μόνη ; See *musica* in Smith's larger *Dict. Antiq.* Comp. Crashaw :

> " Many a sweet rise, many as sweet a fall,
>   A full-mouth *diapason* swallows all ;"

and Milton's *At a Solemn Music*, where he would that we on earth should "answer" the melodies of heaven,

> " As once we did, till disproportion'd sin
>   Jarr'd against Nature's chime, and with harsh din
>   Broke the fair music that all creatures made
>   To their great lord, whose love their motion swayed
>   In perfect *diapason*," &c.

closing. See *Hymn Nat.* 100. So Herbert :

> " Sweet spring, full of sweet days and roses ;
>   A box where sweets compacted lie,
>   My music shows you have your *closes*,
>   And all must die."

[How would you parse *full* here ?]

16. Collins in the beginning of his *Ode* describes how, when Music was yet young,

> " The Passions oft, to hear her shell,
>   Throng'd around her magic cell,
>   Exulting, trembling, raging, fainting," &c.

till at last each one determined to try his own skill. Comp. *Midsummer Night's Dream*, II. i. 150, the well-known line,

> " Music hath charms to sooth a savage breast "

(it occurs in the beginning of Congreve's *Mourning Bride*) ; &c. &c. Porphyry states of Pythagoras : "Κατεκήλει δὲ ῥυθμοῖς καὶ μέλεσι καὶ ἐπῳδαῖς τὰ ψυχικὰ πάθη καὶ τὰ σωματικά.

quell is strictly but the older form of *kill*.

17. *Jubal.* See *Genesis* iv. 21.

shell. This somewhat affected name for a lyre found great favour with our poets from Dryden to the close of the last century. It is of course a Classicism ; comp. *testudo*, χέλυς.

the chorded shell. See Homer's (so assigned) *Hymn to Mercury*, 25-65.

21. [What part of speech is *less* here ?]

33. 25. Comp. Virg. *Æn.* ix. 501:

> " At tuba terribilem sonitum procul ære canoro
> Increpuit."

with which Servius compares Ennius'

> " At tuba terribili sonitu tara tantara dixit."

See Shakspere's *Richard II.* I. iii. 134:

> " With boisterous untuned drums,
> With harsh-resounding trumpets' dreadful bray."

28. [What does *mortal* mean here? See Trench's *Select Glossary*, s. v. Comp.:

> " Come, thou *mortal* wretch."

(*Antony and Cleopatra*, V. i. 63.)]
 alarms. See note, *Prothal.* 158.
 29. Comp. Dryden's " Come if you dare," &c.
 33. Chaucer says of his Squire:

> " Syngynge he was or *flowtynge* all the day."

The "floyte" is mentioned in the *House of Fame.* See Chappell's *Popular Music of the Olden Time*, i. 33-6.
 34. [What does *dying* mean? Comp. *Twelfth Night*, I. i.4
 discovers = simply uncovers. So *Merchant of Venice*, II. vii. 1:

> " Go draw aside the curtain, and *discover*
> The several caskets to this noble prince."

Comp. *dis*robe, *dis*people, *dis*mantle, &c. [In what sense do we use the word *discover*?]
 35. [How does the sense of *hopeless* here differ from that in Shakspere's *Richard II.* I. iii. 152, " The *hopeless* word of ' never to return ' "? Quote parallels.]
 36. " The lute was once the most popular instrument in Europe, although now rarely to be seen except represented in old pictures. . . . It has been superseded by the guitar," &c. (See Chappell's *Popular Music of the Olden Time*, i. 102-3.) See Shakspere, *passim*; Drummond's Sonnet *To his Sister* (in the *Golden Treasury*); *Paradise Lost*, v. 151 ; *Com.* 478 ; *Ode on the Passion:*

> " Me softer airs befit, and softer strings
> Of *lute* or violl still more apt for mournful things."

Sonnet XV. Pope follows Dryden in his

> " In a sadly pleasing strain
> Let the warbling lute complain."

37. *violins.* Violin (= violino) is a dim. of viol, as violoncello of violin. The violin completely replaced the viol in the reign of Charles II. See Chappell's *Pop. Mus.* ii. 467-9.
 41. *dame.* Comp. Milton's *Paradise Lost*, ix. 612 :—

> " Sovran of creatures, universal *dame*."

So often in Shakspere.
 44. *organs.* See Milton's *Paradise Lost*, i. 708, vii. 596; Shakspere's *Tempest*, III. iii. 98, " the thunder—that deep and dreadful *organ-pipe*." The older English poets gene-

rally speak of organs, or a pair (= set) of organs: that is, the word organ denotes but a single pipe. Thus Sandys:

> " Praise with timbrels, *organs,* flutes;
> Praise with violins and lutes."

See Chappell's *Pop. Mus.* i. 49, &c.   Father Schmidt and other famous organ-builders flourished in the latter half of the seventeenth century.   The organ in the Temple Church, London, was built by Schmidt in Charles II.'s time.

33. 47. The audacity of this line may be regarded as a sign of the times, which were not reverent nor humble-minded. See Dryden's *Ode to the Memory of Mrs. Anne Killegrew, passim.* Comp. *Absal. and Achit.* Part I. 831, of the Duke of Ormond's son:

> " Snatched in manhood's prime
> By unequal fates and *Providence's crime.*"

Comp. Waller's—

> " They now assist the choir
> Of angels, who their songs admire."

48. *Orpheus.* See Shakspere's *Two Gentlemen of Verona,* III. ii. 78-81; *Henry VIII.* III. i. 3, &c.; Hor. *Od.* I. xii. 7-12, &c.

50. *Sequacious.* Comp. Sid. *Carm.* xvi. 3: "Quæ [chelys] saxa *sequacia* flectens." Comp. Ovid's "saxa *sequentia,*" *Met.* xi. 2.

52. [What is meant by *vocal breath ?*]

53. Comp. *Alex. Feast,* 170.
      straight. See *L'Allegro,* 69.

34. 55. See note on l. 1, and on *Hymn Nat.* 125.
      60. Comp. Shakspere's *Tempest,* IV. i. 151-6.
      63. *untune* = destroy the harmony, *i.e.* the vivifying principle, of.

ALEXANDER'S FEAST.

SEE INTRODUCTION TO "SONG FOR ST. CECILIA'S DAY."

THIS song was written in 1697, in a single night, according to St John, afterwards Lord Bolingbroke. He states that Dryden said to him when he called upon him one morning: " I have been up all night: my musical friends made me promise to write them an Ode for their Feast of St. Cecilia, and I was so struck with the subject which occurred to me that I could not leave it till I had completed it ; here it is, finished at one sitting."

34. 1. *'Twas at,* &c. There is here a sort of rhetorical ellipse. He means, " It was at the royal feast that what follows happened," or, " The scene of the subject of our Ode was the hall of the royal feast ;" but he boldly omits the explanatory clause. In the well-known words, " We met, 'twas in a crowd," the explanatory clause, in fact, precedes ; but it is often omitted altogether, as here, especially in the beginning of a tale or poem. Comp. Moore's "*'Tis* the last rose of summer."

[What does *for* mean here ?   What other meanings has it ?]
[When was Persia "won" ?   See *Hist. Greece.*]

7. At a Greek banquet the guests were garlanded with roses and myrtle leaves.

9. *Thais.* See Smith's larger *Biog. and Mythol. Dict.* Athenæus is our chief informant about her. According to him, she was after Alexander's death married to Ptolemy Lagi. She was as famous for her wit as her beauty. " Her name is best known from the story of her having stimulated the Conqueror (Alexander), during a great festival at Persepolis, to set fire to the palace of the Persian kings ; but this anecdote, immortalized as it has been by Dryden's

famous Ode [see ll. 123-50], appears to rest on the sole authority of Cleitarchus, one of the least trustworthy of the historians of Alexander, and is in all probability a mere fable."

34. 11. [In what two ways may *youth* in this line be parsed? Which is the better?]

12. *pair* and *peer* (l. 6) are etymologically identical.

16. *Timotheus.* See Smith's larger *Biog. and Mythol. Dict.* This Timotheus is said to have been a Theban. Suidas tells us he "flourished under Alexander the Great, on whom his music made so powerful an impression that once, in the midst of a performance by Timotheus of an Orthian poem to Athena, he started from his seat and seized his arms." The more celebrated Timotheus, "the musician and poet of the later Athenian dithyramb," a native of Miletus, died some thirty years before Alexander's conquest of Persia.

17. *tuneful* See *St. Cecilia's Day,* 6.

35. 21. *began from Jove.* See *St. Cecilia's Day,* 2.

22. *seats.* So, in Latin, *sedes* is used in the plural.

24. [What is meant by *bely'd the god?* Comp. Shakspere's *Richard II.* II. ii. 76-7.]

For this wild story see Plutarch's *Alex.* &c. See *Paradise Lost,* ix. 494-510. In the mediæval romances about Alexander it was not Jove, but one Nectanebus, a refugee king of Egypt, who was the father of the prince : see *e. g.* the fragment of *Alisaunder* edited by Mr. Skeat for the Early English Text Society.

25. *radiant spires.* Comp. Milton's "circling spires."

[Which is the better word with which to connect *on radiant spires?* What does *rode* mean?]

26. Her name was Olympias. See *Class. Dict.*

31. *a present deity.* Comp. Hor. *Od.* III. v. 2 ; *Psalm* xlvi. 1.

37. See Hom. *Iliad,* i. 528-30 :

> " ἦ, καὶ κυανέῃσιν ἐπ' ὀφρύσι νεῦσε Κρονίων
> ἀμβρόσιαι δ' ἄρα χαῖται ἐπερρώσαντο ἄνακτος
> κρατὸς ἀπ' ἀθανάτοιο, μέγαν δ' ἐλέλιξεν Ὄλυμπον."

Virg. *Æn.* x. 115 :

> " Annuit, et totum nutu tremefecit Olympum."

The Latin *numen* means originally a nod (as in *Lucret.* ii. 633).

38. *Bacchus.* See *Class. Dict.*
See Keats' *Endymion,* IV. ; Catull. lxiv. 251-64.

43. *honest face* = handsome face. The epithet is taken from Virgil (*Georg.* ii. 392) :

> " Quocunque deus [Bacchus] circum *caput* egit *honestum.*"

Comp. *Georg.* iii. 81, and *Æn.* x. 133. *Honest-like* is used in Scotland for "goodly, as regarding the person." (*Jamieson.*) Comp. *Absalom and Achit.* Part I. 72 :

> " Seams of wounds *dishonest* to the sight."

44. *hautboys* = oboes (French, *hautbois*, that is *haut-bois*).

53. [What battles had he fought ?]

[Is *fought* a "strong" pret. or a "weak"?]

[What is meant by *to fight over a battle?*]

56. *ardent eyes.* See Cicero's speech *in Verr.* II. iv. 66, of one Theomnastus' madness : " Nam quum spumus ageret in ore, *oculis arderet,* voce maxima vim me sibi adferre clamaret, copulati in jus pervenimus."

[To whom does the former *his* refer ? To whom the latter ?]

36. 59. *Muse.* So Hor. *Sat.* II. vi. 16, 17 :

> " Ergo ubi me in montes et in arcem ex urbe removi,
> Quid prius illustrem satiris *musaque* pedestri ? "

It is sometimes used for a poet. See note, *Prothal.* 159.

36. 61. [Was there ever any difference between *sung* and *sang?* See Latham's *English Grammar.*]

65. *weltring.* See *Hymn Nat.* 124.

[What word is omitted here?] Comp. A. Phillips *To Charlotte Pulteney* (in the *Golden Treasury*):

> " And thou shalt in thy daughter see
> This picture once resembled thee."

&c. &c.

68. *expos'd* = cast out. Comp. Latin *exponere*, Greek ἐκτιθέναι.

69. Comp. Pope's *Elegy on an Unfortunate Lady* :

> " By foreign hands thy dying eyes were closed :
> By foreign hands thy decent limbs composed."

Virg. *Æn.* ix. 487.

With not a friend. A here has its older force ; it = one, a single ; see note to " at a birth," *L'All.* 14. *Not a* is, in fact, a stronger form of *none* or *no.* The negative in this phrase is sometimes *never.*

[What is the force of *with* here?]

71. *revolveing* = Latin *revolvens ;* as in Ov. *Fast.* iv. 667 :

> "Excutitur terrore quies ; Numa visa *revolvit.*"

73. *a sigh he stole* = he sighed privily, or it may be silently. See Shakspere's *Taming of the Shrew,* III. ii. 142 :

> " 'Twere good, methinks, to *steal our marriage.*"

Comp. the phrase " *to steal a march.*" So in Greek, κλέπτειν = to do anything in a thievish, a secret, an underhand manner ; see Sophocles' *Ajax,* 189 :

> " εἰ δ' ὑποβαλλόμενα.
> κλέπτουσι μύθους οἱ μεγάλοι βασιλῆς," κ.τ.λ.

El. 37: δόλοισι κλέψαι σφαγάς, &c. Comp. *Cymb.* I. v. 66 :

> " He *furnaces*
> The thick sighs from him ;"

which is explained by " the lover sighing like furnace " in *As You Like It,* II. vii. 147.

77. *'Twas,* &c. See above, l. 1.

[What does *but* mean here? What other meanings has it?]

to move. Comp. Virg. *Æn.* x. 163, " Cantusque *movete.*" Strictly, the verb applies to the striking or stirring of the strings. Comp. song in Cowley's *Davideis* :

> " Hark ! how the strings awake !
> And though the *moving* hand approach not near," &c.

79. [What does *sweet* here qualify?]

Lydian measures. See *L'Allegro,* 136.

Conversely, love melts the soul to pity, in *Two Gentlemen of Verona,* IV. iv. 101.

82. See Falstaff's catechism, 1 *Henry IV.* V. i.

83. [What is it that is *never ending,* &c. ? What *fighting still,* &c. ?]

85. *worth winning.* So " worth nothing," " worth ambition," " worth thy sight," " worth inquiry," " worth while." (With " worthy " the preposition is generally inserted, but in Shakspere, *Coriol.* III. i. 299, we have " worthy death.") This construction may be explained in this way : the Ang.-Sax. inflection which marked the word governed by *weorth* fell out of use, and its omission was not compensated for by the introduction of the preposition.

36. 88. *the good.* Comp. *Will. of Palerne*, 5075:

> "And eche day was gret *good* give all aboute."

Nowadays we use only the plural form. So we use now only "wages."

89. *the many* = οἱ πολλοί.

96. [What is the force of *at once* here? What does it qualify?]

37. 98. [Why does he say *again* ?]

100. *bands of sleep.* Comp. "*bands* of death," " the *bands* of those sins " (Collect for the 24th Sunday after Trinity), &c. The notes that rouse him are to be very different from those which are to make Orpheus "heave his head " in *L'Allegro.*

108. *see the snakes that they rear,* &c. In *Æn.* vi. 571-3, Tisiphone's left hand is filled with snakes :

> " Continuo sontes ultrix, accincta flagello,
> Tisiphone quatit insultans, torvosque sinistra
> Intentans angues, vocat agmina sæva sororum."

117. *crew.* See *L'Allegro*, 38.

122. *flambeau.* French words were much affected by the English in the latter part of the seventeenth century. See Butler :

> " For though to smatter words of Greek
> And Latin be the rhetorique
> Of pedants counted and vainglorious,
> To smatter French is meritorious."

See Macaulay's *History of England*, I. chap. iii.

125. [How far does this parallel between Thais and Helen hold good?]

128. *organs.* See note on *St. Cæc.* 44.

129. [What is the force of *to* here ?]

133. *the vocal frame* = the speaking structure.

88. 137. [What is the force of *with* here ?]

POPE.

THE details of Pope's life are involved in much obscurity. The part of London in which he was born, his birthday, the circumstances under which several of his works were published, his share in the *Odyssey*, his rupture with Addison, his relation to various notable persons of his time, are all matters of yet unsolved controversy. Some at least of these difficulties result from a certain want of ingenuousness, or, to speak positively, a certain love of petty diplomacy and intrigue which marked his character.

(1) Alexander Pope was born in London in 1688. In his *Prologue to the Satires* he says:

> " Of gentle blood (part shed in honour's cause,
> While yet in Britain honour had applause)
> Each parent sprung."

Elsewhere (in his *Letter to a Noble Lord*) he says, his father " was no mechanic, neither a hatter nor a cobbler, but in truth of a very honourable family ; and my mother of an ancient one." His father, at the time of the future poet's birth, was a wholesale linen-merchant in London. As he was a Roman Catholic, he was debarred from giving his son the best educational advantages the country had to offer. What he could do, he did. Alexander was instructed in the rudiments of Latin and Greek by a Roman Catholic priest, then sent to "a Catholic seminary " at Twyford, near Winchester, then to another in London. When he quitted this last school he was not quite twelve years old. "This," he said to Spence. "was all the teaching I ever had, and God knows it extended a very little way. When I had done with my priests, I took to reading by myself, for which I had a very great eagerness and enthusiasm, especially for poetry ; and in a few years I had dipped into a very great number of the English, French, Italian, Latin, and Greek poets," &c.

His father had retired from business, and settled first at Kensington, and then at Binfield, near Windsor Forest. To Binfield Pope went when his school-days were ended, and there he mainly resided, making occasional visits to London and other places both near and some distance off, till 1716. At an early age he began to write verses ; he

> " Lisp'd in numbers, for the numbers came ; "

he translated ; he imitated. At last in 1709 he commenced his career of fame by publishing his *Pastorals*. Presently (in 1711) followed his *Essay on Criticism ;* then the *Rape of the Lock*, in two Cantos, afterwards increased to four. Pope at once took the first place amongst the poets of the day. This rapid success is to be accounted for not only by the excellence of what he produced (in the eyes of his age that excellence was of the highest order), but by "the plentiful lack" of writers worthy in any sense of the title of poets which then prevailed. The throne of poetry was in fact empty ; it could scarcely be said that there was any one standing even on the steps of it. Pope had no rivals ; he was crowned as soon as he appeared.

> " Well-natur'd Garth inflam'd with early praise,
> And Congreve loved, and Swift endur'd my lays.
> The courtly Talbot, Somers, Sheffield read ;
> Ev'n mitred Rochester would nod the head ;

> And St. John's self, great Dryden's friend before,
> With open arms receiv'd one poet more.
> Happy my studies when by these approv'd !
> Happier their author when by these belov'd ! "

He found many friendly neighbours at Binfield ; and he soon became known and sought after in a far wider society. Addison and Steele welcomed him not only as writers of the *Tatlers* and the *Spectators*, but personally. He formed, however, his more permanent friendships amongst the Tories. He was himself professedly neither Whig nor Tory : his closest friends were Tories ; his views, at least later in life, were thoroughly Whiggish. But Pope, though of a not ungenial nature, was precluded by his physical constitution from any abundant enjoyment of social pleasures. From an early age he was an invalid. At a later period he needed constant nursing. His life was "a long disease ;" see Dr. Johnson's account of his extreme weakness, his deformity, his helplessness. "The tenement of clay" was "o'er-informed ;" it had its revenge. It is impossible not to connect the irritability and tendency to satire which Pope exhibited from his very schoolboyhood with this distressing condition of his body.

(2) But though he was not to be a great social light, he was pre-eminent elsewhere. The world was delighted to know, in 1713, that he proposed to devote himself to the translation of the *Iliad.* The publication of this memorable work began in 1715, and ended in 1720. Then proposals were issued for the translation of the *Odyssey.* In this labour Broome and Fenton assisted him with some classical knowledge which they had gathered at Cambridge, and a mastery of the heroic couplet which they had learnt from himself. This performance seems to have been completed in 1725. Besides these two translations Pope wrote during the ten years, from 1715 to 1725, the *Epistle of Eloisa to Abelard,* and other minor pieces ; and also edited Shakspere, not with much knowledge, but not without taste.

As to his private life, his Homer brought him not only much reputation, but very considerable money profits. "Thanks to Homer," he lived and thrived,

> " Indebted to no prince or peer alive."

In 1716 he removed with his parents from Binfield to Chiswick. There in the following year his father died :

> " Born to no pride, inheriting no strife,
> Nor marrying discord in a noble wife ;"

—Pope is reflecting on Addison here—

> " Stranger to civil and religious rage,
> The good man walk'd innoxious thro' his age :
> No courts he saw, no suits would ever try,
> Nor dared an oath nor hazarded a lie.
> Unlearn'd, he knew no schoolman's subtle art,
> No language but the language of the heart.
> By nature honest, by experience wise,
> Healthy by temp'rance and by exercise ;
> His life, tho' long, to sickness past unknown,
> His death was instant, and without a groan."
> *Prol. to the Sat.*

In 1718 the poet and his mother migrated from Chiswick to Twickenham, or "Twitenham," as he pleased to call it. He beautified his house and little grounds after his heart's content. Within no great distance from him lived, at one time or another, many of his friends—some not always to be so—as Lord Bolingbroke, Lady Mary Wortley Montagu, Lord Peterborough, Lord Burlington. Here, varying his devotion to literature with so much social intercourse as his weakly frame permitted him to enjoy, he passed, not quietly or peacefully, nearly a quarter of a century.

(3) His next great work after the *Iliad* and *Odyssey* were completed was the *Dunciad.* In 1727 he had ridiculed, in his *Treatise on the Bathos, or Art of Sinking in Poetry,* many of the poetasters of the day. Not unnaturally, these gentlemen retaliated to the best of their ability. Pope—not, probably, without hints and instigations from Swift—replied, in 1728, with his famous *Satire* epic. In the following year he re-issued it with copious notes, that secured his sarcasms their proper application. From 1730-7 he continued his war with the Dunces by various contributions to the *Grub Street Journal.* In 1742 he republished the *Dunciad,* with the addition of another book. In 1743 appeared another edition, with Cibber substituted for Theobald as the hero—a change not made without damage to the unity of the poem.

Meanwhile, he had been more nobly busy. The earliest of his *Moral Essays* (the one usually printed last) was published in 1731 ; the latest (the one printed as Epistle II.) in 1735. In 1732 came out the first two books of the *Essay on Man;* in 1733 and 1734 the third and fourth books. To this same period belong the *Satires,* the earliest of which appeared in 1733; the *Epilogue* came out in 1738. In 1737 and in 1741 Pope issued his *Letters,* copies of which had already in some mysterious way been procured and published without authority.

Besides this list of works there is not much more to record. The friends whose successive influence is especially discernible in his post-Homeric works are Swift, Bolingbroke, and Warburton. All these survived him ; but the " thin partition " which latterly divided Swift's "great wit" from madness was broken down in 1740, and converse between the two foremost geniuses of their time for ever closed. Gay and Arbuthnot had passed away some years before. Pope's mother died in 1733. Pope, though not old as years go, began to find himself alone. He saw a new race springing up around him. In 1738, the year in which Pope finished his last poem—the fourth book of the *Dunciad*—appeared Johnson's *London.* In 1741 commenced with *Pamela* the æra of the modern novel.

Pope died on May 30, 1744.

Perhaps no poet ever expressed more successfully what he had to express than Pope.* Many have been gifted with a loftier imagination, with a profounder intuition, with nobler and more passionate sentiments ; but in few have their gifts been more clearly understood and represented. Pope knew his strength, and acted accordingly. He did not waste many long years of his life, as did Dryden, on a kind of literature in which he was not competent to excel ; he scarcely essayed the drama. He quickly abandoned lyric poetry, in spite of injudicious praises given to his *Ode for Musick on St. Cecilia's Day.*

His great aim was to express himself clearly and smoothly. He was ready to receive subjects from his friends, or from preceding writers. He did not care to originate. His business was attractive and lucid expression ; it was to "set" gems, not to create them. When he was yet a youth, his friend Walsh remarked to him that "though we had several great poets, we never had any one great poet that was correct ; " "and he desired me," Pope told Spence, "to make that my study and aim." And so Pope made it ; and few men have succeeded in their "study and aim " as Pope succeeded. Nor is the lesson which Pope's literary life conveys to be undervalued—the lesson of careful and conscientious workmanship. Pope gave always his best. His view of the poetic art may have been narrow, but he acted up to it with a most dutiful observance.

He adopted at an early time one particular metrical form—the heroic couplet, and adhered to it to the end. Perhaps no poet has been so completely a man of one metre. He is said to

---

* Comp. Browning's *Andrea del Sarto:*

> "I can do with my pencil what I know,
> What I see, what at the bottom of my heart
> I wish for, if I ever wish so deep;
> Do easily too—when I say perfectly,
> I do not boast perhaps."

See especially the following lines.

have contemplated writing an epic poem on Brutus, the mythical colonizer of Britain, in blank verse. There are some few blank verses of his composing in Thomson's *Seasons.* But he never really quitted the one vehicle of which he had made himself so famous a master.

Dryden was his great model. Perhaps his highest excellence lies in the same direction as that of Dryden lay—in the power of sketching characters. He, too, was a skilful portrait-painter; but his style is very different from Dryden's. In one instance he has ventured to challenge comparison with his master, in his picture of Villiers, of *Zimri,* forlorn and dying. A careful juxtaposition of the two masterpieces will well illustrate the affinities and the differences of their authors.

RAPE OF THE LOCK.

INTRODUCTION.

A QUARREL had arisen between the family of Miss Arabella Fermor and that of Lord Petre "on the trifling occasion of his having cut off a lock of her hair." One of their and of Pope's friends, a Mr. Caryl, laid the matter before the poet, that his wit might laugh away the clouds that had gathered. The result was a poem of two cantos, describing in a mock-heroic manner the circumstances of the robbery and the battle which ensued. This was published in a Miscellany of Bernard Lintot's in 1711.

"It was received so well," says Pope, in his note to the poem, "that he [the author] made it more considerable the next year by the addition of the machinery of the Sylphs, and extended it to five cantos." The game at Ombre was also inserted, as also the picture of the Cave of Spleen. The piece grew, in fact, from an amusing sketch into an epic on a small scale. Pope's models for this work were Tassoni's *Rape of the Bucket,* and Boileau's *Lectern;* but indeed there is no work of his that belongs more truly to his age than this one. The exquisite raillery with which the poem perpetually sparkles, the familiarity which it exhibits with the epics of antiquity, and the use to which that familiarity is turned, the finished ease of its style, all at once connect it with the age which produced it. Addison called it *merum sal,* that is, "pure wit," in its earlier form. Certainly the additions made, if they do in some degree impair its unity, must not be allowed to deprive it of that happy title.

The spirit of that age found its most complete embodiment in burlesque poetry. It was then in perfect accordance with that spirit that Pope developed and expanded his *jeu d'esprit* into its fuller form. It was thought that supernatural agents were essential to an epic poem. Pope was particularly happy in his selection of such beings. He made use, with certain modifications, of the spiritual system of the Rosicrucians, a sect well known throughout Western Europe in the seventeenth century. This, too, he used with the characteristic light mockery of his age.

The idea of the game at Ombre was suggested by Vida's *Scacchia Ludus.** Vida was a Latin-writing poet who flourished under the smile of Leo X. See *Essay on Criticism,* 697–708. Pope's age, in the somewhat indiscriminate ardour of its Roman classicism, embraced even the Latin poets of the Renaissance. The game *Ombre* was introduced into England about the middle of the seventeenth century from Spain, as its name and the names of its cards show. In Queen Anne's time it was the favourite ladies' game, as Piquet was the gentlemen's, Whist or Whisk that of clergymen and country squires. When it fell into disuse Quadrille, which was a species of it, "obtained vogue, which it maintained till Whisk was introduced, which now," says Barrington, writing in 1787 (quoted in Chatto's *Facts and Speculations on the Origin and History of Playing Cards*), "prevails not only in England, but in most of the civilized parts of Europe."

---

* Vida was not the first verse-maker who celebrated the favourite old game of Chess. A catalogue of the library of Peterborough Abbey mentions "Versus de ludo Scaccorum." See Warton's *Hist. Eng. Poetry,* i. 81, note, Ed. 1840.

U

CANTO I.

39. 1. Comp. beginning of Pope's translation of the *Iliad.*

3. *This verse,* &c. See *Introd.*

39. 4. [What is the force of *ev'n* here? What part of speech is it?]

5. Comp. Virg. *Georg.* iv. 6, 7.

6. [Would there be any difference in the sense if he had written *inspires* and *approves?*]

8. *Belle. Beau* (l. 23, &c.) is almost fallen out of use.

11. Comp. Hor. *Od.* II. xvi. 17.

12. Comp. Virg. *Æn.* i. 11.

13. *Sol.* The tendency to classical names and titles was beginning to be excessive in the early part of the eighteenth century. Phœbus, Titan, Sol, were superseding the simple sun; Chloe, Mary, &c. Cowper may be said to have commenced for us that deliverance from such classicism which Wordsworth completed.

14. *must* = are ordained. See *Lycidas,* 38.

15. *lap-dogs.* There are many references in our literature to these pets of the ladies, from Chaucer's *Prologue* (see the description of the Prioress) downwards.

[What is the force of *the* here?]

16. [What part of speech is *just* here? How can he say they *awake,* if they were *sleepless?*]

17. It would seem that three rings of the bell with a tap on the floor were the signal that the sleeper had arisen.

rung. See note on *blow, Hymn Nat.* 130.

18. The watch was what we should call "a repeater."

19. *prest.* In the preceding line the past participle is spelt *pressed.*

20. *Sylph.* See *Introd.*

22. Comp. *Il Penseroso,* 147.

23. *a Birth-night Beau,* i.e. a fine gentleman, such as were to be seen at the state ball given on the anniversary of the royal birthday. See *Satires of Dr. Donne versified,* iv. 130:

> " Mere household trash! of *birthnights,* balls, and shows
> More than ten Holinsheds, or Halls, or Stowes,
> When the Queen frown'd or smiled, he knows."

Spectator, No. 15: " A ball is a great help to discourse, and a *birthnight* furnishes conversation for a twelvemonth after." See *Spectator,* No. 294, for Feb. 6 (Queen Anne's birthday).

27. He is parodying *Paradise Lost,* v. 35 *et seq.*

care. See note on *sorrow,* in *Lycidas,* 166.

40. 29. *touch'd.* Comp. Lat. *tango;* e.g. Hor. *A. P.* 98.

30. *the Nurse,* &c., *the Priest,* &c. This conjunction is not insignificant of the age. Comp. Dryden's *Hind and Panther,* Part III. 1686:

> " The priest continues what the nurse began,
> And thus the child imposes on the man."

[What is the force of *the* here?]

31. Comp. *Paradise Lost,* i. 781-8.

[What is the force of *by* here?]

32. *the silver token.* See Bishop Corbet's *The Fairies' Farewell:*

> " And though they sweepe the hearths no lesse
> Than maides were wont to doe,
> Yet who of late for cleanlinesse
> Findes sixpence in her shoe?"

and Poole's *English Parnassus,* of Queen Mab:

> " But if so they chance to feast her,
> In their shoe she drops a tester."

See Ellis's Brand's *Pop. Ant., Notes to Fairy Mythology.* Comp. the Story of the Pixies in Keightley's *Fairy Mythology,* p. 303 of Bohn's Edition.

40. 32. *the circled green.* See Tennyson's *Gardener's Daughter;* Dryden's *Hind and Panther,* Part I. 212:

> " As where in fields *the fairy rounds* are seen," &c.

For many other allusions, see Ellis's Brand's *Pop. Ant.*

33. See Chaucer's *Secounde Nonnes Tale,* 12,146, *et seq.* Ed. Wright.

36. *narrow* is used here " proleptically," or anticipatingly, as adjectives are often used in Latin and in Greek. So *propitious* in Canto ii.

[What is the force of *bound* here ?]

37. He does not shrink from parodying the New Testament. See *St. Matthew's Gospel,* xi. 25.

40. [What does *still* mean here ?]

42. *Militia.* There was scarcely yet that sharp antithesis between " the militia" and the army" which prevailed afterwards. The idea of "a standing army" was scarcely yet altogether accepted by the nation. The first " Mutiny Act" was passed in 1689.

44. *the Box:* i.e. at the opera. See below.

the Ring = our " Row." See below, and *Spectator,* No. 15: " She thinks life lost in her own family, and fancies herself out of the world when she is not in *the Ring,* the play-house, or the drawing-room." See Swift's *Cadenus and Vanessa:*

> " To scandal next: 'What awkward thing
> Was that last Sunday in *the Ring?*'"

&c. &c.

46. See Dryden's *Juvenal,* 1st Sat. 184:

> " Some beg for absent persons, feign them sick,
> Close-mew'd in their *sedans* for want of air,
> And for their wives produce an empty *chair.*"

47. "The poet here forsakes the Rosicrucian system, which in this part is too extravagant even for ludicrous poetry, and gives a beautiful fiction of his own on the Platonic Theology of the continuance of the Passions in another state, when the mind before its leaving this has not been well purged and purified by philosophy ; which furnishes an occasion for much useful satire." (Warburton.)

55. See Virg. *Æn.* vi. 653-5. For the passion of the ladies for fine equipages see *Tatler* and *Spectator,* passim.

56. *Ombre.* See below.

41. 73. [What part of the sentence is *safe* ?]

spark. Comp. " flame."

87. *'Tis these.* Comp. Greek ἔστιν οἵ. So in Latin, but perhaps the instance is unique, Prop. IV. ix. 17, 18:

> " *Est quibus* Eleæ concurrit palma quadrigæ ;
> *Est quibus* in celeres gloria nata pedes."

Dr. Johnson, in his *Plan of a Dictionary of the English Language,* 1747, quotes this line as erroneous in syntax, to illustrate the unsettled, ill-regulated state of our language ; but his objection would not seem well-founded. Comp. the Greek idiom. *'Tis* here, as often, is used in a purely rhetorical manner : *'tis these that* is but a more emphatic form of *these.* In such uses *'tis* and *'twas* do not necessarily require numerical inflexion. They serve just to introduce the subject of the sentence ; they need not vary in form according to the number of that subject.

94. [What does *impertinence* mean here? What is its etymological meaning?]

96. [What is meant by *treat* ?] See below, and Prior to Swift: "I have *treated* Lady Harriot at Cambridge, (a Fellow of a College treat!) and spoke verses to her in a gown and cap," &c.

41. 100. They keep re-arranging the affections, so to speak.

Comp. Addison : "Fans, silks, ribbands, laces, and gewgaws lay so thick together, that the heart was nothing else but a *toyshop*."

[What is the sense of *moving* here ?]

101. Warburton quotes from Statius :

> "Jam clypeus clypeis, umbone repellitur umbo,
> Ense minax ensis, pede pes, et cuspide cuspis."

102. *Beau* had been so completely adopted that it formed its plural according to the English rule. In Warburton's edition the French plural appears.

drive : i.e. drive out, expel.

105. [What is meant by *thy protection claim* ? What other meaning might the words have, not here, but with another context ?]

108. "The language of the Platonists, the writers of the intelligible world of spirits," &c. (Pope.)

110. We should rather say "this morning's sun."

112. [What is meant here by *pious* ? What other meaning has the word ?]

113. *all thy guardian can* = all that is in thy guardian's power. Comp. Dryden *apud* Johnson :

> "Mæcenas and Agrippa, who *can* most
> With Cæsar, are his foes."

"The Rosicrucian doctrine was delivered only to Adepts, with the utmost caution, and under the most solemn injunctions of secrecy." (Warburton.)

42. 115. *Shock.* "A rough-coated dog." (Halliwell's *Dict.*) "Shoughs" are mentioned as a species of dog in *Macbeth*, III. i. 94. "I would fain know," writes Locke, "why a *shock* and a hound are not distinct species." The word is cognate with *shaggy*, *shag*-haired. (Shakspere, 2 *Henry VI.* III. i. 367.)

[What difference would our modern usage make in this line?]

121. *Toilet* is strictly the cloth covering the dressing-table ; a diminutive of French *toile*.

128. *Pride.* Comp. *Piers Ploughman*, Prol. 23 :

> "And some putten hem to *pruyde* ; apparailed hem thereafter
> In contenaunce of clothing comen disguised."

So in R. Brunne's *Handlyng Synne, of Pride*, amongst the Seven deadly Sins (Ed. Furnivall, for the Roxburgh Club).

131. [What is meant by *nicely* ?]

138. See *Vicar of Wakefield*, chap. iv.

See *Spectator*, No. 478 ; Prior's *Hans Carvel* :

> "An untouch'd Bible grac'd her toilet ;
> No fear that hand of hers should spoil it."

146. *set* = adjust, arrange. See Swift's *Cadenus and Vanessa* :

> "Dear madam, let me set your head."

CANTO II.

152. [What does *Launch'd* mean here? what is its strict meaning?]

the silver Thames. See Spenser's *Proth.* 11.

43. 161. [What is meant by *strike* ?]

43. 167. *to.* Comp. *Psalm* xv. 4; 2 *Kings* xiv. 10, &c.

173. *sprindges.* See *Hamlet*, V. ii. 317:

> " As a woodcock to my own *springe*, Osrick,
> I'm justly killed with mine own treachery."

175. *insnare* = ensnare. So inquire, enquire, &c. Some persons pronounce " engine " as " ingine."

176. Warburton quotes from *Hudibras*:

> " And tho' it be a two-foot trout,
> 'Tis with a single hair pulled out."

Disraeli, in the *Curiosities of Literature* (in his chapter on " Poetical Imitations and Similarities "), more aptly, from Howell : " 'Tis a powerful sex : they were too strong for the first, the strongest and wisest man that was ; they must needs be strong when one hair of a woman can draw more than an hundred pair of oxen." Howell would seem to be referring to some older proverb or phrase.

186. *twelve vast French Romances* = the works of Calprenede, Mad. Scuderi, La Fayette, and others : e.g. *Cleopatra, Le Grand Cyrus, Clelie, Zayde,* &c. &c. Pope may well call them " vast ;" e.g. *Clelie* appeared in ten volumes of 800 pages each. The English translations were published in huge folios. See especially *Spectator*, No. 37.

193. See Virg. *Æn.* xi. 794-5.

196. *tydes.* Comp. Dryden:

> " But let not all the gold which Tagus hides,
> And pays the sea in tributary *tides*," &c.

[What is meant by *floating* ?]

44. 197. *melting music.* Comp. *Il Penseroso*, 165.

203. *Denizens.* The old French *deinzein* (from *deins,* Latin *de intus*), means properly one who dwells within, *i.e.* within the city, or who enjoys its franchise ; then generally an inhabitant ; then specially a naturalized citizen. Here *his Denizens* = his fellow-inhabitants.

205. [What are the *shrouds* of a ship?] For other meanings of *shrouds* see note to *Hymn Nat.* 218.

207. [What is the force of *insect* here ?]

See *Paradise Lost*, vii. 476-9.

208. *waft:* here in a middle sense. So *wave* in *Il Penseroso*, 148.

in clouds of gold. This use of *cloud* is common enough : *e.g.* see *Paradise Lost*, i. 340: " a pitchy *cloud* of locusts," &c. For *gold* see *Paradise Lost*, i. 483. Comp. " gilded butterfly " (*King Lear*, V. iii. 12 ; *Coriolanus*, I. iii. 65, &c).

210. [What part of speech is *half* here?]

211. *to the wind.* See *Lycid.* 13.

212. *filmy.* Properly *film* means a thin skin or pellicle. See *Paradise Lost*, xi. 412. It is used for a very slender thread : Queen Mab's " lash " was *of film.* (*Romeo and Juliet*, I. iv. 63.) Here *filmy dew* seems to mean the film-like moisture that covers leaves, &c.

glitt'ring textures. Milton's " glittering tissues " (*Paradise Lost*, v. 592). Tissue and texture are radically identical.

213. *dipt—tincture.* See *Paradise Lost*, v. 283 and 285.

218. *Superior by the head.* See Hom. *Il.* iii. 168 :

> " ἤτοι μὲν κεφαλῇ καὶ μείζονες ἄλλοι ἔασιν," κ.τ.λ.

So *Ibid.* 193, 227. We should now rather say "*a* head."

221. *Sylphs and Sylphids.* The feminine form *sylphid* is formed after the analogy of Achæid or Achæad (*Iliad*, v. 424), Troad, &c. Comp. Hom. *Il.* :

> "'Αχαιίδες, οὐκέτ' 'Αχαιοι."

(Comp. Virg. *Æn.* ix. 616.) This *id* or *ad* is also the Greek feminine patronymic sign. Comp. Nereus and Nereid, &c. (The masculine is *ida.* Comp. Atreus and Atreides, &c.) This same termination is also specially used to denote a poem or work on some subject specified in the first part of the word: thus *Thebaid* = poem on Thebes; *Æneid* = poem on Æneas; *Iliad* = poem on Ilium. (*Iliad* = a Trojan woman in *Æn.* i. 480, &c.)

44. 221. This is a parody of *Paradise Lost*, v. 600:

> " Hear, all ye angels, progeny of light,
>   Thrones, dominations, princedoms, virtues, powers."

See also l. 772.

222. *Fays, Fairies, Genii,* are names of Latin origin. *Fays* and *fairies* are romance from the same root, the Latin *fatum.* *Elf* is of Teutonic origin ; *dæmon* of Greek.

223. *spheres.* Sphere—properly = a ball, globe, and then specially a planet (see *Hymn Nat.*)—seems to be used also for a planet's path, or orbit, or circuit, and so for the area or region of its motion ; then generally for any tract or district or province in which any body moves. Comp. Shakspere, 1 *Henry IV.* V. iv. 65 :

> " Two stars keep not their motion in one *sphere.*"

So Gonzalo speaks of the moon's *sphere.* (*Tempest*, II. i. 182. Moon's sphere = moon in *Midsummer Night's Dream*, II. i. 7.) So *Midsummer Night's Dream*, II. i. 153:

> " And certain stars shot madly from their *spheres*
>   To hear the sea-maid's music."

So *King John*, V. vii. 74:

> " Now, now, you stars that move in your right *spheres,*
>   Where be your powers ? "

&c. &c. The general sense occurs in *Antony and Cleopatra*, II. vii. 15: "To be call'd into a huge *sphere* and not to be seen to move in 't," &c. Comp. *orb* in 1 *Henry IV.* V. i. 15:

> " Will you again unknit
> This churlish knot of all-abhorred war,
> And move in that obedient *orb* again
> Where you did give a fair and natural light ? " &c.

(Comp. *orb* in Bacon, *apud* Johnson.) Comp. the uses of " circle," " circuit," " round."

226. [*whiten.* Mention other verbs with this termination. What other force has it ?]

227. *wandring orbs* = meteors. See Shakspere, *passim.* Strictly the term *planets* (see following line) means " wanderers ; " but it is applied to stars that move along regular and calculated courses.

230. See *Paradise Lost*, iv. 555-60, especially 556-7 :

> " Swift as a shooting star
>   In autumn thwarts the night."

Comus, 80-1.

athwart. Comp. across, &c. For the simple word, see *Troilus and Cressida*, I. iii. 15 :

> " Trial did draw,
>   Bias and *thwart.*"

232. See *Paradise Lost*, xi. 244 : " Iris had dipt the woof."

233. *main.* The full phrase is the " main sea ; " so " main flood " (*Merchant of Venice*, IV. i. 72); " the main waters " (*Ib.* V. i. 97).

234. [What is the meaning of *kindly* here ? Comp. " gentle rain," in *Merchant of*

Venice, IV. i. 185. What is meant by "the *kindly* fruits of the earth" in the *Book of Common Prayer*?]

44. 237. [Put these words in their proper order. What objection is there to such an inversion of an English sentence as they now present? Make your answer clear by quoting or making examples.]

[What is meant by the *care of Nations*? What other meaning might the words possibly have? Comp. l. 240.]

Dryden proposed to introduce the guardian angels of kingdoms into his never-written *Arthuriad*. See Johnson's *Life of Dryden*. Dryden charged Blackmore with stealing his subject; "only," he adds, "the guardian angels of kingdoms were machines too ponderous for him to manage." Pope, following Dryden in this respect, as in many others, proposed to use the same supernatural agency in his epic on Brutus; but that, too, was never written.

239. *Fair* was commonly used as a substantive in the latter part of the seventeenth and in the eighteenth centuries, after the French; thus *Spectator*: "Gentlemen who do not design to marry yet pay their devoirs to one particular *fair*;" but it does not seem to have been adopted so far as to have a plural inflection.

45. 245. *A wash*. See *Vicar of Wakefield*, chap. vi.

246. [What is meant by *airs* here? What other various meanings has the word?]

248. Comp. *Spectator*: "She was *flounced* and *furbelowed* from head to foot, every ribbon was crinkled, and every part of her garment in *curl*."

Flounce. See note on *frounced*, *Il Pens*. 123.

Furbelo = strictly a kind of flounce; commonly, the fringed border of a gown or petticoat. "Furbelows, fringe; any ornamental part of a female['s] dress. *Var. dial*." (Halliwell's *Arch. and Prov. Dict.*) Comp. German *falbel*. Perhaps the *-ow* is diminutival. Comp. (hole) hollow, (fur) furrow, morrow (= morning), (sper) sparrow (sperhauke = sparrow-hawk, *Piers Ploughman*, Ed. Skeat, vi. 199). Perhaps the spelling of the word points to some popular attempt at an explanation of it.

251. *slight*. So sleight was variously spelt. We retain the word in the phrase "sleight of hand." In older English it was used much more commonly; *e.g.* see Shakspere, 3 *Henry VI*. IV. ii. 20, &c.

254. *China jar*. China-ware or porcelain "was first introduced into Europe in the beginning of the sixteenth century. . . . For a long time it was erroneously believed that China alone furnished the proper kind of clay necessary for its manufacture, and this circumstance, along with the then extremely rude state of the potter's art in Europe, prevented, for nearly two hundred years subsequent to its first introduction, any attempt towards the fabrication of this article in the west," &c. &c. See *Pop. Encycl*. The great value set upon it about Queen Anne's reign is often referred to by the writers of that time. See Swift's *Directions to Servants*; Pope's

" And mistress of herself, though china fall."

A visit to a china-shop cured ladies of the "vapours:" see *Spectator*, No. 336. See Macaulay's *Hist. Eng.* chap. xi. : "Mary had acquired at the Hague a taste for the porcelain of China, and amused herself by forming at Hampton a vast collection of hideous images, &c. &c. . . . The fashion . . . spread fast and wide," &c. &c. This taste, for which, perhaps there is something more to be said than that it is, in Macaulay's words, "frivolous and inelegant," has still its votaries, but now they are mostly of the opposite sex. See Gay's *Epistle to a Lady on her Passion for old China*.

255. *brocade*. "A stuff of gold, silver, or silk, raised and enriched with flowers, foliage, and other ornaments. Formerly it signified only a stuff woven all of gold or silver, in which silk was mixed. At present all stuffs . . . are so called if they are worked with flowers or other figures." (*Pop. Encycl.*) Comp. Gay:

" Should you the rich *brocaded* suit unfold,
Where rising flow'rs grow stiff with frosted gold."

45. 256. *masquerade.* See *Spectator*, Nos. 8, 14. From the Restoration onwards masquerades were extremely popular. They were suppressed by law in 1724, but presently revived with the connivance of the Government. See Fielding's novels, *passim.*

260. *Fans* were a notable part of a lady's equipment at this time. In a skilful hand they did much execution on manly bosoms. See *Spectator*, No. 102: see especially the passage on the fluttering of the fan. Gay devoted a poem to this fatal engine.

261. *drops* = the *pendants* of l. 286.

265. See *Spectator*, No. 127.

272. [*stop'd*. What is meant by *stop'd* here? *Stopper* and *stopple* are the substantives.]

274. *bodkin* = originally a small dagger, as in *Hamlet*. Here, as in our modern usage, a large blunt needle. It also meant an instrument used in dressing the hair ; see below, l. 561–3 :

> " Was it for this you took such constant care
>   The *bodkin*, comb, and essence to prepare ;
>   For this your locks in paper durance bound."

278. *Shrink.* See *Hymn Nat.* 203.

279. *Ixion.* See *Class. Dict.*

280. *Mill* = chocolate mill. "Chocolate was introduced into Europe (from Mexico and the Brazils) about A.D. 1520. . . . It was sold in the London coffee-houses soon after their establishment, 1650." (Haydn's *Dict. of Dates*.) Mill would seem to have been pronounced *meel.*

46. 284. *orb in orb* = circle in circle. See *The Dunciad*, iv. 79, 80 :

> " Not closer, orb in orb, conglob'd are seen
>   The buzzing bees about the dusky queen."

See note on *sphere.*

285. *thrid*: a various form of *thread.* See *Dunciad*, iv. 256.

288. [What is the force of *birth* here?]

CANTO III.

290. [What is the force of *rising*?]

291. *a structure*, &c. = Hampton Court. It was built by Wolsey on the site of the manor-house of the Knights Hospitallers.

292. In the time of William III. and Queen Anne, Hampton Court was frequently the scene of Cabinet meetings. See Macaulay's *Hist. Eng.* chap. xi. &c.

294. *foreign Tyrants* = Louis XIV.

296. *Tea* was pronounced *tay* till towards the middle of the eighteenth century, a pronunciation still surviving amongst our lower classes. An advertisement in the *Mercurius Politicus* for September 20, 1658, speaks of the new "China drink" as "called, by the Chinians *tcha*, and by other nations tay, alias tea." Locke writes it thé. So bohea was pronounced bohay : see Pope's *Ep. to Miss Blount*, 1715. For other changes in pronunciation see Trench's *English Past and Present.* Tea was first brought into Europe from India by the Dutch in 1610. "That it was known [in England] in the time of the Protector was pretty evident, but it was only used as a regalia at high entertainments. Tea was sold at from six to ten guineas the pound. Thomas Garway, the founder of Garraway's Coffee House, first offered it at a more reasonable price, and in 1657 he advertised tea at fifty shillings a pound." (*Our English Home.*) Waller says wrongly that we owed "the best of herbs," as "the best of queens," to Portugal. It grew gradually into request in England in the latter half of the seventeenth century. Pepys drunk his first dish of tea in 1660. It was still a luxury in Pope's time. See *Tatler* and *Spect.* &c. *passim.* See Disraeli's *Curiosities of Literature*, Chambers' *Book of Days.*

46. 300. Comp. Swift's *Journal of a Modern Lady:*

> " Let me now survey
> Our madam o'er her evening tea,
> Surrounded with the noisy clans
> Of prudes, coquettes, and harridans," &c.

[*the ball—the visit.* What is the force of *the* here ?]

301. *speaks the glory.* See *Lycid.* 173.

305. *Snuff.* "Snuff-taking took its rise in England from the captures made of vast quantities of snuff by Sir George Rooke's expedition to Vigo in 1702." (Haydn's *Dict. of Dates.*) See the "Advertisement" on the Exercise of the Snuff-box at the end of *Spect.* No. 138. A letter in *Spect.* No. 344 dwells on "an impertinent custom the women, the fine women, have lately fallen into, of taking snuff." See Swift's *Polite Conversation:*

" *Col.* [*Atwit*]. Miss, will you take a pinch of snuff ?

" *Miss* [*Notable*]. No, Colonel ; you must know I never take snuff but when I'm angry.

" *Lady Answerall.* Yes, yes, she can take snuff, but she has never a box to put it in."

[*supply.* Is the plural defensible ?]

313. [*thirst of fame.* What should we say ?]

47. 321. *Matadore.* "One of the three principal cards in the games of ombre and quadrille, which are always the two black aces, and the deuce in spades and clubs and the seventh in hearts and diamonds." (Johnson.)

329. *succinct* = "tucked or girded up." (Johnson.) See Milton's *Paradise Lost,* iii. 643 :

> " His habit fit for speed *succinct.*"

330. *halbert* = pole-axe. See Shakspere, *Comedy of Errors,* V. i. 185.

334. *trump* is a corruption of triumph.

335. *sable Matadores.* See l. 321.

336. The game was, as has been said, of Spanish origin.

349. *Pam* = knave of clubs.

353. It will be seen Belinda has now won four tricks.

354. *the field* = the battle, as in Milton, *Paradise Lost,* i. 105 :

> " What though *the field* be lost ?
> All is not lost."

359. *boots* is used personally with regard to *circle and limbs,* impersonally to *that long,* &c. See *Lycid.* 64. So "avails" is used both personally and impersonally.

the regal circle = " the circle of my glory "(Shakspere, *King John,* V. i. 2); "the hollow crown that rounds the mortal temples of a king" (*Richard II.* III. ii. 161).

362. *the globe* = the orb, a symbol of dominion usually accompanied by a sceptre.

48. 368. *strow:* a very common variant of *strew.*

374. *In heaps on heaps.* See *Judges* xv. 16.

376. It will be seen that the Baron has now won four tricks.

380. *Codille* "is when those who defend the pool make more tricks than those who defend the game, which is called winning the codille." (*Boyle.*)

388. *the long canals.* The grounds of Hampton Court were laid out according to the Dutch taste.

392. Comp. Virg. *Æn.* x. 501-5.

394. *the mill* = the coffee-mill. Coffee was introduced into England shortly before the middle of the seventeenth century. "A Greek named Canopius visited Oxford in 1637, and, in preference to the Ipocrase and ale of the College buttery, quaffed a dark decoction strange to the Oxonians. Evelyn perhaps saw him drink the first cup of coffee ever drank in England." (*Our English Home.*) The first coffee-house is said to have been opened at Oxford by a man

named Jacobs, in 1650. See Disraeli's *Cur. of Lit.*, Chambers' *Book of Days*, the *Tatler* and the *Spectator*, passim, Macaulay's *Hist. Eng.*, &c.

48. 395. *shining Altars of Japan* = a bright japanned stand.   Perhaps he used the plural altars because the plural (*altaria*) is the common form in Latin. "All substances that are dry and rigid, or not too flexible, as woods, metals, leather, and paper prepared, admit of being japanned." (*Pop. Encycl.*)   Japan ware was in great esteem at this time.   Swift speaks of a "japan glass," "a standish well japanned," &c.   Probably the art reached us from the island whence it derives the name In the course of the seventeenth century, through the medium of the Dutch.

397. *liquors.*   The plural seems here to be used in a distributive sense ; *liquors* = the several cupfuls or draughts of liquor.

399. [What is the force of *at once* here ?   What other force has it ?]

401. [*hover.*   What would have been the difference in meaning had Pope written *hovers* ?]

402. *fuming.*   So *Paradise Lost*, vii. 600, &c.   The metaphorical sense of the word is now its prevailing one.   Comp. *vapour.*

403. *display'd.*   See *Il Penseroso*, 149.

405. Coffee "much quickens the spirits and makes the heart lightsome," says an old coffee-house handbill.   See Chambers' *Book of Days.*

49. 410. *Scylla.*   See *Class. Dict.*   She must not be confounded with her of the straits of Sicily, a confusion committed by Virgil (*Ecl.* vi. 70), Ovid (*Fast.* iv. 500), and others.   For the story of her crime and its punishment, see Ovid's *Metam.* viii. the beginning.

411. Comp. Ovid, *l. c.* 150 :

" Pluma fuit ; plumis in avem mutata vocatur
    Ciris, et a tango est hoc nomen adepta capillo."

See the poem called *Ciris*, attributed to Virgil, 488 *et seq.*

413. See the converse in Shakspere, *King John*, IV. ii. 219.

416. Comp. Scott's *Marmion*, VI. xii. 1–6 ; *Sir Bevis of Hamptoun*, p. 249 of Ellis's *Early Eng. Met. Rom.* (Bohn's edition), where Josyan arms Sir Bevis.

420. *engine.*   See *Lycid.* 130.

422. [*steams.*   Explain the plural.]

425. *thrice.*   So the Latin *ter* is used.   See *e.g.* Ovid's *Trist.* I. iii. 55.

433. *expir'd.*   This cannot be called a passive participle.   It is, in fact, a past participle active.

434. *Resign'd.*   Observe the absolute use of this word.   [How would you explain the phrase "I was resigned" ?]

439. *shears.*   See Milton, *Lycid.* 75.

440. Comp. *Paradise Lost*, vi. 344–9 ; Wordsworth's *Laodamia* :

" The phantom parts, but parts to re-unite."

447. Comp. *Moral Essays*, II. "On the Characters of Women," 268.
        [How do you scan this line ?]

50. 451. See Virg. *Bucol.* v. 76.

453. *Atalantis.*   The *New Atalantis*, entitled " Secret Memoirs and Manners of several Persons of Quality of both sexes, from the New Atalantis, an Island in the Mediterranean," published in 1709, was in fact a personal satire on certain families well known at the time.   It was written by Mary de la Rivière Manley, a daughter of Sir Roger Manley, Governor of Guernsey.   "Deceived by a false marriage, and then deserted and thrown upon her own resources, she sustained herself by writing and by 'intrigue.'   She died in 1724.   *Atalantis*, 'with a key to it,' was one of the works in Leonora's Library." (*Spect.* No. 37.)   See above, line 186.

454. *the small pillow.*   This was a richly decorated pillow which supported ladies in a

sitting posture when they received visits in their bedchambers. The custom of so receiving visits was introduced from France. *"Courir les ruelles* (to take the run of the bedsides) was a Parisian phrase for fashionable morning calls upon the ladies. The *ruelle* is the little path between the bedside and the wall." (Professor Morley, note to *Spect.* No. 45.) This custom is described with exquisite humour in *Spect.* No. 45.

60. 461. *the labour of the Gods.* See *Laomedon* in *Class. Dict.*

466. *unresisted =* irresistible. Comp. *unreproved, L'Allegro,* 40 ; *Paradise Lost,* iv. 493.

CANTO IV.

472. *ancient ladies =* what are now called old maids. See l. 493.

474. *awry.* Comp. across, athwart, aslant, &c. *= cross-*wise, &c.

manteau, from French *manteau,* or from the Italian town of Mantua. (Comp. milliner from Milan, Italian irons, Leghorn hats.) See *Proceedings of Phil. Soc.* v. 136.

481. [What does *scene* mean here ?]

482. *Spleen =* melancholy, *ennui,* low spirits, hypochondria, ill-humour ; what is vulgarly called "the blues" or "the dismals." A number of the *Spectator* speaks of "the spleen so frequent in studious men," and "the vapours to which the other sex are so often subject." Pope couples "spleen, vapours, and small-pox ;" Swift :

> " You humour me when I am sick,
> Why not when I am splenetic ? "

Comp. "a spleeny Lutheran," Shakspere, *Henry VIII.* III. ii. 99 ; Persius' "petulanti splene cachinno." See *Tatler* and *Spect.* passim. Sir William Temple's *Essay on Poetry :* "Our country must be confessed to be what a great foreign physician called it, the region of *spleen,*" &c.

486. [*all the wind.* In what sense is *the wind* used *here* ?]

51. 487. *grotto =* cave or cavern. "This was found at the entry of the grotto in the Peak," = Peak Cavern. (Woodward *apud* Johnson.) So grot, French *grotte,* Italian *grotta.* The word is said to be a corruption of *crypt.* Mr. Wedgwood, more probably, connects it with Fr. *gratter,* German *grab,* our "grave." The termination is perhaps diminutival. Wedgwood quotes *crottot* as a dialectic form of the French word. "*Grotesque* is the style in which grottoes were ornamented." Pope's grotto at his Twickenham house was a subterranean passage connecting his lawn (on the river-bank) and his garden, which were separated by the road. See Chambers' *Book of Days,* i. 703.

[What part of speech is *close* here ?]

488. [*in shades.* Would *by shades* be precisely the same ?]

Compare or contrast *Il Penseroso,* 28.

490. *Megrim :* French *migraine =* Greek ἡμικρανία (literally a half-headedness). Halliwell quotes from *Chron. Vilodun. :* "A fervent mygreyn was in the ryght syde of hurr hedde." In a plural form the word was used, and still is in the provinces, for "whims, fancies, bad spirits."

491. *wait the throne.* See above, l. 301.

495. *store.* See *Proth.* l. 33.

496. *lampoons :* originally drinking songs.

499. See *Spect.* No. 38. [Explain the force of *Practis'd* here.]

501. *quilt.* See Wedgwood's *Dict.* According to that authority, the *counter* in counterpane is radically the same word.

504. See above. So Zoilus, according to Martial (ii. 16), fell ill to show off his fine bed-furniture :

> " Zoilus aegrotat : faciunt hanc stragula febrem :
> Si fuerit sanus, coccina quid facient?

Quid torus a Nilo? quid Sindone tinctus olenti?
Ostendit stultas quid nisi morbus opes?
Quid tibi cum medicis? dimitte Machaonas omnes.
Vis fieri sanus? stragula sume mea."

51. 509. *snakes on rolling spires.* See *Paradise Lost*, ix. 496-502.
[Explain *rolling.*]

512. *Angels in machines*, i.e. angels coming to succour, angels "interfuturi" (comp. Hor. *Ars Poet.* 191). Comp. the Latin *deus ex machina*; Greek θεὸς ἀπὸ μηχανῆς, of which see Suidas' explanation, quoted by Orelli on Hor. *Ars Poet.* 191.

513 Comp. Milton's *Com.* 526-30; Hom. *Od.* x. 139 *et seq.*

Comp. Burton's *Anatomy of Melancholy*, Part I. Sec. ii. Mem. 1 Subs. 4: "One thinks himself a giant, another a dwarf; one is heavy as lead, another is as light as a feather. . . . One fears heaven will fall on his head; a second is a cock, and such a one Guianerius saith he saw at Padua that would clap his hands together and crow. Another thinks he is a nightingal, and therefore sings all night long; another he is all glass, a pitcher, and will therefore let nobody come near him," &c. &c.

517. [*Pipkin.* Mention other instances of this termination.
like Homer's Tripod. See *Iliad*, xviii. 372-81, esp. 373-77, which Pope translates:

" Full twenty tripods for his hall he fram'd,
That, plac'd on living wheels of massy gold,
(Wondrous to tell) instinct with spirit roll'd
From place to place, around the blest abodes,
Self-mov'd, obedient to the beck of gods."

521. [*past.* What part of the verb is *past* here?]

522. Just as Odysseus was protected by his "good antidote," "which the gods called moly" (*Od.* x. 305), so the attendant spirit declared himself protected by his root of hæmony. *Com.* 629-41.
[Has *healing* here a strictly participial sense?]

523. *wayward Queen:* on the "like man, like master" principle. From the time of Virgil's "varium et mutabile semper foemina" downwards, and long before it, women have been specially so characterized by men poets.

524. *the sex.* This somewhat jaunty phrase was popular in Pope's time. It is perhaps an abridgment of "the fair sex."

525. *vapours.* See above, line 482.

527. [What should we say for *by*?]

52. 533 Comp. Chryses' prayer, *Iliad*, i. 37-42.

535. "Aqua vitæ, distilled with the rind of citrons." (Johnson.) See *Mor. Ess.* II. "Of the Characters of Women," 64:

" Now drinking *citron* with his Grace and Chartres."

See Swift's *Journal of a Modern Young Lady*:

" And then, to cool her heated brains,
Her night-gown and her slippers brought her,
Takes a large dram of *citron-water*."

[What part of the sentence is *like citron waters*?]

536. *at a losing game.* On *losing* see note, *L'All.* 20. Cards were perhaps at their very greatest popularity in England about this time.

538. *head-dress.* On the head-dresses of this time see *Spect.* No. 98.

541. Radically *chagrin* and *shagreen* are the same word. The primitive sense is more discernible in *shagreen.*

52. 546. See Hom. *Od.* x. 19 and 20.

547. [What is meant by *the force* here ?]

549. [What is meant by *fainting fears* ?]

555. [What is the force of *Full* here ?]

556. *vent* is generally a small opening (as Shaksp. *Ant. and Cleop.* V. ii. 352), but not necessarily so.   It is the Fr. *fente* (from Lat. *findo*) the *f* flattened.   Comp. our *fat, vat.*

furies used generally, not specifically, as in *Lycid.* 75.

562. *bodkin.*   See above, l. 274.

565. *fillet* = headband, snood.

568. *Fops.*   " Fop " and " fopling " and " beau " were the special words at this time for what at other times has been called " buck," " dandy."

569. [What does she mean by *honour* ?   Comp. below, l. 652.]

53. 578. [What word in this line would our present usage omit ?]

579. *circling* = encircling.   So *pales* for " impales " (Shakspere, *Cymbeline*, III. i. 19).

581. *Hyde-Park Circus.*   See above, l. 44.

582. *in the sound of Bow*, i.e. amongst the " cits," or in any sort of neighbourhood to Grub Street.   The City was but one large butt for the jests of the " wits ;" while its immediate suburbs were the head-quarters of that pinched and starved fraternity of scribblers between whom and Pope there was never peace.   See *Spect.* No. 34 : " Upon this my friend the Templar told Sir Andrew that he wondered to hear a man of his sense talk after that manner ; that the City had always been the province for satyr ; and that the wits of King Charles's time jested upon nothing else during his whole reign."   " In the early part of Blackmore's time a citizen was a term of reproach ; and his place of abode was another topic to which his adversaries had recourse in the penury of scandal." (Johnson's *Life of Blackmore.*)   After the Restoration, Fashion moved its residence well to the west of the City ; then the "West End" began to be.   See a forthcoming work by H. B. Wheatley, Esq. on Piccadilly and its neighbourhood.

585. *repairs.*   Repair is a very favourite word at this time.

Sir Plume = Sir George Brown, brother of Thalestris (Mrs. Morley).

588. *clouded.*   Comp.

" The handle smooth and plain,
Made of the *clouded* olive's easy grain."

593. [*'tis past a jest.*   What part of speech is *past* here?   Comp. "beyond," and such a phrase as " One may have too much of a joke."]

595. [What is the sense of *again* here ?]

598. Comp. Hom. *Il.* i. 234 *et seq.*

599. [What is meant by *renew its honours* ?]

601. Comp. Virg. *Æn.* i. 387.

[What is the mock-heroic element in this line?]

604. *long-contended* = long contended for.

605. [What is the meaning of *so* here ?]

609. *heav'd* has here the force of a pres. part. pass.

[What exactly does *hung* mean here ?   What other pret. has the verb " hang " ?   Mention other verbs with two prets.   Have any three ?]

54. 619. *marks* = furrows, makes tracks on.

620. Obs. the rhyme here.   See above, l. 296.

622. Comp. the trite lines in Gray's *Elegy*, and Waller's " Go, lovely son."

627. *China.*   See above, l. 254.

628. *Poll.*   See above, l. 584.

630. As were those Cassandra saw and announced.

631. *hairs.*   This plural occurs sometimes in our older writers, where we should rather use the singular in a collective sense.

54. 633. *break* was pronounced *breek* in Pope's time, as the Staffordshire people pronounce it.

635. *uncouth.* See *L'Allegro,* 5.

639. *cruel.* So we use " dear," " savage ; " but these are also used substantively.

CANTO V.

646. See Virg. *Æn.* iv. 330.

647. [What does *graceful* qualify here ?]

55. 651. " A new character introduced in the subsequent editions, to open more clearly the moral of the poem, in a parody of the speech of Sarpedon to Glaucus in Homer." (Pope.) See *Iliad,* xii. 310–28.

See *Spect.* No. 15.

654. The ladies, it would seem, occupied the front boxes, the gentlemen the side. See below, l. 657. See *Epistle to Miss Blount,* of *Pamela :*

> " She glares in balls, *front boxes,* and the Ring."

660. The small-pox was one of the most fearful plagues of society about this time. One of the chief terrors of the day, it is very frequently mentioned by the poets : see Dryden's lines *Upon the Death of Lord Hastings,* his *Ode on the Death of Mrs. Anne Killigrew,* Cartwright's lines *On his Majesty's Recovery from the Small-pox,* &c. &c.

663. *ogle* is of the same root as English *eye,* German *auge,* Latin *oculus,* &c. The notion of sidelong sly glances has attached to the word. See the *Spect.* No. 46, where " an Irish Gentleman " announces his intention of setting up for an ogling-master : " I teach the church ogle in the morning, and the playhouse ogle by candlelight. I have also brought over with me a new flying ogle fit for the Ring, which I teach in the dusk of the evening, or in any hour of the day by darkning one of my windows. I have a manuscript by me called the *Compleat Ogler,* which I shall be ready to show you upon any occasion." Comp. Arbuthnott : " Jack was a prodigious ogler ; he would ogle you the outside of his eye inward and the white upward."

665. *to paint.* See *Spect.* on the Picts, especially No. 41.

668. [How would you emphasize the words of this line ?]

672. *flights.* Comp. *Moral Ess.* ii. 49, 50 :

> " Strange graces still, and stranger *flights* she had,
> Was just not ugly, and was just not mad."

Comp. our use of " flighty," " to fly into a passion."

On *scolding* see *Spect.* Nos. 479, 482 ; *Freeholder :* " A shrewd in domestic life is now become a scold in politics."

673. [What is the force of *may* here ?]

674. *strike,* i.e. produce an immediate impression on. Comp. the use of this word of planetic influence, as in *Hamlet,* I. i. 162 :

> " The nights are wholesome ; then no planets *strike.*"

676. *Prude* is derived from the Latin *probus,* and so is etymologically connected with *prove,* &c. The old French form is *prode,* feminine of *prod.* Comp. Modern French *prud-homme.* On the degradation of meaning see Trench's *Study of Words.*

677. *Virago.* " Melpomene represented like a *virago,* or *manly lady,* with a majestick and grave countenance." (Peacham.)

685. See *Iliad,* xxi. 272–513.

[What does *makes* mean here ?]

687. *Mars.* He means Ares. This identification of the Latin and Greek gods, and consequent treatment of their names as convertible, is a scarcely yet obsolete habit ; but it is hoped that it is at last becoming so.

55. 690. *storms.* This literal sense of the verb is rare.

692. See Milton's *Hymn Nat.* 160

693. *sconce.* Comp. Dryden:

" Golden *sconces* hang upon the walls
To light the costly suppers and the balls. "

According to Wedgwood this word = Low Latin *absconsa* (scil. *candela*), a hidden
light, a dark lantern.

Comp. Hom. *Od.* xxii. 239, of Pallas watching the final struggle of Ulysses with
the suitors :

" αὐτὴ δ' αἰθαλόεντος ἀνὰ μεγάροιο μέλαθρον
ἕζετ' ἀναΐξασα, χελιδόνι εἰκέλη ἄντην."

695. Comp. Virg. *Æn.* ix. 229.

56. 697. *press.* See *St. Mark's Gospel,* ii. 4, &c. ; Shakspere's *Julius Cæsar,* I. ii. 14, &c.
[What does *flies* mean here ?]

699. [*a Beau and Witling.* Is the omission of the art. with *Witling* correct ?]

700. [What is meant here by *dying in metaphor* ?]

701. [Which dies in metaphor, which in song? Where is the metaphor ?]

704. These are among the words of a song in the opera of *Camilla.*

705. *Mæander.* See *Class. Dict.* See Ovid's *Heroides,* vii. 1, 2 :

" Sic ubi fata vocant, udis abjectus in herbis,
Ad vada Mæandri concinit albus olor."

711. Comp. Hom. *Iliad,* viii. 69-73 ; Virg. *Æn.* xii. 725-7 ; Milton's *Paradise Lost,*
iv. 997.

scale and *shell* probably are radically connected.

712. [What is the force of *against* here ?]

723. [What is meant by the *Gnomes* being *to ev'ry atome just* ?]

731. Comp. the account of the sceptre, *Iliad,* ii. 100-8.
[Is there not a generation passed over ?]

57. 745. See *Othello,* III. iii.

746. Observe the hint of ridicule in *Roar'd.*

748. [What old fable is there, where a like result befalls two combatants ?]

753. *the Lunar sphere.* See *Ariosto,* cant. xxxiv. (Pope.) Milton assails this old belief,
which held the moon to be the place where the earth's rubbish was shot. See *Paradise Lost,*
iii. 459-62. He makes that place to be the skirts of the earth. See ii. 418-97.

757. *death-bed alms.* Comp. *Eloisa to Abelard,* where Eloisa speaks of the founding
of " these hallowed walls," from within which she writes :

" No silver saints, by dying misers giv'n,
Here brib'd the rage of ill-requited heav'n."

758. *riband.* The forms ribband and ribbon also are common. Comp. French *ruban,*
Old French *riban.*

759. *courtier's promises.* Comp. Shakspere, *Cymb.* V. iv. 135.

762. *Dry'd butterflies.* Pope seems here, and elsewhere, not to assign their proper
value to entomological and other scientific studies.

tomes of casuistry = the works of the Schoolmen.

705. See *Livy,* i. 16 ; Ovid, *Fast.* ii. 481-512, esp. 503-4 :

" Pulcher et humano major trabeaque decorus
Romulus in media visus adesse via."

766. [What is the meaning of *confess'd* here ?]

767. [What is meant by *liquid* here ?]

768. Like a comet. The original meaning of the word comet is " the long-haired one."

57. 769. See *Class. Dict.* Callimachus wrote a poem on this subject, of which a translation by Catullus is yet extant.

770. *dishevel'd* means etymologically "with hair disordered," = dis-chevelled (French *chevel* ; Latin, *capillus*).

771. *kindling.* So Isaiah xliii. 2 : " Neither shall the flame kindle upon thee." Comp. uses of *burn*, &c.

773. *the Mall.* The upper side of St. James's Park was a favourite place for evening strolls.

776. *Rosamonda's lake,* filled up in 1770, was near where now stand the Wellington Barracks. It was " of oblong shape, and overhung by the trees of the Long Avenue." " It occurs as a place of assignation in the comedies of Otway, Congreve, Farquhar, Southern, and Colley Cibber ;" comp. the present text. (Timbs' *Curiosities of London.*) Swift writes to Stella Jan. 31, 171⁹/₈ : "We are here in as smart a frost for the time as I have seen ; delicate walking weather, and the Canal and Rosamond's Pond full of the rabble sliding, and with skaits, if you know what those are." See a print of this pond in *Old England*, engraving No. 2,397. For the name, it is " referred to the frequency of suicides committed here." (Timbs.) " Beneath the print in the Pennant Collection we read : 'The south-west corner of St. James' Park was enriched with this romantic scene. The irregularity of the trees, the rise of the ground, and the venerable Abbey, afforded great entertainment to the contemplative eye. This spot was often the receptacle of many unhappy persons, who in the stillness of an evening plunged themselves into eternity.'" (*Old England.*) But one can scarcely think that the water derived its name from this ghastly use of it. Rather it was so called because its banks were the haunts of lovers. The name occurs, according to Timbs, but we do not know on what authority he speaks, in " a grant of Henry VIII."

777. *Partridge.* Partridge, an almanack-maker of the day, was a favourite joke with the wits. Swift seems first to have selected him as the representative of the astrological fraternity. See *The Bickerstaff Papers.* In his *Predictions for the Year* 1708, he says : " I have consulted the star of his [*Partridge's*] nativity by my own rules, and find he will infallibly die on the 29th of March next about eleven at night of a raging fever ; therefore I advise him to consider of it, and settle his affairs in time." There appeared presently : " The accomplishment of the first of Mr. Bickerstaff's predictions, being an account of the death of Mr. Partridge, the almanack-maker, upon the 29th instant." Partridge protested he was not dead, but it was no use : see the other papers.

778. *Galileo's eyes.* Telescopes are said to have been first made—not perhaps first invented—by one Metius, at Alkmaer, and about the same time by Jansen, of Middleburg," about 1590-1609. " Galileo imitated their invention by its description, and made three in succession, one of which magnified a thousand times, 1630. With these he discovered Jupiter's moons and the phases of Venus." (Haydn's *Dict. of Dates.*) See *Paradise Lost*, i. 287-91.

779. *wizard.* See note on *Hymn Nat.* 23.

782. *shining sphere.* All the spheres or planets were anciently believed to be contained in one greater sphere. Hence the word *sphere* came to be used generally for the heavens.

[With what word is the negative here to be connected ? What other connexion might it have, if only the words, not the sense, were considered ? What would be the difference in meaning ?]

58. 784. *draw* = attract. [What is the literal meaning of *attract* ?]

786. *after millions slain.* This is the Latin idiom. Comp. " post urbem conditam," " ante Christum natum," &c.

DR JOHNSON.

Dr Johnson's life may be divided into four parts: (i) 1709—1731, (ii) 1731—1737, (iii) 1737—1762, (iv) 1762—1784.

(i) 1709—1731. He was born at Lichfield (commonly then spelt Litchfield), Sept. 18, 1709, the son of a bookseller and stationer. Both his father and mother seem to have been of superior intelligence and aims. They taught him something themselves, and presently sent him to various schools; then two years were spent at home, his father's book-stock providing him with abundant mental food; then, through the kindness of some friend or relative, he was entered a commoner at Pembroke College, Oxford, where he kept terms for about three years.

(ii) 1731—1737. His career at Oxford, all along made distressing by his extreme poverty, was at last cut short by it. He returned home in great gloom in 1731. Fresh pecuniary troubles came with his father's death. Life, not easy before, now grew terribly hard. For some thirty years he was involved in perpetual straits and difficulties. He was an usher at Market Bosworth in Leicestershire; he essayed journalism and literature at Birmingham; he issued proposals for an edition of Politian from Lichfield; he set up a school, his wife, the widow of a Birmingham "mercer," having brought him some £800. All these ways and means failed dismally.

(iii) 1737—1762. At last, accompanied by David Garrick, one of his very few pupils, at this time as destitute as his master, he set off for London, with three acts of a play (*Irene*) in his pocket. For some time but little is known of his course in London; but it is certain that he had to endure the bitterest distresses. He bore them nobly, somewhat hardened and roughened externally, no doubt, but still always with a high fortitude and an inward spirit that never forgot to be truly gentle and tender. He slowly fought his way to fame. In 1738 appeared *London*, which won him the praise of Pope, and first made him generally known. Then he "reported" the House of Commons' debates in such way as was permitted in George II.'s reign, for the *Gentleman's Magazine*, at that time newly started. The *Life of Savage* (Savage and he had walked the streets starving together), *The Vanity of Human Wishes* (1749); *The Rambler* (March 20, 1750—March 14, 1752); *The Dictionary* (published in 1755), *The Idler, Rasselas* (1759), and other works gradually secured for him the foremost literary position of the day. His wife died in 1752, his mother in 1759.

(iv) 1762—1784. His pecuniary troubles, which had by no means ceased with his obscurity, were at last happily ended by the bestowal upon him by the Crown of a well-deserved pension of £300 a year. During this fourth period of his life he was a very literary and social king; no greater ever reigned either in literature or literary society. His private life was replete with benevolences. "His house was filled with dependants, whose perverse tempers frequently drove him out of it, yet nothing of this kind could induce him to relieve himself at their expence. His noble expression was, 'If I dismiss them, who will receive them?'" (Chalmers). His edition of *Shakspere*, certain political pamphlets, *A Journey to the Western Islands of Scotland, The Lives of the Poets* now successively appeared. In 1784, Dec. 13th, full of years as of glory, he died at his house in Johnson's Court, Fleet Street. "On the 20th, his body was interred with great solemnity in Westminster Abbey, close to the grave of his friend Garrick. Of the other honours paid to his memory, it may suffice to say that they were more in number and in quality than were ever paid to any man of literature." (Chalmers).

Of Johnson as an author the estimate commonly formed now widely differs from that of his contemporaries. For his *style*, it abounded in Latinisms both in its vocabulary and in its structure. Perhaps of all English writers he is the least Teutonic, which is as much as to say

x

the least idiomatic. But there is no denying that in his own way he is a great master. If he takes a very low place amongst our idiomatic writers, he deserves a very high one amongst the Latinistic. In his own language he can express whatever he wishes to express with the utmost vigour and with consummate nicety. That language was deliberately adopted in his works in preference to a more truly native tongue. He could and did speak—no doubt he thought—in thoroughly idiomatic English; but out of a false taste, as surely it was, he for the most part in his writings translated the vernacular into something utterly different. An author's conversational style always of course differs from the style of his books: but in Johnson's case there were two separate languages. In the present age, when the Teutonism of our national tongue is certainly more and more prevailing to the complete subordination of all secondary influences, "Johnsonese" is liable perhaps to receive less appreciation than it really deserves. Though highly artificial, and balanced and counter-balanced, epithet for epithet, and verb for verb, to a wearisome degree, yet it was certainly a very potent and effective vehicle of thought. As a *critic*, there are few *dicta* of Dr Johnson's which later judgments do not modify or reverse. His critical code is conventional and narrow. In this respect he was the spokesman of his time. There is in him but little of what is called spiritual criticism; he knows not "art" in that modern sense the Germans have taught the world. He seems scarcely to distinguish between an artistic and a moral purpose; he criticizes always from the moralist's point of view. Of style he is a somewhat severe critic; the value of his remarks must of course depend upon his knowledge of the language; and it may be safely said that his knowledge of the English language was but circumscribed and limited (see the *Dictionary, passim*). His strong Latinistic predilections somewhat disqualified him for this office of criticism. Yet in him as a critic his natural acuteness and power are perpetually manifested; they are, it may be, perverted, but they are there. As an *essayist*, the character of his style is highly detrimental. Such a style is indeed incompatible with success in what was called essay-writing in the last century. It cannot relax, or trifle, or toy Johnson as a writer is always in full dress, and full dress of the stiffest and most unrelenting description. Perhaps even the skilfullest trainer could not make an elephant waltz. To use Goldsmith's figure, Johnson cannot but make even little fishes talk like whales. As a *dramatist* his *Irene* contains some noble sentiments; so do many of the *Ramblers* and the *Idlers*. It is wanting in characterization, in grace, in music, in interest, in humanity. The moral overbears everything else; the *personæ* are but ethical puppets. As a *political pamphleteer*, Johnson failed even in the estimate of his own prepossessed time. His political views were mostly obstructive or retrograde. He was a Tory, a Jacobite, a fierce opposer of American independence. His *poetry* is but a small part of his works. He may perhaps be defined as more of a rhetorician than a poet. He can declaim finely, and with power. He might have produced vigorous satires, had not Providence designed him for something better; but verse is not his natural form of expression. 'As a *lexicographer*, he deserves the gratitude of all English posterity, not for the final excellence of his compilation, but for the splendid beginning it made. Defective as his *Dictionary* is, however grotesque in etymologies, however chaotic the order of its definitions, yet it made an epoch in its department. By this work Johnson was the greatest benefactor of his native language. Many of the definitions are in themselves admirable; the collection of illustrating quotations is most valuable; there is everywhere strong sense, if not always assisted by competent learning.

After all, Johnson's greatest works are his conversations as so happily preserved by Boswell, his most assiduous and faithful retainer. His wide information, his acuteness, his power of language, his trenchant wit, his noble nature show more clearly and brilliantly in them than in any of his more formal productions. Had he but written more as he talked, he would have filled a greater place in our literature than can now be conceded him; he would still and always come home to many who will never know him in his strange literary disguise.

The greatest non-literary service he did his day and all following days was the freeing the profession of literature from the slavery of patronage. He too was in his sphere a Washington, with whatever eyes he regarded that famous leader; he too waged and won a war of independence; he manfully took his stand upon the dignity of Letters, and made his age and country acknowledge that illustrious power. Authors by profession were no longer forced to be parasites. It is true that the time was rife for this emancipation; so Teutonic Europe was ripe for the Reformation; so the Colonies for the Declaration of Independence; but we thank and praise Martin Luther and George Washington; therefore must we thank and praise Samuel Johnson.

LONDON.

INTRODUCTION.

London was published in 1738, on the same morning with Pope's Satire named after that year. It bears evident marks of that period of Johnson's life, in which it was written; see *Life*. It is pervaded by a bitterness, almost inseparable from his then circumstances. For the style, it belongs to Johnson's earlier manner. He had not yet formed that style which especially characterizes him, though many symptoms of it may be detected.

Satires were the height of the literary fashion about the time Johnson came up to London. The master poets of the two preceding ages had given their best energies—one was still doing so—to that form of composition. A young poet in the reign of George the Second wrote a Satire as naturally as one of the time of James I. wrote a play.

London is a free imitation of Juvenal's Third Satire. This Satire had previously been so treated by Oldham, as well as vigorously translated by Dryden.

[Make a short abstract of this poem. Into how many parts would you divide it? Read the original poem side by side with it.]

5v, 2. *Thales.* Juvenal calls his friend Umbricius. Probably enough Johnson is thinking of Savage. Somewhat in the spirit of Thales here did Savage actually leave London for Wales in 1739, fulfilling then a scheme formed some time previously. As to Savage's "injuries," see Johnson's *Life* of him. Perhaps the most grievous were those inflicted by himself.

4. *I praise the hermit.* The Doctor was wiser in 1759, when Prince Rasselas and his sister visit such an one in their search for happiness, "'I have indeed lived fifteen years in solitude,' said the hermit, 'but have no desire that my example should gain any imitators... ... The life of a solitary man will be certainly miserable, but not certainly devout.'" (*Rasselas*, chap. xxi.). See the following note. From the sentiment there mentioned arose a tendency to believe, or at least affect belief, in hermits and hermitages.

5. *From vice and London far.* A belief in the iniquity of towns and the innocence of country life was one of the besetting delusions of the last century of the time of Rousseau and his fellows. In *Rasselas*, written and published in 1759, Johnson speaks more wisely.

7. *Cambria.* The old Roman names for the various countries of Western Europe were much used by poets at this time. According to the poetic creed of the day they were supposed to be more "poetical." Thus England and Wales are superseded by Britannia and Cambria. So Hibernia in l. 9. See Gray's *Bard*, Thomson's famous song *Rule, Britannia*, in his masque of *Alfred*, &c.

8. *St David.* David, who succeeded Dubritius (him who crowned and married Arthur; see Tennyson's *Coming of Arthur*), removed the see from Caerleon to Menapia, which name was presently superseded by his own.

9. Many were doing so at this very time. Smollett arrived in London in 1739, Burke in 1750, Goldsmith in 1756.

woud. From this spelling it seems that *would* was once in danger of being corrupted by *coud*, just as *coud* has actually been corrupted by *would*; for the *l* in *could* is probably due to a mistaken assimilation of the proper form to *would*, where of course the *l* is a root-letter.

X 2

10. The barrenness of Scotland and the poverty of its inhabitants were favourite jests with Englishmen of the last century, especially with Dr Johnson.

14. *a rabble.* "Fielding, in the *Covent Garden Journal,* has an amusing passage on the power of 'the fourth estate,' by which he means the mob." See Knight's *Pop. Hist. Eng.* VII. vi. The offences with which Fielding charges them are pretty much the same as those which distinguish the Roughs of our own day. The Fourth Estate, in his sense of the phrase, is strikingly like what it was, in its ways and in its power.

15. *ambush* = strictly an *in*-lurking, a hiding in a bush. The *a* here answers to the French *e* of *embûche.* The *bush* is the French *bûche,* which is from the Low Latin *boscus,* less changed in the Ital. *imboscare.* Comp. *boskage* (Tennyson's *Dream of F. W.*), *Josky, Boscobel* in Shropshire, &c.

18. *A female atheist.* Pope says of Narcissa (*Moral Essays,* ii. 65, 66) :

> " Now Conscience chills her, and now Passion burns,
> And Atheism and Religion take their turns."

Young's *Love of Fame,* Sat. vi., published in 1728:

> " Atheists have been but rare ; since Nature's birth
> Till now, she-atheists ne'er appeared on earth," &c.

[What part of the sentence is *dead?*]

19. *wherry.* From the oldest Eng. *werian* = our weary, meaning something urged on, say some ; a corruption of *ferry,* Dutch *veer,* Germ. *fähr,* and so connected with *fare,* say others.

wait. See note to *Prothal.* 135.

20. [What is meant by *dissipated* here ?]

22. *silver flood.* See note to *Prothal.* 11.

23. Elizabeth, afterwards Queen, was born at Greenwich, Sept. 7, 1533.

24. See Sir Roger de Coverley's admiration for her, *Spect.* 329.

60. 27. *main.* In *King Lear,* III. i. 6. *main* = main-land. [Explain the word.]

28. Spain was still at this time a most formidable power in the estimation of England and other countries. We were on the verge of a great war with it. See Anson's *Voyages, passim.*

29. *masquerades.* See note to *Rape of the Lock,* l. 256.

debauch'd. In *King Lear,* I. iv. 263, occurs the form *debosh'd.* The word is of Fr. origin. "*Débaucher* faire sortir de l'atelier (qui est *bauche* dans notre vieille langue)." (Brachet.)

excise. "Excise duties are said to have had their origin in this country in the reign of Charles I., when a tax was laid upon beer, cider and perry of home production. The act by which these duties were authorised was passed by the Long Parliament in 1643. This act was adopted and enforced under the protectorate of Oliver Cromwell, and by statute 12 Charles II. c. 24. The duties of excise were granted to the crown as part of its revenue. For a long time this class of duties was viewed with particular dislike by the people, on account of its inquisitorial interference with industrial pursuits, &c." (*Stand. Libr. Cyclop. of Political Knowledge.*) See *The New Litany* in *The Cavalier Songs and Ballads of England:*

> " From being taken in a disguise,
> From believing of the printed lies,
> From the Devil and the *Excise,*
>   Libera nos, Domine."

Marvel :

> " *Excise*
> With hundred rows of teeth, the shark exceeds,
> And on all trades like Cassawar she feeds.'

Johnson in his *Dict.* defines it to be "a hateful tax levied upon commodities, and adjudged not by common judges of property but wretches hired by those to whom excise is paid." The same popular feeling appears in Burns' lines *The Deil's awa' with the Exciseman.* The unpopularity of excise duties had perhaps reached its height some five years before this Satire was published. In the Session of Parliament which commenced in January, 1733, such a storm was raised by the very name of excise as went nigh to shake the monarchy to its foundations. See Knight's *Pop. Hist. Eng.* VI. iv. See also *Kerr's Blackstone's Commentaries,* I. 312—315. Ed. 1857, and Knight's *London,* V. 97—108.

32. [What does *sense* mean here?]

36. *wants* = lacks, is without, *caret* not *eget.* So often in old English, as *King Lear,* I. i. 282, &c.

devote. Devote often occurs in a participial sense, being in fact but an Englished form of the Lat. part. *devotus.* At a later time the word was used as a *verb,* and then there was formed a fresh part. in the common English way, viz. devoted. So with *nominate, situate, derogate* (*King Lear,* I. iv. 302.), &c.

38. [Is there anything *pleonastic* in this line?]

Science. This word had not commonly in the last century the special meaning that now attaches to it. It meant knowledge in the broadest sense; as in Gray's *Elegy:*

" Fair *Science* frowned not on his humble birth."

He here follows Juvenal pretty closely:

"quando artibus, inquit, honestis
Nullus in urbe locus, nulla emolumenta laborum,
Res hodie minor est here quam fuit, atque eadem cras
Deteret exiguis aliquid," &c.

39. *sooths.* So *bath,* where we should now write *bathe,* as in Milton's *Hist. Eng.* Cordelia, hearing of King Lear's coming, "appoints one of her most trusty servants....to array him, *bath* him," &c. The verb *soothe* is not at all connected with the old subst. *sooth,* any more than *bless* is with *bliss.* It is probably from the Gothic *suthjan,* to tickle the ears.

40. [What part of the sentence is *less?*]

41. See Juvenal:

"et pedibus me
Porto meis, nullo dextram subeunte bacillo."

48 *His foes* = the low German invaders of the 5th and 6th centuries = the Anglians or English.

51. *pensions.* In his *Dict.,* published 1755, Johnson's definition of a pension is: "An allowance made to any one without an equivalent. In England it is generally understood to mean pay given to a state hireling for treason to his country." And one definition of a pensioner is: "A slave of state hired by stipend to obey his master." It was not till 1780 that in a bill brought in by Burke the principle was asserted that "distress or desert ought to be considered as regulating the future grants of such pensions, and that parliament had a full right to be informed in respect to this exercise of the prerogative in order to ensure and enforce the responsibility of the ministers of the crown." Till that time the distribution of pensions had lain altogether in the hands of the sovereign and his ministers, and no doubt the patronage was often abused. During the ten years of Walpole's administration, into which an enquiry was ordered by the House of Commons, of £150,000 per annum, paid away to secure support for the government, part had gone in the shape of pensions. The law passed in Queen Anne's reign, and ratified in that of George I., that no person having a pension under the Crown during pleasure, or for any term of years, is capable of being elected or sitting in the House of Commons, would seem to have been utterly set at nought, or at least triumphantly evaded. But the royal patronage was not always abused. In 1762 (some twenty-four years after the publication of *London*) Johnson himself received a well-deserved pension.

52. Johnson's views of the anti-Court party had been somewhat modified when in his *Dict.* he stated of the word Patriot that "it is sometimes used for a factious disturber of the government."

53. *explain away* = strictly, to obscure, or indeed pervert by glosses.

54. The Spaniards, to suppress the frequent smuggling carried on by English vessels in the West Indies, had asserted the right of search on the high seas. "Ships were often illegally detained and their crews sometimes treated with severity." See the story of Jenkins' Ear. It was on the 21st of March, of the year in which *London* was published, that that worthy exhibited his famous ear to the House of Commons, "out of a box in which he always carried it about him, wrapt up in cotton." Although the country generally so completely sympathized with him and what he represented (viz. resistance to the Spanish Right of Search) that it went to war with Spain, there were many who ridiculed his tale, and felt that Spain had some justification for its policy. It is to these Johnson here refers. See Knight's *Pop. Hist. Eng.* VI. chap. vi.

56. [What is the force of *lend* here? What of *confidence?* What "case" is *lie?*]

58. The 2nd of Adam Smith's Four maxims or principles on the subject of Taxation is (see *Wealth of Nations*, published 1776): "The tax which each individual is bound to pay ought to be certain, and not arbitrary. The time of payment, the manner of payment, the quantity to be paid, ought all to be clear and plain to the contributor and to every other person," &c. Certainly the Roman financial economy was far from satisfying these conditions. The *Publicani* were notorious extortioners. And so the corresponding functionaries of modern countries.

farm a lottery. State-lotteries were a favourite mode of raising money for the public service during the whole of the 18th century, and down to the year 1826, when the last one was drawn in England. See Chambers' *Book of Days*, ii. 465—8. An act was made in the 19th year of George III. to license and regulate the Keepers of such offices. See Kerr's *Blackstone's Comment.* Private lotteries were suppressed "as public nuisances" in the reign of Queen Anne. See Knight's *Pop. Hist. Eng.* V. Chap. iii.

farm. The noun *farm* (A. S. feorme) means radically food. "Lands were let on condition of supplying the lord with so many nights' entertainment for his household.... This mode of reckoning constantly appears in *Doomsday Book:* 'Reddet firmam trium noctium'" (Wedgwood). Then, this entertainment being commuted for *money, farm* = so much money, rent; and then by a natural transition, *arm* = the land producing that money or rent; and, as a verb, = to occupy such land; whence in a general sense, to hold or occupy or manage anything for which rent is to be paid. This latter verbal sense is the sense here.

59. *silenc'd stage.* It was in 1737 that Walpole "moved an amendment to the Vagrant Act as far as related to the common players of interludes... Under this bill the Lord Chamberlain might prohibit the representation of plays; and copies of all new plays, additions to old plays, prologues and epilogues, were to be submitted to that officer for the purpose of being licensed." See Knight's *Pop. Hist. Eng.* VI. chap. vi. It was the political personalities which had begun to find a place upon the stage, as in Fielding's *Pasquin*, that led to this interference. Walpole's enactment still remains in force. Some Editions read *licens'd* here, wrongly and feebly. Comp. Horace's *Ep. ad Pis.* 283:

> "Successit vetus his comœdia, non sine multâ
> Laude, sed in vitium libertas excidit, et vim
> Dignam lege regi; lex est accepta, chorusque
> Turpiter obticuit sublato jure nocendi."

63. [Explain *rebellious* here.]
68. Comp. Juvenal:

> "Quid Romæ faciam? mentiri nescio."

61. 72. *The Gazetteer* was the Court newspaper of the time.
73. [Explain *in half his pension dress'd.*]

80. [Explain *to puzzle right.*]

varnish wrong = disguise the proper hue or colour of wrong.   Comp. the phrase "a coloured account."

81. *a spy.*   See Pope's *Satires of Dr Donne versified*, iv. 279:

> "Scared at the grizly forms, I sweat, I fly,
> And shake all o'er, like a discover'd *spy* "—

and *ib.* 158:

> "Then as a licens'd *spy*, whom nothing can
> Silence or hurt, he libels the great man."

Donne writes:

> "He like a privileg'd *spy*, whom nothing can
> Discredit, libels now 'gainst each great man "—

and

> "I shook like a spy'd spy."

83. [What is meant by *social guilt* ?]

Comp. Juvenal :

> "Quis nunc diligitur nisi consclus?....
> Carus erit Verri, qui Verrem tempore quo vult
> Accusare potest."

86. *Marlborough.* In 1708, "exclusive of Blenheim, the duke's fixed yearly income, from offices and emoluments, was very nearly fifty-five thousand pounds ; and the income of the duchess, from her offices at court, was nine thousand five hundred pounds " (Knight's *Pop. Hist. Eng.* V. chap. xxii.). See Johnson's *Life of Swift*: "That is no longer doubted of which the nation was then [in *Swift's Conduct of the Allies*] first informed, that the war was unnecessarily protracted to fill the pockets of Marlborough; and that it would have been continued without end, if he could have continued his annual plunder." As to his parsimony Johnson here, and Thackeray in his *Esmond*, have only too good authority for their attacks, allusive or direct, upon him.

Villiers. See Dryden's *Abs. and Achit.* Part i. 544—568, and Pope's *Moral Essays*, Ep. iii. 299—314, where more famous for his vices than his misfortunes, after having been possess'd of about £50,000 a year, and passed thro' many of the highest posts in the kingdom, died in the year 1687, in a remote inn in Yorkshire, reduced to the utmost misery."

89. [Explain *self-approving day.*   What part of the sentence is it ?]

93. [What is meant by *gen'ral* here ?]

94. *Rome.*   By Rome he means Italy generally.

[Is *common sewer* a metaphor or a simile ?]

97. [Explain *transports.*   Should we use the word in the same way ?]

98. Comp. Juvenal:

> " non possum ferre, Quirites,
> Græcam urbem."

99. See *Spect.* no. 329: "Sir Roger, in the next place, laid his hand upon Edward the Third's sword, and leaning upon the pummel of it gave us the whole history of the Black Prince, concluding that in Sir Richard Baker's opinion Edward the Third was one of the greatest princes that ever sate upon the English throne."

100. [Mention some saints of English birth.]

106. See l. 28.

108. *Gibbet*, Fr. *gibet*, Ital. *giubbette* (which is closely connected with *giubetto*, which is a dim. of *giubba*, which properly means an under-waistcoat) = a halter. Then the framework from which the halter was suspended, in which, the modern, sense Robert of Gloucester uses it, and Chaucer, in his *House of Fame*, i.:

" Cresus that was King of Lide
That high upon a *gebet* dide."

108. *wheel.* Breaking on the wheel, according to Haydn's *Dict. of Dates,* Ed. 1863, "was used for the punishment of great criminals, such as assassins and parricides, first in Germany; it was also used by the Inquisition, and rarely anywhere else, until Francis I. ordered it to be inflicted upon robbers, first breaking their bones by strokes with a heavy iron club, and then leaving them to expire on the wheel, A.D. 1515." Shakspere makes Coriolanus speak of "Death on the wheel" (III. ii. 2). See also *Winter's Tale,* III. ii. 176:

" What studied torments, tyrant, hast for me?
What *wheels?* racks? fires? what flaying? boiling?
In leads or oils? what old or newer torture
Must I receive, whose every word deserves
To taste of thy most worst?"

See *The Traveller,* 435.

62. 113. Comp. Juvenal:

" Augur, schœnobates, medicus, magus; omnia novit
Græculus esuriens; in cælum jusseris, ibit."

A great dislike of the French was one of Johnson's many violent prejudices.

118. See *Spect.* 329: "The glorious names of Henry the Fifth and Queen Elizabeth gave the knight great opportunities of shining and of doing justice to Sir Richard Baker," &c.

119. Comp. Hor. *Ep.* II. i. 156. So Butler, with respect to dress of his time, *Hud.* I. iii. 923:

" And as the French we conquer'd once
Now give us laws for pantaloons,
The length of breeches and the gathers,
Port cannons, perriwigs, and feathers," &c.

gulled. Gull is possibly connected with *guile;* but rather, perhaps, it is the sea-fowl's name used as a verb, in a secondary sense, = to treat as a gull, i. e. as something very stupid.

128. See *St. Matthew's Gospel,* A.V. xxiii. 24, where for "out" is incorrectly printed "at." The Greek is οἱ διυλίζοντες.

129. *awkward.* "Aukwarde, frowarde, peruers. Aukwar, lefte-handed, gauche. Auke, stroke *reuers*" (Palsgrave). The *Promptorium Parvulorum* gives "awke or wrong, Sinister."

131. There were French actors in England as early as the reign of James I. It was probably by a French *troupe* that actresses were first introduced upon our stage; See Prynne's *Histriomastix.* English women do not seem to have "gone upon the stage" till after the Restoration.

133. Comp. Juvenal:

" Melior qui semper et omni
Nocte dieque potest alienum sumere vultum,
A facie jactare manus."

138. Comp. Juvenal:

" Rides; majore cachinno
Concutitur; flet, si lacrimas eonspexit amici,
Nec dolet; igniculum brumæ si tempore poscas,
Accipit endromidem; si dixeris æstuo, sudát."

Æsch. *Agam.* 764—768, ed. Paley:

" τῷ δυσπραγοῦντι δ' ἐπιστενάχειν
πᾶς τις ἕτοιμος· δῆγμα δὲ λύπης
οὐδὲν ἐφ' ἧπαρ προσικνεῖται·

καὶ ξυγχαίρουσιν ὁμοιοπρεπεῖς
ἀγέλαστα πρόσωπα βιαζόμενοι."

141. *dog days.* See *Lycidas,* 138.

143. [What is the meaning of *fix* here? What other meanings has the word?]

153. *commence your lords* Comp. the University phrase, "to commence M.A." The construction is elliptical.

154. [What is the sense of *by numbers* here?]

155. Perhaps no poet has treated Poverty with less mercy than Pope. See the *Dunciad,* passim.

63. 163. Comp. Juvenal:

"Nil habet infelix paupertas durius in se
Quam quod ridiculos homines facit."

169. The Pope, Alexander VI., at the beginning of the 16th century, had assigned to Spain all lands discovered more than 470 leagues west of the Azores.

170. Comp. Hor. *Epod.* xvi.

177. *The groom,* i. e. The great man's great man.

180. [What is the force of *rais'd* here?]

192. *spread.* Comp. the Lat. *sterno,* as frequently in Virgil. So Ovid's *Met.* xii. 550:

"Ille tuus genitor Messania moenia quondam
Stravit."

64. 199. *dome* is used by Pope and Prior also in the simple sense of a house, a building.

200. They pay back, in part at least, what has been paid them for their support in parliament for so selling their souls, for so "their sauls indentin'," as Burns has it (*Twa Dogs,* 148). "Every man has his price," was Walpole's theory, founded on an extensive experience.

206. *the park and play* should rather be *the park and the play.* [What should be the difference in meaning?]

210. *the smiling land.* See Gray's *Elegy,* 63.

211. [What is the force of *rent* here?]

212. Much attention was about this time beginning to be paid to landscape gardening. See, for instance, Johnson's *Life of Shenstone.* When Leasowes had in 1745 come into Shenstone's possession, "he took the whole estate into his own hands, more to the improvement of its beauty than the increase of its produce. Now was excited his delight in rural pleasures, and his ambition of rural elegance; he began from this time to point his prospects, to diversify his surface, to entangle his walks, and to wind his waters; which he did with such judgment and such fancy as made his little domain the envy of the great and the admiration of the skilful; a place to be visited by travellers and copied by designers," &c. Aislabie begun to "lay out" the grounds of Studley Royal (= Fountain's Abbey) about 1720.

218. With the rhyme between *smile* and *toil,* comp. *Dunciad,* ii. 221:

"Now turn to different sports, the goddess *cries,*
And learn, my sons, the wond'rous pow'r of *noise."*

224. *frolick.* See note to *L'Alleg.* 18.

235. [*bursts the faithless bar.* In what sense do we now use *burst?*]

238. In one year ninety-seven malefactors were executed in London; on one morning twenty were hanged. "Hanging-day" came round regularly. See Knight's *Pop. Hist. Eng.* VII. chap. vi. In Butler's time there was a great executing once a month; see *Hudibras,* I. ii. 532.

"Tyburn was anciently a manor and village west of London, in the Tybourn or Brook, subsequently the West-bourn, the western boundary of the district, now incorporated in Paddington.' (Timbs' *Curiosities of London.*) As early as 1196, the execution of London and Middlesex criminals took place on its banks. Then, early in the 15th century, the gallows was for a time brought nearer London, to St Giles'-in-the-Fields. Then again it was removed westward to its old neighbourhood; and there remained till 1783, when the place of execution was changed to Newgate. As to its precise site, it would seem to have been originally Elms Lane, Bayswater (see Map of London); there lay the channel of the old stream; then to have been transferred eastward, and been, at various times where Connaught Square now is, where Oxford Street and the Edgeware Road meet, and thirdly, at the junction of Upper Bryanston Street and the Edgeware Road. See Oldham's *Satires, Imitation of the Third of Juvenal:*

> "Then fatal carts through Holborn seldom went,
> And Tyburn with few pilgrims was content."

65. 243. George II. several times visited his continental possessions, e. g. in 1735, and 1736. These absences made him highly unpopular at home. In 1736 "People of all ranks were indignant at the king's long stay in Germany. The national ill-humour was expressed in pasquinades ... In December the king came home after the public hopes rather than fears had been excited by the belief that he was at sea during a terrible storm in which many ships had been wrecked." See Knight's *Pop. Hist. Eng.* VI. Chap. v.

244. *gaol* and *cage,* strangely different as they look, are probably derived ultimately from the same Latin word, viz. *cavea, gaol* coming from the dim. form. See Ital. *gaiola* = *gabbiuola.* French *geôle.* See Wedgwood, to whom "the origin seems gael, gabh, to take, seize, to make prisoner, hold or contain." But is not the origin rather to be seen in the Lat. *cavus, cavea,* meaning radically much the same as *caverna?* The place where Joshua confined the five kings was literally a gaol. The first notion is that of a hole or hollow. Just such was the Tullianum at Rome; and just such very commonly were the prisons of the mediæval castles. But perhaps *cavus* may be ultimately connected with *capio.*

Alfred's reign is the golden age with many a Satirist and many a historian.

248. *No special juries.* There were no juries at all, in our sense of the word, known in King Alfred's time. Trial by jury, however pertinaciously assigned to him by popular tradition, does really date from the 13th century or thereabouts. According to eminent authorities, as Sir F. Palgrave, it was of Norman rather than of "Anglo-Saxon" origin.

253. *wilds* is perhaps a corruption of *wealds,* = woods, wooded districts. A. S. *weald,* Germ. *wald.* The extent of the Weald of South Kent may still be traced by the place-names ending in *den* and *hurst,* as Tenter*den,* Stan*den,* Sand*hurst,* &c.

VANITY OF HUMAN WISHES.

This piece was published in 1749, the twelfth year of Johnson's London struggles. It was in that same year that Gray finished his *Elegy.*

As *London* of the Third, so this is an imitation of Juvenal's Tenth Satire. There is much difference of tone between the two Satires as well in the originals as in the English versions. The Tenth Satire is not only destructive, it is partly constructive; that is, it is not only satirical, it is also didactic.

The text might well be: "*He gave them their desire, and sent leanness withal into their soul*" (*Psalm* cvi. 15, *the Book of Common Prayer Version*). See Horace's *Od.* I. xxxi.

[See Juvenal's *Tenth Satire,* and Dryden's Translation of it along with this imitation.]

Notice any differences between Johnson's style here and that of *London.* Take any 20 lines of each poem, and compare them together. Can you see any differences in *grammatical structure,* in the *word-order,* in the *language,* &c.?

Into how many parts would you divide this poem?
Add fresh historical illustrations to those successively given by Johnson.]

65. 3. [What is there noticeable about the use of *toil* here?]
6. The hidden pathway of our lives is made yet more dark and difficult by our own wilfulnesses.

7. *vent'rous*. We now use *venturesome*.

9. [What part of the sentence is this clause?]

11. *Stubborn* = radically, as fixed and immoveable as *a stub*. Comp. stock-still.

15. Comp. Pope's *Moral Essays*, ii. 147:

> " Atossa, *cursed with every granted prayer*," &c.

16. [What parts of the sentence are *each gift of nature, each grace of art*?]

17. Observe how much the *predicative* force of the sentence lies in what is grammatically but a subordinate part. Perhaps the style in which such a form of predication is most used—used to a degree of obscurity and frequent misleading—is that of Gibbon ; but it is common in nearly all the writers of the middle of the last century. It is immediately of Latin, ultimately of Greek origin.

66. 22. [What is the force of *of* here?]

25. Comp. Soph. *Antig.* 295—301, *Timon of Athens*, IV. iii. 382—394.

30. *madded* = maddened. The shorter form often occurs in Elizabethan writers, as in Sidney's *Arcadia*: "O villain ! cried out Zalmane, *madded* with finding an unlooked for rival." *Mad* also occurs as a neut. verb = to be mad; as in Milton :

> " The *madding* wheels
> Of brazen chariots rag'd."

So Gray's *Elegy*, 73.

33. *hind*, A. S. *hina*, Scot. *hyne*, used by Barbour, Douglas, &c. See Milton's *Comus*, 174, &c.

This line, as many others in this poem, shows what vigorous English Dr Johnson could write, when for a while forgetting his extreme predilection for "Sesquipedal" Latinisms. See on this point Macaulay's Biog. of him.

37. See Chaucer's *Wyf of Bathes Tale :*

> " Iuvenal saith of povert merily
> The pore man when he goth by the way
> Bifore the theves he may synge and play."

38. *the wide heath*. The heaths around London were about this time, and long afterwards, infested with highwaymen. Hounslow Heath was especially notorious in this respect. See Knight's *Pop. Hist. Eng.* VII. chap. v.

43. [Is the sing. verb correct here?]

46. [Explain *load the tainted gales*.]

49. *Democritus*. See *Class. Dict.* Burton, the author of the *Anatomy of Melancholy*, styles himself *Democritus junior*.

51. *motley* is of the same word-family as *smut, smutch, bysmotered* (Chaucer's *Cant. Tales*, 76), A. S. *besmitan*, &c. For the *s*, comp. Nottingham from Snottengaham, *smelt* and *melt*, &c.

52. [What part of the verb, and what part of the sentence is *feed* here?]

54. *man was of a piece*, i. e. when people were less completely inconsistent and variable than they now are.

a = one. See notes on *L'Alleg.* 14.

56. This is as true as history written by satirists mostly is. Aristophanes was but some 16 years younger than Democritus, and were sycophants and parasites scarce in his time ?

57. Were all the debates of the Bûlé and of the Ekklesia so unexceptionably grave and earnest?

58. The Lord Mayor's show dates from the 15th century. It was in 1453 that the first lord mayor went to be sworn at Westminster. The route then was the river.

67. 62. *Gibe* is from the same root as *gabble*, Old Eng. *gab*, Fr. *gaber*.

63. [What part of the sentence is *to descry*?]

65. [What is the predicate in this sentence?]

68. [What is the antecedent of *where*?]

72. *Canvass* = strictly, to examine by passing the object through *canvas*, or a sieve, to sift. *Canvas* is the Lat. *cannabis*, Gr. κάνναβις, Old High G. *hanf*. Eng. *hemp*.

74. *athirst.* See note on *Eve of St. Agnes*, 2.

79. Comp. Virg. *Georg.* ii. 461, 462.

> " Si non ingentem foribus domus alta superbis
> Mane salutantum totis vomit ædibus undam," &c.

[Explain *love ends with hope*.]

82. See *Vicar of Wakefield*, chap. xx.

84. The *Palladium* was an image of Pallas preserved at Troy, said to have fallen from heaven (as that of Diana at Ephesus; see *Acts of the Apostles*, xix. 35), and believed to have supreme protecting power. See Virg. *Æn.* ii. 165—8 and 227. As the city could not be taken while this divine statue was in it, Diomede and Ulysses plotted how to carry it off. Afterwards it, or what passed for it, was transferred from Greece to Rome, where Metellus signalized himself by rescuing it from being burnt along with the temple of Vesta, in which it was deposited. See Cic. *Phil.* XI. x. 24, where the orator says that Brutus ought to be preserved and supported "ut id signum quod de cælo delapsum Vestæ custodiis continetur : quo salvo, salvi sumus futuri,"

94. [Illustrate from English history of the 17th century.]

97. The act for Septennial Parliaments was passed in 1716. Comp. "Septennial bribe " in Crabbe's *Village*, Bk. 1.

98. [What is meant by *full* here?]

99. *Wolsey.* See Shakspeare's *Henry VIII.* "Thus passed the Cardinal," says Cavendish, "his life and time from day to day and year to year, in such great wealth, joy, and triumph, and glory, having always on his side the king's especial favour."

100. [What part of the sentence is *law in his voice*?]

68. 109. The frown came in 1529 In the spring of 1530 he was commanded to reside within his archbishopric. Early in November of that same year he was arrested at Cawood on a charge of high treason. At the close of that month he died at Leicester Abbey, being then on his way to London, to be put upon his trial.

113. On the brilliancy of Wolsey's establishment see *Hist. Eng.* " Pope Leo himself," it has been said, "scarcely lived with more splendour and magnificence. He became most gorgeous in his dress, retinue, housekeeping, and all other things. He maintain'd a train of one hundred persons, among whom were nine or ten lords. Whenever he appeared in public his cardinal's hat was borne before him by a person of rank," &c. &c.

116. *menial* is strictly an adj. = belonging to a *meiny* (*K. Lear*, II. iv.), or household staff. Thus it is strictly synonymous with Lat. *familiaris*.

118. See note on l. 109.

129. See *Hist. Eng.* sub anno 1628.

130. Harley survived his release from the Tower seven years. It was during this period that he made his famous collection of MSS., afterwards purchased for the British Museum.

131. *Wentworth.* See *Hist. Eng.* for the year 1641.

Hyde. See *Hist. Eng.* for the year 1667.

136. [Is the metre of this line decasyllabic?]

139. *Bodley*, after being employed by Queen Elizabeth on various embassies, falling into disgrace, retired in 1597 to Oxford, his old University, and presently set about restoring the University Library; to whose support and extension he subsequently bequeathed all his property. He died in 1612.

140. "There is a tradition that the study of friar Bacon, built on an arch over the bridge, will fall when a man greater than Bacon shall pass under it. To prevent so shocking an accident, it was pulled down many years since" (Johnson's note). Roger Bacon spent the greater part of his studious life at Oxford, many years of it in confinement, his contemporaries being unable to appreciate his learning and attributing the discoveries he made to Satanic agency. What precisely those discoveries were, it is difficult to ascertain, as Bacon's name has been as thickly surrounded with traditions as that of King Alfred. But it seems certain that both as a man of research and as an original thinker he was one of the greatest if not the greatest, Englishman of the Middle Ages. He died in 1272.

69. 149. *thy cell refrain* = refrain itself with regard to thy cell, refrain from thy cell. So *forbear* is sometimes used. Comp. *muse* in Shaksp. *Temp.* III. iii. 36, &c.

154. Burton considers at length Study as a Cause of Melancholy. See *Anat. of Mel.* I. ii. 3. Subs. 15. Jaques speaks of the Scholar's Melancholy; his was not that; see *As you like it*, IV. i. 10.

160. The age of the Patron was at this very time beginning to pass away, the age of the Public to dawn. No one did more to deliver literature from Patronage than Johnson himself. In his earlier London life he had sorely needed a helping hand; but no such hand was stretched out to him; nor was it so, until he had ceased to need it. See his *Letter to the Earl of Chesterfield*. As books and the ability to read them became more widely diffused, it became less and less important to an author to be supported by some aristocratic name.

162. As to "Hudibras" Butler see the Epigram by Samuel Wesley (the father of John and Charles Wesley):

> " While Butler, needy wretch, was still alive
> No generous patron would a dinner give,
> See him when starv'd to death and turn'd to dust
> Presented with a monumental bust.
> The poet's fate is here in emblem shown:
> He ask'd for bread, and he received a stone."

164. *Lydiat* was a man of various learning, distinguished as a theologian, a chronologer, a mathematician. After a somewhat troubled life, including severe sufferings as a royalist, he died in indigence in 1646.

To say nothing of previous dangers, Galileo was summoned before the Inquisition in 1633, and compelled to renounce his great discoveries and confirmations of Copernicus' discoveries; but his "E pur si muove" (= and yet it moves) sent him to imprisonment. In 1634 his sentence was commuted to banishment to the Episcopal palace at Sienna, and soon after, to the palace of Arceti not far from Florence. Then various bodily ailments, blindness, deafness, want of sleep, pains and aches, came upon him in the midst of his immortal studies. "In my darkness," he writes in 1638, "I muse now upon this object of nature and now upon that, and find it impossible to soothe my restless head, however much I wish it. This perpetual action of mind deprives me almost wholly of sleep." It was in that same year that Milton saw him. "There [in Italy] it was that I found and visited the famous Galileo grown old, a prisoner to the Inquisition, for thinking in Astronomy otherwise than the Franciscan and Dominican licensers thought" (Milton's *Areopagitica*); where by "a prisoner to the Inquisition" is meant not in the dungeons of the Inquisition, but kept under some restraint by the Inquisition. His was what the Latins called a "libera custodia." He died in 1642, a prey to a slowly consuming fever. See Hallam's *Liter. of Eur.* 1600—1650, chap. viii.

168. *Rebellion.* Johnson's extreme Toryism, and his Jacobitism are well-known.

168. *Laud* was arrested in Dec. 1641, condemned by bill of attainder just three years afterwards, and executed in the following month. See *Hist. Eng.*

170. *the plundered palace.* He refers to Woodstock &c. See, in Scott's novel of *Woodstock*, some account of the Commissioners there and how they fared.

The sequester'd rent. There was a special court of *Sequestrators*, whose function it was to discover and fine any favourers of Royalty. Of course in the eyes of Royalists sequestrator meant robber; hence Jeremy Taylor: " I am fallen into the hands of publicans and *sequestrators*, and they have taken all from me." " Sequestrations were first introduced by Sir Nicholas Bacon " (Blackstone).

171. [What is meant by *parts* here ? See *Winter's Tale*, I. ii. 400.]

177. *gazette.* " A paper called the London Gazette was first published, Aug. 22, 1642. The London Gazette of the existing series was first published at Oxford, the court being there on account of the plague, Nov. 7, 1665, and afterwards at London, Feb. 5, 1666."—(Haydn's *Dict. Dates.*)

179. [What interval of time was there between Alexander's landing in the Troad, and his death at Babylon? See *Hist. Greece.*]

182. [*The Danube and the Rhine.* See in your *Atlas* the following places, and in your *Hist. Eng.* some account of the battles fought at or near them : Hochstett, Dettingen, Fontenoy. Add to these]

183. [*This pow'r has praise*, &c. Which is the subject here? What is the antecedent of *that* ?]

184. *The universal charm.* See Young's *Love of Fame, the universal passion, in Seven characteristical Satires.* (1726—8.)

188. We have to thank our Wars, and them only, for our National Debt. The beginning of that monstrous burden dates from the reign of William III. In 1697 it amounted to 5 millions; at the conclusion of the wars of Queen Anne's reign to 54 millions ; at the end of the Spanish War in 1749, when this satire was published, to 78 millions. Since Johnson's time it has increased at such a frightful pace, that it now amounts to some 800 millions—a fine legacy for posterity as for us

70. 192. See Voltaire's *Charles XII.* Charles' reign extended from 1697 to 1718.

193. Voltaire speaks of his "Ce corps de fer gouverné par une âme si hardie et si inébranlable." See the instances he gives.

199. *surrounding kings.* The Tsar of Russia (Peter the Great), the King of Denmark (Frederick IV.), the King of Poland and Elector of Saxony (Frederick Augustus). The dangers surrounding Charles XII. in the beginning of his reign, and the amazing vigour with which he extricated himself from them, call to mind Alexander's earlier career.

200. *one capitulate.* So the king of Denmark in 1700.

one resign. So the king of Poland in 1701.

202. Charles was not content with great victories over the Russians. He conceived the idea of overthrowing that vast empire. In 1707, when the Duke of Marlborough had an interview with him, that shrewd observer no less than consummate general saw that "le véritable dessein du roi de Suède et sa seule ambition étaient de détroner le czar après le roi de Pologne." After Charles had crossed the Dnieper, and his purpose was made manifest, the Tsar attempted to negotiate. " Charles XII., accoutumé à s'accorder la paix à ses ennemis que dans leur capitales, repondit: ' Je traiterai avec le czar à Moscow.' "

209. *cold.* The winter of 1708 was of uncommon severity.

delay. The sing. here is certainly inaccurate; but it is perhaps explicable when the sense is considered. The sense is: "*both* want *and* cold do *not* his course delay."

210. The battle of *Pultowa* was fought, July 8, 1709.

212. " He fled into Turkey, where he met with a hospitable reception. His establishment at Bender was such as became a prince. Though his followers were soon a thousand—numbers from Poland and Sweden joined him every week—they were liberally maintained by the sultan Achmet III., who allowed him 500 crowns a day for his own household."

(Dunham's *Hist. Denm. Swed. and Norway*). Then he began to dream of enlisting Turkey in his great design. "Vizier after vizier he flattered or assailed, according as they aided or opposed his views ; and the seraglio, in which gold brought him creatures devoted to his will, became the scene of innumerable intrigues. The tsar had more gold than he ; and it was distributed with better effect," &c. At last, in 1713, he was removed by force to Adrianople, and thence to Demotica ; whence, despairing of Turkish aid, he made his escape in disguise to Stralsund, 1714. See *Tatler*, No. 155.

220. *A petty fortress.* He was shot dead at Frederickshall on the coast of Norway, on the night of Dec. 11, 1718.

A dubious hand. Whether it was an enemy's ball that struck him down, or that of a traitor friend, remains a vexed question. Voltaire speaks of the story that Siquier assassinated him as "une colomnie renouvelée trop souvent à la mort des princes, &c.," and altogether disbelieves it. Coxe (died 1828) agrees with Voltaire, (see his *Travels in Poland, Russia, Sweden and Denmark*). Clarke, the traveller (died 1822), on the other hand, says : "that he was assassinated seems so clear that it is marvellous any doubt should be entertained as to the fact."

224. *Persia's tyrant.* See *Herod.* vii. and viii.

Bavaria's lord. Charles Albert, Elector of Bavaria, who, on the death of the Emperor Charles VI., laid claim to the Kingdom of Bohemia on the strength of an article in the will of the Emperor Ferdinand I., brother to Charles V.

226. See Grote's *Hist. Greece*, Part II. chap. xxxviii.

230. *sooth.* See *London*, 40.

232. See *Par. Lost*, x. 306—311, esp. 311 :

> "And scourged with many a stroke the indignant waves."

Butler's *Hudibras*, II. i. 845 :

> "A Persian emp'ror whipped his [Cupid's] grannum,
> The sea his mother Venus came on."

71. 234. *lops*, &c. See the story of Dagon.

239. See the play in which Æschylus celebrates the splendid triumph of his country, the *Persæ*, 417—20 (Dindorf) :

> "ὑπτιοῦτο δὲ
> σκάφη νεῶν, θάλασσα δ' οὐκέτ' ἦν ἰδεῖν
> ναυαγίων πλήθουσα καὶ φόνου βροτῶν."

241. France assisted him, and at first he carried everything before him. He seized Passau, and then Lintz ; and so advanced upon Vienna. Presently he was crowned King of Bohemia at Prague, and then elected Emperor at Frankfort.

242. *Cæsarean power.* He would be *Kaiser*. See Bryce's *Holy Roman Empire*.

245. *Fair Austria* = the fair Archduchess of Austria. So in *King Lear*, for example, Burgundy = Duke of Burgundy, France = King of France.

"Her form was majestic, her features beautiful, her countenance sweet and animated, her voice musical, her deportment gracious and dignified." (Macaulay's *Essays*, *Frederic the Great*.)

sets the world in arms. At the Diet of Presburg "the enthusiasm of Hungary broke forth into that war-cry which soon resounded throughout Europe : ' Let us die for our king, Maria Theresa.'"

247. *beacon* is of the same root as *beckon*, &c., and properly means a sign, a signal. See Macaulay's fragment on the *Armada*.

249. *Hussars* = "light cavalry of Poland and Hungary, about 1600." The name was adopted into the British army in 1759.

"The terrible names of the Pandoor, the Croat, and the Hussar then first became familiar to Western Europe."

251. *baffled.* In chivalry, *baffle* was a technical word. See Trench's *Study of Words.*

"The unfortunate Charles of Bavaria, vanquished by Austria, betrayed by Prussia, driven from his hereditary states, and neglected by his allies, was hurried by shame and remorse to an untimely end." He died at Munich in 1745.

252. [*the fatal doom.* What is the force of the article here?]

253. *blame.* See note on *sorrow, Lycid.* 166.

265. Comp. *As you like it,* II. vii. 163—6.

270. *Orpheus.* See *Lycid.* 59. [What is meant by *witness'd* here?]

273. *dictates,* the Lat. *dictata.* We should rather say "dictations," if we used any word of this family.

274. [What is the sense of *positively* here? What is its common sense now? Connect the two senses.]

275. *the still returning tale.* This weakness of old age is a theme Thackeray often touches upon, in a style between tears and laughter.

72. 277. [What is the meaning of *gath'ring* here?]

280. *expence.* Perhaps this old spelling arose from some lurking suspicion, quite groundless, of a connection between this word and *pence.*

282. [Explain *improve* here.]

285. Comp. Horace's *Ep. ad Pis.* 170. The miser has been a favourite subject with both painters and poets. [Mention instances.]

293. See Goldsmith's *Deserted Village,* 107—112.

302. [Explain *mourns* here.]

308. [Explain *superfluous.*]

313. See *Herod.* i. 29—33.

[What is meant here by *descend*?]

317. In the last eight years of Marlborough's life (1714—22), "two paralytic strokes shook his strength, but without at all seriously impairing his faculties;" Johnson's line "was at least a poetical exaggeration ; for he continued to be consulted on all affairs of war or of policy and to attend his parliamentary and other duties until a few months before his death." (*Cabinet Portrait Gallery of British Worthies,* Vol. xi.)

318. See Johnson's *Lives of the Poets, Swift:* "He grew more violent, and his mental powers declined, till (1741) it was found necessary that legal guardians should be appointed of his person and fortune. He now lost distinction. [What does that mean?] His madness was compounded of rage and fatuity ... At last he sunk into a perfect silence, which continued till about the end of October, 1744, when in his 78th year he expired without a struggle."

319. *teeming.* See *Hymn Nat.* 240.

73. 320. *birth* = what is born. So 2 *Henry IV.,* IV. iv. 122, &c. So often *partus* in Latin, as in Cic. *Tusc. Disp.* v. 27: "bestiæ pro suo *partu* propugnant."

321. *Vane.* Lady Vane, the daughter of a Mr Hawes; she married first Lord William Hamilton, and then Lord Vane ; she was the mistress of Lord Berkeley and others. She is the heroine of the *Memoirs of a Lady of Quality,* inserted in Smollett's *Peregrine Pickle.* See Walpole's *Letters, passim.*

322. *Sedley.* The daughter of Sir Charles Sedley, was one of the mistresses of James II. made by him Countess of Dorchester. See Macaulay's *Hist. Eng.* chap. vi. It was certainly not her *beauty* that raised, or ruined her; for this "form that pleased a king" was singularly plain ; but her influence over her lover was supreme. "Personal charms she had none, with the exception of two brilliant eyes.... The nature of her influence over James is not easily to be explained.... Catharine herself was astonished by the violence of his passion."

346. *darkling.* The term *ling* here is not participial, but adverbial. So in *grovelling* &c. See note to *sidelong, Des. Vill.* 29.

353. [What is the meaning of *ambush* here ?]

355. *Secure* here in the sense of the Latin *securus,* as Hor. *Od.* I. xxvi. 3—6:

> "Quis sub Arcto
> Rex gelidæ metuatur oræ
> Quid Teridaten terreat, unice
> *Securus.*"

In this sense verbalized *secure* occurs in *King Lear,* IV. i. 22—a passage which has terribly puzzled commentators.

359. Comp. the prayer which Horace offers for himself at the dedication of a temple of Apollo :

> "Frui paratis et valido mihi,
> Latoe, dones et precor integra
> Cum mente nec turpem senectam
> Degere nec cithara carentem."

361. = for love which can hold or contain nearly all mankind, love of vast capacity.

362. *Sovereign o'er transmuted ill* = sovereign over ill so that it becomes transmuted or changed into good. *Transmuted* is used proleptically. Misfortunes may be made blessings, if borne well and nobly. *Transmute* was a technical term in alchemy.

74. 365. [Should we now use *goods* in this way?]

COLLINS.

William Collins was born at Chichester, the son of a hatter, in 1720. He received education at Winchester school, and at Queen's College, Oxford.

About the year 1744, according to Dr Johnson, he came up to London, "with many projects in his head and very little money in his pocket," which indeed was very much Dr Johnson's own equipment on his first appearance in the metropolis. For some years he led a life of hardships and necessities. "He published proposals for a History of the Revival of Learning;" he designed several tragedies; he undertook to translate, with a commentary, Aristotle's Poetics; but with all these strings to his bow he shot nothing. Like many another *litterateur* of his time he lived often in fear of the debtor's prison. Johnson speaks of visiting him one day, "when he was immured by a bailiff that was prowling in the street." At last he was freed from his pecuniary difficulties by a legacy from an uncle of some £2000—"a sum which Collins could scarcely think exhaustible, and which he did not live to exhaust." Freed from poverty, still direr evils fell upon him—disease, and insanity. After a vain struggle with a terrible despondency which gradually overwhelmed him, he was confined for a time in a lunatic asylum, and shortly afterwards died in his sister's house in his native city.

Like Gray, Collins produced but little ; but concerning him, as concerning Gray, there can be no doubt that he had in him a genuine poetical spirit. His Ode *How sleep the brave* is one of the most exquisite gems of our lyrical literature. Strength does not so much characterize him as a certain fine delicacy and sweetness. His powers of expression were scarcely adequate for his ideas and sympathies; for certainly he lived mostly in the poet's land; his mind was ever there revelling in the fair visions of it. Spenser, "the poet's poet," was his great delight. When the bailiffs were besetting his earthly lodgings, he was often far away in Faerie. He felt and enjoyed more than he could write. In what little he did write, with all its imperfections, it is easy to see how refined and spiritual was his nature.

THE PASSIONS.

INTRODUCTION.

Collins, like Spenser, has but little dramatic power; for his fine imagination abstractions were themselves real and substantial enough ; he does not feel any necessity for clothing them with flesh and blood. Hence in his poems, as in Spenser's, abstractions abound unbodied, as Peace, Evening, Mercy, Simplicity, and the Passions in the following poem. He introduces "airy nothings" in all their airiness; for him they are the real existences. Despair is as forcible a figure in his eyes as the desperate man; the concrete has no advantage over the abstract. Poets of this type are never, and are not likely ever to be, so popular as the dramatic poets. The general taste prefers creations more tangible and solid; it cannot be satisfied with spiritual visions; it wearies of pure airinesses; nor can this preference be justly censured. Collins can only hope. like another greater master of the same poetic order, for "fit audience, though few."

75. 2. *yet.* See note to *Il Penser.*, 30.

3. *shell.* See note on Dryden's *Song for St Cecilia's Day*, 17.

6. [What is meant by *possest* here?]

8. *disturb'd.* Comp. in Coleridge's exquisite lyric *Love:*

> "but when I reach'd
> That tenderest strain of all the ditty,
> My faltering voice and pausing harp
> *Disturb'd* her soul with pity."

10. [What is the meaning of *rapt* here?]

11. *myrtles.* See *Lycid.* 2.

14. *forceful.* Shaks. *Winter's Tale*, II. i. 161—3:

> "Why, what need we
> Commune with you of this, but rather follow
> Our *forceful* instigation?"

So in Collins' *Manners:* "Each *forceful* thought." Comp. in *Ode to Simplicity:* "*forceless* numbers."

16. [What is meant by *expressive power?*]

See Collins' *Ode to Fear.*

25. See Spenser's picture of Despair and his cave, *F. Q.* I. ix. 33—54.

26. [What part of the sentence is *low sullen sounds?*]

76. 32. [What part of the sentence is *at distance?*]

35. So the Lady in *Comus;* see her invocation of Echo.

36. [Explain *where* here.]

37. *close.* See note in *Hymn on the Nativity*, 100.

41. See Dickens' *Great Expectations.* This passage is perhaps somewhat theatrical, and not altogether to be rescued from that novelist's ridicule.

46. See *Revelations* viii—x., of the Seven Angels, to whom "were given seven trumpets," how they "sound."

47. [What is meant by the *doubling drum?*]

49. See Collins' *Ode to Pity.*

55. *veering.* "To veer. Fr. *virer,* to veer, turn round, wheel or whirl about. Cot. It. *virare,* to turn. Rouchi, *virler,* to roll. In all probability from the same root with E *whirl,* whether it directly descends from Lat. *gyrare* or not." (Wedgwood.)

[Is the force of *diff'ring* precisely the same as that of *different?*]

57. *with eyes uprais'd.* Comp. *Il Penseroso*, 39.

59. *sequester'd.* See Gray's *Elegy*, 75.

63. *runnel.* This diminutival form is used by Fairfax, &c. We now prefer *runlet.*

65. *haunted stream.* See *L'Alleg.*, 130.

77. 69. [What noun is represented by *its?* Paraphrase this line.]

alter'd is here used loosely for *other,* or *different,* = Lat. *alius,* as in Sall. *Cat.* 52; "Longe *alia* mihi mens est," and Plaut. *Pœn.* prol. 125;

> "*alius* nunc fieri volo."

71. See Virgil's picture of Venus disguised as a huntress to meet her forlorn sea-beaten son. *Æn.* i. 318:

> "humeris de more habilem suspenderat arcum
> Venatrix."

72. *buskins.* See latter part of the note to *Il Pens.* 102. Add Virg. *Æn.* i. 336, 7, where Venus explains her costume thus:

> "Virginibus Tyriis mos est gestare pharetram,
> Purpureoque alte suras vincire cothurno."

And *Ecl.* vii. 32.

73. [What is the force of *that* here?]

75. *the oak-crowned sisters* = the virginal sisterhood, garlanded with forest leaves, that formed Diana's train.

their chaste-eyed queen. See Ben Jonson's noble *Hymn* to her:

" Queen and Huntress, chaste and fair," &c.

77. *alleys.* The Spirit in *Comus* sings of " cedar'n *alleys*" (l. 991). See also " Yonder *alleys* green" in *Par. Lost*, iv. 626.

peeping from forth. One might say "peeping from out," and so "from forth:" but more commonly perhaps one would say " peeping forth from."

80. [Explain the phrase *Joy's ecstatic trial.*]

81. *viny.* Phineas Fletcher speaks of the "*viny* Rhene" in his *Piscatory Eclogues*, II. xiii.

83. *viol.* See note on *Ode for St. Cec. Day*, 37.

88. *to.* See note on *Lycidas*, 13.

90. *a gay fantastic round.* See *L'Alleg.* 34.

91. He makes Mirth feminine. Comp. Spenser's *Phædria, F. Q.* II. vi. Horace's corresponding deity is *Jocus (Od.* I. ii. 34).

her zone unbound. Hor. *Od.* I. xxx. 5, to Venus :

" Fervidus tecum Puer et *solutis*
Gratiæ *zonis*, &c."

92. [Who is meant by *he*?]

94. Comp. *Par. Lost*, v. 285—7. See note on *Il Penser.* 146.

95. *sphere-descended.* See note in *Hymn Nat.* 125.

99. *that lov'd Athenian bower* = what he calls above Music's *Magic Cell.*

100. Observe the use of both *thy* and *you* in this passage. It would be in vain to look for any such distinctive force as certainly marks the use of these forms in Shakspere and the older writers. (See Abbot's *Shakesp. Gr.* §§ 231—5.)

104. *devote.* See *London*, 38.

108. [Who is this Sister? What stones does he refer to?]

110. *reed.* See note to *Lycid.* 33.

111. *rage* is often used in the post-Elizabethan writers of the 17th century, and in the 18th century writers, for inspiration, enthusiasm. Thus Cowley :

" Who brought green poesy to her perfect age
And made that art which was *a rage*."

78. 112. Handel's *Messiah*, which came out in 1741, was not received at first with any great favour. He died in 1759.

113 and 114. He means the organ. Marvell speaks of ' the organ's city': see his lines *Music's Empire.* See notes on Dryden's *Alexander's Feast*, &c. The humblest musical instrument in the ancient days, he says, was more effective than that great combination of all musical instruments—the organ—is in these days.

116. Collins, as also Gray, had a genuine admiration for Greek art and literature—was a sincere if not a very profound Hellenist. The age in which he lived, as that which preceded it, adored rather what was Latin. Classical, or Classicistic, is too broad a title for what it worshipped.

THOMAS GRAY.

Gray's father, a money-scrivener, is said to have shamefully neglected his duties as the head of a family, being a thorough profligate. His mother, to support herself, assisted by her sister, opened a milliner's shop in Cornhill, London; and there the future poet was born in 1716, on Dec. 26th (so Mitford; Dr Johnson says Nov. 26th, inaccurately—would that it was the only inaccuracy in his *Life of Gray!*) The attachment between Gray and his mother was thus especially close and tender, and so continued to the end of her honoured life. No doubt it was made the more so by the fact that of twelve children Thomas was the only one that survived infancy. Through the help of his mother's brother, then an Assistant-Master at Eton, Gray had the advantage of being educated at that school, and in due course, in 1734, proceeding to Cambridge, to Peter-House, or St Peter's College, about the same time his school-fellows Horace Walpole and West went up, the former to King's College, the latter to Christ Church, Oxford.

In 1738 (the year of Johnson's *London*) Gray quitted the University with the intention of studying Law at the Inner Temple; but no such special career was to be his. His income presently receiving additions from private sources, he found himself possessed of a life-long competency. Thus placed above the fear of penury, he was enabled to devote himself altogether to self-culture. He travelled in France and Italy, amongst the English Lakes, in Wales, in Scotland; he studied Architecture, Botany, the Classics of Greece and Italy and England, besides other literatures, Music, Painting, Zoology, History, Heraldry; in all ways he cultivated and refined his mind. He produced a few finished poems; he wrote delightful letters; he formed many worthy literary schemes. Such was Gray's life. He resided mainly at Cambridge. In 1768 he was appointed Professor of Modern History there, but he never delivered any lectures. There he died, July 20th, 1771. He was buried in Stoke Pogis churchyard, by the side of his mother, whom he had had "the misfortune to survive" (to use his own sad words inscribed on her tombstone) some eighteen years.

It might have been happy for Gray, had he felt some of those sharp goads which perpetually impelled his contemporary Johnson to action. He was certainly the most accomplished man of his time, and he was something much more than accomplished. His learning was not only wide but deep; his taste, if perhaps too fastidious, was pure and thorough; his genius was of no mean degree or order; his affections were of the truest and sincerest. What he wanted was productive impulse; his mind was insatiable in acquiring, it was tardy in creating. In this respect his cloistered life was seriously harmful. He liked neither the place nor its inhabitants, nor professed to like them, says Dr Johnson of his residence at Cambridge. Assuredly neither the place nor its inhabitants gave him that stimulus he needed. The picture his letters paint of the University of his day is dreary and dismal beyond words. So he for the most part spent his days in strenuous idleness so far as production went, his one object self-culture. He heaped up riches; in his own life he distributed but slightly, and his wealth was not of a kind that could be bequeathed. Perhaps few men of such high attainments and of such great powers have achieved so little. His career was one of unfulfilled promise. Perhaps of all our poets Milton and he were of the highest culture. In genius they differ vastly; but in this respect they are alike. The studies of Milton at Horton and in Italy from 1631 to 1639 remind one of Gray at a similar period of his life. Happily for Milton and for us the likeness ends there. Milton turned those studies, so ardently pursued, to noble

political and poetical uses. Fervently as he recognized the duty of self-culture, he acknowledged it but as a means, not as an end :

> "All is, if I have grace to use it so,
> As ever in my great Task-master's eye."

See also that most noble passage in his *Reason for Church Government*, where he describes
with what reluctance he resigned for a time, he could not say how long it might be, the darling
purpose for his life for unwelcome controversies. "But were it the meanest underservice, if
God by his Secretary Conscience enjoin it, it were sad for me if I should draw back." Compare what is said of Gray: " He could not bear to be thought a professed man of letters, but
wished to be regarded as a private gentleman who read for his amusement."

But, while it is to be lamented that Gray did not do more for his own day and for posterity,
let us be grateful for what he did do. That life was not lived in vain that gave us the *Elegy
written in a Country Churchyard*. Besides this he produced some seven Odes, two Translations from the Norse, and a few other pieces of a miscellaneous sort. His fine critical taste as
expressed in his letters, exercised and may exercise a beneficial influence, though the area
over which it acted and acts was and is something confined.

His *Poems* are works of refinement rather than of passion : but yet they are inspired with
genuine sentiment. They are no doubt extremely artificial in form; the weight of the author's
reading somewhat depresses their originality; he can with difficulty escape from his books to
himself; but yet there is in him a genuine poetical spirit. His poetry, however elaborated, is
sincere and truthful. If the exterior is often what Horace might have called over-filed and
polished, the thought is mostly of the simplest and naturalest. When he sees the school of
his youth in the distance, his eyes fill with real feeling, whatever carefully chosen phrases are
on his tongue. His soul was always simple, and true, and tender, and catholic, however
exquisitively select and uncommon the dialect that represents it. And even in this dialect
it must be allowed that there are many felicities. It is not always cold and scholastic. It is
often of finished beauty. It is sometimes itself tremulous with emotion.

THE ELEGY WRITTEN IN A COUNTRY CHURCHYARD.

1. This famous poem was begun in the year 1742, and finished in 1749. It found its
way into print in this latter year, to Gray's annoyance, who thereupon published it himself in
1750. Some stanzas, written originally as part of it but afterwards rejected by the author's
severe self-criticism, are given below in the course of the notes. As to the churchyard, where
it was written or meditated, there is controversy; Stoke Pogis near Slough, where Gray's
mother and aunt resided after his father's death, and Madingley some four miles from
Cambridge, competing for the honour—Stoke Pogis perhaps with the better claims ; but there
is little in the poem to localize it.

2. The *Elegy* is perhaps the most widely known poem in our language. Many phrases
and lines from it have become "household words." The reason of this extensive popularity
is perhaps to be sought in the fact, that it expresses in an exquisite manner feelings and
thoughts that are universal. In the current of ideas in the *Elegy*, there is perhaps nothing
that is rare, or exceptional, or out of the common way. The musings are of the most
natural and obvious character possible ; it is difficult to conceive of any one musing under
similar circumstances who should not muse so ; but they are not the less deep and moving
on this account. There are some feelings and thoughts that cannot grow old and hackneyed.
The mystery of life does not become clearer, or less solemnizing and awful, for any amount
of contemplation. Such inevitable, such everlasting questions as rise on the mind when
one lingers in the precincts of Death can never lose their freshness, never cease to fascinate

and to move. It is with such questions, that would have been commonplace long ages since if they could ever be so, that the *Elegy* deals. It deals with them in no lofty philosophical manner, but in a simple, humble, unpretentious way, always with the truest and broadest humanity. The poet's thoughts turn to the poor; he forgets the fine tombs inside the church, and thinks only of the "mouldring heaps" in the churchyard (see below, note on L 13). Hence the problem that especially suggests itself, is the potential greatness when they lived, of the "rude forefathers" that now lie at his feet. He does not, and cannot solve it, though he finds considerations to mitigate the sadness it must inspire ; but he expresses it in all its awful-ness in the most effective language and with the deepest feeling; and his expression of it has become a living part of our language.

3. The metre of the *Elegy*, had been used, before Gray's time, by Sir John Davies for his *Immortality of the Soul*, Sir William Davenant in his *Gondibert*, and Dryden in his *Annus Mirabilis*, and others; but in no instance so happily as here by Gray. In the *Elegy* the quatrain has not the somewhat disjunctive and isolating effect which it has in those other works where there is continuous argument or narrative that should run on with as few metrical lets and hindrances as possible ; it is well adapted to convey a series of solemn reflections, and that is its work in the *Elegy.*

[What are *the leading thoughts* of the *Elegy?* What stanzas contain each one? How many groups of stanzas are there?

In what other of his poems does Gray refer to himself?]

79. 1. *The curfew.* See note on *Il Pens.* 74. It is a great mistake to suppose that the ringing of the curfew was, at its institution, a mark of Norman oppression. If such a custom was unknown before the Conquest, it only shows that the old English police was less well regulated than that of many parts of the Continent, and how much the superior civilization of the Norman-French was needed. Fires were the curse of the timber-built towns of the middle ages; "Solæ pestes Londoniæ sunt stultorum immodica potatio et *frequens incen-dium.*" (Fitzstephen.) The enforced extinction of domestic lights at an appointed signal was designed to be a safeguard against them. How grotesque in a historical point of view are Thomson's lines:

> "The shiv'ring wretches at the curfew sound
> Dejected sunk into their sordid beds,
> And through the mournful gloom of ancient times
>   , Mus'd sad, or dreamt of better."

parting. See *Hymn. Nat.* 185.

Mitford quotes Shakspere, 2 *Hen. IV.* I. i. 101 :

> "a sullen bell
> Remember'd knolling a departed friend." (Comp. *Marmion*, III. xiii.)

3. *plod.* See Shakspere, *All's Well that Ends Well*, III. iv. 5 ;

> "Ambitious love hath so in me offended
> That barefoot *plod* I the cold ground upon."

5. [What is meant by *on the sight?*]
6. [Is *air* the subject, or the object?]
7. See note on *Lyc.* 28.
droning = dully humming, like a drone. See Browne's *Britannia's Pastorals*, I. iii.

> "But, as it seem'd, they thought (as do the swaines
> Which tune their pipes on sack'd Hibernia's plaines)
> There should some *droning* part be...."

So they send to ask the king of bees to help in their part-song :

> "Who condescending gladly flew along
> To beare *the base* to his well tuned song."

10. *The moping owl.* See Ovid's *Met.* v. 550, of Ascalaphus punished by Proserpine for his too keen observation :

> "Fœdaque fit volucris, venturi nuncia luctus,
> *Ignavus bubo*, dirum mortalibus omen."

12. *reign* = realm ; as in Pope's *Iliad*:

> "The wrath which hurl'd to Pluto's gloomy *reign*
> The souls of mighty chiefs untimely slain."

13. As he stands in the churchyard, he thinks only of the poorer people (comp. below, *passim*) because the better to do lay interred inside the church. Tennyson (*In Mem.* x.) speaks of resting

> "beneath the clover sod
> That takes the sunshine and the rains,
> Or where the kneeling hamlet drains
> The chalice of the grapes of God."

In Gray's time, and long before, and some time after it, the former resting-place was for the poor, the latter for the rich. It was so in the first instance, for two reasons : (i) The interior of the church was regarded as of greater sanctity, and all who could, sought a place in it. The most dearly coveted spot was close by the high altar. (ii) When elaborate tombs were the fashion, they were built inside the church for the sake of security, "Gay tombs" being liable to be "robb'd." (See the funeral dirge in Webster's *White Devil*.) As these two considerations gradually ceased to have power, and other considerations of an opposite tendency began to prevail, the inside of the church became comparatively deserted, except when ancestral reasons gave no choice.

16. [What is the form of *rude* here ?]

17. See *Par. Lost*, ix. 192 :

> "Now when as sacred light began to dawn
> In Eden on the humid flowers that breathed
> Their morning incense," &c.

18. Comp. Hesiod's epithet of the swallow in *Works and Days*, 568 (Göttling):

> "τὸν δὲ μετ' ὀρθρογόη Πανδιονὶς ὦρτο χελιδὼν
> ἐς φάος ἀνθρώποις."

See *Æn.* viii. 455.

19. See *Par. Lost*, vii. 443.

20. [What is the force of *shall* here ? What would *will* mean ?]

21. Comp. Lucret. iii. 894—6 (Lachmann) :

> "Jam jam non domus accipiet te læta, neque uxor
> Optima nec dulces occurrent oscula nati
> Præripere et tacita pectus dulcedine tangent."

Hor. *Ep.* ii. 40. Mitford refers to Thomson's *Winter*, 311.

22. [What is meant by *ply her evening care ?*]

This is probably the kind of phrase which led Wordsworth to pronounce the language of the Elegy unintelligible. Compare his own

> "And she I cherished *turned her wheel*
> Beside an English fire."

23. Comp. Burns' *Cotter's Saturday Night*, 21, Shelley's *Revolt of Islam*, viii. 4.

24. See *Georg.* ii. 523.

26. [What word-form in this line has now fallen out of use ?]

    [What is meant by *furrow* here ?]

80. 27. *afield.* See *Lycid.* 27.

33. [What exactly is meant by *the boast of heraldry* ?]

38. [Explain *trophies.*]

39. See note to *Il Penser.* 157.

39. *aile.* Fr. *aile*, Old Fr. *aisle*, Lat. *axilla*, which means literally a winglet, or little wing. The French spelling was common in Gray's time.

    fretted = strictly, ornamented with frets or small fillets (or bands) intersecting each other at right angles (see *Glossary of Architecture*) ; from the Fr. *fréter*, to cross, or interlace, as the bars of trellis-work. Etymologically, these interlacing bands or "heads" were of iron (Lat. *ferrum*). *Ferrata* in Ital. = an iron grating. See Hamlet's fine use of the word, *Hamlet*, II. ii. 313 :

    "This majestical roof *fretted* with golden fire."

Comp. *Cymb.* II. iv. 38. *Fretful* is of quite different origin.

    vault = arched roof. The word is ultimately derived from the Lat. *volvo.*

40. [What is meant by *swells* here?]

    pealing. See *Il Pens.* 161.

41. *storied.* See *Il Pens.* 159.

    animated bust. Comp. Virgil's "spirantia æra," *Æn.* vi. 847. *Bust* is radically the same word with breast, through the Fr. *buste*, which is a weakened form of the Germ. *brust.* The Germ. equivalent for our *bust* is *brust-bild.*

42. [Is *fleeting* here an adj. or a part.? What is the difference between an adj. and a part.?]

47. Mitford quotes Ov. *Ep.* v. 86:

    "Sunt mihi quas possint sceptra decere manus."

48. [Is there anything at all tautological in this line? Is there in any other line of the *Elegy* ?]

50. *unroll* = Lat. *revolvere*, as in Hor. *Ep.* II. i. 223:

    "Cum loca jam recitata *revolvimus* irrevocati."

So the word *volume* properly applies only to the old shape of books.

51. *rage.* See note to *The Passions*, 111.

53. *purest ray serene.* A favourite word-order with Milton. See note to *Hymn Nat.* 187.

    Mitford quotes from Hall's *Contemplations:* "There is many a rich stone laid up in the bowells of the earth, many a fair pearle in the bosom of the sea, that never was seene, nor never shall bee."

55. Comp. Waller's

> "Go, lovely rose:
> Tell her that's young
> And shuns to have her graces spy'd,
> That hadst thou sprung
> In deserts where no men abide
> Thou must have uncommended died."

Rape of the Lock, 622.

57. It was in 1636 that John Hampden of Buckinghamshire (a cousin of the great Cromwell) refused to pay the ship-money tax, which the misguided king was levying without the authority of the Parliament.

58. See *Hist. Eng.*

    [What is meant by *the little tyrant of his fields* ?]

59. Could a Milton have ever been mute and inglorious? Or would a genius so vast have in some sort overcome all the circumstances that obstructed it? Would he have "grappled with his evil star?" (*In Mem.* lxiii.)

60. The prejudice against Cromwell was extremely strong throughout the 18th century, even amongst the more liberal-minded. That cloud of "detractions rude," of which Milton speaks in his noble sonnet to our "chief of men," as in his own day enveloping the great republican leader, still lay thick and heavy over him. His wise statesmanship, his unceasing earnestness, his high-minded purpose, were not yet seen. As to the particular charge against him suggested here, it need only be remembered that it was not till some time after Charles had raised his standard at Nottingham (Aug. 1642) that Cromwell became of importance. It was not till the spring of 1645 that he became the real head of the army.

61. [What is the main predicate of the sentence beginning here?]

The great age of Parliamentary oratory was just dawning when the Elegy was published. The elder Pitt was already famous for his eloquence.

63. As Walpole's long, peaceful administration (which ended in 1742) had done.

81. 66. *Their growing virtues* = The growth of their virtues.

69. [What is meant by *conscious truth*?]

71. This was but too common a fashion with poets in the days of patronage.

71, 72. [Paraphrase and fully explain these two lines.]

72. Here, in Gray's first MS., followed these four stanzas:

> "The thoughtless world to majesty may bow,
>   Exalt the brave, and idolize success,
> But more to innocence their safety owe
>   Than pow'r or genius e'er conspired to bless.
>
> "And thou who mindful of th' unhonour'd dead
>   Dost in these notes their artless tale relate,
> By night and lonely contemplation led
>   To wander in the gloomy walks of fate:
>
> "Hark, how the sacred calm that breathes around,
>   Bids every fierce tumultuous passion cease;
> In still small accents whisp'ring from the ground
>   A grateful earnest of eternal peace.
>
> "No more with reason and thyself at strife
>   Give anxious thoughts and endless wishes room;
> But through the cool sequester'd vale of life
>   Pursue the silent tenour of thy doom."

And so the *Elegy* was to have ended.

73. Are ignoble strifes confined to towns? are they impossible in villages? See Johnson's *London*, 5 and 6.

madding. See *Van. of H. W.* 30.

77. *these bones* = the bones of these. So *is* is often used in Latin, esp. by Livy, as v. 22: "*Ea* sola pecunia" = only the money derived from that sale, &c.

79. *uncouth.* See note to *L'Alleg.* 5.

rhimes. This word ought to be spelt *rimes.* The *h* was inserted through a mistaken derivation from the Greek *rhythmus.*

[*deck'd.* Why is the final *d* here sounded like *t*? Give similar instances.]

80. Comp. *Lycid.* 21.

82. This was an age much given to elaborate epitaphs and elegies. See W. Thompson's *Epitaph on my Father, Epitaph on my Mother*, Smart's *Epitaph on the Rev. Mr. Reynolds*, Whitehead's *Epitaph on a Marble Pyramid of the Monument of John Duke of*

Argyle, &c., &c. Part of Book iii. of Watts' Poems (died 1748) is "sacred to the memory of the dead," and contains "an Epitaph on King William," "an Elegiac thought on Mrs Anne Warner," &c. Shenstone has an Elegy "on the untimely death of a certain learned acquaintance," &c. Gray himself had contributed to this funereal literature. See also Pope's works, Goldsmith's, &c., and the walls and monuments of Westminster Abbey, *passim*. This style of writing still survives in country places; but happily even there is growing rarer.

84. [Is the plural verb correct here? Explain *rustic moralist*.]

85. At the first glance it might seem that *to dumb Forgetfulness a prey* was in apposition to *who*, and the meaning was "who that lies now quite forgotten," &c.; in which case the 2nd line of the stanza must be closely connected with the 4th; for the question of the passage is not "who ever died?" but "who ever died without wishing to be remembered?" But in this way of interpreting this difficult stanza (i) there is comparatively little force in the appositional phrase, (ii) there is a certain awkwardness in deferring so long the clause (virtually adverbial though apparently coordinate) in which, as has just been noticed, the point of the question really lies. Perhaps therefore it is better to take the phrase *to dumb Forgetfulness a prey* as in fact the completion of the predicate *resign'd*, and interpret thus: "Who ever resigned this life of his with all its pleasures and all its pains to be utterly ignored and forgotten?" = " who ever, when resigning it, reconciled himself to its being forgotten?" In this case the 2nd half of the stanza echoes the thought of the 1st half.

86. *this pleasing anxious being*. See in the fine lines to Life by Mrs. Barbauld (given in part in the *Golden Treasury*):

> "Life! we've been long together
> Through pleasant and through cloudy weather."

89. In this stanza he answers in an exquisite manner the two questions, or rather the one question twice repeated, of the preceding stanza. His answers may, as has been suggested to me by a friend, form a climax. The 1st line seems to regard the near approach of death; the 2nd its actual advent; the 3rd the time immediately succeeding that advent; the 4th a still later time. What he would say is that every one while a spark of life yet remains in him yearns for some kindly loving remembrance; nay, even after the spark is quenched, even when all is dust and ashes, that yearning must still be felt. We would never not be loved. The passion for affection and sympathy can never, never die. Comp. Tibullus' beautiful lines to his Delia:

> "Te spectem, suprema mihi quum venerit hora;
> Te teneam moriens deficiente manu.
> Flebis et arsuro positum me, Delia, lecto,
> Tristibus et lacrimis oscula mixta dabis.
> Flebis; non tua sunt duro praecordia ferro
> Vincta, nec in tenero stat tibi corde silex."

Mitford quotes from Solon:

> "μηδ' ἐμοὶ ἄκλαυστος θάνατος μόλοι, ἀλλὰ φίλοισι
> καλλείποιμι θανὼν ἄλγεα καὶ στοναχάς."

Strangely different was Sterne's wish about his last moments—a wish which accident gratified.

90. *pious* in the sense of the Lat. *pius*. See Ov. *Trist.* IV. iii. 41. Comp. *debitâ lacrimâ* in Hor. *Od.* II. vi. 23.

92. Chaucer's Reeve, saying that old men such as he do not forget the passions of their earlier days, adds, *Cant. T.* 3880:

> "Yet in oure asshen old is fyr ireke [raked]."

Gray himself quotes from Petrarch's 169th (170th in some editions) sonnet:

> "Ch' i veggio nel pensier, dolce mio fuoco,
> Fredda una lingua e due begli occhi chiusi,
> Rimaner doppo noi pien di faville,"

thus translated by Nott:

> "These, my sweet fair, so warns prophetic thought,
> Closed thy bright eye, and mute thy poet's tongue,
> E'en after death shall still with sparks be fraught,"

the "these" meaning his love and his songs concerning it. Gray translated this Sonnet into Latin Elegiacs. His last line is:

> "Ardebitque urna multa favilla mea."

Comp. *The Bard*, l. 122. Mitford quotes Ovid's *Trist*. III. iii. 83, and Propert. II. xiii. 41. No one, I think, has yet quoted Propertius' closely pertinent line (V. xi. 74):

> "Hæc cura et cineri spirat inusta meo,"

with which "Broukhusius" and after him Hertzberg (see Paley ad l. c.) compare Cicero's "Cur hunc dolorem cineri ejus atque ossibus inussisti." Add the well-known lines from Tennyson's *Maud*, I. (xxii. 11):

> "She is coming, my own, my sweet,
>   Were it ever so airy a tread
> My heart would hear her and beat,
>   Were it earth in an earthy bed;
> My dust would hear her and beat,
>   Had I lain for a century dead,
> Would start and tremble under her feet,
>   And blossom in purple and red."

95. [What part of speech is *chance* virtually here?]
    Contemplation. See *Il Pens.* 54.

98. *at the peep of dawn.* See *Comus*, 138—140:

> "Ere the blabbing eastern scout,
> The nice morn, on the Indian steep
> From her cabin'd loop-hole peep."

99. See *Par. Lost*, v. 429, *Arcades*, 50.

100. See Notes to *L'Alleg.* 92, and *Hymn Nat.* 85.

101. The first draught of the poem gave:

> "Him have we seen the greenwood side along,
>   While o'er the heath we hied, our labour done,
> Oft as the woodlark pip'd her farewell song,
>   With wistful eyes pursue the setting sun."

Comp. *As you like it*, II. 1.

103. *His listless length.* So: "if you will measure your lubber's length again," &c. *King Lear*, I. iv. 97.

104. *babbles.* Comp. Hor. *Od.* III. xiii. 15:

> "unde *loquaces*
> *Lymphæ* desiliunt tuæ."

82. 105. *hard by.* See note to *L'Alleg.* 81.
    [To what noun is *now smiling as in scorn* adjectival?]

107. [What part of the sentence is *woeful* here ?]
108. *hopeless* is here used in a proleptic or anticipatory way.
111. [To what noun does *another* refer?]
114. *church-way path.* See *Mids. N. Dream*, V. i. 386 :

> " Now it is the time of night
> That the graves all gaping wide
> Every one lets forth his sprite
> In the *church-way paths* to glide."

The phrase may mean the path leading church-way or church-ward. Or *church-way* may be a corruption of church-hay = church-yard. For *hay*, when it became obsolete, the popular mind, which is always etymologizing in its way (see note to *Hymn. Nat.* 60.), substituted a word it knew. "*Chyrche-haye* occurs in an early MS. quoted in *Prompt. Parv.* p. 221, and was in use in the seventeenth century, as appears from Lhuyd's MS. additions to Ray in Mus. Ashmol." (Halliwell's *Archaic and Prov. Dict.*). *Hay* is the Oldest Eng. *haga*, " 1. a hedge, haw. 2. what is hedged in, a garden, field." (Bosworth). For this word in place-names, see Taylor's *Words and Places.* " In the Seven Dayes, 2625, the chirche-hawe is spoken of." (Way's *Prompt. Parv.* s. v. *chyrche yarde*).

115. *for thou canst read.* Reading was not such a very common accomplishment then that it could be taken for granted. When will it be so everywhere ? All things considered, the present age is far from having any right to vaunt itself over that of Gray.

the lay. This is an odd use of the word *lay.* The men of the latter part of the 17th, and of the greater part of the 18th century, were very ignorant of the older forms, and the older vocabulary of the language ; else, how could the Rowley Poems have been believed in for one second?

116. Here original copy contained this stanza :

> " There scatter'd oft, the earliest of the year,
> By hands unseen are show'rs of violets found ;
> The redbreast loves to build and warble there,
> And little footsteps lightly print the ground."

118. [What part of the sentence is *a youth* ?]
119. Certainly Gray is thinking of himself in these lines, to some extent at least. See the *Memoir* of him.
123. Mitford quotes from Lucretius, ii. 27 :

> " Has lacrimas memori quas ictus amore
> Fundo, *quod possum.*"

THE PROGRESS OF POESY AND THE BARD.

INTRODUCTION.

The Progress of Poesy, as appears from one of Gray's letters to Walpole, was finished all but a few lines at the end in 1755. It was published along with the *Bard* in 1757.

Both Odes met with a very cold welcome. "Even my friends," writes Gray, in a letter to Hurd, "tell me that they do not succeed, and write me moving topics of consolation on this head. In short I have heard of nobody but an actor [Garrick] and a doctor of divinity [Warburton] that profess [Gray's grammar is often worse than dubious] their esteem for them. Oh yes ! a lady of quality (a friend of Mason's) who is a great reader. She knew there was a compliment to Dryden, but never suspected there was anything said about Shakespeare or · Milton till it was explained to her, and wishes there had been titles prefixed to tell what they were about." It says but little for the intelligence of the general reader of George II.'s time that the common charge against these poems was their utter obscurity. It would seem that such leading facts of English History as Gray deals with in the *Bard* were then by no means generally known. A writer in the *Critical Review* thought that the Æolian lyre meant the Æolian harp. Coleman (the elder) and Robert Lloyd wrote parodies entitled Odes to Obscurity and Oblivion. At a later time Gray was persuaded to add elucidatory notes.

It can scarcely be said that these Odes have ever become popular, though they have certainly taken a permanent place in English Literature. Their artificiality is too manifest; there is felt but little of that Pindaric fervour by which they profess to be inspired. A poem should rise noiselessly, like Solomon's temple; "neither hammer nor axe nor any tool of iron" should be heard while it is "in building;" but in these poems one's ear cannot but catch those mechanical sounds, and they grate upon it. Still, these works have their beauties, or they would long since have perished. They are good in parts rather than as wholes. The language, if often somewhat stiff and frigid, is sometimes highly graceful and felicitous. The metre is here and there full of life and beauty. The various figures and groups are not unfrequently portrayed with great force and vigour. In fact one may be sensible everywhere of the hand of a master, though it may be doubted whether that hand is always wisely and congenially employed.

The metre of these Odes is constructed on Greek models. It is not uniform, but symmetrical. Milton's great *Ode* or *Hymn* is written in stanzas, as are Horace's Odes; most of the Odes of Cowley, those of Dryden, Wordsworth's *Ode on Intimations of Immortality from Recollections of early Childhood,* Tennyson's *Ode on the Death of the Duke of Wellington,* are written in an irregular metre, varying from time to time with the thought, grave or light according as the sense is the one or the other; these Odes of Gray's are written in a perfectly regular metre, not in uniform stanzas but in uniform groups of stanzas. The nine stanzas of each Ode form three uniform groups. A slight examination will show that the 1st, 4th, and 7th stanzas are exactly inter-correspondent; so the 2nd, 5th, and 8th, and so the remaining three. The technical Greek names for these three parts were στροφή, ἀντιστροφή, and ἐπωδός—the Turn, the Counter-turn, and the After-song—names derived from the theatre, the Turn denoting the movement of the chorus from one side of the ὀρχήστρά or Dance-stage to the other, the Counter-turn the reverse movement, the After-song something sung after two such movements. Odes thus constructed were called by the Greeks Epodic. Congreve is said to have been the first who so constructed English Odes. This system cannot be said to have prospered with us. Perhaps no English ear would instinctively recognize that correspondence between distant parts which is the secret of it. Certainly very many readers of the *Progress of Poesy* are wholly unconscious of any such harmony. Does anyone really enjoy it in itself, apart from the pleasure he may receive from his admiration of Gray's skill in construction and imitation? Does his ear hear it, or only his eye perceive it? In other words, was not Gray's labour, as far as pure metrical pleasure is concerned, wasted?

For similar historical sketches with that given in the *Progress of Poesy* see Collins' *Ode to Simplicity,* Cowper's *Table Talk,* Keats' *Sleep and Poetry.*

It is perhaps scarcely now necessary to say that the tradition on which *The Bard* is founded is wholly groundless. Edward I. never did massacre Welsh bards. Their name is legion in the beginning of the 14th century. Miss Williams, the latest historian of Wales, does not even mention the old story.

THE PROGRESS OF POESY.

82. 1. *Æolian lyre.* Æolia or Æolis extended along the coast of Asia Minor from the Troad to the river Hermus. The people from whom this strip of coast derived its name, was one of the chief branches of the Hellenic race. They are said to have been originally settled in Thessaly and thence to have spread over various parts of Greece and across the Ægean to

Lesbos and to the mainland. It would seem that it was amongst their Asiatic colonies that Hellenic genius first found artistic expression. Smyrna, one of the places, which severally claimed to be the birthplace of Homer, was originally an Æolian town, though subsequently ' possessed by Ionians. Alcæus and Sappho were natives of Lesbos. Hence one of the chief Greek rhythms, or harmonies, was called Æolian. See Pindar's Αἰολη̈ῗδι μολπᾷ (*Ol.* i. 102), ἐν Αἰολίδεσσι χορδαῖς (*Pyth.* ii. 69, ed. Donaldson). It is with reference to these Pindaric phrases that Gray uses the word; see his own note. He calls this ode a *Pindaric Ode.* So Æolian lyre = lyre of Pindar, or lyre such as Pindar struck. [Perhaps the young reader should be cautioned against confounding the *Æolian lyre* here with the *Æolian harp* often heard of elsewhere, a blunder made by one of the first "reviewers" of this poem. The Æolian of the latter phrase is derived from Æolus the mythical wind-god, and = wind-blown, wind-played. "The invention of this instrument is ascribed to Kircher, 1653; but it was known at an earlier period," (Haydn). See Thomson's *Castle of Indolence;* Collins' *Ode on the Death of Mr Thompson,* and Cowper's *Expostulation.*]

Comp. the beginning of one of Cowley's pieces (in the *Golden Treasury*):

"Awake, awake, my lyre !
And tell thy silent master's humble tale," &c.

3. *Helicon.* See note to *Lycid.* 15.

9. *Ceres' golden reign.* Comp. Virgil's *Flava Ceres* (*Georg.* i. 96), Homer's ξανθὴ Δημήτηρ, *Iliad,* v. 499:

"ὡς δ' ἄνεμος ἄχνας φορέει ἱερὰς κατ' ἀλωὰς
ἀνδρῶν λικμώντων, ὅτε τε ξανθὴ Δημήτηρ
κρίνῃ ἐπειγομένων ἀνέμων καρπόν τε καὶ ἄχνας" κ.τ.λ.

[What is the meaning of *reign* here ?]

10. *amain.* See *Lycid.* 111.
See Hor. *Od.* IV. ii. 8.

83. 12. [What is the force of *to* here ?]

13. "The thoughts are borrowed from the first Pythian of Pindar," (Gray).

14. [Explain *solemn breathing.*] See *Comus,* 555.

15. [What is the power of *the* here ?]
sullen is radically connected with *sole, solitary,* &c.

17. Ares was believed to have his abiding-place in Thrace. [Where exactly was *Thrace* ?] In that country and in Scythia were the chief seats of his worship. Horace speaks of "bello furiosa Thrace," (*Od.* II. xvi. 5). See also *Æn.* iii. 35.

18. *curb* is closely connected with *curve.* [Can you connect the two words in meaning?]

20. [To what subst. does *perching* refer ?]
See Pind. *Pyth.* i. 9—18 :

...... "εὕδει δ' ἀνὰ σκάπτῳ Διὸς αἰετός
ὠκεῖαν πτέρυγ' ἀμφοτέρωθεν χαλάξαις
ἀρχὸς οἰωνῶν, κελαινῶπιν δ' ἐπὶ οἱ νεφέλαν
ἀγκύλῳ κρατί, γλεφάρων ἁδὺ κλαῖστρον, κατέχευας· ὁ δὲ κνώσσων
ὑγρὸν νῶτον αἰωρεῖ, τεαῖς
ῥιπαῖσι κατασχόμενος."

22. [What part of the sentence is *with ruffled plumes* ?]

26. [Explain *tempered.*] See *Lycid.* 32.

27. Gray seems to use *Idalia* here for *Idalium,* for that was the name of the town in Cyprus. *Idalia* was a title given to Aphrodite because of her worship in that town. Comp. her titles of *Erycina, Cytheræa,* and *Cyt21ereis.*

velvet-green occurs in Pope. Johnson censures the phrase, apparently believing it of Gray's invention.

30. *antic.* See *Sams. Agon.* 1325, when the word is used as a personal substantive. In *Faerie Queene,* II. iii. 27, it is used to denote "odd imagery and devices," (Nares). Shak-

spere uses it as a verb in *Ant. and Cleop.* II. vii. 132. For the meaning, what is old and old fashioned is liable to be thought odd, grotesque, fantastic. Milton has the word in its primitive sense in *Il Pens.* 158.

31. *Frisk, brisk, fresco, fresh,* are all closely connected.
frolic. See note to *L' Alleg.* 18.
35. Gray quotes Hom. *Od.* ix. 265:

"μαρμαρυγὰς θηεῖτο ποδῶν· θαύμαζε δὲ θυμῷ."

Comp. Catullus' "*fulgentem . . . plantam*" (lxviii. 70).
38. [What is meant by *sublime* here?]
41. *the purple light of love.* See *Æn.* i. 594:

"lumenque juventæ
Purpureum."

Gray quotes from Phrynichus, the Tragedian, *apud* Athenæum:

"λάμπει δ' ἐπὶ πορφυρέῃσι
παρείῃσι φῶς ἔρωτος."

42. Comp. Hor. *Od.* I. iii. 29—33.
84. 50. *boding. Bode* is cognate with *bid.*
birds of boding cry = what the Latin augurs called *oscines.* See Hor. *Od.* III. xxvii. 11. Cic. *ad Fam.* VI. vi. 7: "Non igitur ex alitis involatu, nec *e cantu sinistro oscinis*, ut in nostra disciplina est, nec ex tripudiis sollistimis aut soniviis tibi auguror; sed habeo alia signa quæ observem."
52. Gray refers to Cowley, *Brutus, an Ode:*

" One would have thought 't had heard the morning crow,
Or seen her well-appointed star
Come marching up the eastern hill afar."

53. *Hyperion.* Properly the strong accent of this word is upon the penult (see the Latin and the Greek poets, *passim*); but the English poets, almost universally, throw it back to the ante-penult, as does Gray here (see *Hamlet*, I. ii. 140, &c.). Classical names were much mis-shapen and mis-pronounced before the Revival of Learning, as it is called; and some of these Romantic irregularities still prevailed even when Classical usages were better known. See the scarcely recognizable Classical names in Chaucer's *House of Fame*, &c. &c. See note on *Delphos* in *Hymn Nat.* 178; add Shakspere's *Postúmus, Andrónicus.*
glitt'ring shafts of war. Comp. Lucretius' *tela diei*, i. 148, &c.
54. Comp. *Æn.* vi. 795:

" Extra anni solisque vias."

56. See *Hymn Nat.* 188.
60. [What is meant by *repeating a chief?*]
62. *feather-cinctur'd* = " girt with feather'd cincture " (*Par. Lost*, ix. 1116).
[Has *loves* an abstract or a concrete signification here? Comp. *sable loves*, Pope's *IV. For.* 410.]
64. *pursue.* Observe this use of the plural with the first of a series of subjects. Warton compares Hom. *Il.* v. 774:

"ἦχι ῥοὰς Σιμόεις συμβάλλετον ἠδὲ Σκάμανδρος."

66. See Collins' *Ode to Simplicity* (by which he seems to mean Poetic Truth and Purity):

" By old Cephisus deep
Who spread his wavy sweep
In warbled wanderings round thy green retreat,
On whose enamel'd side
When holy Freedom died
No equal haunt allur'd thy future feet."

66. *Delphi's steep.* See *Hymn Nat.* 178 and note.

67. See Byron's *The Isles of Greece*, &c.

68. The Ilissus, rising on the north slope of Hymettus, flows through the east side of Athens. See *Atlas* and *Class. Dict.* Socrates and Phædrus are represented in the dialogue called after the latter as strolling up its channel, then as now often quite dry. "Δεῦρ' ἐκτραπόμενοι," says Socrates, "κατὰ τὸν Ἰλισσὸν ἴωμεν, εἶτα ὅπου ἀν δόξῃ ἐν ἡσυχίᾳ καθιζησόμεθα." (*Phædr.* Chap. iii.)

69. The first great metropolis of Hellenic intellectual life was Miletus on the Mæander. Thales, Anaximander, Anaximenes, Cadmus, Hecatæus, &c., were all by birth Milesians. See note to l. 1.

70. The lower course of the Mæander lies through a wide plain, where it wanders at will in that remarkable manner which has made it a type of all curving and winding things. See Selden's Illustr. No. 2 of Drayton's *Polyolbion:* "Intricate turnings, by a transumptive and metonymical kind of speech, are called *meanders;* for this river did so strangely path itself that the foot seemed to touch the head." Fuller's *Worthies, Bedfordshire*, apud Richardson: "But this proverb may better be veryfied of Ouse it self in this shire, *more mæandrous than Mæander*, which runneth above eighty miles in eighteen by land."

73. See *Hymn Nat.* 181—8.

75. *hallow'd fountain.* See Virg. *Ecl.* i. 53.

81. See Collins' *Ode to Simplicity:*

> " While Rome could none esteem
> But Virtue's patriot theme,
> You lov'd her hills, and led her laureate band :
> But staid to sing alone
> To one distinguish'd throne,
> And turn'd thy face, and fled her alter'd land."

The vast interval between the Augustan age and the great Florentine period is here quite unrecognized. Virgil died B.C. 19, Dante was born A.D. 1265. For some thousand years of that interval there had prevailed a deep silence of poetry in Italy; in France and certain neighbouring countries the *Troubadours* and the *Trouvères* had sung their songs. But that in his note quoted to l. 82, Gray mentions Dante, it might have been supposed that like Selvaggi in his memorable distich which Dryden imitated ("Three poets in three distant ages born," &c.), he recognised no great genius between the Augustan and the Elizabethan age; comp. Cowper's *Table Talk*, 556—9. But Gray was a diligent and admiring student of the Tuscan poets.

82. "Chaucer was not unacquainted with the writings of Dante or of Petrarch. The Earl of Surrey and Sir Thomas Wyatt had travelled in Italy and formed their taste there. Spenser imitated the Italian writers ; Milton improved on them." (Gray).

[Of what great countries of Europe is nothing said in this survey ? Why is Germany not mentioned ?]

85. 83. That is, far from the Sunny South.

84. *Nature's darling.* See *L'Alleg.* 133, and note.

85. [Who is the mighty Mother ?]

87. *the dauntless child.* Comp. Horace's

> "non sine dis animosus infans." (*Od.* III. iv. 20.)

88. Mitford points out that this identical line occurs in Sandys' translation of Ov. *Met.* iv. 515.

89. *Pencil* is used here in its proper sense. "Caudam antiqui penem vocabant," says Cicero writing to Paetus, "ex quo est propter similitudinem *penicillus.*" (*Ad Fam.* ix. 22.)

92—94. [What various plays by Shakspere may Gray have in his mind here ?]

95. All Gray's poems show a profound admiration for, and a thorough knowledge of

Milton's Works. He was greatly attracted by the high culture that marks them; his own genius was of the same order, though inferior in degree.

96. See *Ezek.* viii. 1.

97—98. [What books of *Paradise Lost* are referred to?]   See *Par. Lost,* vii. 12.

98. Gray quotes Lucretius' "flammantia mœnia mundi."   (i. 74.)

99. See *Isaiah* vi.

101. In fact it was Milton's political labours, not his poetical, which destroyed his sight (see Sonnet on his blindness,to Cyriac Skinner); but he too delights to connect that physical malady with the splendour of his inner visions. See *Pro Populo Anglicano Defensio Secunda:* "Divinus favor..cælestium alarum umbra has nobis fuisse tenebras videtur." Gray quotes Hom. *Od.* viii. 64,

"ἰφθαλμῶν μὲν ἄμερσε· δίδου δ' ἡδεῖαν ἀοιδήν."

103. Gray "admired Dryden almost beyond bounds." See Mason's *Life of White-head,* quoted by Mitford in his *Life of Gray.*

105. The Heroic couplet was first introduced from Italy into England by Chaucer. Between Chaucer and Dryden it was adopted by many poets as their metrical form. The general French adoption of it gave it a new popularity in this country in the latter part of the 17th century. In Dryden's hands it assumed a new character; it acquired an amazing power and vigour, and a certain novel rapidity of movement. See Pope's *Imit. of Hor. Ep.* I. ii. 267—269.

106. See *Job* xxxix. 19.

111. "We have had in our language no other odes of the sublime kind than that of Dryden on St Cecilia's Day : for Cowley, who had his merit, yet wanted judgment, style, and harmony for such a task. That of Pope is not worthy of so great a man. Mr Mason indeed, of late days, has touched the true chords, and with a masterly hand, in some of his choruses ; above all in the last of Caractacus:

Hark! heard ye not yon footstep dread? &c. (Gray.)"

115. Horace (*Od.* IV. ii. 25) calls Pindar the Dircæan swan.

114. *Pinion,* possibly *pennant* and *pennon, pinnacle, pin, pen,* are all cognate words.

THE BARD.

86. 1. Observe the alliteration.

4. See *King John,* V. i. 72 :

"Mocking the air with colours idly spread."

5. Observe the omission of the first negative here. So sometimes in Greek, as *Thuc.* viii. 99: καὶ αἱ Φοίνισσαι νῆες οὐδὲ ὁ Τισσαφέρνης τέως που ἦκον.

hauberk radically signifies neck-covering armour. *Hau* is a corruption of the A. S. *heals,* the neck. Comp. Scotch *hawse, hals,* &c. *Berk* is from *beorgan* to protect. *Habergeon* is etymologically a dim. from hauberk. See Chaucer's *Prologue,* 76. The Low Latin form was *halsberga.* See note to *Haburyone* in *Prompt. Parv.*

7. *nightly,* see note to *Hymn Nat.* 179.

11. It was in the Spring of 1283, that English troops at last forced their way among the defiles of Snowdon. Llewellyn had preserved those passes and heights intact till his death in the preceding December. The surrender of Dolbadern in the April following that dispiriting event opened a way for the invader; and William de Beauchamp Earl of Warwick at once advanced by it. See Miss Williams' *Hist. of Wales.*

There is much "poetical license" in the topographical description of this scene. The details cannot be realized. Probably the height on which the bard stands is meant for Pen-maen-mawr. See *Lycid.* 52. Snowdon is of course used here in a very wide sense.

11. *shaggy.* See *Lycid.* 54.

13. *Glo'ster.* Gilbert de Clare, Earl of Gloucester and Hereford, had, in 1282, conducted the war in South Wales; and after overthrowing the enemy near Llandeilo Fawr, had reinforced the King in the North-west. See Miss Williams' *Hist. of Wales*, chap. xxii.

14. *Mortimer.* Edward de Mortimer actively co-operated with the King in North Wales. It was by one of his knights, named Adam de Francton, that Llewellyn, not at first known to be he, was slain near Pont Orewyn.

[What is meant by *couch'd* here? Why is *d* pronounced as *t* at the end of this word?]

18. *haggard.* See note to *Hymn Nat.* 23.

19. [Is *loose* predicative here, or adjectival?]

"The image was taken from a well-known picture of Raphael, representing the Supreme Being in the vision of Ezekiel." (Gray.)

20. See *Par. Lost*, i. 537:

     "Shone like a meteor streaming to the wind."

22. [What is meant by *the deep sorrows of his lyre?*]

26. *hoarser* = perhaps, with continually .increasing hoarseness, hoarser and hoarser; so sometimes the compar. in Latin, as *latior* in Hor. *Ep. ad Pis.* 209. Or *hoarser* may mean with unwonted hoarseness, hoarser than they are wont to be; so also the compar. in Latin sometimes: e. g. *senior* an elderly person, one that is older than he was, as we say.

27. See Introduction.

28. *soft Llewellyn's lay* = the lay celebrating the mild Llewellyn. 'Many bards celebrated the warlike prowess and princely qualities of the sons of Gruffydd; and, on the death of Llewellyn, Dafydd Benfrus, Bleddyn Fard and Gruffydd ab yr Ynad Coch composed elegies.' (Miss Williams' *Hist. Wales*). See also Woodward's *Hist. Wales.* The hard names introduced here, with one exception, are drawn from the old annals or traditions of the Cymric muse. Of *Hoel's* songs some are said to be extant; of those of Cadwallo and of Urien there is nothing preserved. Of course Gray is not here referring to these old bards; he but appropriates their names. No name *Modred* is found in the old bard lists; but it is a name only too conspicuous in the old Arthurian story. Malory writes *Mordred.* Looking at the context, it would be better to take *Llewellyn* here for a bard.

87. 34. [Where exactly is this mountain?]

35. *Arvon.* Caernarvon = Caer yn Arvon = the camp in Arvon. This name was given to the place about the close of the 11th century. The old name was Caer Seiont, the Roman Segontium.

38. The Welsh name for Snowdon signifies the eagle's crags.

44. *griesly.* Grisly, A S. grislic, Germ. grösslich.

48. *tissue.* See *Rape of the Lock*, 212, and note.

"See the Norwegian Ode (the Fatal Sisters)." (Gray.)

49. *the warp* = the threads stretched out parallel in the loom, ready to be crossed by the *woof* or *weft* (the woven, inserted thread). The phrase here therefore is not quite accurate. Strictly neither the warp nor the woof can be said to be weaved or inwoven. But perhaps "weave the warp and weave the woof" is but an emphatic way of saying "weave the warp and woof" = "weave the web." Comp. l. 53.

54. See *Eng. Hist.* s. a. 1327.

57. See Shaksp. 3 *Hen. VI.* I. iv.

60. [What part of the sentence is *the scourge of heaven?*]

88. 72. [What is meant by *azure realm?*]

Z 2

77. The older writers say Richard II. was starved to death. "The story of his assassination by Sir Piers of Exon is of much later date." (Gray.)

82. See *Hist. Eng.* s. a. 1398. It is certain, however, that some one who was believed to be King Richard was living in Scotland as late as 1417. "The English writers of the period all speak vaguely on the subject of Richard's death." See *Annals of England*, ii. 400.

85. [Over how many years did the Wars of the Roses extend?]

87. The oldest part of the Tower is said to have been built by Julius Cæsar without any authority.

89. 98. See *Eng. Hist.* A D. 1291.

99. Horace speaks of Virgil as "animæ dimidium meæ." (*Od.* I. iii. 8.)

101. See above, 43—48.

106. *skirt* and *shirt* are closely akin to each other, and to *short*.

109. It is probable that Arthur himself belonged to that branch of the Keltic race which, when the English came over, was settled in the South or South-West of the island—in what is now called Somersetshire. But in the course of what are queerly called "the Dark Ages," and the Early Middle Ages, he had become regarded as the great Prince of the whole Keltic race.

110. Henry VII's paternal grandfather was Sir Owen Tewdwr of Penmynydd in Anglesey. This Sir Owen's mother (Gwenllian Serch Rhys ab Gruffydd) was of royal British blood. See Miss Williams' *Hist. Wales*, chap. xxv.

all hail. Hail in this phrase is not a verb, though it has come to be thought so, but is either (i.) an adj., the A. S. hæl. Comp. the A. S. version of *Matt.* xxvi. 49: "hál [hál is a cognate form] beo ðu," of *Matt.* xxvii. 29: "hál waes ðú." In this case *all* here is an advb.; see note on *Prothal.* 56. Or (ii.) a subst., the A. S. hǽlu or hǽlo; in which case *all* is of course adjectival. The latter would seem to be the later interpretation of the word. The *Prompt. Parv.* gives "heyl, seyde for gretynge. Ave, Salve." From this "hail" was formed the verb *heilin* to say "hail," to greet, Lat. *salutare. Hale, heal, health, healthy, whole,* are all cognate words with *hail.*

[What is the force of *genuine* here?]

113. [Give the names of some of these *dames* and *statesmen.*]

114. *In bearded majesty.* See *Beard* in the Glossary attached to Fairholt's *Costume in England.*

115. See Johnson's *London,* 24.

118. [What poets are here referred to?]

121. *Taliessin* was one of the bards who celebrated the exploits of Urien Rheged a Cymro of North Britain in the first half of the 6th century. See Miss Williams' *Hist. Wales,* c. vii. There is no authority for connecting him with Arthur, as Mr Tennyson does in his *Holy Grail.*

122. [Explain this line.]

125. [What is the subject of *adorn?*]

126. See *Faerie Queene.* Introductory stanzas to Book i.

128. See *Il Pens.* 102.

90. 137. See *Lycid.* 169.

GOLDSMITH.

1. **1728—52** Oliver Goldsmith was born at Pallas, in Forney parish, co. Longford, Ireland, Nov. 29, 1728, the son of a clergyman, whose portrait, as given in that of Village Preacher drawn by his son, is well known to everybody. To his elder brother Henry he afterwards dedicated *The Traveller*. He was sent to some local school, and in time (in 1744) to Trinity College, Dublin, but he does not seem to have cut a very good figure as a pupil and scholar. After his leaving the University, his friends proposed various schemes for his future life, which were frustrated by his masterly thoughtlessness.

2. **1752—6.** At last, in 1752, with the assistance of his friends he reached Edinburgh, to study medicine. Then he passed over to Leyden, to study anatomy and chemistry; but the gaming-table had more attractions for him. Then he travelled, a very vagrant, about Europe; through Flanders, France, Switzerland, Italy, dependent during at least part of his tour upon what he could earn with his flute or beg by the way. In 1756 he landed at Dover.

3. **1756—9.** Arrived in London, matters went hard with him. He was usher in a school, assistant in a chemist's shop, medical practitioner, literary hack. In 1759 he won some distinction by his *Present State of Polite Literature in Europe*. Though his distresses were by no means over, nor indeed were ever to be, or could ever be, so incurable was his improvidence, with 1759 began better times; Goldsmith had found his work.

4. **1759—74.** In 1760 his fame was extended by his *Citizen of the World;* in 1764 by *The Traveller*, 1766 by *The Vicar of Wakefield*, 1770 by *The Deserted Village*, 1773 by *She Stoops to Conquer*. During these years he took his place as one of the literary leaders of his time. He became a conspicuous member of the Johnsonian circle. But his improvidence never failed to embarrass his circumstances. In the spring of 1774 his difficulties reached a crisis. Mental distress aggravated an attack of a disease to which his habits, at times severely sedentary, had rendered him liable; his illness was made worse by injudicious self-doctoring. In the height of his fame he died, March 25, 1774.

As a prose writer few English writers have been endowed with a happier gift of style than Goldsmith; and few writers illustrate better than he how great is the power of a happy style. Perfect ease is his characteristic. Not a trace of effort is ever perceptible. Indeed his danger is of an opposite sort; for traces of carelessness may be detected only too often. There is a world of difference between writing easily, and writing free-and-easily—a difference often forgotten by attempters of the easy style. Goldsmith never mistakes the one for the other; he never sinks into vulgarity. With all his charming familiarity he yet never takes liberties with his readers, or exposes himself to liberties from them. Other characteristics are lucidity, idiotism, aptness and felicity of language. Such were the attractions of his style that they served as a complete apology for very serious defects in many of his works. They served to make his *History of England*, his *History of Rome*, his *History of the Earth and Animated Nature*, popular for more than two generations, and still give a wonderful fascination to those so-called histories. "Nullum [scribendi genus] quod tetigit, non ornavit." It is difficult to conceive of any theme which his style could not have rendered palatable and sweet. He was a very literary Midas; he could transmute to gold whatever he touched.

Literature was his profession. He tried other means of livelihood in vain. He wrote much and variously, charming always. To us of to-day he is best known as a *Novelist* and a *Poet*.

As a novelist, to whom is he not known, and known with delight? The *Vicar of Wakefield* as a story abounds in improbabilities and incoherences; indeed as a story it is worth very little ; neither as a picture of what it professes to paint, English domestic life, can it be pronounced of great value; but it has created at least one fellow-creature for us with a truthfulness, a humour, a pathos almost incomparable. The Vicar can never be forgotten. He is a permanent part of the population of the world. Neither can the unceasing kindness of nature, the true gentle sympathy with the joys and the sorrows of men, the love not blind but still considerate and pitying which inspire and animate that portrait, ever be forgotten. "It is not to be described," writes Göthe to Zelter in 1830, "the effect which Goldsmith's *Vicar* had upon me just at the critical moment of mental development. That lofty and benevolent irony, that fair and indulgent view of all infirmities and faults, that meekness under all calamities, that equanimity under all changes and chances, and the whole train of kindred virtues, whatever names they bear, proved my best education." Surely one may look leniently on Goldsmith's shortcomings as a constructive artist, as one may shrink from passing any bitter sentence upon the frailties of his life, when one is refreshed and purified by his high wisdom and never-failing charity. If without offence I may use the words, I would say that his sins which were many should be forgiven, for he "*loved much.*"

As a poet, grace marks Goldsmith rather than power—"sweetness" rather than "light." In accordance with the dubious theory of his age, he attempted what was called didactic poetry. Both *The Traveller* and *The Deserted Village* have a didactic purpose. So far as that purpose predominates, they fail as poems, if not also as philosophical treatises. But happily Goldsmith's practice was better than his theory. Moved by a true poetic instinct, he often forgets his text; he intermits his preaching or his argumentation; and turns his powers to properer uses. Goldsmith is certainly one of our most charming descriptive poets. One cannot readily mention any pieces of domestic scenery that deserve comparison with those he has given us. Crabbe essayed to follow in his train; but, great as are his merits, he can scarcely be equalled with his master. In his facts Goldsmith is well-nigh as faithful as Teniers; in sentiment and in spirit he excels him.

THE TRAVELLER, OR A PROSPECT OF SOCIETY.

This poem was begun during Goldsmith's wanderings abroad. The first sketch is said to have been sent from Switzerland to his brother Henry in Ireland. Perhaps what is called the first sketch was only the opening passage in which he talks of himself and home, and of his brother. Certainly there is something abrupt in the relation of that passage to the main part of the poem—in the transition from those personal thoughts to the thesis proposed to be treated of - from the home-sick wanderer to the abstracted philosopher. See ll. 31—62. Probably other parts were written during his subsequent travels. Johnson, to whom what was written was shown when Goldsmith and he became acquainted, recognized the merit of it and urged its completion. Johnson himself wrote l. 420, and the concluding ten lines, except the last couplet but one. t was published towards the end of 1764.

In the title, for *prospect* we should rather say *view; Society* is employed in a much broader sense than is now the common use of the word. The nominal object of the poem is to show that, as far as happiness is concerned. one form of government is as good as another. This was a favourite paradox with Dr Johnson. Whether he or Goldsmith really believed it, may be reasonably doubted. Of course it is true that no political arrangements, however excellent, can secure for any individual citizen immunity from misery; it is true also that different political systems may suit different peoples, and further that every political system has its special dangers; and it is true, again, that what constitution may be adapted for what people is often a question of the profoundest difficulty; it is true, lastly, that no civil constitution relieves anyone enjoying the benefit of it from his own proper duties and responsibilities· but it is assuredly not true that there is no relation whatever between the government of a country and the happiness of its inhabitants. A government can, as it pleases, or according to its enlightenment, make circumstances favourable or unfavourable to individual development and happiness. So *a priori* one would suppose; so *a posteriori* one sees that it is. The political indifferentism set forth in *The Traveller* is in fact merely paradoxical. Fortunately one's enjoyment of the poem does not depend upon the accuracy of the creed it professes.

91, 1. [Describe the course of the *Scheld*. Why is it called *lazy*?]
    Slow. See Boswell's *Johnson*, chap. lxiii.
    2. *Wandering Po*. =the ancient Lat. *Padus*, Ligurian *Bodencus*, Greek *Eridanus*. Virgil refers to its terrible floods; See *Georg.* i. 481, iv. 372.
    3. [Where is Carinthia?]
    6. [Explain *expanding to the skies*.]
    11. [What part of the verb is *crown*?]
    13. Comp. *Des. Vill.* 149—162.
    17. *crown'd*. Comp. *Psalm* xlv. 11.
    19. *pranks* = Welsh *pranc*, a frolic.
    21. There are many negligences of style in this poem, as always in Goldsmith's writings. The echo of the word *stranger* in l. 16 has scarcely died out of the reader's ear before here it occurs again. So *bending* and *bend* in ll. 48 and 52. Comp. the double recurrence of the word *ill* in *Des. Vill.* l. 51:

                "*Ill* fares the land, to hastening *ills* a prey;"

where the fact that in the former case it is an advb., in the latter a subst., rather makes matters worse.
    23. Cowper must have had this passage, consciously or unconsciously, in his ear when he wrote l. 100 *et seq.* in his lines *On the receipt of my Mother's Picture out of Norfolk*.
  92. 27. [Explain *the circle bounding earth and skies*.]
    32. *me*. See note to *L'Alleg.* 25.
    33. [Why is the *d* in *plac'd* pronounced as *t*?]
    34. *an hundred*. See note on *Des. Vill.* 93.
    35. [What part of the sentence is *cities*?]
    41. [Explain *dissemble*.]
    [How would you analyze *all it can*?]
    42. *these little things*. See l. 40.
    45—49. See ll. 34—36.
    48. [Explain *bending*.]
    swains. *Swain* was the poet's word for *peasant* in the last century. It is of Teutonic origin, and means properly a young man, then a servant; cf. παῖς, *garçon, knave,* &c
    [What does he mean by *dress* here?]
    50. [What part of the sentence is *creation's heir*?]
    52. As if the reckoning of his treasure was his work.
    53. [What is meant by *fill* here?]
    55. [How would you explain *to* here?]
    57. *sorrows fall*. *sorrows* = signs of sorrow, *i. e.* tears.
    64. [What is the government of *to find* here?]
  93. 72. See *Alex. Feast*, 88.
    74. [What is meant by *his* here?]
    77. [What difference in the meaning would *will*, instead of *shall*, make?]
    84. *Idra* = Idria in Carniola, a town amidst mountains on the river Idria. Near it are the famous quicksilver mines.

84. *Shelvey* = gently sloping. See *Merry IV. of W.* III. v. 15.

85. *rocky crested* is really one word.

87. With the use of the word *Art* here comp. Johnson's first definition : "The power of doing something not taught by nature or instinct." In ll. 146 and 304 *arts* = the Fine Arts.

90. *either* is not very accurately used here ; the *ther* is properly dual. It is as if *uterque* should be used for quisque, ἑκάτερος for ἕκαστος. But this careless use of *either* is not so unfrequent : thus Bacon *apud* Johnson : "Henry VIII, Francis I. and Charles V. were so provident as scarce a palm of ground could be gotten by *either* of the three but that the other two would set the balance of Europe upright again," &c. So Wither, &c. So *neither* in the Auth. V. of *Rom.* viii. 38, &c. But perhaps *either* may be justified here by supposing the "blessings" just enumerated, to be considered as divided in a two-fold manner : (i.) the one prevailing, (ii.) the others, which are cast into the shade by that prevailing one.

95. *the favourite happiness.* Comp. Pope on the Ruling Passion, *Moral Essays*, 1.

98. *peculiar pain* = its proper pain, the pain that especially results from that "fav'rite good."

108. *in gay theatric pride.* The stage often borrows similes and metaphors from nature ; here nature is made indebted to the stage !

109. [What "part of *speech*," and what part of the sentence is *between* here ?]

111. See Virgil's splendid panegyric on his Italy in the second *Georgic*, 136—176.

94. 113. Thus cherries (*Pruni Cerasi*) were imported by Lucullus, &c. &c.

114. Comp. *Tusc. Disp.* V. xiii. 37 : "arbores et vites et ea quæ sunt humiliora neque se tollere a terra altius possunt."

115. [*blooms.* Explain this word here.]

119. *the kindred sail.* Obs. the proleptic use of the adj. So often in Greek and Latin ; as Soph. *Antig.* 881, ed. Dindorf :

"τὸν δ' ἐμὸν πότμον ἀδάκρυτον οὐδεὶς φίλων στενάζει.

120. [Explain this line. Which is the emphatic word?]

122. *winnow* here = waft, blow, with no notion of separating and sifting as commonly. Of course the word is directly connected with *wind*. Obs. the use of this verb in *Par. Lost*, v. 269 :

> "then with quick fan
> *Winnows* the buxom air ;"

i. e. strikes the air as if winnowing, in a winnowing or fanning manner. Ultimately, *fan* and *winnow* are connected.

127. *manners* in the sense of the Lat. *mores.*

132. Genoa and Venice and Florence reached their commercial prime about the close of the Middle Ages.

135—138. [Of what architects, painters, sculptors, is he thinking ?]

139. Two of the main causes, certainly, of the decay of Italian commerce were the discovery of America, and that of the sea-route to India.

143. [What is meant by *skill* here ?]

144. [What is meant by *plethoric ill* ?]

95. 167. *bleak* and *black* are primitively identical words. The radical notion is *pale.* *Bleach* = to make *bleak.* Here *bleak* has its secondary meaning of *chill, cheerless.*

170. From the 15th century downwards the Swiss were the chief mercenary soldiers of Europe. See *Hamlet*, IV. v. 97.

178. [What part of the sentence is *the lot of all* ?]

181. [Explain *deal* here.]

182. *loath.* See note to *London*, 40.

187. *trolls.* One of Johnson's definitions of *troll* is : "to fish for a pike with a rod which has a pulley towards the bottom, which I suppose gives occasion to the term." He quotes from Gray :

"Nor drain I ponds the golden carp to take,
Nor *trowle* for pikes, dispeoplers of the lake."

The word is akin to *thrill, drill,* Germ. *trollen,* Fr. *trôler,* &c.

187. *finny.* See *Rape of the Lock,* 174. This application of the word to the sea itself is bold, and perhaps unique ; as if *squamigerum* or *squamosum* should be applied to the sea !

190. *savage.* We now confine this word as a substantive to members of the human species.

191. [What part of the sentence is *every labour sped?* Parse *sped.* What does the word mean?]

193. *him.* See *me,* l. 32.

Comp. Burns' *Cotter's Sat. Night.*

196. *platter* is of course derived from *plate.*

198. *nightly.* See note on *Hymn Nat.* 179.

96. 202. *enhance.* Lit. forward, put forward. The stem is the Lat. *ante.*

206. *close and closer.* Perhaps = closer and closer; but the former comparative inflection is omitted for euphony's, or for the metre's sake, just as one adverbial inflection is omitted in "safe and nicely," *King Lear,* V. iii., "fair and softly," *John Gilpin,* &c.

216. *supplies* = satisfies.

221. [What is the force of *level* here?]

224. The *of* serves to make *once a year* adjectival to festival. It has the force of *ly* in *yearly.* *Once* is treated as a subst. = one occurrence.

232. [Can *fall* be justified here? What led him to write so?]

235. Such "morals" as "play" in the *Tatler* and *Spectator.*

97. 243. Compare *Tristram Shandy,* end of Book 7.

244. *tuneless.* See below, ll. 247, 248.

253. *Gestic* is cognate with *gesture, gesticulate, jest* (originally *gest*), *gest* in Spenser's *F. Q.* Scott speaks of the "gestic art" in *Peveril of the Peak,* chap. xxx.

256. [Explain *their world.*]

259. Obs. this definition of what is here called *honour.*

262. *traffic,* derived ultimately from Lat. *trans,* and *facio,* is said to mean originally "something done beyond," *i. e.* beyond the seas. With the use here comp. "*commercing* with the skies," *Il Pens.* 39, where see note.

264. Comp. Horace of the Greeks, (*Ep. ad Pis.* 324):

"Præter laudem nullius avaris."

273. *tawdry.* This word is said to be derived from *Saint Audrey* (= Saint Ethelreda), at the fairs held on whose days gay finery, especially laces, was sold. In Spenser's *Shepheards Calendar, April,* it has scarcely acquired its depreciatory sense :

Binde your fillets faste,
And gird in your waste,
For more finenesse, with a *tawdrie* lace."

277. [What is the meaning of *cheer* here? What other meanings has the word?]

98. 285. See Andrew Marvell's bitter satirical description of Holland in his *Character of Holland.* He most unjustly taunts the Dutch with what they might and may well be proud of—the vigour and industry which rescued and protected their country from the sea.

286. *rampire* = the old French form *rampar.* This form occurs often, if not generally, in the Elizabethan writers. So in *Tim. of Ath.* V. iv. 47. "Our *rampired* gates." So Chapman, &c. Holland, in his translation of Pliny, writes *rampiar.* Milton uses the form *rampart* (*Par. Lost,* i. 678).

288. *bulwark* = etymologically, bole-work, that a rampart made of tree-trunks. *Boulevard* is but a corrupted form of *bulwark.* "Les boulevards de Paris n'étaient sous Louis XIV. que l'enceinte même [= le terre-plein des ramparts] de Paris" (Brachet's *Dict. Etym.*).

291. "A stranger can have a full impression of this [the critical condition of certain parts of the provinces] only when he walks at the foot of one of those vast dykes, and hears the roar of the waves on the outside, 16 or 20 feet higher than his head." (Murray's *Handbook to North Germany, Holland*, &c.)

302. [Is *are* defensible here?]

304. [What is meant here by *convenience?*]

305. See what the Vicar says on the dangers of a commercial community, in *V. of Wakefield*, Chap. xix.

312. [What *lakes* are there in Holland?]

313. The Roman *Belgica* included a vast number of various tribes, lying between the Sequana (Seine) and Matrona (Marne) in the West and the Rhine in the East. That tribe, which was settled nearest the Holland of Goldsmith's and our day, was the Batavi, a branch of the Chatti. It was settled between the two great branches of the Rhine. Lucan speaks of its furious warlike ardour (i. 431):

> " Batavique truces quos ære recurvo
> Stridentes acuere tubæ."

It was a Teutonic race, as were other tribes comprised in Belgica. According to Tacitus' account, North-western Germania was occupied by the Ingævones. The "Belgic sires" of the text is therefore a somewhat loose phrase.

316. *now.* In the 16th century they had fought stoutly against the same domineering enemy as England had withstood; in the 17th they had contested with England the queenship of the seas. But perhaps Goldsmith here refers to the fact that the Dutch are our nearest kinsmen. They belong to the same Low German race as ourselves. Their language and our own resemble each other very closely. They are our brothers; the Germans and the Danes are but cousins.

318. [What does he mean by *courts the western spring?*]

319. *Arcadian pride.* Arcadia, perhaps most noted in the Greek and Latin writers for the stupidity of its inhabitants (see *Juv.* vii. 160, and Mayor's note), was about the time of the revival of learning adopted as the ideal of rural beauty. It became the favourite "scene" with pastoral poets and romancists, as with Sanazzaro, Sidney, &c.

320. *Hydaspes.* The name is a corruption of the Sanscrit Vitastâ, "which is probably preserved in that of one of its modern titles, Behat. Its present most usual name is Jelum." (Smith's *Dict. G. & R. Geog.*). This river was reached by Alexander. It was the subject of many wild tales; hence Horace's "fabulosus" (*Od.* I. xxii, 8). One was that it ran gold and gems.

320. *brighter streams*, &c. In Goldsmith's time there was still a touch of silver in the Thames at London, as it may now be hoped there may be yet again.

324. That is, the extremes of climate cannot be palpably realized there by the happy proprietor; they can only be imagined.

325. [What "part of speech" is *stern* here?]

327. *port.* So "lion-port" in Gray's *Bard*, 117.

349. 333. *boasts these rights to scan* = boasts that he scans these rights, that he takes his part in the discussion of public questions.

345. It was just at the time of the publication of *The Traveller* that Wilkes was issuing the *North Briton.*

346. [What is meant here by *round her shore?*]

348. [Parse *fire* here.]

351. *fictitious.* We should rather use *factitious* in this sense. [What is the sense?]

358. *wrote.* It may often seem as if the pret. of strong verbs was used as the past part.; but in fact the pret. seemingly so used is the past part. with its proper ending cut off. Thus the part. *found, bound, drunk*, &c., identical in form with the pret. of the verbs to

which they belong, are in reality curtailed forms of *founden, bounden, drunken,* &c. *Broke, spoke,* &c., as past part., are defensible; being merely shortened from *broken, spoken,* &c. Of *write* the more common form of the part. was *writen,* as in Chaucer's *Cant. Tales,* 12052:

> " Sche never cessed, as I *writen* fynde,
> Of hire prayer."

Writ would be correct enough. See Shakspere *passim* (with whom *writ* is the favourite form of the pret. also). So *wrete* in *Rom. of Partenay,* ed. Skeat, 6401. So *ywrite.* For the form *wrote,* and similar forms, they are probably the result of a false analogy. As *find* makes pret. *found,* part. *found, write,* &c., has been conjugated similarly. Shakspere uses *wrote* in *Ant. and Cleop.* III. v. 11, and *Cymb.* III, v. 2; and also "thou hast fell" (*King Lear,* IV. vi. 54); "has took" (*Pericles* I. iii. 35). Sterne has "had rose"; see the Death of Le Fevre in *Tristram Shandy.*

362. *the great.* This was a very favourite phrase about Goldsmith's time. See for instance Hume's essay on *The Middle Station of Life,* Johnson's *Letter to the Earl of Chesterfield,* &c. The Greeks and Romans used to speak of the good, the best, in the same sense.

365. The literature of the last century abounds with apostrophes to Liberty. That theme was the great common-place of the time. Goldsmith has his laugh at it in the *Vicar of Wakefield,* chap. xix. See Cowper's *Task,* v.

100. 375. Hear the Vicar on Monarchy, *V. of W.,* chap. xix.

380. [Read carefully the history of England about the time of the accession of George III., and illustrate this paragraph.]

386. See *V. of W.,* chap. xix.: "What they may then expect may be seen by turning our eyes to Holland, Genoa, or Venice, where the laws govern the poor, and the rich govern the law."

391. These are precisely the views enunciated by the Vicar; see the above-cited chapter.

patriot. See note on *London,* 53.

394. Perhaps he is thinking of Oliver Cromwell; see note on Gray's *Elegy.*

401. See the *Deserted Village, passim.*

411. *Oswego.* This river runs between Lakes Oneida and Ontario, as Niagara between Ontario and Erie.

412. It is said that the thunder of Niagara may be heard for 20 miles.

416. [What is meant by *Indian* here? Explain how the word comes to have that meaning.]

431. Comp. *Par. Lost,* i. 254—7.

436. *Luke's iron crown.* Goldsmith "dormitates" here. Of two brothers, Luke and George Dosa, who were engaged together in a desperate peasant war in Hungary in 1514, it was George, not Luke, who suffered the torture of the iron crown. See Nares' *Glossary;* and Boswell's *Johnson,* chap. xix.

iron crown. "The putting on a crown of iron, heated red hot, was occasionally the punishment of regicides and rebels." See *Rich. III.* IV. i. 59. See Nares; and Boswell's *Johnson,* chap. xix.

Damiens was executed with frightful tortures for his attempt on the life of Louis XV., 1757. His limbs were torn with red-hot pincers, &c. See *Hist. France.*

THE DESERTED VILLAGE.

The Deserted Village was published in May, 1770, six years after *The Traveller,* four after *The Vicar of Wakefield.* It ran through six editions before the year closed. In any period of English Literature such a poem would have won, and have deserved, notice; in the period of its appearance it stood almost alone. Goldsmith's was the one poetical voice of that time. No other poems besides his, published between Gray's *Odes* and Cowper's *Table Talk*, can be said to have lived. It is no wonder the *Deserted Village* was so widely popular. The heart of the people was not dead, though something chill and cold. It warmed towards a presence so genial, so graceful, so tender.

Here, as in his other poem, Goldsmith entertained not only an artistic but also a didactic purpose. He wished to set forth the evils of the Luxury that was prevailing more and more widely in his day. This is a thrice old theme; but indeed what theme is not so? No doubt the vast growth of our commerce and increase of wealth in the middle and latter part of the last century especially suggested it in Goldsmith's time. Possibly enough in handling it Goldsmith made some blunders; the work could scarcely be his, if it were free from blunders. He has often been taunted by later critics with his false political economy; and it has been pointed out how he was propagating his errors at the very time when Adam Smith was first preaching the truths of that great science. Errors he undoubtedly commits—errors of fact and errors of interpretation. He was wrong in his belief that England was at the time of his writing rapidly depopulating. In the dedication of his poem to Sir Joshua Reynolds, he admits that the objection will be made by him and "several of our best and wisest friends" "that the depopulation it deplores is nowhere to be seen, and the disorders it laments are only to be found in the poet's own imagination. To this," he says, "I can scarcely make any other answer than that I sincerely believe what I have written; that I have taken all possible pains in my country excursions, for these four or five years past, to be certain of what I allege, and that all my views and enquiries have led me to believe those miseries real, which I here attempt to display." But it certainly was not the case. He was obviously wrong in ascribing this supposed depopulation to the great commercial prosperity of the time. Whatever sentimental, whatever real objections may be urged against Trade, it cannot be denied that it multiplies and widens fields of labour, and so creates populations. Large towns with their myriad inhabitants are the offspring of commerce. Goldsmith and his age disbelieved in large towns; they thought such unions of men mere conspiracies of vice; they held, to invert the text, that wheresoever the eagles were gathered together, there the carcase would be. And large towns do include great and wide miseries; but to say that they are signs of present depopulation is to contradict their very definition. Goldsmith's fallacy lies in identifying Trade and Luxury; see the poem *passim*. Observe the mere phrase "Trade's unfeeling train." Again, the picture drawn of the emigrants in their new land is certainly much exaggerated. Such experience as befalls the hero of *Martin Chuzzlewit* is very much what Goldsmith conceives to await all emigrants. He sees the tears and the agonies of the leave-taking; and surely no one can make light of these sorrows; but he sees nothing of the hope and confidence that lie beneath such distresses, however severe and temporarily overwhelming. He forgets that even those earliest and saddest of emigrants, though "some natural tears they shed, yet wiped them soon." He knows not, or he ignores, the happier side of the exile's prospects. He cannot fancy his hearth blazing as brightly on the other shore of the Atlantic as in the old country, or picture any "smiling village" there with gay swains and coy-glancing maidens. He imagines only swamps and jungles, and whirlwinds and sunstrokes, and wild beasts and worse wild men, and shrieks and despair. See ll. 341—358, and *Traveller*, 405—422.

But he is not always in the wrong. His attacks on Luxury, when he really means Luxury and not something else in some way associated with that cardinal pest, are well-deserved and often vigorously made. And when he deplores the accumulation of land under one ownership —how "one only master grasps the whole domain"—and how consequently the old race of small proprietors is exterminated—how "a bold peasantry, their country's pride" is perishing, he certainly cannot be laughed down as a maintainer of mere idle grievances. One may agree with him in his view in this matter, or one may disagree; but it cannot be denied that here he has a right to his view—that this is a question open to serious doubt and difficulty. I suppose there are few persons who will not allow there is something to regret in the almost total disappearance of the class of small freeholders, however much that something may seem to be com-

pensated for by what has come in their place. The present experience of Belgium, of Switzerland, of certain parts of Germany, certainly says much in their favour. (See Mill's *Polit.
Econ.* Book II. Chaps. vii. and viii.) As the question is generally discussed by Political
Economists, it lies between small farms and large farms—between *la petite culture*, and
la grande culture; most English writers, with one most distinguished exception, till lately
at least, declaring for the latter. As it presented itself to Goldsmith, it lay between small farms
and large parks—between a system of small ground-plots assiduously cultivated, and wide
estates reserved for seclusion and pleasure. He saw, or thought he saw, tracts of land
reclaimed not from wildness but from cultivation, that they might form sometimes an artificial
wilderness, always some idle and unproductive enclosure. "Half a tillage," as it seemed,
"stinted the smiling plain;" and in his eyes there was no smile possible for the plain like that
of the waving corn, which is, as it were, the gold-haired child of it. Then, like the gentle
recluse Gray, and like the bright day-labourer Burns, he felt much sympathy with the merriments and sadnesses and interests of the common country-folk. Their life was precious to
him; and he could not bear to think that the area of it was being narrowed, that for them no
more the blazing hearth should burn where it had been wont, not because they were dead, but
because they were ejected wanderers.

It is from this sincere sympathy, apart from all theories and theorizings, that the force and
beauty of this poem spring. When Goldsmith thinks of the decay or destruction of those
scenes he prized so highly, a genuine sorrow penetrates him, and he gives it tongue as in this
poem; he becomes the loving elegist of the old yeomanry. It may or it may not have been
well, that that order should have passed away; but its passing must be wept for. Often it
may be well for our friends to leave us; but certainly we sigh sadly when they go. But
Goldsmith was assured it was not well that that old order should be uprooted; therefore
his grief is aggravated; and with his tears there are mixed shame and indignation.

101. 1. *Auburn.* There is a village of this name, sometimes spelt Albourne, in Wiltshire
(some 8 miles N.E. of Marlborough), which some Gazetteers identify with the scene of this
poem, quite fancifully.

2. *swain.* A favourite word in the Poetic Diction of the last century.

4. *parting.* See the *Elegy*, 1.

9. [Explain this use of *on*.]

102. 12. [What is here meant by *decent?*]

13. See *Cotter's Sat. Night,* 81.

16. *remitting.* In the same absolute way ἀνίημι is used by Attic writers and by Herodotus; *e. g.* Soph. *Philoct.* 764:

$$\text{`` } ἕως ἀν \underset{\bar{ῃ}}{}$$
$$τὸ\ πῆμα\ τοῦτο\ τῆς\ νόσου\ τὸ\ νῦν\ πάρον.''$$

[What is the force of *lent* here?]

17. *train.* A most frequent word in Goldsmith's Poems.

18. [Explain *led up.*]

19. *circled.* Comp. *went round* in l. 22. So *circle* and *circulate* of the wine-cup.

21. *gambol* is connected with Fr. *jamb,* Ital. *gamba,* Low Lat. *gamba.* *Gammon* is a
congener. For the form, it is perhaps due to the Fr. *gambiller,* to kick about.

25. [What is meant by *simply* here? What is the common meaning now?]

27. *smutted.* See note on *motley.*

29. *sidelong.* Sidney uses "sideward" (*Arcad.* iii.). Holinshed has the form *sideling-
wise.* Probably the *long* is a corruption of the adverbial termination *ling*, which yet survives
in *groveling* and *darkling.* So *flatlong, headlong, endlong.* Comp. *noseling.* In oldest
English the term occurs in the forms *linga* or *lunga*; thus *bæclinga* = backwards, *handlunga*
= hand to hand. In Lowland Scotch the form is *lins,* as in *hafflins* (*Cotter's Sat. Night,* 62),

aiblins (*Twa Dogs*, 147), *darklins*, *backlins*, &c. See a paper by Dr Morris in *Philol. Soc. Transactions* for 1862—3.

34. *were*. Comp. the famous FUIMUS *Troes*, FUIT *Ilium* (*Æn.* ii. 318).

35. *the lawn*. See Gray's *Elegy*, 100.

40. *stints thy smiling plain* = deprives thy plain of the beauty and luxuriance which once characterized it. A various form of *stint* is *stunt*.

42. Obs. the alliteration here.

43. *glades*. *Glade*, ultimately connected with *glitter*, denotes a break or open space in a wood, where the light shines.

44. *hollow sounding*. Goldsmith does not hyphen or link together the parts of his compounds; see below, 360; *Traveller*, 85.

    bittern. See *Isaiah* xiv. 23, xxxiv. 11.

45. *lapwing*. *Lap* = *flap*.

51. *fares the land*. So below, 295.

52. [What does he mean by *men decay*? That they decay *morally*, or *numerically*? See the following lines.]

53. See *Cotter's Sat. Night*, 165:

        " Princes and lords are but the breath of kings."

Comp. *For a' that and a' that:*

            " A prince can mak a belted knight,
                A marquis, duke, and a' that;
                But an honest man's aboon his might,
                Guid faith, he mauna fa' that."

103. 55. See *Introduction*.

57. Perhaps it was most nearly so in the 15th and 16th centuries.

58. *rood* is but another form of *rod*, which to begin with denoted the pole used in land-measuring. So *perch* is properly a measuring pole (of less length than the *rod*). In ecclesiastical language Rood = the Cross. (So there is no idea of any transversity in the Greek σταυρός.) Hence *Holyrood*, *rood*-loft, by the holy *rood* (*Rich. III.* III. ii.), *Roodee* (at Chester), &c.

60. [Why *her*?]

66. *unwieldy*. Spenser uses *weeldlesse* in *F. Q.* IV. iii. *Wieldly*, obsolete now, occurs in Chaucer's *Troil. and Cress.*

74. *manners* = Lat. *mores*. See *Trav.* 230.

76. *forlorn*. See note in *Hymn Nat.* 196. *lorn* is connected with *lose*. Comp. *rear* and *raise, chair* and *chaise*, &c.

84. [What part of the sentence is *my latest hours to crown*?]

92. [What part of the sentence is *I felt*?]

93. *an hare*. Our present rule that *a* rather than *an* is to be used before a word beginning with a consonant or a sounded *h* is of comparatively modern date. In Oldest English (what is commonly called A.S.) the shortened form does not occur. In Medieval writers *an* is the more common form: thus in the *Ormulum* we find *an man*, in Mandeville's *Travels*, *an hors*, &c. (Stratmann); but *a* also is found. The distinction between the numeral and the article was only then completely forming. In Chaucer's writings it seems fairly formed; he has *oo, oon, on* for the former; *a* and *an*, as now, for the latter. Before *h* he commonly prefers the form *an*, as *an hare* (*C. T.* 686), *an holy man* (Ib. 5637), *an housbond* (Ib. 5736) &c. This was perhaps due to French influence. In the Authorized Version of the Bible we have *an house* (1 *Kings* ii. 24, and often elsewhere), *an husband* (*Num.* xxx. 6, &c.), but also *a husband* elsewhere, *an hundred* again and again, *an host*, *Psalm* xxvii. 3, *an hair, an habitation, an hand, an hymn,* &c., &c., but *a horse*. It must be remembered that the language of the A. V. is older than the time of James I.; it belongs rather to the age of Henry VIII., in some points perhaps to a still older age, as the Wickcliffite translation had much influence on all succeeding versions. Shakspere's usage is pretty much that which is

now followed ; as "a hauke, a horse, or a husband." *Much A. about N.* III., Fol. of 1623,— "a hare," 1 *Hen. IV.* I. iii. But with regard to many words custom fluctuated. In the case of the word *hare* perhaps euphony would seem to favour the fuller form of the article.

95. [What part of the sentence is *my long vexations past?* Translate the phrase into Latin, and Greek.]

104. 100. [What does *age* mean here?]

> *hounds and horns. Titus Andr.* II. iii. 27.

105. *surly* is probably cognate with *sour.*

106. *spurn* is connected with *spur*, which means radically a foot-mark. In the primitive sense of to push away with the foot, *spurn* is common in Shakspere, as *K. John*, II. i. 24, &c.

107. *latter end.* A common Bible phrase, *e.g.* Prov. xix. 20.

109. Comp. *Vanity of H. W.* 293.

115. *careless* = Lat. *securus*, and old Eng. *secure*. See *Van. of H. W.* 355.

118. [What part of the sentence is *to meet their young?*]

121. *bayed.* Bay is from the old French *abayer* = aboyer, "de *ad. baubari.* De là le subst. *abois*, proprement extrémité où est réduit le cerf, le Sanglier, sur les fins, lorsque les chiens l'entourent en aboyant" (Burguy).

122. *the vacant mind.* So Shaksp.

> "The wretched slave
> Who with a body fill'd and *vacant mind*
> Gets him to rest," &c.

Comp. Lat. *vacuus.*

[Give other instances of this use of *spoke.*]

124. *pause*, is used technically of "a stop or intermission in music" (Johnson). It is often employed in our older writers in this sense of the nightingale's singing.

126. *fluctuate in the gale.* Comp. the common use of *float*, which is *ultimately* connected with *fluctuate, flow*, &c.

128. *bloomy* is used also by Milton and Dryden.

130. *plashy* = puddle-like. Comp. the Dutch *plas*, and our *splash.*

132. [In what other senses is *mantling* used?]

135. [What part of the sentence is *she* here?]

137. *Copse* = coppice = old Fr. copeiz, which is derived from *couper*, which is derived from the Lat. *colaphus* a fist-blow, (Brachet).

[*The garden.* Why *the?*]

139. [What is meant by the *place disclose?*] Comp. Wordsworth's *To a Highland Girl at Inversnaid:* "These trees—a veil just half withdrawn."

140. *mansion* = the Lowland Scotch *manse;* but last century poets use it in a general sense. *Mansio* was properly the house of the lord of the manor.

105. 141. See the *Traveller*, 10—22. Comp. Chaucer's *Prologue*, 479—530.—Crabbe sketches the opposite sort of parson in his *Village*, Book I:

> "And doth not he, the pious man, appear,
> He 'passing rich, with forty pounds a year?'
> Ah! no; a shepherd of a different stock,
> And far unlike him, feeds this little flock," &c.

142. Forty pounds seems to have commonly been a curate's income about the middle of the last century. Churchill, when a curate at Rainham, "prayed and starved on forty pounds a year," to use his own words.

[Explain *passing* here.]

143. See *Heb.* xii. 1.

> *Remote from towns*, &c. See *London*, 6, &c.

144. *place, not* village or place of abode, but = post, position. The word was especially used of political appointments; comp. *place-man, place-seeker,* &c.

146. Like the famous Vicar of Bray.

[Explain *to* here?]·

148. [What part of the sentence is this line?]

155. *The broken soldier.* Comp. "fracti bello," Æn. ii. 13, "infractos adverso Marte," Æn. xii. 1; see also Hor. *Sat.* I. i. 5.—Campbell's *Soldier's Dream*:

"And fain was their *war-broken* soldier to stay."

bade. Bidden and *Bid* (as *Merch. of V.* II. v. 11) are the common, and the correct forms. See note on the *Traveller,* 358.

156. *talked the night away.* Comp. the exquisite phrase in Callimachus' Epigram (in the Greek usage of the word) on hearing of the death of his friend Heracleitus:

ἐμνήσθην δ' ὁσσάκις ἀμφότεροι
ἥλιον ἐν λέσχῃ κατεδύσαμεν.

157. [What is the force of *done* here?]

159. [What is meant by *glow* here?]

162. [What is the precise meaning of *charity* here?]

171. *parting.* See Gray's *Elegy,* 89.

172. *dismayed* = strictly, deprived of might, un-strengthened.

174. *fled the struggling soul.* See *V. of H. IV.* 149.

181. [What part of the sentence is *the service past?*]

106, 189. [Explain *cliff* here?]

198. *truant* is said to be of Keltic origin. In Breton there is *truant* "gueux, vagabond" (Burguy). In Kymric *tru,* miserable. Hence Medieval Latin formed *trutannus.* The old meaning was simply a vagabond. Then it came to mean wandering away from the place where one ought to be, the place of one's duty, which is commonly its sense in Shakspere. In *Merry W. of W.* V. i., it occurs in the special sense in which it is now generally used: "Since I plucked geese, *played truant,* and whipped top, I knew not what 'twas to be beaten till lately." (Comp. *micher,* 1 *Hen. IV.* II. iv.) In mod. Fr. *truand* = vagrant.

201—4. These two couplets furnished Webster with mottoes, and something more, for his two excellent pictures.

205. *aught* = simply, a-whit; as *awhile* = a-while, *another* = an-other, &c.

207. *The Village all,* &c. So Ovid uses *vicinia* for *vicini: Fast.* ii. 655:

"conveniunt celebrantque dapes vicinia supplex."

Comp. *Twa dogs,* 125:

"When rural life, o' every station,
Unite in common recreation."

208. *cypher* and *zero* are probably various corruptions of one and the same word. See Max Müller's *Chips from a German Workshop.*

209. *tides* = here times, seasons; as in *King John,* III. i. 85:

"Among the high *tides* in the Calendar," &c.

"*Christ-tide,* I pray you," says Ananias in the *Alchemist,* when Face talks of Christmas. We still speak of *Whitsuntide;* and have a proverb that "time and *tide* wait for no man," when perhaps *tide* has the secondary meaning of opportunity. *Tide* is cognate with Germ. *Zeit.* What is now the common meaning of the word—a meaning derived from the primitive sense—would scarcely be pertinent here.

[What is meant by *terms* here?]

210. *gauge* = measure the capacities of vessels. *Gauger* has acquired the special meaning of one who so measures vessels containing excisable liquors.

221. *nut-brown draughts.* As if we should say "pale draughts" for "draughts of pale ale."

226. Etymologically *parlour* belongs to the same group with *parliament, parlance, parley,* and *parole.* The common stem is the Low Lat. *parabolare.—Parlour* originally denoted the speaking-room of a monastery, that is, the room where conversation was allowed, called also *locutorium.* The word seems now to be beginning to fall out of use, superseded by *dining-room* and *breakfast-room.*

[What is meant by *the parlour splendours,* &c.?]

Of this department of village life Goldsmith could write from abundant experience. See the account of his early days given by Irving and by Forster. He had certainly often made one in such a company as he depicts at the *Three Pigeons* in *She Stoops to Conquer.*

107. 229. [What is the sense of *debt* here?]

232. *the twelve good rules.* See Crabbe's *Parish Register,* Part i. of the pictures possessed by "the industrious swain:"

> "There is King Charles and all his golden rules
> Who proved Misfortune's was the best of schools."

These rules were: 1. Urge no healths. 2. Profane no divine ordinances. 3. Touch no state matters. 4. Reveal no secrets. 5. Pick no quarrels. 6. Make no companions. 7. Maintain no ill opinions. 8. Keep no bad company. 9. Encourage no vice. 10. Make no long meals. 11. Repeat no grievances. 12. Lay no wagers. Jonson wrote rules for the Devil Tavern (close by Temple Bar on the river side).

the royal game at goose = perhaps, the game of the Fox and the Geese, but why called *royal?*

235. *chimney* here = fire-place. See note to *L'Alleg.* 111.

239. [What part of the sentence is *obscure?*]

241. Comp. Horace's "addit cornua pauperis" of the wine-jar (*Od.* III. xxi. 18). See *Tam o' Shanter,* 57.

243. *The farmer's news.* The farmer's necessary visits to the neighbouring market town would naturally make him the newsman.

The barber's tale. The endless garrulity of barbers who, at least in the country, practised as surgeons also, is a perpetual matter of joke or disgust with the novelists of George II.'s time. So too in the *Arabian Nights,* &c.

244. *woodman.* Now = a tree-feller, once = sportsman, hunter; as in *Merry W. of W.,* V. v.: "Am I a *woodman,* ha? speak I like Herne the hunter?" So *Meas. for Meas.* IV. iii. 170, *Cymb.* III. vi. 28., *Comus,* &c.

the woodman's ballad = some praise of the greenwood, or perhaps some tale of Robin Hood, the hero of foresters. Perhaps it was not till after the middle of the last century that *Ballad* acquired what is now its general meaning, viz. a narrative piece. Johnson in his *Dict.* gives no special sense. Formerly it denoted a song of any kind, as in *As you like it,* II. vii. 148:

> "And then the lover
> Sighing like furnace, with a woeful *ballad*
> Made to his mistress' eyebrow."

Older writers call *Solomon's Song* the *Ballet of Ballettes.* Chaucer speaks of the birds singing *ballads and layes* (*Dreame*).

246. *lean to hear.* Comp. Wordsworth's exquisite lines of a far other listening:

> "And she shall lean her ear
> In many a secret place
> Where rivulets dance their wayward round," &c.

248. [Explain *the mantling bliss.*]

A A

250. Comp. Jonson's "O leave a kiss but in the cup," &c.   It was also a Greek custom; see Bekker's *Charicles*, Sc. ii.

254. *gloss* is probably from the same root as *glass*.   This *gloss* is quite distinct from the *gloss* which means an explanatory note.

258. Comp. *Par. Lost*, V. 899, *Hamlet*, I. v. 77.

266. See *Introduction.*

268. *an happy land.*   See note to "an hare," above, l. 93.

269. [Explain *freighted.*]

108. 276. [What part of the sentence is *pour* ?]

277. Comp. Hor. *Od.* II. xv.

280. Comp. l. 40.

281. But "sports" are not always "solitary" in the Squire's park! See the Introduction to *The Princess*, &c. &c.

283. He seems to mean that the country does not keep back the amount of its own products that is needed for its own consumption, but exports and barters away what is necessary it should retain for what is altogether superfluous.

284. *for*, i. e to be exchanged for.

285. [Explain *all* here.]

286. [What is the force of *the fall*, as compared with *its fall* ?]

288. [What is meant by *secure to please* ?]

295. [What does he mean by *bless* here?]

296. [What part of the sentence is this line?]

298. *vistas* = orig., views, prospects, sights, from the Lat. *video.*

305. The enclosure of Commons, a measure by no means always dictated by mere greed, but sometimes in the highest degree prudential and considerate, has always been an extreme popular grievance. See Latimer's *Last Sermon preached before King Edward VI.*, *Ballads on the Condition of Eng. in Hen. VIII. reign*, &c., Part I. ed. Furnivall, p. 54, &c., &c.   Some 1600 or 1700 Inclosure Acts are said to have been passed before the beginning of the present century.   Goldsmith ignores the fact that "half a tillage stinted the plains," where the old Commons lay extended.   If the enclosure were made without proper compensation to the Commoners, then assuredly nothing can be more shameful.

109. 316. *artist* = here our artisan.   Contrariously *artisan* was formerly used somewhat in the sense of our *artist*; as in the *Guardian*:

> "Best and happiest *artisan*
> Best of painters, if you can,
> With your many-colour'd art
> Draw the mistress of my heart."

"What are the most judicious *artisans* but the mimicks of nature?"   Wotton's *Architect*, apud Johnson's *Dict.*.   See also Trench's *Sel. Gloss.*

319. *dome.*   See note to *London*, 199.

336. *she left her wheel.*   See Mrs Browning's *A year's Spinning.*   Burns' Bessie is wiser; see his lines *Bessy and her Spinnin Wheel.*

344. *Altama* = the Altamaha or Alatamha in Georgia, U. S.   Bancroft mentions a settlement made on it near Darien by certain Gaels; see *Hist. United States*, II. 1008, 12mo. ed. 1861.

    to.   See note to *Hymn Nat.* 132.

345. He seems to forget that there are other parts of America besides the Tropical. For a description of the New World made in a very different spirit, see Kingsley's *Westward Ho!*

346. [What part of the sentence is *terrors* ?]

352. [What does he mean by *gathers death* here?]

355. "This is a poetical licence; the American tiger, or jaguar, being unknown on the banks of the Alatamha." Mitford.

110. 357. *tornado* and the Eng. *turn* are ultimately from the same root.

358. *landschape*. The oldest English form is *landscipe*. The second syllable is cognate with *shape*, *ship*, *scoop*, *skiff*, the Greek σκάπτω, &c.

360. *grassy vested green*. Comp. "short-grass'd green," in *Tempest*, IV. i. 83.

367. *thefts of harmless love*. So Lat. *furta*, as *Catull*. LXVIII. 140, of Juno's wrath:

"Noscens omnivoli plurima *furta* Jovis."

And *Georg*. IV. 345, of Cyrene's attendant Nymphs down in the sea-depths:

"Inter quas curam Clymene narrabat inanem
Vulcani Martisque dolos et dulcia *furta*."

363. *gloom'd*. See l. 318.

368. *seats* = Lat. *sedes*. See l. 6.

378. Was the lover never able to go too?

386. [What does he mean by *things like these* ?]

394. [Parse *sapped their strength*.]

111. 399. *anchoring* = lying at anchor, *not* in the act of anchoring.

402. He seems to distinguish between *shore* and *strand*, making *strand* mean the beach, the shore in the most limited sense of the word. *Shore* and *shores* are often used very loosely; as "He left his native shore" = he left his native land, &c. There is no etymological reason for any such distinction. *Shore* is ultimately connected with *shear*, *shears*, *shire*, *share*. *Strand* is the Oldest Eng. *strand* a margin or border.

413. Comp. Wither's fine lines to his Muse from *the Shepherd's Hunting*:

"And though for her sake I'm crost,
Though my best hopes I have lost,
And knew she would make my trouble
Ten times more than ten times double,
I should love and keep her too
Spite of all the world could do.

*   *   *

She doth tell me where to borrow
Comfort in the midst of sorrow,
Makes the desolatest place
To her presence be a grace," &c. &c.

418. *Torno's cliffs*. The heights around Lake Tornea in the extreme N. of Sweden ?
Pambamarca. A mountain in South America, near Quito.

422. Comp. *Progress of Poesy*, 54—62.

426. *Very blest*. The common English rule is to use the adv. *very* with other advs. and with adjs., the adv. *much* with part. *Blest* here may be regarded rather as an adj. than a part.

429. [What does he mean by *self-dependent power* ?]

ROBERT BURNS.

1. 1759—1784. ROBERT BURNS was born some two miles to the south of Ayr, Jan. 25, 1759, (the year in which Handel died, Johnson's *Rasselas* was published, Goldsmith first began to make way against adverse fortune). His father, a small farmer, lived a somewhat hard struggling life; but he did not let his difficulties prevent his doing all he could for the education of his children. His own example and influence, both moral and intellectual, were of more advantage than much formal schooling. Even of formal instruction he gave them much himself. In 1766 he removed to Mount Oliphant Farm; 11 years afterwards to Lochlea, where he died in 1784. When that event happened, Robert and his brother Gilbert had for some years worked under him on the farm. The poet had already begun to feel and to reveal his talent. He had written the *Death of poor Mailie; O Mary, at thy window be;* and several other short pieces of no mean order.

2. 1784—1786. On the death of the father, the children—two sons and two daughters—stocked a farm on their own account; but "spem mentita seges," and it did not go well with them. It was early in this period that Robert first met Jean Armour. Scarcely less important perhaps in the history of his development was the state of polemics in his neighbourhood. The New Light or the Rationalists, as they were called, and the Auld Light or Evangelists, were struggling for the mastery. Thus, at this time, all Burns' nature was stirred within him. His wit and humour no less than his love-passionateness were all aroused, and found for themselves fervent and brilliant expression. He soon became locally famous, but his pecuniary fortunes grew worse and worse; and his amour brought him much distress and shame. He determined to leave the country. To raise money to pay his passage to Jamaica, he published a volume of the various poems he had written the last few years. His local fame spread at once into national. When now on the point of sailing, he received a letter from a Dr Blacklock of Edinburgh, which excited in him hopes of success at home; so he abandoned his voyage. Perhaps it might have been better for him if he had gone.

3. 1786—1789. At Edinburgh Burns found himself an object of curiosity and wonder rather than frankly recognised as a fellow, or a superior, in the world of letters. He was the gorilla of a season. Little did his condescending patrons dream how great, with all his ignorance of conventionalisms, he really was—how much of the "divine air" there was in him; but no doubt they were civil and friendly according to their lights. His visit to Edinburgh was of no advantage to Burns; it rather tended to vulgarise him. His genius produced nothing worthy of it during his stay in the midst of that society. A bright time seemed dawning for him when in 1788 he took a lease of the farm of Ellisland on the banks of the Nith in Dumfriesshire. The following twelve months were certainly the happiest of his life. He married his Jean. *Of a' the airts the wind can blaw; O were I on Parnassus' Hill; I hae a wife o' my ain*—all songs written at this time—tell their own tale of content and bliss. Would that the sunshine could have lasted !

4. 1789—1796. In August 1789 Burns received an appointment in the Excise. This was surely an evil thing. It did not perhaps produce, but certainly it expedited his ruin. From this time all is decline and fall. He presently (in 1791) gave up the farm which was proving a failure, and resided in Dumfries; habits of hard drinking gradually prevailed over him; that choicest treasure of all, self-respect, began to desert him. It was not without frequent remorses that he sank so low, not without intermissions of a higher and nobler life. Some of

his best songs were composed during this period. The end could not be long in coming. In July 1796 he died, a splendid wreck.

Of the lyric poets, pure and simple, of British literature, Burns is certainly the chief. Few songs in the language, in whatever dialect, equal, very few indeed surpass, the best of his. In no writer has the passion of the moment, let it be what it would, love or wrath or anguish or despair, moulded itself into words more completely reflecting it—words of greater intensity or burning more fiercely. His love-songs are ablaze with passion ; his humorous pieces are one inextinguishable laughter ; his despondent shed around them a darkness that may be felt. In many respects it is obvious to couple him with Byron, different as they were in birth, and education, and associations. They were both in an eminent degree "bards of passion and mirth." If for wit the palm be given to Byron, as perhaps it should justly be, Burns is the greater master of passion. No song of Byron's can compare for fire and flame with *Ae fond kiss and then we sever.* In humour too the superiority lies with the Scotch poet. With all his quick radiant fancy there was in him a certain grand tenderness and indulgency of nature, which saved him always from savagery. He never confounded vile men with humanity, gross instances with the entire genus. His nature was singularly free from morbidness. Rude and uninstructed and ill-regulated it was in some ways; but frank, generous, noble it was always, and these fine traits are omnipresent in his poetry. Light that could satisfy his spirit he never saw, or saw only in sparse glimpses; but indeed of whom can much more be said? Of some darkness at least that prevailed around him he was quickly conscious, and did what in him lay to dispel it. He spoke out plainly and vehemently, never, to do him mere justice, with profane and godless lips; for he was of a really reverent and worshipping soul, and wherever he recognised what was good and beautiful he bowed his face to the ground before it. It was quite consistent with, nay, dissociable from, this habit of obeisance, that wherever he beheld what was mean and foul he assaulted it, though it might stand in the high place itself. The intrinsic virtue of his nature is shown in that seeing around him so much that was truly ignoble and vicious, he was never corrupted into a mere cynic and satirist ; but to the end, with whatever sad lapses of practice, held firm his faith in true manliness and honour. His was a life of much spiritual disorder and tumult. Often he beat his wings wildly against the bars of the world as he saw it ; in calmer moments he sang out his pain, and whatever joy there might be, in notes that must for ever awaken a responsive thrill in the bosom of mankind.

Perhaps no poet ever more truly sang "because he must" than Burns. To the ordinary eye there was but little in his early surroundings to evoke a poetical spirit. To call him wholly uneducated is of course a mistake ; his mental faculties had much care bestowed upon them; he was born in an intellectual country; and such gross unculture, if I may use such a word, as marks many a well-to-do farmer, and others than farmers, in England was happily not possible for him; but still it seemed as if everything was against his turning out a poet. Pope, the idol of the time, could not be inspiring to such a nature as that of Burns. Cowper began to write only two or three years before Burns himself. What in the shape of composition most moved his genius was the balladry of his native land, the old popular songs, which had long died out in England, but were still to be heard across the Border. How active their influence upon his mind, his works show everywhere. For a genius so rich and abundant, a slight outward inspiration sufficed. As to the themes of his poetry, he wanted no teaching ; he found them all around him, in the ploughlands, in the cottages, in all creation as it lay around his own door.

It is only as a lyric poet that Burns was great. He is said to have meditated writing a comedy, but nothing came of it. Indeed dramatic poetry, and epic also, would have demanded a higher culture than Burns could boast. Moreover, his genius does not seem to have lain in those directions. In this respect Burns may be regarded as the apotheosis of the poetry of Scotland; in which country no poet other than lyric of the highest order has yet appeared.

All Burns' best pieces are written in his native dialect. He knew English—that is, the dialect of education and of literature—well, and could write in it fluently and with vigour; but it was not his vernacular, and he could not express in it with the essential sensitiveness and delicacy the ideas and emotions that called for an outlet. So strangely intimate in the art of poetry is the connection between thought and language, that no language in any sense foreign can suffice for the representation of inmost and purest thought; no translation is endurable. Whenever Burns writes in general English, he becomes comparatively languid and ineffective. David with the sling and stone of his youth can more than match even Goliath; with Saul's armour on, he is but as, or less than, any other Hebrew; and so Burns with his native Ayrshire, and his acquired English. He essayed again and again to write in the latter; but nature was stronger than all his efforts.

COTTER'S SATURDAY NIGHT.

This piece was written in 1785. The friend to whom it is addressed was one into whom Burns had been brought into connection in the Auld and New Light Controversy. The poet wrote this epitaph for him:

> "Know thou, O stranger to the fame
> Of this much lov'd, much honour'd name,
> (For none that knew him need be told)
> A warmer heart death ne'er made cold."

It is easy to see in this piece the influence of Gray, of Goldsmith, and of Pope: see the notes; but easier still to observe the freshness and originality of it. There are few, if any, "interiors" in our literature that rival the one given here for truthfulness, and sincere but not exaggerated sentiment.

The language is partly Ayrshire, partly English. The more homely passages are written in the poet's vernacular; in the more exalted he uses a less familiar tongue. No doubt he made this distinction deliberately; he feared to degrade his higher themes by colloquial associations. It must be remembered that in Burns' time provincial dialects were commonly believed to be mere distortions and corruptions of the national language; whereas a wiser philology teaches us rather that the national language is a corruption of them, at least of some one of them. To say that Ayrshire is a deterioration of English, would be as ridiculous as to insist that Ionic, or Doric, or Æolic is a corruption of Attic; or that the Langue d'oc is a corruption of French.

Cotter is defined by Jamieson to mean "one who inhabits a cot or cottage, dependent on a farm," and referred to barbarous Lat. *Cottarius*, Fr. *Cottier*. But it has not the technical sense of the Fr. *Cottier*. "In its original acceptation," says Mill (*Pol. Econ.* i. 383, Note, ed. 1857), "the word 'Cottier' designates a class of sub-tenants, who rent a cottage and an acre or two of land from the small farmers. But the usage of writers has long since stretched the term to include those small farmers themselves, and generally all peasant farmers whose rents are determined by competition."

112. 1. See *Introduction.*

4. [What is the grammatical construction of this line?]

5. *lays* was a favourite word with the poets of the last century; *e.g.* Pope's *Prol. Sat.*
138:

> "Well-natured Garth inflamed with early praise,
> And Congreve loved, and Swift endured my *lays*," &c.

Gray uses it for an epitaph, see *Elegy*, 115. The sense is generally somewhat vague. Radically, *lay* is probably of the same root as the Germ. *lied*, a song.

6. *the lowly train*. See *Des. Vill.* 252. *Train* also was a favourite 18th-century word. Goldsmith uses it some half-dozen other times in the *Des. Village*; thus "trade's unfailing train," "the busy train" of remembrance, "the harmless train" = the old innocent villagers, "the vagrant train" = beggars, "the gorgeous train" = a brilliantly dressed crowd, "the loveliest train." The radical meaning of the word is something drawn along. It was properly used of a body of retainers following their chief.

See Gray's *Elegy*.

9. *I ween*. Perhaps the difficulty of satisfying the severe rhyming exactions of the Spenserian stanza may partly account for the liberal use of archaic words and forms, and of superfluous phrases by all writers of it. Spenser himself takes strange liberties.

See Johnson's *London*, 6.

10. *sugh* is also written *souch, sough, sowch, swouch*, with perhaps slight variations of meaning. Burns uses *sough* for a *sigh* in his lines *On the Battle of Sherriffmuir*:

> " My heart for fear gae *sough* for *sough*
> To hear the thuds," &c.

Sough is used in Prov. Eng. for a murmuring. The root is seen in the Low Germ. *suchten*, the Oldest English (= A. S.) *sican*. Comp. *sike* in the *King's Quair*, &c. *Suck* is of the same word-family.

12. *frae*. Perhaps this is one of the many signs of Norse influence, which appear in Lowland Scotch; for the Icelandic form of the prep. is *fra*. The Mæso-Gothic form is *fram*; see Skeat's *M. G. Gloss*. There was however an Oldest Eng. *fra* We shorten our Eng. *from* into *fro* in the phrase *to and fro*, and perhaps in the word *fro-ward*.

[What is the syntactical construction of this and the following line?]

15. *moil* is derived from the Fr. *mouiller*, which comes itself from the Lat. *mollis*. The succession of meanings seems to be: (i) to moisten or wet; (ii) to stain with moisture, to soil; (iii) in a *neut.* sense, to be soiled, to grow dirty; (iv) to grow dirty with toiling, with dust and sweat; (v) to toil. For (ii) see Spenser's *Hymn to H. Love*:

> " Then rouze thy selfe, O Earth ! out of thy soyle
> In which thou wallowest like to filthy swyne.
> And doest thy mynd in durty pleasures *moyle* !"

So Chapman and Hakluyt. In sense (iii), it is used in Westmoreland. See Halliwell's *Dict. Arch. & Prov. Words*. In the last sense it is common enough in the literature of the 17th and 18th centuries, and still in the provinces, as in Lancashire; see Peacock's *Lonsdale Glossary*. "They toil and *moil* [this is a common conjunction] for the interest of their masters, that in requital break their heart." (L'Estrange, *apud* Johnson.) So Dryden :

> " Now he must *moil* and drudge for one he loathes."

17. *the morn* = *tomorrow* in South-Tweed English. *Morrow* and *morning* are both "diminutives" from *morn*. More usually, the N. Tweed English prefers the diminutival form. The *to* in *tomorrow* is said to be a corruption of *the* or *this*. The vowels in *morrow* attract and assimilate the neighbouring vowel. Perhaps similar is the explanation of *mistress* as compared with *master, vixen* with *fox, Jenkins* with *John*, the pronunciation of *women* (Chaucer sometimes writes *wymmen, Prol.* 213), as compared with that of *woman*, &c.

18. Comp. Gray's *Elegy*, 3.

21. See the *Elegy*, 23.

toddlin. In N. Tweed English the *d* of the pres. part. has dropped off altogether : in S. Tweed Eng. the *d* has been corrupted into *g*, through the influence of an old substantival ending, viz. *ing*. The oldest Eng. (= A. S.) part. terminated in *-ende*, as *tellende, lvbbende, gangende*, &c., also in the Northumberland dialect *-ande*. In 14th-century writers of England the pres. part. ends variously in *-and*, *-end*, *-inde*, *-inge*, and *-ynge*, *-yng*. In the English of Scotland *-nd* and commonly *-and* prevails; thus in Barbour's *Bruce*, occur *slayand*, *destroyand*, *swonand*, *assailyeand*, &c. *-Ing* with Barbour is a substantival ending, *e.g.* xiv. 1168, &c. Dunbar in *The Thistle and the Rose* has *variand*, &c. This final *d* dropping off, come the forms *toddlen*, *fichterin*, *blinkin*, *rantin*, *sueeshin*, &c. So *an'* for *and*.

    stacher, also written *stakker* and *stagher*, = stagger.

    22. *fichterin* is the Scotch form answering to the English *fluttering*.

    23. *ingle* = fire, fire-place. The word is used in Northumberland. Jamieson connects it with Gael. *aingeal*, Lat. *ignis*.

    wee bit ingle. Scotch omits the prep. which in Southern English would link the two substantives: it uses *wee bit* adjectively. So *way bit* in Northumb.

    wee is not uncommon in provincial Eng. Simple speaks of his master Slender's "little *wee* face" in *Merry W. of W.* I. iv. 22. It is perhaps of the same root as the Germ. *wenig*. In Lancashire is found the form *weeny*; see Peacock's *Glossary of the Hundred of Lonsdale*.

    24. *wifie*. Scotch is particularly rich in diminutival forms.

    26. *carkin* from "A. S." *Care* = *care*, with which word probably it is radically cognate. *Care-ærn* is a prison. The Latin *carcer*, Greek ἕρκος, may be of the same root. *Cark* is found in Elizabethan writers, as Sidney, Spenser, &c.; as *Faerie Q.* I. i. 44:

> " devoide of careful *carke*."

    27. *Toil* seems to have been pronounced *tile*, or something like *tile*, in the last century. In Johnson's *London*, 219, it rhymes with *smile*, as here with *beguile*.

    [*labor*. Is this spelling correct ?]

    113. 28. *belyve* = presently. Chaucer has *blyve*; Robert of Gloucester, *blive*, *belive*. So Spenser, who has also *bylive*. *Belive* is used in Lanc. "Cf. Dan. *oplive* = to quicken, enliven, and the two senses of our Eng. *quick*." (Coleridge's *Gloss. Ind.*)

    bairns. *Bairn* is a later form of Oldest Eng. *bearn*. In *Death and Life* (*Percy Folio MS.* iii. 59), *barnes* = 'children of men' = mankind.

    30. *ca'* = drive; strictly call, drive with calling or shouting. So Globe Edition of *The Works of Burns*, p. 32:

> " Tell him if e'er again he keep
> As muckle gear as buy a sheep,
> O bid him never tie them mair
> Wi' wicked strings o' hemp or hair !
> But *ca'* them out to park or hill,
> And let them wander at their will."

Comp. Kingsley's song:

> " Go, Mary, go, and *call* the cattle home."

Perhaps, however, the root is quite different from that of the Eng. *call*. Jamieson refers to Dan. *kage*, 'leviter verberare.'

    tentie is a corruption of *attentive*. *Tent* is used in Lancashire both as a subst and a verb. 'Take tent' occurs in Ben Jonson's *Sad Shepherd*, 'the dialect of which is in a great measure northern' (Nares). *Tent* in *Hamlet* II. ii. end, and *tent* in *Coriol.* III. ii. are both different words.

    rin. The Mæso-Gothic—that is, the oldest extant Gothic—form is *rinnan*. See Skeat's *M. G. Gloss.*

    31. *cannie* is probably from the same root as *can*, *ken*, Mæs. Goth. *kunnan*.

    neebor town. See note to *Prothal.* 112.

    34. *braw* = *brave*, in the sense of *fine*. As often in Shaksp., *e.g. Hen. V.* IV. iv. 40: "*brave* crowns." See Trench's *Sel. Gloss.*

35. *Sair-won* = dear-won, hard-earned.

penny-fee = wages paid in money (Jamieson). *Penny* is used vaguely for *money*. A *penny-wedding* is a wedding at which the guests contribute money for their entertainment, a matrimonial ἔρανος. A *penny-friend* is one who has money in view in his friendship. *Fee* here = hire, wages. Of both words the most primitive meaning is *cattle*; Comp. Lat. *pecunia*.

deposite. Obs. the accentuation. So on the other side the Tweed you may hear *cómmittee, ásylum, mágazine,* &c.

38. *speirs* is from the Oldest Eng. *spirian* to tread on the heels (*spur* and *spurn* are of the same family), to track, investigate, &c. *Speer* is in use in the Northern counties of England. For an instance of it in literature, see *Percy Fol. MS.* ii. 528, *Guy and Cole-brande:*

> "And euer he *sperred* priuilicke
> How they ffared att Warwicke
> And how they liued there."

40. *uncos* = uncouth, *i. e.* unknown things = news; see note to *L'Alleg.* 5.

44. *amaist* = almost. [Explain how almost (= all-most) comes to mean *nearly*].

gars = makes, compels. The word is common in the North counties of England: see *John de Reeve*, a Northern Tale, scene partly in Durham, in the *Percy Fol. MS.* 564:

> "And if you be sturdy and stout,
> I shall *garr* you to stand without
> Ffor ought that you can say."

It is of Norse extraction.

the new. In Southern Eng. we should not use the article here.

47. *younker.* Shakspere uses this word in a contemptuous sense, as 1 *Hen. IV.* III. iii. 90: "what, will you make a *younker* of me?" Chapman uses it for *youngsters;* which form has superseded it in Southern English. *Youngling* is used of all young animals, most commonly of non-human; but see l. 155. Perhaps the Elizabethan *younker* had often the secondary sense of gallant, &c.; comp. the Greek νεανιεύομαι. Trench compares the Germ. *junker* (see *Sel. Gloss.*). For the form, perhaps *younker* is but a various form of *younger*. We speak of an *elder;* why not of a *younger?* We say colloquially "juniors" as well as "seniors." In *Merch. of Ven.* II. vi. 14, the 1623 Fol. reads "a *yonger* or a prodigall." Comp. *hang* and *hanker, segment* and *sect,* &c. Trench makes the Germ. junker = Jung-Herr, which is surely a derivation worthy of medieval etymology.

48. *eydent* = diligent. This word is current in Northumberland; see Halliwell's *Prov. & Arch. Dict.* Jamieson gives as other forms *ithand, ythen, ythand.* It is of Norse origin.

49. *jauk* = trifle. Jamieson refers it to Isl. *jack-a* "continuo agitare," or Teut. *gack-en* "ludere." Could it not be a corruption of *joke?*

50. [*alway.* Is this form strictly correct?]
He here passes from the "oblique" to the "direct" form of narration. So Virg. *Æn.* viii. 293, *Par. Lost,* iv. 724, &c.

51. *duty* is here used in a concrete sense = expression of dutifulness. Comp. Spenser, *F. Q.*

> "They both at once
> Did *duty* to their lady as became."

The expression of piety meant here is prayers.

52. *gang.* The Oldest Eng. *gangan,* Dutch *gaan,* Germ. *gehen. Gang* is still common in N. Prov. Eng. The subst. *gang* (= a company, usually of villains) meant originally a band of persons *going together;* comp. *Acts of the Ap.* ix. 2, xxii. 4. Comp. *gangway.* Strange, but it seems true, that the name of the Indian river *Ganges* is ultimately cognate.

54. *aright.* Comp. *aloft, across, athwart,* &c.

59. *the conscious flame.* This was a favourite use of *conscious* in the last century—a use derived from the Latin poets ; e. g. *Catull.* lxiv. 24, when the apple, given a maiden by her lover and hidden away in her bosom, being forgotten, slips out as she too hastily starts up on her mother coming in :

> " Illud prono præceps agitur decursu,
> Huic manat tristi *conscius* ore rubor."

Ovid's *Heroid.* xviii. 105, &c. [What is the exact force of *conscious* here, and in such uses ?]

62. *hafflins* = half. On the adverbial term *lins,* see note in *Sidelong, Des. Vill.* 29. See *The Holy Fair:*

> " Altho' his carnal wit an' sense
> Like *hafflins*-wise o'ercomes him
> At times that day."

hafflin = half grown (see *Jamieson*) is either a distinct cognate word or this same advb. used adjectively, as *darkling* and *groveling* are used.

64. *ben* = the inner part of the house, from the Oldest Eng. *binnan* within; in Dutch *kom-binnen* = to "walk in ;" *binnen-kamer* = inner room, &c. See *Waverley Novels, passim.* *To bring far ben* = to treat with the utmost respect and hospitality, lit. to admit to the very *penetralia* of one's house. The opposite of *ben* is *but.* See *The Holy Fair:*

> " Now *butt* an' *ben* the Change-house fills
> Wi' yill-caup [ale-cup] commentators."

In houses where there is but one room, and in this room a low partition-wall or screen running between the door and the fireplace in Lowland Scotch called *hallan*—just as is often the case in England in the chief room of village ale-houses (*e. g.* in the immortal "Rainbow" in *Silas Marner;* see chap. vii.)—*ben* meant the space on the fire-side, *but* that on the door-side of this *hallan* or screen.

65. *Strappan. Strapping,* and a subst. *strapper,* are common words in the English provinces.

takes. So in Bacon's *Ess.* xxxvii., see Wright's *Gloss.* (*Golden Treas. Series Ed.*) &c. Kindred is the use of the word for "to affect violently as by witchcraft," as several times in Shakspere. Indeed perhaps this latter was the older sense, and the former but derived from it, just as *fascinate* and *bewitch* have come to be used in a quite general meaning. [Give instances of *take* in the sense of *captivate* in the colloquial Eng. of to-day.]

66. *no,* the "A. S." *na.* is commonly used in Lowland Scotch as the negative adverb. In Southern English we prefer the compound word *not,* "A. S." *ndht* = ne-áht; comp. French *ne point, ne pas.*

67. For the father's conversation, comp. Tennyson's *Brook.*

cracks = talks. So *crack* as a subst. in *The Holy Fair,* &c. Shakspere uses the verb in the sense of to boast, as in *Love's L. L.* IV. iii. 268 :

> " And Ethiops of their sweet complexion *crack.*"

Comp. *Cymb.* V. v. 177 :

> " Either our brags
> Were *crack'd* of kitchen-trulls or," &c.

Perhaps *crack* in such phrases as "a crack player," &c. = cracked = boasted, *i. e.* who is a common subject of boasting.

kye. In Oldest Eng. (= "A. S.") the sing. was *cu,* the plur. *cy.* Robert of Brunne has pl. *kie* (Stratmann). Perhaps *kine* was a double plural. = kie-en; or perhaps it was another form of the pl. formed straight from the sing., cu-en = ķine. In the Romance of *Alisaunde apud* Weber *kuyn* is used; l. 760:

> " Oxen, schep, and eke *kuyn*
> Mony on he dude slen."

In *Vis. P. P.* 4076, ed. Wright is *kyen.* The old Frisian pl. is *kij.*

114. 68. *youngster.* The termination *ster* is said to be properly *fem.*, as still in *spinster;* thus *younger* or *younker* would = *puer, youngster = puella.* But this feminine force seems to have decayed at a very early period.

69. *blate*, also written *blait, bleat* = bashful. It is from Oldest Eng. *bledᵹ* gentle, slow, sluggish (Bosworth). Layamon uses it.

laithfu' = loathful = reluctant, unwilling, shy. We use *loath* in a much stronger sense.

72. *lave* is from the Oldest Eng. *laf* = what is *left* (from *leave*, "A. S." læfan, as *reliquus* from relinquo, λοῖπος from λείπω).

80. *in others' arms.* Comp. l. 38.

93. *soupe* (or, sup), here means the *milk*, the liquid element in the entertainment. The word is used generally for "spoon-meat." The Oldest Eng. *supar* is akin to Germ. *saufen* *Sup, supper, soup, sop,* are all ultimately connected.

hawkie denotes properly a cow with a white face. So in Northumb. *Bawsand* was used of an animal with a white spot on its forehead. *Crummie* for a cow with crooked horns.

94. *hallen.* See note on *ben,* l. 64. The word is said to be connected with *haell,* "the stone at the threshold."

96. *weel-hain'd* = well-spared, carefully kept. Primitively *hain* perhaps = to hedge or enclose. See *haining* and *hainite* in Jamieson.

kebback = cheese, from Gael. *cabag.* So *mattock* from Kel. *madog.*

fell = tasty; strictly, biting, in which sense it is used in Northumb. In the general Eng. usage *fell* has only a bad sense, and is applied only to living things and to feelings and actions, or to other things with a moral reference.

99. *towmond* = tolmond or tolmonth = twal-month, twelve-month. *Towmond auld* is made into one word, viz. *towmondall* = a yearling. (Jamieson.)

sin' lint was i' the bell = since flax was in flower. She means that the cheese was a year old *last* flax blossoming, as we might say. Strictly *sin'* should be *when;* but it is easy to see how *sin'* was employed. Obs. how, conversely, in Latin *quum* sometimes = *since*, and in Greek how ἐπεί, as in Æsch. *Agam.* 40.

103. *ha'-Bible*, strictly the hall-Bible, *i. e.* the Bible kept in the hall or chief room (not what we call the hall), was used generally for what is called in England the Family Bible.

104. *bonnet.* See note to *Lycid.* 104.

105. *lyart* = grey, or mixed grey, Hamlet's "sable-silvered." *Liard* is used for a grey horse in Old Eng.

haffets = temples; = perhaps the middle of the head, lit. half-heads, from "A. S." *healf-heafod*, 'the fore part of the head' (Bosworth).

115. 107. *wales* = chooses. M. G. *waljan;* Germ. *wåhlen.* The word is found in Old Eng.

109. [What does he mean by *guise* here?]

113. *beets the flame* = supplies the flame with fuel. See Burns' *Ep. to Davie, a brother Peat:*

> " It warms me, it charms me
>   To mention but her ['my darling Jean's'] name:
> It heets me, it *beets* me,
>   And sets me a' on flame."

Betan fyr is found in Oldest Eng. in this sense. So in Chaucer, *C. T.* 2255 :

> " I wol do sacrifice and fyres *beete*."

Originally, *betan* = to better, to mend, &c. The root appears in *better, best, boot,* &c. See *Piers Pl.* VI. 239, Clar. Press, ed. Skeat.

117. [Find the passages referred to in these two stanzas?]
135. See *Revelations* xviii.
126. [What is the meaning of *theme* here?   What is its more common use?]
133. [Where is *Patmos*?]
138. See Pope.
143. *society* = social enjoyment, *not* company.
144. [What is meant by *sphere* here?]

116. 149. *The Power.* So Dryden, *Pal. and Arc.* iii. 267, of Diana :

> " *The Power*, behold ! *the Power* in glory shone
>   By her bent bow and her keen arrows known."

150. *stole.* See note to *Il Pens.* 35.
154. *take off.* Comp. *start off*, ἀποβαίνω, *discedo,* &c.
     [What is the force of *off* here?
165. See *Des. Vill.* 53.
166. See Pope, *Essay on Man,* iv. 247.
168. So the last century believed.
182. *Wallace.* Burns' admiration for Wallace was profound. The feeling was partly local perhaps, for Wallace was an Ayrshire hero, but it was also national.

THE TWA DOGS.

This piece was written in 1786.

Here Burns gives his humour play. The tables are turned, and a couple of dogs discuss with fine discernment and powerful moral sense the lives and fortunes of their masters. In sincerity and depth the dialogue is certainly superior to that by Cervantes between Scipio and Berganza "dogs of the Hospital of the Resurrection in the city of Valladolid, commonly called the dogs of Mahudes." (See Cervantes' *Exemplary Novels.*) In this latter work there is much shrewd observation, and worldly knowledge ; but the true pathos that underlies Burns' poem is wanting. Perhaps in no one of his works are Burns' breadth of sympathy, upright manliness, and practical wisdom better shown. Even like Saint Francis, he sees in all creation his fellows ; or, as Wordsworth of himself in a certain mood, Burns might say ;

> " To her fair works did Nature link
>   The human soul that through me ran."

He was the "poor earth-born companion and fellow-mortal" of the mouse ; in the fate of the Daisy, down-turned by the plough, he saw his own ; and so here, these canine critics, are they not dogs and brothers? Does he not shew that in lives beyond the outwardly human all there may be humanity?

> " My heart has been sae fain to see them,"

says Luath, after most genially describing the New Year's merry-making :

> " That I for joy hae barkit wi'. em."

There is no affectation in the picture he gives of cottage life ; there is neither any little-minded discontent, nor yet any over-strained laudation. He sees keenly enough the distresses that beset the humble tenant; but he sees with equal clearness compensating happinesses. His eyes are not dazzled by rank or riches.

> " Regem non faciunt opes,
> Non vestis Tyria color
> Non frontis nota regiæ,
> Non auro nitidæ trabes. "

All that can really brighten and ennoble life may be found, he thinks, in the cottage; for mere tinsel and trappings he does not care:

> " To make a happy fire-side clime
> To weans and wife ;
> That's the true pathos and sublime
> Of human life. "

Thus Burns, whilst a national and a universal poet, is yet in a special sense the poet of the peasant.

117. 1. The place meant here is a part of Ayrshire—elsewhere Burns calls it *Coila;* see *Globe Ed.* p. 79. There are several *Kyles* in Scotland, *e. g.* Kyle Akin, Kyle of Bute, Kyle Durness, Kyle Rea, Kyle Shin, Kyle Sutherland, Kyle Tongue. The word properly signifies a sound, a strait. Jamieson mentions in connection with it the Gael. *caolas,* and the Isl. *Kyll* "gurges." With regard to its use in Ayrshire, perhaps it originally denoted the strait between Arran and the opposite mainland, now called the Firth of Clyde, and then became attached to that mainland. Then the name so given to the Ayrshire shore was popularly explained as derived from some old King, just as Britannia from Brutus, Italia from Italus, &c. &c. *Coil* is mentioned in *The Black Book of Caermarthen*:

> " Whose is the Grave on the slope of the hill?
> Many who knew it do not ask.
> The grave of *Coel*, the son of Cynvelyn. "

(M. Arnold quotes a neighbouring verse in his *Study of Celtic Literature.*) ' Boece tells us : "*Kyl* dein proxima est vel *Coil* potius nominata, a Coilo Britannorum rege ibi in pugna cæso," and a circular mound at Coilsfield, in the parish of Tarbolton, on the highest point of which are two large stones, and in which sepulchral remains have been found, is pointed out by local tradition as his tomb. The name of "Auld King Coil" is also perpetuated in the crags of Kyle, the burn of Coyl, and the parish of Coylton.' (Glennie's *Essay on Arthurian Localities.*) So Buchanan says of *Coila* (which he places between *Glottiana* and *Gallovidia*), that the British king, Coilus, overthrown by the Picts and Scots, "regionem in qua pugnatum est de suo nomine celebrem fecit," (*Rerum Scot. Hist.* Lib. iv.). This name occurs also in Geoffrey of Monmouth's *List of old British Kings,* chap. xix., after "Catellus *Coillus.*" He makes another Coillus, son of Marius, and father of Lucius, the first Christianized king of Britain. A third is mentioned as the father of the famous Helena, whom Constantius married, of which wedlock came Constantine. This last monarch Spenser mentions in his *Chronicle of Briton Kings,* in *F.Q.* II. x. 58 and 59, deriving the name Coylchester from him. It is by no means intended to suggest that this so common an old Keltic (it would seem Gaelic) king's name is really derived from *Kyle,* but only that that derivation was the reason for localizing him in Ayrshire. In the old days chroniclers and tradition-mongers were the mere victims of any similarity of names.

'Twas in, &c. See note to *Alex. Feast,* 1.

4. [With what *subst.* does the part. *wearing* "agree?"]

5. *thrang* = busy. So in Lancashire, where is used the form *throng* also. Lite-

rally = pressed, crowded (from A.S. *thringan*). Of course the common Eng. *throng* = a crowd is closely cognate. Comp. the secondary sense of ὅχλος, as in Eur. *Med.* 337 :

"ὅχλον παρέξεις, ὡς ἔοικας, ὦ γύναι – "

and how the Lat. *turba* is used.

6. *forgather'd.* This prefix—*for*— was once very common in Eng.; see the instances given by Stratmann. It answers to the Germ. *ver.*

8. *keepit.* So in the *Brus: redressyt, governyt, enbuschyt,* &c.

9. *lugs* = ears; so in North Eng. It also = the handles of pitchers. Comp. Gr. οὖς, ἀμφῶτις, and the use of *aurts* in *Georg.* i. 172. *Lug,* according to Wedgwood, is properly "the flap or hanging portion of the ear." "To *lug* a thing along is probably to pull it along by an ear or any loose part employed as a handle, but it might be to trail, or drag along the ground, as Swiss *lugger.*" *Luggage, lug-sail, lugger,* are all connected with *lug.*

11. *whelpit* = whelped. [What part of the verb is it here ?]

12. [What place is meant?]

14. [What is the force of *the* here ?]

16. *the fient a pride* = perhaps, the "devil a bit" of pride. Or does it mean "the devil take pride," as the negative is so sufficiently given by the following "na"? *A* is very common for *have.* Were the former the sense, perhaps the phrase, would rather be "fient a bit," or "fient hait," or "deil hait" (as in the *Antiquary,* chap. 44, when Edie Ochiltree is asked what he hopes to get from Lovel for his services : "*Deil haet* do I expect.") But, of course, that sense is possible enough—perhaps it is preferable; *a* = *of,* and *the fient* = fiendish, or devilish little = not a whit. Comp. *Twelfth Night,* II. iii., where Maria says of Malvolio : "*The devil a puritan* that he is, or anything constantly but a time-pleaser." In this and such uses the phrase, *the devil,* denotes excess, and so may be used either as a violent intensive, or a violent negative. Thus, "Thou most excellent devil of wit," in *Twelfth Night,* II. v. end, = thou superlative wit, &c. The negative sense is common in the old plays, &c. With this twofold use springing out of that idea of *excess,* comp. the use of *male* in Latin, and δυσ- in Greek—*e. g.,* see what the commentators say of "*male* pinguis" in *Georg.* i. 105. Comp. "*male metuo*" in Ter. *Hec.* III. ii. 2 = "I am terribly afraid," and "*male* raucus," *Hor. Sat.* I. iv. 66, on the one hand, with "*male* sanus," "statio *male* fida carinis " (*Æn.* ii. 23), on the other. Observe the two senses of δυσέρως. Usually when this very strong English phrase is used in a negative sense, it is placed first in its clause, or sentence.

18. *messin,* "a dog of mixed breeds." Gloss. *Burns,* Globe Ed. Jamieson suggests two derivations : (i.) from Messina, "whence this species was brought;" (ii.) from the Fr. *maison.* Halliwell gives "messet" = a cur, as used by Hall in his poems, 1646, and "still in use."

18. *smiddie.* Obs. the German form *Schmiede.*

20. *tawted* = shaggy, unkempt, Other forms are *tawtie* and *tatty.* Jamieson connects it with the Islandic word for to *tease* wool.

duddie, ragged. *Dudds* = garments, strictly = rags. So *dudes* in North Eng.

21. *stan't* = stand it = go on standing. In this use of *it,* on which see note to *trip it, L'Alleg.* 33, there is often the idea of continuance.

22. *stroan't.* So Launce's dog Crab, when he had "thrust me himself into the company of three or four gentleman-like dogs under the duke's table." *Two G. of V.* IV. iv. beg.; only in Cæsar's case there was no offence.

23. *the tither. Tither,* the prov. Eng. *tother,* is a crasis of *the other:* so *tae* of the one. In course of time the meaning of the initial *t* was forgotten, and the words used as primitive. Thus, *Old Mortality,* chap. xiii.: "Wi' the pistol and the whinger in *the tae* hand, and the Bible in *the tother,*" &c. It is possible, however, that *the tother* = that other, &c.

collie = a country dog. A word of Gaelic descent, according to Jamieson.

24. *billie* = companion, good fellow. See *Minstrelsy of the S. B., passim.* So in North of Eng.

27. Luath was the name of Cuchullin's dog in Ossian's *Fingal.*

28. When he adds *Lord knows how long*, he is no doubt thinking of the doubts that prevailed of the genuineness and the authenticity of Macpherson's *Ossian.* Certainly it might well be questioned whether there was more Ossian or Macpherson in them.

29. *gnst* = sagacious. Perhaps derived from Old Fr. *gas*, which Roquefort and also Burguy connect with *gab*. Could it possibly be derived from *sagacious, sagax*, by decapitation? Comp. *centum* from *decem-tum, van* from *avant, drake* from *ened-ric, tent* from *attend*, &c., &c.

30 *lup.* The old strong pret. Mause uses the corresponding part. in her famous quotation : "'Through the help of the Lord I have *luppen* ower a wall." (*Old M.*, chap. xiv.)

sheugh = trench. Another form is *seuch.*

118. 31. *sonsie* is from *sons* or *sonce,* a word of Gaelic origin, meaning prosperity, good luck, &c.

baws'nt. See note on *hawkie, Cotter's S. N.* 93. See Wedgwood *s.v.*

33. *towzie* = shaggy.

35. *gawcie* = large, thick. In the *Holy Fair* it means plump, comfortable-looking :

> " In comes a *gaucie* gash guidwife,
> An' sits down by the fire."

36. *hurdies* = hips.

38. *pack.* The idea is the same as in *thick*, and in our *" close* familiarity."

unco. See note *L'Alleg.* 5.

39 *whiles.* This is an old noun-case used adverbially; so *needs, whilom, seldom;* so often in Greek and in Latin.

snowkit. The *Prompt. Parv.* gives "snokyn or smelling, K. P. *nicto."* Mr. Way quotes from the Ortus ; " Nicto, to *snoke*, as houndes dooth when following game," and from Goulman: " Indago to *snook*, to seek or search, to vent, to seek out as a hound doth." In this sense *snook* is used in Lincolnshire.

40. *moudieworts* = moles. Other forms are *mowdiewarks, modywarts.* These forms are mere variations, and *mole* is in fact but a corruption of the first syllable of *mould-warp* = mold or earth thrower or caster. Shakspere has *moldwarp* once, 1 *Hen. IV.* III. i. For the dropping off of the *warp*, comp. *map* for mappe-monde = mappa mundi), *canker* for canker-worm, &c.

howkit = holked = digged. The root is seen in *hole, hollow.*

43. *daffin* = fun, folly, &c. The word is used in Northumb. *Daft* occurs in various dialects for *foolish, stupid.* See *Piers the Plowman*, I. 138, ed. Skeat:

> "Thou doted *daffe*, quod she, dulle arne thi wittes."

Chaucer's *Clerke's Tale :*

> " Beth not *bedaffed* for your innocence."

Daffe in *Prompt. Parv.* is defined as = " dastard, or he that spekythe not yn tyme." Mr. Skeat, in his Clar. Press *P. P.* Glossary, points out that *deaf* is cognate.

44. [What is the common Eng. form of *knowe?* Quote, or find, similar instances of liquefaction.]

50. *ava* = *av-a'* = *of all*, much in the sense of the common Eng. *at all.* This phrase, from its very nature, is used only in questions (direct and indirect), in conditional, and in negative sentences ; comp. the use of the indef. *quid* in Latin, *du tout* in French. For the form the Scotch and the French approach each other most nearly. *At all* is an adverbial form of *all*, used with certain restrictions ; comp. Lat. *omnino*, Gk. πάντως. *At* is frequently so employed to form adverbs, as *at length, at last, at first*, &c. With *at all* comp. especially

at least. *All* in negative and quasi-negative sentences often has the sense of *any;* so πᾶς (as the N.T. οὐ δικαιωθήσεται πᾶσα σάρξ κ.τ.λ.—*Rom.* iii. 20), *omnis* (as in *sine omni*, etc., in Plaut., Ter., and Ovid). Thus *at all* = in any wise, anyhow. Lowland Scotch adverbializes *all* by means of the prep. *of.* In *Cant. Tales*, 5628, the prep. *in* is used. But, perhaps more probably, *ava* = Anct. Eng. *awa, ava,* always, ever. Comp. Mæs. G. *aiw*, Lat. *ævum*, Gr. αἰών.

51. *racked rents* = rents raised to the greatest possible amount; lit. rents strained, drawn out to the utmost. Comp. *M. of Ven.* I. i. 180 :

> " Try what my credit can in Venice do,
> That shall be *rack'd* even to the uttermost."

rent is close cognate with *render*, Low Lat. *rendo*, Lat. *reddo*.

52. *kain* or *cane*, or *canage* = "a duty paid by a tenant to his landlord in kind," as "cane cheese," "cane fowls," &c. (Jamieson). Kain bairns = children paid as tribute by witches to their lord the devil. See *Bord Minst.*

stents = "assessments, dues" (Gloss. *Burns*, Globe Edn.). Jamieson derives the word from *extendere* in the sense of "æstimare, appretiare." Comp. *cess* from *assess*. The *Promp. Parv.* gives "stente or certeyne of valwe ordrede and other lyke (of value or dette), *taxacio*."

54. *at the bell.* Comp. *Marmion*, III. xxix. :

> " Blithe would I battle, for the right
> To ask one question *at* the sprite—"

57. *steeks* = interstices, reticulations; strictly = *stitches. Steek*, or *steik, stitch, stick*, are all various forms from Ancient Eng. *stician*. With *stick* and *stitch*, comp. *brig* and *bridge*, *læccan* and *latch, thack* and *thatch*, &c.

58. *keeks* = peeps. The word is used in Northumb. *Intueri* is the equivalent given by the *Promp. Parv.* In Dutch there is *Kijken.*

[*Geordie.* Give other instances, both ancient and modern, of coins being called after the monarchs uttering them.]

59. [*its.* Try to explain the use of *its*].

but is a shortened form of *butan* = be-outan = except.

61. *stechin* = cramming. "O. Teut. staecken, stipare." (Jamieson.)

[What is the exact force of the imperfect Present tense here?]

62. *pechan* = stomach.

63. *ragouts* = radically, things to revive the appetite. The stem of the latter syllable is *gustus.*

trashtrie. For the *trie*, the *t* is an "auxiliary (inorganic) consonant," as the *d* in gender, Fr. *gendre, number*, &c., *i.e.* trashtrie = trashrie. (See Peile's *Introd. to Greek and Latin Etymology*, Lect. xiv.); the *rie* or *ry* is a termination with a collective, and so sometimes a generalising force. Comp. *chivalry, cavalry, infantry, peasantry, heraldry, yeomanry, Irishry, rivalry, Jewry, gentry;* so *pastry*. Comp. Fr. *gaucherie, causerie*, &c. So *wastrie* in the following line. Comp. Lowland S. *snastry.*

65. *wonner* = wonder, here in a contemptuous sense. So elsewhere Burns uses *ferlie.* Comp. how *uncouth*, βάρβαρος, Fr. *outré*, &c. come to have a bad meaning. Whatever is unusual and so excites surprise is apt to be despised. These words express the very spirit of conventionality. "I am surprised, or astonished, or amazed, at your conduct," as a rule, = "I am much dissatisfied with it."

66. *elf.* Comp. the sense of δαιμόνιος, as in *Iliad.* ii. 190:

> δαιμόνι', οὔ σε ἔοικε κακὸν ὣς δειδίσσεσθαι.

Similar perhaps is the history of *wight;* see Trench's *Select Gloss. s. v.*

69. *painch.* So *hainch.*

110. 71. *fash't* = troubled. It is used in Northumb. It is from the Fr. *facher.*

[What is the force of *eneugh* or *enough* here?]

72. *sheugh* or *seuch* = a furrow, a ditch; see above, l. 30.

73. *dyke* = wall. So in some parts of England. Radically, *dike* is connected with *dig*, and denotes perhaps first the ditch dug (= Lat. *fossa*), then the mound, formed of the earth thrown up out of the ditch (= Lat. *agger*, also *vallum* when stockaded).

76. *smytrie* = "a numerous collection of small individuals" (Jamieson). The stem is *smyte*, a small bit, a particle; for the *rie* see above on *trashtrie*.

 duddie, see above, l. 20.

77. *darg* or *dark* is said to be a corruption of *day-wark*.

77. [What is the grammatical construction of *nought but his han' darg*?]

78. *in thack an' rape* = under a good roof. *Thack* = thatch. *Rape* or *rap* or *raip* = rope; in this phrase, the rope with which the thatch was fastened on to the rafters and walls.

81. *maist* = most = here, almost.

82. *maun.* Other forms are *mon*, *mun*, *mune*. In one form or another the word prevails in North English dialects in the sense of the Southern *must*. It is an Old Norse verb.

82. *o'*. We should say *with*; but we say "he died of a fever," &c. For various old uses of *of*, see Wright's *Bible Word-book*.

85. *buirdly* or *burdly* = "large and well-made;" so Jamieson, who makes it of Icelandic origin.

 chiels, radically, = children, then *servants* (comp. *puer*, πᾶις, *knave*, *garçon*, &c.), then, generally, fellows.

 hizzies = huzzies = housewives.

87. *negleckit.* It is not uncommon in England to hear imperfectly-educated persons say "objec," "subjec," &c. In all languages, both in their literary and their provincial forms, such signs of a desire for easier articulation may be found. See Max Müller's *Lectures on the Science of Language*, 2nd Series.

92. *brook* = badger.

94. Comp. *Chevy Chase:*

  "For Widrington my heart is woe," &c.

96. *thole* = suffer, from Ancient Eng. *tholian.*

Burns is here doubtless thinking of certain bitter experiences of his own youth during his father's tenure of Mount Oliphant farm.

[What is the common Eng. name for such an agent as is called a *factor* here?]

snast = abuse, from the "Sueo-Gothic," according to Jamieson.

98. *poind* = distrain, lit. *pound*, shut up, from Ancient Eng. *pyndan*, to shut up.

104. *poortith* = poverty. Another form is *purtye* (Old Fr. *pourté*). Perhaps *poortith* is formed from this form *purtye*, the *-th* being a secondary substantival affix, the French form being Englished by this affix, so common in English words, as *youth* (= young-th), *tealth, length, strength, tilth*, &c. Comp. bountith.

120. 105. [What is there noticeable in this line as compared with the common English usage? How would you explain it?]

110. *blink.* In common English *twinkling* is used for a very short space of time.

112. *grushie* = "of thriving growth." Another form used is *grush*. It is from the same root as *gross, grow, great*, Germ. *gross*, &c. In Old. Eng. *gross* = simply, large, as in *King Lear*, IV. vi. 14.

113. *just.* This adverb is now so commonly used by Scotchmen, as to be specially characteristic. Such phrases as "it was just delightful," "I was just weary of it," &c., at once indicate the nationality of the speaker. An Englishman qualifies certain adverbs as *now*, *enough*, by *just*; and also verbs, as "I just touched him," &c.; with *adjs.* he scarcely uses it at all.

115. *nappie* = fine ale. Strictly, nappy is an adj. signifying strong—"noppy (as ale is), *vigoureux*" (Palsgrave). Burns speaks of a "nappie callan" = strong boy. In a song called

The Tale of the Cobbler and the Vicar of Bray, ascribed erroneously to "Hudibras" Butler, is the phrase *nappy ale:*

> "A dozen of your *nappy ale*
> Will set 'em right again."

Halliwell and Wright in their ed. of Nares' *Glossary* quote from *Harry White's Humour,* 1659:

> "M.P. wisheth happy
> Successe and ale *nappy,*
> That with the one's paine
> He the other may gaine—"

An old 'Borough' proverb runs:

> "The nappy strong ale of Southwark
> Keeps many a gossip frae the kirk."

But commonly the *ale* is understood; comp. Lat. *merum, mulsum,* Gr. ἀκρατος, and especially Eng. *Stout.* Halliwell and Wright apparently (see l. c.) derive *nappy* from *nap,* as = nap-inspiring, sleepy-making. Johnson makes it = spumy, frothy, from *nap* down, &c. Lye, quoted by Johnson, refers it to A. S. *nappe,* a cup.

122. *ferlie* = wonder. The word occurs in Old English, and in Northumberland now. *Fer-lie* is the Ancient Eng. *faer-lic* = *fear-like.*

123. [When is *Hallowmas?* Derive, and illustrate the name.]
See Burns' *Halloween.*

124. *kirns* = Harvest-home feasts. See the phrases *cry the kirn,* and *win the kirn,* and *kirn-dollie apud* Jamieson.
See Burns' *Scotch Drink:*

> "That merry night we get the corn in!
> O sweetly then thou reams the horn in!
> Or reeking on a New-year mornin
>   In cog or bicker,
> An' just a wee drap sp'ritual burn in
>   An' gusty sucker."

126. [How can the *singular verb* be defended here?]

127. *blinks* = glances. Comp. "ae *blink* o' the bonie burdies" in *Tam o' Shanter.* So in common English *twinkle,* as in Dryden's *Don Sebastian:* "I come, I come; the least *twinkle* had brought me to thee." How different Burns' *blinker* (= a bright-glancing girl) from the Eng. *blinkard.*

slaps, as *hits* in *Love's L. L.* IV. i. 109—141.

131. *ream* = cream. The A. S. is *ream.* Perhaps the prefixed *c* is due to the weakening of *r* sound in Eng.—is, in fact, a compensation, some ringent sound being felt to be onomatopeically necessary. Hence in Lowland Scotch, where the *r* has not suffered such debilitation, the *c* has not been required.

reeks = smokes. Comp. Germ. *rauchan.*

133. *luntin* = smoke-emitting. Jamieson refers the subst. *lunt* to "Teut. *lonte,* fomes igniarius" = fuel, or "kindling," or "eldin."

mill = "a snuff-box, properly of a cylindrical form." So Jamieson, who connects with "Isl. *mel-ia* contundere, the box being formerly used in the country as a *mill* for grinding the dried tobacco leaves." But it is not necessary to go to Islandic for the root. "Miln" is found in Ancient English. Comp. Germ. *mühle.*

134. [To which subject does the predicate strictly apply? Quote other instances of such a *zeugma*].

135. *cantie* = cheerful. A word of Gaelic extraction, according to Jamieson.

crackin = chattering, gossiping. So in Norfolk (Halliwell). Often = talking boastfully; see note to *Cotter's S. N.* 67.

crouse = "merry, brisk, lively, bumptious." So Halliwell, who connects with *crus* wrathful—as in *Havelek*, 1966, where it has much the sense of *cross*.

· 136. *rantin.* See l. 24.

· 142. *fawsont* = "seemly." Gloss. *Burns*, Globe Ed.

121. 147. *ablins.* See note to *sidelong, Des. V.* 29. For the derivation, comp. Gk. δυνατῶς. *thrang.* See l. 5.

a = on. See note to *L Alleg.* 20.

148. *indenting* = selling; strictly, bargaining—as in 1 *Hen. IV.* I. iii. 86:

> "Shall we buy treasure? and *indent* with fears,
> When they have lost and forfeited themselves?"

The word is now not used except in its literal sense. The secondary sense arose from some custom of *notching* the edges of the parchment or paper on which contracts were drawn up. "The term indenture implies that the deed is of two parts, that is, two parts or copies exactly alike, and that the two parts were divided by the line to afford additional means of authentication." (*Standard Libr. Cycl. of Pol. Knowledge.*)

149. *haith* = faith, as in the following line. There is no class of words more liable to corruption than those containing *oaths*. With them affectation and caprice have their fullest sway. A perpetual tendency prevails to disguise the oath, as it were—to make the mere form of it nonsense. Observe such strange shapes as '*slud, zounds, oons*, &c., &c. Even so little outrageous an expression as "in faith" becomes *i'faith, faith, faix*, &c.

151. [*gaun.* What part of the verb is *gaun*?]

155. *daft.* See note, l. 43.

162. *guitar* is ultimately derived from the Gk. κιθαρά.

nowt = cattle; here bulls. Other Scotch forms are *nout* and *nolt* (used for black cattle]; see Jamieson. Comp. Eng. *neat*, Isl. *naut.*

163. See *The Traveller*, 152.

165. *bouses.* See "*bouzing* can" in *Faerie Q.* I. iv. 22, "quaff and *bowze*" in Harington's *Epigrams* (quoted in Nare's *Gloss.*, ed. Halliwell and Wright), "*bousy* poet." *apud* Dryden, "sup and *bowse* from horn and can" in Keats' lines on *The Mermaid Tavern*. Johnson quotes Dutch *buysen.*

drumly = muddy. The word is used in Northumb. (Halliwell) as a verb—in *Highland Mary:*

> "Ye banks and braes and streams around
> The Castle o' Montgomery,
> Green be your woods, and fair your flowers,
> Your waters never drumlie."

169. *hech.* Comp. *heigh-ho*, as in Amiens' song in *As you like it*, II. vii.

Dear sirs is a sort of wondering appeal to the world in general, just as *Ye gods, Great Heavens*, &c. to Heaven. The plural *sirs* occurs in Author. Version of the *Acts of the Apostles*, xiv. 15, &c., &c. In the Elizabethan poets it is sometimes used in addressing ladies. There is no etymological reason why it should not be so.

173. *aback* = on back = backward. Chaucer has this form.

176. *billies.* See above, l. 24.

177. *thae* = these.

178. *Fient.* See above, l. 16. *hait* = "the least thing." (Gloss. *Burns*, Globe Ed.) = whit, aught, A. S. aht, awhit. *Fient haet* = devil a bit. In l. 206 there is *deil haet.*

179. *timmer.* The *b* in the common form *timber* is merely auxiliary; see note on l. 63. *Timmer-man* = carpenter, &c. Here perhaps *timmer* = fences.

180. *limmer* = mistress. This word, used generally in a disparaging sense, is seemingly connected by Jamieson with *limm* = *limb*, i.e., a limb of Satan, a devil's limb. Comp. *imp*. But such a derivation seems much to be doubted. Ben Jonson uses *limmer*, *Sad Shepherd*, II. ii.

182. *Ne'er a bit.* See note to *Alex. Feast*, 70.

122. 185. *steer* = common Eng. *stir.*

188. [*The gentles.* Mention other adjectives that are treated so completely as substantives as to receive a plural inflection.]

189. [What is meant by *starve* here ?]

194. *for a'.* See note to *Hymn Nat.* 73.

197. *sturt* = *start*, *startle*, and so trouble, vex. See *Halloween*, of the bold Jamie Fleck :

> " He marches thro' amang the stacks,
> Tho' he was something *sturtin.*"

201. [How do you " scan " this line ?]

202. *dizzen* = a dozen " cuts " of yarn = a hank or hesp.

203. [Explain *warst* here.]

204. *e'n down* = downright. With the use of *even* comp. that of *flat* in such phrases as " a *flat* contradiction."

205. *lank* = languid. A. S. *hlanc* = lean, meagre. Germ. *Schlank.*

206. *deil haet.* See above, l. 178.

209. Horse Races have been our great national sport since the time of the Restoration at least.

213. *Cast out* = quarrel. *Outcast*, a quarrel (Jamieson). Wyntown uses to "cast words " in this sense ; comp. Swedish *ord kastas.* In " cast out," as used in the text, the object of the verb is omitted ; the " out " gives intensity. With this use of " cast " comp. Lat. *jacere* in such phrases as "in feminas inlustres probra jecerat." (Tac. *Ann.* xi. 13.)

214. *sowther* = solder (lit. make solid).

216. [What " part of speech " is *past* here ?]

218. [Explain *great* here. Comp. " great friends."]

220. [What part of the verb is *run* here ?]

jads. Wedgwood connects *jade* with the Lat. *ilia* through the Span. *ijada*, and so makes the radical meaning a panting broken-winded horse, one that "ilia ducit." (Hor. *Ep.* I. i. 9.)

221. Comp. *Rape of the Lock*, 297—306.

123. 223. *lee-lang* = livelong. See note to *sidelong*, *Des. V.*, and *Phil. Soc. Transactions* for 1862—3.

227. [Is there anything noticeable in the language of this line ?]

230. *gloamin*, A. S. *glomung.*

235. See *Cotter's S. N.* 154.

WILLIAM COWPER.

1731—1749. WILLIAM COWPER was born at Great Berkhamstead, Hertfordshire, Nov. 26, 1731. His father, the rector of that place, was a descendant of Sir William Cowper, the friend of Hooker. His mother, whose maiden name was Anne Donne, could trace her pedigree back to a royal house (see *On the Receipt of My Mother's Picture*, l. 108). For the pronunciation of his surname, up to the beginning of the 17th century, says his latest biographer, 'the name had been spelt *Cooper*, and it has never been pronounced otherwise by the family.' John Cowper of James I.'s time 'altered it probably in affectation of the Norman spelling "Cupere" or "Coupre," as the names appear in the roll of Battle Abbey. Many of the family, however, retained the old spelling for some time after. In Lord Campbell's *Life of Chancellor Cowper*, we have one or two letters signed "Wm. Cooper."' (Globe Ed. of *Cowper's Works*, xxi. note). It was the future poet's misfortune to lose his mother when he was but six years old; but he never lost the fondest memory of her. He was presently sent to a school at Market Street, and then to Westminster. Amongst his Westminster schoolfellows were Thornton, Lloyd, Colman and Churchill. His experience of public school life seems to have been bitter; see his *Tirocinium*. His bodily frame was not robust; he was of a highly sensitive disposition. Such a boy was ill fitted for the public school life of that time, perhaps for the public school life of any time.

2. 1749—1763. After leaving school, he was articled to an attorney for three years, but he preferred 'giggling and making giggle' with certain lady cousins to law studies. Then he took chambers in the Temple with the design of continuing, or really beginning those studies. Here some twelve years drifted away. At last his friends procured him an appointment in the Civil Service; this from nervousness he resigned; they procured him another—that of clerk of the journals to the House of Lords. A parliamentary dispute made it necessary for him to appear at the bar of the House of Lords to entitle him to the office. Before this necessity his strangely nervous nature succumbed. Towards the end of 1763, his reason giving way, it became advisable to commit him to complete medical care and supervision.

3. 1763—1780. After remaining some seven months in the house of Dr Cotton, at St Albans, his mind in some degree recovered its balance; but he was a changed man. He had undergone a great reaction. He had discovered with shame and remorse the frivolousness of his London life, and altogether shrunk from renewing it. Not unnaturally, he ran now into an opposite extreme, and was for a life devoted to religious exercises. At Huntingdon he became acquainted with the Unwins—a clergyman, his wife, and a son. In 1765 he became an inmate of their house. Mr Unwin being thrown from his horse and killed the following year, in 1767 Cowper and Mrs Unwin removed to Olney, a village on the Ouse in Buckinghamshire, well known by the poet's subsequent descriptions, that they might enjoy there the ghostly ministrations and counsel of the Rev. John Newton. There can be little doubt that Newton's society was harmful for Cowper. Newton was a man of a vigorous mind, of sincere piety, of genuine kindliness; he was certainly attached to Cowper; but, as compared with Cowper, it must be allowed that he was of a hard and unsensitive nature. In his earlier life he had been a slave-dealer. Such a man was ill-fitted

to deal with so delicate a temperament as that of his new parishioner. He might know how to train trees, but his hands were too robust and rude for flowers. Cowper's old disorder soon began to threaten him with a second attack. In 1773 the threat was fulfilled. 'Calvinistic doctrine and religious excitements threw an already trembling mind off its balance, and aggravated a malady which but for them might probably have been cured' (see 'Introductory Memoir' to Globe *Cowper*, p. xlii). Some six years passed before Cowper was himself again. In 1779 he was delivered from his well-meaning but injudicious director and friend, by that gentleman's presentation to the living of St Mary Woolnoth, London. It was after his Newton's departure, that Cowper, finding much leisure at his disposal, commenced writer.

4. 1780—1800. The decad beginning with the year 1780 was the great productive period of Cowper's life. In 1780 he wrote *The Progress of Error;* in the winter, 1780—1, *Truth, Table-Talk, Expostulation.* His first volume of Poems was published in 1782. It was when he was in the midst of these literary labours that Lady Austen first visited Olney. Their acquaintance ripened into the warmest friendship. In 1782 her ladyship came to reside in the village, and for some two years made Cowper's life bright with her gay sprightly presence. Would that that good angel had come to him sooner, and abode with him longer! The evil spirits that haunted Cowper were banished for the time. There was no hour for them, when Lady Austen played her harpsichord and sang, or enlivened the very air with her pleasant converse and sympathetic humour. It was she who told him the story of John Gilpin; and gave him the *Sofa* for a theme. Unhappily, this cheerful intimacy was abruptly ended in 1784. It would seem that there arose some jealousy between Lady Austen and Mrs Unwin; and Cowper, having to choose between his old friend and the new, did his duty firmly, with whatever sorrow. *The Task* was published in 1785, along with the *Tirocinium.* His next great work was his translation of *Homer;* this was published in 1791. Meanwhile, Mrs Unwin and he had removed to Weston, about two miles from Olney.

Presently his old malady began to return. During the last six years of his life it prevailed almost without intermission. In 1796 Mrs Unwin died, but he seemed almost unmoved; indeed his gloom could not be made deeper. In March, 1779, he wrote that most forlorn and unhoping poem, *The Castaway.* On April the 25th, 1800, his troubles ceased for ever.

Cowper was distinguished not only as a poet but as a letter-writer; indeed, in the epistolary literature of England he deserves and occupies the first place. His only rival is Horace Walpole; and when we consider first how different their lives were, how much fuller of suggestion and material Walpole's was, how seemingly dull and uninspiriting Cowper's, and, secondly, what license Walpole allows himself in his remarks and criticisms, how to be piquant he spares nothing and nobody, how, on the other hand, Cowper will not let an ill-natured word escape his pen, one cannot but claim for Cowper the praise of superior originality. He has succeeded in making the most eventless and unsuggestive life interesting, and this by no meretricious means—by no false colouring or extravagant ornament.

In his poems as in his letters truthfulness is one great characteristic charm of Cowper. The service he did to English literature by this thorough sincerity can scarcely be exaggerated. Perhaps his place in the history of our literature is higher than that he holds in that literature itself. In an age of poetic conventionality, of shallow theories, of soul-less practice, it was Cowper that inspired our poetry with a higher and nobler tone. Cowper began the needed reformation, which Wordsworth and Coleridge and Scott achieved. In this work he had one great coadjutor—Burns. The Ayrshire ploughman and the Buckinghamshire recluse, differing widely in character and genius, were in fact great allies. Their lives are alike in nothing but sadness. As poets they lived and worshipped the same sovereign mistress—

Truth. They would not prate of nature without knowing her; they would not pretend to passions of which they were unconscious; they would not take any part in the tricked-out masquerades of their day. It is pleasant to know that before his last attack of despondency overcame him, Cowper read Burns' volume of poems with much enjoyment. Lightness and grace may sometimes be wanting in Cowper's poetry, but that virtue of truthfulness is never wanting. Perhaps no writer is so absolutely free from affectation of every sort. Indeed his language occasionally suffers from his anxiety to be quite unartificial.

HEROISM.

This piece was published in Cowper's 1st volume, 1782.

124. 1 & 2. [Is there anything pleonastic here?]

7. *unctuous.* The metaphorical use of this word [what is that use?] is now-a-days almost superseding the primitive use. Johnson in his *Dict.* gives no instance of the secondary use.

9. [What part of the sentence is *hopes* ?]
11. *on a day.* See *L'Alleg.* 14.
13. *teem'd.* So *King Lear*, I. iv. 303:

> "If she must *teem*,
> Create her child of spleen,"

&c. Esp. comp. 1 *Hen. IV.* III. i. 26:

> "Diseased nature oftentimes breaks forth
> In strange eruptions; oft the *teeming* earth
> Is with a kind of colic pinch'd and vexed
> By the imprisoning of unruly wind
> Within her womb; which for enlargement striving
> Shakes the old beldam earth, and topples down
> Steeples and moss-grown towers."

See *Hymn Nat.* 240. From *teem* is derived *team*, or *teeme* as Spenser spells it. See *Pro-thal.* 63.

15. See the famous letter of the younger Pliny to Tacitus on his uncle's death (vi. 16).

21. *van* is from the Fr. *avant.*

25. *uninform'd* = uninspired with life, containing and developing no seeds. Comp. *inform'd*, *Par. Lost*, iii. 593:

> "Not all parts like, but all alike *inform'd*
> With radiant light, as glowing iron with fire."

and *o'erinformed* in *Abs. and Achit*, Part i.:

> "And *o'er-informed* the tenement of clay."

idle. Comp. Virgil's use of *segnis* in *Georg.* i. 72:

> "Et *segnem* patiere situ durescere campum."

125. 32. Strictly (but *pictoribus atque poetis*, &c.) he should have said *herds*, not *flocks*, or should have used some other part. than ruminating. [What is meant by *ruminant*? What animals belong to the genus *Ruminants*?]

41. *lure* = strictly, bait. Comp. Germ. *luder*.

65. *scourges*. It will be remembered that Alaric frankly assumed the title of the *Scourge of God*.

ON THE RECEIPT OF MY MOTHER'S PICTURE OUT OF NORFOLK.

Cowper says that he had more pleasure in writing this poem than any other of his except one, that one "Addressed to a lady who has supplied to me the place of my own mother—my own invaluable mother—these six-and-twenty years." (Probably the lines to Mrs Unwin, beginning *Mary! I want a lyre of other strings.*)

The letter, acknowledging the receipt of the Picture, is dated Weston, Feb. 27, 1790: "My dearest Rose whom I thought withered, and fallen from the stalk, but whom I find still alive: nothing could give me greater pleasure than to know it, and to learn it from yourself. I loved you dearly when you were a child, and love you not a jot the less for having ceased to be so. Every creature that bears any affinity to my mother is dear to me, and you, the daughter of her brother, are but one remove distant from her. I love you therefore, and love you much, both for her sake, and for your own. The world could not have furnished you with a present so acceptable to me, as the picture which you have so kindly sent me. I received it the night before last, and viewed it with a trepidation of nerves and spirits somewhat akin to what I should have felt, had the dear original presented herself to my embraces. I kissed it and hung it where it is the last object that I see at night, and of course the first on which I open my eyes in the morning. She died when I completed my sixth year; yet I remember her well, and am an ocular witness of the great fidelity of the copy. I remember too, a multitude of the maternal tendernesses which I received from her, and which have endeared her memory to me beyond expression. There is in me I believe more of the Donne than of the Cowper; and though I love all of both names, and have a thousand reasons to love those of my own name, yet I feel the bond of nature draw me vehemently to your side. I was thought in the days of my childhood much to resemble my mother, and in my natural temper, of which at the age of fifty-eight I must be supposed to be a competent judge, can trace both her and my late uncle, your father, somewhat of his irritability; and a little I would hope both of his and of her—I know not what to call it, without seeming to praise myself, which is not my intention, but speaking to *you* I will even speak out, and say—*good nature*. Add to all this, I deal much in poetry, as did our venerable ancestor, the Dean of St Paul's, and I think I shall have proved myself a Donne at all points. The truth is, that whatever I am, I love you all," &c. &c.

126. 1. *O that*, &c. This is an elliptic phrase for "how I wish that, &c." So in Lat. *si*, in Greek *εἰ*, are used, the principal verb being understood. "O" here is in fact a sign *expressing* a longing—a written representative of a sigh—a simpler, less developed way of uttering an emotion of regret; it has really contained in it both subject and predicate.

2. *but roughly*. In this and like phrases of recent and present English, the *but* has scarcely its full force. It rather tempers and qualifies the adverb or adj. with which it is used; whereas, radically, it should intensify. Thus "but roughly" is a softened way of saying "roughly;" strictly, it should be a more violent way; it should mean "roughly and nothing

else" — altogether roughly. *But* then in such uses strictly = nothing but = the Northern *nought but* or *nobbut* = only, merely. For instances of the pleonastic introduction of these last-mentioned equivalents into the same sentence with it, see *Shakespearian Grammar*, § 130. To this elliptic use of *but* there is something similar in that of the Greek ἀλλά in such passages as

ὦ θεοὶ πατρῷοι, συγγένεσθέ γ' ἀλλα νῦν.

10. [For what substantive does *it* stand here ?]

127. 16. *as*. This the common old usage, though now confined to poetry. In fact what is now expressed by the addition of *if* was once expressed by the subjunctive mood. See note to *Hymn Nat.* 81. For another instance in modern poetry see Hood's lines, "We watched her," &c. :

> "So silently we seemed to speak,
> So slowly moved about,
> *As* we had lent her half our powers
> To eke her being out."

19. *reverie* is derived from the French *rêver*, and so radically = dream ; but is limited to mean "a waking dream," the Gr. ὕπαρ.

29. *hearse*. See note to *Lyc.* 151.

33. *Adieus*. So *beaus*, *Rape of the L.* 653.

35. *pass my lips*. Comp. the Homeric phrase : ποῖόν σε ἔπος φύγεν ἕρκος ὀδόντων.

37. Comp. Tacitus' "Quod quisque vult, credit facillime."

46. Cowper's father d. 1756. Southey does not mention the date.

50. *bauble* is ultimately connected with *babe*.

coach is cognate with *couch*.

56. "I can truly say," said Cowper, nearly fifty years after his mother's death, "that not a week passes (perhaps I might with equal veracity say a day) in which I do not think of her : such was the impression her tenderness made upon me, though the opportunity she had for showing it was so short.'

128. 58. *nightly*. See note to *Hymn Nat.* 179.

67. [What is meant by *humour* here ?]

71. *numbers*. This was a conspicuous word in the poetic verbiage of the last century, which was attacked, by precept and also in his earlier works by example, by Wordsworth. See Johnson's *Lives of the Poets, passim*.

97. This line is taken, as Cowper points out, from Garth's *Dispensary*.

98. [What part of the sentence is *on the dangerous tide of life* ?]

108. Cowper's mother, through the Hippesleys, of Throughley, in Sussex, and the Pellats, of Bolney, in the same county, was "descended from the several noble houses of West, Knollys, Carey, Bullen, Howard, and Mowbray ; and so by four different lines from Henry III., King of England."

SAMUEL TAYLOR COLERIDGE.

(1) 1772—1794. COLERIDGE was born at Ottery St Mary, Devonshire, Oct. 21, 1772— Scott was born the year before, Wordsworth the year before that—the son of the Vicar and Head-Master of the King's School there. In 1782 he was sent to Christ's Hospital; in 1791 to Jesus College, Cambridge; in 1794 he left the University for good without taking a degree, after a curious escapade shortly before.

(2) 1794—1800. Cambridge deserted, Coleridge joined Southey at Bristol in a scheme for founding a Pantisocratic State at Susquehannah. Both men marrying—they married sisters—this fine bubble burst. Presently, for good as for evil, Coleridge's ardent radicalism sobered down. In 1797 he published a volume of poems in concert with his old school-friend Charles Lamb. About the same time he became acquainted with Wordsworth. That was the year of his greatest poetic productiveness. In 1798, that famous Volume, the *Lyrical Ballads*, was published. That same year Coleridge was enabled through the kindness of certain friends (the Wedgwoods) to set off for a sojourn in Germany.

(3) 1800—1816. He returned to England in 1800. He lived at divers places—London, Keswick, Calne, Malta, Rome—formed various literary schemes, devoted himself to various intellectual pursuits.

(4) 1816—1834. In 1816, his wife and family living up in the Lake country, Coleridge was received into the house of Mr Gillman, a surgeon residing at Highgate, that what could be done might be done to cure him of his excessive use of opium. There he remained to the end of his life. There he sat "as a kind of Magus, girt in mystery and enigma, his Dodona oak-grove . . . whispering strange things, uncertain whether oracles or jargon." (Carlyle's *Life of Sterling*.) To this last period of his life belong his *Two lay Sermons*, *Aids to Reflection*, *On the Constitution of Church and State according to the Idea of each*; but probably he exerted his greatest influence at this time through his conversations, or rather monologues. "He had, especially among young inquiring men, a higher than literary, a kind of prophetic, or magician, character." After a four years' long illness, on July 25, 1834:

> " Every mortal power of Coleridge
> Was frozen at its marvellous source;
> The rapt one, of the godlike forehead,
> The heaven-eyed creature sleeps in earth."

Poetry was with Coleridge but one of many pursuits; he did not take the Muse to him for better and for worse, and cleave only to her. It was only in his young manhood that he devoted himself to her; in the latter periods of his life political and critical and religious questions mainly occupied him. What of poetry he produced was of a singularly exquisite quality; but his works are a collection of fragments rather than complete achievements. He was for ever designing and plotting, not acting. He was conscious of his weakness in this respect, but had not strength to overcome it. He was a living Hamlet, full of the most splendid thoughts and the noblest purposes, but a most incompetent doer. "Carmen reliquum," he notes at the end of *The Three Graves, a fragment of a Sexton's Tale*, "in futurum tempus relegatum. To-morrow! and To-morrow! and To-morrow!" At the end of his introduction, 1816, to

Kubla Khan, or a Vision in a Dream, a fragment, he adds : "Yet from the still surviving recollections in his mind, the Author has frequently purposed to finish for himself what had been originally, as it were, given to him. Αὔριον ἄδιον ἄσω; but the to-morrow is yet to come." And it never came. The incompletion of *Christabel* is a severe loss to our literature. The two parts we happily possess are of wonderful beauty and power. They were the immediate inspiration of the *Lay of the last Minstrel.* ("It is to Mr Coleridge," writes Scott, "that I am bound to make the acknowledgement due from the pupil to his master"); and certainly Scott himself never succeeded in surrounding any one of his works with so fine an atmosphere of glamour and romance. Moreover, Coleridge's spiritual insight is incomparably profounder than that of Scott; he sounds depths of feeling and of thought beyond the reach of the Northern minstrel's plummet. In the scanty amount of what he produced Coleridge reminds one of Gray (see *Memoir of Gray*); but the causes of sterility were different. Gray suffered from fastidiousness; Coleridge rather from an overwhelming abundance of interests and ideas. "His mind," writes Southey, "is in a perpetual St Vitus' dance—eternal activity without action." If no man can serve two masters, still less can he serve half-a-dozen. "Ex pede Herculem;" in such a way we must be content to infer how splendid an artist was here in Coleridge.

THE ANCIENT MARINER.

Wordsworth gives the following account of the composition of this poem. "In reference to this poem, I will here mention one of the most noticeable facts in my own poetic history, and that of Mr Coleridge. In the autumn of 1797, he, my sister, and myself started from Alfoxden pretty late in the afternoon, with a view to visit Linton and the Valley of Stones near to it; and as our united funds were very small, we agreed to defray the expense of the tour by writing a poem to be sent to the *New Monthly Magazine* set up by Phillips the bookseller, and edited by Dr Aiken. Accordingly, we set off, and proceeded along the Quantock Hills, towards Watchet, and in the course of this walk was planned the poem of the 'Ancient Mariner,' founded on a dream, as Mr Coleridge said, of his friend Mr Cruikshank. Much the greatest part of the story was Mr Coleridge's invention; but certain parts I suggested; for example, some crime was to be committed which should bring upon the Old Navigator, as Coleridge afterwards delighted to call him, the spectral persecution, as a consequence of that crime and his own wanderings. I had been reading in Shelvocke's *Voyages* a day or two before, that while doubling Cape Horn, they frequently saw Albatrosses in that latitude, the largest sort of sea-fowl, some extending their wings twelve or thirteen feet. 'Suppose,' said I, 'you represent him as having killed one of these birds on entering the South Sea, and that the tutelary spirits of these regions take upon them to avenge the crime.' The incident was thought fit for the purpose, and adopted accordingly. I also suggested the navigation of the ship by the dead men, but do not recollect that I had anything more to do with the scheme of the poem. The gloss with which it was subsequently accompanied was not thought of by either of us at the time, at least not a hint of it was given to me, and I have no doubt it was a gratuitous after-thought. We began the composition together, on that to me memorable evening; I furnished two or three lines at the beginning of the poem, in particular:

> 'And listened like a three years' child,
> The Mariner had his will.'

These trifling contributions, all but one, Mr C. has with unnecessary scrupulosity recorded, slipped out of his mind, as well they might. As we endeavoured to proceed conjointly (I speak of the same evening), our respective manners proved so widely different, that it would have been quite presumptuous in me to do anything but separate from an undertaking upon which I could only have been a clog. We returned after a few days from a delightful tour, of which I have many pleasant, and some of them droll enough recollections. We returned by Duburton to Alfoxden. The 'Ancient Mariner' grew and grew till it became too important for our first object, which was limited to our expectation of five pounds; and we began to think of a volume, which was to consist, as Mr Coleridge has told the world, of poems chiefly on supernatural subjects, taken from common life, but looked at, as much as might be, through an imaginative medium Accordingly I wrote 'The Idiot Boy,' 'Her Eyes are Wild,' etc., and 'We are Seven,' 'The Thorn,' and some others."—*Memoirs of William Wordsworth, by Christopher Wordsworth, D.D.*

See also Coleridge's *Biographia Literaria*, Chap. xiv.

"Not only in matters of speculation," writes Mr. W. Rossetti, in his *Prefatory Notice* to his edition of Coleridge's *Poems*, "but in poetry as well, Coleridge has been assailed as an unmeasured and disingenuous borrower: for instance, the *Ancient Mariner*—which yields to none of his works in the salient appearances of originality—has been stated by De Quincey to be founded on a passage in the writings of Shelvocke the circumnavigator." It will be seen from the extract just given from Wordsworth, that Coleridge's obligation to Shelvocke was no new discovery of De Quincey's. Whatever may be the value of other charges of plagiarism against Coleridge, this certainly is worthless enough. Coleridge draws a certain amount of material from Shelvocke, and that is all. If his doing so is to destroy his character for originality, then Shakspere, and most other writers, must be wholly condemned in the same respect. Is an architect bound to make his own bricks? Is a painter bound to create his own models? With detectives of the De Quincey sort there is scarcely an author who does not run a chance of being taken up for a thief and a robber. The passage in Shelvocke, which is most to the point, is this: describing his voyage between "the streights of le Mair" and the coast of Chili, he says they saw no fish, "nor one sea-bird, except a disconsolate black Albitross, who accompanied us for several days, hovering about us as if he had lost himself, till Hatley (my second captain), observing in one of his melancholy fits that this bird was always hovering near us, imagin'd from his colour that it might be some ill-omen. That which, I suppose, induced him the more to encourage his superstition was the continued series of contrary tempestuous winds, which had oppress'd us ever since we had got into this sea. But be that as it would, he after some fruitless attempts at length shot the albitross, not doubting (perhaps) that we should have a fair wind after it." (Shelvocke's *Voyage round the World by the way of the great South Sea*, &c., London, 1726.)

In Rossetti's edition of Coleridge's *Poems* will be found the older version of the *Ancient Mariner*—the version published in *Lyrical Ballads*, 1798. It differs from the later, the commonly current version, in its orthography, which is more archaic; and secondly, in its larger admission of the horrible: for instance, Death, "that woman's mate," or "her fleshless Pheere," as the earlier reading runs, is described with an overflowing ghastliness, and so the movements of the defunct bodies towards the end of the voyage. A taste for such details prevailed about the close of the last century; the time of "Monk" Lewis, 'Apollo's Sexton,' and Mrs Radcliffe who dealt freely in

" Nocturnos lemures portentaque Thessala."

Coleridge happily quite outgrew that blood-curdling appetite. Also, he came to the conclusion that there was nothing spiritually effective in spelling "ancient" with a y, or appending an e to mariner.

This poem was by no means received with enthusiasm. Its "Pre-Raffaelitism" was not to the satisfaction of the age. Like many another great work in the beginning of a new æra, it had to create the taste by which it was to be approved.

PART I.

130. 1. *It is, &c.* See note to l. 1 of *Alexander's Feast.*

5. *bridegroom.* The *groom* here is a corruption of Ancient Eng. *guma* = a man.

8. *mayst.* The pronoun, radically contained in the verb, is not independently expressed. See note to *L'Alleg.* 104.

11. *loon.* This word is still in use in provincial dialects, Shakspere has it in *Macbeth,* V. iii. 11 :

"The devil damn thee black, thou cream-faced *loon.*"

Dryden in *The Cock and the Fox :*

"But the false *loon,* who could not work his will
By open force, employed his flattering skill."

12. *eftsoons.* See *Prothal.* l. 55.

131. 32. *bassoon.* Fr. *basson* = the *bass* instrument.

35. *minstrelsy.* Certainly Ritson was right in asserting that *minstrel* in the late Middle Ages and in the 16th century = musician, as against Percy who in the 1st edition of the *Reliques of Ancient Eng. Poetry* claimed for it a far wider meaning. Scott therefore uses the word and its cognate somewhat inaccurately of the *ballads* of the Scottish border and in *The Lay of the Last Minstrel.* Here it is used correctly. See 2 *Kings* iii. 15, *Matt.* ix. 23. In *Psalm* lxviii. 25, the Auth. V. reads "the players on instruments," where the Prayer-Book gives "the minstrels." With the present passage comp. *The Taming of the Shrew,* IV. ii. 185, of Petruchio's grotesque wedding :

"Hark! hark! I hear the *minstrels* play."

38. In Yorkshire, and perhaps elsewhere, the pret. of *beat* is pronounced *bet,* which is the more effective pronunciation here.

41. *he.* With this personification comp. the Greek *Typhon.*

55. *clifts* here = clefts. Spenser uses it for *cliffs.*

62. *swound.* So Drayton's *Heroical Epistles :*

"Still in a *swound* my heart revives and faints."

This form is still common in East Anglia (Halliwell). The A. S. verb is *swunan,* the Old High Germ. *swindan.*

[Explain the simile.]

132. 64. *thorough.* Puck uses this fuller form in *Mids. N. D.* II. i. 3, &c. In the advb. it is generally used.

75. [What is meant by *shroud* here ?]

76. *vespers* = simply, evenings, as in *Ant. and Cleop.,* IV. xiv. 8 :

"They are black *vesper's* pageants."

77. *whiles.* So *Much A. ab. N.,* IV. i. 221, 2 *Corinth.* ix. 13, &c. In Lowland Scotch *whiles* is very commonly an advb., as *Twa Dogs,* 221.

PART II.

83. So Herodotus declares of the exploring fleet sent out by King Nechos that the sun rose first on the left, and then presently on the right. If it was so, that fleet must have doubled what we now call the Cape of Good Hope. The Ancient Mariner's ship seems to have turned round somewhere near the Antartic circle, and so come back Northward. The "good South wind" (see l. 71) begun to blow as they emerged from the ice zone.

92. [What case is *'em* here?]

133 97. [With what part of the sentence is *like God's own head* connected?]

98. *uprist.* This is a weak preterite form = *up-rised.* (Chaucer uses *npriste* as a subst. in *Cant. Tales,* 1053: .

> "And in the gardyn at the sonne *upriste*
> Sche walketh up and down wher as hire liste.")

A common provincial form of the pret. of the simple verb is *ris,* shortened from *rist.*

104. [What is meant by the *furrow* following free?]

109. A common provincial pronunciation of *break* is *breek.*

111. [What part of speech is *all* here?]

116. Southey has the same words rhyming together, of a similar becalming in his *Inchcape Bell:*

> "Her sails from heaven received no motion,
> Her keel was steady in the ocean."

117. *a painted ship, &c.* Comp. *Hamlet,* II. ii. 502, when Pyrrhus' sword

> "seemed i' the air to stick:
> So *as a painted tyrant,* Pyrrhus stood,
> And like a neutral to his will and matter
> Did nothing."

So of Iphigenia, all dumb and helpless, in Æschylus, *Agam.* 233, ed. Paley:

> "πρέπουσα θ' ὡς ἐν γραφαῖς, κ.τ.λ."

120. [What is the force of *and* here? Comp. *Rich. III.* II. i. 103.]

125. Comp. *Rich. III.,* I. iv. 32.

127. *about, about.* See *Macb.* I. iii. 33.

130. *the death-fires* = Corpse candles, Fetch-lights, or Dead men's candles. See Ellis' Brand's *Pop. Ant.*

134. 133. [*nine fathom deep.* So we say *a five-pound note, a two-foot rule, a three-mile walk,* &c. How would you account for the absence of the usual number-inflection in these phrases?]

PART III.

144. *glazed. Glaze* is simply a modified form of *glass,* used as a verb.

152. *wist.* So 1 *Hen. VI.* IV. i. 180. It is the pret. of *wite* to know; comp. Lat. *novi.* Cognate are *wote* I wot, and *wisse* to instruct. See Skeat's *Piers Pl.* (Clar. Press *Gloss.*). Cognate too is the adv. *iwiss* (often corrupted into *I wiss.* Sir W. Scott seems so to mistake; see his *Gloss.* to *Sir Tristrem,* where he explains " Y wis and nought at wene" = " I know certainly and do not speak at guess"), the A. S. *gewiss.*

155. *dodged.* This word was once considered dignified enough. Johnson quotes from South: "The consideration should make men grow weary of *dodging* and shewing tricks with God."

158. *with black lips baked.* See *Lament. of Jerem.* v. 10.

135. 184. *gossameres.* 'Gossomer. Properly God-summer. G. der sommer, fliegende sommer, sommer-fäden (summer-threads), Marien faden, unsrer lieben frauen fäden, from the legend that the gossomer is the remnant of our Lady's winding-sheet, which fell away in fragments when she was taken up to heaven. It is this divine origin which is indicated by the first syllable of the E. Term.' (Wedgwood.)

136. 223. The talking oak compares the passing soul of the "Stormy Brewer" to a stork.

PART IV.

234. *never a saint.* See note to *Alex. Feast,* 69.
137. 245. *or ever.* See note to *Hymn Nat.* 86.

PART V.

138. 295. See 2 *Hen. IV.* III. i. 6.
297. *silly.* See note to *Hymn Nativity,* 92.
302. *dank* is closely connected with *damp.* Milton uses the word several times, as in his translation of Hor. *Od.* I.
310. *anear* is a corruption of *on near,* the *on* standing in a quasi-prepositional relation to the advb. of place. The word is still current in Somerset (Halliwell).
140. 358. *adropping.* See note to *a Maying, L'Alleg.* 20.
367. [What is the force of *on* here?]

PART VI.

142. 427. *belated.* = made late. The prefix *be-* converts an adj. into a causative verb. Give other instances of this force of *be-.*] See *Par. Lost,* i. 783.
144. 512. *shrieve. Scrifan* is A. S. = to receive confession. *My soul,* seemingly the direct object, is therefore strictly the case of the nearer object. Similarly *confess* is used.

PART VII.

145. 535. *ivy-tod.* "*Tod,* a bush generally of ivy. In Suffolk, a stump at the top of a pollard." Halliwell, who quotes from Drayton :

> "And, like an owle, by night to goe abroad,
> Roosted all day within an ivy *tod,*" &c.

Jamieson refers it to Isl. *tota ramusculus.*
540. *a-feard.* The *a-* is a corruption of the oldest English *of,* which strengthens the simple verb; so *ἀπό* and *ab* sometimes in Gk. and Lat. Comp. *a-hungred (af-yngred, Piers Pl.* vi. 269), *a-weary,* &c.
146. 565. [What is the force of *go* here?]

SCOTT.

(1) 1771—1789. WALTER SCOTT was born in Edinburgh, Aug. 15, 1771,—which lies midway between the birth-years of Wordsworth and Coleridge. Delicate health led to his passing his boyhood in the country—in the Borders, at Sandy-knowe, and at Kelso. He was presently sent to the High School, and then to the University, of Edinburgh.

(2) 1789—1805. He commenced his man's career as a lawyer; but literature soon began to prevail with him. He studied German, which was then an almost unknown tongue in this country, and translated some German pieces (Bürger's *Leonore* and *The Wild Hunts-man*, Göthe's *Götz von Berlichingen*, publ. 1799); he collected ballads, and composed himself in the ballad style (see *Minstrelsy of the Scottish Border*, publ. 1802 and 1803); he read old mediæval romances, and edited one of them (*Sir Tristrem*, publ. 1804). Meanwhile, in 1797, he married Charlotte Margaret Carpenter, the daughter of a French refugee. In 1799 he was appointed Sheriff of Selkirkshire; in 1804 he removed from Lasswade to Ashestiel.

(3) 1805—1814. In 1805 appeared the first great fruit of all his past studies, the *Lay of the Last Minstrel*, which made him at once the most popular writer of the day; no greater contrast to the reigning school of poetry can be conceived. It was followed by *Marmion* in 1808, *The Lady of the Lake* in 1810, and other less successful 'lays.' As the novelty of the style wore off, the imperfections of his poetry became apparent. Moreover a greater master of the art, Byron to wit, began to attract all ears to himself. He "beat" Scott, to use Scott's own phrase when asked why he quitted the poetical field. To turn to his private life : in 1805 he entered into partnership with James Ballantine, a rising Edinburgh printer—a connection kept studiously secret; in 1806 he was appointed a clerk of the Court of Session ; in 1811 he bought land on the banks of the Tweed, near Melrose, and began the erection of Abbotsford.

(4) 1814—1832. In 1814 Scott, finding his popularity as a poet on the wane, set himself to finish a tale in prose, which he had begun some nine years before, and thrown aside as of no promise. This was no other than *Waverley, or Sixty years since*—with the publication of which commenced the most brilliant period of Scott's life. He had at last discovered where his strength lay. In the next six years appeared his other masterpieces, *Guy Mannering*, *Rob Roy, The Antiquary, Old Mortality*. These immortal works were followed by others inferior only to them. Amongst other results was a very considerable income. Scott made various additions to his estate. His hospitality was unbounded. He was baroneted in 1820. A terrible financial reverse befell him in the winter of 1825—6, a time of wide-spread commercial distress. The firm of Ballantine and Co. failed for some £117,000. The bankruptcy of another publisher, Constable, involved Scott in losses and engagements to the amount of some £60,000. Scott did not allow himself to be prostrated by these severe blows. He bore up nobly against them ; there was in him no slight element of that high chivalrous nature, which he delighted to pourtray in his writings. So, though now in his fifty-fifth year, this "knight without fear and without reproach" armed himself with stern resolve for the struggle. His remaining years were spent in this same struggle. All that he could do to redeem himself he did, and it was much ; but his adversities were too strong for his physical strength. Early in 1830 he suffered a stroke of paralysis ; still he toiled on. In April 1831 came a second attack. Some months later he visited Malta and Naples and Rome, in the hope that change and a milder air might recruit him. During this tour he still worked at Romances; but his mental powers were rapidly decaying. He was brought back to England in June, 1832, a mere wreck physical and intellectual. In the following September he at last rested from all his labours.

As a poet, the "virtue" and power of Scott appear best in his songs. Of these many are of the highest excellence, and may even take rank with some of Shakspere's. They come from the very depths of a deep passionate nature, that never in any other form so openly confessed its inmost character, but was for the most part reserved and seemingly conventional They are the very cries of Scott's most secret spirit; sometimes, as he writes them, he becomes almost inarticulate with feeling; at least, he cannot find current words that are adequate to his emotion. This is the real explanation of those wild burdens, composed of strange fancy-woven melodious syllables, that he used in his Lyrics with such a weird effect (as "Eleu Loro" in "Where shall the lover rest," &c. *Marmion*). They are the voice of Nature herself, speaking a certain mysterious tongue of her own, not according to any human grammar. Shakspere, too, often has recourse to these rudimentary sounds—this primitive, unorganised language; and so other Elizabethan poets, often with a most pathetic accent. During the latter part of the seventeenth century and during the eighteenth these refrains are unknown—a significant fact. The poets of those days felt no need of any mystic utterances. They could say well enough all they had to say in the ordinary speech. It was a sign of the revival of a profounder poetry about the beginning of this century, that once more the imperfectness of the current dialects was felt, once more men were visited by thoughts too deep for received phraseologies. Scott was no supreme master of language like Wordsworth, or Shelley, or Coleridge. He could not utter the thoughts that arose in him with any fine subtilty of analysis. When his nature was deeply stirred within him, it found its relief in melodized unworded sounds, which in fact often speak more significantly and deeply than the seemingly distincter utterances to which they form a sort of diapason.

In his longer pieces Scott's poetical genius shines less manifestly. One reason is that his "Lays" were for the most part inspired by other than poetical motives. The writer's object in them is antiquarian and historical, both in their form and in their subject-matter. For their form, he aims at reproducing the Metrical Romances of Chivalry. It is true that he does not quite succeed in doing that—it was impossible that he should succeed; but that is his aim. His ambition was to be what he calls a 'Minstrel'—to be a Trouvère. He adopted with certain variations the favourite measures of those mediæval rhapsodists; he threw himself with the utmost ardour into their times; he recalled the scenes and forms of life amid which they lived. The *Lay of the Last Minstrel* is a fine poetic handbook of the Middle Ages, as Scott could see them. It is the work of an enthusiastic archæologist with no contemptible gift of measure and of rhyme, rather than of a purely poetizing spirit. It displays much imaginative power, but it is rather historical imagination than artistic. So in *Marmion* we have six brilliant chapters describing the life of the early sixteenth century—the Castle, the Convent, the Inn, the Camp, the Court, the Battle. To convey information about an olden time, which had supreme fascinations for Scott, is in short the prime impelling purpose of these infant Epics. Apollo lays aside his singing-robe, and leaving the heights of Parnassus for the Professor's chair delivers glowing, though not always accurate, lectures on the Manners and Customs of the Middle Ages. In these labours of revival and imitation and learning, Scott's creative power never at all worthily expressed itself. It is a most notable fact that his wonderful gift of humour found no place for itself in them. It cannot be said that they contain a single figure in any way comparable with those numerous real living and moving human beings that spring into life in his prose works. They are indeed rather echoes than voices. The only poetical form which could possibly have comprehended Scott's genius in all its breadth was the Dramatic. Dramatic power, in the untechnical sense, he possessed in the highest degree. It is difficult to believe that, had he lived in the Elizabethan age, he would not have ranked high amongst the "old masters" of our drama, to whom as towards his spiritual brothers he felt himself always strongly drawn in his sympathies. He is one of the very few who since Shakspere's time have seemed to be endowed with something of Shakspere's nature. But, as it proved, he could express himself in the dramatic form even less worthily than in the metrical romance. It would seem as if every great age and every great genius have their own form of expression, which dies with them. The Drama in Scott's time was an obsolete thing, incapable of resuscitation; with all Scott's dramatic faculties he could not write dramas. The one shape in which all the richness of his genius was to be revealed was the Novel. The Novel was for his day and for him what the Drama was for Shakspere and his age. There all his various talents were to find free play—his descriptive and narrative powers, his shrewd observation, his tragic intensity, his lyrical excellence, his infinite humour. Perhaps our own day supplies us with a somewhat parallel instance of failure in the Drama, technically so styled, by one possessed of the highest dramatic spirit in the more general sense of the word. *Adam Bede* is certainly worth a whole tribe of *Spanish Gipsys*, great as is the interest of the *Spanish Gipsy*. It may be remembered that Dickens essayed play-writing with but slight success.

CADYOW CASTLE.

Scott composed this piece the Christmas of 1801 when visiting at Hamilton Palace, Lanarkshire. It has this interest: that it is the first "work in which he grapples with the world of picturesque incident unfolded in the authentic annals of Scotland." It is inserted here from a wish not to omit Scott's name in this collection, and an unwillingness to represent him by any fragment of a poem; certainly it cannot be regarded as of any great intrinsic merit. It is the work of a 'prentice hand; but the works of such 'prentice hands as Scott must not be neglected.

Cadyow or Cadzow Castle was the old baronial seat of the Hamiltons. It stood, where its ruins may still be seen, on the banks of the Evan some two miles from the junction of that stream with the Clyde. Close by are some remains of the Caledonian forest that once covered the whole of southern Scotland.

For accounts of the assassination of the Regent Murray (Jan. 23, 1569—70), see Robertson's *History of Scotland*, Book V., Scott's *Tales of a Grandfather*, chap. xxxii. The ballad follows the facts pretty closely. The murderer escaped to France. In the civil wars of that country an attempt was made to engage him, as a known desperado, in the assassination of the Admiral Coligni; but he resented it as a deadly insult. "He had slain a man in Scotland," he said, "from whom he had sustained a mortal injury; but the world could not engage him to attempt the life of one against whom he had no personal cause of quarrel."

148. 1. [What is the meaning of *abode* here?]
  Cadyow was dismantled at the close of the Scotch Civil Wars for its devotion to the cause of Queen Mary.
  2. [What is the force of *Gothic* here? In what other senses is the word used? See Trench's *Study of Words*.]
  4. *revel* is etymologically but a various form of *rebel*.
  6. [Explain *so* here.]
  10. *vaults.* See Gray's *Elegy*, 39.
  12. *Evan.* See Introduction.
  [What is the force of *hoarser* here? Is it the same as in Gray's *Bard*, 26?]
  14. [What "part of speech" is *minstrel* here?]
  15. Scott was at this time busy completing his *Minstrelsy of the Scottish Border*.
  17. *thou.* He uses *thou* here, rather than *you* as in l. 14, because he wishes to be more pointed and emphatic. All this stanza is given to the description of the *thou*—the Right Hon. Lady Anne Hamilton.
149. 27. As at his own Abbotsford in later years.
  31. *ashler.* Fr. *pierre-de-taille*, Ital. *Pietra riquadrata*, Germ. *Bunderwerke, Quaterstein.* Various forms of the word are achelor, ashlar, aschelere, astler, &c. See *Gloss. of*

Arch., which work quotes, amongst other passages from *Hist. Dunelm. Scrip. tres*, CLXXX: "et erit [murus] exterius de puro lapide, vocato *achiler*, plane inscisso, interius vero de fracto lapide, vocato *roghwall.*" Chambers' *Etym. Dict.* suggests a Celtic derivation, but it looks anything but satisfactory.

32. *battled* = battlemented.

33. *keep.* Fr. *donjon.*

It may perhaps be doubted whether Castle chapels were ever surmounted with spires. Such ornaments would have made excellent marks for the enemy. But *spire* here may = the turret pinnacles.

37. [Explain *their.*]

40. *bower.* See *Prothal.* 93.

43. *route.* The *e* belongs to the old Eng. form; see *Palsg. apud* Wedgwood, and also to the old Fr., which Brachet derives from the Eng. *rout.* According to Wedgwood, this *rout* is connected with rout, "to snore, to bellow as oxen," and denotes first, a confusion, tumult, and then a mob. It is certainly of the same house with the Germ. *rotte.* *Rout* = a defeat, is of different origin.

50. *scud* is connected with A.S. *scéotan,* our modern *shoot.* The grammatical construction here is noticeable, *scud* not usually governing an object. case without a preposition to help it. Comp. the boating phrase "to shoot a bridge." *Walk* is used in a similar way, when people speak colloquially of "walking a country." So "walked the waves," in Milton's *Lyc.* 173, where see note.

53. See *Introduction.*

60. *the Mountain Bull.* "There was long preserved in this forest the breed of the Scottish wild cattle, until their ferocity occasioned their being extirpated about forty years ago. Their appearance was beautiful, being milk-white, with black muzzles, horns, and hoofs. The bulls are described by ancient authors as having white manes; but those of latter days had lost that peculiarity, perhaps by intermixture with the tame breed." (Globe Ed. of Scott.) See Scott's note to *Castle Dangerous.* This breed survives now only at Chillingham Castle in Northumberland.

62. *swarthy* is cognate with Germ. *schwartz.*

150. 68. *sound the pryse.* The Prise was the note or notes blown at the death of the stag. See *Sir Tristrem*, Fytte Third, xli. :

> "He blew *priis* as he can
> Thre mot other mare."

i.e. three notes or more. *Sir Eglamour of Artois*, 298—300 (*Camd. Soc.*) :

> "Then had Syr Egyllamoure don to dedd
> A grete herte, & tan the hedd,
> The *pryce* he blewe fulle schylle."

According to some, the *pryce* consisted of "two longe notes and the rechate." See notes to *Syr Gawayne*, p. 322. The word, like nearly all other words in English connected with the chase, is Norman-French. It is in fact the same word with the Fr. *prise*, lit. a capture, and our *prize.*

72. *dight.* A. S. *dihtan,* to arrange, dress, &c.

[What is meant by *cheer* here?]

73. *clan* is a Keltic word, of the Gadhelic branch. Gael. and Irish *clann.*

78. [Explain *still* here.]

81. *Claud* = Lord Claud Hamilton, second son of the Duke of Chatelherault and "Commentator" of the Abbey of Paisley; a firm adherent of Queen Mary, for whom he fought at Langside.

83. *buxom.* See note to *L'Alleg.* 24.

85. *Woodhouselee* was on the bank of the Esk, near Auchendinny. The final syllable is *lea* a meadow.

87. *hearths.* Obs. the plural.

89. *wan, wane, want,* the negative prefix *un,* Lat. *vanus,* are all of the same family.

91. *sate.* Perhaps this *e* was originally added to shew that the chief vowel was long. The A.S. pret. is *sæt.* We now pronounce the *a* short, and have dropped the final *e.*

94. See Introduction. Bothwellhaugh had been pardoned for his part taken at Langside, but amerced of his property. The lands so forfeited were bestowed upon one of the Regent's favourites.

151. 101. *wildered* = bewildered; but this word is scarcely ever now used in its strict sense

108. *Arran brand.*

110. *resistless. Less* (= A. S. *los,* connected with our *loss, lose,* not with our *less*) is not often compounded with verbs. Besides *resistless* occur *ceaseless,* and *hireless;* Gower has *haveless.* See *Stud. Man. Eng. Lang.,* Lect. vi.

110. *headlong.* See note to *D. Vill.* 29.

111. *poniard* = Fr. *poignard* = It. *pugnale* = Lat. *pugio.*

112. *jaded.* See note to *Twa Dogs,* 220.

steed is akin to *stud,* A.S. *stod.*

117. *selle,* the Fr. *selle.* See *Faerie Q.* II. ii. 11, &c.

120. *carbine* = Fr. *carabine,* old Fr. *calabrin,* from *calabre,* an old stone-hurling engine, whose name was afterwards transferred to the musket. So *musket* originally denoted a sparrow-hawk.

124. *drink.* So *bibere aure* in Latin, as Hor. *Od.* II. xvii. 32 :

> "Sed magis
> Pugnas et exactos tyrannos
> Densum humeris bibit aure vulgus."

125. *quarry.* Fr. *curée,* Lat. *corata,* "viscères et poumons d'un animal, de *cor* cœur; la curée étant proprement les poumons et les entrailles du cerf que l'on donne aux chiens après la chasse." (Brachet). *Quarrel,* a dispute, is a quite distinct word—from Lat. *querela.*

o'er dale and down. A favourite phrase in the old Metrical Romances.

127. *base-born* = bastard. See *apud* Wedgwood, who derives from the Gael. *baos,* lust, fornication, " a bast ibore " (Rob. Gl. 516), " begetin o bast" (Arthur and Merlin), " born iu baste " (Hall).

129. [*Linlithgow.* Where exactly is this town?]
    [What is meant by *side* here?]

131. *bigot.* Derived by some from *Visigoth* (see Taylor's *Words and Places*); by others, from Span. *bigote* moustache (*hombre de bigote* = man of spirit and vigour); by others it is held to be pretty much identical with the Flem. *beguin,* the common stem being the Ital. *bigio* = grey, the word referring originally to the dress worn by certain religionists in the 13th century (see Wedgwood's *Etym. Dict.*).

152. 135. [Explain *settled.*]

137. *hackbut* or hagbut = "the arquebus with a hooked stock." (Fairholt's *Costume in England, Gloss.*) "Arquebus is said to be derived from the Italian arca-bouza (corrupted from *bocca*) signifying *a bow with a mouth.* Hackbut, or hagbush, is perhaps from the old German hakenbüsche, *a hook and gun,* or any cylindrical vessel." (Eccleston's *Eng. Antiq.*)

bent = cocked. A word, properly applying to a bow, is here transferred to a gun. Many terms of the old artillery were transferred to the new. See note on *carbine,* l. 120.

The carbine with which the Regent was shot is still preserved at Hamilton Palace.

140. *Scottish pikes and English bows.* "In all ages the bow was the English weapon of victory, and though the Scots, and perhaps the French, were superior in the use of the

spear, yet this weapon was useless, after the distant bow had decided the combat." (Scott's "Advertisement" to *Halidon Hill*.)

141. *Morton.* James Douglas, Earl of Morton, was the chief of Darnley's accomplices in the murder of Rizzio.

144. [What part of the sentence is *clan*?]

Macfarlanes. Lennox Highlanders.

145 *Glencairn* = Earl of Glencairn, "a steady adherent of the Regent." (Scott's note.)

Parkhead = George Douglas of Parkhead, a natural brother of Morton. Cf. l 141

147. *Lindesay* = Lord Lindsay of the Byres, "the most ferocious and brutal of the Regent's faction, and as such was employed to extort Mary's signature to the deed of resignation presented to her in Lochleven Castle." So Scott's note. See also *Tales of a Grandfather*, chap. xxxii. and the *Abbot*, chap. xxii.

149. *pennon'd spears.* "*Pennon*, a small flag at the head of a knight's lance" (Fairholt). *Pennant* is a various form.

150. [Explain *plumage*.]

153. *visor* = "the moveable face-guard of a helmet" (Fairholt). From the Fr. *vislere*, which is of course ultimately from *video*. *Visard* is cognate.

155. *truncheon* is the Fr. *tronçon*, from *tronc*, Lat. *truncus*. The termination is dim., as in *báton*, *musketoon*, &c.

157. *sadden'd* = made serious. Comp. Rosalind's "*sad* brow and true maid," *As you Like it*, III. ii. 228.

161. *parts.* See Gray's *Elegy*, l. 1.

166. [What part of the sentence is *love* here?]

167. As Llewellyn in the Welsh version of one of the oldest tales of the Indo-European race. It had been recently told in English in a pleasing manner by the Hon. W. R. Spencer:

> "'Hell-hound! my child's by thee devoured,'
> The frantic father cried;
> And to the hilt his vengeful sword
> He plunged in Gelert's side."

See the whole version in Chambers' *Cycl. of Eng. Lit.* ii. 380—1. For references to old foreign versions, see Dasent's *Popular Tales from the Norse*.

broaches. *Brooch* is cognate.

170. [What part of the verb, and what of the sentence, is *roll*?]

153. 173. This is a strange use of *groan* for *groan out*, *groan away*.

felon's is virtually an adj. here. [Quote similar phrases.]

189. [What is the meaning of *for* here?]

WILLIAM WORDSWORTH.

(1) 1770—1791. WILLIAM WORDSWORTH was born at Cockermouth, in Cumberland, April 7, 1770, the son of the law agent to Sir James Lowther. He was educated at Hawkshead School, Lancashire; whence, in 1787, he proceeded to St John's College, Cambridge. The University seems to have had few attractions for him; he was *in* Cambridge, by no means *of* it; see Books III.—VI. of the *Prelude*. The better part of his nature was not stirred at all there. Neither the studies of the place nor the society excited interest or admiration. He lived his own life, read the books of his own choice—Spenser, Chaucer, Milton (see *Prelude*, Bk. III.)—enjoyed much his vacations, feeling always that he "was not for that hour, nor for that place." In the summer of 1790 he made his first continental tour, passing through France, then in the first wild hopes of the Revolution, to Switzerland. Early in 1791 he passed his examination for the degree of B.A., for which ordeal he had prepared himself, it seems, by reading Richardson's novels; with so litttle respect was he inspired for the rites of the University.

(2) 1791—1797. Released from Cambridge, he led for some years a somewhat unsettled life, but a life of steady observation, and thought, and development. He travelled in Wales, in France, in South England, in Yorkshire, and the Lake country. His most important sojourn was in France. In the aspirations and hopes of the Revolutionists he was an ardent sharer; he thought that the world's great age was beginning anew; and with all his soul he hailed so splendid an æra; see his lines on the *French Revolution as it appeared to enthusiasts at its Commencement*, a passage from the *Prelude*, (printed separately in Coleridge's *Friend*):

> "Bliss was it in that dawn to be alive,
> But to be young was heaven."

The ultimate degradation of that great movement by wild lawlessness, and then by most selfish ambition, alienated Wordsworth's sympathy from it; in its earlier progress it awoke and aroused him infinitely more than any event of the age; it was the chief external event of his life. He returned to England with reluctance towards the close of 1792. In 1795 a friend, by name Calvert, dying, left him some £900—a very memorable bequest, as it left Wordsworth, a plain liver, and a high thinker (see Sonnet *Written in London*, Sep. 1802), in a position to obey his lofty nature, free from sordid cares. With help in addition of £1000 from his father's estate, his sister, to whom had come a legacy of £100, and he set up house together at Racedown, Dorsetshire. This sister was to the end a most congenial and inspiring presence; see his poems *passim*, especially *Lines composed a few miles above Tintern Abbey, &c., July* 13, 1798. From Racedown they removed in 1797 to Alfoxden near Nether-Stowey, Somerset, to be near Coleridge, then residing at the latter village. It must be mentioned that Wordsworth had published in 1793 two little volumes of poetry, entitled *Descriptive Sketches* and *The Evening Walk;* but they cannot be called Wordsworthian. The poet's formation was only then beginning.

(3) 1797—1814. In the influential sympathetic companionship of his sister, and of his new-found friend Coleridge, Wordsworth's spirit soon began to express its real self. With 1797 begins the prime poetic period of his life, culminating with the publication of the *Excursion* in 1814. To this period belong

His share of the *Lyrical Ballads*, 1st Ed. 1798, 2nd 1800.
The Prelude, written 1799—1805, not published till 1850.

Peter Bell, written 1798, not published till 1819.
The Waggoner, written 1805, not published till 1819.
Ode on Intimations of Immortality from recollections of Early Childhood,
    written 1803—1806.
Ode to Duty, written 1805.
The White Doe of Rylstone, written 1807.
Song at the Feast of Brougham Castle, written 1807.
Nearly all his noble *Poems dedicated to National Independence and Liberty.*
Many of his *Miscellaneous Sonnets.*
The Excursion, published 1814.

The three years 1798, 1799, 1800 were by far the most productive lyrically of Wordsworth's life. From 1799 to 1814, he was mainly busy with his great philosophical poem, to be called *The Recluse,* "containing views of Man, Nature, and Society," of which the *Prelude* is the "ante-chapel," the *Excursion* the Second Part of the main work. (Of the First and Third Parts only one book was ever written, and this has never yet been published!) See Preface to the *Excursion.* Around this *magnum opus* his minor pieces, "properly arranged," "will be found by the attentive Reader to have such connection with" it-"as may give them claim to be likened to the little cells, oratories, and sepulchral recesses, ordinary included in" "Gothic churches."

As a theorist, Wordsworth set himself to overthrow the narrow conceptions of poetry that prevailed at the close of the last century. The revolutionary spirit was working in him. In poetry, as in society, there was much barren conventionalism; and he was moved to rebel against it. He put forth a famous manifesto in 1800 in the Preface to the Second Edition of the *Lyrical Ballads*—as famous in its way as the *Declaration of Independence.* He certainly did well to be angry with the school of Pope; but it cannot be denied that his indignation led him into some strange paradoxes, into which the sounder criticism of Coleridge declined to follow him. While justly attacking the limits within which the language of poetry was confined in the last century, he went so far as to deny there should be any limits at all. See Coleridge's *Biographia Litteraria.* Happily his practice did not coincide with his theory in its extremest form. Though in one or two of his earlier poems he attempted to make it do so, he grew wiser. His instinct was better than his doctrine.

Both his theory and his practice met with a very cold reception, or rather with a very warm one of opposition. It was by very slow degrees that he won for himself an audience. To the end it was, and is, but "few," but then, as now, it was "fit." The finer spirits of the time recognised the excellence of his genius.

For the facts of his domestic life: the winter of 1798—1799 he spent in Germany with his sister, part of the time with Coleridge also; see his *I travelled among unknown men.* In 1799 he settled amongst "his native mountains," living first at Town End, Grasmere, then at Allan Bank, then temporarily at the Parsonage, from 1813 to the end of his life at Rydal Mount. Meanwhile, in 1802, he married his cousin Mary Hutchinson, the Phantom of delight with

> "Eyes as stars of Twilight fair,
> Like Twilight's, too, her dusky hair.
> But all things else about her drawn
> From May time and the cheerful Dawn."

In 1803 he visited Scotland (see *Memorials of a Tour in Scotland,* 1803), and made the acquaintance of Scott, then known by his *Minstrelsy of the Scottish Border.* In 1813 he was appointed Distributor of Stamps for Westmoreland. His official duties were happily not oppressive; the salary was now extremely welcome, as his wife had borne him two children (a son and a daughter), and his poems brought him but little money.

(4) 1814—1850. The last 36 years of Wordsworth's life passed for the most part serenely and calmly. His means enabled him to enjoy what he most dearly loved—various

tours at home and abroad, for he was a confirmed "wanderer." He visited Scotland twice more, Holland, Belgium, France, Ireland, Italy, Wales. His merits as a poet were daily more and more truly appreciated. In 1842 he received a pension from the Crown; in the following year upon Southey's death he was appointed Poet-Laureate. To this period belong

> *Laodamia* (written 1814).
> *Artegal and Elidure* (written 1815).
> *Dion* (written 1816).
> *Ode to Lycoris* (written 1817).
> *Ecclesiastical Sonnets.*
> *The Egyptian Maid, or the Romance of the Water Lily.*
> &c., &c.

He died full of years and of honour in 1850.

> "The moving accident is not my trade,
> To freeze the blood I have no ready arts;
> 'Tis my delight, alone in summer shade,
> To pipe a simple song for thinking hearts."
>
> HART., *Cap. Well.* Part II.

Wordsworth is essentially the poet of reflection and thought. Of dramatic power and of epic he possessed little. Dramatic writing he essayed with but mean success. He vaguely meditated a great epic poem after the manner of Milton, or rather of Spenser; see *Prelude*, Book I:

> "Time, place, and manners do I seek, and these," &c.

But he lacked objective faculty. His genius was altogether introspective and interpretative. He loved to look on the face of Nature, but to him this face was precious as the index of the soul. It was the meaning of things he cared for, not the things themselves. It was the inner voice that he heard, and echoed. Like Spenser, he was most eminently a spiritual poet. In the mere description of Nature many writers have surpassed him: many have reproduced more effectively her terrors and her loveliness, and portrayed her visible lineaments with greater grace and power; but no one has ever entered so far into the secrecies of her heart or partaken so deeply of her inmost communings.

> "Love had he found in huts where poor men lie,
> His daily teachings had been woods and rills,
> The silence that is in the starry sky,
> The sleep that is among the lonely hills."

Everywhere he heard her deep mysterious speech. There was no rock, no flower, no creature in short, human or other, in the wide world, but for him it was one of Nature's words. What he cultivated in himself was a calm quiet mind, vexed by no tumults such as might make that pure refined voice inaudible to him.

The utterances of Nature that his ear caught or seemed to catch he expressed for our hearing, always with much dutiful care and profound sincerity, sometimes with a wonderful force and beauty and an exquisite distinctness of thought and of phrase.

It is not surprising that the works of one who wrote so much should vary considerably in merit. Perhaps no poet is more unequal than Wordsworth. It may be said that he was instant in season and out of season; he wooed the Muse at all hours, and she was not always in the humour. But it is also true that few poets have left behind so much that is thoroughly excellent. Some of his smaller pieces are simply perfect. Whatever may have been his poetical theories, however vehemently he may have protested against the over-elaborateness and artificiality—the unspontaneity—of the school of Pope, it is certain that he was himself a most scrupulous and careful workman. His best pieces both in structure and phraseology are finished and refined to the utmost. He is a conscious artist. His view of his labours was too high to permit recklessness or negligence. His language in his highest efforts is singularly choice, often abounding in "curious felicities" as Coleridge points out. He acted up to the noble maxim he himself inculcates in his own exquisite manner:

> "Give all thou canst; High Heaven rejects the lore
> Of nicely calculated less or more."

ODE ON INTIMATIONS OF IMMORTALITY FROM RECOLLECTIONS OF EARLY CHILDHOOD.

This noble poem was written partly in 1803, partly in 1806. The following extract forms so valuable a commentary upon it that, in spite of its length it must be given here :

" This was composed during my residence at Town-End, Grasmere. Two years at least passed between the writing of the first four stanzas and the remaining part. To the attentive and competent reader the whole sufficiently explains itself, but there may be no harm in adverting here to particular feelings or experiences of my own mind on which the structure of the poem partly rests. Nothing was more difficult for me in childhood than to admit the notion of death as a state applicable to my own being *. I have said elsewhere :

> 'A simple child
> That lightly draws its breath,
> And feels its life in every limb,
> What should it know of death?'

" But it was not so much from the source or animal vivacity that *my* difficulty came, as from a sense of the indomitableness of the spirit within me. I used to brood over the stories of Enoch and Elijah, and almost persuade myself that, whatever might become of others, I should be translated in something of the same way to heaven. With a feeling congenial to this, I was often unable to think of external things as having external existence, and I communed with all that I saw as something not apart from, but inherent in, my own immaterial nature. Many times while going to school have I grasped at a wall or tree to recal myself from this abyss of idealism to the reality. At that time I was afraid of mere processes. In later periods of life I have deplored, as we have all reason to do, a subjugation of an opposite character, and have rejoiced over the remembrances, as is expressed in the lines *Obstinate Questionings*, etc. To that dream-like vividness and splendour, which invests objects of sight in childhood, every one, I believe, if he would look back, could bear testimony, and I need not dwell upon it here : but having in the poem regarded it as a presumptive evidence of a prior state of existence, I think it right to protest against a conclusion, which has given pain to some good and pious persons, that I meant to inculcate such a belief. It is far too shadowy a notion to be recommended to faith as more than an element in our instincts of immortality. But let us bear in mind that, though the idea is not advanced in Revelation, there is nothing there to contradict it, and the Fall of man presents an analogy in its favour. Accordingly, a pre-existent state has entered into the popular creeds of many nations, and among all persons acquainted with classic literature is known as an ingredient in Platonic philosophy. Archimedes said that he could move the world if he had a point whereon to rest his machine. Who has not felt the same aspirations as regards the world of his own mind? Having to wield some of its elements when I was impelled to write this poem on the 'Immortality of the

---

* It is said that this, the first stanza of *We are Seven*, was composed by Coleridge.

Soul; I took hold of the notion of pre-existence as having sufficient foundation in 'humanity for authorising me to make for my purpose the best use of it I could as a poet."—*Memoirs of William Wordsworth, by Christopher Wordsworth, D.D.*

The main idea of this Ode is treated in a very remarkable piece by Henry Vaughan, a Platonic poet of the seventeenth century. See *The Retreat*, in the *Golden Treasury*, No. lxxv. :

> " Happy those early days, when I
> Shined in my angel-infancy !" &c.

Compare too Shelley's *Lament, Golden Treasury*, No. cclxxxv. :

> "O World ! O Life ! O Time !
> On whose last steps I climb,
> Trembling at that where I had stood before ;
> When will return the glory of your prime ?
> No more—O never more.
>
> Out of the day and night
> A joy has taken flight :
> Fresh spring, and summer, and winter hoar
> Move my faint heart with grief, but with delight
> No more—O never more."

See also Wordsworth's own lines *Composed upon an Evening of Extraordinary Splendour and Beauty*, 1818, stanza iv. :

> " Such hues from their celestial urn
> Were wont to stream before mine eye,
> Where'er it wandered in the morn
> Of blissful infancy." &c.

One may compare too Hood's lines, *I remember, I remember*, last stanza :

> "I remember, I remember
>   The fir-trees dark and high ;
> I used to think their slender tops
>   Were close against the sky :
>
> It was a childish ignorance,
>   But now 'tis little joy
> To know I'm farther off from heav'n
>   Than when I was a boy."

On the metrical structure of this Ode, see Introduction to Gray's *Odes.*

Wordsworth seems to use *Immortality* in the title rather in the sense of *Eternality*, perhaps because the latter properer word is scarcely now current. It is used by Udall, and Sir T. More ; see *Richardson.*

[Into what parts would you divide this poem ? What are the leading ideas ?]

154. 4. *Apparelled.* To *apparel* is strictly to put like to like, to suit ; from the Fr. *pareil,* Lat. *parilis* (from *par*).

6. [Is *of yore* used here quite in the ordinary sense ?]

21. *tabor* comes ultimately from the root *tap, τυπ,* &c., and so means strictly something beaten. The form is Provençal = Fr. *tambour ;* see *Bible Word-book. Tabret* is a dim. Fr. *tabouret. Tambourine, timbrel,* τύπανον or τύμπανον are cognate words.

155. 25. *the cataracts* = the Ghills, and Forces, and Falls of his loved Lake country.

27. *the echoes.* See *Adonais,* 127.

28. *the fields of sleep* = the yet reposeful, slumbering country side. It is early morning, and the land is still as it were resting.

31. *jollity.* See *L'Alleg.* 26.

32. Comp. *Robin Hood and the Monk:*

> " Hit befell on Whitsontide,
> Early in a May mornyng,
> The son up faire can shyne,
> And the briddis mery can syng.
>
> This is a mery mornyng, said litulle Johne,
> Be hym that dyed on tre,
> A more mery man than I am one
> Lyves not in Christianté.
>
> Pluk up thi hart, my dere mayster,
> Litulle Johne can say,
> And thynk it is a fulle faire tyme
> In a mornynge of May."

Such May raptures abound in our older poetry.

38. *jubilee* = shout of joy, Lat. *jubilæus* from *jubilum,* used by Silius Ital. *Pun.* xiv 475:

> " Et lætus scopulis audivit *jubila* Cyclops."

40. As at Greek and Roman banquets. When Alcibiades arrives in the *Symposium,* it is said ἐπιστῆναι ἐπὶ τὰς θύρας ἐστεφανωμένον αὐτὸν κιττοῦ τέ τινι στεφάνῳ δασεῖ καὶ ἴων, καὶ ταινίας ἔχοντα ἐπὶ τῆς κεφαλῆς πάνυ πολλάς. See Excursus on *The Chaplets,* in Bekker's *Gallus.*

43. [What "case" is *herself?*]

50. And so his heart still leaps up when he " beholds a rainbow in the sky ;" see his famous lines.

54. *pansy,* Fr. *pensée* from *penser* = the thought-flower.

56. [Explain the phrase *visionary gleam.*]

58. See l. 5.

59. The transition of thought here is perhaps somewhat abrupt. There was an interval of more than two years between the writing of st. iv. and that of st. v.

This idea of our ante-natal existence found much favour with Socrates and Plato, and their school ; see *Phæd* chap. xviii (72 E), *Meno, Rep.* x. 617, &c. The doctrine of Metempsychosis, an extension of this doctrine, is said by Herodotus to have been first held by the Egyptians ; see ii. 123: πρῶτοι δὲ καὶ τόνδε τὸν λόγον Αἰγύπτιοί εἰσι οἱ εἰπόντες ὡς ἀνθρώπου ψυχὴ ἀθάνατός ἐστι· τοῦ σώματος δὲ καταφθίνοντος ἐς ἄλλο ζῶον αἰεὶ γινόμενον ἐσδύεται. κ.τ.λ.

156. 72. [What is meant by *Nature's priest?*]

85. Compare, or much rather contrast, Pope's *Essay on Man,* ii. 275—82:

> " Behold the child, by Nature's kindly law,
> Pleas'd with a rattle, tickled with a straw ;
> Some livelier plaything gives his youth delight,
> A little louder, but as empty quite :
> Scarfs, garters, gold, amuse his riper stage,
> And beads and prayer-books are the toys of age :
> Pleas'd with this bauble still, as that before,
> Till tir'd he sleeps, and Life's poor play is o'er."

The child Wordsworth had specially in his mind here was Hartley Coleridge ; see his lines "To H. C., six years old." See *Memoir of Hartley Coleridge,* by his brother, especially the account of Ejuxria.

86. *pigmy* = pygmy. Gr. πυγμαῖος = of a πυγμή's length. A πυγμή = the distance from the elbow to the knuckles, = 18 δάκτυλοι, about 13¼ inches.

88. [Explain *fretted* here.]

102. *cons. Con* is from Ancient Eng. *cannian,* as *ken* from *cannan.*

157. 103. "*humorous stage*" = stage on which are exhibited the humours of mankind, that is, according to the Elizabethan usage, their whims, follies, caprices, odd manners. For this Elizabethan sense of the word, see Shakspere, *Merry Wives of W.,* Ben Jonson's *Every Man in his Humour,* &c. See *Nares.* In its modern acceptation, *humour,* confined rather to words, implies a conscious, deliberate whimsicality, a sense on the part of the actor of the ridiculousness of what he does, an intentional and well-appreciated incongruity.

104. *persons* = Lat. *personæ.*

110. [What is meant by *yet* here ?]

117. This line was omitted in a later edition. It is wanted for the rhyme's sake.

127. [Explain *custom* here.]

129. *embers. Ember-day* is of quite different origin. See *Wedgwood.*

141. See *Introduction.*

158. 143. *falling from us, vanishings* = fits of utter dreaminess and abstraction, when nothing material seems solid, but everything mere mist and shadow.

[What is the force of *us* here ?]

151. See Plat. *Meno.*

155. *moments,* i. e. but moments, nothing more than moments.

159. 189. *heart of hearts.* Hamlet's phrase is *heart of heart* (III. ii.).

190. [What does *only* qualify here ?]

191. See *Lines on revisiting the banks of the Wye.*

192. *fret.* Comp. in Keats' *In a drear-nighted December :*

"They stay their crystal *fretting*"

Of the 'bubblings' of the frozen brook.

193. *I tripp'd lightly as May.* Comp. Homer's Ἀργυρόπεζα Θέτις.

199. [What is meant by *race* here ?]

LAODAMIA.

See Catull. lxviii. 79 et seq., Verg. *Æn.* vi. 447, Ovid's *Heroides.*

Laodamia was the type of over-powering passion with the ancient poets. See especially the passage in Catullus, ll. 107—110. Thus her story was well fitted to convey the lofty teaching which Wordsworth here associates with it. No doubt it was this suitability that specially suggested and recommended it to him. In another respect it would attract Wordsworth, viz. for that sympathy between Nature and man and the invisible which it declares. The highest animate existences, and also inanimate things, feel with and for the human sufferer. Such a belief in a continuous sympathy throughout creation, in the wholeness and unity of the world, the great poet delighted to entertain. See his lines *Written in Early Spring :*

"To her fair works did Nature link
The human soul that through me ran."

Of all Wordsworth's poems perhaps no one is more marked by a certain sustained loftiness of thought and language, and a supreme calmness of tone. He has here caught something of the majestic simplicity of Greek art. Hermes has touched him with his wand, and inspired a certain marvellous grace and quiet. It is a poem of "depth," not of "tumult." (l. 75.)

159. 1. The first Edition of this stanza ran thus

> "With sacrifice before the rising morn
> Performed, my slaughtered lord have I required;
> And in thick darkness amid shades forlorn,
> Him of the infernal gods have I required."

11. Comp. Verg. *Æn.* vi. 48—50, of the Sibyl as the god descends upon her:

> "sed pectus anhelum,
> Et rabie fera corda tument; majorque videri
> Nec mortale sonans."

160. 27. Comp. Verg. *Georg.* iv. 501.
    36. *boon* meant originally a prayer, Anc. Eng. *ben*, Dan. *bon*.
161. 66. In the earlier editions

> "Know virtue were not virtue, if the joys," &c.

    72. [What are the emphatic words in this line?]
    78. *Sojourn*, Anc. Fr. *sojourner*, Prov. *sojornar*, Ital. *soggiornare*, Lat. *sub-diurnare*.
    79. This rescue is the subject of Euripides' play, *Alkestis*. See also Milton's last sonnet.
    83. See *Class. Dict.*
    90. See Shelley's *When the lamp is shatter'd:*

> "When hearts have once mingled,
>   Love first leaves the well-built nest;
> The weak one is singled
>   To endure what it once possest.
> O Love, who bewailest
>   The frailty of all things here,
> Why choose you the frailest
>   For your cradle, your home, and your bier?"

162. 101. Comp. Verg. *Æn.* vi. 637—65.
    105. Comp. *Æn.* vi. 639:

> "Largior hic campos æther, et lumine vestit
> Purpureo, solemque suum, sua sidera norunt."

    120. [Where was *Aulis*?]
    See Æschyl. *Agam.* 184—249, Eurip. *Iphigenia at Aulis*, Lucret. i. 84—101.
163. 150. Comp. *Par. Lost.* viii. 588—94.
    158. The first version ran:

> "Ah! judge her gently who so deeply loved!
> Her who in reason's spite yet without crime
> Was in a trance of passion thus removed,
> Delivered from the galling yoke of time
> And these frail elements, to gather flowers
> Of blissful quiet 'mid unfailing bowers."

164. 167. [What is the force of *fondly* here?]

BYRON.

1. 1788—1807. GEORGE GORDON BYRON was born in Holles Street, off Oxford Street, London, Jan. 22, 1788, the son of Captain John Byron of the Guards by his second wife Catherine Gordon, an Aberdeenshire heiress. The Byrons traced their descent from a Ralph de Burun of Doomsday Book. They were ennobled by Charles I. for services done him in the Civil Wars. The future poet's father, a reckless spendthrift and rake, after running through his wife's fortune, left her to maintain herself and their son, and shortly afterwards took himself off to the Continent, where he died at Valenciennes, in 1791. Mrs Byron—she had no claim to the title of "Honourable" which her son subsequently gave her, nor ever had—retired with the boy to Aberdeen. There they lived on but scanty means till 1798, when on the death of his great uncle he succeeded to the family title and estates. His formal education, began at the Free school at Aberdeen, was now continued at a school at Dulwich, and then at Harrow. During his Harrow days he fell in love with Mary Chaworth, daughter of his neighbour at Newstead; but she thought of him but as a schoolboy, and married a Mr Musters. From Harrow he went up in 1805, to Trinity College, Cambridge; where he passed two years, studying occasionally but consuming his time for the most part in boxing, swimming, fencing, pistol-practice, and in other practices much less laudable.

2. 1807—1812. In 1807 appeared *Hours of Idleness*, a volume of poetical pieces of little intrinsic merit, and of as little promise. A disparaging critique of these *Hours* in the *Edinburgh Review* stirred their author to revenge, and the result was his *English Bards and Scotch Reviewers*, published in 1809. That same year he took his seat in the House of Lords, and for a time meditated a political life. At this time he resided mainly at Newstead Abbey, living somewhat wildly. Possessed with a passion for travel, he quitted England for two years, visiting Portugal, Spain, Albania, Greece. On his return he published the first two Cantos of *Childe Harold*, which he had written during his tour, and at once found himself famous.

3. 1812—1816. During the next four years Byron enjoyed an amazing popularity as a poet, and in London Society. The *Childe* was followed by a series of tales, or Eastern Romances: *the Giaour, the Bride of Abydos, the Corsair, Lara, the Siege of Corinth, Parasina.* These in a great measure owed their form to the influence of Scott's "lays"; but they were of a far different spirit. In January 1815, Byron married Miss Milbanke. Just twelve months afterwards, shortly after the birth of a daughter, she separated herself from him and on grounds not commonly known, but which in the eyes of judicious friends seemed quite satisfactory and indeed decisive, declared she would never live with him again. The public of the day was all of a sudden inflamed, for whatever reason, with a similar disgust and indignation. Out of the midst of this outcry Byron, partly perhaps puzzled and astonished, partly scornful and cursing, partly it may be conscience-bitten and remorseful, withdrew to the continent, never, as it proved, to return.

4. 1816—1824. He lived some months in Switzerland, with the Shelleys; then at Venice, when his life was of unbridled licentiousness; then at Ravenna; then at Pisa, and lastly at Genoa. In 1819 he became connected with the Countess Guiccioli. Through her relatives he was associated with the revolutionary party then secretly agitating Italy. When the Greek insurrection against Turkey began, he allied himself with it with the utmost ardour.

He resolved to support it not only with money but with personal aid; and in July 1823 sailed from Genoa for that generous purpose. Meanwhile, his pen had not been idle. He had written the latter two Cantos of *Childe Harold*, all his Dramas, *Beppo*, the greater part of his unfinished *Don Juan*, besides other pieces.

He was not long to be with his Greeks. For some seven months he devoted himself to their cause with all his energy, and is said to have shown a wonderful aptitude for managing the complicated intrigues and plans and selfishnesses which lay in the way. His health was already somewhat broken when he left Italy. In the Spring of 1824 it gave way altogether under his self-imposed fatigues. On April the 19th after a twenty-four hours lethargy ensuing upon an attack of inflammation of the brain, he said "Now I shall go to sleep," and died.

In Byron's life there is certainly much that needs apology, if apology could be found. It must be remembered also that there is much that calls for compassion. He inherited a wilful headstrong nature, which it must be owned was confirmed rather than subdued or regulated by what early lessons he received. To the end of his life he was a spoilt child—to the end wayward and wild and undisciplined. The presiding spirit of his ancestral demesnes seemed to have passed into his blood. There was something of Robin Hood in him—something of a native lawlessness and defiance. Self-control he never learnt; with all his triumphs he was never "victor sui." Hence the nobler part of his nature was often obscured. To him

"deus fit dira cupido."

The British public treated him as injudiciously as did his mother—first fondly petting, then in a fury fiercely slapping him. He was blessed and cursed with a most unwise, a well-nigh fatal abruptness. After he left England, the society of the high-minded Shelley was no slight benefit to him. After he parted from Shelley his life was for a time utterly sensual. But through all that degradation what was noble in him was only eclipsed, not extinguished. The last months of his life show his better self awaking. They were spent generously and well, and, had his life been prolonged, might have proved for him the beginning of a higher æra.

As a poet, Byron professed himself a partisan of Pope, and his first successful essay is after the manner of Pope; but no writer belongs more thoroughly to the early nineteenth century and all its movements than he. In one respect it might have been better for him, had he really followed his professed master, viz. in careful workmanship. His productions are often wanting in finish. He did not "file" and perfect enough; in this regard as in others he is the son of his time. He is of the Revolution. His age is fallen and base, to his thinking. This thought filled him with contempt and scorn for it. This same belief made Shelley an earnest, though perhaps a somewhat wild, reformer; it made Byron only cynical, and destructive so far as he was active. His spirit found its most congenial expression in a kind of poetry that allowed it the utmost freedom of style, where he could praise or mock, be refined or coarse, terrible or grotesque, comic or tragic or farcical, as his mood was. Undoubtedly *Don Juan* is the best and fullest representation of Byron's nature, as that nature was in the prime of his life. His most abundant wit, his consummate mastery of language and of metre, his beliefs and still more his disbeliefs are all shown there as in a clear glass. His models in this familiar style were Italian; they provided him with just what he wanted. His *Tragedies* reflect only part of him, and in that part is much affectation and, it must be said, much superficiality. He often mistook for high philosophical melancholy what was in fact only remorse. If Hamlet, and not his uncle, had murdered his father, one would see another reason for his declaring all the uses of this world weary, stale, flat and unprofitable. His *Tales* enjoyed a vast popularity. Certainly there are passages in them of exquisite beauty, which will live as long as anything their author ever wrote; but, as a whole, they have not so much life in them as have those "lays" of Scott's which they cast for the time so completely into the shade. Scott's pieces, if they are not thrilled by the passionateness which permeates those of his successor in the throne of poetry, are also free from the extreme morbidness that marks those; and their comparative merits are now recognized. Marmion has outlived the Corsair. The latter two Cantos of *Childe Harold* are of "a higher mood" than the former. This superiority of the 3rd cant ₁ at least was undoubtedly to a great extent due to the companionship and influence of Shelley. As a whole, the work wants unity. It is a collection of splendid passages, and is for the most part only known by excerpts. Byron lacked one of the highest faculties of the artist—that of construction. He was incapable of forming a noble and complete design, and executing it carefully and faithfully. He wrote from hand to mouth, so to speak. No one could tell, and he perhaps less than any one, what a Canto or an act might bring forth. He leapt something recklessly on his Pegasus' back, and rode anywhere, often to evil places, often in a wild fashion. Of his shorter pieces many are beyond praise. He was essentially a lyrical poet. His songs for their beauty, their sweetness, their intensity can never be forgotten.

PRISONER OF CHILLON.

This piece was written in 1816, shortly after Byron's leaving England for the last time. He was then living with Shelley, of whose influence the third Canto of *Childe Harold*, also written about this time, bears signs.

Byron knew little or nothing of any actual captive, when he wrote this piece. The mere sight of the dungeon suggested it. Not till afterwards was he familiar with the story of the illustrious prisoner Bonnivard. There is no resemblance at all between Byron's hero and that historical one; except that they were both imprisoned in Chillon. Bonnivard was confined only 6 years, from 1530 to 1536 (he had been confined before at Grolée for 2 years, 1519—21); the cause was political, not religious; no brothers shared his fate. Byron afterwards celebrated him in a sonnet; which see.

This poem belongs to the close of what may be called the *Tale* or *Romance* period of Byron's life. He had not yet discovered that style of which he was to be such an especial master. In that style *Beppo*, written the year after the *Prisoner*, was his first essay. In the *Prisoner* the influence of Scott's example is yet acting. What is still more noticeable in it is the influence of Coleridge and Wordsworth. Byron was perpetually laughing at the Lake School, as it was somewhat strangely called; he accused Wordsworth of unintelligibility and also of renegadism, and Coleridge of unconsciously turning into a metaphysician. But for all his derision the greatness of these poets was really felt by him. The traces of them perceptible in his writings at this time are perhaps mainly due to Shelley, who was to begin with an intense Wordsworthian, though estranged from the great master by what he regarded as his political tergiversation.

This poem cannot be pronounced a masterpiece; to say nothing of several lapses and carelessnesses, there is a want of concentration in it; the purpose of the poem is somewhat vacillating. But it is a capital specimen of Byrons vigour and *verve*. The passage in which he tries his power of language to the utmost and displays best how remarkable that power was is Stanza IX.

105. 4. "Ludovico Sforza and others. The same is asserted of Marie Antoinette's, the wife of Louis the Sixteenth, though not in quite so short a period, grief is said to have the same effect; to such, and not to fear, this change in *hers* was to be attributed." (Byron)—See 1 *Hen. IV.* II. iv. 393: "Thy father's beard is turned white with the news." On which see Steevens' note, who quotes from Nashe's *Have with you to Saffron Walden*: "Looke and you shall find a grey haire for every line I have writ against him; and you shall have all his beard white too, by the time he hath read over this book."

10. *bann'd.* This is an unusual, though perhaps a not unnatural use of this word. It is commonly used only of *persons*; here it is used of *things*; as if one should say in Latin—it would scarcely be correct Latin—"aqua et ignis Galli interdicebantur" instead of "aqua et

igne Gallis interdicebatur" or "aqua et igni Gallos interdicebant.' *Ban* (i) properly means to proclaim, from the High Germ. *bannan* (see *Brachet*); then (ii) to outlaw or otherwise sentence by proclamation (as Gloucester proposes to have Edgar proclaimed in *King Lear*, II. i. 62); then (iii) generally to curse. For (i) see Robert of Gloucester, *apud* Richardson :

> " Of ys rounde table ys *ban* aboute he sende
> That eche a Wytesonetyd to Carleon wende."

Hence *bandon* = command, power ; the early English lover says of his mistress Alysoun ·

> "I am in her *bandoun*."

Hence *abandon* = to give up or resign to anyone's power. So *bans* or *banns* of marriage = proclamation, public announcement. For (ii) obs. the word *bandit* = one proclaimed, and *banish* &c. For (iii), Udal has "to *ban* and execrate himself," Turberville "they *banne* the sunne, they curse the moone," Shakspere "Fell *banning* hag" (1 *Hen. VI.* V. iii. 42), "lunatic *bans*" opp. to "prayers" (*King Lear*, II. iii. 19) &c. With the use here, which is of course a variety of (ii), comp. *bans* in *Par. Lost*, IX. 925.

[*forbidden*. What is the effect of *for-* here ?]

11. *this*, &c. There seems some carelessness of style here, such as often marks Byron's writings. *This* should be *it*, or line 12 should be omitted altogether. As the text stands, line 12 is pleonastic.

22. The indefinite or aoristic preterite might be better here, as in lines 19 and 25.

Seal is lineally connected with *sign*. The *l* in seal is from the dim. *sigillun*, It. *sigillo*.

25. *dungeon* is a various form of *donjon*, the Provençal *dompnhon*, which leads to the Lat. *dominionem* (see *Brachet*). Diez however derives the word from Keltic *dûn*.

26. Probably *wreck* and *frango* (frag.) are of the same ultimate root. The *w* answers to the *f*.

27. [Explain of *Gothic mould*.]

> "The dungeon of Bonnivard is airy and spacious, consisting of two aisles, almost like the crypt of a church." (Murray's *Handbook for Switzerland, &c.*)

30. According to Murray's handbook, "it is lighted by several windows, through which the sun's light passes by reflection from the surface of the lake up to the roof, transmitting partly also the blue colour of the waters."

166. 32. *crevice* and *crevasse* are cognate. The root is in the Lat. *crepo* (so *arrive* from *ripa*).

34. [What is the force of *so* ?]

35. See *L'Alleg.* 104, *Mids. N. D.* II. i. 39.

38. *Canker* and *cancer* are the same word.

40. *this new day*. See below, Stanza xiv.

45. *score*, cognate with *scar, scaur, shear, shore, sheer*, means properly a *notch* or mark for keeping count.

53. Comp. *Par. Lost*, i. 61—64.

55. *fetter'd*. Fetters are strictly foot-shackles, Lat. *pedica, foot-ers*, which becomes *fetters* by assimilating vowel-sympathy. Hand-shackles, Lat. *manicæ*, were called strictly *manacles; hand-cuffs* is a sort of comic term; but both *fetters* and *manacles* are used in a quite general way; and so *gives* or *gyves* (as "with gyves upon his wrist" in Hood's *Eugene Aram*), which seems strictly to have denoted some foot-bond ; thus Tyndall *apud* Richardson : "He that hath his feete in fetters, gives or stockes must first be loosed or he can go, walke, or run to."

57. [What is meant here by *the pure Elements of Earth* ?]

63. So the voices of Arctic explorers. When Franklin, then Lieutenant, was heading an expedition from the Stations of the Hudson's Bay Company to the mouth of the Coppermine River to join Parry if possible, who had sailed from England in 1819, he with a few attendants

went on in advance of Dr Richardson and others. When the party was re-united, "the Doctor" says Franklin, "particularly remarked the sepulchral tone of our voices, which he requested us to make more cheerful, if possible, not aware that his own partook of the same key." See Milner's *Gallery of Geogr.* i. 84.

167. 71. *ought* here has a past sense; and strictly, it is a preterite,= owed; but it is commonly used as a present; see note on *went. Prothal.* l. 139; *Durst*, also strictly a pret., is used sometimes in a present, sometimes in a past sense.

[What would *I ought to have done*, mean?]

91. [What is meant by *below* here?]

95. [What is the force of *had stood* here? How would you explain this usage? Comp. the Latin usage, as in Hor. *Od.* II. xvii. 28.]

97. *To pine* must be connected with *formed* in l. 93.

101. *forced it on.* He speaks of his spirit as of a drooping soldier.

168. 107. *Lake Leman.* So Cæsar, *Bell. Gall.* i. 8. Elsewhere this lake is called *Lausonius* and *Losannensis.* Perhaps the root is that from which comes the Greek λίμνη, and also the English place-name *Lymne*, the Roman name of which (founded no doubt on some native name) was *Portus Lemanis.*

118. So in some of the Cornish mines the workers hear the sea beating about them.

121. *sky* = radically, something shading or covering, a cloud, &c. Probably *sky*, *shade*, σκία are all from the same prime root.

122. *the very rock hath rock'd.* The subst. *rock* and the verb *rock* are of altogether different extraction. The root idea of the subst. is something *broken*, (*rock* and *broken* are in fact cognate); that of the verb *movement.* The word-play might better have been avoided. And so the play in the next line on the literal and the metaphorical—the physical and the moral—forces of *shake* and *shock*, which are really but various forms of one word.

131. [What is meant by *the like* here?]

169. 148. *gnash.* This word is no doubt an *onomatop*, expressing the sound made by striking or clashing the upper-jaw teeth against those of the lower-jaw; here it seems to mean to break by violent bitings—by clashing the teeth fiercely and madly against the chain; to crash with the teeth, to craunch furiously as one might say of a lion.

150. *scorp, shape, ship, skif*, σκάπτω, Lat. *cavo* are all ultimately akin.

152. *boon* = originally, a prayer. See in another form in Wordsworth's *Force of Prayer:*

"What is good for a bootless *bene?*"

(The A. S. form is *ben*, the Danish *bon*). Then = that which is prayed for, (so *wish* = object of one's wishes), and so = a favour, a deed of grace.

155. *within my brain it wrought.* See *Christabel:*

" And to be wroth with one we love
Doth work like madness in the brain."

Macbeth, I. iii. 149:

"My dull brain
Was *wrought* with things forgotten—"

Wrought would seem to be formed from *wroked = worked* (so briddes and birds, κραδία and καρδία &c).

162. [How can the *chain* be called *empty?* Could you speak of an *empty* piece of string?]

163. [What is the force of the possessive case here?]

172. *Yet.* See note to *Il Penser.* 30.

[What does *held* mean here?]

175. [What difference of meaning is there between *he was withered* and *he wither'd?*]

170. 189. *those he left behind.* There is much delicacy in this plural. By such a fanciful multiplying of the survivors the elder brother prevents self-intrusion; himself and his lone-

liness are, as it were, kept out of sight, and forgotten. There is a not unlike sensitiveness in the Scotch phrase "them that's awa" of some single lost one. The grief is softened by vagueness. So too the Greeks used the plural.

194. [What part of the sentence is *eye?*]

225. *franctic* =, etymologically, phrenetic, frenzied. See Butler's *Hudibras:*

> "What oestrum, what *phrenetic* mood
> Makes you thus lavish of your blood?"

Harvey speaks of madmen as *phreneticks.*

171. 251. He is saved from that deadly torpor, described with such masterly power in the IXth stanza, by the song of a bird, just as the Ancient Mariner is delivered from a like stagnancy by the sight of the fishes disporting themselves. The sympathies of his nature are awakened once more. His heart softens. He lives again.

172. 294. Comp. Wordsworth's *Daffodils:*

> "I wandered lonely as a cloud
> That floats on high o'er vales and hills."

173. 317. *fell* is a verb of "incomplete predication" here; so in "fell ill."

331. A thoroughly Wordsworthian line.

336. *the blue Rhone.* The Rhone does not become "blue" till it leaves the lake at Geneva. It enters it of the common colour of glacier streams.

340. *skimming.* Comp. Virgil's use of *rado*, as Æn. v. 170:

> "Ille inter navemque Gyæ Scopulosque Sonantes
> *Radit* iter lævum interior—"

174. 351. Comp. *Ancient Mar.* 272—91. Wordsworth's *Song at The Feast of Brougham Castle*, 141—6.

378. Comp. Lovelace's famous lines "Stone walls do not a prison make," &c.

KEATS.

1. **1795—1817.** JOHN KEATS was born Oct. 29, 1795, in Moorfields, London. His father, employed in some large livery stables there, had married his master's daughter. Killed by a fall from a horse in 1804, he left his widow, who survived him six years, a moderate competency. John was sent to school at Enfield, when he learnt some little Latin and Classical Mythology, and was then apprenticed to a surgeon in Edmonton. In 1812, during his apprenticeship, a great æra was made in his life by the perusal of the *Faerie Queene.* Deep called unto deep; Keats felt that he too was a poet. In 1815 he came up to London "to walk the hospitals." At this time he made the acquaintance of Leigh Hunt and other notable men of the day. He began to form a dislike to his appointed profession. This arose partly from the extreme nervousness of his nature—he mistrusted his skill as an operator—partly no doubt from his growing devotion to his own proper art. 1817 he published a little volume of poems.

2. **1817—1821.** This volume attracted little, or no general notice. But Keats had now made his election. He was fully conscious of the high requirements of the work he had chosen, and of his own imperfections. In 1818 was published *Endymion.* This poem, with all its many faults, gave unmistakeable signs of a genuine poetic power, and of aims and strivings of the loftiest order. It met with simply infamous treatment from the *Quarterly Review,* and *Blackwood's Magazine,* and other, minor serials. The author was told to "go back to his gallipots," and that "a starved apothecary was better than a starved poet." And this, in the face of an extremely touching preface, in which he had frankly acknowledged his many shortcomings. The story that these brutal reviews shortened Keat's life is happily without foundation. They were too coarse to wound him; he thoroughly despised them. He went on steadily toiling to satisfy somewhat better his own high ideal—in his own words, "fitting himself for verses fit to live." And the progress he made was grand. In *Hyperion* a true master is apparent. But meanwhile, consumption, an hereditary disease, which in 1818 had laid low one of his brothers, began to undermine him. His delicate health was no doubt made worse by certain love troubles. He had become attached with all the vehemence of his nature to a lady at Hampstead. His passion was returned; but his pecuniary position seemed at this time hopeless. What little money he had received from his mother was gone; he had abandoned the medical profession; his literary prospects were anything but bright. Moreover, he was much dissatisfied with his own poetic performances. All these things broke him down. As a last chance, it was arranged that he should winter in Italy. In September, 1820, he sailed for Naples, accompanied by his true friend Severn, a painter of rising fame. From Naples he went to Rome, only to die. There for some weeks he lay bed-ridden, more than "half in love with easeful Death," not calling him

> "Soft names in many a mused rhyme
> To take into the air my quiet breath,"

but calling him eagerly, often somewhat wildly. At last the call was answered. "Thank God, it has come," he said, rejoicing at the near release from all his pains of body and mind.

This was on the 27th of February, 1821. He was buried in the Protestant Cemetery; where some eighteen months afterwards Shelley too, his fervent elegist, was laid.

> ὦ μέλεος ἥβης σῆς, 'Ορέστα, καὶ πότμου
> θανάτου τ' ἀώρου. ζῆν ἐχρῆν σ' ὅτ' οὐκέτ' εἶ.

Keats had not reached his poetic prime when he died. The work he has left behind him is marked by numerous signs of youthfulness. It is florid, luxuriant, often wild and wanton. He was only just beginning to learn the great duty of restraint, of pruning, of selection. Few geniuses have been more liberally endowed by nature; it is not perhaps too much to say that amongst the many great poets of this century Keats was pre-eminently, if not solely, the one of epical power; but he was only just learning how to manage his splendid property. To begin with, he was a very prodigal, a mere lavisher; he scattered his pearls and gems recklessly around him, and had no sense of any noble economy. His education was all along very imperfect. His school-training was inadequate. Leigh Hunt, his chief friend and counsellor when he came up to town, was not of sufficient culture and judgment to guide him. The critics, instead of trying to direct and promote his growth, simply mocked and abused him. Indeed England gave but a queer welcome to her brilliant son. What Keats above all things wanted was a wise education. Perhaps for no man that ever lived would the thorough study of "the Classics," especially of Greek Literature, have been more beneficial. With Greek art, so far as he knew it, he deeply sympathised; see especially his *Ode on a Grecian Urn*, and the *Sonnet on first looking into Chapman's Homer*, but there is scarcely a poem in which this sympathy is not shown. There was in him the keenest sense and enjoyment of beauty; and this gave him a fellow-feeling with the great Greek masters. He recognised in them the most perfect representers of the beautiful, and this, so far as literature went, through translations. Happily he could know their plastic art better through the specimens treasured up in the British Museum, of which he was an earnest rapturous visitor. But it was only one side of Greek art that he saw. He saw its beauty; but he did not see its purity, its self-restraint, its severe refinement. He did not learn from it that the fancy must not be merely indulged. A knowledge of Sophocles might have impressed this lesson upon him. His one great delight in English Literature was a dangerous model for him. Spenser as a writer suffers from diffuseness, amd exuberance. No doubt years, had they been granted him, would have taught him repression and control. Certainly he was beginning to grow wiser in this respect. *Hyperion* is a hopeful advance upon *Endymion*. The flowers do not lie so tanglingly thick there; the pathway is not encumbered with them; one is not choked with sweet odours; one's eyes are not dazzled and blinded with a monstrous blaze of colours. Clearly, he was gathering a better understanding of his art. The Apollo, of whom he had sung so sweetly but so wildly, was revealing himself to him; the Muses were becoming known in their serene, not showy beauty, draped gracefully, not in any garish colours.

But who would part with what he has left us, let the faults be what they may? No works of our literature are more truly poetical; none more completely carry one away into an ideal realm, where worldly noises come to the ear, if they reach it at all, subdued and deadened; none breathe out of them, and around them a more bewitching atmosphere. His song as one hears it is like that of the nightingale as he heard it:

> "My heart aches, and a drowsy numbness pains
> My sense, as though of hemlock I had drunk,
> Or emptied some dull opiate to the drains
> One minute past and Lethe-wards had sunk."

Not without reason Shelley, apostrophizing Keats, calls the nightingale 'thy spirit' sister

ST AGNES' EVE.

1. The chief incident of this poem is founded on a popular superstition. The belief which in Scotland is associated with Halloween, or the Eve of All Saints' Day, was in England attached to the vigil of St Agnes, whose feast was celebrated on January the 21st. It was thought that, if certain rites and forms were observed, maidens might be vouchsafed a sight of their future husbands. The accounts of these requisite ceremonies vary. See Chambers' *Book of Days*, also Ellis' Brand's *Pop. Antiq.* It is impossible to say when such a notion became connected with St Agnes. Her legend is "one of the oldest" of the church; see Mrs Jameson's *Sacred and Leg. Art;* her effigies are as old as any, next to those of the Evangelists and Apostles; but in the story of her martyrdom, in the Diocletian persecution, there is no sign of the matrimonial interest that is found at a later time adding to her popularity. For other legends that gathered around her, her name is no doubt answerable. It was impossible that it should not suggest "agna," and that, consequently, lambs and she should not be allied. In Tennyson's lines, called *St Agnes' Eve*, the speaker, some saintly nun, wins through prayer and faith a vision of the Heavenly Bridegroom.

Other incidents of the poem seem to have been drawn from *Romeo and Juliet*, perhaps from Chaucer's *Troilus and Cressida*, and also, it may be, from the old Haddon Hall story of the elopement of Dorothy Vernon with her true lover, John Manners.

2. The poem abounds with the beauties, and with the faults, that characterize Keats. It need not mar one's enjoyment of it as a poem that its archæology is somewhat inaccurate. Scott himself is by no means perfect in this respect. If we are not introduced into the veritable medieval world, at least we are taken out of our own present workaday atmosphere; we are borne away into a land of enchantment; we feel the very air of Romance blowing around us; we too are "hoodwinked with faery fancy."

176. 1. *St Agnes' Eve*, Jan. 21.

2. *for all his feathers.* See note in *Hymn Nat.* 73.

a cold. So *King Lear*, III. iv. 84, &c. In 13th and 14th century writings occur the forms acolden, to grow or make cold; akelen, accolded, and acold, part. &c. (Stratmann). See in the *Ancren Riwle*, Ed. Morten, p. 404: "Idel acoaldeth and acwencheth this fur" = Idleness cooleth and quencheth this fyre. The *a* here is a corrupted form of an intensive prefix *af* or *of*. So in *a-hungred*, which in *Piers Ploughman*, vi. 269, appears as af-yngred (comp. A. S. *of-hingrian*, and see Skeat's, Clar. Press, *P.P.* Gloss.). So *afered, afraid, atheist, ago* (see note to *Hymn Nat.* 155), *aweary* (as *Mids. N. D.* V. i. 257, &c.), &c.

5. *beadsman* = strictly, prayers-man. The term often denoted one who in return for obligations received gave his benefactor the benefit of his prayers. Hence often beadsman = almsman. So the "blue-gowns" of Scotland are called *King's Bedesman;* see the *Antiquary.* As for prayers being looked upon as a return for material kindnesses, comp. the yet extant phrase in "petitions": "and your petitioners will ever pray, &c." See in the N.T., *St James* v. 15, Shakspere, *passim.* For the form of the word, in *Piers Pl.* is found *bedeman* (see iii. 41 and 46 in Clar. Press Ed.), in the *Ancren Riwle, beodeman.* The final *e* of *bede* represents the old plural inflection. When that inflection was superseded by *s*, then came in the form *bedesman.* For the derivation, *bede* is connected with *bid, beadle,* &c. *Bead,* = a little ball, is *bede* itself in a secondary sense. *Bidding-prayer* is strictly a tautologue, if we may use such a word (comp. *analogue*).

told. See note to *L'Alleg.* 67.

6. *rosary* = (i) a rose-bed. See Virgil's "biferique *rosaria* Pæsti" (*Georg.* iv. 119). (ii) a rose-chaplet, a garland. Jeremy Taylor speaks of "rosaries and coronets." (iii) a selection of prayers. Comp. such book-titles as the *Crown Garland of Golden Roses, Foliorum Centuriæ, The Evergreen,* &c. (iv) a string of beads; see note on *bedesman,* l. 4.

Comp. Tennyson's *St Agnes' Eve:*

> "My breath to heaven like vapour goes;
> May my soul follow soon."

7. *censer* is shortened from the Fr. *encensoir,* Lat. *incensorium.* [Give other instances of such abbreviation.]

8. [Explain *without a death.*]

12. *meagre* is from the Lat. *macer,* as *eager* from *acer* (*vin-ager* = vinum-acre).

13. *degrees* is here used in its radical sense. *-gree* is from the Lat. *gradus.*

15. [What does he mean by *purgatorial rails*?]

16. [What is meant by *dumb* here?]

[*orat'ries.* What letter does the apostrophe represent here? What other letters does it occasionally represent?]

17. *fails.* Comp. *In Mem.* ii.:

> "I seem to *fail* from out my blood."

18. *hoods. Hood* is cognate with *head.*

mails. This *mail* (quite distinct from *mail,* Fr. *malle* = trunk or bag, especially one for letters, which is of Teutonic origin) is ultimately from Lat. *macula,* in its secondary sense of a hole, an interstice, a mesh; which sense it has for instance in Ovid's *Her.* v. 19, where Œnone speaks of her old pastimes with Paris:

> "Retia sæpe comes *maculis* distincta tetendi."

Hence *macula,* becoming *macla,* becoming *maille,* the Eng. *mail,* denotes steel-ring armour; then, generally, steel armour of any kind.

21. *flatter'd.* Leigh Hunt breaks out into an ecstasy on the use of this verb here. He says, the old man thinks the music is for him as well as for others, &c. &c.; see *Imagination and Fancy.* But probably Keats uses the word somewhat vaguely—he is not a very accurate writer—for *softened,* Lat. *solvit.* Comp. Dryden's *Dufresnoy apud* Johnson: "A consort of voices supporting themselves by their different parts make a harmony, pleasingly fills their ears, and *flatters* them." Johnson defines *flatter* in this usage, as, "to please, to sooth." This sense, he says, is "purely Gallick." Etymologically, *flatter* is closely akin to *flatten, flat,* &c.

177. 31. *chide.* The A. S. *cidan,* whence *chide* = to strive, quarrel, brawl. Whence *chide* of any clamour, or noise, as of dogs, as *Mids. N. D.* IV. i. 119, of a flood, *Hen. VIII.* III. ii. 197 (comp. the reading *chiding* in *Othello,* II. i. 12), &c. With the sense here comp. the use of *bray,* as in *braying trumpets, K. John,* III. i. 303.

32. *the level chambers.* Comp. *the level matting* in l. 196.

37. *argent* = silver-bright, gleaming.

revelry = revellers. See note to *trashtrie, Twa Dogs,* 63.

38. *tiara* is a Persian word, brought into Europe by the Greeks. See Æsch. *Pers.* 661:

> "βασιλείον τιάρας φάλαρον πιφαύσκων."

Of like antecedents, and perhaps of much the same meaning, except that the τίαρα was used specially of the king's head-dress, were κυρβασία and κίδαρις, or κίταρις. For κυρβασία see *Herod.* v. 49, where Aristagoras speaks depreciatingly of the Persian trowsers (ἀναξυρίδες) and κυρβάσιαι. *Turban,* too, is of Persian origin. Here it would seem that *tiara* refers to the ladies' head-dresses.

40. *triumphs.* See *L'Alleg.* 120.

43. [Explain this use of *brooded*. Can you illustrate it from the Latin or the Greek?]

45 [How would you explain *as* here?]

49. *upon*, &c. So Tennyson's *Mariana*: "Upon the middle of the night." Virgil's "nocte super media" (*Æu.* ix. 61)

52 *supine* = lying on the back   See l. 54. So the Greek ὕπτιος. Contrast pronus, πρηνής. From the complete relaxation of the attitude comes the secondary sense of indolent. "The fourth cause of errour," says Sir Thomas Brown, in his *Vulgar Errors*, "is a *supinity* or neglect of enquiry, even in matters wherein we doubt, rather believing than going to see."

54. *for.*   The construction is according to the analogy of *pray for*, &c.

60. *tip-toe* = excited.   See *Hen. V.* IV. iii. 42.

178. 70. *hoodwink'd* = strictly, hooded or covered as to the eyes, i. e. blinded: see *All's Well that Ends Well,* IV. i. 90; *Romeo and Juliet*, I. iv. 3:

> "We'll have no Cupid *hoodwink'd* with a scarf, &c."

So the simple *hooded* in *Meas. for Meas.* V. i. 358; comp. *hoodman.* For *hood* see l. 18. *Wink* in this compound seems = that which winks, the eye, though, as a simple word, it does not appear to occur in that sense. Perhaps it is shortened from *winkers*. *Blinkers* is used for eyes in the dialect of "slang."

faery = Fairy land; as in the title of Spenser's poem.

all amort.   See *Taming of the Shr.* IV. iii. 36, &c. Probably, as Nares suggests, a corruption of *alamort.* Fanshawe writes *alamort* in his translation of the *Lusiad*, v. 85.

71. [What is the force of *to* here?]

75. *on fire.* In *aflame* the *on* is corrupted.

77 [What is meant by *buttress'd* here?] *Buttress* and *abutment* and *butt* are all cognate.

82 Comp. the visit of Romeo and his friends to the house of the Capulets.

84. *citadel* is the Ital. *citadella*, dim. of *citta.*

90 *beldam* So 1 *Hen. IV*, III. i. 32, &c. Perhaps the *bel* = *belle* is used ironically, perhaps euphemistically Johnson says that in Old Fr. the word "signified probably an old woman, as *belle âge*, old age." But *belle âge* scarcely illustrates *belle dame*. In English we can speak of "a fair age," "a good age," "a good old age;" but we couldn't say "a good or a fair man" for "a good-aged man." *Goodman* and *goodwife* mean something very different.

94. *hall-pillar.* From the words immediately following it would seem that Keats uses *hall* here in the modern acceptation, for a vestibule; not in the medieval, for the chief room of the house.

179. 100. *dwarfish.* *Dwarf* is the later form of the Ancient English *dweorh* or *dweorg* = crooked.

101. *fit* is perhaps connected with *fight*. It is quite a distinct word from *fit*, the adj., also used substantively, which is from the Fr. *fait.*

105. *gossip* = god-sib, strictly, a god-kinsman, or a kinsman with respect to God, that is, in a religious sense; a sponsor at one's baptism, a godfather or godmother. On the corruption of meaning see Trench's *Eng. Past and Pres.*

116. See the extract from the *Translation of Naogeorgus*, apud Brand:

> "Then commes in place St Agnes' Day, which here in Germanie
> Is not so much esteemde nor kept with such solemnitie:
> But in the Popish Court it standes in passing hie degree,
> As spring and head of wondrous gaine, and great commoditee.
> For in St Agnes' church upon this day while masse they sing,
> Two lambes as white as snowe the nonnes do yearely use to bring:
> And when the Agnus chaunted is upon the aulter hie,
> (For in this thing there hidden is a solemne mysterie)

> They offer them. The servants of the pope when this is done
> Do put them into pasture good till shearing time be come.
> Then other wooll they mingle with these holy fleeces twaine
> Whereof, being ssonne and drest, are made the pals of passing gaine."

120 See Reginald Scot's *Discovery of Witchcraft*, Book xii. chap. xvi. p. 145, of Ed. 1665: "Leonardus Vairus saith that there was a Prayer extant whereby might be carried in a sieve water or other liquor. I think it was clam clay, which a crow taught a maid that was promised a cake of so great quantity as might be kneaded of so much flour as she could wet with the water that she brought in a sieve, and by that means she clam'd it with clay, and so beguiled her sisters, &c. And this Tale I heard among my grannams maids, whereby I can decipher this witchcraft."

121. You should be Oberon himself.

125. *mickle.* The Ancient Eng *micel* or *mycel,* Old Eng. *moche,* Mod. Eng. *much.*

129. *urchen,* strictly = a hedgehog, coming ultimately from the Lat. *ericius,* is used jocosely for a child. The father

> "Must needs express his love's excess
> With words of unmeant bitterness."

See *Christabel,* conclusion to Part II., where with the consummate philosophical and poetical power combined which characterizes him, Coleridge discusses such whims of speech.

crone means strictly a crooning or groaning sound. As if a beggar should be called *a whine.*

133. *brook* is oddly used here. *Brook,* from the Anct. Eng. *brucan* (comp. Germ. *brauchen,* Lat. *fruor, fructus*), means to use, to bear, to endure. *He scarce could brook tears* must mean "he could scarcely tolerate tears," certainly not "he could scarcely refrain from tears."

180. 136. [*like a full-blown rose.* What is the point of the simile? What verb, or verbal does the phrase strictly qualify?]

153. *fang'd.* *Fang* is strictly that which seizes or clutches. Probably *finger* is of the same root.

156. *passing bell.* It was called also the soul bell. See Ellis' Brand's *Pop. Antiq.* Ellis quotes from the *Advertisements for due Order,* &c. 7 Eliz.: "Item, that when anye Christian bodie is in passing that the bell be tolled, and that the curate be speciallie called for to comforte the sicke person; and after the time of his passinge to ringe no more but one shorte peale," &c. He mentions "the present national saying:"

> "When the bell begins to toll,
> Lord have mercy on the soul."

158. *plaining.* So *plaint.* The stem is Lat. *plango.*

162. *betide* is from Anct. Eng. *tidan* to happen. *Tidings* = what happens, occurrences; then an account of what happens.

weal. So *wealth,* as in the *Book of Common Prayer:* "Grant her in health and *wealth* long to live."

169. [*pale enchantment.* How would you explain the epithet?]

171. Evident reference is made to the fearful storm which swept over the woods of Broceliande, the night of that day when Merlin revealed his charm to his mistress and was tree-prisoned for ever. But Keats seems to be confusing that story with some other. See Tennyson's *Vivien.*

181 177. *cater* is the Old Fr. *acater,* Mod. Fr. *acheter,* Low Lat. *acceptare.*

180. = "Utinam nunquam resurgam."

181. *hobble* is formed from *hop.*

188. *amain.* See Lycid. 111.

193. *like a mission'd spirit* = like a spirit commissioned to succour the old woman.

196. *matting.* The poet should mean the rushes that were strewn over the medieval floor; see a *Hen. IV.* V. v. 1, *Tam. of the Shrew* IV. i. 48, &c.; but matting can scarcely denote them. See note on *carpet*, l. 251.

199. *ring-dove.* The cushat or wood-pigeon, is so called from a white line that runs round its neck.

fled. Many neut. verbs in Eng have past part. used in an active sense. In this respect as in many others, the affinity between English and Greek is noticeable. *Fled* here = φυγούσῃ. It could not be translated into Latin by any one word; imagine such a form as *fugita.* The only verbs in Latin which have past participles with an active sense are what are termed deponent verbs: thus *dead* is exactly represented by *mortuus*, *risen* by *ortus*, *started* (on a journey) by *profectus*, &c.

202. [What do you think is meant by *visions wide?*]

204. *voluble.* See it in its more literal sense in the form *volubil* accented on the penult, in *Par. Lost*, iv. 594:

> "Whether the prime orb
> Incredible how swift, had thither roll'd
> Diurnal; or this less *volubil* earth
> By shorter flight to the East had left him there," &c.

Elsewhere Milton uses *voluble.*

206. When the tongue-bereft Philomela of the old Greek story was transformed into a nightingale, her tongue was restored her, or she might have died such a death.

182. 208. *casement* = strictly, the *case* or *frame* of the window. *Case* radically means that which contains or encloses, the ultimate stem being the Lat. *capsa.*

212. [What is the force of *of* here?]

213. *tiger-moth.* See Wood's *Nat. Hist.*, Insects.

216. [What does *shielded* mean here? What other meanings does it sometimes bear?]

shielded scutcheon. Strictly this phrase is tautologous; for *scutcheon* or *escutcheon* is the Old Fr. *escusson*, which is from the Lat. *scutum.* (Comp. *espérer* with *sperare*, *espace* with *spatium*, &c. Cognate is *esquire*, Old Fr. *escuier* from *scutarius.* The form from which *escusson* immediately comes is *scutionem; scutionem* corrupted gives *scution*, whence *scusson*, or with the prosthetic vowel *escusson*, Mod. Fr. *ecusson*, see Brachet's *Dict. Etym. de la L. Fr.* Technically *scutcheon* = a heraldic shield; so *achievement*, commonly corrupted into *hatchment* (here there is a radical reference to the service in return for which the armorial ensigns were granted). Keats somewhat inaccurately uses *scutcheon* here to denote simply armorial bearings.

218. *gules* = red colour, represented in engraved shields by vertical lines. See *Hamlet*, II. ii. 477, of "heraldry," with which Pyrrhus was smeared:

> "Head to foot
> Now is he total *gules*, horridly trick'd
> With blood of fathers, mothers, daughters, sons," &c.

In *Timon of Athens*, IV. iii. 59, the misanthrope bids Alcibiades

> "With man's blood paint the ground, *gules*, *gules*."

The ultimate stem is that Lat. *gula* the throat.

According to Mr Millais' illustration, this exquisite passage is founded on a falsity. The light of the moon would not be strong enough to reflect the colours of the window. One feels a wretched iconoclast for saying so.

221. *amethyst* = violet. Commonly a violet-coloured precious stone, so called primitively because it was believed to have the virtue of preventing drunkenness.

222. *a glory.* So *nimbus*, and *aureola.*

229. *bodice.* Formerly *bodies*, from fitting close to the body, as Fr. *corset*, from

corps. "A woman's bodies, or a pair of bodies, corset, corpset." Sherwood's Dict. "Thy *bodies* bolstred out with bumbast and with bagges." Gascoigne in R., i. e. "Thy bodice stuffed out with cotton" (Wedgwood). Ben Jonson writes *bodies*, see an *Elegie:*

> "The whalebone man
> That quilts those *bodies* I have leave to span,"

for probably here *those bodies* = that bodice: but it is possible it may = those boddices. Laced boddices seem to have been the mode in the first half of the eighteenth century. See Fairholt's *Costume in England.*

230. *attire.* See note on Lycid. 146.

231. *mermaid* = sea-maid. *Mer* is of the same family as the mor in *Ar-mor-i-ca* and in *Mor-ini*, the Lat. *mare*, Eng. *mar-iner*, *mar-ish* or *mar-sh*, &c.

237. Prosaically, the epithet *poppied* should perhaps be attached to *sleep*, rather than to *warmth*, but indeed *warmth of sleep* is but a phrase for *warm sleep*, like 'Cato's virtue for 'the virtuous Cato,' 'Hercules' strength' for 'the strong Hercules,' &c. See Georg. i. 78 :

> "Lethæo perfusa papavera somno."

[What does he mean, do you think, by *poppied* ?]

239. *the morrow-day. Morrow* strictly = *morning*, the *-ow* = *-ing*, both being diminutival. But the strict sense has been forgotten, as in *Tomorrow-night.*

240. = unread, and so unopened. Mohammedans would no more care to peruse the Christian Scriptures, than Christians those of Mohammed.

242. See Tennyson's *Ulysses.*

183. 244. *stolen.* See note on l. 199.

[What does *so* mean here ?]

247. *tenderness.* Comp. "tender-taken breath" in Keats' Last Sonnet, "a gentle sigh," *lenis* of sounds in Latin writers, &c.

251. *carpet.* So in l. 360. But in the Middle Ages *carpets* in the modern sense were almost unknown. What were called *carpets* then, were our table-cloths, as in *Tam. of the Shrew*, IV. i. 57. The only exception seems to have been that sometimes in palaces carpets were laid down in "my lady's chamber." "Isabella, queen of Edward II., had a black carpet in her chamber at Hertford," &c.; see *Our English Home.* Floor-carpets (obs. the significance of this compound) were not *common* till the 17th century.

255. This was a carpet in the medieval sense.

257. *Morphean.* The accent *ought* to be on the penult. as in the case of *Orpheus* in *Par. Lost*, iii. 17.

amulet, of Arabian origin, strictly = something carried. *Talisman* is of Greek origin, and strictly = something consecrated.

261. This may serve to illustrate *In Mem.* xxviii.

263. *lavender'd. Lavender*, Fr. *lavande*, derives its name from the usage here referred to.

265. *candied* is said to be derived from the Pers. *gand* = sugar. So that *sugar-candy* is simply tautologous, as *Brown Bess* (see Blackley's *Gossip about Words*), *Mount benjerlaw* (where ben = law = Mount), &c.

quince is the Fr. *coing*, Old Fr. *cooing*, Prov. *codoing*, Ital. *cotogna*, Lat. *cotonea* (see *Brachet*), which comes from *Cydonia*, the name of a town in Crete.

gourd is from the Fr. *congourde*, Lat. *cucurbita* (from *curvus*).

267. *syrops.* Fr. *sirop*, Low Lat. *sirupus*, Arab. *sharab*. *Shrub* and *sherbet* are cognate—are in fact but various forms of *syrup.*

268. *argosy* is derived from *Argo* the famous old Greek ship; or, more probably, from *Ragusa* the famous late medieval port (at its greatest prosperity 1427—1440).

269. [Where are *Fez* and *Samarcand* ?]

270. Samarcand is described as a populous and prosperous city by the Spanish traveller Clavijo in the beginning of the 15th century.

276. *seraph*   How completely "artists" have ruined the word *cherub* as a term of endearment!

277. *eremite*.   Of this word *hermit* is a corruption.   Comp. ἀναχωριτής and *anchorite*.

184. 284. *salvers* =radically, tasting-dishes (so Wedgwood), or perhaps savers, safe-keepers.

285. i.e. the fringe shows bright in the moonlight.

288. *woofed* here loosely for *woven*.

289. *hollow*, i.e. resounding.   See note on this word in *Hymn Nat.* l. 178.

292. See it in Keats' Poems, ed. 1868, or that of 1871 (ed. W. Rossetti) or in the *Golden Treas. of Songs and Lyrics.* It would seem to have been rather the name of the old poem, than the old poem itself, that inspired Keats' piece. The old poem, written originally by Alain Chartier in the early 15th century, translated into English by Sir Richard Ros, consists mainly of a somewhat prolix conversation between an obdurate lady and her lover, at the close of which she goes away indifferent to dance and play, he desperate to tear his hair and die. A copy of the English version may be seen in Chalmer's *British Poets*, vol. i. 518, and also in *Political, Religious, and Love Poems*, ed. by Mr. Furnivall for the Early English Text Society. For some account of Alain Chartier see Besant's *Early French Poetry*, chap i.

293. [How would you explain *touching the melody* ?]

309. *tuneable*.   See *M. N. D.* I. i. 182;

> "Your tongue's sweet air
> More *tuneable* than lark to shepherd's ear," &c.

(Complete nonsense is made of these words in Steeven's glee, by breaking off the connection of *air* with its predicate).   On *-ble* see note to *variable, Proth.* 13.

185. 318. See Keats' Sonnet, *Bright star! would I were steadfast as thou art.*

325. *flaw-blown*.   *Flaw* = gust, blast, as often in Spenser.

330. Here Madeline really wakes.

333. *unpruned* = untrimmed.   *Prune* is ultimately from the stem *propago*.   See *Cymb.* V. iv. 118.

> "His royal bird
> *Prunes* the immortal wing, and cloys his beak,
> As when his god is pleas'd."

336. A somewhat fantastic piece of blazonry.

346. *wassailers*.   *Wassail* is said to be derived from the Ancient Eng. drinking salutation *wces-hael* = good health to join.

349. *Rhenish*, see *Mer. of Ven.*, I. ii. 102; *Hamlet*, I. iv. 10.
       mead.   Milton uses the form *meath, Par. Lost*, v. 345.

186. 355. *darkling*.   See note to *Des. Vill.* 29.

358. The arras of Henry V's bed was embroidered with scenes of hunting and hawking. See *Our Eng. Home.*   Read M. Arnold's *Tristram and Iseult.*   Best of all, go and look at the old tapestry still hanging in the Earl's bed-chamber and the dressing-room belonging to it at Haddon Hall.

SHELLEY.

1.   1792—1811.   Percy Bysshe Shelley was born Aug. 4, 1792, at Field Place, near Horsham, Sussex, where his father resided till his succession to the Baronetcy in 1815. He was sent to minor schools, and then to Eton, and thence in 1810 to University College, Oxford. From his earliest years he shewed great independence of mind and spirit; indeed he never accepted things as he found them, because he found them so, but from the beginning he boldly asked for reasons, and protested when they could not be or were not given, and if somewhat wildly and over sanguinely, yet always with the utmost generosity and the purest purpose, schemed reformations. He says that even at school he vowed thus with himself:

> "I will be wise,
> And just, and free, and mild, if in me lies
> Such power; for I grow weary to behold
> The selfish and the strong still tyrannize
> Without reproach or check."
>
> *Revolt of Islam.* Dedication.

And this vow to the end of his life he did his best to keep. At Oxford, his vigorously sceptical spirit expressed itself in certain theological discontents. The authorities of that day could not, or did not believe in "honest doubt." Shelley's dissatisfactions and enquirings were answered summarily by a sentence of expulsion.

2.   1811—1818.   Thus Shelley at the age of 19 was sent adrift. There seems to have existed but imperfect sympathy between him and his own family at this time; though he received some pecuniary allowance from his father, he resided little, or not at all at home. It could not be good for him to be thrown so completely upon his own unassisted judgment; and the only wonder is that the consequences were not quite disastrous. Happily he had great, though not sufficient, protections in his own noble nature and sincere philanthropy. He made an unfortunate marriage with Harriett Westbrooke, a school-girl of 16. The young couple lived at various places—at Edinburgh, York, Keswick, Dublin, in the Isle of Man, North Wales, North Devon, Killarney, London. Shelley studied and speculated and theorized; he wrote also some few poems, of which *Queen Mab* was the chief. Towards the close of 1813 his wife and he parted. Her subsequent life is sad enough; let charity draw a veil over it till its end in suicide in November, 1816. Meanwhile Shelley had formed a fresh connection with Mary Godwin, a truer helpmate, whom after Harriett's death he married. Their pecuniary distresses were relieved in 1815, by an arrangement with his father, just then become Sir Timothy, by which he was to receive £1000 a year. He still lived a somewhat nomad life; he visited Switzerland; then resided awhile in South Devon, at Clifton, at Bishopgate Heath, near Windsor Forest; visited Switzerland again; then settled for some time at Great Marlow. During these various wanderings he wrote *Alastor*, and the *Revolt of Islam*, besides various minor poems. His genius was more and more definitely and brilliantly displaying itself. But he began to find his country but little congenial. The shamefulest calumnies about him were circulating everywhere. Lord Chancellor Eldon de-

prived him of the guardianship of his own children by his first wife. His hopes and dreams of a more truly free and enlightened time seemed to find nothing to sustain them.

Tennyson in one of his poems, after speaking with high pride of this English land, declares that he would quit it if ever the praises he bestows should cease to be due.

> "Should banded unions persecute
>   Opinion, and induce a time
>   When single thought is civil crime
> And individual freedom mute;
>
> Tho' Power should make from land to land
>   The name of Britain trebly great:
>   Tho' every channel of the State
> Should almost choke with golden sand:
>
> Yet waft me from the harbour mouth,
>   Wild wind! I seek a warmer sky,
>   And I will see before I die
> The palms and temples of the South."

To Shelley that dire condition of things appeared to be existing. So he quitted England. There was already in exile another illustrious poet. It must be said that to Byron and to Shelley, and also to Keats, their country was a harsh stepmother.

3. 1818—1822. The rest of Shelley's life was passed in Italy—at Milan, Leghorn, Venice, Ferrara, Bologna, Rome, Naples, Pisa, lastly at Spezzia. During this period his greatest works were written, not to mention minor pieces; in 1819 were composed his great dramas *Prometheus Unbound*, and *The Cenci*, in 1820 his exquisite *Ode to a Skylark*, in 1821 that most generous and noble Elegy *Adonais*. In Italy, 1822, he was drowned in a squall off Via Reggio in the gulph of Leghorn. His remains, restored by the waves a fortnight afterwards, were, according to an Italian law relating to things washed up by the sea, burnt on the shore, where they were found. The ashes were deposited in the Protestant Cemetery at Rome, where lay his loved little son, his "lost William,"

> "In whom
> Some bright spirit lived, and did
> That decaying robe consume,
>   Which its lustre faintly hid."

There too lay Keats. Shelley's widow lived worthily of him till 1851.

Shelley found the time "out of joint;" but he did not cry

> "O cursed spite
> That ever I was born to set it right!"

Rather he addressed himself to the task of reformation with zeal and delight. There are many points of similarity between Shelley and Milton, in their geniuses, in their tastes, even in the facts of their lives. They were both idealistic, not realists, and lyrical rather than dramatic; they were both intensely Greek in their literary sympathies; they were both ardent social, religious, and political reformers. The error of both of them as reformers arose out of their too sanguine hopes of their fellow-men. Out of the generosity of their natures they calculated on others acting with the same denial, the same single-mindedness, the same purity of soul as moved and guided themselves. As to the practicability of the reforms advocated it would be decidedly unfair to couple Milton with Shelley. It is true that Milton's schemes mostly proved at the time abortive; but certainly they cannot be stigmatized as wild and dreamy. Some of his measures did in time become facts; and some may in some sort be even now becoming so. Whereas Shelley can scarcely be rescued from the charge of fancifulness and unreality. He had less knowledge and less judgment than his great predecessor. He set about reforming the world before he well understood its case, at an age when the really impossible seemed possible. He had faith enough in his cause and in his fellow-man to make the removal of mountains seem easy; but the mountains were huge and of deep roots, and scarcely even quaked for all his efforts. His early rupture with the English world lost him all the advantages which a fuller experience of it and a longer intercourse with it might have given. That world was no less estranged from him than he from it. It misunderstood and misinterpreted him throughout his career. It covered him with its opprobrium. Assuredly he was not the man that world painted. It by no means followed that because Shelley did not repeat the ordinary creeds and even mocked at them, he believed in nothing. Shelley was never in his soul an atheist; it was simply impossible with his nature that he should be; what he did deny and defy was a deity whose worship seemed, as he saw the world, consistent with the reign of selfishness and bigotry.

Shelley's poetry bears the impress of his eager, spiritual nature, and also of his vexed, peaceless life. When those vexations are remembered and also that he was cut off when not yet "in flushing," the works he has left behind move wonder and astonishment at the splendour of his genius. Without doubt he is one of the foremost of English poets. Scarcely one has possessed in a higher degree the gifts of language and of melody. Few indeed have heard

> "The still sad music of humanity,"

and echoed it with such fine feeling and exquisite modulation as he. If ever any poet, he heard that subtle sphere-music Plato speaks of, and made it in some sort audible for mankind. There was much in common between his genius and that of Wordsworth. Certainly of his contemporaries Wordsworth influenced him most, however the conservatism of Wordsworth's maturer years shocked and alienated him. Would that he had had something of Wordsworth's patient, faithful workmanship! In other respects he was perhaps the better endowed by nature. His poetic faculty is livelier and more vigorous. It droops or falls less often—is less subject to prosaic intervals. Guidance and control it sometimes wants, not ever life and power. His eyes pierced, so far as a man's may, through the material world, to the eternal world which lies beyond and onward. Indeed the material world did but furnish him with the means of expression; what he would express was not its nor of it. His visions were not of earth; to his spirit one may speak as he to the lark in his famous ode :

> "Higher still and higher
> From the earth thou springest
> Like a cloud of fire;
> The blue deep thou wingest,
> And singing still dost soar and soaring ever singest."

All the fairnesses of the earth were dearest to him as imaging yet more exquisite and diviner beauty.

> "He will watch from dawn to gloom
> The lake reflected sun illume
> The yellow bees in the ivy-bloom,
>   Nor heed nor see what things they be ;
> But from these create he can
> Forms more real than living Man,
>   Nurslings of Immortality."

Prom. Unbound.

ADONAIS.

Keats died at Rome on the 27th of Dec. 1820 according to Shelley's Preface, on Feb. 23 1821 according to Lord Houghton's *Memoirs*, on Feb. 27 according to Mr W. M. Rossetti's *Prefatory Notice*, on Feb. 24 according to Hole's *Brief Biog. Dict.*, on Feb. 21 according to Leigh Hunt's *Autobiography*. Shelley, then living at Pisa, was moved to lament him by profound sorrow and indignation. He had seen in Keats' earlier works much that was re-pugnant to his own taste; but he considered "the fragment of 'Hyperion' as second to nothing that was ever produced by a writer of the same years." His indignation was stirred by the report that Keats' illness was caused by the attacks of certain ruffianly reviewers in England—a report that had little or no foundation; not that his reviewers had not been ruffianly, but Keats had too much strength of mind to be "snuffed out" by any article.

With this Elegy should be compared, or contrasted, *the Epitaph on Bion* commonly ascribed to Moschus, Milton's *Lycidas*, Tennyson's *In Memoriam*. A careful study will show Shelley's intimate acquaintance with the Greek piece just named, as also his familiarity with the first Idyll of Theocritus, and the last Eclogue of Virgil.

187. 3. *So dear a head.* A classicism; comp. Horace's "tam cari capitis" (*Od.* I. xxiv.). So frequently the Gr. κάρα. In English cattle are commonly counted as so many "head"; hence the use of the word in the *Dunciad:*

> "A hundred *head* of Aristotle's friends."

5. *thy obscure compeers* = thy fellow hours not made memorable by any such great sad event as has marked you and is ever to be mourned by you.

10. Comp. Theocr. i. 66, Virg. *Ecl.* x. 9, 10, Milton's *Lyc.* 50—55.

11. See *Psalm* xci. 6.

12. *Urania.* In the Greek mythology Urania was the Muse of Astronomy, "and was represented with a celestial globe, to which she points with a small staff" (Smith's *Class. Dict.*). But Milton, who uses the old mythology in a very independent manner, sometimes re-shaping or at least re-adjusting it (see note to *L'Allegro*, l. 2), makes Urania (literally, "the Heavenly one") the spirit of the loftiest poetry; see *Par. Lost*, vii. 1—20, especially the earlier lines:

> "Descend from heaven, *Urania*, by that name
> If rightly thou art called," &c.

where the "if" shews he was consciously using the name in a new sense. Comp. "Heavenly Muse" in *P. L.* i. 6. Shelley follows Milton in this changed nomenclature, as indeed in other matters, for he was an intense admirer of that great master (see below ll. 30—6). Comp. also Tennyson's *In Memoriam*, xxxvii. Horace in his dirge for his friend Quintilius invokes *Melpomene.*

13. Comp. Virgil's picture of Cyrene amidst her nymphs.

16. *Re-kindled.* *Kindle* is radically cognate with *candle.*

18. Perhaps he is thinking particularly of the *Ode to the Nightingale:*

> "Darkling I listen; and for many a time
> I have been half in love with Easeful Death,
> Call'd him soft names in many a mused rhyme
> To take into the air my quiet breath.

> Now more than ever seems it rich to die,
> To cease upon the midnight with no pain,
> While thou art pouring forth thy soul abroad
>   In such an ecstasy !
> Still wouldst thou sing, and I have ears in vain—
> To thy high requiem become a sod."

27. Comp. *Rom. and Jul.* V. iii. 101—5, also *Alastor*, of the departed Poet:

> "Silence, too enamoured of that voice,
> Locks its mute music in her rugged cell."

188. 29. [What part of the sentence is *pride* ?]

32. See any history of Charles II.'s reign.

36. Who are the other two? Homer and Virgil, or Homer and Dante? Probably Shelley means the former pair. Comp. Dryden's lines, "Three poets in three distant ages born, &c." See note to Gray's *Progress of Poesy*, l. 81. The Drama is not included in these surveys, or Sophocles and Shakspere could not be omitted.

37. This is a very obscure stanza. It seems to mean: not all poets have essayed such lofty flights as Milton, i. e. attempted Epic poetry, but some have wisely taken a lower level, i. e. attempted Lyric poetry, and are still remembered as Lyric poets, as for instance Gray or Burns; others, attempting a middle flight, have been cut off in the midst of their work, as Spenser, whom

> "Ere he ended his melodious song
> An host of angels flew the clouds among
> And rapt this swan from his attentive mates
> To make him one of their associates
> In Heaven's faire Quire."

Others yet live, of whom nothing definite can yet be said, e. g. Shelley himself, Byron.

48. A graceful reference to one of Keats' own poems; see *Isabella*, when the "sad maiden" has found her lover's body, and carried the head away with her, and tenderly dressed and shrouded it: she

> "For its tomb did choose
> A garden pot, wherein she laid it by
> And cover'd it with mould, and o'er it set
> Sweet Basil, which her tears kept ever wet.
> And she forgot the stars   *   *
>
>   *   *   *   *   *
>
>   but in peace
> Hung over her sweet Basil ever more,
> And moisten'd it with tears unto the core."

49. *true love tears.* See *Rich. II.* V. i. 10. *True love* is a corruption of *troth love*.

51. *thy extreme hope* = spes extrema.

52. *blew.* This *blow*, Lat. *floreo*, connected with *bloom*, *blossom*, Germ. *blühen*, is quite distinct from *blow*, Lat. *flo*.

[What is there noticeable in the word order?]

55. Keats arrived from Naples at Rome in the late autumn of 1820.

See *Childe Harold*, IV. lxxviii. et seq.

61. Comp. *the Giaour:*

> "He who hath bent him o'er the dead," &c.

63. *liquid* = calm, serene; as in *Georg.* iv. 59, "per æstatem *liquidam*," *Æn.* x. 272 "*liquida* nocte."

189. 65. *twilight chamber.* See *Hymn Nat.* 188, *Il Penser.* 133.

67. *trace* = to mark out, to conduct him along, lead by a track.

69. *the eternal Hunger* = Death.

70. [Explain *pale rage.*]

75. Obs. the pastoral language; comp. *Lycidas.*

80. Does *after their sweet pain* mean after their birth—after the pains they endured when first feeling the joy of being? Birth was all that heart was to give them.

81. *nor.* The Pisa Edition reads *or.*

84. *our sorrow.* See *Lyc.* 166.

90. With this use of *outwept* [Explain it] comp. Tennyson's *Tithonus:*

> "The vapours *weep* their burden to the ground."

With the whole simile, comp.

> "Whose thunder is its knell."

91. *starry dew.* Comp. Tennyson's *Talking Oak:*

> "All starry culmination drop
> Balm dews to bathe thy feet."

The stars were supposed to distil dew. So from the moon "vaporous drops profound" were thought to "come to ground;" see *Macbeth*, III. v. 25.

93. *profuse.* Obs. the accent. So in the *Ode to a Skylark*, l. 5.

94. *anadem.* Comp. Hippolytus' offering to his mistress Artemis:

> "ἀλλ' ὦ φίλη δέσποινα χρυσέας κόμης,
> ἀνάδημα δέξαι χειρὸς εὐσεβοῦς ἄπο."

96. [What is the force of *would* here?]

97. *reeds.* So Lat. *arundo*, as Virg. *Æn.* iv. 73, &c.

99. = and dull the fierce fire of her grief by contact with his death-cold cheek. As if the heart-flame would be allayed by a physical chill!

barbed = radically bearded. By a metaphor the jags on the heads of an arrow or "fishing-hook"—"the points which stand backward to hinder them from being extracted" (Johnson)—were called "beards"· so *barbed* = fanged, and so generally = piercing, cruel.

190. 100. *alit.* Anc. Eng. *alihton.* The simple verb occurs in the *Book of Common Prayer:* "O Lord, let thy mercy *lighten* upon us."

102. i.e. which made it welcome to both the minds and the hearts of men, that won it approval from both their careful judgments and their warm, eager feelings.

105. *quenched its caress* = chilled the warm kiss it gave. The splendour kissed; but Death, rather than Adonais, received the kiss.

107. *clips* = embraces, contains, holds. So in Shakspere, as *Ant. and Cleop.* V. ii. 362:

> "No grave upon the earth shall *clip* in it
> A pair so famous."

Anct. Eng. *clyppan.*

113. See the Song to Sorrow in *Endymion:*

> "O Sorrow,
> Why dost borrow," &c.

117.
> "While barred clouds bloom the soft-dying day,
> And touch the stubble-plains with rosy hue."
>
>   Keats, *To Autumn.*

Comp. *Ant. and Cleop.* IV. xii.

119. See Keats' poems, *passim.*

127 Comp. *Epitaph. Bionis*, 30:

> "Ἀχὼ δ' ἐν πέτρῃσιν ὀδύρεται ὅττι σιωπῇ
> κοὐκέτι μιμεῖται τὰ σὰ χείλεα."

132. See the preceding quotation.

133. *she.* Some editions wrongly, indeed- nonsensically, read *he.* See the story of Echo in *Class. Dict.*

191. 137. *Kindling. Kindle* is a favourite word with Shelley; see ll. 16, 78.

144. Other flowers too, not only the Hyacinth and the Narcissus, fade for grief.

145. He is thinking of the *Ode to the Nightingale;* see the quotation given in the note to l. 18.

149. This is the reading of the Pisa Edition. The common texts put the comma after *youth,* not so well.

150. Comp. Æs. *Agam.* 49—54, of vultures hovering wildly over their desolated nest.

151. [What is the force of *of* here?]

152. See Introduction.

154. Comp. the famous passage in the *Epitaph. Bionis,* 106—11 :

> "αἰαῖ ταὶ μαλάχαι μὲν ἐπὰν κατὰ κᾶπον ὄλωνται
> ἠδὲ τὰ χλωρὰ σέλινα τό τ' εὐθαλὲς οὖλον ἄνηθον,
> ὕστερον αὖ ζώοντι καὶ εἰς ἔτος ἄλλο φύοντι·
> ἄμμες δ' οἱ μεγάλοι καὶ καρτεροί, οἱ σοφοὶ ἄνδρες,
> ὁππότε πρᾶτα θάνωμες, ἀνάκοοι ἐν χθονὶ κοίλᾳ
> εὕδομες εὖ μάλα μακρὸν ἀτέρμονα νήγρετον ὕπνον."

Also Spenser's *Shep. Cal.* xi.

157. [Explain the *airs.*]

160. *brere* = briar; here, thicket.

169. So the *Epitaph. Bionis* :

> "καὶ σὺ μὲν ὦν σιγᾷ πεπυκασμένος ἔσσεαι ἐν γᾷ,
> ταῖς Νύμφαισι δ' ἔδοξεν ἀεὶ τὸν βόστρυχον ᾄδειν·
> πῶς δ' ἐγὼ οὐ φθονέοιμι; τὸ γὰρ μέλος οὐ καλὸν ᾄδει."

192. 172. [What is meant by *this spirit tender?*]

174. So "one that dwelt by the castled Rhine" called the flowers,

> "Stars that in Earth's firmament do shine."

177. *knows* = has the power of gathering knowledge.

179. *sightless* = invisible; so *Macbeth,* I. v. 50 vii. So *viewless, Meas. for Meas.* III. i. 124.

188. *urge* = follow closely, press fast after. See Hor. *Od.*

> "Urget diem nox et dies noctem."

191. *Mother,* i. e. Urania ; see above.

192. And allay with tears and sighs the wound at thy heart—a wound yet more grievous than that which slew Adonais.

193. So the Pisa edition. The common text omits *with,* which alters the sense entirely —into nonsense.

195. *their sister,* i. e. the echo who is mentioned in l. 15 as singing over his songs to Urania and the others.

196. *holy silence* = sacro silentio, Hor. *Od.* II. xiii. 29. The Latin phrase meant such a silence as was observed at the time of sacrifice, when men "favoured with their tongues."

199. Comp. Shelley's lines :

> "Swiftly walk over the western wave,
> Spirit of night," &c.

193. 208. See above, l. 14.

211. Comp Virg. *Ecl* x. 48, 9:

> "Ah! te ne frigora lædant!
> Ah! tibi ne teneras glacies secet aspera plantas!"

213. *they never could repel* = that would not be repelled, that for all the roughness she encountered was yet steadfast in her purpose to visit her perished darling (l. 46).

219. It is the opposite in *Laodamia*, 66—8.

225. Comp. above, l. 105.

227. Comp. Bion's *Epitaph. Adonidis*, 42:

> "τοσσοῦτόν με φίλησον, ὅσον ζώει τὸ φίλημα."

238. *the unpastured dragon in his den* = the ferocious, savage critic; comp. l. 243, *Unpastured* = unfed, Lat. *impastus*, as Æn. ix. 339

> "Impastus ceu plena leo per ovilia turbans—
> Suadet enim vesana fames—manditque trahitque
> Molle pecus mutumque metu, fremit ore cruento."

240. *mirror'd*, not = reflected, but rather reflecting; strictly, mirror-furnished, bearing the shield in which folly saw its own face.

194. 245. *obscene*, Lat. *obsceni*, as in Æn. xii. 876.

250. He refers to Byron's *English Bards and Scotch Reviewers.*

259. Lighting up the earth so brightly that it is not possible to see the stars—scattering the clouds that cover the earth, &c.

262. Comp. Virg. *Ecl.* x. 19.

263. *magic mantles.* Comp Arion's request to the sailors bent on murdering him, "περιιδέειν αὐτὸν ἐν τῇ σκευῇ πάσῃ στάντα ἐν τοῖσι ἑδωλίοισι, ἀεῖσαι. (Herod. i. 24.) Milton speaks of a "poet, soaring on the high reason of his fancies, with his garland and singing robes about him." (*Reason of Church Government.*) See also the *Tempest.*

264. This name for Byron is suggested by the title of his "Romaunt"—*Childe Harold's Pilgrimage.* Byron was commonly identified with his Pilgrim; in the 4th Canto he accepts the identification: see his letter to Hobhouse prefixed to that Canto.

The visits here paid are purely figurative. Only Severn was actually with Keats at his death.

265. His fame makes a sort of vast splendid canopy over his head.

267. Shelley thought Byron of a more generous nature than he really was. Byron treated Keats' death as something of a jest; see *Don Juan*, xi. 60:

> "John Keats—who was killed off by one critique
>   Just as he really promised something great,
>   If not intelligible—without Greek
>   Contrived to talk about the gods of late,
>   Much as they might have been supposed to speak.
>   Poor fellow! his was an untoward fate!
> 'Tis strange the mind that fiery particle
>   Should let itself be snuff'd out by an article."

and his lines, *Who killed John Keats?*

269. Does he refer especially to the suppression of the insurrection of 1803, and Moore's lines on the fate of Robert Emmett, one of its leaders? See amongst the *Irish Melodies, Oh, breathe not his name,* and *When he who adores thee,* and *She is far from the land.* (The lady referred to in the latter two songs was a daughter of Curran.) The "lyrist" is "sweetest" perhaps: but one cannot sympathize with "her saddest wrong." That rising of 1803 was utterly wild and foolish; and "marked by an act of peculiar atrocity." See Knight's *Pop. Hist. of Eng.* vii. 425—7, 2nd Ed.

271—96. With this picture of Shelley himself, comp. *Alastor, passim* ; see also *Hymn to Intellectual Beauty.*

276. *Actæon-like.* See Ovid's *Metam.* iii. 138 et seq.

195. 291. Comp. the Bacchic θύρσος. See Eur. *Bacch.* 80, ed. Dind. :

"ἀνὰ θύρσον τε τινάσσων κισσῷ τε στεφανωθεὶς
Διόνυσον θεραπεύει."

297. Comp. *As you like it*, II. i. 50, also Cowper's *Task, The Garden*, 108.

298. [What is meant by *partial* here ?]

306. His enemies pronounced him a very Cain; those who knew him better held far other views.

307. This stanza means Leigh Hunt.

308. As was Priam's ; see *Il.* xxiv. 163.

310. Comp. Milton's *Epit. on the admirable dramatick Poet William Shakspeare*, 7—17.

313. Leigh Hunt was Keats' earliest and chief poetical friend and adviser.

315. Shelley explains in his *Preface* why the true generous Severn is not introduced here. He did not know "the circumstances of the closing scene" till too late to celebrate Severn's conduct.

196. 321. Comp. extract from Byron to l. 267. See Preface to *Endymion.*

325. [Explain this line.]

See Shelley's *Preface*, on the critics of his day. There too he singles out the special miscreant : "Miserable man ! you, one of the meanest, have wantonly defaced one of the noblest specimens of the workmanship of God. Nor shall it be your excuse that, murderer as you are, you have spoken daggers but used none."

343. Comp. Eur. *Hippol.* 190—8, *Polyeid.* Frag. 8 :

"τίς οἶδεν εἰ τὸ ζῆν μέν ἐστι κατθανεῖν,
τὸ κατθανεῖν δὲ ζῆν κάτω νομίζεται ;"

(comp. Arist. *Ran.* 1022, and 1404.) See also Milton's *Sonnet on the Religious Memory of Mrs Catharine Thomson.*

197. 356. He can never become worldly, and mean, and heartless.

[What is meant by *slow* here ?]

358. *in vain*, i. e. without true wisdom and nobleness, not so as to be "a crown of glory." (Prov. xvi. 31.)

360. i. e. he cannot now outlive all noble impulses and enthusiasms.

362. See above, l. 120.

367. The reading *morning* of some editions is wrong.

370. See *In Mem.* xlvi.

373. Comp. Wordsworth's *Ode on Intimations*, &c. 120.

381. See Spenser's *Hymn to Beauty*, especially stanza 7, et seq.

382. Comp. Spenser :

"The duller earth it quickneth with delight,
And life-full spirits privily doth powre
Through all the parts that to the lookers sight
They seeme to please."

Chaucer's *Knight's Tale*, 2156.

383. *successions* is here used in a concrete sense.

385. *as*, i. e. according as.

198. 395. *there*, i. e. in the region above the earth (l. 193) attained by the lofty-minded.

399. *Chatterton.* Coleridge also (see his *Monody on the Death of Chatterton*), and Wordsworth (see his *Resolution and Independence*), seem to have been deeply impressed by

Chatterton's genius and fate. Keats dedicates his *Endymion* to his memory. Whatever the absolute merits of his writings, they are simply astonishing productions for a youth of sixteen. He was not eighteen when he ended his unhappy life (Born Nov. 20, 1752; Died Aug. 25, 1770).

401. *Sidney.* Born 1554, Died 1586. See Spenser's *Astrophel*, and also his *Ruines of Time.*

404. *Lucan.* Born 39, Died 65. He was scarcely "by his death approved." There was no escape for him; and after his infamous unfaithfulness to his fellow conspirators he deserved none. His *Pharsalia*, though farther advanced towards completion than *Hyperion*, is unfinished.

410. See *Isaiah* xiv. 9—10.

412. *blind* = dark. So often the Lat. *cæcus*, Gr. τύφλος.

414. These individual empires are scarcely consistent with the absorption spoken of above.

417—20. This seems to mean: Traverse the universe in fancy; see how vast it is, what a mere atom of it is this world of ours.

422, 23. I cannot explain these two lines.

199. 424. See *Childe Harold*, IV. lxxviii—clxxiv.

442. See Shelley's *Preface:* Keats "was buried in the romantic and lonely cemetery of the Protestants in that city, under the pyramid which is the tomb of Cestius, and the massy walls and towers, now mouldering and desolate, which formed the circuit of ancient Rome. The cemetery is an open space among the ruins, covered in winter with violets and daisies. It might make one in love with death to think that one should be buried in so sweet a place."

444. The Pyramid of Caius Cestius. See Murray's *Rome.*

447. *Like flame,* etc. i. e. in shape.

450. The cemetery had only lately been made.

453. If any wound is healed, or healing, do not renew it.

459. Shelley was to become it—"What Adonais is"—in a few months.

200. 462. Life is like some gaudy crystal canopy, through which the true colour of the skies above cannot be seen.

465. *Rome's azure sky,* &c. Nothing material can adequately express eternal beauty. The finest works of all the arts, and the exquisitest scenes of nature are but feeble representations of it.

472.   "Out of the day and night
                               A joy has taken flight."

474. There is terrible peril in mutual love, for the loved one may be lost; also in love which wins no response there is dire distress and pain.

480. Comp. Wordsworth's *Ode on Intimations*, &c. *passim.*

482—2. i. e. through all creation.

484. *as each are,* &c. He means: "as they are, each one, &c."

485. *the fire for which all thirst* = the celestial fire, the light of eternity.

490. i. e. those who shrink from quitting the earth, from soaring up in thought at least into the empyrean.

495. The sign was soon answered.

INDEX.

A.

A, 233, 284, 315, 371.
Aback, 371.
Ablins, 371.
Accord, 209.
Acold, 406.
Adieus, 377.
Adjectives used proleptically, 291.
Adropping, 383.
A-feard, 383.
Afford, 215.
Afield, 329.
Against, 206.
Agast, 224.
Aile, 329.
Alarmes, 211, 281.
Ale, 206.
All amort, 408.
Alleys, 324.
Amain, 263, 335, 409.
Amaist, 361.
Ambush, 308.
Amethyst, 410.
Amulet, 411.
Anadem, 418.
Anagram, 278.
Anear, 383.
Anow = enow, 263.
Anthems, 253.
Antic, 335.
-Ard, 215.
Argent, 407.
Argosy, 411.
Aright, 362.
Artist, 354.
As, 224.
Ashler, 386.
Assoile, 209.
Astrology, 249.
Atalantis, 298.
Athirst, 316.
Attire, 411.
Aught, 352.
Augusta, 274.
Ava, 367.
Awful, 217.
Awkward, 312.
Awry, 299.

B.

Baffled, 320.
Bairns, 360.
Ban, 400.
Barb, 418.
Barbican, 274.
Barge, 273.
Base-born, 388.
Bassoon, 381.
Bauble, 377.
Bauldricke, 212.
Bawson't, 367.
Be-, 219 383.
Beacon, 319.
Beadsman, 406.
Beet, 363.
Beldam, 408.
Belle, 269.
Belman, 248.
Belyve, 360.
Ben, 362.
Beside, 229.
Bespeke, 263.
Bested, 244.
Betide, 409.
Bigot, 388.
Billies, 371.
Blame, 216.
Blate, 363.
Blaze, 261.
-Ble, 206.
Bleak, 344.
Blink, 369.
Blinks, 370.
Bloomy, 351.
Blow, 223, 253.
Board, 209.
Bodice, 410.
Boding, 336.
Bodkin, 296.
Bonnet, 263, 363.
Boon, 397, 407.
Both, 227.
Bouses, 371.
Bout, 243.
Bower, 208, 240, 387.
Braw, 360.
Brere, 419.
Bridegroom, 381.

C.

Broaches, 389.
Brocade, 295.
Brooding, 233.
Brook, 369, 409.
Brutish, 228.
Buirdly, 369.
Bulwark, 345.
Buskind, 249.
Buskins, 275, 323.
But, 368.
Buxom, buchsom, 234, 387.
Byas, 277.
Byde, 210.

Ca', 360.
Cage, 314.
Candied, 411.
Canker, 259, 401.
Cannie, 360.
Cantie, 371.
Canvass, 316.
Carbine, 388.
Carkin, 360.
Carpet, 411.
Casement, 410.
Cater, 409.
Cease, 216.
Censer, 407.
Center, the, 225.
Chagrin, 308.
Chariot, 217.
Cherubim, 221.
Chest, 229.
Chide, 407.
Chiels, 369.
Chimney, 242, 353.
China, 295.
Circled, 349.
Citadel, 408.
Clan, 387.
Clinches, 275.
Clip, 418.
Close, 221, 323.
Closing, 280.
Cloysters, 252.
Coach, 377.
Comet, 303.

Con, 396.
Consecrated, 227.
Consent, 249.
Consort, 223, 251.
Copse, 351.
Cotter, 358.
Crackin, 371.
Cracks, 362.
Cranks, 235.
Crevice, 401.
Crew, 285.
Crone, 409.
Crop-full, 242.
Crouse, 371.
Crude, 255.
Crue, 237.
Cruel, 301.
Curb, 335.
Curfew, 248, 327.
Cynosure, 240.
Cypher, 352.

D.

Daft, 371.
Dank, 383.
Darg, 369.
Darkling, 320, 412.
Darksom, 215.
Dative, the ethic, 235.
Dear, 255.
Death-fires, 382.
Debauched, 308.
Debonair, 235.
Deil haet, 372.
Delphos, 226.
Demure, 246.
Denizens, 293.
Deposite, 361.
Devote, 309, 324.
Diapason, 280.
Dight, 238, 253, 387.
Dim, 227.
Discovers, 281.
Dishevelled, 304.
Dismayed, 352.
Ditties, 258.
Dodged, 382.
Dog-days, 313.
Dome, 313, 354.
Draw = attract, 304.
Drugget, 273.
Drumly, 371.
Duddie, 366, 369.
Dunce, 272.
Dungeon, 401.
Dwarfish, 408.
Dyke, 369.

E.

Eftsoones, 208, 381.
Either, 344.
Elf, 368.

Embers, 396.
Engine, 264, 298.
Enhance, 345.
Enranged, 210.
Entrayled, 207.
Ere, 219, 242.
Eremite, 412.
Essex, Earl of, 211.
Even down, 372.
Every, each, 262.
Excise, 308.
Expence, 320.
Exposed, 284.
Eydent, 361.
Eyn, 229.

F.

Fable, 266,
Faery, 408.
Fair, 295.
Fans, 296.
Farm, 310.
-Fast, 221, 218
Fawsont, 371.
Fayes, 230.
Fayre, 205.
Featously, 207.
Ferlie, 370.
Fettered, 401.
Fillet, 301.
Finny, 345.
Fit, 408.
Flambeau, 285.
Flasket, 207.
Flashy, 264.
Flawblown, 412.
Flights, 302.
Flocke, 206.
Flounce, 295.
Fond, 245.
Footing, 262.
Fops, 301.
For, 218.
For-, 227, 249, 350, 366.
Forceful, 323.
Forfeit, 215.
Foulded, 226.
Frae, 359.
Frame, 279.
Franctic, 403.
Freakt, 266.
Fret, 396.
Frisk, 336.
Frolick, 234, 313, 336.
Frounc't, 250.
Furbelo, 295.

G.

Gadding, 259.
Galileo's eyes, 304.
Gambol, 349.
Gang, 361.

Gaol, 314.
Gareish, 251.
Gars, 361.
Gauge, 352.
Gawcie, 367.
Gazette, 318.
Genius, 227, 252.
Gestic, 345.
Gibbet, 311.
Gibe, 316.
Glades, 350.
Glaze, 382.
Gloamin, 372.
Globe, 221.
Glory, 410.
Gloss, 354.
Gnash, 402.
Goodly, 208,
Gossemeres, 382.
Gossip, 408.
Gourd, 411.
Grain, 246.
Great, the, 347.
Griesly, 339.
Grisly, 228.
Grotto, 299.
Grushie, 369.
Guitar, 371.
Gules, 410.
Gulled, 312.

H.

Hackbut, 388.
Haffets, 363.
Hafflins, 362.
Haggard, 339.
Hairs, 301.
Halcyons, 218.
Hallen, 363.
Harbinger, 216.
Hard by, 240, 332.
Harness, 230.
Hath, 242.
Hauberk, 338.
Hautboys, 382.
Hawkie, 283.
Head-dress, 300.
Headlong, 388.
Hearse, 377.
Hech, 371.
Hence, 232, 244.
Hercules, Pillars of, 211.
Here, 221.
Herse, 266.
Hight, 274.
Hind, 315.
Hinges, 222.
His, 230, 233.
Hobble, 409.
Hollow, 226, 412.
Honest, 283.
Hoods, 407.
Hoodwinked, 408.

Hopeless, 281.
Horrour, 226.
Hurdies, 367.
Hussars, 319.

I.

IAMBICKS, 278.
Idle, 375.
In, 267.
Increase, 271.
Influence, 218, 242.
Ingle, 360.
Intervall, 272.
Its, 221.
Ivy-tod, 383.

J.

JACK O' THE LANTERN, 241.
Jaded, 388.
Japan ware, 298.
Jollity, 235, 395.
Jubilee, 395.
Junkets, 240.
Just, 369.

K.

KAIN, 368.
Kebback, 363.
Keep, 387.
Kercheft, 231.
Kindling, 304.
Kirns, 370.
Kye, 362.

L.

LAMPOONS, 299.
Landschape, 355.
Landskip, 239.
Lank, 372.
Lap, 243, 265, 367.
Lap-dogs, 290.
Laureat, 266.
Lave, 363.
Lawn, 219, 350.
Lay, 333.
Lays, 358.
Lee, 207.
Lee-lang, 372.
Lemures, 227.
Lies, 240.
Limmer, 372.
Liquid, 417.
List, 264.
Liveries, 238.
Loath, 344
Loon, 381.
Loth, 211.
Lottery, 310.

Lubbar, 242.
Lucky, 257.
Luntin, 370.
Lure, 376.
Lute, 273, 281.
Lyart, 363.
Lydian aires, 243.
Lydian measures, 284.
Lyre, Æolian, 334.

M.

MAB, 240.
Madded, 315.
Madding, 330.
Mail, 407.
Main, 294, 308.
Mall, the, 304.
Manners, 344, 350.
Mansion, 351.
Manteau, 299
Masquerade, 296, 308.
Matadore, 297.
Maun, 369.
Maying, 234.
Maze, 230.
Mead, 412.
Meagre, 407.
Meed, 261.
Megrim, 299.
Menial, 316.
Mermaid, 417.
Messes, 240.
Messin, 366.
Methinks, 208, 273.
Mickle, 409.
Midst, 215.
Militia, 291.
Mill, 370.
Minstrelsy. 381.
Mirror'd, 420.
Moil, 359.
Monstrous, 266.
Moon-loved, 230.
Morn, the, 359
Mortal, 281.
Motley, 315.
Moudieworts, 367.
Mould, 223.
Muse=poet, 211, 222, 256, 283.

N.

NAPPIE, 369.
Ne'er a bit, 372.
Negative, the double, 207.
Negleckit, 369.
Neightour, 209.
Never a, 383.
Nightly, 226, 249, 338, 345, 377.
Nightsteeds, 230.
No, 362.

Noise, 221, 243.
Nowt, 371.
Numbers, 377.

O.

OF, 205, 208.
Ogle, 302.
On hye, 207.
Oozy, 222, 267.
Ore, 267.
Or ere, 219.
Or ever, 383.
Organ, 223.
Organs, 253, 281, 285.
Orient, 229.
Orus, 229.
O that, 376.

P.

PACK, 367.
Paint, 302.
Pair, 283.
Pale, 252.
Pale-ey'd, 226.
Pall, 249.
Pansy, 395.
Paramours, 206.
Parlour, 353.
Parting, 227, 349, 352.
Partridge, 304.
Parts, 389
Patriot, 347.
Pencil, 337.
Penny fee, 361.
Pensioners, 245.
Pensions, 309.
Perfect infinitive, 244.
Perfet, 261.
Pide, 239.
Pigmy, 396.
Pinion, 338.
Pious, 331.
Plaining, 409.
Plashy, 351.
Plat, 248.
Platter, 345.
Pledge, 263.
Poind, 369
Point of dawn, 220.
Pollute, 216.
Pomp, 243.
Poniard, 388.
Poortith, 369.
Posy, 207.
Pranks, 343.
Press, 303.
Preterites, strong and weak, 219, 283.
Prevent, 216.
Profaner, 251.
Proof, 253
Pride, 302.

Q.

QUAINT, 227, 265.
Quarry, 388.
Quell, 280.
Quills, 268.
Quilt, 299.
Quince, 411.
Quips, 235.

R.

RADDLE, 308.
Rage, 329.
Ragouts, 368.
Rampire, 345.
Rathe, 265.
Ream, 370.
Rebecks, 240.
Redemption, 214.
Reed, 324.
Reeds, 418.
Reek, 370.
Rekindled. 416.
Release, 215.
Remitting, 349.
Rents, racked, 368.
Resistless, 388.
Revel, 386.
Reve'ry, 243, 407.
Reverie, 377.
Rhenish, 412.
Rhyme, 256.
Riband, 303.
Rin, 360.
Ring-dove, 410.
Rood, 350.
Rosamonda's lake, 304.
Rosary, 407.
Route, 387.
Rugged, 233.
Rush, Friar, 241.
Rutty = rooty, 205.

S.

SABLE-STOLED, 229.
Sair-won, 361.
Savage, 345.
Scale, 303.
Science, 309.
Score, 401.
Scourges, 376.
Scrannel, 264.
Scud, 387.
Scutcheon, 410.
Seats, 283, 355.
Secure, 321.
Sedge, 263.
Self, 244.
Sequacious, 282.
Sequestered, 323.
Seraph, 412.
Session, 225.
Set, 224.
Severall, 230.

Sex, the, 300.
Shaggy, 339.
Shapes, 233, 245.
Shatter, 255.
Shears, 298.
Shell, 280, 323.
Shelvey, 344.
Shend, 209.
Sheugh, 367.
Shew, 207.
Shore, 355.
Shrieve, 383.
Shrink, 296.
Shrinks, 228.
Shroud, 229, 257.
Shrunk, 264.
Sicken, 223.
Sidelong, 349.
Sightless, 419.
Silly, 220, 383.
Skirt, 340.
Sky, 402.
Smiddie 366.
Smutted, 347.
Smytrie, 369.
Snowkit, 367.
Snuff, 297.
Sock, 243.
Sojourn, 397.
Sol, 290.
Sonsie, 367.
Sooth, 319.
Sooths, 309.
Sorrow, 267, 418.
Soupe, 363.
Sovereign, 217.
Spangled, 215, 207.
Spark, 291.
Speirs, 361.
Sphear, 216.
Spheres, 294.
Spirit, 204
Spleen, 299.
Spread, 227.
Sprindges, 502.
Spurn, 351.
Spy, 311.
Stacker, 360.
Stechin, 368.
Steer, 372.
Stents, 368.
Still, 267.
Stole, 246.
Store, 207, 242, 299.
Storied, 329
Straight, 282.
Strand, 355
Strayed, was, 262.
Streit, 239.
Strikes, 217.
Stubborn, 315.
Substantive, verbal, 228.
Suburbian, 275.
Sugh, 359.
Sullen, 335.
Supine, 408.

Supinely, 272.
Surly, 351.
Swain, 343. 349.
Swans, 207.
Swart, 265.
Swarthy, 387.
Swindges, 225.
Swound, 381.
Sylph, 290.
Syrops, 411.

T.

TABOR, 394.
Tale, 238.
Taper, 243.
Tawdry, 345.
Tawted, 366.
Tea, 296.
Teem, 208.
Teeming, 320.
Tenderness, 411.
Tentie, 360.
Terrour, 225.
Thack and rape, 369.
Thae, 371.
Thames, silver, 205, 273, 292.
The, 253.
Thole, 369.
Thrang, 371.
Thrid, 296.
Tiara, 407.
Tides, 352.
Timmer, 371.
Tiptoe, 408.
Tissue, 339.
To, 207, 223, 250, 324, 354.
Toddlin, 359.
Toil, 315, 360
Toilet, 292.
Tornado, 355.
Towsie, 367.
Trace, 418.
Traffic, 345.
Train, 349.
Trashtrie, 368.
Treat, 292.
Tree, 219.
Trim, 208, 239.
Tripod, 300.
Triumphs, 100, 242, 407
Troll, 344.
Truant, 352.
True-love, 4 7.
Truncheon, 389.
Tuneable, 412.
Tuneful, 283.
Twilight, 227, 251.
Tympany, 278.

U.

UNCESSANT, 260.
Unco, 367.

Uncos, 361.
Uncouth, 233, 267, 302, 330.
Undersong, 209.
Unexpressive, 222, 267.
Unpastured, 420.
Unpruned, 412.
Unreproved, 237.
Unresisted, 299.
Unroll, 329.
Unsphear, 249.
Unsufferable, 215.
Urchen, 409.
Urge, 419.
Use, 260, 265.

V.

Van, 375.
Vapours, 300.
Varnish, 311.
Vaults, 329, 386
Veering, 323.
Vein, 215.
Vent, 301.
Vent'rous, 315.
Vertuous, 260.
Viol, 324.

Violins, 281.
Virago, 302.
Vistas, 354.
Vizor, 389.
Voice, 220.
Voluble, 410.

W.

Waft, 267.
Wait upon, 209.
Wale, 363.
Warble, 243.
Warbling, 273.
Wan, 388.
Wardrop, 259.
Warp, 339.
Wash, 295.
Wassailers, 412.
Weal, 409.
Weanling, 259.
Wee, 360.
Weeds, 242.
Welter, 256.
Weltring, 222, 284.
Went, 262.

Wheel, 312.
Wherry, 308.
Which, 212.
Which the, 205.
While, 208, 215.
Whiles, 367, 381.
Whilom, 210, 273
Whist, 217.
Wifie, 360.
Winnow, 344.
Wisard, 260.
With, 215.
Wonner, 368.
Wont, 210, 215.
Woodman, 353
Woud, 307.
Wroth, 225.

Y

Ychained, 224.
Ycleaped, 233.
Yet, 207, 245, 323, 402.
Yon, 247.
Yore, 245.
Youngster, 363.
Younker, 361.

.

THE END.

www.ingramcontent.com/pod-product-compliance
Lightning Source LLC
Chambersburg PA
CBHW022011110726
47901CB00006B/1477